THE TENNESSEE MOUNTAIN MAN

George Moon

Order this book online at www.trafford.com
or email orders@trafford.com

Most Trafford titles are also available at major online book retailers.

Printed in the United States of America.

ISBN: 978-1-4669-8691-6 (sc)
ISBN: 978-1-4669-8690-9 (hc)
ISBN: 978-1-4669-8689-3 (e)

Library of Congress Control Number: 2013907291

Trafford rev. 05/22/2013

www.trafford.com

North America & international
toll-free: 1 888 232 4444 (USA & Canada)
phone: 250 383 6864 • fax: 812 355 4082

Acknowledgments

The Tennessee Mountain Man contains two battle maps drawn by the noted illustrator, Ralph Baldino. I was fortunate to be able to commission him as he was in the midst of preparing a public viewing of his excellent pen-and-ink art.

Special thanks must go out to my wife, Marilyn, who spent countless hours working with me editing the book. She had to use every ounce of experience she gained while employed at the *Daily Journal* in Kankakee, Illinois. My writing style would drive any editor up the wall, and she stayed the course.

Contents

Preface

Before hearing the gnashing of teeth, I want to apologize to all the Civil War buffs. While finding the Civil War a compelling subject, I am by no means qualified to write its history.

Most of what is included in the story was taken from the excellent Internet site, Wikipedia, the free encyclopedia. Other sources were *Captains of the Civil War: A Chronicle of the Blue and the Gray* by William Charles Henry Wood; *Personal Memoirs of Ulysses S. Grant* by Ulysses S. Grant; *Killing Lincoln: Lincoln's Last Hours* by Charles A. Leale, MD; *1861: The Civil War Awakening* by Adam Goodheart; *The Civil War: A Narrative: Volume 1: Fort Sumter to Perryville* by Shelby Foote; *Battle Cry of Freedom: The Civil War Era* by James M. McPherson; *History of the Civil War, 1861-1865 (Oxford History of the United States)* by James Ford Rhodes; *The Story of a Common Soldier of Army Life in the Civil War, 1861-1865* by Leander Stillwell; and the noted Civil War documentary by Ken Burns. All of which allowed me to cobble together the battles fought in Virginia in which the Seventh Tennessee regiment took part.

That being said, my story is about Jack Leffingwell, a character taken from my first book, *Reno's Funmakers.*

The story takes place in 1861, five years after his marriage to Abigail Adams, the daughter of Hyrum Adams, a Methodist minister and fellow conductor with the Underground Railroad.

Troubles down at Fort Sumter, South Carolina, and President Lincoln's subsequent decision to send seventy-five thousand troops into the South caused Tennessee to reluctantly join the secessionists. Jack Leffingwell, against slavery in any form, felt duty bound to side with others from Wilson County and wear the butternut colors of the Dixie faithful.

An active participant in transporting runaway slaves to freedom, he finds himself in a railroad car destined for Virginia and ending up fighting as part of Robert E. Lee's Army of Northern Virginia. The story takes him through the Virginia battles until wounded by an exploding shell and sent to Robertson Hospital in Richmond, Virginia, with amnesia and no memory of a prior life before the incident.

Unaware of being married, he is enchanted by the beautiful and exotic young nurse, Grazyna McCracken-Kaminski, who lost her husband at the first battle of Manassas without consummating her marriage.

Jack Leffingwell found favor with Gen. Stonewall Jackson because of his sharpshooting skill. The ubiquitous Jackson liked the idea of shooting the enemy from a mile away. So much so, he gave the marksman a telescope to attach to his rifle, which made the deadly shot arrive from an even farther distance. Upon hearing of Leffingwell's condition, Stonewall took a personal interest in assuring the finest treatment available. At the time, it was Captain Sally Louisa Tompkins and the Robertson Hospital.

It was there at Robertson's where Jack met Grazyna and fell under her spell. They soon became lovers and planned for a life together once the war ended. Jack's wife, Abigail, made the arduous journey to Richmond to visit her husband and found a man who did not know her. One look at Grazyna told Abigail she had a rival. With a husband who had no memory of their life together, Abigail took solace in the doctor's claim that Jack's memory will return someday. She had no choice, with children who needed her, but to return to Statesville.

Through the efforts of his friend, Abel Strawn, Jack received orders to report for active duty back at the Fredericksburg camp. Prior to leaving the hospital, the mountain man learned Grazyna was with child and promised to ask his wife for a divorce.

Grazyna died after the delivery of their baby boy, whom she named Jozef. She also made Jack promise to return to Statesville so that Jozef could have a family. The crestfallen mountain man swore he would honor her last wishes; and shortly thereafter, when Robert E. Lee surrendered at Appomattox, Jack, Jozef, and sharpshooter friends Abel Strawn, Melvin Kaufman, and his new wife, Hope, made the six-week trip to Tennessee in a covered box wagon.

Abigail, deeply in love with her husband, accepted Little Jozef into her family. Jack, in turn, learned of Abigail's inheritance of the property adjoining their own and now had two farms, which had been neglected the past four years. He set about making the overdue repairs and planting, all the while finding pieces missing from his amnesia puzzle. He did, however, begin to notice the inner beauty of Abigail, and as the weeks passed by, her outer beauty stirred his emotions.

Yes, he fell in love with his wife for a second time. Whether or not Jack Leffingwell completely regained memory of his past life cannot be told at this writing. Bits and pieces seem to crop up each week, and collectively, doctors were satisfied with their original prognosis.

The couple repeated their wedding vows with Abigail's father, Rev. Hyrum Adams, conducting the ceremony.

Other characters from my first novel become interwoven into the story, especially Yalata, Jack's Choctaw Indian friend. Yalata and his wife, Ailana, had taken Jack's horses and cattle for safekeeping and watched over his family while he was away fighting the Union army.

Filled with human emotion, the fast-moving story covers four years during the Civil War and the Seventh Tennessee regiment's stay in Virginia. While centering on the activities of Jack Leffingwell and those around him, the reader is introduced to several other characters, both real and fictional, that help tie the story together.

Chapter One

The winds of change are now blowing
from the South

The Gilf Kebir mountain ridge extends across the countries of Egypt, Libya, and Sudan. Several caves can be found in these mountains which contain ancient paintings depicting the conditions and life at the time. In southwest Egypt, near the border with Libya, there is a cave containing rock paintings with images of people swimming. At first, this appears to be impossible, but not when you consider the area was more fertile during the Ice Age some ten thousand years earlier. A dramatic climate change since then brought about the arid Sahara we are familiar with today.

Perhaps the ancient cave artist painted symbols and images he recalled when sitting on the bank of a great river, no longer in existence. His drawings and paintings only prove one thing for certain, that things change, albeit, in this case, over thousands of years.

We live our lives in a constant state of flux or change. Whether, it is accomplished in a matter of seconds, as with earthquakes, tsunami, and floods, or over years through the relentless march of evolution, the certainty of change is forever with us. In the case of human beings, our physical presence changes over time as we grow older. Our plans and those of society, in general, constantly undergo change. When it comes to humans, one thing basically remains the same. Our human nature and character is the same today as it was ten or a thousand years ago. I've often made the statement that *people never change*. My philosophy in this matter might allow one possibility—a Christian conversion. Most often, even that results in a person reverting to his basic character, after the fact.

Jack Leffingwell has been happily married for five years. His love for Abigail only deepens and grows stronger each day. They now have a daughter, christened Sarah Jane, and Abigail is once again expecting—this time hoping for a boy. Jack is so pleased with his life that the work necessary to make the farm successful has become just another joy. Hyrum Adams couldn't be more proud of his daughter and son-in-law. Outside of ministering the church, he spends a goodly amount of personal time spoiling his granddaughter.

The widow, Minnie Rosenthal, who sold Jack the property he now farms, frequently visits Abigail and shares a cup of tea with her. She looks on Abigail as a granddaughter. The union they have created, undoubtedly, has made her remaining years enjoyable. The fact her farm adjoins the Leffingwell spread makes it easier to include her as part of the family when traveling to church each Sunday morning.

It's plain to see why the Leffingwell family has become a major part of the community and been held in high regard and respect by all its citizens. They offer hospitality to anyone who comes to their door and freely help those in need. Jack Leffingwell has his own singular respect from the town's families. So much so, the mothers encourage their sons to be like him when they grow up. The life Jack now lives, while more important than any other, differs somewhat from his true character of being a mountain man. The love of his former wilderness independence and hunting, fishing and trapping, is part of Jack's nature and will never change. In the quiet time of the evening, when the crickets call their mates, he sometimes sits on the front porch and dreams of stalking game with Yalata, his Choctaw Indian friend. Such reveries, however, quickly disappear once Sarah Jane crawls onto his lap and falls asleep. With his daughter snuggled in his arms, he returns to his thoughts and recalls the events responsible for the miracle he is holding and the sunshine in his heart.

He remembers when he was a conductor for the Underground Railroad abetting runaway slaves to find freedom. One occurrence stands out among all the others. That was when he ferried Wilbur Littlefield and his family across Lake Chickamauga; and how excited their son, Leroy, was to ride a horse for the first time, even though he had to ride double with his sister, Celia. Jack harkens back to leading them through the Cumberland Plateau on their way to Cardwell Mountain and the miles of caverns beneath. It seemed like only yesterday, waiting for the next conductor to arrive to take the Littlefields to Statesville and the Methodist church. He could envision the excitement he felt when Abigail Adams showed up and how her stunning beauty was exposed when she removed her hat to wipe her brow. He was moonstruck from the very first time he saw her. Looking back, he recalled how difficult it was to break through her shield of resistance just to win civility toward him.

The memory of meeting her father, Hyrum Adams, and how kind he was to a mountain stranger is vivid in Jack's mind. The minister turned out to be the wisest of all. Hyrum immediately saw beneath the problem his daughter had and encouraged Jack to never give up on winning her heart. Jack's daydream popped like a bubble when Abigail opened the screen door and sat down next to her husband and sleeping daughter.

"A penny for your thoughts," Abigail whispered so as not to wake Sarah Jane.

"Oh, I was just thinking how blessed I am to have you and Sarah Jane," Jack replied.

Jack had more on his mind but needed to talk to Hyrum before disclosing any of it. Now, more than ever, the country faced the possibility of war. While against slavery, and all its variations, Jack was still a Southerner and, more likely as not, be against the North should a conflict come to pass.

"I felt Little Jack move just before I came out. I hoped he'd do it again so you could feel him, but I think he went to sleep." Abigail smiled.

"You always refer to the baby as he. Darling, I will be just as happy to have another daughter," Jack said reassuringly.

"I know, but a mother can tell. This little guy is a boy. I can tell by the way I'm carrying him," Abigail stated with conviction. With that, she gently lifted Sarah from her father's lap and went back inside to put her in bed. Jack gave a heavy sigh and rose from the homemade rocker and joined them.

* * *

Abraham Lincoln was elected the sixteenth president of the United States on November 6, 1860. His victory was earned primarily by the vote in the North. There were three other candidates on the ballot, and the voting broke down somewhat like the following:

Republican Party .... Abraham Lincoln:
1,866,452 votes
Democrat Party .... Steven A. Douglas:
1,376,957 votes
Southern Democrat Party.......... John C. Breckinridge:
849,781 votes
Constitutional Union Party .... John Bell:
588,789 votes

The Republican candidate won the presidency with 180 electoral votes, compared to the 123 of the all the others combined. There's no question that the election was actually one of the North against the South. In fact, no ballots were cast for Lincoln in ten of the fifteen Southern slave states. No sooner, as the election became official, South Carolina adopted an ordinance declaring its secession from the United States of America; and by February 7, 1861, six other states adopted similar decrees.

On April 12, 1861, South Carolina demanded that the United States Army abandon its facilities in Charleston Harbor. Brig. Gen. P. G. T. Beauregard, the first general of the newly formed Confederate States of America, was in command of the Confederate forces in Charleston. Beauregard energetically directed the strengthening of batteries around Charleston Harbor, concentrating on Fort

Sumter. The Union commander, Maj. Robert Anderson, refused to vacate and anxiously awaited reinforcements. After President Lincoln notified South Carolina governor Frances W. Pickens that he was sending supply ships to reinforce Fort Sumter, the Confederate bombardment commenced from artillery batteries surrounding the harbor. Major Anderson had no choice other than evacuate the fort.

Following the battle, Lincoln called for seventy-five thousand volunteers to suppress the rebellion. With that, an additional four states declared their secession and joined the Confederacy.

Tennessee governor Isham Harris favored secession, but the state had a strong pro-Union sentiment. In February 1861, a referendum for secession was defeated by a 54-46 percent margin. Only after Lincoln's call to suppress the rebellion did Tennessee voters change their minds and approve a referendum on June 8, 1861, becoming the last state to join the Confederacy.

* * *

The next morning, after breakfast, Jack saddled his horse and rode to the Methodist church in Statesville in order to discuss with Hyrum the war and pray for the future. Jack was too emotionally torn to think clearly, and Hyrum always had sound views in times of crisis. Jack's horse, Rambler, cavorted, cantered, and pranced about, celebrating another opportunity to enjoy the spring morning's crisp, refreshing air. The tall chestnut was purchased as a yearling and grew into an astonishing animal, far beyond what anyone expected. It had a smooth, ambling gait and incredible stamina. When it cantered, it exhibited a natural rocking-horse motion, quite pleasant to the rider. Jack, hopefully, planned to use Rambler to sire a breed of horses with similar traits. Looking across the pasture, Jack saw three of Rambler's foals running in tandem with their mothers. It was the beginning of his project and vision for the future. As horse and rider crossed the rippling stream, Jack's surroundings never seemed more beautiful. Spring wildflowers were promising the advent of warmer days. Lining the stream, a virtual prism of colors met his eye, including Purple Larkspur, Jack in the Pulpits, Black-eyed Susan, and Fire Pink, a hummingbird favorite. In his undeveloped land, near the standing hardwood trees, he beheld even more vibrant colors decorating the landscape, making Jack think. *Such beauty can only be the handiwork of the unseen and loving Creator.*

It was too early for many of the townsfolk, demonstrated by their darkened windows. Hyrum, on the other hand, was an early riser, and his kitchen window illuminated a bright yellow glow.

"Good morning, Jack. What brings you out so early?" Hyrum greeted and asked. "Can I offer you some breakfast?"

"No, thanks, I ate just before coming over here," his son-in-law answered.

"I hope you don't mind me eating in front of you. I know you'll take a cup of coffee," Hyrum said as he poured another cup. "Sit down and take a load off."

A period of silence followed while Jack tried to formulate his concerns into the proper words. The two men have been comfortable with each other from the beginning, and Hyrum continued eating his breakfast until Jack began to explain his visit.

"This war is going to change all our lives. The country is never going to be the same," Jack averred. "There has always been talk about breaking away from the Union, but each time I felt that, it was just that, talk."

"I know what you mean, son. I've thought there was a possibility, but hoped we all could settle our differences without seceding the Union and going to war because of it. The South has felt animosity toward the North for a long time, way before Andrew Jackson was president. I think most of it had to do with tariffs.

"Britain could supply the country with merchandise at lower prices than Northern manufacturers could compete against. Originally, tariffs were passed to protect the Northern manufacturers. This resulted in less goods purchased from Britain and, thus, less money for Britain to buy cotton from the South. The tariff also allowed the Northern manufacturers to raise their prices. The Southern states were forced to pay higher prices for goods from up North, with reduced revenue from Britain. That had a drastic effect on the Southern economy and caused cotton states to think about secession. When Andrew Jackson got elected, he lowered the tariff, but not enough to change economic conditions in the South. The talk about secession has gone on ever since. Now it has finally happened."

"Who do you think will win the war?" Jack honestly asked.

"Nobody wins in war. In the final outcome, just look at what each side has to offer. The North has more people, more manufacturing to make armaments, more railroads, and more money. The South believes it has more cause. We will eventually lose," Hyrum said regretfully.

"The South has better fighters," Jack stated.

"The Indians were better fighters, and look where that got them," replied Hyrum.

"Tennessee has called for volunteers. Most of my neighbors are signing up. What's happening here in town?"

"From what I've been told, the younger men are also enlisting. They really don't have a clue of what they're in for. I'm not going to speak out one way or the other. That decision will be a personal resolution for each individual."

"How would you feel if I volunteered?" asked Jack.

"I would be concerned for your safety and how the decision affects Abigail and the children. You notice I said children. I'll have two grandchildren before the snow flies. Have you said anything to Abigail?"

"Not really. She always can tell what's on my mind, but hasn't brought up the subject."

Hyrum knew what Jack's decision will be. He put his arm around his son-in-law's shoulder and walked him to the sanctuary. Two men knelt and prayed to the God who will eventually be on both sides in the war. Jack left the house of the Lord and rode back to the farm, more contented with his decision. He unsaddled his prize chestnut stallion and released him to the corral. He will face the hardest part of his decision once he enters the house. Abigail was sitting at the dining table peeling potatoes. The tears in her eyes said it all. She knew without being told that Jack was going to war on the side of the South.

"Why, Jack, don't you think we can win without you?" Abigail said mockingly. "It's a volunteer army. You don't have to go. Think of what you leave behind. You're going to have a son this fall and may never see him. Is that what you want?"

"You, of all people, know I don't want those things," he replied. "It's something buried deep within my soul. It's patriotism for my people. If I didn't join them, I would feel that I deserted my duty. I couldn't live with that. Can't you understand? It's a part of what makes me a man."

Abigail wiped her tears with her apron, rose from the table, and carried the potatoes to the kitchen stove. After filling the pan with water, she said, "Dinner will be in about an hour." It was their last conversation on the subject.

Chapter Two

The Tennessee Brigade received orders to travel to Virginia

The call went out from Camp Trousdale in Sumner County, and soon, a cohesive assemblage began to form. Statesville volunteers were part of the group from Wilson County. Other unforced men of free will arrived from neighboring counties and, shortly thereafter, became part of the Seventh regiment, mustered into Confederate service during the month of July 1861. Men of various stripes composed the unit with officers primarily older and experienced with service, either military or legislative.

Colonel Robert Hopkins Hatton was the field officer for the Seventh Tennessee Infantry Regiment. A lawyer, politician, and United States congressman, the thirty-four-year-old Hatton believed that the Union should be preserved and opposed secession. When President Lincoln called for volunteers to invade the Southern states, Hatton reversed his position and formed a Confederate military unit, the Lebanon Blues, and became part of the

Seventh Tennessee. While bivouacked at Camp Trousdale, Jack Leffingwell distinguished himself as a sharpshooter, using his Whitworth rifle. Made in England, the rifle allowed Jack to consistently hit targets over two thousand feet away. Colonel Hatton was impressed and asked Jack to form a group of sharpshooters to accompany the regular infantrymen. They would later be asked to pick off and eliminate Union artillery gun crews. Long-range marksmanship isn't wasted on the front lines. Jack could do a better job from a farther distance away. The first keen rifleman he selected was Abel Strawn. In Jack's view, Strawn was only limited by his weapon. When it came to marksmanship, he was every bit as good as Jack. Three more were added during the next week, making a total of five superior riflemen. They included Lomas Chandler, John Henry Bickford, and Ihme (pronounced *Eye-me*) Mueller (a German immigrant who could hardly speak English but can shoot the eye out of a squirrel at one thousand feet). Later, they became known as the Favorite Five and were respected by most of the troops.

Idleness is the beginning of all vices
—Proverb

Any military commander understands the problems caused by idleness. It serves as the main reason to keep the troops busy, even if the work makes little sense and is basically without visible value. Accordingly, the Seventh regiment is kept busy from dawn to dusk. In addition to being drilled six hours a day, they formed work crews and maintained the camp to the satisfaction of the officers. One thing to be said about the Tennessee Brigade is, they slept like babies. At the end of another strenuous day,

Abel and Jack sat in front of their pup tent. Abel took the time to light his pipe and stare into the gradual darkness, searching for the first star of the evening. Tonight, Jack used what daylight remained to write to Hyrum Adams.

"When are we ever going to fight in this here war?" Abel interrupted. "I didn't sign up to just drill and dig ditches."

"Never is too soon for me," replied Jack. "Are you a married man, Abel?"

"I suppose you can call it that. It's a long story. Do you really want to hear it?"

"Only if you want to tell it," Jack replied.

"I was born and raised in Lebanon, Tennessee. My Pappy is the Methodist minister there. The church folk provided a house for the preacher and his family. Ours was next door to the church. All in all, it isn't a mansion or anything like that, but respectable. It seems like the parishioners don't want the other churches showing up their preacher or his family. Well, that's another story. I always had my eye out for one of the girls in town. She never gave me a second look until one day she wanted to talk to me about something real important. You got to remember, I'm the preacher's son and raised strict. The most I ever did was hold her hand once. So she comes to me and says she is going to have a baby and the father won't marry her. She asked me for a big favor. She asked me if I would say the baby is mine and marry her. I always thought she was the prettiest girl in town, and naturally, marrying her had been my dream for a long time. After we got hitched, she finds out she wasn't having a baby after all. She started seeing her old boyfriend again but wanted to stay married to me. It gave her admiration. The whole thing made me sick. I couldn't eat, I couldn't sleep, and I couldn't live like that. So I wrote my father a note, telling him the truth about her, and joined the Seventh Tennessee."

"Have you heard from your father since you left?"

"Not a word as yet," Abel replied as he tapped his pipe against the sole of his boot.

"Life wouldn't be worth a plug nickel if anything happened to my marriage with Abigail. These last five years have been a true blessing. She has given me a beautiful little daughter and tells me that I'll have a son before the snow flies."

"She sounds like a wonderful woman," Abel complimented.

"I don't mean to be butting in, but if I was you, I'd write your father and tell him how you're doing," advised Jack.

The following morning, the camp was buzzing like a dynamo with unfocused energy. The Tennessee Brigade received orders to travel to Virginia. Soon, they will participate in a war destined to continue for the next four years—an American war, in which Americans killed each other, burned American towns, and, in the view of President Lincoln, was necessary in order to give the United States the chance for rebirth. For the most part, the Tennessee Confederates will be transported to Virginia by railcar. Passing through towns and villages found the sides of the tracks lined with ladies waving handkerchiefs. Old men and young boys were displaying banners and holding up signs. The more populated communities supported brass bands playing Dixie, a fitting send-off for their heroic volunteers. Most, of which, had never been more than twenty miles away from home. The excitement of it all made their blood course through their bodies and throb in their ears, while the boxcars swayed and rattled, transporting them to their ill-fated calling.

"At least we won't have to drill all day," a voice came from the corner of the boxcar.

"You're right, but just wait until we get to Virginia. They'll probably drill our ass off," answered someone from the other side of the car.

Jack Leffingwell had found a place to squat down and lean back against the side. His eyes were shut and thoughts indistinguishable. The click and bump of the rolling train served to encourage the hypnotic stupor. He was comforted in the knowledge that, by now, Abigail had received his letter.

July 9, 1861
Dearest Abigail,

Separation is teaching me a painful lesson. Your absence gnaws at the pit of my stomach, and the only way to dispense melancholy is to constantly be busy. Colonel Hatton takes every opportunity to see that we all are active from when the rooster crows until the old owl hoots at night. Nights are the time I miss you the most. Your tender touch has always renewed my soul no matter how frustrated or tired I am. This may sound strange, but as I wake in the morning, there is a second when I feel your presence as if you are there with me.

My trusty Whitworth rifle earned me a promotion the first week here. Five of us are now called sharpshooters and won't have to be in the front line of battle, should we ever have one. I'm not sure exactly how they plan to use us, but from what I hear, this war will be over in three months, so whatever they decide won't be for very long.

The food is tolerable, and my comrades mostly likable. I share a pup tent with a fellow sharpshooter by the name of Abel Strawn. Don't know much about him except that he comes from a Methodist family and his dad is a preacher. He doesn't seem to care about praying at night, so I don't say mine out loud.

Let me know everything that happens with you and Sarah and remember that I love you with all my heart.

Your loving husband,
Jack
P.S. I plan to write your father tomorrow.

On July 25, 1861, Jack Leffingwell and his fellow Tennessee volunteers reached Staunton, Virginia, and were joined by Col. George Earl Maney's First and the Fourteenth Tennessee infantry regiments. From that point, and throughout the war, they were known as the Tennessee Brigade of Northern Virginia and served under Brig. Gen. Samuel R. Anderson. This group of loyal Southern men and boys will remain together throughout the war, until the surrender at Appomattox.

From Staunton, the men wearing Confederate gray proceeded to Big Spring, in Page County, and set up camp. Much to their chagrin, the routine of drilling six to eight hours a day had resumed. Located in the heart of the Shenandoah Valley, the landscape reflected the splendid beauty of the Blue Ridge Mountains and serpentine flow of the Shenandoah River.

The Shenandoah River is a tributary of the Potomac River. It is nearly sixty miles long, with two branches of one hundred miles each, twisting through Virginia and West Virginia. Along with its tributaries, it drains the central and lower Shenandoah Valley on the west side of the Virginia's Blue Ridge Mountains and the Eastern Panhandle of West Virginia.

Twenty years hence, near the Confederate encampment, the largest series of caverns in the Eastern United States will be discovered. A mysterious domain of stalactites and stalagmites is destined to make the area world famous.

Jack Leffingwell was promoted to corporal and ordered to keep the sharpshooters together, rather than dispersed among nearly two thousand soldiers. Rumor travels like the wind, and they soon learned they were part of Gen. Robert E. Lee's army. Once the news became fact, the drill routine received considerably less complaining. The sharpshooters practiced two hours each day. That time was subtracted from their six hours of marching and drill. There was little resentment, since a marksman could, someday, save their lives.

In mid-August, Jack received a responding letter from his wife, Abigail. Most mail from home has a way of brightening a soldier's outlook and assuages the loneliness. Unfortunately, history tells us that a Confederate soldier writes four letters to every one he receives. Jack sat on his cot and opened the anticipated epistle. Abel remained silent while Jack absorbed the words, hoping it will be read aloud, once he finished.

July 17, 1861
My Darling Husband,

The letter of July 9 was most welcome. Your absence is so distressing for me and Little Sarah. Sometimes I feel as though my heart will break and the simple act of breathing becomes a difficult task. You will be proud to know that I've come to understand why you cannot just stand by and be a spectator in this war brought on through no fault of our own. You, my husband, are a good man, and only active participation will suffice the love you have for our country.

The most curious thing happened yesterday. I was awakened by the sound of horses walking about and the fluttering sound only such animals can make. Opening the curtains, to get a better look, my eyes revealed Indians, of all things. One of which resembled your friend Yalata, but I must confess, it was difficult to clearly see him due to the heavy morning ground fog. He rode around the farm as though he was going to purchase it and finally dismounted and walked into the barn. A few minutes later, he reappeared and climbed back on his pinto and led the others away. I was able to count twenty braves, however, there may have been more. You know how they like to remain unseen.

What does it all mean? Nothing was taken, yet the leader didn't come to the door. I'm sure he knew I was watching him. Quite unnerving, I must say. Father was puzzled by it as well and told me to tell you about it and you will understand.

I'm making my best effort to exist here without my tender husband. To be honest, there are times I think it can't be done. Little Jack will be born in three months. No telling what I'll do when he comes. You can rest assured that, whatever it is, it will be the best for our family.

Keep yourself safe for me and Sarah and return to us soon.

Your loving wife in this world and the next,
Abigail

"Do you have any idea who those Indians were?" asked Abel, after Jack read the letter aloud.

"I think so. I have a friend, who is a Choctaw, who lives twenty-five or thirty miles south of my farm," Jack said.

"You're saying that real American Indians live right next to you? I thought the Indians were moved to the reservations."

"We still have some in Tennessee," Jack asserted. "The Chikamaka live in and around the Cumberland Plateau. They're made up of people from several Indian tribes. The Cherokee, Choctaw, Creek, and Mohawk, among others, came together to fight settlers taking their property. For years, they resisted and battled the army, only to lose and withdraw, relinquishing their territory. After the towns of Running Water and Nickajack were destroyed by government troops, the survivors retreated to the hilly terrain of Black Bear Mountain, now known as the South Cumberland Plateau. They pledged to hold that land at all costs, resolving to die in its defense if they could not live there in peace. The Chikamaka remained in their mountainous stronghold, and the US Army lost its enthusiasm to attempt their removal. To do so would be a Pyrrhic victory, and they knew it.

"They assimilated into American society but handed down their own traditions and identity—being ever suspicious of the government and anyone else who trespassed. It was there I first met Yalata. He was recently married to the daughter of a Cherokee chief. The Cherokee are strong on tradition, and Yalata had to be accepted by the entire council before receiving permission to marry Ailana.

"When I showed up, with a deer across my saddle, he welcomed me to sit by his fire. Apparently, it is a traditional requirement to welcome the first visitor after marriage. My folks didn't raise any fools. I told Yalata the deer was a wedding present, and we have been friends ever since.

"While I was living the life of a mountain man, I became a *conductor* for the Underground Railroad. Yalata assured me free and unmolested passage to Caldwell Mountain. In my permitted time, Yalata and I would hunt, fish, and trap animals for fur. I took the pelts to the trading post and split the money with him."

By this time, Lomas Chandler and Ihme Mueller had joined Jack to listen to the discussion about Indians. Lomas was fascinated, having never been beyond his counties' border. While Ihme had never seen an American Indian, he did sail the Atlantic Ocean, shoveling coal into the liner's steam generating furnace. The ship he worked on also had sails, to take advantage of favorable winds. It took over two weeks to reach America. Ihme had a story or two to tell, once his turn came about. John Henry Bickford chose to lie on his cot and sleep.

"I believe the visitors on my farm were Yalata and some of the other braves. He knew I would enlist in the army to fight the Northern invaders and was sizing up the farm to defend Abigail and the property," Jack said assuredly. That night Jack wrote Abigail and repeated his opinion.

August 10, 1861
My Darling Abigail,

Receiving your letter is like the sunrise after a storm. I kiss you every night before I go to sleep and again each morning when I awaken. You please me so much, it makes me a better man. Understanding me proves you are a celestial being who was tricked into marrying a poor mortal.

The Tennessee Brigade has yet to see any action. I confess there are times when I hope it will stay that way. But other times, I wish something would happen to end the boredom. There is one fellow in my group who hates President Lincoln and all Northerners. He also hates the slaves and calls them dumb monkeys. Fortunately, the other men don't share his kind of hatred. He knows I was with the Underground Railroad. Thus far, he doesn't risk criticizing me for it.

I wrote your father, but we moved before it could be mailed. Here, at Big Spring, they pick up mail once a week and take it somewhere else to be mailed. Your father's letter is enclosed with yours.

The Indians you saw must have been Yalata and his braves. Don't be frightened. He probably was sizing up the farm to protect you. When the war is over, you must let me go hunting with him. I don't have any more information to tell you right now. God bless you, Sarah Jane, and the baby on its way.

All my love forever,
Jack

* * *

The Battle of Cheat Mountain

On Tuesday, September 10, 1861, the Tennessee Brigade was alerted to make ready for a march to West Virginia. Their mission will be under the direction of Gen. Robert E. Lee. This will mark the first battle of the

Civil War in which the gentleman general led troops in combat. His objective was to secure the Union-held fort, named Fort Milroy, atop Cheat Summit. The fort offered an excellent view of the surrounding area, including the Staunton-Parkersburg Turnpike, which crossed about one hundred feet below. Union forces began construction of the fort in July, and due to its high elevation, it faced a number of winter-related miseries. Snow began to fall in August, and even horses froze to death by mid-September. Even though it was believed to be impregnable, due to the precipitous descent and dense laurel growth, General Lee devised a complicated plan to attack in a five-column assault. It required complete cooperation from those officers serving under him.

Conditions couldn't have been worse. The summer had been, for the most part, wetter than usual in a normally wet region. Mountain roads were muddy and unserviceable; the streams were overflowing and cold enough for ice to form. Attempts to avoid the soggy mountain roads by traveling through the mountain wilderness promised to offer severe punishment for those who tried.

Such conditions made it almost impossible to feed the Southern soldiers. Supply wagons sunk to their hubs in mud. Many Confederate commanders wished to abandon their entrenchments and move to a more accommodating location. The inclement weather contributed to heavy outbreaks of measles and fever, depriving units of needed manpower. Without food and medical supplies, it was almost impossible to prevent the spread of disease or control such illnesses. In fact, over one-half of Lee's army was too sick to fight. In spite of the present situation, General Lee held firm to his battle plan.

Under the command of Col. Samuel R. Anderson, a Mexican War hero from Davidson County, the Tennessee Brigade moved along the elevations west side and succeeded in securing the turnpike as it crossed the last ridge of Cheat Mountain. They had moved so silently that they surprised unsuspecting Union soldiers and captured them with a successful enclosing maneuver. An inordinate amount of Federal artillery crews where struck from a long distance by Confederate marksmen. A particular sharpshooter hit his targets with a bullet that made a ghostly whistle, finding its mark. Jack Leffingwell used the Whitworth elongated bullet responsible for creating that eerie screech, the sound which frightened recipients knowing they might be killed by someone over a mile away.

Now that the other columns had achieved their positions, all that remained was for Col. Albert Rust, the combative razorback, handy with his cane, to attack the fort. Lee's first step was to reconnoiter the area, but even that simple task became onerous. The Gray Fox could not get General Loring, known as Old Blizzards for his battle cry, to do so. That, in itself, was foreboding enough to have warned Lee of impending disaster. Lee decided to personally search out the routes through the mountains that could flank the fortified Union positions. When the weather broke enough to allow suitable reconnaissance, Lee discovered he could not unite his forces, located on both sides of the mountain, unless they directly attacked the fort itself.

Unfortunately, Rust's assault was doomed from the beginning. He had informed Lee of finding a pathway up the mountain from his own personal reconnaissance of Cheat Summit. It was that information which made Lee decided to attack the fort in the first place. It turned out to be false. For thirty miles, the soldiers under Rust were forced to march single file through the wilderness. By climbing, hacking, and wading, as rain continued to pelt them, they slowly drew near their goal. The troops were hungry and tired and in miserable condition by the time they reached Cheat Summit. Instead of attacking immediately, Rust encountered Federal supply wagons, less than a half mile away. Led by Union colonel Nathan Kimball, they were coming with three hundred men to supply and support the fort. Rust engaged them in the dense woods, lost his nerve, and ordered a retreat. His men willingly retreated, throwing away their rifles and abandoning equipment. All Rusk would say later was that he had become convinced he was facing an overwhelming force. At that point, there was nothing left for Lee to do but pull back to winter quarters.

For his failure at Cheat Mountain, Lee was returned to an advisory position by Jefferson Davis. All his life, Lee had lived with gentle people, where kindly sentiments and consideration for the feelings of others were part of the noblesse oblige. One trait that became clear in his West Virginia operations, and one that would follow him throughout the war, was Lee's inability to discipline rebellious, subordinate officers.

The Tennessee Brigade returned to Big Springs and awaited their next orders. Shortly after their return, they were attached to Gen. Stonewall Jackson's brigade. With Jackson, on January 4, 1862, they participated in the expedition to Bath, Virginia, and destroyed the railroad bridge near that point. Skirmishes were small and loss of life minimal.

Controlling the Shenandoah Valley was of prime importance to General Jackson and the Confederacy.

Jackson drove the Union forces out of Bath and into Hancock, Maryland. Stonewall didn't want to leave Virginia, so he chose not to pursue them. It became the start of what was to be known as Jackson's Romney Campaign.

Later, the Tennessee volunteers went to Winchester, then Yorkville, by way of Fredericksburg. They encountered small losses in the move from Yorkville to Richmond.

Jack and the other sharpshooters had performed admirably at Cheat Mountain and caught the eye of General Jackson. He liked the idea of fighting the enemy a mile away from their lines.

"Corporal Leffingwell?" asked the general's aide.

"Yes," Jack replied.

"Compliments of Gen. Stonewall Jackson," the aide announced as he handed Jack a package. "Will there be an answer?" said the aide.

"Tell the general thank-you," said Jack as he unwrapped the package and held up a telescope.

Abel Strawn walked over as Jack was taking sight of his surroundings through the general's gift. Curiosity got the best of all four marksmen, and they formed a circle around Jack.

"Now what the hell does he want you to do with that?" questioned John Henry.

"I'm not positive, but I think he wants me to find a way to attach it to my rifle," Jack suggested.

* * *

Meanwhile, in Lebanon, Tennessee, a serious conversation was taking place between the Methodist

Church minister, Rev. Joseph Strawn, and a young woman named Amanda, who also shared the minister's surname.

"I haven't heard from Abel since the day he joined the army," the minister disclosed. "You've been a stranger to both me and the church ever since I married you and Abel. What brings you here today?"

Tears began to swell up in the pretty girl's eyes, and she confessed, "Oh, Rev. Strawn, I've been a terrible person. I've dishonored Abel and the church."

The minister placed a consoling arm around her shoulder and said, "Go ahead and cry, it's good for the soul."

And cry she did. It was a long-lasting lamentation, with animallike sounds, as her mournful wailing expelled the pent-up evil with each sob. The minister's handkerchief was useless. He led her to the sink so the cold water might wash the redness from cheeks and eyes.

Returning to a chair, Amanda continued, "I've made love to another while married to Abel."

"Was Abel aware?" he asked.

"Yes, that's why he left and joined the army," she asserted.

"I must ask you again. What brings you here today?"

"I want Abel back. I don't want him to hate me. I want to beg his forgiveness," she wept.

"And this other person, where might he be today?" the minister asked.

"I don't know. When I told him I wouldn't see him anymore, he left town," answered Amanda.

"Perhaps he, too, joined the army," Rev. Strawn conjectured.

"If he did, it will be on the side of the North, he hates the South," she stated.

"Well, daughter, we can't worry about him now. I'll write to my son and explain what has happened. Hopefully, the letter will, somehow, find its way to him. In the meantime, you move in with your parents. It isn't safe to live alone nowadays."

"I don't want to move back home for a lot of reasons," she said. Rev. Strawn didn't ask why; he just said, "Then you move in with my wife and me. After all, Agnes is your mother-in-law."

Living with Abel's parents allowed Amanda to rebuild her self-esteem. It seemed as though her past was only a bad dream and didn't really exist. Attending church, obviously, became second nature, and Amanda grew to enjoy it as part of her new life. Many girls her age found themselves living under similar circumstances. Amanda was soon included among them as their friend. They prayed each day for Abel's safety and to hear from him soon.

Those prayers were answered when the postal carrier delivered the reply to his father's correspondence. All three excitedly gathered in the parlor as Joseph put on his half-rimmed spectacles and read the letter.

October 12, 1861
Dear Father,

Your letter finds me in good health and stationed in Virginia with the Seventh Tennessee regiment. I am part of a five-man sharpshooter team led by a man from Wilson County, named Jack Leffingwell. He is pro-Union and, before he got married, was a conductor in the Underground

Railroad helping runaway slaves find freedom. Something you may know a little about. I've never met a man I admire more, excluding you, sir. He's a true mountain man and here only because Mr. Lincoln sent troops to invade the South.

Remember how I used to win all the turkey shoots and every other shooting contest? Well, I now know that was because Jack Leffingwell wasn't entered. He can hit a target a mile away. He tries to make me feel better by saying it is because of the rifle he got from England, but when we switch rifles, he can still beat me. I am proud to be called his friend.

Amanda knows how I feel about her. If she really cares for me, all is forgiven. Tell her I'll write her first chance I get. Also, tell Mother I love her.

Your obedient son,
Abel

Women weep when they're happy and weep when they're sad. This time the eyes of Agnes and Amanda fill with tears because they are happy.

Chapter Three

Disease was a major factor in the death of Civil War soldiers

Life in the Confederate base camp or, for that matter, any Civil War army camp was susceptible to boredom and disruption, not to mention the constant fear of disease. And as the Mormon inspirational leader, George Quale Cannon is quoted as saying, "For when men labor they keep out of mischief," a constant activity would serve to do just that. The average soldier's day began at five o'clock in the morning when awakened by reveille. After the first sergeant took roll call, the men ate breakfast, and then prepared for their first of as many as five drill sessions during the day. Here the men would learn how to shoot their weapons and perform various maneuvers they may need in battle. Drill sessions lasted approximately two hours each and, for most men, were exceptional exercises in monotony. Regardless, it was believed by officers and military brass to be the best inoculation against potential problems. When the soldiers didn't drill, they cleaned the camp, built roads, dug trenches for latrines, and gathered wood for cooking and heating.

Armies on both sides were constantly on the lookout for clean water, especially when in the field. The lack of potable water was a problem that led to widespread disease. Disease was a major factor in the death of Civil War soldiers. The science of medicine was distressingly, incredibly deficient, and they lived under conditions that were likely to make them sick. There was no chance to get the kind of medical treatment which a few years later would be routine. While the typical soldier's main concern was being killed by an enemy bullet, disease accounted for the demise of three out of five Union combatants and two out of three Confederate fighters. Half of the deaths from disease were caused by intestinal disorders, mainly typhoid fever, diarrhea, and dysentery. Most of the remainder died from pneumonia and tuberculosis. Both governments did their best to provide proper medical care for their soldiers; thus far, even the best was not very good.

In the beginning of the war, soldiers were fed relatively well. Their daily ration in 1861 included at least twenty ounces of fresh or salt beef, or twelve ounces of salt pork; more than a pound of flour; and a vegetable, usually beans. Coffee, salt, vinegar, and sugar were provided as well. When armies were moving fast and supply trains could not reach them in the field, supplies became limited. In the field, soldiers saw very little beef and only a few vegetables. They subsisted on salt pork, dried beans, corn bread, and hardtack, a flour, and water biscuit. Hardtack became the food of last resort if nothing else was available. The biscuits were often infested with maggots and weevils after storage. When hard-pressed, soldiers would dunk them in hot coffee and, when the insects floated to the surface, brush them away. Outbreaks of scurvy were common due to a frequent lack of fresh fruits and vegetables.

In the minds of the soldiers, coffee was, by far, the most important staple. Men pounded the beans between rocks or crushed them with the butts of their rifles to obtain grounds with which to brew the strong pick-me-up. Although most Federals were well-supplied with coffee, the Confederates were often forced to make do with substitutes made from peanuts, potatoes, peas, and chicory.

Army regulations called for the camps to be laid out in a fixed grid pattern, with officers' quarters at the front end of each street and enlisted men's quarters aligned to the rear. The camp was arranged along the lines the unit would form when engaged in battle, with each company displaying its colors on the outside of its tents. Regulations also defined where the mess tents, medical cabins, and baggage trains should be located. Often, however, lack of time or a particular hilly or narrow terrain made it impossible to meet army regulations. The campgrounds themselves were often appalling, especially in the South where wet weather produced thick mud for extended periods in the spring and summer; in the winter and fall, the mud turned to dust.

* * *

Jack Leffingwell and the other marksmen occupied a tent designed to accommodate six soldiers. In the summer, most troops slept in canvas tents. At the beginning of the war, both armies used the Sibley tent, named for its inventor, Henry H. Sibley, who later became a Confederate brigadier general. He was probably influenced by the Great Plains American Indian tepee, since his design consisted of a large cone of canvas, eighteen feet in diameter, twelve feet tall, and supported by a center pole. The tent had a circular opening at the top for ventilation and a cone-shaped stove for heat. Although designed to fit a dozen men comfortably, army regulations, in its wisdom, assigned about twenty men to each tent, leading to cramped, uncomfortable quarters. When ventilation flaps were closed on cold or rainy days, the air inside the tent became fetid with the odors of men who had limited access to clean water in which to bathe. For the more hardy souls, a fast-moving creek served as the bathtub; however, that also was subject to good fortune if one happened to be located nearby. As the war dragged on, the Sibley was replaced with smaller tents. The Union army favored the wedge tent, a six-foot length of canvas, draped over a horizontal ridgepole, and staked to the ground at the sides, with flaps that closed off one end. Southern forces also found it necessary to change to a smaller shelter. Federal blockades limited imports of many essential items, and as canvas became scarce in the South, lots of Confederate soldiers rigged open-air beds of straw or leaves.

Winter has taken root and nights have become frosty, requiring some mode of external heat, in order to prevent hypothermia. The marksmen have it better than most. In the corner of their tent resides a Franklin stove, a generous gift from Lomas Chandler. When asked how he came by the stove, Lomas told them he won it in a poker game. In an intimation of disbelief, the others accepted his answer. No one was willing to challenge him on it and lose such a wonderful furnace during the Virginia winter. Ihme Mueller had engineered a smoke stack and manual damper, and the dwelling could be maintained quite warm with a minimal amount of kindling. Jack Leffingwell was probably the most suspicious of the gift, but it allowed his feet to warm up and that was enough to assure his silence. The Tennessee mountain man was also basking in the warm glow of the news of his newborn son. All who knew him had shook his hand and extended sincere compliments. Abigail's letter had been opened and reopened several times since he received it, and as he lay back on his cot, Jack prepared to read it once more.

November 12, 1861
Dearest Jack,

Congratulations, dear husband, you are the father of a beautiful baby boy. I've named him Jack Junior. You'll be pleased to know he was born in the house his father built. Minnie Rosenthal helped me a great deal, and Father and Old Dr. Campbell were there as well. Young Dr. Campbell is off somewhere in the war. I've gotten most of my strength back, but Grandma Minnie still won't let me do much by myself. Praise Jesus, I'm the only one that can nurse Little Jack.

They now post the names, at the post office, of those killed. It's a frightening thing and makes me want you home now. Father keeps telling me the Lord will protect you by the amount of faith we have in him. I find myself on my knees more than once each day. Father's Sunday sermon was about being prepared. He thinks the Union army will soon be in Tennessee. I hope for once he is wrong.

No sign of Indians since that first day. There are times, though, when I feel as if I'm being watched. It's kind of spooky.

Words can't describe how much I miss you, Jack. I miss your touch, I miss your smell, and I miss the way I feel with you in bed at night. I think I'm blushing.

Your faithful wife,
Abigail

"Have you written back to your wife?" asked Abel.

"Not yet. I need to get some paper and envelope," Jack replied.

"Don't trouble yourself, Jack, I'll get what you need tomorrow," Lomas offered.

"I appreciate the offer, Lomas, but I need to go to the commissary anyway for other things." He liked Lomas, yet there always seemed to be a little larceny whenever he got involved. "Was that thunder I just heard?"

"I think you're right. We're going to get some more rain," Abel said as he gathered the catch basins to capture rainwater. Rainwater is God's gift from nature, and the men planned to use it for shaving and, most important of all, make coffee in the morning.

"Looks like it's going to rain all night," Abel conveyed as he shook off water after returning to the tent. "We might as well just relax because we sure aren't going anywhere tonight. How about you, Lomas, are you playing poker?"

"Naw, I think I'll give it a rest. The boys are kind of upset with me at the moment. They even went as far as accusing me of cheating."

That brought smiles to those who heard him. The sound of raindrops pattering overhead gave a soothing accompaniment to the scene of five Southern men relaxing on their cots. Thoughts of war were in abeyance as the wick of their lantern emitted comforting illumination and corresponding shadows against the walls. Once each man was occupied with his individual thoughts, John Henry arose from his folding bed and approached Jack.

"You said you needed this," he stated dispassionately and handed Jack writing paper and an envelope.

"Thanks, John Henry, I'll pay you back tomorrow."

Of all people, under that roof, John Henry was the last one Jack expected to offer anything out of pure goodness. He knew John Henry would rather not have him praise this act of kindness, so Jack spoke no further. A few moments later, the mountain man from Tennessee sat up and took pencil in hand and began to write his wife.

December 21, 1861
My Darling Wife,

You have made me the proudest soldier in the Southern army. It's been said that a man has earned the right to howl at the moon for three reasons: the day when he has successfully completed the most important job he has ever undertaken, the day he gets married to the woman he loves, and the day his son is born. Because of you, I have howled three times. The first two I kind of kept to myself for fear of scaring you half to death. The latter, my sweet, got the attention of the entire camp. My day was filled with slaps on my back and handshakes until my hand got so tired I could no longer grip another.

As you know, I view my absence as God's will. Little Jack must wait a bit longer before he meets his father, but please tell him how much I love him. Your father must be fit to be tied. I'm confident Little Jack will get to know his grandfather very well.

Thank Minnie Rosenthal for me. It would please me greatly if she stayed with us rather than travel between each other's farm. She must be a comfort to you, and we love having her with us. She's just like family.

Not much is happening here since General Jackson's expedition to Bath, Virginal. We spend our time practicing and doing drills. Being a marksman pays dividends. We only drill once a day, and the rest of the time is spent at target practice.

It seems colder in Virginia than Tennessee. There is a lot more rain here as well. We will have services on Christmas and probably sing hymns. Nothing like our celebrations at home with your father and Minnie Rosenthal.

The fellows want to hit the hay, so I'll turn down the lamp and close for now. Just remember, my empty arms remind me that I need you as I need breath. Give Sarah and Little Jack a kiss for me.

Your loving husband,
Jack

On February 24, 1862, the Seventh regiment was ordered to Manassas, Virginia, and was joined by the First and Fourteenth from Tennessee. These three Tennessee regiments remained in the same brigade throughout the war, being the only Tennessee regiments to spend their entire term of service in the Virginia Theater. The march was about sixty miles as the crow flies, but considering the terrain and travel routes, it amounted to more. Thomas Jefferson is quoted as saying, "The sovereign invigorator of the body is exercise, and of all the exercises walking is the best." The cadre of those soldiers now marching would beg to differ with him. It rained most of the journey, further making the junket more unpleasant.

* * *

The diverse climate of Virginia has five different regions. They are the Tidewater, Piedmont, Northern Virginia, Western Mountain, and Southwestern Mountain. Some areas, for example, have long growing seasons and rarely winter temperatures below zero, while winters on the northern Blue Ridge frequently produce bitterly cold temperatures like those in the North. Annual rainfall totals vary from a sparse thirty-three inches in the Shenandoah Valley to more than sixty in the Southwestern Mountains.

Virginia's climate results from global weather patterns that are modified by the state's diverse landscape. The Atlantic Ocean and its river of warm water, commonly called the Gulf Stream, play a dominant role in differentiating amounts of precipitation. Winter storms generally move, or track, from west to east and, in the vicinity of the east coast, move northeastward paralleling the coast and the Gulf Stream. This shift northeast results, in part, from the tendency of the storm to follow a pathway between the cold land and the warm Gulf Stream waters. When this occurs, moisture-laden air crosses Virginia from the east and northeast. The eastern slopes and foothills of the Blue Ridge Mountains are the principal recipients of the moisture. Such storms can also produce record snowfalls along the northern section of the Blue Ridge.

The high-reaching Appalachian and Blue Ridge mountain systems also help to control Virginia's climate. Their influence originates with a similar rainfall pattern, evident along the mighty mountains of the far western part of North America. Great quantities of rain fall on these western slopes as moist air from the Pacific Ocean flows eastward, rises, condenses, and precipitates. As the air flows down over the eastern gradients, very little rain falls and a rain shadow pattern results. A rain shadow is a dry area on the lee side of a mountainous area. The mountains block the passage of rain-producing weather systems, casting a *shadow* of dryness behind them. As the warm moist air is pulled by the prevailing winds over a mountain, it condenses and precipitates on the top or windward side. The air then descends on the leeward side but has lost much of its initial moisture, leaving a rain shadow behind the mountain. Sometimes the airflow originates from the east creating rain shadows on the other side of the mountains. Either situation makes the Shenandoah River valleys the driest portions of the state. When the airflow is from the west, the valley is in the rain shadow of the Appalachian Mountain; when the airflow is from the east, the valley is in the shadow of the Blue Ridge Mountains.

The complex pattern of rivers and streams drain the precipitation and modify the pattern of moist airflow. These river systems drain Virginia's terrain in all four directions. Depending on the direction each river or stream flows will determine the influence it has on rainfall. An upward movement of airflow over river drainage could increase rainfall as the elevation rises.

Much of the Commonwealth rainfall results from storms associated with warm and cold fronts. Storms mostly move parallel to the Appalachian or the Blue Ridge Mountains, the coastal zone, and the Gulf Stream, all of which have a northeast trend. When sufficient cold air invades Virginia from the west and northwest, frontal storms may cause heavy snowfalls. The average winter does not have a major coastal snowstorm, and heavy winter snows usually are confined to the mountainous areas of the state. Some of the heaviest snowfalls in the Eastern United States occur in the Appalachians of West Virginia, just a few miles west of Virginia. More than one hundred inches fall annually in this area; but Virginia, being in West Virginia's snow shadow, receives only a fraction of this amount.

Virginia is also the recipient of an occasional hurricane and tropical storm. Such storms derive most of their energy from the warm ocean surface. Once reaching Virginia, these storms move in a general northeasterly track and, like frontal storms as they move along this route, intensify. They rarely appear before June or after November, known as the hurricane season.

Thunderstorms occur in every month of the year although most common in the moist, warm air of summer. And they are most likely to occur during the warmest part of the day, usually beginning in late afternoon until after midnight.*

* * *

The hike to Manassas was accompanied by either rain or drizzle most of the way. Temperatures rarely got above forty degrees during the day and thirty at night. Because of mired roads, the soldiers walked on the grassy edges; however, supply trains were bogged down and unable to keep up with the column. This meant food supplies were in short order and limited to what was carried by the troops. That, unfortunately, consisted mainly of hardtack. Under better weather conditions, it would have been possible for the soldiers to live off the land, albeit, not at present. At the end of each day, when the troops made camp, attempts were made to gather wood and start a fire. Tents were always a few miles behind and ingenuity resulted in crude shelters being made using rain slickers and outer clothing placed on top of a tree branch framework. Once a fire got started, the luckier soldiers were able to dry out and keep warm. Jack Leffingwell had real-life experience in such situations, and he and the marksmen shared an enviable overhead shelter.

---

* *(Reference Virginia's Climate by Bruce P. Haden and Patrick J. Michaels/ University of Virginia Climatology Office/climate@virginia.edu)*

"I should have joined the cavalry," John Henry said gravely. "They at least get to ride on these marches."

"That wouldn't work for me," returned Lomas, "I'm afraid of horses."

"I was on a horse ever since I was three years old. My father believed you weren't a gentleman unless you could ride," John Henry replied.

While the men sat under the protection of their rain shield awning, the fire smoldered until it reached the intensity so that, when another log was placed on top, it sizzled and spit until dry enough to burst into a glowing flame. And as the rain sprinkled, in a steady fashion, Abel placed billycans under runoffs to catch plenty of drinking water.

"If we had some coffee, we could boil the water over our fire," Abel said hoarsely.

"I got some coffee," Lomas responded while rummaging in his knapsack.

"Lomas, you never cease to amaze me," Jack said laughingly.

"Hell, that's nothing, Jack, I even got some tinned meats and candy for dessert. That ought to make the hardtack taste better."

"With a feast like that, we probably won't even eat the hardtack. Dare I ask how you came by all this?"

"Don't ask," Lomas said firmly.

Lomas obviously came by these things from the sutler, a civilian provisioner, attached to the army post at the previous camp. Sutlers are purveyors of all goods not issued by the army. They offer tobacco, candy, tinned meats, shoelaces, patent medicines, fried pies, and newspapers. Sutlers were known for their steep prices; regardless, soldiers desperate for cigarettes, sweets, and news from home were willing to use their pay for these treats. Everyone knew Lomas didn't purchase these items, so the question as to how he came by them was left unanswered. That night, five well-fed fighting men relaxed, some with another item provided by Lomas Chandler—tobacco.

"Why did you ever join the army, Lomas?" asked Abel Strawn.

"It was kind of a matter of convenience most of all. Things were getting a little hot for me back home. It got so I was being blamed for anything that went wrong or got stolen. I'm not saying I never did any of those things, but I sure as hell didn't do all of them. The time had come for me to change the scenery, and Abe Lincoln gave me the answer when he sent in the Yankee troops and Tennessee seceded from the Union. I figured I could enlist and keep out of any danger. Guess I was wrong with that one."

"How about you, John Henry. What made you end up here with us?"

In spite of not liking the way the question was posed, John Henry, usually reluctant to commit to conversation, said the following, "I'm sure as hell not here to free the slaves. We have slaves. In fact, as far back as I can remember, my father had slaves and treated them right, as long as they didn't act up. The Bickfords have been a well-respected family in Tennessee for generations. Someone had to join up if only to keep up our reputation. My father was getting old and needed to stay home and run the plantation. The responsibility fell on me. I refused to go. My father insisted."

"With the importance of your family and all, how come you didn't join up as an officer?"

"I had a commission. My father bought it for me. I rejected it just to embarrass him."

Jack Leffingwell looked up and said, "Back home we call that cutting off your nose to spite your face."

"Looking at it that way, you might be right. I comfort myself knowing people will talk about it and say, 'What kind of a father would send his only son to war without an officer's commission?'"

"Looks like the rain has stopped," said Abel. "We better get some shut-eye before they blow reveille."

They all chimed in to say, "Thanks for the tinned meat, Lomas."

Sleep comes easy to those with a pure heart. Not every sharpshooter shares such a status, but as Benjamin Franklin is quoted, "Fatigue is the best pillow," and they all are painted with that broad brush.

At five o'clock in the morning, the buglers blaring reveille wakened over a thousand men. The sharpshooters stirred, used the latrine, and prepared for roll call. As expected, breakfast was spare and a good meal won't be anticipated until the supply wagons catch up. Unless, of course, Lomas Chandler had more surprises up his sleeve. Today the morning fare was hot black coffee and hardtack. That is, until Lomas Chandler showed up and whispered, "Don't let anybody see these or I'll have the whole army after my ass."

With that, several fried pies were divided among the occupants of last night's shelter. In the South, fried pies were known as crab lanterns and popular in nearly every Southern kitchen. Lomas Chandler was the purveyor of pies made with peaches, perhaps the tastiest of all. Conversation was limited as the Confederate sharpshooters savored the taste of their flavorful endowment.

With breakfast over, the brigade was back on the route to Manassas. The rainclouds separated and a brilliant sun beamed overhead, uplifting the enthusiasm to the point that the column broke out in song. They sang their favorite marching song, and when it came to "In Dixie Land I'll take my stand / to live and die in Dixie," soldiers seemed to shout the words. "Dixie" was the most popular song for Confederate soldiers on the march, in battle, and at camp. The song was also a favorite of President Abraham Lincoln; he asked that it be played at some of his political rallies in spite of it raising the feathers on some of his constituents.

Chapter Four

First major battle of the war was Manassas, also called Bull Run by the Union

After sending troops into the South, resulting in Confederate secession, President Lincoln took executive control of the hostilities and sought an overall strategy to put down the rebellion quickly. As commander-in-chief, he took it upon himself to employ unprecedented powers. They included disbursing funds before appropriation by Congress, suspending habeas corpus, and the arrest and imprisonment of thousands of suspected Confederate sympathizers. In all these cases, he was supported by Congress and the Northern public.

Lincoln imposed a blockade on all the Confederate shipping ports, a concept devised by Gen. Winfield Scott, the seventy-four-year-old general-in-chief designed to win the war with as little bloodshed as possible. Scott's plan called for a Union blockade of the main ports which would weaken the Confederate economy. Once that was affected, Scott purposed the capture of the Mississippi River which would split the South. Lincoln overruled Scott's warnings that his new army was not ready for an offensive operation because public opinion demanded an immediate attack.

In terms of war strategy, Lincoln articulated two priorities: ensure that Washington was well defended and conduct an aggressive war effort that would solidify the demand in the North for prompt, decisive victory. Major Northern newspaper editors actually expected victory in ninety days. He also knew that to communicate better with his generals, he had to be familiar with the nomenclature and tactics of war. To learn the technical military terms, Lincoln borrowed and studied *Elements of Military Art and Science* from the Library of Congress. No matter how competent he became in this area, he failed to gain the respect of many of his top generals.

Lincoln appointed Gen. Irvin McDowell to command the Army of Northeastern Virginia and pressed Gen. Winfield Scott, his superior officer, to order him to advance on Confederate troops stationed at Manassas Junction. Educated at the College de Troyes, in France, before graduating from West Point, McDowell never before commanded troops in combat and was concerned about the untried nature of his army. In addition, the native Ohioan may have been somewhat unsure of his own ability. Nevertheless, he was reassured by President Lincoln, himself beleaguered by impatient politicians and citizens in Washington, wishing to see a quick battlefield victory over the Confederate army.

"You're green, it is true, but they are green also! You are all green alike," reassured Lincoln.

Against his better judgment, McDowell commenced the campaign and departed Washington with the largest field army yet gathered—about thirty-five thousand men.

Initially, the attack was successful; but after Confederate reinforcements were introduced, the South won the day. McDowell's army retreated in a chaotic fashion, running in the direction of Washington.

General McDowell was replaced. And the aged Winfield Scott retired. Lincoln, suddenly aware of the threat of a protracted war and the army's need for organization and training, appointed Gen. George B. McClellan general-in-chief. That turned out to be another disappointment for the embattled president. McClellan took several months to plan and attempt his Peninsula Campaign, much longer than Lincoln wanted. The plan was to capture Richmond by moving the Army of the Potomac by boat to the peninsula and then overland to the Confederate Capital. McClellan's repeated delays frustrated not only Lincoln but the Congress as well.

Another point of contention was McClellan's stance that no troops were needed to defend Washington. Lincoln insisted on holding some of the troops in defense of the capital. McClellan considered the president a fool and lean-witted and continued to drill and train the soldiery, consistently overestimating the strength of Confederate troops.

Lincoln finally had enough. The Army of the Potomac and the western forces, under McClellan's command, accomplished very little, at a time when action was paramount. As the winter wore on, Lincoln and the Union waited impatiently for a conclusive engagement. McClellan showed no inclination to move. In an effort to push matters, Lincoln issued General War Order No. 1 on January 27, 1862. This order, besides unnecessarily telling the armies to obey orders, directed that a general movement of land and sea forces against the Confederacy be launched on February 22, 1862. Many thought he issued such an order only to get McClellan off the dime.

* * *

The Seventh Tennessee regiment reached the Manassas camp the first part of March and spent the rest of the winter training and preparing for battle. Once again, their quarters were a canvas tent designed to accommodate six persons. With only five in the team, the extra room made for additional creature comfort. Daytime temperatures were now in the upper forties; however, at night it bordered on freezing. Ihme Mueller had constructed a crude wood burning firebox out of discarded pots and pans—not as functional as a Franklin stove, yet capable of removing the nighttime chill.

Most of the camp news was only rumor, and soldiers learned about the war in letters from home. That, too, was sometimes sketchy, due to movement of the brigades and combat interruptions of mail delivery.

Now, at day's end, Jack Leffingwell sat up on his cot and penned a letter to Abigail. It's been said that a soldier writes three letters for every one he receives, which is understandable, considering the amount of time he has on his hands when not actually engaged in combat. The others cleaned and oiled their weapons, a frequent activity and obligation of the riflemen.

"How come you're not playing poker?" Ihme asked Lomas. "Can't you find a game?"

"There are plenty of games, Ihme, but I have to find the right one," replied Lomas. "You see, my daddy always told me that in every poker game, there's a patsy. After a half hour, if you don't know who the patsy is, you're the patsy. I'm always looking for a game with more than one patsy."

"Did you fine one?"

"Sure did, but they're not playing tonight. I think everybody is out trying to borrow more money. We're going to play again tomorrow."

"What do you do with all your winnings?" Abel asked.

"Oh, when it begins to pile up, I send it to my mother," Lomas stated frankly.

His answer seemed to satisfy the rest, since they already concluded that an Irish boy would do just that. No other ethnic group is so closely identified with the Civil War and the immediate aftermath as Irish Americans. Over one hundred fifty thousand joined the Union army. Statistics for those joining the Confederacy is unclear. We know for sure that a great deal of the South was settled by Irish immigrants, and it stands to reason, many enlisted to defend their newfound homeland. In the North, centers of Irish settlements were primarily the larger cities, i.e., Boston and New York. During the Civil War, over one-half million Americans claimed to have been born in Ireland. The Irish faced periods of severe economic difficulties. Especially when the new immigrants were singled out for the distrust and hatred of their fellow Americans; No Irish Need Apply was a frequently seen placard above the doors of factories, shops, warehouses, and farms.

The Irish were primarily distrusted because they were Catholic, and there was much opposition in the country to the Church of Rome. This prejudice led indirectly to the boil-over of tempers in July 1863 when the first official draft was held in the North. A crowd of mostly immigrant laborers gathered at the site of the draft lottery. As names were called, and those not wealthy enough to purchase a substitute were required to join up, the mob's temper flared. Full-scale rioting lasted for three days, with larger cities caught up in a rampage of looting, burning, and destruction. Most rioters were frustrated Irish laborers who could not get jobs; and their targets were draft officials, as well as free blacks living in the North, who seemed able to get jobs that the Irish were denied. Armed troops were required to leave the fighting at Gettysburg to bring the cities back to peace and quiet. Such events did little to help the image of the Irish in America until years after the war, and an inordinate length of time before ugly anti-Irish prejudice faded.

"Hey, Lomas, did you know our Lord was Irish?" John Henry asked with a smile.

"How do you figure that?" returned Lomas.

"Well, he was thirty years old, not married, and still lived with his mother."

When the good-natured kidding was over, Lomas said, "I could have got married lots of times. I just couldn't find the right girl. Every time I thought I found her, another would show up and I decided I wanted her instead." Turning to Jack, Lomas asked, "How do you know if it's the right girl?"

"I knew the very first time I saw Abigail," Jack replied. "I could never get her off my mind. I could be chewing on a twig, sitting on a riverbank, with my line in the water, and never stop thinking how lucky I am to be married to her. Don't get me wrong, I still am a man and enjoy looking at a pretty filly as much as the next guy, but there is no chance she could ever take the place of Abigail."

"Someday I hope to meet a colleen who's a real steph. I think then I can be faithful to one woman," Lomas insisted.

"What's a steph?" Abel asked.

"Glad you asked. A steph is the most amazing, beautiful, and irresistible girl you will ever meet. She has a heart of gold, will never let you down, and stays loyal for life. You can call at 2:00 a.m., and no matter what she is doing, she will be by your side in five minutes. She is always the life of the party, makes everyone laugh, and is ready to go out and have a good time at a moment's notice. Once you meet a steph, you will love her forever."

"I got some bad news for you, Lomas. You ain't ever going to get married," John Henry added.

Jack went back to writing his letter to his wife.

March 2, 1862
Dearest Abigail,

I learned a new word today. It's Irish and describes you to a tee. The word is steph, and it means beautiful girl, among other things, that I'll tell you when I get home. We are now stationed at Manassas, Virginia. It took about a week to walk here, and the weather was undesirable most of the way. The last day things brightened up, and we sang songs the rest of the way. It made me proud to be part of these men. Our news is mostly rumors, so you can't believe everything you hear. They tell me we can buy a newspaper at the sutler's shop. I'll probably pick one up tomorrow.

I'm so very sorry Sarah Jane and Little Jack don't have me to help you raise them. I know you are doing a fine job, but it bothers me nevertheless. It's been so quiet the last few weeks, you never can tell there's a war going on. I can't complain about not fighting though. It's a whole lot safer this way. They tell me that Col. Robert Hatton will be promoted to brigadier general and take command of the Tennessee regiment. He's a good old boy from Lebanon, Tennessee, and well-liked by all. If he gets the promotion, it will make all of us happy.

I got a letter from your father last week. He seems to be holding up under it all. He went on and on about his grandchildren. Next to you, I believe he is my best friend. He treated me so well from the first day we met.

Write me soon, sweetheart. I live for your letters, and don't worry about their delivery, just keep them coming.

With eternal love,
Jack

The Tennessee regiment in Virginia was unaware of most of the activities taking place back home. And to a large extent, a major portion of the battles took place there; only Virginia saw more. Tennessee was also the last of the Southern states to declare secession from the Union. Even then, the state remained divided on the decision. Prior to Abraham Lincoln's call to send seventy-five thousand Northern troops into the South, Tennessee was pro-Union. All noise to secede was voted down by a large margin. Only after Lincoln's action did a majority vote take place. The people in East Tennessee continued to be firmly against the move to leave the Union and remained loyal. Thus, Tennessee, and its torn allegiance, became the northern border to the newly formed Confederacy.

Defending Tennessee was of extreme importance because of its rivers and railroads. Roads were virtually impassable in winter, and the lines of internal communication mostly came from either water or rail. In addition, the state had a heavy reliance on northbound riverboats to receive staple commodities from the Cumberland and Tennessee valleys. The responsibility of protecting Tennessee, as well as a five-hundred-mile line extending from western Virginia to the border of Kansas, fell upon Jefferson Davis's appointee, Gen. Albert Sidney Johnston. To protect a lateral railroad, where it crossed two rivers in Tennessee, and yet respect Kentucky's neutrality, the Confederates had built Fort Henry on the Tennessee River and Fort Donelson on the Cumberland River, just south of the boundary between the two states. The idea of using the rivers to breach the Confederate defense line in the West was well-known; Union gunboats had been scanning Confederate fort-building on the twin rivers for months before the campaign.

The Battle of Forts Henry and Donelson

Brig. Gen. Ulysses S. Grant, at the time an inconspicuous district commander at Cairo, Illinois, had, meanwhile, proposed a river expedition up the Tennessee to take Fort Henry. After some hesitancy on the part of Gen. Henry Halleck, a plan was approved for a joint army-navy expedition consisting of fifteen thousand men, under Grant, and supported by armored gunboats and river craft of the U.S. Navy, under Flag Officer Andrew H. Foote, to "take and hold Fort Henry." While President Lincoln prodded and squabbled with General McClellan to take action in Virginia, the Union war machine was finally on the move in the west.

Grant moved Union forces, on river transports, down the Mississippi River and landed his troops below Fort Henry and, together with Foote's naval force, advanced against the Confederate position. The fort was poorly situated on a floodplain and virtually indefensible against gun boats, with many of its guns underwater. As Grant approached, the Confederate commander sent most of his men to Fort Donelson. Muddy roads delayed Grant's advance; nevertheless, Foote plunged ahead with seven heavily armed gunboats and, in a short firefight, instigated the defenders of Fort Henry to surrender. The fort's colors were lowered before Grant's infantry reached the action. The Tennessee River now lay open and unimpeded to Federal gunboats all the way to northern Alabama.

Fort Donelson, on the Cumberland River, was more defensible than Henry; and Foote's navy assaults on the fort were ineffective. After receiving considerable damage, the gunboats withdrew. Grant realized that any success at Donelson would have to be carried by the army without strong naval support. Any conquest will mainly require action on land. Grant's army marched cross-country and attempted immediate assaults on the fort from the rear. They, too, were unsuccessful. From all indications, it looked to Grant that in order to take the fort, he may have to revert to a siege or a military blockade of the fortress and the area around it.

Grant recovered from the temporary reversal and was able to rally his troops and resume the offensive. In addition, the initial fifteen thousand Union troop strength was increased by ten thousand reinforcements. Although the weather had been mostly wet up to this point in the campaign, a snowstorm arrived the night of February 13, with strong winds, bringing temperatures down to ten degrees and depositing three inches of snow by morning. Guns and wagons were frozen to the earth. Because of the proximity of the enemy lines and the active sharpshooters, the soldiers could not light campfires for warmth or cooking; and both sides were miserable that night, many having arrived without blankets or overcoats.

Despite their unexpected naval success, the Confederate generals were still gloomy about their chances of holding the fort. In another late-night council of war, they decided to try their escape plan. On the morning of February 15, the Confederates launched a dawn assault on the still-unprotected right flank of the Union line. The attack started well, and after two hours of heavy fighting, men were able to push Federals out of the way and open the escape route. For the first time in the West, Union soldiers heard the famous and unnerving rebel yell. Even though Confederate general Pillow saw that his attack was successful and the escape route open, he believed he should regroup and resupply his wing before pushing forward and, to the amazement of the other commanding officers, ordered his men back to their trenches. Fearing the Union soldiers were being heavily reinforced, Generals Floyd and Buckner ordered the entire force back inside the lines of Fort Donelson.

The Confederate hesitation allowed General Grant to seize the moment and retake the ground lost that morning. By nightfall, rebel troops were driven back to their original positions. Grant began planning to resume his assault in the morning, however, for some unexplained reason, neglected to close the escape route that was opened earlier.

Nearly one thousand soldiers on both sides had been killed, with about three thousand wounded still in the field; some froze to death in the snowstorm due to the aforementioned lack of proper clothing.

Initially, the Confederate generals were happy about the day's performance and considered it a victory. As the day wore on, their resolve began to weaken. Thinking of consequences of Union reinforcements and another full-scale attack, they determined such an event would result in over 75 percent casualties. Any large-scale escape would be difficult, since most of the river transports were currently conveying wounded men to Nashville and would not return in time to evacuate the command. The next scenes were reminiscent of a Max Sennett slapstick comedy. General Floyd realized that he was about to be captured and would probably be tried for his alleged previous misconduct by the North. He promptly turned over his command to General Pillow, who also feared Northern reprisals. Pillow passed it, in turn, to General Buckner, who had no choice but agree to remain behind and surrender the army. Pillow quickly bid his adieu and escaped in a small boat across the Cumberland during the night. Floyd hightailed it the next morning on the only steamer available, taking his two regiments with him. Disgusted at the show of cowardice, a furious Nathan Bedford Forrest announced, "I did not come here to surrender my command." He stormed out of the meeting and led about seven hundred of his cavalrymen to escape the fort. Forrest's horsemen rode toward Nashville through the shallow icy waters of Lick Creek, encountering no enemy and confirming that many more could have escaped by the same route, if guards were not posted to prevent any such attempts.

Buckner agreed to surrender the garrison with twelve to fifteen thousand troops and its forty-eight artillery pieces. Capture of Forts Henry and Donelson were the first significant Union victories in the war and opened two great rivers as avenues of invasion to the heartland of the South. Grant was promoted to major general, second only to Henry W. Halleck in the Western theater.

* * *

The usual ennui of the Manassas, Virginia, base camp was relieved and abuzz with the rumor about Robert H. Hatton being promoted to brigadier general and assigned to head up the Tennessee regiment. Though born in Ohio, early in his life, his family moved to Tennessee. He graduated from the Cumberland University and School of Law and, after passing the bar exam in 1850, established a successful practice in Lebanon, Tennessee.

Hatton believed that the Union should be preserved and initially opposed secession. However, after President Abraham Lincoln called for volunteers to invade the Southern states, Hatton took umbrage, changed his position, and formed a Confederate military unit, the Lebanon Blues, which became a part of the Seventh Tennessee.

He and his wife Sophie attended the Methodist Church in Lebanon and were an outstanding and well-respected family in the community. A Methodist of the strictest order, Hatton had an aversion to both dance and drink. After an unsuccessful run for governor, Hatton was elected to the Thirty-sixth Congress of the United States and served as chairman of the Committee on Expenditures in the Department of the Navy.

"Colonel Hatton is from your hometown. Do you know him personally?" Jack Leffingwell asked Abel Strawn.

"I don't, but my father does. The Hatton family attends our church, and his wife is on some of the ladies' committees. They're good people and well-liked by everybody. He comes from a church background, his father is also a Methodist minister. You can sure tell because he never misses a chance to stand in the pulpit. I guess he was sick when he was young and darn near died. It left him with a slight twitch in the corner of his mouth. If he gets worked up, he needs a handkerchief to wipe the spittle."

"Sometimes you can get ahead of yourself when you talk, and it causes you to stutter," Lomas added.

"Don't get me wrong, Colonel Hatton is a very good speaker and doesn't stutter. It's just a twinge at the corner of his mouth."

Jack was smiling when he added, "The Bible says Moses had a speech impediment. When God told him to free the Israelites from slavery in Egypt, Moses replied, 'But my Lord, never in my life have I been a man of eloquence, either before or since you have spoken to your servant. I am a slow speaker and not able to speak well' [Exodus 4:10]."

"Damn it, I didn't say he had a speech impediment. I said he had a tic, like a nervous disorder at the corner of his mouth."

"Yeah, in Germany, I too knew a man who also stuttered all the time," Ihme replied jokingly.

"The hell with you guys, you'll find out on your own," Abel shouted and walked outside to cool off. A fine mist of rain had started, and with the wind picking up, it made him squint as he searched the sky to see how severe the pending storm will be.

A canvas tent isn't the best protection in a storm with high winds, and the sharpshooters collectively held on to their fluttering domicile and managed to keep it grounded. The same couldn't be said for many others when their shelter took to the air and was carried away. Some soldiers had to double up until their tents were found or replaced. Others slept in the open air and hoped it didn't rain again until more suitable accommodations were found.

Because of the storm damage, morning drills were cancelled. The troops were set about to locate and replace missing tents and, like always, patrol and clean up debris. After dinner, the soldiers were expected to make good use of their time, and reveille will recommence at five in the morning.

Once he saw that Mason Poor had a newspaper in his bedroll, Jack became an advocate for offering emergency use of their tent. Lomas wanted to charge him rent by the day, but was voted down. John Henry claimed they didn't have the room. Abel knew the Poor family. They lived on a small farm outside of town. Wilson, the father, raised seven children, five boys and two girls, on fifty acres and a garden. He and his wife, Molly, lived under reduced circumstances most of the time and labored just to keep the wolf from the door. The girls were always quiet, but had singular beauty, mostly hidden by flowered dresses made from feed sacks, patterned just for that purpose.

The family came to church every Sunday and brought something either cooked by the women or handmade by the men. Many times, such items were either sold or bartered outside the sanctuary. Molly Poor's pies were a favorite among the more affluent parishioners, and Wilson and his sons crafted brooms, an item every household required. Each year, a couple acres were set aside for sorghum or broom corn. The plant is an annual and, from a distance, looks like sweet corn in the field. Upon closer examination, there are no cobs, just a large tassel on the top. That tassel is the part of the plant used for making brooms.

Many homes still cooked in a huge fireplace. Wood had to be carried in for the fire, and the ashes had to be carried out. In between, the fire required tending to provide just the right flame, coal, and heat. All in all, it's a big and messy job. A good broom was an important tool in keeping the hearth area clean. The Poor family made excellent sweepers; in fact, nearly every household in Lebanon had at least one made by Mason or his sons. Due to the nature of the raw material and the manner in which it's used, brooms wear out—a problem easily rectified the next Sunday at church. Ten percent of the proceeds were donated to the church and the remainder used to buy seed and help the Poors get through winter.

"I notice you have a newspaper in your duffel bag. How old is it?" Jack inquired.

"It's about two weeks. A fellow in the tent next to ours gave it to me. I don't read that good, but I took it anyway. Would you like to read it?" answered Mason as he handed the *Richmond Enquirer* to Jack.

"Yeah, it's the best way to tell what's going on with the war, if you can trust or believe what they print," Jack replied as he took the newspaper from him. The marksmen were confident Jack would recount with them any worthwhile news, so they went on with their own personal obligations, making sure they didn't disturb the concentration of the reader.

After about an hour, Jack looked up and said, "The editorial says we lost Fort Henry and Donelson to the Yankees, but somehow, it was perceived as a victory for our side. You all can figure that one out by yourself. To me, no matter how courageous we were and valiantly we fought, it's hard to see it as a victory. The way I look at it, surrendering those two forts eliminates our first line of defense and gives the Yankees free reign on the Tennessee River. There's not much mention of losses in men and matériel, and you know there had to be plenty. John Henry, you've got a good feel in that area. How much do you think we actually did lose by surrendering those two forts?"

"About fifteen thousand men taken prisoner, another twenty thousand stand of arms, at least fifty pieces of artillery and heavy guns, anywhere between three thousand to four thousand horses, and whatever was in the commissary stores," John Henry replied.

"The paper says our casualties were light," Jack added.

"Well, we probably lost less than the Yankees just by the nature of the fight. Our boys were behind the defenses of the forts. Nevertheless, I'd think we lost, about one thousand killed and three times wounded," said John Henry.

"What will they do with fifteen thousand prisoners?" inquired Lomas.

"They will put them on boats and ship them up North to a prison camp," replied John Henry.

"What other victories did we have?" Lomas asked sarcastically, quickly pointing to the paper.

"This is an interesting article about how we acquired the ironclad ship renamed *Virginia*," Jack said. "I'll tell you what it says."

"On April 20, 1861, and for reasons puzzling to the South, the Federals withdrew from the naval yard at Gosport, Virginia. The Union was in full control of the yard; therefore, making the decision to evacuate was one of the most extraordinary actions of the war. The rebel soldiers, with no heavy guns to mount in batteries, were powerless to capture the place. The evacuation was done so hurriedly that the best part of the valuable material, abandoned at the yard, fell into Confederate hands. Apparently, the dry dock was rigged to explode, but the fuse failed to ignite the gunpowder, leaving two thousand guns of all descriptions uninjured, three hundred of them being new Dahlgren guns of various calibers. The magazine, with great numbers of loaded shells and 150 tons of powder, had already been confiscated.

"Besides the guns, machinery, steel plates, castings, construction materials, and ordnance, stockpiles, in vast quantities, came into the possession of our troops. The gunpowder was carried to Richmond, and the navy yard was taken over immediately by the Confederates. An excess of 1,195 large-caliber guns were captured. These armaments furnished the batteries of the Confederate forts from Norfolk to New Orleans and were found on all the rivers of the South. Without them, it is difficult to see how our Dixie comrades could have armed either their forts or ships. Prior to the evacuation, the Union troops destroyed or partially destroyed several vessels. These included the *Pennsylvania*, the *Delaware*, the *Columbus*, the frigates *Merrimac*, *Columbia*, and *Raritan*, also the sloops-of-war *Germantown* and *Plymouth*, and the brig *Dolphin*. The old frigate United States was left intact and was afterward used by the Confederates as a receiving ship."

The Battle of the *Merrimac* (christened CSS *Virginia*) and the *Monitor*

The large steam frigate *Merrimac* was scuttled and sunk. She was set on fire and burned to her copper line and down through to her berth deck, which, with her spar and gun decks, also suffered severe burn damage. She was immediately raised, and the South's fortunes improved when they found gunpowder in her magazine (put up in airtight copper tanks) to be in good condition. It was later used in her engagements in Hampton Roads. Steps were directly taken by the Confederate authorities to convert the Merrimac into an ironclad. At that time, it was believed that the possession of an iron-armored ship was a matter of the first necessity. Such a vessel could navigate the entire coast of the United States, prevent all blockades, and made the prospects of their regular navy more successful.

Naval history was made on March 8, 1862, when our beloved South's first ironclad steamed down the Elizabeth River into Hampton Roads to attack the wooden-sided U.S. blockading fleet anchored there. She was christened CSS *Virginia*, but in common usage, retained its original name of *Merrimac*. After ramming and sinking the twenty-four-gun steam-sailing sloop *Cumberland*, the *Virginia* headed for the fifty-gun frigate *Congress*. The Yankee navy was in awe as she fired shot and shell into her with devastating effect, while the shot from the *Congress* glanced off her iron-plated sides, without any apparent damage.

When darkness came that evening, the Confederate ships did not leave, but lay in wait to resume their attack in the morning. At dawn, a strange-looking tower was seen sliding over the waters bearing the flag of stars and stripes. It was the *Monitor*, which, during the previous night, had come in from the sea and, by the light of the burning *Congress*, had been seen and reported by one of the Confederate pilots. We knew of the Union ironclad from the Yankee newspapers and also learned she had been in momentary danger of floundering during a twenty-four-hour passage from Sandy Hook to Cape Henry, while just in ordinary reef topsail breeze. The Virginia steamed toward her and engaged the battle. For nearly two hours, shell and shot was exchanged at close quarters with no perceptible damage to either vessel.

A great deal was learned regarding the design of both vessels. It took the cumbrous *Virginia* several minutes to turn and expose her broadside, and during this maneuver, the *Monitor*'s turret was whirling around like a top; and by this easy working of her turret, and with her precise and rapid movement, was a design worthy of admiration. The ships passed and repassed very near each other, the *Virginia* frequently delivering a broadside at a distance of only a few yards, with no great effect. The captain of our *Virginia* knew the turret of the *Monitor* was impenetrable to our shot and shell. The next move was to run the *Monitor* down. Because of the difficulty maneuvering the Virginia, we would need nearly a mile under full steam for the necessary headway. The gunners and armorers gang had all their posts assigned. They were equipped with sledgehammers, large wedges, crowbars, heavy chain, and whatever else was available to wedge the turret and keep it from revolving. The boatswain's gang, manned with heavy hawsers and chain cables, was prepared for another possibility. If they could hook her securely to the *Virginia*, she can be walked away to Norfolk, whether the turrets revolved or not. As the *Virginia* rushed forward under full steam and drew near the *Monitor*, she abruptly turned tail and fled for more shallow water. She needed only ten feet draught against our twenty-two. By way of emphasizing our victory, the *Virginia* fired five more shells at the *Monitor*, whereas, at such a distance, made it only a symbolic gesture.

"I'd call that a real victory," said Abel.

"I'm not so sure," Jack said. "It pointed out that the Yankee ironclad had a better design that ours."

"They turned tail and ran, better design or not."

With that comment, Ihme Mueller entered the conversation. "That's true, but if they shot a torpedo at us, the *Virginia* would have sunk like a rock. She was assembled in the roughest way, still, the fatal defect in her construction was that the iron shield extended only a few inches below the waterline. She was lucky that a wayward shell amidships didn't strike her lower extremities. If that had happened, her career was over. To top it all, she drew twenty-two feet of water, in every respect, ill proportioned and top-heavy, making her nearly impossible to manage."

"All this talk makes me wish I had learned to read better," Mason Poor added.

"You got time to do that, Mason, I'm glad you brought the newspaper with you," Jack responded frankly.

"Is there anything else of interest?"

"Not much other than Abe Lincoln created an income tax. It's 3 percent of incomes of under $600 and 5 percent of incomes over $10,000," Jack read. He is also printing paper money they call greenbacks to take the place of coins and gold. If this war goes on for any length of time, old Jefferson Davis will probably do the same thing."

"Well, that will be a first. I've seen bank drafts, script, and coins, but never paper money. It's understandable there may be a shortage of coins because metal is needed for the war. Times sure are changing. As far as I'm concerned, bring back the good old days," Abel said honestly.

Chapter Five

"I think we're in for one hell of a battle,"
Jack answered firmly.

There was a noticeable change in the camp's atmosphere over the past few days. The tone among soldiers began to be more subdued. Normally raucous and loud after dinner, men now have become more quiet and thoughtful. It was something you couldn't exactly put your finger on, yet undeniably there. An emerging transformation was taking place which Jack perceived almost on the first night. Yes, there is definitely something in the air. It's been said, men in battle have a sixth sense when it comes to danger; and if the surroundings at the Manassas camp could be tested and analyzed, it would be found to be exactly the cause of the attitudinal shift. The announcement came after breakfast and roll call. All quarters were to prepare to move out the next morning.

A misty rain began to fall while the Seventh regiment stood at attention. An airy white fog appeared each time a soldier exhaled, acknowledging the cold morning. Mountain air, coupled with the presence of mizzle, resulted in a temperature of under fifty degrees. Jack and the sharpshooters were curious why their drill sergeant took a few steps back after shouting formation. All questions were answered when newly appointed Gen. Henry Hatton appeared, riding a dappled gray mount and shouting, "Look, smart men, we march to defend our capital against the Yankees." Words of that nature could be heard up and down the columns as Hatton urged his grizzled charger with the heel of his boots. Hatton had the mien of one comfortable with leadership and his personal visit, this particular morn, went a long way, building trust among the troops.

"That's the first time a general ever took time to talk to the plain troops," said John Henry.

"I think some of them do talk to the commons, but this is the first we ever saw," Abel answered. "What do you think, Jack?"

"I think we're in for one hell of a battle," Jack answered firmly.

* * *

Shortly after the battle of ironclads, CSS *Virginia* and USS *Monitor*, President Lincoln removed General McClellan as general-in-chief and made him commander of only the Army of the Potomac purportedly so that he would be free to devote all his attention to the move on Richmond. When McClellan arrived at Fort Monroe, the army had 50,000 men; nonetheless, Lincoln allowed a buildup that grew to 121,500 in order to remove "inefficient troop strength" as an excuse for more delay.

The fort was identified as a strategic defense location from the earliest days of the Colony of Virginia.

After establishing the settlement of Jamestown in 1607, the colonist efforts were directed at the site of Old Point Comfort for the purpose of coastal defense. To begin with, they built Fort Algernon; and as numerous years went by, the more substantial facility of stone was completed in 1834 and named in honor of U.S. president James Monroe. While most of Virginia became part of the Confederacy, Fort Monroe remained in Union hands.

In 1862, the fort was used as a transfer point for mail exchange. Mail sent from states in the Confederacy, addressed to locations in the Union, had to be sent by flag of truce and could only pass through at Fort Monroe where the mail was opened, inspected, resealed, marked, and sent on. Prisoner of war mail from Union soldiers in Confederate prisons was also required to be passed through this point for inspection.

Union General McClellan's First Pitched Battle of His Peninsula Campaign

The continuing presence of the Union Navy base at Fort Monroe enabled Federal water transports from Washington, D.C., to land unmolested and gave great support to General McClellan's Peninsula Campaign.

After Lincoln issued a direct order for McClellan to engage the enemy, the reluctant general began the first large-scale offensive in the Eastern theater. The operation was an amphibious turning movement intended to capture the Confederate capital by circumventing Robert E. Lee's Army of Northern Virginia.

McClellan's troops moved up the Virginia Peninsula, reaching within a few miles of the gates of Richmond, only to be surprised by Confederate general John B. Magruder's defensive position, maintained along the Warwick River. General Magruder's troops held the line for thirty days, dashing McClellan's expectations for a quick advance. His initial hopes foiled, McClellan ordered his army to prepare for a siege of Yorktown; however, just before the siege preparations were completed, the Confederates, now under the direct command of Joseph E. Johnston, began a withdrawal toward Richmond. Johnston's departure was making slow progress on the muddy roads; so to give more time for the bulk of his army to break away, he detached part of his force to make a stand at the large earthen fortification of Fort Magruder, located on the Williamsburg Road near Yorktown.

The battle of Williamsburg was the first pitched battle of McClellan's Peninsula Campaign, in which nearly 41,000 Union and 32,000 Confederates took part. Confederate causalities at Williamsburg were 1,682; Union 2,283. McClellan categorized his first significant battle as a "brilliant victory" over superior forces. However, the defense of Williamsburg was seen by the South as a means of delaying the Federals, which allowed the bulk of the Southern troops to continue withdrawal toward Richmond.

Confederate general Johnston, who had retreated up the peninsula to the outskirts of Richmond, knew that he could not survive a massive siege and decided to attack McClellan. His original plan was to attack the Union right flank, north of the Chickahominy River, before additional Union troops, marching south from Fredericksburg, could arrive. It was later learned the Yankee reinforcements had been diverted to the Shenandoah Valley and would not be bolstering the Army of the Potomac. With this knowledge, Johnston decided to attack the two Union forces south of the Chickahominy River and leave them isolated from the other three companies.

If executed correctly, the Confederate general would engage two-thirds of his army, about 51,000 men against the 33,000 men of the enemy forces. His attack plan called for the divisions of A. P. Hill and Magruder to distract the Union forces north of the river while General Longstreet and D. H. Hill were to advance on separate roads at a crossroads known as Seven Pines (because of seven large pine trees clustered at that location). The Union division farthest forward, under Brig. Gen. Silas Casey, was manning the earthworks a mile west of Seven Pines. The fact that it consisted of only 6,000 men, and the least experienced in the detachment, gave an excellent potential for success. If they could be defeated, the remaining corps, to the east, could be pinned against the Chickahominy and overwhelmed. The resulting battle became known as the Battle of Seven Pines.

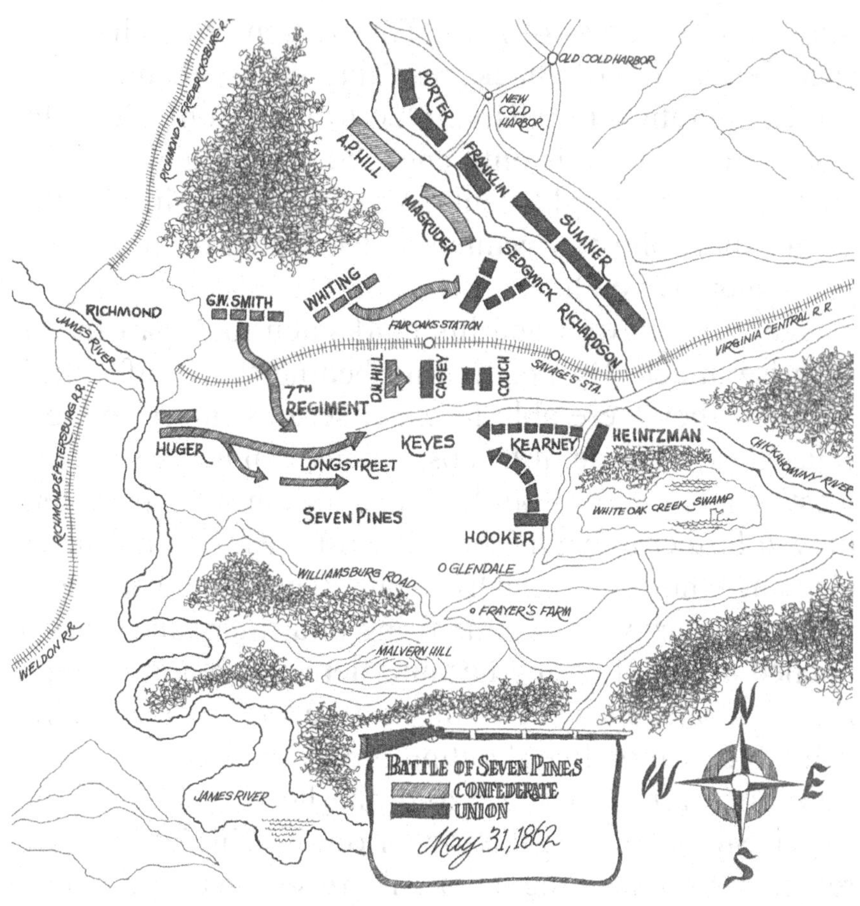

The plan was mismanaged from the start. Johnston chose to issue his orders to Longstreet orally. The other generals received orders in writing, but they were vague and contradictory. Longstreet chose to modify his orders without informing Johnston. Rather than taking his assigned avenue of advance, his column joined Hill's, which not only delayed the advance but also limited the attack to a narrow front with only a fraction of its total force. Making matters worse, for both sides, was a severe thunderstorm on the night of May 30, which flooded the river, destroyed most of the Union bridges and turned the roads into a morass of mud. The written orders had not specified a time of attack, resulting in less than desired forces operating in unison. Due to their confusion, the Confederate generals only engaged four brigades of the thirteen on their right flank so they did not hit with the power that Johnston wanted concentrated on this weak point in the Union line.

Jack Leffingwell and his marksmen took part in the surprise attack. By positioning behind the Confederate artillery, they were able to exact serious injury to Gen. Silas Casey's Federal troops. Abel Chandler assumed a location a few yards from Jack, and the other sharpshooters moved farther down the line. It wasn't as wide a front as General Johnston originally detailed, but the other troops were yet to arrive. Once the firing of artillery and musket opened up, the fighting became fierce. Looking through his telescope, Jack took aim at a Federal officer riding behind the Union line shouting orders. Jack couldn't hear him; however, experience told him he would be a good target. Slowly pulling the trigger of his Whitfield, it gave recoil and sounded the report. There seemed to be a long interval before contact was made, like a moment frozen in time and space, then the officer flew from his horse with both arms and legs extended. With that, Jack picked out an artillery crew and dispatched the fuse lighter. Moving the telescope image to the left, he spotted a soldier handing shells to his crew. For a moment, the Tennessee mountain man was taken aback. The lad appeared to be no older than twelve. Jack had heard the Yankee army had many youngsters employed. This was the first time he actually saw one. He was unmoving for a moment, then General Hatton gave the order to charge; and the Confederate front line burst forward, sounding the rebel yell and Jack snapped back to the matter at hand. The first wave was momentarily repelled, and General Hatton was heard cursing, “Where the hell are the other brigades?”

Casey’s line, even though manned by inexperienced troops, fought fiercely for possession of their earthworks, resulting in heavy casualties on both sides. He sent for reinforcements, even so, Union general Keyes was slow in responding. Eventually, the mass of Confederates broke through, seized a Union redoubt, and Casey’s men retreated to the second line of defensive works at Seven Pines. The entire camp was captured with all its tents standing and great quantities of all the usual army stores, including hundreds of small weaponry. Later that afternoon, Gen. D. H. Hill, now strengthened by reinforcements from Longstreet, hit the secondary Union line near Seven Pines, which was manned by the remnants of Casey’s division, along with the third and fourth Federal corps.

Hill organized a flanking maneuver, sending four regiments from Longstreet’s command to attack Keyes right flank. The attack collapsed the Union line back to the Williamsburg Road, a mile and a half beyond Seven Pines. The fighting died out by early evening.

Over the past two days, constant rain and heavy winds had grounded the Union aerostats or observation balloons. Two such airships were launched as the fighting began to slow down. Abel spotted one of them as it rolled up from behind a hill across the river.

“Would you take a look at that,” he exclaimed. “The Yankees are going to attack us from the sky.”

“I doubt it,” Jack followed. “More than likely, they want to look at our positions and determine our troop strength.”

“Let’s pick ’em off,” suggested Abel.

"You can if you want to. As far as I'm concerned, there's been enough killing for one day. That guy up there probably isn't even armed."

Abel was captivated and watched the slow-moving inflatable until his neck muscles started to ache, finally asking, "What keeps it up?"

"I read where certain gasses are lighter than air, and when they are used to fill the balloon, it tends to rise up. I don't think the Yankees are using those gasses, they're probably just heating the inside air."

"I wonder how long they can stay up there."

"Until the air inside cools down," Jack, who was now watching the balloon slowly drift above the river, replied.

"Yeah, I know, but how long would that take?"

"Can't say for sure, just watch and time it yourself," Jack suggested.

"I can't do that, my neck hurts too much."

Jack noticed that his friend was in a talkative mood. More than likely, it was due to stress relief and gladness to still be alive, after the pitched battle ended. A complete range of emotions can be found under these circumstances. There are those that laugh, perhaps a little too loud, and others who cry, thinking of the escape from death and their loved ones back home. The Tennessee mountain man experienced all the emotions, but was the silent type. He understood and held no predisposition against any of the others.

"I wonder how the guys made out," Abel mused. "Guess we won't find out until this here scuffle is over."

"Yeah, you're right there. My bet is that the generals have another skirmish planned first thing in the morning, and they will be working out the strategy on both sides of the Chickahominy tonight."

"It's field rations tonight," Abel said while reaching in his duffel bag and pulling out a piece of hardtack. "I'll bet you money that little turd Lomas is eating in style while we're stuck with this crap."

At that moment, a soldier came running along the line with a large container of hot steaming coffee and shouting, "Hold out your cups, boys, and get it while it's still hot."

"Have you heard any news about the battle? Did we win?" questioned Jack.

"From what I heard, so far, it looks like there's no conclusive winner. You boys were winning in the beginning, howbeit the Yankees brought in reserves and kind of evened things up," the soldier replied. "The big news is, General Hatton got killed and Gen. James Archer took command of the brigade. We are now part of A. P. Hill's division."

"Gen. Henry Hatton killed," Abel mused. "We were just talking to him less than two hours ago. He rode by to encourage the troops and say how proud he was of us."

"Well, shortly after that, he was shot in the head and died before he hit the ground. I got to get moving. There's a lot of us Southern boys need hot Java mud."

After giving the marksmen refills, the young regular dashed down the line.

"That sure proves that death can come to you at any time. General Hatton probably thought the fight was over for the day, but a Yankee sniper had other ideas," Abel said out loud. "You give much thought to dying, Jack?"

"Not too much until I got married. Since that day, I must confess it crosses my mind quite frequently. My father-in-law once told me that if you don't know how to die, don't worry yourself about it. Nature will tell you what to do on the spot. Mother Nature will do this job for you perfectly. Don't think too hard on the subject. We trouble our lives with concern about death, and death with concern about life. One torments us, the other frightens us. It's not against death we prepare ourselves. That is too momentary a thing. A short time of suffering, without consequences, without harm, does not deserve any particular precepts. To tell the truth, we prepare ourselves against the arrangements of death. He said we should organize to live the proper life and that, and the Lord, will take care of all of it."

"Do you think he's right?" asked Abel.

"Of course he's right, but we are only human and can't help worrying about such things. During these times, the best thing we can do is remember to keep our heads down and don't give the Yankees an easy target."

* * *

The Civil War caused a shifting attitude toward death

Death took on a new meaning because of the American Civil War. The conflict dramatically changed the course of American society by transforming attitudes toward death and practices surrounding the dead body. The incredible numbers of young men who died during the war, the problems associated with disposal of their bodies, and the rhetorical and symbolic efforts to make sense of the lives lost had profound consequences for our sensibilities and institutional structures.

Prior to the Civil War, we were quite familiar with the presence of death and intimate with the consequences in our homes and communities. The crude death rate in the antebellum period was around 4 percent in the populated

Northern cities and likely higher in the South. Most people lived into their late thirties, if they survived the exceedingly dangerous early years of life. Chances of dying in childhood were also exceedingly high. Infant mortality hovered around 20 percent of live births, and roughly 10 percent of individuals between one year and twenty-one years died from a wide range of causes. Despite this close and personal awareness of human mortality, the Civil War presented a radically different set of experiences. First and foremost, this conflict produced more deaths than any other war in U.S. history. The total number of deaths for both sides, in the four-year period, was over six hundred thousand, including those who expired in battle or later by wounds and/or disease. Disease was actually more threatening to soldiers than mortal wounds on the battlefield. Nearly twice as many men died as a result of poor health in camps and hospitals than from combat. Afflictions such as diarrhea, malaria, smallpox, typhoid fever, pneumonia, and measles wiped out large numbers of men on both sides. Because of the incredibly poor conditions in camps, such as inadequate shelter, contaminated water supplies, unhealthy diet, and a limited knowledge about proper sanitation and hygiene, a deadly disease could sweep through the ranks with devastating results. As the war progressed, both sides worked hard to improve the living conditions of soldiers and patients. Due to an easier access to the material aspects, the North became more advanced in achieving their goals.

Regardless of the arduous incidence of death in life during the antebellum years, the Civil War posed new challenges for those affected by the present carnage. New attitudes reflected distinct modifications of how Americans made sense of death and the disposal of the dead. In the midst of war, unorthodox views on death and the dead body emerged out of entirely unparalleled experience with human violence, suffering, and mortality here in America. The Civil War forced us to reconsider the appropriate treatment of the dead, as well as to reconceptualize the symbolic meanings of the dead body. With brutally slaughtered masses of bodies or hopelessly diseased soldiers dying in hospitals or camps, the conventional patterns of disposal, as well as established attitudes about communal duties, religious rituals, and personal respect in the face of death, have changed. What counted as proper and appropriate in an earlier time was often impossible during combat. Soldiers attempted to provide some kind of burial for fallen comrades who perished during a battle, even if this meant simply covering bodies with dirt or placing the dead in common graves. The details of burial depended on a variety of circumstances, including which side won a particular battle and which was assigned burial duty. Victors had the luxury of attending to their own dead with more care and attention, if time permitted. The losing side had to retreat from the battlefield, leaving the fate of the dead and wounded to the winners. They were treated as most enemies are treated, with indifference and disrespect. Often, Union armies assigned African Americans to burial duties. Soldiers on both sides feared disposition of their dead body if left to the enemy. The desire of both combatants, to be identified after burial, led to soldiers pinning their name in their uniform and carrying identification on their person. Burial duty was an undesirable task which no one wanted and shirked by the soldiers. As the war continued, dead bodies were sometimes buried without their boots, shoes, and other items, growing more difficult to obtain. Such reclaimed items were frowned upon by the rank and file, however, not so much by a soldier marching barefoot.

American attitudes to the Civil War held a belief in the recovering powers of violent death, and that redemption of both the individual and society would follow, after the mass sacrifice by their young heroes. Others grew hardened to the savagery and suffering taking place on American soil. For those people, including soldiers themselves, the meaning of death had nothing to do with religious notions like regeneration or redemption.*

* * *

The subsequent morning, the Confederates renewed their assaults against the Federals (who had brought up more reinforcements and now fought from strong positions) but made little headway. Both armies tested each other until shortly before noon, at which point the Confederates withdrew. As usual, the ever-cautious General McClellan assessed that the rebel forces greatly outnumbered his own; thus, the Union army did not counterattack.

Both sides claimed victory with roughly equal casualties, but neither side's accomplishment was impressive. George B. McClellan's advance on Richmond was halted, and the Army of Northern Virginia fell back into the Richmond defensive works. Union casualties were 5,031 (790 killed; 3,594 wounded; 647 captured or missing) and Confederate 6,134 (980 killed; 4,749

---

* *(Adapted from http://www.deathreference.com/Ce-Da/Civil-War-U-S.html)*

wounded; 405 captured or missing). The battle was frequently remembered by the Union soldiers as the Battle of Fair Oaks Station because that is where they did their best fighting; whereas, the Confederates, for the same reason, called it Seven Pines. It was at the crossroads of Seven Pines that the heaviest fighting and highest casualties occurred.

(Even though the battle ended in a virtual draw, in a war of attrition, the Confederacy is destined to lose. In 1862, the United States had approximately thirty million people. The North had three times the population of the South. Twenty million versus nine million of which four million were black slaves. A long siege or protracted war rings the death knell for the South. The Confederacy must strike convincingly and capture Washington, D.C., quickly, or the gallant effort will be for naught. That will be General Lee's obsession; however, history tells us it never happened and the Confederacy placed its hopes in winning assistance from either England or France. That, too, did not materialize.)

The most historically significant incident of the battle occurred when Confederate general Johnston was struck in the right shoulder by a bullet, immediately followed by a shell fragment hitting him in the chest. He fell from his horse unconscious and, with a broken right shoulder blade and two broken ribs, he was evacuated to Richmond. Shortly thereafter, Gen. Robert E. Lee was named commander of the Army of Northern Virginia.

Despite claiming victory, McClellan was shaken by the experience. He redeployed most all of his army to continue his plan for a siege and capture of the Confederate capital but lost the strategic initiative. While the Union troops sat passively outside of Richmond, Gen. Robert E. Lee devised a plan; and for the next seven days, between June 25 and July 1, 1862, he drove the Federal Army back to the James River and saved the capital. It would take two more years before the Union army got that close to Richmond, and three years before it finally captured it.

The Seventh regiment was held in reserve until the end of June. Primarily, the time was considered rest and recuperation. A time to unwind and let the combat stress and fatigue wash away so they would be ready for the next mission.

The marksmen were back in communal togetherness, living in a tent provided them by the base commander. Taking part in a common, but life-threatening endeavor has unanimously bonded unpredictable friendships between diametrically different personalities. John Henry Bickford, the cynic and bigot; Lomas Chandler, the likable Irish leprechaun; Ihme Mueller, a German immigrant whose command of English was just enough to be confused most of the time; and Abel Strawn, Jack's first army friend, made up the group.

Jack Leffingwell sat with his legs crossed, in the yoga position, and wrote on paper resting atop a small barrel. He was finishing the letter to Abigail started a couple of days earlier.

May 31, 1862
My Darling Wife,

Today certainly is not the best day of my life. Me and the sharpshooters shot Union artillery soldiers all day. Without a doubt, this is the most fighting I've seen thus far. It's only at night do I realize I've killed one of God's beings. Perhaps it's someone with a family like mine. I'm told that if I don't kill them, they will kill me. After the fighting ends, I think how this affects my immortal soul. I can only go on believing that what I'm doing will bring me home to you and the children sooner.

General Hatton was killed today. Apparently, shortly after he commended me and the other sharpshooters. It came as a shock since we were talking to him barely an hour before.

Jack Junior must be getting close to walking by now. Sarah Jane is probably ready for schooling. I can't wait to see them both. Do you tell them about their mountaineer father?

One regiment has been reassigned back to Tennessee. I hoped we would be as well, but the officers tell me that I won't see Tennessee until the war is over. I don't know if I can hold out until then, but I don't think I have any deserter blood in me.

I haven't received any mail for a long time. With the war going on and moving all the time, it's not surprising. Keep writing me anyway. Just knowing you are writing keeps me going.

With eternal love,
Jack

Chapter Six

During the occupation, anyone who disagreed with Union policies was subject to arrest

Tennessee spent most of the war under Union occupation. General Grant had cut Tennessee in half. The middle and west portion of the state was controlled in the spring and summer of 1862; while East Tennessee, having the most Union sympathizers, wasn't taken until later the following year. At first, the Union army supported a policy of "live and let live" with the Confederate partisans; however, this position hardened, as many Southerners continued to profess pro-Confederate views. The situation deteriorated to the point thereupon when West Tennessee general William T. Sherman was placed in command of Memphis. He ordered all unloyal establishments closed, an action that naturally made the situation worse.

Anyone who disagreed with Union policies was subject to arrest. Ordinary citizens could be arrested for a variety of charges such as smuggling, spying, or even comments critical of the Union. Union officials also conducted random searches of homes, looking for evidence of Confederate support.

Food shortages were widespread as farms were periodically raided by soldiers who were foraging for sustenance. To make matters worse, seasonal planting was disrupted along with normal harvests. Armies frequently camped on private land or confiscated private property for military use. Livestock, homes, and crops were taken by the army without any consideration to the owner. Often, soldiers demanded livestock as well as every potato, onion, and any other winter vegetable. Servants' lives were threatened if they didn't turn over all the milk and butter on the premises. In short order, many families became impoverished and uprooted. Refugees traveled to the larger cities seeking protection and food, only to be viewed by the locals as filthy and degenerate criminals or beggars.

Statesville was no exception to the occupation and the rape of property in the town and its outlying farms. Two of the town's three churches were appropriated for military purposes as well as the schoolhouse. Being the oldest building, Hyrum Adam's church was spared. Union soldiers did purloin Hyrum's horse—an act of thievery that nearly broke his heart. The saddened preacher stood at his window and watched a Union officer remove the saddle and tack from the steed he was riding and place it on Hyrum's pet, then mount up and ride off with his own charger in tow. Hyrum, obviously, owned a better animal. The in-your-face robbery tested the man of God, but his faith sustained him. He now had no way to visit parishioners and those who were ill. Trips to see his daughter and grandchildren now would entail a four—or five-mile trek, a difficult ordeal for a man of his age.

Abigail suffered a similar fate. The Leffingwell farm was raided more than once. The first plundering gave a minimal amount of bounty. The cattle and horses disappeared before the arrival of Northern troops. Abigail woke up one morning and was shocked to find they had vanished without a trace. The fields were also bare except for a stand of winter wheat whose grain was in head but still very green. All that remained was her flock of chickens and a small vegetable garden in a plot behind the house. During the day, most of the chickens ran wild in search of food. Toward evening, they returned to the barn to roost. The cackling in the morning signaled Abigail to gather eggs, an activity she shared with a delighted Sarah Jane. Minnie Rosenthal is now living with Abigail. The two women decided it was the best arrangement when the occupation took place. It was fortunate Minnie lived there on the morning a Federal scouting party made an uninvited visit.

The morning clouds were just breaking apart. Abigail and her daughter had returned from the barn with fresh laid eggs when the sound of meandering hoofbeats in front of the porch made Abigail open the front door. It was four Union soldiers, making up a scouting party, looking for anything usable for the military.

"Where's your animals?" asked the lieutenant. "Don't tell me you haven't got any because your barn gives you away."

"All the animals were taken," she replied.

"How about vegetables and milk?" the Federal soldier persisted.

"You've picked us clean. We have none in good supply. There's barely enough for the children and a grandmother," Abigail returned. "Would you take food from the mouths of babies?"

"You're breaking my heart, and you're also lying. I know you Southern trash would steal pennies off a dead man's eyes, so don't get smart with me, bitch, or I'll show you what's for," he said angrily. "When we came by here a few weeks ago, you had a stand of winter wheat nearly ready for harvest. Today, it's been gathered, and the field is barren. Where's the wheat? I know you have it hidden someplace. I'll tell you what. We'll be back tomorrow and you better have something for me, or I'll take something else as payment. When I come back tomorrow, you had better have it ready for us."

"I don't have the wheat, but I could bake you a loaf of bread," Abigail said as her voice began to quiver.

"We're not here for a loaf of bread, like you Southern whores hanging around our camp. We want your stores to help feed the United States Army of the Union," said the lieutenant. He could see that Abigail was frightened, all the same, he still believed she was lying. He also took notice of her honest and desirable good looks. No matronly farm wife stood before him. Instead, it was a fetching young mother in unadorned beauty. She would be dazzling dressed up for the ball, he thought to himself. His musing ended as one of his group appeared from the barn with a large squawking red hen tied to the saddle.

"Looks like chicken for supper, Lieutenant," he shouted while you could see the whites of his horses' eyes, as it shied sideways, unhappy about the unwanted flapping visitor. "I also found five eggs."

Looking back at Abigail, the lieutenant said, "Just remember what I told you. If you don't have the wheat, I might take something else from you."

There was little doubt as to what he meant, and the laughs and joking of the Yankee soldiers removed any uncertainty. Jack had left her with a pistol to use for their personal protection. Firearms were forbidden by the occupation; subsequently, it was discovered and confiscated during the first Union army inspection.

After supper, the family gathered together for prayer. It had become an everyday event—this time, they sought the Lord for their own protection, along with the prayers for Jack.

The Union scouting party rode away at a fast clip. Their image gradually faded because of the dirt cloud created by the horses' hoofs. Confident their departure was dramatic enough, they slowed down to a normal gait. After ten minutes or so, a private asked, "Where'bouts are we going to camp tonight, Lieutenant?"

"Let's just follow the road until we come to the creek. We can ride along the stream until we find a suitable spot."

"That sassy farm gal sure is good-looking. I wouldn't mind taking a poke at her myself," the private stated. "With a husband gone for nearly two years and stuck on that farm, she should be about ripe for the pickings."

"You can forget about that, Private Nolan. That little lady is mine," the lieutenant replied. "I'll save the old one for you."

"Ugh, I'm definitely not that horny yet. Hey, look up yonder. It's got a nice stand of hardwoods and water close by."

The leafy glade was more than suitable. Several hardwood branches had fallen from the last windstorm and, dried in the hot Tennessee sun, were ideal for making a fire. The larger branches were stomped on to form logs, to be used once the fire took hold. Water from the creek was soon boiling, and the soldier who stole the fluffy feathered Rhode Island red hen placed his boot on the chicken's neck and gave a swift jerk removing its head. Even dead, the chicken remained animated with wings flapping and bouncing around for short while. No doubt, that's where the saying, "He ran around like a chicken with its head cut off," came from. However, this particular producer of large brown eggs would see her nest no more. When the water was boiling, the hen was immersed for several minutes, a technique to make feather plucking easier.

"Sure wish we had a fishing pole, those innards would make good bait," said one of the soldiers.

"Just toss them into the creek. We're feeding the fish today," the feather plucker said as he ran a sharpened wood skewer through the hen and positioned the bird above the fire.

Lieutenant Jason Cartwright was from Chicago, Illinois. His father, one of the city's politicians, used his influence and money to give Jason an officer's rank. By having a son in the military, especially while the Union was at war, enhanced his prestige among his political peers. And for Jason, an officer's rank not only paves the way for promotions but also, in his own mind, cuts a figure the ladies can't resist. Under normal circumstances, he probably is right; however, unfortunately for Jason, his personality causes him to be dismissed by those around him. His men learned, early on, that flattery is the shortest path to take when dealing with this officer.

Roasted chicken, complimenting the usual fare scouting parties carry with them, made for a pleasant evening. The men laid out their bedrolls adjacent to the fire; and looking up at a sky, speckled with countless stars, made sleep come easier this warm Southern night. Soon the sound of crickets calling for mates was joined by that of three snoring soldiers. All three regulars were from Ohio and enlisted when they heard the call from President Lincoln. Like most in the North, they planned for only a three-month duty. Ninety days certainly was enough time to tame the upstart rebels and bring them back into the Union, with their tail between their legs. The war has been going on for two years now; and that hasn't happened, in addition, it doesn't look as though it will any time soon.

It took a little longer for Lieutenant Cartwright to doze off. His mind was occupied with thoughts of the beautiful woman he will see tomorrow. Once he finally slept, those thoughts turned into sensual dreams of the flesh, making for a restless slumber. He was the first to wake up the following morning. He lay awake, watching the dawn emerge, until he heard one of the others stir.

"Let's get some water hot and have coffee," he said, while still in a reposed position. The sound of the lieutenant's voice brought the other two soldiers out of their reverie, and soon the scouting camp blossomed with activity.

"Ain't anything better than hot coffee in the morning," said Thomas Tuttle, the soldier who made it.

"I can think of one thing better," another responded.

"I'll go along with that myself," Tuttle agreed.

Clear water in the fast-moving stream provided the group the means to wash up and shave. Last night's fire still had glowing coals and more than hot enough to heat the chilling liquid from the creek. There was less noise and frivolities this morning, due to each man's personal thoughts about the pending revisit to the farm.

Any laughter was, most likely, resulting from their nervousness.

A summer sun, unshielded by clouds, made the horses' coats glisten during the silent ride back. Off in the distance, the morning hawks were still aloft in search of breakfast, and in spite of the growing heat, dew still covered the grass along the dirt road.

Once the farmhouse came into view, three Yankee soldiers found their throat dry, and swallowing became difficult. So much so that they passed a canteen to each other and took a long pull.

Jason Cartwright rode slightly ahead, occupied with erotic possibilities. They arrived at the same time as the previous day and waited in front of the veranda steps.

Abigail appeared on the porch with a freshly baked loaf of bread and Sarah Jane pressing against her side. The lieutenant dismounted and asked, "Well, what do you have for me?"

"I only have this bread, there is nothing else here on the farm," she answered.

Cartwright quickly bound the steps and said, "Then let's move this inside."

Then, calling to Thomas Tuttle, he gave him orders to take hold of the little girl and show her his knife.

"The lady and I have a little business inside."

The threat to harm Sarah Jane put the bewildered mother in a shocking daze; and as the lieutenant confronted her, Abigail felt his hand lock onto her wrist, with the force of superior physical strength, moving her toward the door. Her heart was pounding so hard it made her ears ring. The unbelievable circumstance was making her feel faint. Struggling to free her wrist from his grip, she didn't see the changed expression in Cartwright's eyes. At first, they were narrow and sinister; now they became pop-eyed, like something unaccountable happened. You could see the whites both above and below the irises. There was another event that occurred only seconds before. Following a faint whishing sound, a Choctaw war arrow now extends from both sides of the lieutenant's neck. He fell to his knees, gasping for breath, futilely reached out for something to give support, and rolled over, dead. An Indian battle cry echoed through a nearby wooded area, causing goose bumps on the three men dressed in navy blue uniforms.

Minnie Rosenthal ran to Sarah Jane and extricated her from the astonished Yankee soldier; while Abigail stood with her back against the front porch wall, shielding her eyes from the ghastly scene.

The three noncommissioned soldiers were now petrified and nervously looked about for an unknown and hidden enemy.

"What are we going to do now, Tommy?" asked the youngest of the group.

There was a short pause to clear his thoughts before Private Thomas Tuttle replied, "We need to strap the lieutenant to his horse and get back to the post."

"What are we going to tell the captain?" asked another.

"We sure as hell won't tell him everything," Tuttle stated drily.

It was obvious the trio had never experienced a situation like this previously. Even with all three helping, their clumsiness in securing Lieutenant Cartwright gave them away. Perhaps the fear of another attack added to their ineptitude; nevertheless, eventually, the lifeless body seemed secure enough to remain on the horse while they rode back to the base camp.

“Don’t forget your bread,” Minnie Rosenthal shouted sarcastically as the soldiers turned to leave the farm. If there was a response, it wasn’t heard because these militiamen had only one thing on their mind—to get the hell out of there and do it fast.

It took until she was seated at the kitchen table before Abigail began to cry. Her sobs were deep, like those of a wounded animal, and uncontrolled, even with Minnie Rosenthal there to comfort her. The danger was over, but all Abigail could utter was to repeat, “Jack, Jack, Jack. Oh, where are you, Jack?” After assuring the children their mother was okay, Minnie made a pot of hot tea and sat with Abigail until long shadows began to form.

“Jack must never learn about what happened here today. I know him too well. He would leave the army and hunt down and kill the other three Yankee soldiers. And that, too, would ruin our lives,” Abigail declared. “He has enough to worry about just keeping alive.”

* * *

Meanwhile, at the Union army base camp, General Sherman got wind of his scouting party returning with its officer dead and tied to the saddle.

“You mean to tell me my officer was killed by Indians. I’ve been led to believe the Indians in these parts are peaceful. In fact, we have Choctaw Indians as part of this regiment. Bring me the three soldiers who took part in the mission and also an Indian soldier. I need to find out more about the arrow that killed Lieutenant Cartwright,” General Sherman issued the orders while lighting a slim cigarillo.

Shortly thereafter, a meeting was held with the three principal witnesses and a Choctaw corporal.

"In your own words, tell me what happened, Corporal Tuttle," the general asked the nervous soldier.

"Well, sir, the scouting party was traveling west of Statesville when we came upon a field of winter wheat that looked like it was recently harvested. So the lieutenant said we should have a look at the farm to see if it was being stored. So we headed over there, and a woman comes out and cusses out the Union and us soldiers. She tells us that she doesn't know where the winter wheat went. She said that she has a loaf of freshly baked bread and we were welcome to it. Then, Lieutenant Cartwright dismounts and walks up the steps to retrieve the bread, and an Indian arrow hit him in the neck. They were hiding in the woods, screaming like hell . . . oops, pardon my language, sir, but it sounded like there were hundreds of them.

"We grabbed the lieutenant and headed back to the post as fast as we could. That's about the thick of it," Thomas Tuttle replied, holding his breath, and finished with a deep sigh.

"Are you sure that's the complete story? How about you, other men, is that all that happened?" questioned the general as both soldiers nodded yes.

General Sherman turned to his Choctaw aide and said, "Corporal Paul, have you seen the arrow. Can you tell me anything about it?"

"I have seen the arrow, General Sherman. It is not the usual war arrow. It was marked for revenge and used if rules have been violated."

"If someone disrespects the family or tribe, a revenge arrow might be used to kill the guilty party," answered the tawny corporal. "I know of no other reason."

Sherman walked to his desk and sat down. With his hands to his face, his fingers began massaging his temples as if to ease a headache. He finally looked up and said, "Make out your report, Corporal Tuttle, and say that Lieutenant Cartwright was killed in a skirmish with the enemy."

"Are we going to do something about those Indians?" Tuttle asked.

General Sherman gave Corporal Tuttle a menacing glare and replied, "There's something wrong with the whole story, and I'm not risking a war with the Choctaws while fighting another with the Confederacy. You just do as you're told and keep your nose clean, if you understand my meaning."

(William Tecumseh Sherman has been called the first modern general, recognized for his outstanding command of military strategy. A businessman, educator, and author, this pragmatic individual is perhaps best known for his infamous march to the sea, in which a scorched earth policy was conducted. Sherman's program went beyond burning crops to deny food supplies. His strategy involved the destruction of anything that might be useful to the enemy, including shelter, transportation, and communication.

Sherman's unusual given name never failed to attract attention. Tecumseh was the name of the great chief of the Shawnees

Indian tribe. A heroic figure in American Indian history, Tecumseh lived a life of war and battled against the continuing encroachment of Americans into Indian Territory. He formed a large tribal confederacy of Shawnee and others that opposed the United States. Living a life on the move, Tecumseh found himself in Tennessee fighting alongside the Chickamauga faction of the Cherokee against the government and rebel settlers in their region. Tecumseh met his demise in Upper Canada [modern-day Southern Ontario] during the Battle of the Thames River in the War of 1812.

General Sherman was given his name by his father who fancied the great Indian chief. It's been reported that Sherman was only named Tecumseh until the age of nine or ten, at which time his foster mother, a devout Catholic, took him to be baptized by a Dominican priest who named him William. Sherman himself wrote in his memoirs that his father named him William Tecumseh and had him baptized by a Presbyterian minister as an infant. And he was given the name William at that time. One thing is certain, his friends called him Cump.)

Chapter Seven

Nothing can bring a real sense of security
into the home except true love.

—Billy Graham (b. 1918), American evangelist

Abigail recovered from the episode enough to write her husband. She was well aware of the undependable mail systems and the fickleness of deliveries due to the war. She truly needed the comfort of communicating with Jack, albeit written, instead of in person.

June 12, 1862
Dearest Husband,

I'm unsure if they keep you abreast of the happenings in this terrible war. The Union army has occupied Western Tennessee since the fall of Fort Henry and Donelson this spring. The military has taken over the church buildings and schoolhouse in town. Fortunately, Father's church wasn't wanted. It was probably because the other buildings were newer. They did steal Father's horse. You remember how he loved that animal, and the Union officer took it just for himself. Old Mrs. Clarkson had a nineteen-year-old plug that was retired to the field for its remaining days. Bless her heart, she couldn't put it down and offered it to Father. The spectacle is sad to watch. Obviously, he can't pull the carriage, and Father must walk him half the time he rides. Father visited us the other day and said it took over an hour to get here.

All the animals are now gone, and I think it has something to do with that visit by the Indians. Another strange thing happened recently. The winter wheat was in full head, and everybody kept an eye on it, waiting for the time to harvest. One morning, when we got up, the field was barren and recently picked. In the house, it can only be seen from the children's bedroom, so Minnie and I can't say for sure when it all happened.

The revolver you left us for self-protection was discovered and confiscated by the Federals during an inspection of the premises. The occupation forbids us owning sidearms.

The children are growing like weeds. We talk about you every day and miss you so much.

We are making out in spite of the occupation. Sarah and I still have the chickens and gather eggs every day. I have no idea what they're eating, but they still are fat and sassy. About twice a week we find food at the back door. I know the Indians are putting it there. I once chided you about your Indian friend, and now, they are keeping your family alive. How wrong a person can be? I pray the day will come when I can apologize for my stupidity.

Darling, please keep yourself safe and return to us as fast as you can. We love you.

With everlasting devotion, I remain your faithful inamorata and wife,

Abigail

* * *

The Seven Days Battle

Gen. Robert E. Lee was now on the attack. In what was known as the Seven Days Battles, from June 25 to July 1, 1862, Lee drove McClellan and the invading Army of the Potomac away from Richmond and into retreat down the Virginia Peninsula. Jack Leffingwell and the sharpshooters of the Seventh Tennessee Infantry Regiment were now part of James J. Archer's brigade, under the command of Gen. A. P. Hill's Light Division, so named because it traveled light and was able to maneuver and strike quickly.

The bulk of McClellan's army was arrayed in a line south of the river. And while the army straddled the rain-soaked Chickahominy, Lee determined its northern flank was vulnerable to a well-planned attack. His strategy was to attack the Union flank north of the river. This would concentrate about 65,500 troops to oppose 30,000 Federals. The plan called for Stonewall Jackson to begin the strike on the north flank early on June 26. A. P. Hill's Light Division was to advance when he heard Jackson's guns, clear the Union pickets from Mechanicsville, and then move to Beaver Dam Creek. Gens. J. Longstreet and D. H. Hill were to pass through Mechanicsville and support Jackson and A. P. Hill. South of the river, the Confederates were to feign an attack on the four Union corps.

Lee's complex plan fell apart immediately. Jackson's men were worn-out from their recent campaign and lengthy march, running over four hours behind schedule. By early afternoon, A. P. Hill grew impatient and began his attack without orders—a frontal assault with eleven thousand men. Federal forces had extended and strengthened their right flank and fell back in concentrate along Beaver Dam Creek. Jack Leffingwell and the marksmen, being part of A. P. Hill's advance unit, faced fourteen thousand well-entrenched soldiers, aided by thirty-two guns in six batteries. Union forces repulsed the repeated Confederate attacks and delivered substantial casualties.

When Stonewall Jackson finally arrived late in the afternoon, he ordered his troops to bivouac for the evening, ignoring the major battle raging within earshot.

The embryo of another McClellan miscalculation was taking shape. The proximity of Jackson's men to the Federal right flank caused McClellan to withdraw after dark to a point-five miles east. He viewed that the Confederate buildup threatened his supply line via the railroad north of the Chickahominy and decided to shift his base of supply to the James River. Confederate general Lee's diversionary tactic of feigning attack on the four Union corps south of the river worked like a charm. McClellan reported to Washington that he faced two hundred thousand Confederates and, without the railroad to supply his army, would be forced to abandon his siege of Richmond.

Gen. A. P. Hill, now with Longstreet and D. H. Hill behind him, continued his attack; but the assault was beaten back with more heavy casualties.

Overall, the battle was a Union tactical victory, in which the Confederates suffered heavy casualties, achieving none of their specific objectives, due to the seriously flawed execution of Lee's plan. An outside observer would be justified in attributing blame to Gen. T. J. Jackson's lack of initiative. Instead of over sixty thousand men crushing the enemy's flank, only about fifteen thousand men saw action. Their losses were four times that of the Union. One thing in favor of the Confederates, however, was the beginning of McClellan's strategic debacle in withdrawing his army to the southeast and never regaining the initiative.

On the morning of June 27, A. P. Hill's division had moved across Beaver Dam Creek, finding the former Union line lightly defended. Although fatigued from the previous day's battle, they preceded eastward and approached Gaines's Mill at about the time that D. H. Hill's men were engaged and held up by skirmishes with Federal sharpshooter troops. By early afternoon, D. H. Hill ran into strong opposition, deployed along the swampy terrain, another major obstacle against the advance, and, from that point, made little headway.

Gen. A. P. Hill was ordered to pursue the fleeing enemy. He, instead, attacked an entrenched Union position, losing about two thousand of his thirteen thousand men. Combined with the attacks at Mechanicsville, the previous day, the Light Division had lost over a quarter of its men. When Longstreet arrived to the southwest of A. P. Hill, he saw the difficulty of attacking over such terrain and delayed until Stonewall Jackson could attack on Hill's left. For the second time in the Seven Days Battle, Jackson was late. D. H. Hill attacked the Federal right and was held off. He, too, decided to await Stonewall Jackson's arrival. Jackson finally reached Hill's position in the early afternoon and began his assault at around 4:30 p.m. The battle appeared to be a stalemate until after dark when the Confederates mounted another attack, poorly coordinated; but this time, it collapsed the Federal line. In the wee hours of June 28, Union forces withdrew across the Chickahominy, burning the bridges behind them. For the second day, Lee's forces were able to continue fooling McClellan south of the river by minor diversionary attacks. The Confederates occupied sixty thousand Federal troops, while the real action happened north of the river. In spite of heavy losses, Gaines's Mill was the only clear-cut tactical victory for Lee in the Peninsula Campaign. Through the whole ordeal, McClellan must have been guided by his malignant star. Consistently believing to be outnumbered by the enemy resulted in losing opportunities, one after another, until he precipitously decided to abandon his advance on Richmond.

The Seven Days Battles ended the Peninsula Campaign. Lee withdrew his army to the defenses of

Richmond. Despite heavy casualties and clumsy tactical performances by Lee and his generals, Confederate morale skyrocketed and Lee was emboldened to continue his aggressive strategy.

The Seventh Tennessee regiment suffered severe losses. Lt. Col. John K. Howard was killed in the battle, along with every single field officer. In addition, forty-three Tennesseans died on the battlefield and another twenty-six, sometime later, from their wounds. For the most part, Jack Leffingwell and his marksmen were positioned behind Confederate artillery, offering a modicum of protection; however, they did not circumvent the fusillade and were subjected to exploding cannon shot and Federal sharpshooters. Nevertheless, to escape such violent clashes unscathed bordered on a miracle. Jack knew it and gave thanks to the Lord on every occasion. After the Seven Days Battles, the others as well began joining Leffingwell, spending more time on their knees in prayer. The regiment returned to the Richmond base camp to rest exhausted nerves and await orders. They later learned that Col. John A. Fife was captured by the Union army and Capt. Samuel G. Shepard was promoted to major.

Accepting the fact that Union forces failed to take Richmond, President Abraham Lincoln gave up the idea of personally commanding the army and named Maj. Gen. Henry Halleck general-in-chief. Halleck had been successful for victories in the west. Lincoln wanted Halleck to be proactive in directing the Federal armies and take advantage of the superior numbers of the North. While Halleck proved useful as a military advisor, he disappointed Lincoln by never taking responsibility for strategically directing the forces. Halleck was useful in serving as a channel of communication between Lincoln and the other generals. Lincoln knew he can win a war of attrition, but to do so would require both armies in direct contact over a period of time. If that happened, Lanchester's law guaranteed it, since, all else being equal, the advantage in numbers increased by the square root, instead of just being linear. Confederate general Robert E. Lee, Lincoln's crafty antagonist, made certain that situation didn't happen.

Virginia weather was hot this time of year; and with rain falling nearly every day, it felt sultry, particularly at night. The sharpshooters returned to the same tent occupied before the Seven Days Battles and were able to enjoy the accouterments they personally constructed. Once established in the Richmond base camp, Jack managed to procure a copy of the *Enquirer*, perhaps the most popular of Richmond newspapers. At this time, Richmond boasted four news journals: the *Enquirer*, *Dispatch*, *Examiner*, and the *Whig*. During the Civil War, the Confederate newspapers in Virginia served as vital, if often faulty, sources of reporting on the conflict, organs of national propaganda, and as venues in which to attack or defend the administration of President Jefferson Davis.

At the outbreak of the war, Virginia had about 120 newspapers being published. Two years into the war, only 17 of the state's papers were still in print. There were numerous causes. Many newspaper personnel joined the army, adding to the existing severe labor shortage. Then as the conflict continued, the cost of newsprint, lead typeface, glue, and other supplies spiraled out of control. Finally, the Union occupation of Northern Virginia closed more papers or converted them into organs of their own.

Despite political and social differences, the Richmond papers adopted a tone of unflagging patriotism. They always depicted loyal Confederates as virtuous, moral, and respectable people. On the other hand, dissenters and those who complained of wartime conditions were disreputable and unpatriotic. Regardless, the first obligation of the wartime press was to report the war, which was no easy task given the era's transportation and communications. Confederate military and civilian officials censored war news, mainly through their monopoly of the telegraph. This sometimes forced the papers to supplement their lack of news from Confederate authorities with reports from Northern papers and, on occasion, embellish rumors to make them newsworthy. Rumor always proliferated on both sides of the war. Jack knew most information around camp was tainted by that fact. He depended mostly on news in Abigail's letters and Virginia papers, if he could obtain them. He was reading the *Richmond Enquirer* when Abel Strawn lifted the flap of their tent and entered.

"Have we won the war yet?" Abel said halfheartedly.

"Not yet," was the reply.

"Anything else interesting?" asked Abel.

"Yeah, this is kind of interesting. A fellow by the name of William Bruce Mumford was hanged at the New Orleans mint for pulling down the Stars and Stripes. Earlier, Yankee forces landed in the undefended city and pulled down the Stars and Bars over the mint on Esplanade Avenue. William Mumford was among the Confederate loyalists who took exception to the Yankee flag, so he chopped it down, amid a shower of grape from Union warships, and dragged it through the street, until it was nothing but tatters, by the time he got through with it. Although the city was not officially occupied at the time of this incident, the mint was a federal building. Army general Benjamin Butler decided to make a salutary example out of the incident to quell any possible civil unrest, especially after the New Orleans picayune glorified the act as both patriotic and a call to resistance. When Mumford was hung from a flagstaff projecting from one of the windows under the front portico of the mint, he became a Southern martyr. President Jefferson Davis called the act coldblooded murder and issued an order condemning General Butler, and even his officers, to death."

"Don't you wish we got hold of one of them Yankee newspapers just to see how many lies they told? They probably say that Mumford was a general leading a treacherous army of savage traitors. I don't know about you guys, but I think we better win this here war or we all might get hanged," John Henry surmised.

"What do you think, Jack?" asked Lomas Chandler.

"Oh, I don't think they'd take it that far," answered Jack. "It does make a fellow think though, doesn't it?"

"What else is in that damn paper?" asked Ihme while leaning closer to Jack.

"There's a story about Isabella Marie Boyd. She's best known as Belle Boyd or Cleopatra of the Secession. Well, she's in jail again for spying. They've got her locked up in the Old Capitol Prison in Washington. Apparently, she operated from her father's hotel in Front Royal, Virginia, and provided valuable information to Gen. Stonewall Jackson. The Yankees had her under observation, but her boyfriend was a Union officer and she would get him to spill the beans and Belle figured a way to pass the information to the Confederate army. What you guys will like most about her happened on July 4, 1861, when a band of Union soldiers saw the Confederate flag hung outside her house. They tore it down and hung a Union flag in its place. This made her angry, and when one of them cursed at her mother, Belle pulled out a pistol and shot the man down. She was later exonerated; nevertheless, sentries were posted around the house and officers kept close track of her activities. That arrangement led to a lot of familiarity and allowed her to charm one of the officers, a Capt. Daniel Keily, into revealing military secrets. The Yankees threatened her several times with hanging, but it didn't intimidate her one bit. She continued to spy and give our boys the information, until she got caught again and put back in jail."

"Do you think they will hang her?" asked Lomas.

"Probably not. I don't think the Yankees need news like that, so close to the Washington capital."

John Henry Bickford, always a little taciturn, seemed unusually quiet and laid-back. By now, the team knew him well enough to not be offended. Today seemed a little different to Abel Strawn who said, "What's bothering you, John Henry, got something caught in your craw?"

"Not really, I've been thinking about getting a new pair of boots. These old brogans are beginning to leak. I was just thinking that I might volunteer for the next burial party." The others made no comment. They all knew what he meant and found it macabre. That was John Henry, and no one was surprised.

The gathering started to stir when a moaning wind picked up and their fire, in front of the tent, began to spit from rain hitting the dying flames. They liked it when Jack relayed what he read in the paper. In fact, they liked it better than reading it themselves because Jack had a way about him to make it more interesting. He seemed to elaborate on aspects of a story, making it thought provoking. Tonight was no exception; and the marksmen felt, if they lost the war, they might be hanged.

Chapter Eight

A horse and carriage is like a jail break for ones feet

It wasn't unusual for Abigail to witness women and children driving wagons, loaded with furniture and household necessities, leaving the area in search of a safer place. Besides the threat of Union soldiers, the occupation also brought lawlessness from traveling bands of brigands and guerilla groups. Such assemblages were composed of army deserters and a variety of outlaws. Women, with their husbands away fighting the war, were helpless to defend the farm, their children, or themselves and became evacuees hunting for harborage. Many were eyewitness to family members being horsewhipped for not taking the oath of allegiance to the Union. A little of that kind of treatment went a long way toward deciding to seek sanctuary elsewhere. Some traveled farther South, while others sought refuge in more populated areas, where Union forces were garrisoned. Those who lived in the garrisoned towns found themselves directly under the enemy's thumb and subject to constant scrutiny, but there were compensating advantages. Army authorities were anxious to preserve order around their military posts, provided police and fire protection, health services, and courts of law. They doled out free provisions to the needy and permitted the operation of schools, churches, and markets. People in the garrisoned towns, therefore, could live a relatively normal life despite the war that raged all around them. In the countryside, by contrast, there was famine, anarchy, and violence. Federal foraging squads stripped the farms of crops and livestock. Local government collapsed, law enforcement evaporated, and in that vacuum of authority appeared bandit gangs that preyed ruthlessly on inhabitants. Traveling about became so dangerous that most rural people simply stayed at home.

For most Tennesseans, the occupation was a devastating experience. Many secessionist citizens, appalled by the prospect, fled at the approach of the Yankees and lived as refugees in the Deep South for the duration of the war. Those who stayed faced the agonizing decision of whether, and to what extent, to resist the enemy. The great majority did resist to some degree; the boldest went beyond defiant words and noncooperation to engage in active resistance: smuggling, spying, and even guerrilla warfare, however, at the risk of retaliation.

Abigail had a sample of malevolent behavior on the part of a Union scouting party and its officer. She refused to think where such barbarousness may have led, were it not for a Choctaw arrow. No Union soldiers have visited the farm since the incident and the knowledge of unseen, but ever-present benefactors make coping with the current life much easier. In Statesville, schoolhouses and churches were closed and served for the pleasure of the Yankee military. Only Hyrum Adams's church remained open and attended by town parishioners. Those living in the outlying areas either have no way to travel or fear to do so. In time, more of the devout will visit the Hyrum's church because their own is no longer available.

There are times Abigail yearns for her church and the like-mindedness of its fellowship. She misses the sorority of other women her age and, not the least, playing the church organ. Resolved to forgo these desires, until a future time, she made the most of her surroundings and gave thanks for the children and Minnie Rosenthal.

The Tennessee morning broke to a cloudless sky and promised another sweltering day. Outside, the weather appears to be calm but Jack's barometer is slowly falling; and when that occurs, there's a good chance the long dry spell will soon be over. However, if it continues, another hot dusty wind might blow again, adding to their discomfort. (Around the globe, such winds take the shape of dust and sandstorms and are called by such names as simoon or harmattan.) Abigail spent another restless night and was up early and checked in on her daughter. She found Sarah awake and said, "Let's gather the eggs early this morning, dear. It looks like we're in for another hot day." When Sarah was washed and dressed, they grabbed their baskets and headed for the barn.

Taking notice of the cracked earth, Sarah asked, "Why is the ground breaking that way?"

"It's cracking because it's too dry. We haven't had any rain for a while, and that's what the ground does. The cracks will go away once it rains." That seemed to satisfy the inquisitive child, and she ran ahead to open the barn door. The hinges squeaked as Sarah pulled it open and felt the warmth inside. Rays of brightness streamed through the windows, illuminating the rows of hens sitting on straw nests. They began to cackle their displeasure as Abigail coaxed each one up in order to collect their eggs. All except the two nests at the far end. These hens were sitting on fertilized eggs soon to be hatched. Sarah was never satisfied until she looked in each nest for herself. As Abigail ran her hand under and gently lifted the hens, Sarah made her inspection. Once satisfied there were no baby chicks today, her attention was drawn to the sound of a feint nicker. Standing in one of the stalls was a bay-colored horse.

"Mother, it's a horse," Sarah shouted, while taking hold of Abigail's hand and leading her to the stall.

"It most certainly is, dear," said Abigail as she ran her hand along the horse's rump and on to the withers. The animal was very gentle and gave little reaction to her inspection other than the fluttering sound of another nicker. Attention was primarily given to the hay placed in the feed box. Abigail drew her attention to the bales of hay stacked in the adjoining cubicle and the sack of oats, obviously placed there sometime during the night.

"Is he ours to keep?" Sarah asked with excitement.

"I believe it is, sweetheart, and it's a girl, not a boy. It's also a miracle."

"Then let's call her Miracle," said Sarah.

Abigail was no newcomer when it came to horses. She determined the mare was about five years old by inspecting its teeth. The art of determining the age of horses by inspection of the teeth is an old one. It can be developed to a considerable degree of accuracy in determining the age of young horses. As a horse grows older, it becomes less reliable. Basically, a horse has two sets of teeth, one temporary called baby or milk teeth and one permanent. The permanent teeth are larger, longer, darker, and do not have the well-defined neck joining root and gum that temporary teeth do.

Age determination is made by a study of the twelve front teeth, called incisors. The two central pairs, both above and below, are called centers, pincers, or nippers. The four front teeth adjacent to these two pairs are called intermediates, and the outer four teeth are designated as corners.

The four center permanent teeth, two above and two below, appear as the animal approaches three years of age, the intermediates at four, and the corners at five. Young permanent teeth have deep indentures in the center of their surfaces, referred to as cups. These cups are also commonly used as a reference to determine a horse's age. Those in the upper teeth are deeper than those below; hence, they do not wear evenly with the surface or become *smooth* at equal periods of time. In general, the cups become smooth in the lower centers at age six and the others each year until a *smooth mouth* appears at about age eleven.

Sarah couldn't wait to tell Grandma Rosenthal and came running into the house shouting, "Grandma Minnie, we got a horse and I named her Miracle."

"Land's sake, child, hand me those eggs before you drop them. Now what's all this about a horse?"

"Just ask Mother, and she'll tell you all about it. Here she comes now," said the ebullient Sarah Jane.

"What's all this about a horse?" Minnie asked Abigail.

"It's true, Minnie, we have one in the barn."

"How in heavens did it get there?"

"It must have been Jack's Indian friends. They probably feel as though we won't be bothered anymore because of what happened to the Yankee soldier, and left it for us to travel to town and back. They may be right. Since that day, we haven't seen hide or hair of Union soldiers. It's as though they've been ordered to leave us alone," Abigail surmised.

A great deal of what Abigail said was true. General Sherman suggested that the soldiers give the Leffingwell family a lot of space, and the same was to hold true for the father, Hyrum Adams. I believe what he actually said was, "Give the preacher a long tether and leave that woman alone. I don't want a damn war with the Choctaws! The one I got is plenty, right now."

That evening, after prayers, Abigail and Minnie burned the candle's wick to the end discussing how their lives will be changed having a horse for transportation. In the morning, they will uncover the carriage and try to figure out how to hook it up to the horse. The phaeton was a two-seat double buggy and able to haul other things as well.

Tiny particles of dust could be seen, floating in the shafts of sunlight, as the two women removed the tarpaulin covering the buggy for the past two years. Upon closer scrutiny, it appeared to be in good shape. The harness tack was found lying in the back of the gig. The puzzled look on Abigail's brow forced a smile from Minnie Rosenthal, and after inspection the harness, she said, "Looks like everything is here. Don't worry about hooking it up. I was strapping pulling tack on horses before you were born." That brought a sigh of relief from Abigail who was beginning to show beads of perspiration on her forehead.

"Let's open the doors to this barn and cool it off a little. We're in for another Tennessee snow melter today, and left unvented, it'll be suffocating for the animal. There's not enough wind to twirl a single leaf, but with everything wide open, the horse ought to be more comfortable. We can make it rain-tight again if it storms. What's that over yonder?" Minnie asked, pointing to a covered pail resting in the corner by the door.

After inspecting, Abigail said, "It looks like black grease or something like it."

"Jacob always called it bear grease. We can use it to lubricate the wheel hubs so as to make them roll easier," said Minnie. At that point, the two women backed the mare out of her stall and led her to the adjoining corral. Miracle reacted to her somewhat limited freedom by running the fence line with her head held high and tail arched. She let out with a whinny, followed by a nicker, and walked slowly to Abigail and nuzzled her apron pocket. Abigail had forgotten the apple, meant for Miracle, which she had placed there before leaving the house.

By the time Minnie made breakfast and the children dressed and fed, the little household was ready to launch their first journey to Statesville. The August sun was straight overhead, often hidden by fleecy white cumulus clouds, giving comfort to those beneath. Miracle appeared to conduct her responsibilities without noticeable effort and at times acted as though she thoroughly enjoyed traveling the dirt road leading to town. The breeze from open-air travel refreshed both women as it fanned against their faces. Just riding in the carriage was complete joy for Sarah, and, Little Jack had fallen asleep. Abigail had to pass by the schoolhouse in order to reach her father's church and, in so doing, came into the view of Union soldiers standing in front.

"You see what I see? That's a mighty fine horse for a Johnny Reb wench to be driving," said a soldier sitting on a chair and leaning back against the building.

"Yeah, but I recognize that woman. We got orders not to bother her, and it came from General Sherman himself. I sure as hell don't want him skinning my ass, so I'll be leaving that one alone," said another.

"I remember now. Word has it, she has something to do with the Indians. She's a princess or something like that," recalled the first soldier. "One of our officers took an arrow in the neck for coming on to her."

"Did it kill him?"

"Deader than a doornail," said the other.

Abigail drove the gig around to the back of the church and pulled into a shed standing with its double doors wide open.

"I think it's best we not flaunt our good fortune," said Abigail as her father, hearing their arrival, opened the backdoor of the church and stepped outside.

"Praise the Lord and his many blessings," said Hyrum after observing the fine horse standing in his shed.

"Grandpa, we have a horse, and I named him . . . I mean her, Miracle," Sarah shouted excitedly.

"I see that, darling. Let's everybody go into the house, and you can tell me all about it," Hyrum replied.

Once inside, the joyous reunion continued. Abigail and Sarah explained their discovery in the morning and how Minnie was able to hook up the harness and attach it to the carriage. They told him how easy Miracle pulled them to town and all the things they will be able to do, now that they have transportation. The Union soldiers have shown a sudden lack of interest in the farm, and now, they have this beautiful horse. Hyrum told his daughter about a similar indifference regarding his own movements although Federal soldiers were showing up in the congregation on Sunday. For all Hyrum knew, they just might be spying.

"I don't think so, Father, it's more than that, it's coming from higher-ups."

Minnie had been talking with Mrs. Riberty and reentered the room while the conversation continued on the subject. She interjected, "The rumor round the feed store was that an order came down from General Sherman himself. I think it's because of what happened that day at the farm."

"I believe you're right, Minnie. But whatever the reason, the hand of the good Lord has left imprints on the whole matter."

"Amen to that, Rev. Adams," Minnie proclaimed.

The happy gathering shared in familial fellowship until the shadows began to grow longer. Abigail and Minnie needed to get back to the farm before nightfall and take care of their excellent equine gift. Before leaving, everyone held hands, and Hyrum led them in prayer for Jack and an end of the terrible war.

The temperature had cooled quite a lot from when they left that morning; and during the hour remaining of daylight, Abigail and Sarah managed to give Miracle a bath, use the currycomb, and fill her oat bucket before calling it a day. That night, the household had their first restful sleep since the incident of the Choctaw arrow.

Chapter Nine

In the confrontation between the stream and the rock,
the stream always wins—not through strength
but by perseverance.

—H. Jackson Brown, Jr.

Lee Responds to Union General Pope's Arc across Northern Virginia

On June 26, President Lincoln placed Maj. Gen. John Pope in command of the newly constituted Army of Virginia. Pope had reasonable success in the West and apparently enough for the administration to elevate him to the important command. His initial action was to have the Union army form an arc across Northern Virginia and gradually move South against Robert E. Lee. Its right flank, under Maj. Gen. Franz Sigel, was positioned at Sperryville on the Blue Ridge Mountains; its center, under Maj. Gen. Nathaniel P. Banks, was located at Little Washington; and its left flank, under Maj. Gen. Irvin McDowell, was at Falmouth on the Rappahannock River. Part of Bank's corps, Brig. Gen. Samuel W. Crawford's brigade and Brig. Gen. John P. Hatch's cavalry, were stationed twenty miles beyond the Union line, at Culpeper Court House.

General Lee responded to Pope's strategic act by dispatching Maj. Gen. Thomas "Stonewall" J. Jackson with fourteen thousand men to Gordonsville on July 13. On July 27, Jackson was reinforced by Maj. Gen. A. P. Hill's division with another ten thousand men. The Seventh Tennessee regiment, with Jack Leffingwell and his marksmen, was ordered to march sixty miles to become part of that group. Three days from the point of departure, they were embedded in the division and informed of Hill's responsibilities in the forthcoming action.

On August 6, Pope marched his forces South into Culpeper County with the objective of capturing the rail junction at Gordonsville. He believed such action would draw Confederate attention away from Maj. Gen. McClellan's withdrawal from the Virginia Peninsula.

The Old Man, a name given by his troops as a sign of respect, sent Stonewall Jackson on the offensive. He attacked Pope's vanguard, under General Banks, before the entire Union Army of Virginia could be brought to bear on his position at Gordonsville.

* * *

The Old Man wasn't the only nickname given to Robert E. Lee. In the early stages of the war, the public viewed Lee as too cautious in battle and gave him the moniker Granny Lee. It was this patience, misinterpreted as reluctance to fight, which enabled Lee to keep the Union forces at bay for almost four years.

Lee was born the son of Henry "Light Horse Harry" Lee, the ninth governor of Virginia. Light Horse Harry or Henry Lee III was an early American patriot who served as a cavalry officer in the Continental Army during the Revolutionary War. Later promoted to major general, he accompanied President George Washington to help suppress the infamous Whiskey Rebellion in Western Pennsylvania. His eulogy of Washington, to a crowd of four thousand at the first president's funeral on December 26, 1799, is remembered today: "First in war, first in peace, and first in the hearts of his countrymen." Henry Lee suffered severe financial reverses from failed investments during the Panic of 1796-1797 and was forced to spend a year in debtor's prison. Badly injured in a political riot in Baltimore, Lee suffered extensive internal injuries as well as head and face wounds, affecting his speech. Secretary of State James Madison arranged for Lee to travel to the West Indies in an effort to recuperate from his injuries. He never returned and died when Robert was eleven years old.

Robert E. Lee was raised in the pleasant environment of the antebellum south, a place where genteel manners were expected. His mother grew up at Shirley Plantation, one of the most elegant homes in Virginia. Bobby Lee's great-grandparents were prominent colonists and one of Virginia's first families originally arriving from England in the early 1600s. It's no surprise that Robert E. Lee had a gentle outward disposition with honor being an upmost attribute.

Lee entered West Point in the summer of 1825 and graduated second in his class, having never incurred a demerit during his four-year course of study. He chose engineering as his major field and graduated a military engineering officer. Working out of Washington, D.C., he performed various duties in Michigan, Ohio, Upper Mississippi, and Missouri river projects. While stationed at Fort Monroe, Lee married Mary Anna Randolph Custis, great-granddaughter of Martha Washington by her first husband, Daniel Park Custis, and step-great-granddaughter of George Washington. The ancestral lineage of both Lee and his wife was significant in its historical context.

Lee had distinguished himself as an exceptional officer throughout the United States, Mexican-American War, and as superintendent of the United States Military Academy. The death in 1857 of his father-in-law, George Washington Parke Custis, created a serious crisis, as Lee had to assume the main burden of executing the will. The Custis estate was in disarray, with vast landholdings and hundreds of slaves balanced against massive debts. The plantations had been poorly managed and were losing money. Lee took several leaves of absence from the army and became a planter and, eventually, straightened out the estate. The Custis last will called for emancipating the slaves within five years; however, state law required they be funded in a livelihood outside Virginia. That was impossible until the debts were paid off. They were all emancipated by 1862, within the five years specified.

When Virginia declared its secession from the Union in 1861, Lee chose to follow his home state, despite his personal desire for the Union to stay intact and the fact that President Abraham Lincoln offered him the command of the Union army. As time went on, Robert E. Lee became known as the Great Tycoon by his staff, Bobby Lee or Marse Robert by friends, and the King of Spades, given to him by his soldiers because of his propensity to have them *dig in* when things got tough.

* * *

After defeating Banks, Jackson then wanted to move on Culpeper Court House, twenty-six miles north of Gordonsville and the focal point of the Union arc about Northern Virginia—a move, if successful, which would keep Pope's army from uniting. This would also allow Jackson to fight and, hopefully, defeat each of the Union Corps separately. Jackson's march on Culpeper Court House was hindered by the severe heat wave over Virginia at the beginning of August, as well as by his characteristic secrecy about his plan, which caused confusion among his divisional commanders as to the exact route of advance. As such, the head of his column had only progressed eight miles by the evening of August 8. The Federal cavalry quickly returned to Pope and alerted him of the Confederate advance. In response, Pope ordered more troops to Culpeper Court House to reinforce Banks, and Banks was ordered to maintain a defensive line on a ridge above Cedar Run, seven miles south of Culpeper Court House.

The Battle of Cedar Mountain

On the morning of August 9, Jackson's army crossed the Rapidan River into Culpeper County, led by Maj. Gen. Richard S. Ewell's division, followed by Brig. Gen. Charles S. Winder's division, with Maj. Gen. A. P. Hill's division in the rear, and Lt. Col. Samuel G. Shepard now in command of the Seventh regiment.

Having spotted Federal cavalry and artillery on the ridge above Cedar Run, northwest of Cedar Mountain, Brig. Gen. Jubal Early (Ewell's division) brought up his guns and began an artillery duel between the opposing forces. General Early's infantry formed a line on the eastern side of Culpeper-Orange turnpike on the high ground of the opposite bank of Cedar Run. As the rest of Ewell's division arrived, they formed on Early's right and deployed six guns on the ridge of the mountain. Another division formed on the left. More troops formed in a wheat field on the far left. Artillery filled a gap on the road between the two divisions. A. P. Hill's division, including Lt. Col. Samuel G. Shepard's Seventh regiment and Jack Leffingwell's marksmen in Company H, were still trudging up the turnpike and ordered to stand in reserve on the Confederate left.

The Federals formed a line on a ridge above Cedar Run, with another brigade forming the Union right in a field across from yet another Union division on the Union left, east of the turnpike. Two regiments were kept in reserve in the rear.

The artillery fight began to wane around 5:00 p.m. Confederate brigadier general Charles S. Winder was struck by a shell fragment while attempting to direct his troops. He had been ill that day and was taken onto the field in an ambulance wagon. Winder's left arm and side were torn to pieces, and he died a few hours later. As a result, command of the division devolved on William Taliaferro, who was completely ignorant of Jackson's battle plan. Dispositions on his part of the field were still incomplete; another brigade was isolated from the main Confederate line, with its flank dangerously exposed to the woods. The Stonewall Brigade was to have come up to support them, but remained a half mile distant behind the artillery. Before leadership could properly be restored to the division, the Union attack began.

Two Union divisions were sent against the Confederate right. Their advance was swift and threatened to break the Confederate line, prompting Early to come galloping to the front from Cedar Mountain, where he was still directing troop dispositions. Early's stabilizing presence and the raking fire of the Confederate guns halted the Union advance on the Confederate right.

On the left, the Union attacked Winder's division, sending one brigade directly at the Confederate line and another brigade through the woods on a flanking movement. Emerging from the woods, the Federals came directly into the flank of the First Virginia Infantry, who, under pressure from attack on two fronts, broke for the rear. Capitalizing on their advantage, the Federals pushed on, not waiting to reform their lines, rolling through the outflanked Confederates until they found themselves in Taliaferro's and the artillery's rear. The Stonewall Brigade came up and was swept aside by the Union troops before it had a chance to react. Jackson ordered the batteries withdrawn before they were captured, at the same time, Taliaferro and Early's left were hit hard by the Union advance and threatened to break. At this dire point, General Jackson rode to that part of the field to rally the men and came upon his old brigade, finally being brought up to reinforce the line. Intending to inspire the troops there, he attempted to wave his sword; however, due to the infrequency with which he used it, it had rusted in its scabbard and couldn't be dislodged. As the story goes, undaunted, he unbuckled the sword from his belt and waved it over his head, scabbard and all. He then grabbed a battle flag from a retreating standard bearer and yelled at his men to rally around him. The Stonewall Brigade, heartened by their commander, launched into the Union troops and drove them back. By this point, the Union soldiers were becoming tired and disorganized, with their ammunition nearly gone. Without any support, they were unable to follow up on their initial success. In their eagerness, the Stonewall Brigade pursued the Federals as they fell back; however, soon found themselves beyond the Confederate line, and they, too, without support. The Federals reformed and attacked, driving the Southern rebels back. The actions of the Stonewall Brigade gave enough time for the Confederate line to reform and A. P. Hill's troops to come up, filling the gaps from Winder's broken regiments. Jackson ordered Hill and Ewell to advance. The Union right immediately collapsed. The Union left began to waver at the sight of the right's retreat and was broken when a Confederate brigade charged down Cedar Mountain. Before dark, the Union line was in full retreat. In a last ditch effort to help cover the infantry's retreat, Union general Banks sent two squadrons of cavalry at the adversary's line. They were met with a devastating volley from the rebel infantry, posted behind a fence on the road, allowing very few to escape. The Confederate infantry hotly pursued the retreating Federals, nearly capturing Union generals Bank and Pope. After a mile or so of pursuit, and darkness setting in, Jackson grew weary. Not sure of the location of the rest of Pope's army, the pursuit was called off—the right decision—considering that around 10:00 p.m., additional Union troops arrived effectively covering Banks's retreat. Losses were high in the battle: three men from Wilson County's Company H were killed and a total of thirty-four men were lost from the Seventh regiment.

Casualty Estimates for the Battle of Cedar Mountain*

	Total Casualties	Wounded	Killed	Captured/Missing
Union	2,353	1,445	312	594
Confederate	1,338	1,107	231	—

*Also known as Slaughters Mountain or the Battle of Cedar Run.

Stonewall Jackson maintained his position for two days; then, after receiving news that all of Pope's army had arrived at Culpeper Court House, he fell back on Gordonsville to a more defensive position, behind the Rapidan River.

As in many battles, Lady Luck played her significant role. Weather and poor communications had robbed Jackson of the initiative in the fight, and he was taken by surprise and nearly driven from the field. The fortuitous arrival of Gen. A. P. Hill, when it appeared that the battle was lost, staved off defeat. From that point, the numerical superiority of Southern troops helped drive the Federals from the battleground.

Jackson's division settled in at Gordonsville for a brief respite and break in the fighting while they awaited Pope's advance. However, the newly appointed Union general-in-chief Henry Halleck became apprehensive; and with Jackson on the loose, wreaking havoc against his troops, he called off Pope's advance on Gordonsville. Almost as soon as Jack Leffingwell, and the others in Company H, began to relax and recuperate from the previous battle, they were ordered to march to Manassas, Virginia.

The rain had finally stopped, and an unnerving silence came over the camp as the troops prepared to depart. It was in the predawn hours and the Alice blue moon gave a ghostly shine amid wispy clouds, making the scene appear somewhat surreal. Soldiers had experienced this phenomenon before and discounted it as prebattle nerves, but tonight, somehow it seemed different. Perhaps it was an omen or the phantasm of ill fate.

"I don't feel good about this trip," Abel said to Jack. "Don't it feel kind of spooky to you?"

"I know what you mean," Jack replied. "Did you say your prayers last night?"

"Always, Mother," answered Abel.

As the dawn arrived, the situation became more ordinary and returned to a typical day on the move. The morning is always very forgiving, and soon the lines broke into song while tramping toward their destination.

By this time, Union general Pope had united his disheveled army and awaited reinforcements. Gen. Robert E. Lee had organized his Army of Northern Virginia into two *wings* of about fifty-five thousand men. The right wing was commanded by Maj. Gen. James Longstreet, and the left by Stonewall Jackson, who also directed the Cavalry Division under J. E. B. Stuart. On August 13, Lee sent Longstreet to reinforce Jackson. The combined Confederate forces now outnumbered Pope's, and Lee planned to use the advantage to outflank and cut off Pope's army before the whole of McClellan's forces could be brought to bear.

From August 22 to August 25, the two armies fought a series of minor skirmishes along the Rappahannock River. It was like two heavy weight boxers feeling each other out before landing vicious haymakers. Rain had swollen the Rappahannock to the point where Lee was unable to cross it. Union reinforcements were beginning to arrive from the peninsula, and General Lee knew he soon would lose numerical advantage. Up to this point, both adversaries learned each other's plans by intercepting messages. Pope ascertained that Lee's plan was to trap him against the swollen river and withdrew to the northern bank along the Orange and Alexandria Railroad. Always able to fire his imagination and think out of the box, General Lee devised a different and much bolder plan. In the words of Wordsworth, Lee had "that inward eye which is the bliss of solitude." His plan called for Stonewall Jackson and J. E. B. Stuart, plus half of the army, to commence a wide turning movement through Thoroughfare Gap in the Bull Run Mountains and outflank Pope's line at the railroad junction. General Longstreet's forces following close behind.

Union general Pope took notice of Jackson's move, but still assumed it was pointed toward the Shenandoah Valley. Instead, Stonewall Jackson covered nearly sixty miles in two days, came in behind Pope, and destroyed the massive Union supply depot at Manassas Junction, slipping away unmolested. The frustrated Union general marched his forces back and forth for two days searching for the elusive Confederates. Jackson, meanwhile, had marched his divisions north to the first Bull Run battlefield and took defensive positions behind an abandoned railroad embankment. The defensive position was a good one. Heavy woods allowed the Southern allies to conceal themselves, while maintaining good observation points. They were able to oversee the approach roads for Longstreet to join Jackson, and routes for retreat, should that occasion arise.

Pope attacked by a series of frontal assaults which were repulsed with heavy casualties. When reinforcements arrived from McClellan, they were ordered to charge

Jackson's right flank in the south. By this time, Longstreet's column had burst through Thoroughfare Gap and deployed on Jackson's right, blocking the Yankee move. Now, both wings of Lee's army were on the battlefield.

The next day, Pope renewed his attacks against Jackson, thinking him to be retreating. Lee seized the moment to catch the Federals in an exposed position and sent Longstreet along the Warrington Turnpike to catch Pope's flank, while it was out in the open. The Confederates loaded and fired their deadly musketry as fast as men could shoot. The sounds of battle were deafening, and the Union soldiers were commanded into the blazing inferno of flashing sparks from a thousand rebel rifles, sizzling from continuous use. Hundreds of Pope's men fell that day, sacrificed because of another miscalculation. The Federal army soon retreated from the field, and a defeated General Pope led it back to Washington, having to fight nearly every step of the way. The friendless general was relieved of his command on September 12, and his army merged into the Army of the Potomac, under McClellan.

Casualty Estimates for the Pope's Northern Virginia Campaign*

	Total Casualties	Wounded	Killed	Captured/Missing
Union	16,054	8,373	1,724	5,958
Confederate	9,197	7,627	1,481	89

*Also known as the Second Manassas or Bull Run Campaign

With a major victory under his belt, Lee immediately began his next campaign. On September 3, his Army of Northern Virginia crossed the Potomac and tramped toward a fateful encounter with the Union Army of the

Potomac at Sharpsburg, Maryland, and Antietam Creek. It was to be the first battle on Northern soil. By this time, the proud Seventh regiment of Tennessee was down to 350 men with effectives of less than 100. John Henry Bickford was mortally wounded at Manassas and buried on the field with over 1,300 rebel heroes. John Henry died while sporting his recently purloined boots, and once again, they didn't make it to the grave.

Lee's army consisted of 55,000 active troops, including cavalry brigades. He set up camp near Fredrick, Maryland, and, to maintain inertia, sent Stonewall Jackson to capture an isolated Union garrison at Harper's Ferry. Lee had learned that the Federal garrison had not retreated after his incursion into Maryland; and since he had the inordinate advantage of troop numbers, he decided to surround the force and capture it. He divided his army into four columns, three of which converged upon the designated target. After Confederate artillery was placed on the heights overlooking the town, the Union commander surrendered the garrison of more than twelve thousand soldiers. Jackson took possession of Harper's Ferry and led most of his soldiers to join up with Lee at Sharpsburg. The capture of Harper's Ferry provided the Southern coalition with a large amount of supplies, including clothing, shoes, thousands of small arms and ammunition, and over seventy pieces of artillery. The remainder of Lee's army then crossed South Mountain and headed for Hagerstown, about twenty-five miles to the northwest.

McClellan's rejuvenated Army of the Potomac consisted of about ninety thousand men and marched northwest from Washington to intercept Gen. Robert E. Lee's Army of Northern Virginia with half the manpower. McClellan was in pursuit of the Southern army, but unknowing he had a two to one advantage, he traveled at a snail's pace—a typical performance by the overly cautious Union general. At times, McClellan's excessively restrained behavior was one of the traits which frequently frustrated President Lincoln.

Nobody can argue that McClellan wasn't lucky. While inspecting an abandoned Confederate camp, Union soldiers found a copy of Lee's order for company movements, giving the routes, objectives, and times of arrival. McClellan was given the best of windfalls and an unmatched opportunity to defeat Lee's scattered forces, if he moved quickly through the exposed gaps. McClellan dawdled for nearly a day, during which time Lee eventually learned of his lost orders and sent all available forces to hold the gaps. Accordingly, it was nightfall on September 14 before McClellan found his way across South Mountain. By then, Lee had retreated to Sharpsburg on Antietam Creek, where he dug in and prepared to fight.

On September 16, McClellan dispatched Union general Joseph Hooker to confront Lee's outnumbered coalition. Hooker's assault on Lee's left flank resulted in the bloodiest single day in American history. Attacks and counterattacks eventually pierced the Confederate center; regardless, the Federal advantage was not followed up. Later, Union general Ambrose Burnside's corps finally got into action, crossing the stone bridge over Antietam Creek and rolled up the Confederate right.

Burnside failed to perform adequate reconnaissance of the area, and instead of taking advantage of several easy fording sites out of range of the enemy, his troops were forced into repeated assaults across the narrow bridge, which was dominated by Confederate sharpshooters on high ground. By noon, McClellan, unaware of the intense burden Burnside faced, was losing patience. He sent a succession of couriers to motivate Burnside to move forward. The battered general sent each dispatch rider back with a request for reinforcements, which McClellan refused. Finally, a portion of Maj. Gen. A. P. Hill's Confederate division had completed the occupation of Harper's Ferry and arrived at a crucial moment. At last, Burnside broke through the resistance at the bridge and secured a crossing. While he began to climb the slopes toward Sharpsburg, he was told of the enemy moving a strong force against him. Actually, it consisted of only elements of A. P. Hill's division numbering less than two thousand men; however, Union troops had difficulty identifying them because of battle smoke and some of Hill's men were wearing portions of Union uniforms captured at Harpers Ferry. In their confusion, the Federals fell back. Unsure of the size of the Confederate force attacking his left, Burnside ordered a withdrawal to the creek. Whether by twist of fate or just plain luck, the fragment of A. P. Hill's division appeared in time to head off more Union assaults and even counterattacked, saving the day.

By failing to commit his forces to battle on September 15 and 16, the meticulous McClellan squandered the chance to exploit his superior numerical advantage. On September 17, he gave a piecemeal commitment of only a portion of his command during the battle and failed to deliver a knockout blow to destroy Lee's army. His decision not to renew the battle on September 18, with the same, if not greater opportunity as the previous day, allowed General Lee to withdraw safely to Virginia's protective clime.

Antietam was not the decisive victory Lincoln had wanted; nevertheless, it gave him the opportunity to strike at the Confederacy both politically and economically. On September 22, he issued the preliminary Emancipation Proclamation, declaring that the Federal government would, after January 1, 1863, consider slaves, in any state in rebellion against the Federal government, to be free. Although the battle ended in a stalemate, Lee's army left the battlefield and McClellan remained, thus technically, making him the victor. As a result, the prospect of England or France intervening in the war on behalf of the Confederacy was eliminated.

Despite expansive wording, the Emancipation Proclamation was limited in many ways. It applied only to states that had seceded from the Union, leaving slavery untouched in the loyal border states. It also expressly exempted parts of the Confederacy that had already come under Northern control. Most importantly, the freedom it promised was contingent upon a Union military victory. While the president opposed slavery, he was not an abolitionist and stated publically that the war was being fought over secession, with the slavery question only incidental. Lincoln's proclamation did not immediately free a single slave, but it did change the character of the war.

Starting on January 1, 1863, every advance of Federal troops expanded the domain of freedom; and the acceptance of black men into the Union army and navy resulted in two hundred thousand black soldiers and sailors fighting for the North by the time the war ended.

Gen. Robert E. Lee had become tenacious as a spotted hyena, and, at the same time, also knew his army needed rest to maintain both emotional and physical strength. With McClellan showing no interest in an immediate confrontation, Lee ordered a rest at Berryville, Virginia.

Chapter Ten

We must teach our children to resolve their conflicts with words, not weapons.

—William Jefferson Clinton

Many times Abigail felt as though a nervous breakdown was just around the corner. Her husband had been gone for two years, and the interval between letters was unpredictable. The Union occupation disrupted her life to the point that she was uncertain about the future prospects of living in Statesville or even Tennessee for that matter. The best houses were commandeered for lodging Federal soldiers, and the schools and churches closed and turned into military functions.

Hyrum Adam's church was one of the exceptions. It was allowed to continue, but closely monitored by the Northern occupiers. Ever since General Sherman's edict, those wearing blue uniforms showed respect for the minister and his family. In fact, they even tipped their hat to Abigail and Minnie Rosenthal when the women were in town on errands.

Still, care must be taken so as not to make comments critical to the Union. Free speech no longer existed, and those who vocally disagreed with present policies were arrested and their homes thoroughly searched. Soldiers assigned to such details were not careful when hunting through the houses. Complete sets of dishes were smashed. Some were keepsakes and irreplaceable antiques. Returning home, owners often found doors smashed, windows broken, and excrement left on the walls. Adding insult to injury, they were heavily fined and forced to take the amnesty oath of loyalty to the Union. It was a time many women wished they were men and could join the army to fight these occupying devils.

Abigail, fortunate to escape a serious episode, had similar desires, even so, tried to concentrate on more positive activities. She had a thought of something she could do constructively and planned to discuss it with her father on Sunday. It had become a pleasant routine of going to church, playing the organ, and sharing lunch with Hyrum when services were completed. Hyrum looked forward each week to seeing his daughter and especially the two grandchildren. To Hyrum, God is good and Sundays only prove it.

The luncheon fare this week was chicken and noodles, created by the hands of Minnie Rosenthal. Most parishioners lost their livelihood due to the war and subsequent occupation. Farms were periodically raided by soldiers foraging for food. Farmers were unable to plant or harvest crops, thus eliminating any chance for marketing their wares. Donations to the church primarily consisted of vegetables planted in small gardens, other types of foodstuffs, and items handcrafted. Hyrum's personal needs were minor; therefore, a major portion of the foodstuffs were redistributed among the more needy families.

Hyrum gave thanks for the meal and turned to Minnie Rosenthal, saying, "I think you outdid yourself on the chicken and slicks." The term *slicks* was given to the noodles. Actually, they weren't like most noodles we think of today. Instead, they were thicker, longer, and wider. Minnie made noodle dough, rolled it out, and cut it into the aforementioned strips. Next, she covered the dough strips with a dish cloth and allowed them to sit for the time it takes to finish boiling the chicken. After which, the slicks are added and allowed to cook an hour longer. For Hyrum, the finished product was a dream come true.

"Is everything still okay at the farm?" Hyrum asked his daughter.

"Yes, Father. Our getting the mare has made a wonderful difference, and having Minnie Rosenthal with me is truly the Lord's blessing. I don't think I could have made it this far without her. The children think the world of her. It's almost like having a mother with me."

Abigail's statement was made in total innocence, yet it brought back an eye-twitching memory of his departed loved one. The minister reached for his water glass and took a sip, hoping no one noticed the hurt his heart refused to abandon. It was only an instant before Hyrum regained composure and asked, "What was it you wanted to discuss with me daughter?"

"Well, now that we have Miracle, I'm able to travel to Statesville whenever I wish. And for a long time now, I've wanted to contribute something to our cause. The first thing that came to mind was nursing at one of the

Confederate hospitals. Until now, with the occupation and all, I think I missed my chance."

"Don't take this wrong, my dear, we love you for it. With your tender mercies, I'm not sure you could hold up taking part in a man's arm and leg being sawed off, let alone all the distressing other scenes attached to war. Consider it a blessing you missed the chance." Abigail had only considered giving medication, cleaning wounds, and changing bandages. Her father was right about the rest of it. She would faint at the sight of that much blood and trauma.

"Well, I'd like to teach school. All the town schools have been shut down, and most of the church activities discounted. I could, let's say, teach the children two days a week and give homework for the time in between. The children still have their textbooks, and we can meet in the church Sunday schoolroom."

Hyrum was silent while digesting his daughter's idea and then said, "I've thought about and prayed for the children many times lately. While most of them have been lucky enough not to have witnessed any battles, they still are with soldiers all around and witness their parents' fear of the occupation. Others were unfortunate enough to see the war up close. Battles often happened on their own farms and in their hometowns. Those children experienced sheer terror, and some have experienced the tragic loss of family members. The children of Statesville are lucky having never witnessed this war firsthand. Most likely, in their view, this occupation has given them joy by shutting down the churches and school. That perhaps is the most dangerous position in which they could find themselves. We all need boundaries, and especially the children. Attending school not only educates, but it also gives order to their lives at a time when they need it most. Abigail, I think you have an excellent idea, and I shall announce it this coming Sunday. That will give us some information as to how many will attend."

Before returning home, Abigail walked to the post office and read the most recent list of war casualties. None was posted for Wilson County, and she gave a short prayer of thanks. A lot has happened today, and she was anxious to get back to the farm and write Jack.

September 29, 1862
Dearest Husband,

You'll be proud to hear that your wife will probably soon be teaching school in Statesville. I've just returned from meeting with Father, and he promised to mention it Sunday next. Ever since this occupation, the children have been without the anchor they need to help develop their character as well as book learning. I want to contribute something to our effort here in Tennessee, and teaching, at the moment, is the best I can consider. Oh, how I miss your counsel in matters like this. You always seem to do the right thing when the rest are wringing their hands. The mysterious gift now gives me the ability to travel back and forth and take Sarah Jane with me. Our daughter will benefit from being with the other children in a social setting. As far as book knowledge is concerned, she has gotten a great deal here at home. Grandma

Rosenthal offered to tend to Little Jack while I'm gone.

Do you remember the girl who made your first curtains, Maryellen Riberty? Of course you do. She was the one that's overly endowed. Well, her parents own the general store in town. Maryellen and I have gotten to be friends, and the last time we were in town, she gave me the end bolts of cloth from the store. There wasn't enough on each one to make a woman's dress, but Minnie Rosenthal has made dresses for Sarah Jane. That woman is a genius. We have the best-dressed little girl in the whole state. I make certain everybody knows her clothes are made from scraps, else they will think we are too ritzy and just showing off. I've had to pray about that in case I'm feeling too proud.

I know how you feel about slavery, but a lot of people in Tennessee own them; and once we were occupied by the Union, they just took off and went to the Union camps. People call them contraband. So many have showed up outside the camps, white folks in town are getting nervous about it. Mind you, I know none of this firsthand. I get my information from Maryellen. Father says it could very well be true. Outside of all that, there isn't much of interest to relate. I miss you so much. There are times I think I'll go crazy without you here to touch and hold. Father says it's all in God's plan for us. I wish God would concentrate more on other people.

Your devoted wife,
Abigail

* * *

The Seventh Tennessee regiment withdrew from Antietam Creek and trudged over forty miles to Berryville, Virginia, for a much-needed breather, caused by the stress of battle. Most of all, the Southern protagonists needed to recover from the rigors of mental fatigue. They have faced the enemy in mortal combat and bravely fought, in some cases, hand to hand using their rifles as a club. Battle scenes of this nature will come back to them in nightmares for many weeks to come. Today, however, the column rolls along singing favorite marching songs. There was one in particular the Southern soldiers loved to sing, entitled, "Goober Peas." It is a rollicking song timed perfectly for the march.

Sitting by the roadside on a summer's day, chatting with my messmates passing time away,

Lying in the shadow underneath the trees, Goodness how delicious, eating goober peas!

Peas! Peas! Peas! Peas! Eating goober peas! Goodness how delicious, eating goober peas!

When a horseman passes, the soldiers have a rule, to cry out at their loudest, "Mister here's your mule."

But another pleasure enchantinger than these, is wearing out your grinders, eating goober peas!

Peas! Peas! Peas! Peas! Eating goober peas! Goodness how delicious, eating goober peas!

Just before the battle the General hears a row, He says the Yanks are coming, I hear their rifles now,

He turns around in wonder, and what do you think he sees, The Tennessee Militia, eating goober peas!

Peas! Peas! Peas! Peas! Eating goober peas! Goodness how delicious, eating goober peas!

I think my song has lasted almost long enough, the subject's interesting, but rhymes are mighty rough

I wish this war was over when free from rags, and fleas, we'd kiss our wives and sweethearts and gobble goober peas!

Peas! Peas! Peas! Peas! Eating goober peas! Goodness how delicious, eating goober peas!

* * *

The Berryville camp was located in the upper Shenandoah Valley about eleven miles south of what later will become West Virginia. Resting in the base of the Blue Ridge Mountains, with the Potomac River north and the James River south, makes it ideal for rejuvenating battle-worn troops. Dense forests encircle the area, and running mountain streams ripple and twist through and around the camp. Because of the abundance of slope forests, many log cabins serve to house the South's finest. Jack Leffingwell and the marksmen hoped to be assigned a cabin rather than the old standby, the six-man tent. That was not to be; however, the camp commander pointed out an area and gave them the option to build their own cabin. He went on further to free them from drills while the cabin is being constructed. Jack readily accepted the offer.

Dense spruce fir stood near the assigned area, making it convenient for hauling logs. For the next two weeks, from dawn to dusk, the sound of saw and ax was heard as the log shelter began to take shape. The work was hard, but inspiring, and served to ease the horrific thoughts of battle from their minds. The physical labor prompted a good night's sleep and, for the most part, was uninterrupted by nightmares.

Jack Leffingwell was the only one in the crew who has built a log home, and his experience was very helpful to the rest. One of the most important things was to guard against termites. They made certain to pack a lot of sand over their foundation. Lomas Chandler couldn't understand why everybody was so concerned about such things, since they will have to give up the dwelling once they are called to battle and, probably, never get it back.

"If you do anything, it's important to do it to the best of your ability, no matter what it is," Ihme said. The rest shook their heads in agreement. And that is exactly what they did. Upon completion, the cabin, built with their own hands, turned out to be one of the best in the camp and the envy of the neighborhood. Lomas, once again, provided another Franklin stove, which, déjà vu, he won in a poker game. The weather has noticeably cooled, especially at night, with temperatures dropping into the low forties, making the stove quite useful and well appreciated.

The landscape is slowly surrendering to the advent of winter and has burst into a kaleidoscope of color. Maple, ash, oak, and hickory display vibrant hues of red, orange, bronze, and rust before releasing them in the prewinter tradition. The leaves of the beechnut trees persist in winter, but soon they will dislodge their fruit. The oily-sweet meat of beechnuts is a favorite of the area fauna including opossum, black bears, and white-tailed deer. Similarly, the shagbark hickory will soon spill their ripened seeds to the delight of squirrels, raccoons, and chipmunks. The hickory shed not only its leaves but also its bark. It's not surprising this unusual tree produces a most difficult hard-shelled nut.

The pending winter is recognizable by changes in the wildlife, especially wild boar that has grown a much-denser fur and an increased mating desire, as evidenced by sows giving birth in the spring and the gestation period being approximately four months. Another inhabitant is the black bear who begins extra effort to fatten up before hibernating. They need to gain at least thirty pounds to last them through the winter fast. October or November is the time they enter their dens located in hollowed-out trees, under logs, rock piles, caves, or culverts. Indigenous black bears hibernate for three to five months, during which time their heart rate drops from forty to fifty beats per minute to as low as eight. White-tailed deer also have a winter routine. Their coat thickens and turns from reddish-brown to grayish-brown. Males won't shed their antlers until all females are bred, usually from December to February, and their spotted offspring appear in early to midsummer.

Now that the cabin is built, the riflemen have resumed drills which consisted of early-morning marches and the afternoon taken up with target practice. The majority of rebel soldiers have been issued new Enfield rifles, not as popular as the Springfield Model 1861. Considering many soldiers were using hunting rifles from home and even shotguns, the new combat weapons were greatly appreciated. The Confederates imported more Enfields during the war than any other type of rifle, buying from private contractors and gun runners. The British government refused to sell them once they believed the Confederacy could not win the war. The Enfield rifle was their companion from 1862 until the surrender in 1865 and saw action in all the major battles. Jack Leffingwell was partial to his Whitworth rifle and declined acceptance of the new Enfields. He believed that if his life depended on the rifle, his faith rested with the long-distance Whitworth. Thus far, his decision has proven to be correct.

Returning from target practice, the sharpshooters ate supper then entered their cabin. A few pieces of firewood gave enough heat to make them comfortable. Abel Strawn glanced at each of his companions and said, "We are stinking up the place. Did anybody notice how bad it smelled at our table? When the wind blew, I had to hold my breath. We need to take a bath . . . real bad."

"We washed our face and hands," replied Lomas. "That's all army regulations require."

"You're right, Lomas, but that's not what Abel is referring to. Our bodies stink, and one other thing, we can never get rid of the lice unless we have a bath," Jack added.

"Well, there ain't no place to take one," Lomas said frankly.

"Like hell there isn't. We have a clean, fast-running stream not more than a hundred feet away. That would be a perfect place to use the bars of hard soap they issued us. And if Abel and I take a bath there and the rest of you guys don't, then you will have to sleep outside," Jack stated with conviction. Reluctantly, the others found the hard soap and a towel, stripped down to Mother Nature, and made a dash for the creek. A world record had to have been set that day, if there was such a thing, as the soldiers jumped in, up to their chest, and scrubbed dry skin until it turned pink. They continued bobbing underwater until the suds were gone and kept eyeing Jack for his permission to get back to the cabin. Once Jack nodded, they hopped like kangaroos over the small stones lining the stream, in an attempt to ease the pain on the bottoms of their tender feet. Entering the cabin was like heaven, as the warm air overcame the chattering of teeth, while each man finished using their towel.

"What happened to you, Ihme? Did you run into the rabbi on the way back?" Lomas asked jokingly. They all had shriveled from the stream's cold water.

"I didn't see any rabbi," Ihme answered seriously, bringing a round of laughter from the others.

Bathing was not a daily activity in a military camp. By regulation, soldiers were only required to wash hands and face for inspection. Whatever else they wanted to wash was up to them. Most of the time, the only available water came from a creek or river, and usually, it was too cold for comfort. As a result, they didn't wash often. There was one thing worse than the smell of dirty men; it was the infestation of lice. Every camp was affected because if one man had them, then everybody else tended to have them. It was agreed among the marksmen that regular bathing was the lesser of two evils. It came down to a choice between five minutes in cold water versus all day scratching, picking, and itching with lice.

Once the men settled down, they began to yawn and found it difficult to keep their eyes open anymore. A gentle form of tiredness gradually took hold and began to influence their capacity to stay awake.

"I don't know about you guys, but I'm going to hit the hay," said Abel. "There isn't anything better than a bath and a warm bed that's more conducive for a good night's sleep."

"I can think of one thing," Lomas replied. "That's the warm body of a woman there beside you." The dwell of silence spoke for the rest.

"How come you never got married, Lomas?" asked Jack.

"I guess I just never found the right girl. Seems like just when I think I found her, another pops up and I go with her. There was one that could have been, but I missed my chance. This beautiful gal moved into the house across the street from where I was living, and I couldn't wait to get to meet her. One night I noticed she left her shades up and you see in real good. She must have gotten home from work. Well, I about fell over. She took every stitch of clothes off and walked around naked. There never was a more perfect body than the one she paraded around the room. The funniest thing about it all was this went on every day. Once she got home from work, she never wore any clothes. Man, I was hot to trot, and after two weeks, I had to ask her for a date. When I finally mustered enough courage to go over there, they told me she had died."

"What from, pneumonia?" asked Abel. You could barely hear Lomas's answer due to the rollicking.

"Very funny," Lomas said. "That was a true story."

"How about you, Jack, I'll bet you've known more different kinds of women than all of us put together, you being a mountain man and traveling for the railroad and all," prodded Lomas.

"I've had a few experiences, but none to compare with my wife, Abigail," Jack thoughtfully replied. "She was a preacher's daughter and straighter than a Choctaw arrow. For the longest time, I choked on my words before they ever came out. In her presence, my heart beat harder than a blacksmith's hammer striking hot iron and just as loud too, or at least, it seemed like it. When we first met, I don't think she liked me . . . my kind of men weren't ever allowed into her life. Thankfully, her father knew her a whole lot better than me and told me never to give up trying to win her over. I'll never forget the day she said yes, and on our wedding night, she gave me a gift for which a man is always beholden."

Lomas turned to Abel and whispered, "What did he mean by that?"

"She was a virgin, dumb ass," Abel softly replied.

That evening, the intermittent sounds of a sprinkling rain was heard by those within, as it gently fell upon the cabin roof. Those inside have trod pliantly down the steps of sleep until they found themselves in the arms of Morpheus. Benumbed by their slumber, the only sounds heard were those of a whisper-soft snore. It truly was the velvet sleep of the just. The Franklin stove released a report of its own as an acrobatic flame danced atop a slow-burning ember. All said, it was a perfect ending for a peaceful day, that night, in the mountains of northern Old Dominion.

* * *

I'm reminded of the quote by Chris LeDoux, American country music singer-songwriter, and rodeo champion, "And takin' a bath in the creek. That's the stuff that really made it worthwhile. Anybody can stay in a hotel."

Chapter Eleven

If you go long enough without a bath, even the fleas will leave you alone.

—Ernie Pyle

The next day was Sunday, giving the soldiers a day off from military drills. After breakfast, Jack and Abel attended church services. Those in the congregation formed a circle around a cheerful bonfire and were sitting on logs and reading excerpts from the King James Bible. The service was led by a divinity student, himself the son of a Tennessee Methodist minister. Abel particularly enjoyed singing the hymns, and it seemed to Jack that he knew most of them by heart. The two Tennesseans always felt a little better after attending such services and returned to the cabin in a good mood. As they went through the required menial activities for the remainder of the day, i.e., cleaning their weapons and doing laundry, a knock was heard at the door.

"It ain't locked, come on in," Lomas shouted.

Standing in the doorway was a typical Johnny Reb, wearing the Confederate gray uniform and carrying a long-distance rifle. He was obviously nervous and removed his hat before saying, “I was ordered to report to you guys about living here.”

“This cabin is for sharpshooters, son,” said Abel in an advising manner.

“Well, I’m a sharpshooter,” the stranger replied, with a little more confidence.

“So you’re a sharpshooter, huh? What exactly can you do? How far can you shoot? Having a rifle doesn’t always make you a sharpshooter,” Abel added.

“I can shoot the eye out of a squirrel at over a thousand feet,” the soldier proudly announced.

“That’s only a little over three hundred yards. What can you do at three thousand feet?” Abel asked.

“I might be able to hit the squirrel,” he answered sheepishly.

“That fellow sitting over there can shoot the eye out of a squirrel at a thousand yards,” Abel said as he pointed at Jack.

“Then he must be Jack Leffingwell,” returned the stranger. Now, everybody likes to be stroked now and then, and Jack was no exception. The offhanded compliment prompted him to join in the conversation.

“What’s your name and where are you from?” Jack asked.

“My name is Melvin Kaufman, sir, and I’m from Watertown, Tennessee, although we move quite a lot when my Pappy looks for work,” Kaufman replied honestly.

“Melvin, we need to take a vote whether or not we want you here. Do you understand? Our lives depend a lot on each other, and we all have to trust any newcomer,”

Jack said. "Have a seat on that log over there while we take a vote."

Jack shut the door and turned to the others.

"What do you guys think? We lost John Henry Bickford at Manassas and probably could use another hand. Before we vote, I'm sure you know how John Henry would have voted." Actually, no one cared that much about John Henry, especially after the way he acquired his new boots. It seemed like Jack was using a little psychology on the team. The Tennessee mountain man had always defended the abused and downtrodden and, to do otherwise, would not be part of his nature.

"Ihme, how do you vote?" asked Jack.

"I don't want to vote first, ask somebody else," Ihme responded.

"I'll vote," Abel interjected. "I vote that he can stay." Lomas spoke next and said, "He can stay, but he has to pay rent." That brought smiles. Then Jack voted in favor of the newcomer and turned back to Ihme who said, "I don't care one way or the other."

"I'll take that as a yes vote and making it unanimous," Jack affirmed.

Melvin Kaufman remained on the log, sitting with his hands clasped to his chin, until the door reopened. Looking up, he beheld the towering presence of Jack Leffingwell who stated, "We voted to accept you, Melvin, but there's something you must do before we allow you to come inside. You gotta take a bath first."

"Take a bath, hell, there ain't no place to take a bath," Melvin uttered.

"There's a creek a short piece in that direction," Jack conveyed and pointed to his right. "In case you don't have hard soap, here's a new bar. Don't forget to wash your hair and scrub every inch of your body. When you get finished, dry off and come back. It's nice and warm inside." With that, Jack slowly closed the door and sat down on his cot. The others did likewise while trying to smother their smiles.

"It's a hell of a lot warmer than when we took our baths," Lomas offered. "But I'm not anxious to take another right away."

As an afterthought, Jack reminded them to make sure Melvin checks his bindle for lice. If he finds any, then to wash the whole kit and caboodle.

When Melvin returned, Lomas, always one for a little fun, made him pass inspection by each member before he could go to his bunk. That night, when the bugler blew taps, the tenderfoot slept deeply, making darkness very brief, and reveille come much too early.

The following day, it was back to the old routine: breakfast, marching drills, and target practice. Target practice gave the crew a chance to evaluate Melvin's long-range accuracy. The distance Jack and Abel practiced was never tried by the new arrival. Instead he displayed exceptional precision at the targets resting between four hundred and five hundred yards way. That was good enough to receive a few slaps on the back and be told, on his way back to the cabin, that he was a pretty fair rifleman. They were back in time to break down, clean and oil the weapons, wash their face and hands, then head for the cook tent to eat supper. Tonight's bill of fare consisted of salt pork, johnnycakes, some kind of greens, swamp cabbage stew, coffee, and of course hardtack biscuits. Not very appetizing, but when men are hungry, the menu transforms into just short of ambrosia. Like the old adage goes, "Hunger is the best seasoning."

With their bellies tight and satisfied, the sharpshooters returned to the inviting, warm domicile to relax for the remains of the day. All except Lomas Chandler, who heard about a poker game nearby and walked over to check it out. Abel lay back on his cot with his hands behind his head and asked, “Hey, Melvin, what got you into this god-awful war?”

“Y’all will probably laugh, but I joined up to get three square meals every day. It seems like my family has always hit it tough. We never owned much, and Pappy took whatever work was available. There were seven of us, counting Mom and Pappy. Two brothers and a little sister never made it to the age of three, another died when it was born. I never did find out whether it was a boy or girl. We lived where Pappy got work. Lots of times it was for a plantation owner, and they let us have one of the shacks and took rent from the money Pappy earned. We all mostly walked with our heads down because people would look at us with contempt and called us white trash. Two of my baby sisters died because Pappy couldn’t get the doctor to come look at them. The plantation owner was afraid they might have something his slaves would catch. In his mind, his slaves were worth a hell of a lot more than any white trash baby. I know lots a people feel sorry for the slaves, but not me. The ones I know have it a hell of lot better than we ever did. They got a place to stay, plenty of food and clothes, and some even had their own gardens. I know they eat good because some of their women are as big as a $40 cow. If they got sick, there was a doctor looking at them faster than you could say, ‘Who shot John?’ One thing they all said about Pappy was, he sure wasn’t lazy. He worked harder than the widow’s fan in church during the month of July. Pappy was just uneducated and the unluckiest man on the face of the earth. We needed money, and when this here war broke out, I heard they paid twelve dollars a month and gave you food and board. Me being the oldest, I had to spit quick or die, so I joined the army. Ever since, I've been sending ten dollars a month home to my mom. The last thing I heard was, the slaves all ran away and plantation owners are now hanging up Help Wanted signs. Pappy sure ain't the only one unlucky in this family."

"Melvin, you have one thing them slaves don't have, and that's freedom. You can get up and move to another town to look for work. I'm sorry for your family's loss of the little ones. I have two of my own, so I can share your pain. All the same, sometimes slaves have their children sold, like a bushel of corn. They just come into their house, take them away, and ship them to who knows where. The same holds true for everybody in the family. If you don't have freedom, you don't have anything," Jack frankly remarked. At that moment, the door opened and Lomas stepped inside.

"Did you find the poker game?" Ihme asked.

"Sure did. I told them that I don't play very well and I'll need to be taught what the rules are. They lit up like a Christmas tree and said for me to come early next week and they'll teach me. They probably had a couple of heavy losers tonight, so they couldn't get me in the game." Lomas happily conveyed.

"Lomas, I know the rules of poker. I'll teach you if you want," Melvin offered. That brought a couple of snickers, and Jack said, "You don't want to play with Lomas, he's a card sharp and was just setting them up."

"How could you say that?" Lomas bemoaned. "I wouldn't take advantage of one of our own."

"You're a good pal. Sometimes I even believe you. Still, bottom line, it's against my better judgment. It isn't because you're a bad person. I think you just can't help it. You do have one asset more than most people, and that's my friendship," Jack assured him as he folded Abigail's most recent letter and returned it to the cigar box he kept for that purpose. Next, he opened the newspaper Melvin had stashed in his bindle when he arrived. It wasn't a very recent edition, nevertheless newer than the last one Jack read. Once Melvin figured out which sharpshooter was the crew leader, he offered it to Jack in hopes of winning an ally. Apparently, it worked, and Melvin not only secured top-notch living quarters, he also made a friend.

"Listen to this," Jack began to read about an explosion at the Union Allegheny, Pennsylvania, arsenal. When he finished reading, the listeners' opinions ranged from "It serves the Yankees right" to "How awful the tragedy was, especially for the young girls and women."

"We sure are lucky having a couple of literary types like Jack and Melvin here to keep us informed about the goings-on," Abel noted while winking at Ihme.

"I ain't no literary type. I brung the paper in case somebody here wanted to read it," Melvin confessed. "For your information, I can write my name."

"I think General Lee should send spies to blow up the Yankee arsenals. That would give them less bullets to shoot at us and give them a taste of what they're doing to our homes," Ihme suggested.

"That'll never happen, Ihme. Old Bobby Lee is too principled for that kind of warfare. That wouldn't be gentlemanlike," Lomas responded.

"You can't be a gentleman when fighting a war. Those Yankee generals could care less about civilians getting killed. Just look at Sherman. He believes in total warfare against everybody on the opposing side in order to end the war quicker," Abel added.

It was similar to so many other conversations among soldiers during a war in which varied opinions ran the gamut. Patriotism always fans the flame, in favor of hostilities, until reality comes into focus. The sharpened details quickly release our flared nostrils and stir the beginning buds of remorse. After two horrible years, the excitement and enthusiasm has vanished and, in its place, drudgery to perform the required duty. Soldiers now look forward to the end rather than the beginning of this costly war.

* * *

Casualties, during the war, weren't confined only to the battlefield. The single worst civilian disaster took place at the Allegheny Arsenal on September 17. Situated on thirty acres of land, bordering the Allegheny River in Lawrenceville, Pennsylvania, the arsenal was an important supply and manufacturing center for the Union army. The need for cartridges, during the Civil War, increased civilian employment to over 1,100 workers. Cartridge manufacturing was conducted in a main munitions factory, which employed 158 workers, mostly women. At 2:00 p.m. that fateful day, the arsenal exploded, shattering windows in the surrounding community and heard over two miles away in Pittsburgh. As Col. John Symington, the arsenal commander, made his way to the site, he heard a second explosion, followed by a third. By the time the fire was extinguished, the ammo lab was reduced to smoldering rubble. Many of the girls working there had left their benches to collect their wages, planning to return afterward. Seconds later, they ran screaming from the building with clothes on fire, faces blackened, and unrecognizable. Some jumped from the windows, while others were trampled underfoot by panic-stricken workers trying to leave the ghastly scene. Corpses were found riddled by shells, cartridges, and lead minié balls. Bodies as well as stray limbs, bones, and scraps of clothing were found hundreds of feet from the horrific tragedy. Most of the victims were never identified and had to be buried in a mass grave.

Generally speaking, most people believed the cause of the explosion was a metal horseshoe striking a spark that touched off loose gunpowder in the roadway near the plant, which then traveled onto the porch, where it set off several barrels of gunpowder. A coroner's jury put the blame directly on Col. John Symington and his subordinates. It claimed they allowed loose powder to accumulate on and around the roadway. Finally, in a military inquiry into Colonel Symington's conduct, the same witnesses, who appeared before the coroner, changed their testimony, creating discrepancies between the two hearings. In the end, the army found Colonel Symington innocent of wrongdoing, and the court concluded that the cause could not be satisfactorily ascertained.

It was common practice in the North to employ women and young girls to make cartridges at arsenals, a number of which were located in urban areas. Even though the work was viewed to be outside what middle-class Americans considered appropriate for women, more females sought after positions that were available. The work was both dirty and dangerous, but they showed no compunction not to perform it. The work was simple and repetitive, but it required extreme care. Cartridge-formers had to place lead balls in paper tubes, fill the tubes with gunpowder, and then tie up the loose ends. The agility of a women's touch gave a uniform cartridge, plus, as opposed to men, horseplay was less likely with a female crew. Accordingly, Federal arsenals and private contractors relied heavily on female labor. The women workers quickly learned to negotiate the politics of their new workplaces, and that better jobs and more pay went to those who were friendly with their male supervisors. Harassment complaints were few and far between, understandably, for fear of losing the job.

The Union army was reluctant to hire women, especially young women, to serve as nurses in field hospitals, feeling their presence might disrupt discipline.

Conversely, believing that women and girls were more obedient than men, they turned a blind eye when it came to arsenal work; and though many thought the work degraded the fairer sex, armory workers themselves were more motivated by wage earning than idealism.

Another consequence of the arsenal explosions and horrific scene of lost lives and destruction was shocking the populace into realizing what war really looked like. It brought about concern of the bloody conflict, now engaged in Southern fields, towns, and homes, moving to Northern cities such as Pittsburgh, New York, and Boston—a very disturbing vision for those who considered the war a novelty and ending in three months.

The explosion at Allegheny wasn't the last tragedy at a munitions factory. On June 18, 1864, the city of Washington, D.C., was startled by an explosion at the nearby arsenal. Responders found that the hundred-foot-long building or shed, called the laboratory, was blown up and on fire. When the fire was extinguished, a horrific scene of death awaited. Under the building's metal roof were seething bodies, mangled, scorched, and charred beyond identification. The disaster claimed twenty-one victims, of which only three or four were identified. Burnt bodies and limbs were placed in a large box and later buried in a mass grave. Fortunately, most of the 250 workers, mainly female, were able to escape. The cause may have been a spark, accidentally falling on inflammable items near the building, and the flames spreading into the laboratory, where women were assembling signal rockets.

With the knowledge of having inflammable substances so near a building, filled with human beings, the verdict of the coroner's inquest severely criticized the arsenal superintendent, charging him guilty of culpable carelessness and negligence.

Chapter Twelve

Friendship is Love without his wings!

—Lord Byron

As 1862 draws to an end, the Union has taken control of New Orleans as well as the northernmost slave states. Missouri, Kentucky, Maryland, Delaware, and West Virginia were now in Federal hands. Gen. Robert E. Lee's incursions into Union territory were repulsed, and his C. S. A. army forced to retreat. Even when Confederate forces went into Kentucky, they soon found they were not welcome, a major surprise considering their close proximity. All in all, the year was considered the high-water mark for the Southern Alliance. From this point forward, General Lee's efforts were more difficult to implement. Leadership in Washington had become much better organized and stood in direct contrast with that of the South. Conditions in the Confederate army worsened. Casualties had significantly reduced military manpower; the response from a request for more troops was inadequate. The remaining soldiers were exhausted from long marches and frequent battle and badly in need of shoes and boots. The war of attrition was beginning to pick up speed.

* * *

By now, Abigail was acclimated into the teaching activity and pleased that more children appeared each day in her classes. What delighted her most was the children were learning the essentials. You can actually witness them gain knowledge by observing their glowing facial expressions. Reasons for children becoming eager to attend school were unclear; perhaps the cause of this mystery had something to do with the fact that school was taken away from them by the occupation. There are many things we humans take for granted, until they are gone. At that point, we realize their importance. As the adage goes, "You never miss the water 'til the well runs dry."

At the Leffingwell farm, Abigail was surprised to hear a knock on her door shortly after breakfast. Minnie Rosenthal rose from the table and went to see who it was. After an unusually long period of silence, Abigail questioned in an increased tone, "Who is it, Minnie?"

"You had better come," Minnie suggested softly.

Standing in the doorway was Yalata and his wife, Ailana. Each carrying rather-large sacks. A quick glance beyond the porch revealed the curious absence of any horses.

"Come in, please come in," Abigail welcomed upon arriving to the rescue of a startled Minnie Rosenthal.

"We've come to visit and bring you more food," Ailana said in broken accents.

"We were just finishing breakfast. Have you had breakfast this morning?" Abigail asked clumsily. She was nervous in the presence of her tawny benefactors.

"Yes, we have eaten earlier," Yalata answered.

"Then come in the kitchen and have coffee with us. Minnie, put on another pot for our guests." Extending the sacks each carried, Yalata said, "These are for you."

Once they all were seated, Ailana turned to Sarah Jane and stated, "You have a beautiful daughter."

"Thank you. She is a blessing to us. Especially since Jack is away fighting in the war."

"Have you heard from him recently?" Yalata asked, taking a sip of the steaming brew.

"Yes, apparently they are on a break from fighting and now at camp in Virginia."

"This war is foolish. What does he win when it is over? A Choctaw would never fight in such a war, both sides lose no matter who wins. Have the bluecoats bothered you?"

"No, not since that first day," said Abigail. Yalata's facial expression slightly changed, but it was still hardly noticeable. To a keen observer, his eyes might divulge the emotion of satisfaction by their flash of twinkle.

"You have a beautiful house," Ailana remarked.

"Come, let me show you around," Abigail said proudly, taking her hand and walking to the steps leading upstairs. Yalata was curious about them from the moment he first entered the house. It was a novelty for log cabin homes to have a second story, and he was interested in how it was constructed.

"We are using this level for the children's bedrooms, and of course, Minnie Rosenthal or I sleep up here if the children are ill."

"Minnie Ro-sen-thal is your mother?" Ailana asked inquisitively.

"No, she is just a dear friend. She's living with us to help me with the children while Jack's away. I'm hoping she stays with us after Jack gets back. She's like a grandmother to the children."

"You are fortunate to have such a woman," Ailana stated.

While Abigail took her guests on tour, Minnie cleared the breakfast table, and she and Sarah Jane washed the dishes. It's hard to tell which one was more stunned by having Choctaw Indians as guests. Minnie had yet to recover from fright, and Sarah Jane remained in a state of awe. The visit was cordial and lasted for about two hours. Yalata offered suggestions to improve the garden, and Ailana gave Abigail several herb roots before they left. Their horses were housed in the barn and were soon retrieved and mounted. The Leffingwell family stood on the porch waving as the visitors rode away.

"I'm not ashamed to admit that I'm glad they're gone. They scared me half out of my wits," Minnie honestly uttered. "That's the first time I saw an Injun up close. All I could think of was us getting scalped."

"Oh, Minnie, those days are long gone. Yalata and his wife are friends and have saved our lives."

"That may be so, but I still remember the days when Jacob and I first got married and those savages were raiding farms and scalping folks."

The three, on the distaff side, reentered the house and took seats in the living room, still flustered by the surprise visit. Turning to Minnie, Abigail said, "I've got to write Jack about this day. You can certainly tell that Yalata and his wife, Ailana, are noble people from very good families.

They are keeping us all alive in these terrible times, and if it wasn't for Jack's friendship with them, there's no telling what would have happened to us."

"If you ask me for my two cents . . ." Minnie was about to reply when Sarah excitedly stated, "I can't wait to tell my friends at school. We were visited by real Indians, and they were actually inside our house."

"Sarah Jane, their visit is a secret. We can't talk about them, calling on us, with anyone right now. Your father wants us to wait until the war is over before we tell a soul," Abigail instructed. The look on Sarah Jane's face said it all. She remained taciturn the rest of the day, carrying it over on the ride to church the next morning.

With the visit fresh on her mind, Abigail found it impossible to sleep until she conveyed the happening in writing to her husband.

November 25, 1862
Dearest Jack,

Guess who paid a visit today. You'll be surprised to hear that Yalata and Ailana paid their respects this morning. It came as quite a surprise to all. They brought more food, and Ailana gave me some herb roots to plant next spring. What a noble couple. They almost exude royalty. I suppose that comes as no surprise since Ailana was the daughter of a chief and Yalata, a chief himself. Nevertheless, it's all new to your family. Sarah Jane still is awestruck and couldn't wait to tell her friends. After I explained you wanted us to keep it a secret, she hasn't spoken since. I'm sure she will get over it once we go to church tomorrow. Grandma Minnie was beside herself. All she could think of was, we were going to be scalped. She and her husband battled Indians during years past, and that might be hard to forget for her.

It's been almost two years since you've gone, and it seems like a lifetime. Little Jack is growing like a weed and into everything. Minnie thinks it's cute and spoils him to the point that I almost give up. Then he will crawl onto my lap, give me a kiss, and all is forgiven. At night I weep for you missing these years.

Teaching school is going well. My class has grown a lot from the first day. Several of the mothers help setting up the classroom and stay, making sure discipline is maintained. You can actually see the children learn by the expression on their faces. I thank God for this endeavor. It keeps me busy and gives less time for my melancholia.

Somewhere in Minnesota, the Sioux Indians revolted and killed a farmer and his family. Apparently, the government subsidy was late and it was a bad year for their crops. No one would give them credit to buy food, so to avoid starvation, they went on the warpath. Now, President Lincoln has sentenced over three hundred of them to be hanged. I haven't heard that the execution was carried out as yet. You may get something about it in the local papers. I considered the subject taboo during Yalata's visit; however, I felt he knew all about it.

Just a short letter this time, darling. Still excited over the visit. I'll write more once I calm down.

Your loving wife,
Abigail

* * *

Through the sharp air a flaky torrent flies, mocks the slow sight, and hides the gloomy skies; the fleecy clouds their chilly bosoms bare, and shed their substance on the floating air.

—George Crabbe

Back at the Confederate camp near Berryville, Virginia, the weather has turned because of a cold front dropping down from Canada. Snow flurries appeared the night before, and due to small crispy flakes, only an inch has accumulated. At times, a swirling wind creates a whiteout, but as yet, nothing to indicate a major storm was imminent. Melvin Kaufman was heard stomping his feet outside before the cabin door was quickly opened.

"Sure it's nice not living in a tent with it snowing like it is," he said while shaking his army coat. "Guys at the post commissary said we have about one inch already."

"Hell, that ain't much," Lomas chided. "Getting only an inch of snow is like winning a nickel in a poker game. We need at least six inches before it amounts to anything. Did they say how much is expected?"

"Nope," Melvin replied as he handed Jack a newspaper. "They said the paper was only two days old, so what's in it should be up to date."

"Thanks, Melvin, I owe you one," Jack said comfortably, then plopped down on his bunk.

By noon, the snow had tapered off, leaving a bright ivory blanket over the mountain slopes and valleys so that the only object seen was a hawk soaring high above, waiting to spot the first dark movement below. During breakfast, it was announced that drills were cancelled for the day, leaving soldiers to their own devises until reveille the next morning. The sharpshooters choose to remain inside their comfortable log cabin and occasionally feed sticks into the Franklin stove. It came as no surprise having the day off, so to speak, because many soldiers were without proper clothing and shoes. In fact, many had no shoes at all. Considering all else, it was good for them to lie back and rest upon the oars. Melvin offered to venture out and see what the Post Exchange had to offer. Lomas gave him a quarter to buy rock candy, and Jack, five cents for the latest *Richmond Enquirer*. Besides playing poker, Lomas had a sweet tooth and loved candy. Practically any kind would do: red hots, molasses taffy, horehound hard candy, jelly beans, fish rock candy (plain rock candy shaped like a fish), and Necco wafers (a flat confection with a chalklike taste, he preferred clove flavored). Lomas loved them all.

The article about 330 Santee Sioux Indian men sentenced to be hanged caught Jack's eye first. It went on to tell that President Lincoln commuted the death sentence of 284 of the warriors, while signing off on the execution of 38 men to be hanged on December 26, in Mankato, Minnesota. It will be the largest mass execution in U.S. history. Were it not for fear of a backlash from England and France in favor of the Confederacy, Lincoln would have hanged all 330.

The Dakota War

The Sioux Uprising, or Dakota War, came about after an insufficient crop the previous year and failure of the Federal government to make payment of money and food, as pledged by a treaty in which Indians turned over a million acres of their homeland to live on a reservation. The crop failure came as no surprise considering most of the land in the Minnesota River valley was not arable, and hunting could no longer support the Dakota community because the reservation had little game. U.S. officials claimed the payments were delayed because of preoccupation with the Civil War.

Throughout the late 1850s, treaty violations by the United States and late or unfair annuity payments by Indian agents caused increasing hunger and hardship among the Dakota. Those trading with the Dakota had demanded that the government give the annuity payments directly to them; the Dakota preferred the annuities directly from their agent for the Bureau of Indian Affairs, Thomas J. Galbraith. Galbraith, in turn, was unwilling to distribute food to the Indians. Under existing conditions, the traders refused to provide any more supplies on credit. Negotiations had reached an impasse, and Indian women and children were starving to death. Finally, on August

16, the treaty payments to the Dakota arrived in St. Paul, Minnesota, and were brought to Fort Ridgley the next day, but too late to stop violence.

On August 17, 1862, a young Dakota and three others killed five settlers while on a hunting expedition looking for food. That night, a council of Dakota decided to attack settlements throughout the Minnesota River valley to try to drive whites out of the area. Throughout the day, Sioux war parties swept the valley killing numerous settlers. The onslaught resulted in over eight hundred settlers killed and just as many taken captive as slaves, some of which, subsequently, were tortured to death.

Minnesota militia and volunteer infantry were sent to quell the uprising and found themselves roundly defeated. Invigorated by initial success, the Dakota continued their offensive and attacked several other communities, but did not attack Fort Ridgley because of its heavy defenses. Instead, they turned toward the town, killing settlers along the way. By the time they reached New Ulm, residents had organized defenses in the town center and were able to keep the Sioux at bay. Dakota warriors did penetrate parts of the defenses, enough to burn much of the town. That evening, a thunderstorm dampened the warfare and prevented further attacks; the pause allowed soldiers, stationed at Fort Ridgley, to arrive and help residents build additional barricades pending another onslaught. It was during this period, the Dakota finally attacked Fort Ridgley, thus limiting the ability of the American forces inside to aid outlying settlements, as a result, subjecting farms and small villages to further carnage.

Bodies of many settlers, killed by the Indians, still remained unburied on the battlefield. A detachment of about 170 men was sent from Fort Ridgley to find survivors, bury the American dead, and report on the location of Dakota Sioux fighters. After burying 54 bodies, the detachment had spotted no Sioux and, feeling safe, made camp in an area called Birch Coulee. The Dakota Sioux planned to ambush the troops in the morning, thinking only the cavalry was present and easily destroyed. The Birch Coulee campsite was not easily defensible, since the Indians could approach from all sides and still remain under cover. In the morning, the Indians commenced their ambush, killing thirteen soldiers and wounding at least forty-seven others and killing most of the cavalry's horses. Only two Dakota were killed in the melee.

The sounds of the battle could be heard from Fort Ridgley, about sixteen miles away, so Colonel Sibley, the forts commanding officer, sent out a relief party of 240 men. They soon found themselves surrounded by the Sioux and sent back for more reinforcements. Colonel Sibley returned with additional troops and an artillery brigade. The shelling forced the Sioux to disperse, and Sibley entered the camp to encounter a sickening sight, with thirteen men and ninety horses dead, forty-seven men severely wounded, and others exhausted from a thirty-one-hour siege without water or food. The battle of Birch Coulee was the most deadly for the United States forces in the Dakota War of 1862.

It took repeated appeals for aid before President Lincoln appointed Gen. John Pope to quell the violence. Lincoln hesitated making the decision for fear sending troops might weaken his forces in the Civil War. As soon as companies were formed, Pope's troops were dispatched. After the arrival of a larger army force, the final large-scale fighting took place at the Battle of

Wood Lake on September 23, 1862. With the aid of a six-pound cannon, Pope's regiments were deployed in a skirmish line and charged against the Dakota Sioux, the greatest light infantry force the world has ever known, and defeated them overwhelmingly. Most of the Sioux fighters surrendered shortly after the battle and were held for military trials, which took place in November. On November 5, 1862, in Mankato, Minnesota, a court-martial held that 303 Santee Sioux were found guilty of rape and murder of hundreds of settlers and sentenced to be hanged. For reasons mentioned earlier, President Lincoln, the Great Emancipator, purposed to hang 38 Santee Sioux, also remove every Indian from the state, and provide Minnesota with two million dollars in Federal funds.

In April 1863, the U.S. Congress abolished the reservation, declared all previous treaties with the Dakota Sioux null and void, and undertook proceedings to expel the Indian people entirely from Minnesota. To that end, a bounty of $25 per scalp was placed on any Dakota Sioux found free within the boundaries of the state.

Skirmishes with the Indians were not over. They continued both large and small until well after the American Civil War; in fact, the last may have been in 1923 between Utes and Mormon settlers.

* * *

"Looks like Honest Abe is fighting more than us Southern boys," remarked Jack, after reading the story to the others. "It took the Union army to make those Sioux Indians surrender."

"Yeah, but they ended up getting hanged," reminded Abel. "I still think that might be our lot if we lose." That comment seemed to bring everyone a little closer to hear what Jack might say.

"I don't think Lincoln will consider hanging the Confederate soldiers because we're in a recognized war and the Europeans would come to our aid. He probably wants it over as much as we do. I can't imagine how we will come back together once it is over. That will be up to the politicians. It surely will be a mess with all those slaves free and cities needing to be rebuilt. It's going to take fifty years or more to get things back to normal. We probably will never see it."

"My grandmother used to tell me and my brothers a poem about the Kilkenny cats every time we'd end up fighting. This here war reminds me of it," Lomas lamented.

"How does it go?" asked Melvin.

"As I remember, it went something like this," Lomas replied.

There once were two cats of Kilkenny,
Each thought there was one cat too many,
So they fought and they fit And they scratched
and they bit
'Til, (excepting their nails
And the tips of their tails)Instead of two cats
there weren't any![*]

"There's a lot of truth in that one," Ihme chimed. "We're just like those two cats. We'll just keep on fighting each other until we both lose."

---

* *(http://en.wikipedia.org/wiki/Kilkenny_cat)*

"Abigail would call that a pyrrhic victory," Jack added. "One which has a devastating cost to the victor."

"Boy, I never want to marry a smart woman, I'd never know what she was saying," Lomas stated and, without intention, stirred in more opinions from the others.

"You don't need to worry. If she is so smart, she'll never marry you in the first place," Melvin chimed.

"Who shook the monkey tree?" Lomas replied. Melvin fitted in with the rest and could dish it out, as well as take it, when it comes to kibitzing. Between Lomas and Melvin, it's hard to keep a straight face. There were not many frowns when they're around.

"Anything else about the war?" Abel inquired.

"Not much more than we already know. A couple of editorials about how great the Confederacy is and why the Union is wrong. There is one story telling how hypocritical Lincoln is when he frees some of the slaves and then allows General Grant to expulse all the Jews from his cabinet." That seemed to tweak interest, so Jack proceeded to read the article aloud.

"On November 9, 1862, Gen. Ulysses S. Grant initiated one of the most blatant episodes of anti-Semitism in nineteenth-century American history. Convinced that Jews, as a class, violated every regulation of trade established by the Treasury Department and also department orders, Grant expelled them from the Department of the Tennessee (an administrative district of the Union army of occupation composed of Kentucky, Tennessee, and Mississippi); and within twenty-four hours, they would no longer be allowed in the department. Post commanders will see to it that all this class of people be furnished passes and required to leave, and anyone returning after such notification will be arrested and held in confinement until an opportunity occurs of sending them out as prisoners. No passes will be given these people to visit headquarters for the purpose of making personal application of trade permits.

"Grant believed that the black market in cotton was primarily organized by Jews and ordered that no Jews be permitted to travel on the railroad southward, into the Department of the Tennessee, from any point, nor were they to be granted trade licenses.

"The immediate cause of the expulsion was the raging black market in Southern cotton. Both the North and South remained dependent of each other economically. Northern textile mills needed Southern cotton. The Union army itself used Southern cotton in its tents and uniforms. Although the Union military command preferred an outright ban on trade, President Lincoln decided to allow limited trade in Southern cotton. To control that trade, Lincoln insisted it be licensed by the Treasury Department and the army. As commander of the Department of the Tennessee, Grant was charged with issuing trade licenses in his area. As cotton prices soared in the North, unlicensed traders bribed Union officers to allow them to buy Southern cotton without a permit. Nearly every colonel, captain, or quartermaster was in a secret partnership with some operator in cotton. In the fall of 1862, Grant's headquarters were besieged by merchants seeking trade permits. When his own father appeared one day seeking trade licenses for a group of Cincinnati merchants, some of whom were Jews, Grant hit the ceiling. A handful of the illegal traders were Jews, but the vast majority was not. Obviously, the famous general harbored a prejudicial opinion against those with Jewish heritage.

"When illegal trading continued, Grant issued his draconian Order No. 11 on December 17, 1862. Literally interpreted, it was an order to remove all Jews from Kentucky, Tennessee, and Mississippi. His subordinates enforced the order at once in the area surrounding Grant's headquarters in Holly Springs, Mississippi. Some Jewish traders had to trudge forty miles on foot to evacuate the area. In Paducah, Kentucky, military officials gave the town's thirty Jewish families, all long-term residents, none of them speculators, twenty-four hours to leave.

"Jewish leaders reacted to Grant's violation of the U.S. Constitution and wrote the president and traveled to Washington, D.C. After meeting with President Lincoln, Grant's order was rescinded. Expulsion of the Jews was unquestionably a grave mistake, yet Grant received the Jewish vote when he ran for president. That says a lot for the man who was once a clerk in his father's leather store rose to be general of the Union armies and then president of the United States—all accomplished in just seven years.

"Grant disliked red meat and refused to eat chicken or, for that matter, any fowl at all. The sight of blood made him ill, so if he had to eat meat, it must be charred flat and black. His favorite foods were pork and beans, fruit, and buckwheat cakes. Grant was known to have an aversion to any kind of profanity (unusual for a general in the army), and no off-color stories were allowed in his presence. He probably wasn't the kind of guy the gang wanted to go out with on a Saturday night. The night Lincoln was assassinated, General Grant and his wife were in New Jersey to see their children. They had previously given President and Mrs. Lincoln their regrets to join them at the Ford's Theater. Were it not for the previous engagement, no doubt Grant would have been in the theater box with Abraham Lincoln and faced a similar fate."

"I don't get it. Here we are fighting the Yankees and we still carry on trade with them because they need our cotton. It just doesn't make sense. If you're at war with somebody, you don't try to help them out," Abel lamented.

"No doubt General Lee doesn't agree with it either, but this type of action is done by the politicians and they apparently ignore the war. They must look at it as two separate events," Jack replied as he folded the newspaper and slid it under his pillow, to be read completely at a later time. Melvin Kaufman had pondered the fact General Grant was furious over illegal trade and couldn't grasp the reason why he blamed the Jews. Having experienced, firsthand, prejudice because he was poor, he could identify with intolerance and bigotry. He didn't recollect ever seeing a Jew, though he always heard they were unliked and couldn't be trusted. Turning to Lomas, he asked, "Do you know why Jews are not liked?"

"Sure, they killed our Lord, Jesus Christ. That's what my grandmother told me, and I've yet to find her wrong about anything."

That was giving Melvin a headache as he attempted to assimilate the answer and comprehend its meaning.

"You're telling me that those Jews were kicked out because they killed the Lord. How can that be if Christ was killed a thousand years ago?"

"I don't claim to understand it all, I just told you what my grandmother said," Lomas responded with a sigh.

"Who wants hot coffee?" Ihme asked while he placed a kettle of water on top the Franklin stove. The others all wanted to be counted in. Lomas Chandler's smile secretly told them he would be able to lace each cup with a little spirits. After the coffee was brewed, Ihme made certain he left room in each cup as he poured the pungent brew. Lomas then made the rounds adding the pick-me-up bracer, most likely rye whiskey, since it came disguised in a plain brown bottle. When everyone had a firm grip on their steaming cup, Lomas raised his, saying, "Here's mud in your eye."

That evening, the Tennessee sharpshooters consumed time with a variety of items stirred into the conversation. Irish coffee put them all in a congenial state of mind and enhanced their fraternal attitude. Melvin Kaufman was the exact opposite of John Henry Bickford and seemed to be a perfect replacement. His curious honesty only gained the others acceptance and favor. Suppressed yawns and slightly closed eyelids signaled the evening was coming to an end. Soon quietness will take over and leave the men to their own thoughts. They say that direction comes to us in a whisper to the soul. We need silence in order to hear it. Everyday sounds tend to block out the angel's whispering voices.

"Tell Melvin about the fairies," Ihme nudged Lomas and then turned down the top blanket on his cot.

"Some other time, it's getting kind of late," Lomas replied.

"What about the fairies?" Melvin asked. "Are they real?"

"Of course they're real. Everybody in Ireland knows the fairies are real. I've never seen them myself, mind you, but my grandmother has seen them many times. She told me fairies were born when the first baby laughed. The laughter broke into a thousand pieces, and each piece grew into tiny fairies. They live where flowers grow, where water ripples over rocks and form crystal clear pools. It's there where most fairies can be found, but you must be a child to see them. Grown-ups, perhaps, can see them, only if they are a child at heart. They appear early in the morning or late at night, when the torch of the fireflies light their way."

Melvin was fascinated and called to Jack, "Do you believe fairies are real?"

"I've seen a lot of strange things in my life. Things I couldn't readily explain. I believe in God and never personally seen him although I've experienced his closeness several times. All I can truthfully say is, if fairies aren't real, they ought to be."

Melvin took that as a yes and made up his mind to be more alert next time he was in places where fairies reside. That night, his dreams were occupied with tiny creatures in the shape of humans with wings like a dragonfly, flitting around the room. With most of his comrades now sawing wood, Jack took the quiet time to write Abigail.

November 27, 1862
Dearest Abigail,

We have a new recruit in the fold, a fellow by the name of Melvin Kaufman. Do you remember the Kaufmans that lived just outside of Statesville? They seemed to be hard up most of the time and moved when the war started. They were Melvin's aunt and uncle. Sure is a small world when you come to think about it.

There's not much going on here at the moment, but rumor is we will be moving soon. So far, I haven't picked up on where it will be. We got our first snow yesterday, and it made me happy to be living in a log cabin instead of the tent.

The fighting, here in Virginia, has caused problems with mail shipments. We sometimes wait two weeks or more before letters get out. That doesn't stop me writing, but might take a while before you get them.

I heard from your father the other day. He confirms the fact that you are doing a good job teaching the children. That comes as no surprise, my darling, for you are a special woman, besides being beautiful, the smartest this mountain man has ever known.

No matter how cold it is outside, all I have to do is think about you and I'm warm as toast. You're my daylight at night and the air I breathe, my first thought in the morning and last in my nighttime prayers.

When this letter gets mailed, it will be part of a package. I finally had my picture taken. Photographers seem to follow us wherever we go. Pictures of battle must be popular and worth a lot of money to the newspapers. I had to wait in line over two hours to have my own taken. Now you have something to show the children.

Little Jack can see what his father looks like, and Sarah Jane can refresh her memory.

I pray the Lord keeps us in the center of his will and reunites us soon.

With my eternal love, your husband,
Jack

Chapter Thirteen

So all day long the noise of battle roll'd among the mountains by the winter sea.

—Alfred, Lord Tennyson

The Battle of Fredericksburg and Marye's Heights

The next morning, the Seventh regiment received orders to make ready and join General Longstreet at Fredericksburg, Virginia. Lincoln had replaced McClellan with Maj. Gen. Ambrose E. Burnside who, subsequently, responded to the president's call for immediate action with a bold plan relying on quick movement and deception. He would concentrate his army in a visible fashion—feigning a movement on Gordonsville and its intersecting railroads, vitally important to the Confederacy. Then he would rapidly shift his army southeast and cross the Rappahannock River to Fredericksburg, hoping to confuse General Lee as to his true intentions. President Lincoln preferred a direct attack on Lee's forces; all the same, he reluctantly approved the plan and cautioned Burnside to move with great speed. No doubt, due to concern that none of this would fool his Southern nemesis with the salt-and-pepper beard—a beard that is gradually growing whiter each day the war continues.

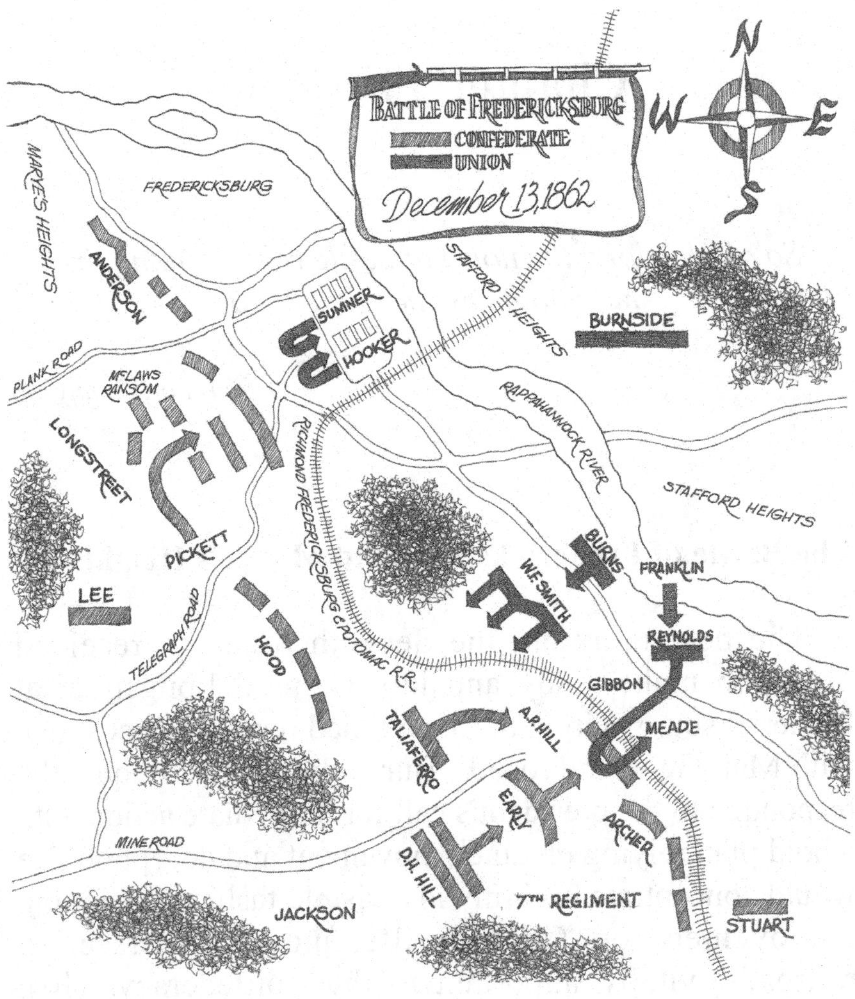

Burnside organized his Army of the Potomac into three divisions with each including infantry corps, cavalry, and artillery. The total force numbered 120,000 men of which he planned to have 114,000 engaged in the coming battle. Robert E. Lee, on the other hand, had about 85,000 men with 72,500 ready for combat.

The Union army began marching in mid-November; and the first elements reached Falmouth, Virginia, located on the north bank of the Rappahannock River on November 17, 1862. Burnside had ordered pontoon bridges sent to the front and assembled for a quick crossing. The army arrived before the bridges. Rather than cross the river at that point by what means he could devise, Burnside decided to wait for the pontoon bridges and cross in mass. When Robert E. Lee saw how slowly the Federals were moving, he directed all of his army toward Fredericksburg. All of Confederate general Longstreet's corps had arrived and was placed on the ridge known as Marye's Heights, west of the town, with other commanders' troops stationed to the left, right, and directly behind. Stonewall Jackson, who was harassing Yankees in the Shenandoah Valley, anticipated Lee's need and marched his troops twenty miles a day to arrive on November 29. Jackson's divisions were deployed downstream from Fredericksburg to prevent Burnside from crossing.

When boats and equipment for a single pontoon bridge finally arrived on November 25, it was much too late for the Army of the Potomac to cross the river without opposition. Even so, had Burnside attacked, he would only face Longstreet's division, about half of Lee's army because the others had not arrived at that point. By waiting until the full complement of bridges were in place, Burnside squandered his opportunity. He also miscalculated Lee's defenses and decided to cross directly at Fredericksburg. To his credit, Burnside positioned 220 artillery pieces east of the Rappahannock along a ridge known as Stafford Heights to prevent Lee from mounting a major counterattack. On December 11, Union engineers began to assemble the pontoon bridges, located in strategic areas, for maximum troop movements: two north of the town center, one on the southern end, and three farther south, near the confluence of the Rappahannock River.

Those constructing the bridge, directly across from the city, came under punishing fire from Confederate sharpshooters. Artillery attempts to dislodge the sharpshooters failed, and Burnside finally dispatched landing parties over in the pontoon boats to secure a beachhead and rout the rebel marksmen. Fighting proceeded in the streets as the engineers completed the bridges. Union gunners sent more than five thousand shells against the town and the ridges to the west. By nightfall, the Union occupied the town, going about destroying buildings and looting—behavior that enraged Lee and native Virginians. River crossings south of the city were successful as sniper fire was suppressed by five batteries of Union artillery. The Yankee accomplishment forced Stonewall Jackson to recall his divisions from down river positions and join his main defensive lines south of the city.

The Union army was now poised for the main attack. His plan called for major divisions, consisting of sixty thousand soldiers, to assail the southern flank of Lee's defenses, with a secondary corps charging the northern end. His generals awaited the orders to commence. When Burnside issued the orders, his subordinates found them vague and confusing. After a cursory inspection of Lee's southern flank, Burnside demurred and ordered his generals to keep their men in position, but send a division to seize the high ground around Hamilton's Crossing, a critical supply base for Confederate troops camped near Fredericksburg. A division of about 4,500 men under the command of Union major general George G. Meade began moving out in a dense morning fog with Brig. Gen. John Gibbon's division following on its right rear. Initially traveling parallel to the river, once they turned to face the Richmond Road, the Federals began to be struck by enfilading fire from the Virginia Horse Artillery, under twenty-four-year-old Confederate major John Pelham. Pelham held his ground until ammunition began to run low, at which point he withdrew. Stonewall Jackson's main artillery batteries had remained silent in the fog during this exchange, but the Union troops soon began to receive direct fire from five batteries atop Prospect Hill. Jackson's artillery stalled Meade's advance, short of his initial objective; however, Meade's troops soon resumed forward movement, even though Jackson's force of about thirty-five thousand men were hidden on the wooded ridge at his front. Stonewall Jackson's formidable defensive line had a flaw. There was a six-hundred-yard gap between the brigades of Gen. James H. Lane and Gen. James J. Archer—a triangular patch of the woods that extended beyond the railroad and covered with thick underbrush and swamp.

Meade's first brigade entered the gap, climbed the railroad embankment, and turned into the underbrush, striking Confederate general Lane's brigade in the flank. Following immediately behind, Meade's third brigade turned left and hit Confederate general Archer's flank. As the gap widened from pressure on the flanks, thousands of Meade's men reached the top of the ridge. At that point, they ran into Confederate general Gregg's brigade. Many of Gregg's men were taken by surprise. Some had even stacked arms while taking cover from Union artillery and, not expecting attack, were killed or captured unarmed. Gregg, in a state of confusion, mistook Yankee soldiers for fleeing Confederate troops and ordered his men not to fire on them. When reality set in, Gregg dashed to the front of the skirmish line, only to be shot in his spine and die two days later. Confederate reserves moved into the battle from behind Gregg's original position. The previously defeated Southern brigades were inspired and rallied to form a new defensive line in the gap.

Now the Federal troops were receiving fire from three sides and could not withstand the pressure. After an unsuccessful attempt to flank a Confederate battery, the Union troops fell back. Further attacks by the Federals now lacked a gap to exploit; and though they fought commendably, in some cases hand to hand, they failed to regain a breakthrough. With their ammunition depleted, the Union soldiers were forced to withdraw back across the railroad embankment. The Confederates now launched a counterattack and, though ordered not to pursue beyond the railroad, chased the retreating Union troops from the woods into the open fields, where they became easier targets for Union artillery fire. The Southern Coalition withdrew back to the safety of the hills south of town. Only skirmishes and artillery duels continued until dark, but no major attacks took place. Jack Leffingwell and the other marksmen were stationed along the line confronting the railroad and right flank of the previously repelled Union brigades.

While the main battle moved north to Marye's Heights, the sharpshooters were still engaged in a continuous contest of dueling artillery. Each side held elevated positions in order to fire against the enemy, while not endangering their own troops. The deafening thunder of raging battle had given way to artillery exchanges and the cracking sound of sharpshooter rifles. The shouts and screams of courageous assault have changed to murmuring pleas for help from the wounded, still on the battlefield. A fog began to move over the combat area, giving it an eerie appearance. It was like a dark undulating ocean with writhing bodies waving and bobbing from side to side. Both factions were in a time warp waiting for a signal to move on the field, tend to their wounded, and bury the dead. As yet, none has been given. Now, fog, mixed with the remaining smoke of battle, would make it more difficult for those with the unpleasant task.

Jack Leffingwell paused for a moment to allow his Whitworth rifle to cool down when Ihme Mueller crawled alongside.

"How's your ammo holding out? Mine's practically gone, so I'm heading to the stocking boxes, and I can bring you back some for the Whitworth," Ihme shouted. Jack removed his earplugs, even though he got the gist of what Ihme asked.

"I guess I am running a little low. Thanks, I'd appreciate it," he returned. The German marksman crawled away, and Jack began to scope the artillery area for a target. The telescope displayed the back of a Union artilleryman loading a shell. He was in the center of Jack's crosshairs; all the same, the mountain man found it difficult to shoot someone in the back and waited until the soldier turned. When he did so, Jack froze in his tracks. There was no mistaking it. The potential target was Leroy Littlefield, the young son of Wilber Littlefield, whose family Jack had conducted to freedom nearly seven years ago. War or no war, he was unable to pull the trigger.

Leroy Littlefield had lived with his parents in Canada until the news of Fort Sumter at Charleston Harbor, South Carolina. Although the family was free from the plantation life in Georgia, the shroud of guilt was never gone. The fact they were fugitives from the United States remained a constant part of who they were. Canadian winters presented another hardship for a family from the Deep South, especially young Leroy, who enjoyed running barefoot across Georgia cotton fields. Leroy never really accepted his new home, and once the Civil War started, a deep desire to return home blazed in his heart. Motivated by the words of Frederick Douglas, Leroy came home to join the army.

> *Once let the black man get upon his person the brass letter, U.S., let him get an eagle on his button, and a musket on his shoulder and bullets in his pocket, there is no power on earth that can deny that he has earned the right to citizenship.*
>
> *—Frederick Douglas*

At first, having blacks in the Union's war effort was met with trepidation by army officials and Abraham Lincoln himself. It begged the question as to how effective black soldiers would actually be in the heat of battle. Nevertheless, by mid-July 1862, Congress passed laws allowing African American enlistments. Prior to the congressional acts, state and local militia had already been enlisting blacks in order to increase their own troops. Leroy signed up in Cincinnati, Ohio, and, after continuous requests, found himself part of General Burnside's Army of the Potomac and transferred to an artillery brigade.

The discharged shell from the Union cannon was no different from all the rest. Its booming blast was intermixed with those on both sides; nonetheless, the resounding whistle was much louder, even when wearing earplugs. The concussion was intense as the shell exploded a few feet behind where Jack was stationed. Ihme was unfortunate enough to be returning with more ammunition and died instantly from discharged shrapnel. A large fragment glanced off the side of Jack's head, leaving him with a bleeding wound. The shock had rendered him unconscious; however, he was still alive. Alerted by the shell striking so near, the medics were quick on the scene. After a cursory examination of Ihme, one of the medics said, "This one is gone, how about the other guy?"

"I know him. It's Jack Leffingwell from the Seventh Tennessee regiment. He's still alive but out cold. I can't seem to be able to wake him up. Let's get him over to triage, they'll know what to do with him. Bring along his Whitworth rifle, he'll be needing it when he wakes up." The doctor in the triage area examined the unconscious Tennessean and bandaged his head wound.

"He appears to be in a coma. The field hospital probably won't be able to give proper treatment for someone in this condition. We can't leave him here. Let's arrange for him to be transported to Richmond. There's a medical wagon heading south in the morning," the doctor ordered. At that moment Gen. Stonewall Jackson was ridding the battle lines to encourage the troops and made a stop at the triage area. Not known for his friendliness with subordinates, he took the time to check the condition of Jack Leffingwell, his favorite sharpshooter. After being told of Jack's situation, Stonewall jotted something on a piece of paper, signed it T. J. Jackson, and handed it to the triage doctor.

"Make sure you take him there and see that his rifle and scope go with him," the famous general instructed and rode off in a gallop.

* * *

Having taken the city of Fredericksburg, Union general Burnside prepared to move forward on the northern end of the battlefield. Confederate artillery fire continued to descend on the city in spite of it being covered by a heavy fog. Burnside, erroneously assuming the assault on the southern end of the Confederate line would be the decisive action of the battle, ordered his generals to seize the high ground to the west. To do so would require crossing over open fields and scattered houses, fences, and gardens, restricting movement of battle lines. In addition, a canal, standing two hundred yards away, served as a barrier which would cause troops to funnel themselves into columns in order to pass over its three narrow bridges, further inhibiting the desired battle line. West of Fredericksburg was a low ridge known as Marye's Heights, rising about fifty feet above the level land. Actually, the ridge was composed of several hills and ravines, from north to south. The location of the Union's attack was protected by a four-foot stone wall, enhanced in places with log breastworks and abatis, giving General Lee a perfect infantry defensive position. Confederate major general Lafayette McLaws was assigned to hold that position and had about two thousand men on the front line and another seven thousand in reserve, at the crest and behind the ridge.

The fog lifted about 10:00 a.m., and Union general Sumner gave his order to advance. The Federals progressed slowly through artillery fire, crossed the canal in columns over the narrow bridges, and formed in position, with fixed bayonets, behind the protection of a shallow slope. In a perfect line for battle, they advanced up the muddy slope until they were cut down by repeated rifle fire, at about 125 yards from the stone wall. While survivors clung to the ground, a second brigade followed with even worse casualty rates. Realizing that their tactics were not working, the Union generals considered a massive bayonet charge to overwhelm the defenders; but as they surveyed the front, they realized the first two divisions were in no shape to move forward again. In a last ditch effort, two more divisions were sent over the same path of those previously fallen and ended with the same horrific results.

By midafternoon, General Burnside had failed to make progress on both flanks of the Confederate defenses. A few more futile attempts were made, ending with the same results. A total of fourteen individual charges, with men moving over and around fallen comrades, reached no closer than fifty yards of the rebel lines. On December 14, both armies remained in position until General Burnside asked General Lee for a truce to attend to his wounded. A request graciously granted by the King of Spades, Gen. Robert E. Lee. The next day, the Federal forces retreated across the Rappahannock, and the campaign came to an end. Fighting on the southern flank produced roughly equal casualties, yet still favoring the Confederates four thousand to five thousand. The northern flank was a complete rout with eight Union casualties for each Southern defender.

Casualty Estimates for the Battle of Fredericksburg and Marye's Heights*

	Total Casualties	Wounded	Killed	Captured/Missing
Union	12,653	9,600	1,284	1,769
Confederate	5,377	4,116	608	653

*Casualty data obtained from http://en.wikipedia.org/wiki/Battle_of_Fredericksburg.

The South was ecstatic over the brilliant victory and, along with the Confederate newspapers, bestowed accolades on the genius of Gen. Robert E. Lee. The Gray Fox, noticeably jubilant, took a measured time to bask in his popularity before resting his army. The Confederate army of Northern Virginia took up winter quarters near Fredericksburg for a needed period to repose and recuperate from the intensity of the most vicious battle thus far.

Chapter Fourteen

We are healed of a suffering only by experiencing it to the full.

—Marcel Proust

Sally Louisa Tompkins was called the Angel of the Confederacy. She was born into a wealthy family at Poplar Grove in Matthews County, Virginia; and when her father died, her mother moved the household to Richmond, Virginia. Even at a young age, Sally had an intrinsic desire to care for those in need. She could often be found tending to families with illness, whether free or slave. Living a comfortable life on her large inheritance allowed her to devote more time to such efforts.

When the first major battle of the Civil War took place near Manassas Junction, Virginia, people on both sides expected the war to end quickly. In fact, those of Northern persuasion were so confident of victory that thousands of civilians traveled from Washington, D.C., to watch the battle. They brought picnic baskets and champagne, as if they were going to a sporting event. But soon, the terrible reality of war became clear to both sides. The bloody battle ended in a Union defeat, and the Northern army and spectators were forced to make a hasty retreat back to Washington. Even though the South won the First Battle of Bull Run, the high number of casualties took the Confederacy by surprise. Richmond's hospitals were filled with injured men, and hundreds of others still needed medical attention. In desperation, Confederate president Jefferson Davis asked the people of Richmond to care for wounded soldiers in their homes. Sally Tompkins was one of many people who responded to this call for volunteer nurses. She convinced a local judge, John Robertson, to let her turn his home in downtown Richmond into a hospital; and after collecting supplies and recruiting six staff members, she opened the Robertson Hospital on July 31, 1861.

In the early days of the war, both the Union and Confederate armies actively discouraged women from serving as nurses. Many men with traditional values felt that nursing was not an appropriate activity for women. They did not want "refined ladies" to be subjected to the horrors of war by treating sick, wounded, and dying soldiers in army hospitals. Confederate nurses faced special problems. Since most of the fighting took place in the South, they were often forced to move patients and, occasionally, entire hospitals in order to remain behind the battle lines. The South also suffered from shortages of food, clothing, and medical supplies throughout the war—making the nurse's job even more difficult.

Within a few weeks of asking Richmond residents to care for wounded soldiers in their homes, Confederate officials became concerned that many soldiers were remaining in private hospitals in Richmond rather than returning to active duty with the army. As a result, Jefferson Davis issued an order that placed private hospitals under the control of military officers. Sally Tompkins met with the Confederate president and requested that he return control of Robertson Hospital to her. On September 9, 1861, Davis made Tompkins a captain in the Confederate army so that she could run her hospital without violating his earlier order. Sally Tompkins, thus became the only female officer in the Confederate army.

For the next four years, Tompkins and her staff ran the most successful hospital on either side of the Civil War. Even though Robertson Hospital usually treated the most seriously injured men, it had the highest survival rate of any hospital. Out of 1,333 patients who stayed there between the time it opened and the end of the war in 1865, only 73 died. In addition, a higher percentage of the soldiers treated there returned to action than in any other Confederate medical facility. Despite her success, Sally Tompkins refused to accept any salary for her work. Instead, she used her family's money and government rations to supply the hospital.

Gen. Thomas "Stonewall" J. Jackson was aware of Robertson Hospital's success, having met Sally Tompkins in Richmond, while she visited the Confederate president, Jefferson Davis. General Jackson had the reputation of being a stern taskmaster, yet his men loved him. He also kept his more compassionate emotions hidden from view; even so, occasionally, they can be witnessed, as in the case of Jack Leffingwell, his favorite marksman, and his insistence that he be treated at Robertson Hospital.

To say that Sally Tompkins ran a tight ship would be an understatement. She insisted her nurses wear a uniform of her design and no jewelry. It was important they appear plain to the patients in order for them to concentrate on their recovery, rather than flirting or making advances. The nurse's cap was white and covered the entire head, similar to the habit worn by nuns. Each nurse wore a white apron with a large frontal pocket, for which to place items necessary to perform her duties, such as thermometers and pencils—all to make her more efficient without drawing attention to her person. Most of all, she insisted on cleanliness. Patients were bathed regularly, and nurses had to wash their hands if they came in contact with either patients' items or the patients themselves. Of all her rules and regulations, this one perhaps was the most responsible for her splendid recovery record.

Jack Leffingwell was carried into the hospital on a stretcher, held by two medics, and placed on a gurney to await a preliminary examination by a doctor. After a cursory inspection, the doctor turned to Sally and said, "His head wound is serious, but he seems to be healing well. It will require a daily change of bandages and application of ointment. I'm mostly concerned by him being in coma. We'll just have to wait on that until he comes around."

"When do you think that will happen?" Sally asked.

"I'm not sure, these things are tricky and I've had no personal experience with this condition. What I've been told is, he might wake up today or a week from now. Try to get him to drink some chicken broth, and if he doesn't come around soon, we may need to force feed him." That suggestion made Sally grimace. The young doctor then asked, "Why was he brought here?"

"It does seem peculiar. General Jackson personally wanted him treated here. The general must believe he is important to the cause." As the doctor shrugged and walked away, Sally called for two nurses. Rachel Crabtree and Lillian Walters quickly responded. Rachel was a unhappy woman in her early forties whose husband just disappeared about ten years ago—leaving her with a teenage son, now serving in the Confederate army general headquarters. Lillian Walters, about ten years her senior, was married to a minister and active in her church. She donated her time at Robertson Hospital to do her part in the war effort.

"I want him bathed completely, and I mean completely. If there is a part of his anatomy you feel reluctant to wash, let me know and I'll do it for you."

The other nurses were smiling when Grazyna (pronounced *Gra-zee-na*) brought in a large pan of warm water and a bar of soap.

"Sally wants you to remove his clothes and give him a bath," they chimed.

Grazyna Kaminski was a true daughter of Delphi, and her beauty rivaled that of Aphrodite. Her high, pronounced cheekbones gave evidence of Mongol invasions into Poland centuries ago, a time when the Tartars conquered most of the known world and assimilated into the general population. This historical intermixing with Slavic and other Europeans has resulted in some beautiful women with fascinating features. Grazyna's full lips and unique eyes capture glances wherever she appears. From a distance, she seemed to have epicanthic eyes, but a closer look reveals it was only an illusion. Her eyes were sparkling blue and beautiful.

Sally Tompkins took Grazyna under her wing after a tragedy in the young girl's life. Grazyna's young husband, Capt. Michael James McCracken, was called to service immediately after the nuptials were performed. He was killed in the First Battle of Bull Run, leaving a young widow from an unconsummated marriage. For nearly two years, Grazyna was a premature spinster in black, with all the natural desires of her gender outwardly suppressed, a rare flower of womanhood whose bud remains unopened.

"You're going to need more hot water. I'll go fetch some while you remove his clothes," said one of the nurses. At that moment, Sally Tompkins returned and wasn't pleased with their progress, not a desirable situation for the original two nurses.

"Let's get cracking, girls. There are other patients here still waiting for medicine," Sally coaxed with a smile; however, they knew she was unhappy and quickly began pulling off Jack's trousers while Grazyna unbuttoned his shirt. In doing so, she noticed something in the front pocket, removed it, and placed it in her apron pouch.

"He certainly is a tall one," the older nurse commented. "He must be six foot four at least. We haven't had many this tall. In fact, he might be the tallest we ever had."

"You forget, Lillian, remember the young man we treated this spring, the one who had his leg removed?" Rachel remarked.

"That's right, he was very tall," Lillian agreed as she helped sponge the legs of the lifeless soldier—making certain to save his private part for the young widow, who was currently concentrating on the upper torso. She wasn't fooled by the other two. They were having fun with her, and Grazyna delayed bathing beyond a certain point so as not to be trapped by their prank.

"I'll be right back," Grazyna announced and left to get another pan of hot water. Outfoxed, the two remaining nurses were determined in their ploy and slowed the pace until Grazyna returned.

"Don't be afraid of that thing, Grazyna, he's in a coma, so it can't hurt you," Rachel said cloyingly. "I bet this is the first time you ever touched one."

"You're right, Michael and I waited until we were married," Grazyna agreed.

"Then he goes and gets himself killed. You poor sweet girl, here, let me do it," Lillian said, reaching for the washcloth.

"Thanks, Lillian, there's no need now, I'm almost finished."

"Anyway, it isn't bad when that thing is flaccid although if he were awake, it would be a different story altogether," Rachel added.

"How you talk, Rachel. You're supposed to be a proper Southern belle who would never let such words escape her lips," Lillian scolded.

"We all act like well-born ladies when the gentlemen are around. When it's just us girls, we're no different than all the rest," Rachel honestly responded.

Sally showed up shortly thereafter, accompanied by an orderly, and the two of them wheeled the bathed soldier's gurney to another room.

"You girls can go about your regular duties. Grazyna, check in on him every so often to see if he comes out of his coma."

While Robertson Hospital stands out as perhaps the leader in patient recoveries and one of the best in Richmond, Virginia, it's being compared against a very low level of the bar. The North and South went to war with inadequate preparations for handling the wounded, and both sides totally underestimating the amount and severity of casualties. As a result, hospitals were hastily improvised, manned by inexperienced medical officers and dependent upon untrained nurses. High mortality figures reflect the fact that surgeons had no antiseptics. Anesthesia was just coming into general use and drugs were inadequate, especially in the South, where drugs and other medical supplies were growing scarcer each day the war continues. A study of such figures reveals that most soldiers died from disease, and death from wounds was about the same as deaths on the battlefield. Were it not for most soldiers being young and having high powers of resistance and recuperation, the situation would have been even more appalling. The most common treatment for arm and leg wounds was amputation. With antiseptic methods unknown at the time, a wounded man was lifted on the operating table and the surgeon quickly examined the wound and settled upon cutting off the injured limb. Some ether was administered if it was available. Cleanliness such as hand washing and nail scrubbing was never practiced before operations or in dressing recent wounds.

During battle, the largest proportion of wounds was caused by minié balls. These were fired from single-shooter and muzzle-loading rifles. Such bullets weighed an ounce or more, and the guns from which they were fired would kill a man nearly a mile away, producing very large ugly wounds. When a minié ball struck a bone, it shattered the contiguous bony structure. Civil War surgeons never failed to infect the part with their dirty hands and instruments, whenever they removed the bullet. The importance of sterilizing surgical implements was unknown; surgeons merely washed the instruments with water and wiped them dry to prevent rusting.

Without knowing exactly why, Sally Tompkins's fetish for cleanliness played a major role in the success of Robertson Hospital.

Another long, laborious and wearisome day was finally coming to an end. Sally was making her final rounds and looked in on the coma patient to find Grazyna sitting at his bedside.

"Has he shown any signs of coming around?" Sally whispered.

"Not to my knowledge. What do the doctors say?"

"They said all we can do is wait. Most of them feel that he will come around sooner or later. All the same, I don't think they really know. These physicians are inexperienced and have never witnessed someone in a coma firsthand. I've a mind to call headquarters and get a message to General Jackson about our current situation. Stonewall cares a great deal about this patient and may have ideas to help," Sally replied earnestly. At that point, Grazyna stood and gathered her belongings, saying, "If you don't have anything more for me, I think I'll head home and get some rest."

"Please do just that, my dear. I'm so proud of all you girls, especially you, Grazyna. Working as a nurse in a military hospital, during war, is the most strenuous job I can think of. Do you still live with your parents?" Sally knew that she did. "If you ever want to change that situation, remember, I have a room for you in my house and you're welcome to it, free of charge. That is, if you can stand to live with an old hussy like me."

"I may fool you someday, Sally, and take you up on that offer," Grazyna replied.

That night, while she was undressing for bed, Grazyna found the small Bible in her apron's front pocket. There were other pieces of paper between the pages, even so, she was too tired to read them. She simply placed the Bible in her nightstand's drawer and planned to return it to the hospital in the morning.

Two days later, when they were preparing to force-feed the patient, Jack awoke from his coma and said quietly, "Where am I?" Those three words created quite a stir as the lifeless body suddenly came alive. Needless to say, the heart of the attending nurse pounded with so much excitement, and she was unable to speak for a moment.

"You're at Robertson Hospital. How do you feel?" she said at last.

"I think I'm hungry." Then after a short time to gather his thoughts, he asked, "Why am I here?"

"You were wounded at Fredericksburg," she responded. "I'm going to tell Captain Tompkins and see about getting you something to eat. Don't try to get up, just relax until the doctor takes a look at you."

Jack was in a quandary. Trying to recall any past events drew a frustrating blank and began to give him a throbbing headache. He knew this wasn't a bad dream, but that was about as far as he could conceptualize. The young doctor and Jack's food tray arrived in a dead heat. Hunger compelled the Tennessee sharpshooter to prioritize food before conversation. Jack dug in like a famished wolf.

"I never knew hospital food tasted so good," said the smiling doctor as he took the chair beside Jack's bed.

"It doesn't," replied the nurse. "My mother used to say hunger is the best seasoning, and he's proving her right."

After scraping the last remnants from the bottom of the bowl, Jack asked, "What was that I just ate?"

"You've been in a coma for a few days, and I don't want you to have solid food for a while. Solid food might be too much for your digestive system right now. As for what the food was, it looked to me like it was gruel and some other soft stuff. How did it taste?"

"Kind of bland, not much taste to it. Still and all, I was so hungry it could have been made from things you find under flat rocks and I wouldn't have cared."

"Do you know why you are here?" asked the doctor.

"I thought I heard somebody say I was injured at Fredericksburg," Jack recalled.

"That's right. What do you remember about Fredericksburg?" the doctor inquired.

"I don't remember anything."

"Do you recall who some of your fellow soldiers are?"

"I can't remember anyone. It all seems so strange," replied Jack.

"What is your name and rank?" the physician further questioned.

"I don't remember. I can't remember who I am," Jack earnestly stated.

"Well, don't let that bother you too much. It's not unusual, in your type of injury, for memory loss to occur. It may take a little time for those things to come back to you. Your head wound is healing properly so that isn't a problem. I do want the bandages changed each day, and tomorrow, feel free to move around a bit. I'll see that a nurse is assigned to help you navigate the premises."

Alone in the room, Jack was swimming in a river of fog. The harder he tried to recall the past, the deeper he was consumed by the shadowy abyss. His situation was bewildering, as if set adrift from his bearings. It also was draining and made him sleepy, even though he spent the last few days in the Land of Nod. Before surrendering to the bed, he had the urge to use the lavatory and saw, across the room, a door ajar. A little unsteady at first, Jack found his way in and sat down.

Sally Tompkins had assigned Grazyna to look after the new patient and supervise a walk around the property as exercise. When she looked in on him, he was nowhere to be found. The lavatory door was shut, and she quickly put two and two together.

"Are you okay in there?" she asked while gently tapping on the door.

"I'll be out in a second," Jack answered.

Jack washed his hands and slowly walked back to the bed. He lay back with his fingers folded behind his head and asked, "Who's the top dog around here?"

"That would be my boss, Capt. Sally Tompkins, she runs the hospital."

"Why do you call her captain? Is she an officer in the Confederacy?"

"Yes, she was commissioned by President Jefferson Davis himself, that's why," Grazyna conveyed. "You're supposed to stay in bed until tomorrow, and then we need to go for a walk. I was on my way to see Sally before I checked in on you. Did you want to talk to her about something?"

"I guess it can wait. Do I get to eat again today, or was that my three square meals?"

"Supper will be served in an hour, but you probably won't like it. They have you on a semiliquid diet. I've never met a patient who really cares for it." Grazyna was smiling. "I'll see you tomorrow morning. Right now I must go find Sally."

At that moment, Sally had a visitor. Apparently her message reached Stonewall Jackson. Her visitor was Maj.

Gen. Walter Shaw, head of the Confederate medical corps, who arrived from headquarters to personally examine Corp. Jack Leffingwell.

"I understand the patient is in a coma," the general stated in a serious manner.

"Not any longer, he came around this morning. Still, he has no memory of who he is or why he is here," Sally conveyed.

"Concussion does funny things to our brains. He will need a thorough examination to see if there's been significant damage," Major General Shaw said, with authority.

"This hospital deals with wounds to the body. We have no experience with cerebral science," stated Sally.

"None of us here in the Confederacy has sufficient experience in that area. Most of the work, as with any breakthroughs in medical knowledge, has been developed in Europe. We learn by reading the publications and attending lectures by those most familiar with medical state of the art. Concerning our patient, we just need to do all that we can and hope for the best," the general frankly returned.

"I'll be staying at the Exchange Hotel while I'm here and would like to examine Corporal Leffingwell tomorrow morning."

"I will make certain everything is arranged," Sally assured. "I do have one question. I'm curious as to why General Jackson is so interested in the patient."

"That has puzzled me as well. I think the general is impressed by Corporal Leffingwell's marksmanship and his Whitworth rifle."

"That still seems out of balance with the amount of attention he is prescribing," Sally commented.

"Did I mention that Corporal Leffingwell saved the general's life with a shot fired nearly a half mile away? Apparently, a Yankee sharpshooter had the general in his sights, but the bullet only struck his saddle. Then, while he reloaded and adjusted his aim, Leffingwell put a Whitworth bullet between his eyes. Whether or not Leffingwell is that good, I cannot confirm, though, the general thinks he is, and that's good enough for me."

Major General Shaw, though outwardly modest, posted outstanding credentials. He was a four-year graduate from the Medical University of South Carolina; studied two years at the medical University of Edinburgh, Scotland; and returned to South Carolina University as lecturer and instructor. Shaw held commission in the United States Army, serving as major in the U.S. medical corps. When the Civil War began, Shaw joined the Confederacy and performed similar duties as with the Union army. Today, there are not many doctors more qualified to treat the young amnesia patient.

* * *

> After the Medical University of South Carolina was chartered in 1823, it became the first medical school in the Deep South. It was founded as a private, proprietary institution by members of the Medical Society of South Carolina and served without outside financial support until the state assumed ownership of the school in 1913. During the period just before the Civil War, a physician received minimal surgical training. The average medical student trained for two years or less,

received practically no clinical experience, and was given virtually no laboratory instruction. Nearly all the older doctors had little formal education and attained their status by serving as apprentices.

In Europe, four-year medical schools were common, laboratory training was widespread, and a greater understanding of disease and infection existed.

In America, the perception that doctors or surgeons knew how to perform amputations, or any other kind of surgery, is wrong. The average student who had just graduated was severely limited in surgical experience. When the Civil War started, there were very few experienced surgeons to handle battlefield wounds. In many cases, those performing amputations had only on-the-job training.

Chapter Fifteen

Amnesia is as if the previous world didn't exist. And now each day Jack Leffingwell feels as though he's just starting over.

Grazyna brought breakfast the following morning. She wanted to tell Jack that their walk was suspended due to the arrival of Major General Shaw. On the tray were scrambled eggs, roasted potatoes, sausage, grits, and a side dish of peaches (obviously canned), plus hot coffee.

"Looks like they took you off the liquid diet. I'm sure you'll like this much better," Grazyna stated formally as she laid the tray on a side table next to Jack's bed. "The exercise is postponed until after Dr. Shaw examines you."

"When will that be?" Jack questioned.

"I believe it will be sometime later this morning. I'll be back after I make my rounds. Is there anything else you need right now?"

"I can't think of anything. I might need seconds of this breakfast."

"I can't help you there. You might ask Captain Tompkins, but you're chances are very slim," Grazyna said jokingly and left the room.

Jack had just finished eating and pushed back from the side table when he heard a muffled conversation outside the door. Shortly thereafter came a polite knock, and Sally Tompkins and Major General Shaw entered the room.

"Good morning, Jack, I want to introduce General Shaw. He is here to help you regain your memory," Sally announced.

Jack recognized the uniform stars before turning his gaze to Shaw's compassionate smile.

"Don't get up, son," the general said. "Military protocol is suspended when the soldier is ill or in the hospital." Shaw dragged a chair over to where Jack sat and said formally, "I need to ask a few questions. You may think some of them are stupid, but they're necessary to evaluate the degree of injury you've sustained. What recollection do you have of when you were wounded?"

"None, sir, I found out about that here in the hospital."

"I've been told you were in deep sleep when they brought you in. Do you recall waking up?"

"Yes, sir, but I had no idea where I was."

"Do you recognize the woman standing by the bed?"

"Yes."

"Who is she?"

"She is Capt. Sally Tompkins, sir. I've been told that she runs the hospital."

"Yes indeed, she does just that. Can you remember anyone else here at the hospital?"

"Yes, sir, there's a nurse named Grazyna, who brought me breakfast this morning, and two others, but I didn't catch their names."

"What regiment are you with, Soldier?" Dr. Shaw probed with vigor.

"I honestly don't know, General. I have no memory of who I am. Previous things in my life seem to have disappeared completely."

Shaw seemed to be satisfied with their conversation thus far. He feels as though he can make a reasonable diagnosis of Jack's type of amnesia and conveyed, "This will take time; nevertheless, I believe you will eventually retrieve that part of your past life which for now, is gone."

"How long will it take?" Jack questioned.

"That I can't say exactly. It could come back this morning, next week, next month, or next year. If it's any comfort, I personally believe it will be sooner rather than later." The sound of sliding chairs and more muffled conversation was heard by nurses loitering outside the door. They have had plenty of training registered by those sounds and slowly walked away.

Sally Tompkins and Dr. Shaw walked unhurriedly back to the office. Sally poured them both a glass of water and asked, "All kidding aside, can we help Corporal Leffingwell here at Robertson's?"

"I feel certain you can care for him better than most. You see, we basically just have to wait and let the body repair itself. The patient isn't suffering from visible wounds, and his amnesia definitely appears to be a result of shock and a corresponding neurotic reaction. The activities of events following the trauma are remembered. That's a good thing. Events preceding the trauma are forgotten, still, his language skills are good and response time is quick. These are indicators of no permanent brain damage. I'm diagnosing Corporal Leffingwell as having retrograde amnesia, and his prognosis is good. Do you wish to add something to my report to General Jackson?"

"I don't believe so. I'm still trying to figure out how to make his visit with us unobtrusive for the rest of the hospital," Sally said softly.

"He doesn't require special attention, and his regiment is inactive for the winter. Time is the only medication required. Just let him roam the grounds when the weather gets better. Walking and physical activity sometimes allows for the mind to rest itself and release constricted memory. I'll explain this in my report, and I feel certain Stonewall Jackson will support us."

* * *

The Army of Northern Virginia has taken winter quarters just outside of Fredericksburg after engaging in the most violent battle in the Commonwealth. The Union army was thwarted in their attempt to capture Richmond and forced to pull back to Washington, D.C., after sustaining heavy losses. Union casualties were vastly greater than those of the South and demonstrated how inept and disastrous Federal general Burnside's tactics were. While fighting on the southern flank produced roughly equal casualties, the northern flank was completely lopsided, with about eight Union casualties for each Confederate. The Richmond Examiner described it as a "stunning defeat to the invader, a splendid victory to the defender of the sacred soil." Confederate general Robert E. Lee, whose demeanor is normally reserved, became more flamboyant and outwardly jubilant. The victory, once again, demonstrated the tactical superiority of the Southern general, astride a white horse named Traveler.

Reactions were just the opposite in the North, and both the army and President Lincoln came under strong attacks from politicians and the press. Burnside was desperate to restore his reputation and the morale of his Army of the Potomac. He certainly had to know how disgraced it presently stood and, like those with dampened egos, had to make the proverbial "just one more attempt." He planned a surprise crossing of the Rappahannock River south of Fredericksburg to flank Robert E. Lee. At the same time, Union cavalry would cross the Rappahannock some twenty miles north and strike south into Lee's rear, destroying his supply lines.

When President Lincoln learned of this plan, he put a stop to it because he felt it was too risky. So Burnside revised his plan by reversing the original sequence. Instead of crossing the Rappahannock south of Fredericksburg, he intended to move upstream and cross due north of the Chancellorsville crossroads. The altered plan aimed at a closer, quicker crossing of the river. Union engineers would push five bridges across. Already, fifteen pontoons were on the river, nearly spanning it; and with five more, it was amply sufficient. After that, two grand divisions would be over the river in four hours. Meanwhile, another grand division would distract the rebels by repeating the December Crossing at Fredericksburg. It all looked good on paper, but unfortunately, the weather was unseasonably mild and with it came rain. Before long, the earth was soaked and the riverbanks had the appearance of a quagmire.

Burnside began at once to bring up his artillery, which had the effect of making a perfect mortar bed. For a considerable area around the ford all day, the men worked in the rain but to little purpose. Quite a number of cannon were advanced near the ford; but the storm wouldn't abate and the artillery, caissons, and even wagons were swamped in the mud. The storm had delayed Burnside's movements, giving Lee ample time to line the other shore with his army, though there was no attempt to interfere with his crossing except from the sharpshooters, who peppered away on all occasions. No doubt Lee was hoping Burnside would affect a crossing. With a swollen river in his rear, it would have been a sorry predicament for the Union army indeed. Burnside finally became resigned to his fate and gave the order for the army to retire to its quarters. General Burnside was relieved of command a month later, following an unsuccessful attempt to purge some of his subordinates from the army and the humiliating failure of his Mud March. Lincoln replaced him with Maj. Gen. Joseph Hooker on January 26, 1863.

* * *

Abel Strawn had just received the answer to his request for passes to visit Jack Leffingwell at Robertson Hospital. Lomas Chandler was first to learn where Jack was and offered to obtain passes. Still, Abel decided to take the long way around and go through proper channels. The original sharpshooters were now down to three and one newcomer, Melvin Kaufman. John Henry Bickford and Ihme Mueller are buried somewhere on the battlefield.

"Our passes are good for forty-eight hours from point of departure. We need transportation from here to Richmond and back, or we'll spend the time walking. Lomas, I'm turning to you for help. All I can say is try to keep it as legal as possible. We don't want to spend the winter behind bars."

"It will be my pleasure to arrange everything, and if anyone ends up behind bars, I promise it will only be Melvin Kaufman," Lomas returned with a silly grin.

"I ain't going. I want to see Jack as much as anyone, but I ain't so stupid as to risk jail time," Melvin honestly returned.

"Lomas is pulling your leg, Melvin. Nobody's going to jail," assured Abel.

Lomas came through, as promised, by working out a deal with a wagon driver who traveled to Richmond on a daily basis. He primarily transported spare parts needed by the army in order to repair artillery guns and caisson wheels. Under normal circumstances, the forty-five-mile trip took eight hours, and with a little monetary persuasion, the driver said it could be done in six. It was arranged to leave the base at 6:00 a.m., shortly after breakfast, and reach Richmond sometime after noon. That would give the sharpshooters plenty of time to locate the hospital and visit Jack. The wagon driver would then pick them up at six the following morning to return to the base camp. Remarkably, that schedule fit well with the wagon driving entrepreneur. He could deliver his cargo to the military repair facility, reload the mended items from a previous trip, and return to the Fredericksburg campsite the next day.

At breakfast, the future travelers were cheerier than usual, anticipating the journey; and the fact that it all was perfectly legal gave them a carefree attitude. The weather was mild for this time of year, but it was still January and coats were a welcome requirement. With their pass documents safely inside their shirt pockets, the group walked over to the maintenance building and found the wagon and team waiting for them.

* * *

"Are you up to a little exercise this morning?" Grazyna asked while standing in the doorway with a soldier's winter coat draped over her arm.

"Wait until I get my shoes on," Jack replied. Actually, after his warm breakfast, he was about to doze off.

"This is the largest coat I was able to find. I hope it fits okay. Although it's a nice sunshiny day outside, it's still too cold without a coat. A walk outside will do you a lot of good—the fresh air and all," she said confidently. Looking up to meet Jack's eyes, she continued, "You're even taller than I thought. We nurses noticed that the day you came in. I've only been here about two years, and you hold the record as far as I'm concerned. How tall are you?"

"I really don't know exactly. I do know that I can keep eating apples after everybody else has to quit."

Grazyna smiled and pushed open the outside door leading to the Robertson's courtyard. Even though the weather was unseasonably mild, a cold rush of air opened Jack's sinuses and made his eyes water. Grazyna took a deep breath and said, "I just love walking in the wintertime. The cold air clears my mind and renews my spirit."

"Walking outside seems natural to me as well. Maybe it has something to do with me being a soldier." Across the courtyard, people were sitting on benches and taking advantage of the bright sun.

"Straight ahead, there's an empty bench. Let's sit for a while," Grazyna imparted while nudging Jack with her shoulder. The bench she chose was positioned in a manner so as the bright sunshine didn't hit them directly, eliminating the necessity to squint or hold up a hand to shield. She seemed to light up when surveying the grounds and said enthusiastically, “I just love Robertson’s courtyard and gardens. It’s particularly beautiful in the summertime when the flowers are in full bloom—almost celestial, like the Garden of Eden.”

Not recalling where or when, Jack felt as though he had seen other places even more idyllic.

“Are you from Richmond?” he asked.

“Yes, from Claysville, that’s just south of the capital but still in the greater Richmond area. My family originated from Poland. Grandfather Kaminski came here for a better life. Once he got settled, he sent for my grandmother and their son, who later became my father. When my father reached adulthood, he, too, sent for his fiancée, who later became my mother. My mother and father were both born in Poland. I was born here in the Commonwealth. Were your parents born here in America?”

“I have no idea,” Jack answered frankly. “I was just wondering. You have an unusual name.”

“Grazyna isn’t that unusual in Poland, but here in Virginia, there aren’t many girls with that name. Jack, are you married?”

“I honestly don’t know.” Jack realized the line of questioning was part of his therapy, but it’s beginning to enervate him. “Can we dispense with questions about my history and just talk to each other like normal people?”

“Please realize that I’m only trying to help you,” quavered Grazyna.

“I’m sorry, dear, it’s just so frustrating not being able to remember my past,” Jack explained. “Let me ask you something, are you married?”

“I was, but my husband was killed at Manassas,” Grazyna volunteered.

"I'm sorry to hear that. I didn't mean to pry or bring up anything painful. Please forgive me."

"It's been two years since Michael was killed. We really didn't have a traditional marriage. He was called immediately after the wedding ceremony, and two days later, I was a widow."

Jack was curious whether or not their marriage was consummated but would never ask. "You're still a young girl, and once this war is over, some lucky guy will come along."

They sat in silence for several minutes, and finally Grazyna said, "I believe this is enough fresh air and exercise for one day. Let's head back to the hospital."

After returning to the hospital, Jack, though tired from the walk and fresh air, felt an unexplained emotional letdown. His disappointment brought on a feeling of emptiness, similar to the way he felt when first attempting to recall his past. This, however, was different and central to his weariness was Grazyna McCracken, his amenable nurse. His bemusement was suddenly interrupted when Sally Tompkins appeared and announced, "Mr. Leffingwell, you have company. There are three comrades of yours here to visit."

Jack's attention was drawn to three grinning faces of men wearing Confederate gray and striding forward with handshakes and back slaps. He had absolutely no idea who they were and just sat on the edge of his bed as though in a trance. The three sharpshooters were prewarned about Jack's condition and schooled to pose their questions accordingly. With that in mind, they kept questions primarily regarding the hospital stay. Abel felt they each needed to introduce themselves as though meeting for the first time and took the lead, "Jack, my name is Abel

Strawn. You and I are friends and in the same Seventh regiment from Tennessee." Each took turns making similar introductions and received a response of "Glad to meet you." Abel explained about their forty-eight-hour pass and the fortunate means of transportation. Jack, constrained by lack of memory and unfamiliar faces, did the best he could to hold up his end of the conversation. Soon, storytelling filled most of the visit, with each friend giving account of their most embarrassing situations and asinine decisions. Their visit marked the first occasion, the Tennessee mountain man laughed, since coming to Robertson Hospital. Generous humor always makes time pass swiftly, and the dinner hour came about before they knew it.

"My golly, look what time it is. We better call it a day, and let you have supper and get some rest," Abel said thoughtfully.

"I'm very glad you guys stopped by. I can't remember when I had a better time. No pun intended," Jack said honestly. At that moment, Grazyna walked in carrying Jack's dinner tray. Three jaws dropped like a rock, and the marksmen began stammering their farewells, with eyes locked on the awesome beauty.

"I think Jack is the luckiest guy on the face of the earth. That nurse is the most beautiful woman I've ever seen. Did you catch her eyes?" said Lomas as the trio opened the outside door and left the building.

"Looking from the ground up, I never got that far," Melvin answered.

"The shame of it all is, Jack's a married man with the love of his life waiting for him back home. When we get back to camp, I'm going to write Abigail to let her know he's all right," Abel imparted.

"Are you going to tell her about his amnesia?" Lomas asked.

"Yes, don't you think I should?"

"I guess so. Not to change the subject, I'm starved, and we need a place to sleep tonight," Lomas responded.

"A church is our best bet. Let's find the nearest one and ask for help. Remember, my father is a Methodist minister, and that should carry a lot of weight." After asking directions to the nearest Methodist church, the three marksmen began walking along the suggested course. It was mutually agreed that the trip to Robertson Hospital was worthwhile, even though Jack had no idea who they were. His still being alive and not physically maimed was satisfying enough, and all three concluded the amnesia would soon heal itself. Before long, the unusually mild temperature made the need for their topcoats excessive; and with beads of sweat running down their cheeks, they removed and carried the coats across their arms.

"Boy, am I thirsty," Lomas declared.

"You're always thirsty," Abel replied.

"For the life of me, I don't know why you would say a thing that. I only drink on two occasions: when I'm thirsty and when I'm not," Lomas said, laughing. "Wait, do my eyes deceive me? Is that a tavern sign up ahead?" Hanging over the walkway and supported against the building by a wrought-iron frame was a wooden placard painted in bright colors with the words Eagle Inn and Tavern.

"Let's stop and have one for the road," Lomas said with a grin.

"I thought we were looking for the Methodist church." Abel was a little piqued.

"Remember what the Bible says, 'A man hath no better thing under the sun, than to eat, and to drink, and to be merry.' I'm certain all three can be found inside this fine-looking establishment." With that, Lomas pulled open the heavy wooden door; and almost at once, the pungent aroma of cigar smoke filled their lungs. From the laughter and shouting, you could tell that the Eagle was a favorite here in Richmond. Melvin's eyes were drawn to the top of the room where heavy smoke clung like a cloud. Its density, heaviest at the top, gradually diminished toward the bottom. Melvin would never say, but this was the first time he had ever been in such an establishment. He definitely was psyched out and now knew why men were drawn to it.

"What will you have, boys?" the bartender asked while wiping the bar top directly in front of them.

"Three beers," Lomas chimed with a smile on his face. He turned and said something to Melvin, but it wasn't heard due to the constant din around them. The bartender delivered three foaming mugs and moved quickly down the bar to pour whiskey into the shot glasses of the more serious imbibers. One of whom popped it down with a single gulp and slid off his stool and walked over to the three Confederate soldiers.

"Let me shake your hands. The Commonwealth couldn't be more proud of you fellows. Did you see any action against Burnside?" the visitor was well on his way to being drunk.

"Yes, we did. In fact, we are here in Richmond to visit a comrade who was wounded in the battle, and unfortunately, we lost another from our outfit," Abel answered.

"I'm truly sorry to hear about the man you lost. I'm not sure what they tell you boys, but you kicked Lincoln's ass and saved the capital and probably the whole damn war. By the way, my name is Johnson, Clyde Johnson, and I'm one of the editors with the *Richmond Enquirer*. Have you read the piece we wrote about you guys and the battle defending our soil?"

"Not yet, we're at winter quarters now, and it takes a while for the newspaper to get around the base camp," Lomas answered.

"Well, when it finally gets to you, make sure you boys read it. I know you'll like it. Did I mention that my son is serving in the army? He's stationed here in Richmond, and we're all quite proud of him. Not everybody sees action on the battlefield. A great many do their part by supporting the effort behind the lines, so to speak." With that Johnson turned to the bartender and shouted, "Hey, Charlie, keep 'em coming over here and put it on my tab."

"Thanks, we sure do appreciate it. Can you tell us how far the Methodist church is from here?"

"When you go out the door, just turn to the left and keep heading that way. The church is about a quarter mile or so. Do you know the minister?"

"Not really, we will need a place to sleep this evening and thought they might put us up for the night. We head back in the morning," Abel replied.

"They got rooms here at the Eagle," Johnson said and called the bartender over to their side of the countertop. Once he arrived, Clyde Johnson whispered, "These fine young men need a bed tonight. Put the bill on my tab. That's the least we can do for the heroes of our beloved South." The barkeep seemed to agree and gave a nod to the marksmen.

Clyde Johnson's tab was actually paid by the *Enquirer* for expenses in search of news items. Oddly enough, most of Johnson's stories originated from the Eagle Inn and

Tavern. The bartender made certain the most expensive rooms were provided for the sharpshooters. It put another three dollars on the *Enquirer*'s tab. As the night wore on, the trio moved to a table, and a platter of sandwiches eventually found its way to them. By then Lomas lost his appetite and continued drinking beer; however, Abel and Melvin made short work of the comestibles. The room remained in a gay mood until nearly two o'clock in the morning. Finally, the barkeep herded the last patron out the door, then dropped three keys on the soldiers' table and pointed to the steps leading upstairs.

Remarkably, the trio was bright-eyed and bushy tailed when their conveyance left the maintenance building and headed back to Fredericksburg.

"Looks like we might get a little rain. There's a canvas tarp back there with you in case you need it," the driver announced. The team of horses gave a jerk, and the return trip was on its way.

Chapter Sixteen

It's been said that you can tell how much a woman cares for a man by the way she cooks for him.

On a blustery winter morning, in mid-January, Maj. Gen. Walter Shaw stomped the snow from his boots and entered the hospital. His was calling on Jack Leffingwell to observe, firsthand, any progress made recuperating his past memory. Because of the importance placed on the patient's well-being by his commanding officer, Shaw established a schedule of visiting every two weeks. His first stop was to report his presence at the front desk, then confer with Sally Tompkins, and meet again with her after examining Jack. With the initial aspects of the routine completed, Dr. Shaw called on his patient.

"Good morning, Jack, how have you been feeling?"

"I feel great, but I think I'm getting claustrophobic. The walls are closing in on me," Jack replied with a chortle.

"I guess, for a man like yourself, you would start to feel a little hemmed in. Have a look outside. Take it from me, it's quite undesirable on the other side of these walls and try to resolve your complaints to the good fortune of being inside, where it's warm and homelike."

"I didn't mean that as a grievance, it's just at times I get the strange feeling that I belong outside rather than inside."

Dr. Shaw made a mental note of what Jack said and asked, "How is the food?"

"I've got no complaints there, unless they don't put enough on the plate." Jack knew portions were under the control of availability and kept the little secret he shared with Grazyna. She added more whenever she got the chance and recently began bringing homemade Polish pastry.

"I understand you received visitors the other day."

"Yes, some men from my regiment. They were very entertaining, and we all had a good time," Jack replied.

"Did you recognize any of them?"

"I now know who they are, yet as far as recognizing them, I don't recall ever seeing them before."

"Eventually, you will be able to recall all of your past memories, it's going to take time and one day it will happen. Unfortunately, I can't predict the exact time; nevertheless, I'm positive it will happen. All you need to do is keep the faith," assured Dr. Shaw before walking out of the room to look for Captain Tompkins.

Once again the two met in Tompkins's office to exchange observations and confer about any changes in future treatment. Dr. Shaw shared what Jack had said about preferring to be outside rather than inside and believed it may, somehow, serve as a clue to his past.

"Amnesia is a confusing malady. When you talk to Jack, he seems like a perfectly normal person, yet he draws a blank about anything before coming here. I've never met anyone with amnesia, and it's hard for me to believe such patients are actually sick," Sally honestly stated.

"The patient isn't physically ill. He has a mental illness caused by shock, literally as well as emotionally. Let's see, how can I explain it better? We've all experienced the frustration of entering a room and forgetting what we were going to do or say. These situations are memory lapses and perfectly normal. The brain has compartmentalized the thought, and the present activity has temporarily blocked it. Of course, we only have a short-term mental obstruction; nevertheless, it is a form of temporary amnesia. Now, when it comes to our patient, Jack Leffingwell, the percussion of the exploded shell has caused his brain to compartmentalize his past. That, too, may be temporary; however, we in the medical profession cannot accurately define the term temporary, as it relates to amnesia, and that is what's so confusing and frustrating."

Their conference basically ended at that point, and Major General Shaw made his excuses pledging to return in two weeks or as soon as there is any breakthrough with Jack's memory loss.

At about the same time Dr. Shaw left the building, Grazyna entered Jack's room holding up a small brown paper bag and said, "Guess what I have."

"It's a watermelon," Jack answered jokingly.

"No, silly, it's some paczki [pronounced *pawnch-kee* or *punch-kee*]." Paczki is a traditional deep-fried, round, spongy yeast cake filled with jam or another sweet filling and covered with powdered sugar or icing. In Poland, paczki is usually eaten on the last day of carnival, similar to Fat Tuesday, the day before Ash Wednesday.

“I made it especially for you. Let me know how you like it when I come around later today.”

“What, no exercise today?”

“Not today, it’s too cold and snowing very, very hard. You might catch pneumonia.”

“I doubt it. I’m a lot tougher than you think. I am going to miss our walk though.” After he said that, Jack wondered if she took it the wrong way. He seemed to always fall short of not encouraging her friendship beyond a professional amicability. Perhaps, he, too, wanted it to go further than what’s considered acceptable.

“Maybe tomorrow we can chance it, though I think the snowdrifts will be pretty deep,” Grazyna offered. “I’ll send someone in with hot coffee. It’ll go good with the paczki.”

Alone again, Jack began to smell the tantalizing aroma coming from the brown bag. His willpower was about as weak as a rained-on bee, and he removed a paczek (singular for paczki) and took a large bite before the coffee arrived. The mouthwatering flavor overwhelmed the Tennessee sharpshooter for he had never tasted anything like it. It sure wasn’t crabapple pie. He heard the squeaking wheels of the coffee cart and poked the remaining pastry in his mouth just as it rolled in the room.

* * *

Back in Statesville, Tennessee, all the talk was about the big battle down in Murfreesboro, called the Battle of Stones River, by the Union. Of the major battles in the Civil War, Stones River had the highest percentage of combined casualties for both armies. The battle itself was inconclusive; however, two Confederate attacks were repulsed by Federal forces before the Southerners withdrew from the field. The Confederate retreat gave a much-needed boost to the Union morale especially after the earlier setback at the Battle of Fredericksburg in Virginia. It also dampened Confederate aspirations for control of Middle Tennessee. Union major general William S. Rosecrans' Army of the Cumberland challenged Confederate general Braxton Bragg's Army of Tennessee in a sustained clash from December 31, 1862, until January 2, 1863, resulting in 24,645 total casualties.

Each army had similar plans of attack—that is, to attack the other's weakest flank. While Federal general Rosecrans was working out details, Braxton Bragg's troops struck first. The massive assault overran a Union wing; however, reinforcements allowed for the defense to stiffen, preventing a total collapse. Perhaps Bragg's biggest mistake occurred on January 2, 1863, when he ordered an assault on the well-fortified Union position, located on an elevated tract of land to the east of Stones River. Faced with overwhelming artillery, the Confederates were repulsed with heavy losses. Fearing Rosecrans was receiving reinforcements, Bragg chose to withdraw his army. Actually, the choice of Murfreesboro to base his army was curious from a military standpoint, since it offered no particular advantages for defense. The only explanation might be because it was a center for strong Confederate sentiment, and Bragg and his men were warmly welcomed and entertained. Located in a rich agricultural region, Bragg might have planned to provision his army while using the position to block a potential Federal advance on Chattanooga. In any case, a move farther south to the Duck River Valley, or north to Stewart's Creek, would have made it easier to defend and, in all probability, result in victory. Nevertheless, it is what it is, and another step closer for Union forces to capture the entire state.

* * *

At the Methodist church in Statesville, Abigail was putting the final touches to lessons she intended to teach, once students arrived. The attendance had grown to the point where she needed to solicit more help. Her father advised she continue instructing the youngest children and he would call out for help by the congregation to instruct those older. The farm, her two children, Minnie Rosenthal, and teaching school occupied her thoughts during the day, but at night—oh, those long, wakeful, agonizing nights—found her yearning for the presence of her husband. The glint in a young girl's eye was long gone. Still beautiful, Abigail was beginning to reveal the facial worry lines of premature aging. Changes, unnoticed by those around her, could not escape the attention and watchful eye of Hyrum Adams. All fathers become wistfully saddened when they first notice their grown daughter exhibit aging. At times, while watching Abigail teaching class, Hyrum's heart aches and his vision was blurred by tears from longing for a happier time. This war had caused his faith to be tested again and again. As to why the Lord would allow such a terrible tragedy to ever take place had no acceptable answer.

On the days Abigail taught school, she had developed the habit of walking to the post office, reading the bulletin board, and checking for mail before returning home. Not seeing any names from Wilson County on the casualty list raised her spirits, and today, there was a letter waiting for her. She didn't recognize the handwriting, but it had military markings and that was enough to quicken her heartbeat. There was no waiting until she got home. Abigail dashed to her father's house to read the curious missive. Hyrum was in his study when he heard his door open and someone hurry inside. Rising from his chair, he walked to the parlor and found Abigail, with trembling hands, struggling to open the letter.

"It's not from Jack. I can tell from the postmark it has to do with the army," she told her father as she removed the message from its envelope.

"Read it aloud, dear," said Hyrum, whose interest was worked up by his daughter's actions.

January 1863
Dear Mrs. Leffingwell,

My name is Abel Strawn. I am a friend of your husband and in the same Tennessee regiment. First of all, Jack is unhurt and in good health. He is, however, in the Robertson Hospital in Richmond, Virginia. He was wounded from a cannon ball explosion during the Battle of Fredericksburg. It gave him a minor bump on the head but also left him with amnesia. Me and two other men, from his squad, visited him a day ago and found him in good spirits. He didn't recognize us or remember anything prior to the explosion. He does remember everything after, and I'm sure he will remember us from now on. The doctor told me that he expects a full recovery, but couldn't predict when Jack's memory will return.

I know how unpredictable correspondence is with the war and all and hope this letter reaches you before you worry about not hearing from Jack. I must repeat, Jack is okay and only has the memory problem. The army is in winter quarters now and hopefully for an extended time. Maybe by then Jack will be cured. In the meantime, don't fret too much about not hearing from him.

I will close by repeating, Jack is okay and in the hospital only because of the memory problem. I'm writing you the first week in January but never could remember the date.

Yours truly,
Abel Strawn

"I must go to him, Jack needs me," Abigail spoke out loud.

"You just can't pick up and go, sweetheart. We are in a war, and preparations and approvals are required for anyone wanting to travel any distance," Hyrum explained. "We know by the letter that Jack's condition isn't life threatening."

"My place is with him now. Please help me, Father, I must get to Robertson Hospital as soon as possible."

"All right, we will need papers to pass through the military lines. Our best bet is to visit Governor Johnson. A pass signed by him should be accepted by both Union and

Confederate guards. We will probably encounter problems traveling to Nashville from here. Be that as it may, about all we can do is put faith in the Lord to protect and guide us there. It's a trip of forty miles, and that means spending one night on the road, not the most desirable place to be."

"I'll write the governor tonight and explain my situation. If he gets my letter, at least he will have time to consider my request," Abigail said with conviction.

"Your mode of transportation must be determined and the hospital notified of your pending visit if . . . if we are successful with all the other stumbling blocks," said Hyrum.

The day after Abigail mailed letters to Robertson Hospital, in Richmond, Virginia, and to Governor Johnson, in Nashville, she and her father embarked on the trip to the state capital. Maryellen Riberty assured Abigail that she would check on Minnie Rosenthal, Sarah Jane, and young Jack every day. Life took unexpected turns. At one time Maryellen was Abigail's main rival and, now, her best friend. Hyrum planned for the trip to Nashville to last no longer than one week. That would allow for time on the road, arranging a meeting with the governor, and the return trip to Statesville. He had borrowed a one-horse chaise from a well-to-do parishioner. The four-wheeled gig was lightly constructed and would go easy on Miracle, yet make good time.

When the January dawn broke, it found the wayfarers well on their way. Early morning offered a cloudless day, making the awning a welcome part of the carriage. Miracle appeared to be handling her burden with ease and gave an occasional soft whinny and blow. Hyrum had assumed the attitude of silent prayer, and Abigail satisfied herself by taking another required step in order to visit Jack.

"The last time I drove to Nashville, I had your mother with me. We both were so excited to be going to the big city. I had to attend a Methodist conference, and your mom was thrilled by the whole experience." Abigail held tightly on to her father's arm and gave it an affectionate squeeze.

"I wish Mom had lived to see me married and she have grandchildren," Abigail whispered.

"You think I spoil your children. Compared to your mother, I am a piker." Hyrum spotted a grassy knoll ahead and said, "Looks like a nice place to rest Miracle and have a bite to eat. What's in the basket?"

"I know there's fried chicken because I made it myself. As far as anything else, it's going to be a surprise."

Hyrum pulled to a stop under a large oak tree and released Miracle from her harness. The gentle horse tossed her head as if to say thank-you and strolled a short distance to nibble grass, still green in the Tennessee winter. Inspection of the basket revealed the predictable fried chicken and a loaf of freshly baked bread, a jar of blueberry jam, six apples, and canned carrots. The bonanza forced Hyrum to exclaim, "It's a meal fit for a king." Abigail poured a pan of water from the kegs in the back of their carriage and presented it to the grateful mare before reattaching her to the harness. As the midday sun began its descent, they were back on the road and continuing their journey.

* * *

The mideastern part of Virginia was experiencing a significant rise in temperature for this time of year. Old-timers referred to it as the January thaw. Nearly everywhere you looked, snow was melting and icicles were slowly disappearing due to their steady drip to the earth below.

At Robertson Hospital, Grazyna wiped the foggy window and peered at the outside thermometer. Noting that it registered over fifty degrees, she smiled to herself as her thoughts focused on another walk with the tall soldier from Tennessee. He now was in her self-communication every idle moment and often occupied her more pleasant dreams. In the beginning, she dismissed feelings beyond that of patient and nurse. As that became more difficult, she considered discussing it with Sally Tompkins. In the back of her mind, Grazyna knew what that outcome would be. By now she was aware Jack Leffingwell was married—knowledge he could not recollect. At this moment in time, while gazing through the window, the beautiful young widow was in a mental quagmire. Torn between right and wrong, she resolved to continue and let the pieces fall where they may.

"Would you like to take a walk?" Grazyna asked while passing through Jack's doorway.

"What's in the sack?" Jack answered her question with one of his own.

"It's a surprise," she purred. "You didn't answer my question."

"My answer is, of course! Especially, if that's the only way I get to see what's inside that big bag."

"Well, you had better put on your boots. It's really warm outside, and the yard is soaking wet," she recommended.

As Jack pulled on his walking boots, he caught a whiff of Grazyna's natural essence. He stopped for a split second to savor the scent and wondered how a woman could smell so good without the help of cologne. The closest match he could determine would be fresh raspberries. After recollecting raspberry jam on his breakfast toast, he was able to make the comparison.

"Better bring your jacket just in case it turns cooler this afternoon. You won't need it for awhile, but better safe than sorry," she advised.

Yesterday the Robertson's grounds were covered with a snowy blanket of white. Today, patches of green were interspersed across the landscape where the crystal coating had melted. And Grazyna was right. Jack's boots left a temporary imprint in the spongy grass and water occasionally was an inch deep.

"Where are we going?"

"Do you see where the stand of woods ends? Well, just beyond that point the caretaker's cabin is to the left," she replied.

"I didn't know there was one. You can't see it from the hospital."

Once they reached beyond the tree line, the cabin came into view. It seemed to be divided into two parts. A large barn door indicated that part of the cabin held landscaping tools; and the portal, on the other side, presented the living quarters. It was easy for Jack to determine Grazyna had been there before. She reached above the doorframe and retrieved the key.

"'Step into my parlor,' said the spider to the fly," Grazyna said laughingly as she unlocked the door. "Do you know Mary Howitt's poem?"

"Can't say that I do," Jack replied.

"It's a children's favorite. I think I read it first when I was in grade school. It's a warning against those who use flattery and charm as a front for potential evil. Mary

Howitt is a heroine for most young girls. She was educated at home, and after her marriage, she and her husband wrote over 180 books."

"Not only beautiful, the lovely nurse is well-read," Jack had absolutely no idea why he said such a thing. Subconsciously, it was like a toe in the water or a probe designed to study her reaction.

"Have a seat on the couch while I set the table," Grazyna said formally as she began removing the contents from the sack. "I have made us ham sandwiches and a plate of pierogies. There is beer to drink and a little Polish vodka to finish the lunch. You can come sit at the table now, while I heat up the pierogies." Grazyna examined the stove to see if any wood remained under the burner grate. Pleased to have found some, she quickly lit them, replaced the grate, and sat the pan holding the pierogies on top. They were sizzling in short order and steaming once they found their way to the table. Satisfied with her handiwork, Grazyna said, "Let's eat."

The room was shuttered with very little daylight coming in. Jack suggested opening them, but Grazyna preferred to keep it dark. She brought candles and said that they would make it more romantic. Jack concluded she was concerned that illumination from the cabin might appear odd to any onlookers. The romantic idea didn't pass without notice and bodes well for a special afternoon.

"These are delicious. What are they?" Jack exclaimed after taking a bite of the pierogi.

"They're called pierogi, and the first thing my mother taught me to make. She said it is the most popular food in Poland—next to ham, that is. They're made of thinly rolled dough and filled with a variety of things. I use ground meat, mushrooms, sauerkraut, and cabbage.

Cooking takes two steps. First, they are boiled like a dumpling and then pan-fried like a pancake. You can fill them with berries, if you want, and serve them as dessert. So today, my sweet, I've prepared you an authentic Polish lunch." The term, *my sweet*, was spoken so nonchalantly that, to Jack, it was as appropriate as morning and dew. When Grazyna leaned forward to light the candles, her dress was stretched against her body, exposing the outline of her ample form. The sight was so arousing, fanning his emotional flame, that Jack averted his eyes and looked away. Grazyna witnessed his response and gently patted Jack's arm before taking her seat.

During the meal, conversation consisted mostly of small talk until Grazyna looked deep into Jack's eyes and said, "I've planned this moment for a very long time. We haven't had a caretaker here for over a year. The place has remained empty ever since he joined the Confederate army. Sally gave me the key and asked me to keep it tidy . . . clean and dusted. I sometimes spend the evening here, depending on my mood, and I thought it would make a perfect place for us to meet and unwind. You must know that I love you, Jack. I think it happened the first day I saw you. I also believe you share similar feelings for me. Let's not rationalize our situation right now, instead, let's finish the meal, have some vodka, and enjoy the rest of this point in time."

Jack carried his snifter of vodka to the couch, and Grazyna brought hers to the sink, sipping as she washed what few dishes there were. Jack, entranced by her immodest statement, noticed the bedroom door, left ajar, when she put aside their coats. His mind was spinning in search of what his next move should be. Amnesia left him without previous experience to draw on. The vodka was beginning to dull his senses, all except one, the emotional desire to make love to his lovely inamorata—now washing dishes at the sink. The rest was like a dream. A dream each of them would have the rest of their lives. Grazyna blew out the candles, save one, and walked over to Jack and took his hand. A single flame lit the way to the bedroom, and after a prolonged kiss, their intimate desire was satisfied that afternoon.

"How long have I slept?" Jack questioned after finding Grazyna awake and beaming her pleasant smile.

"Not too long. You must have needed it, and I didn't have the heart to wake you." The candle had burned down, but enough remained to make out images in the room. Grazyna had pulled the sheet up to her chin, and Jack ran his hand under and touched her naked body.

"Did I hurt you?"

"No, silly. You were wonderful."

Her nakedness once again heightened his passion, and there never were more willing partners to embrace and repeat their love act. The miseries the other nurses had cautioned Grazyna about never happened. In fact, just the opposite took place. She would describe it as exquisite pain, during which she chose to be silent. This time, at the climax, she let herself go and audibly moaned so loud Jack had concern for her well-being. His anxiety vanished when they both broke out in laughter and lay panting side by side. Grazyna rolled over on her side, presenting a reverse view of her contour, and Jacked noticed the bruise just above the union of her buttock cheeks.

"How did you hurt yourself?" he questioned, while running his hand over the area.

"I didn't, it's a birthmark. My grandmother called it my Mongolian blue dot," Grazyna answered while turning to face him. “It’s an ancestral thing dating back to when the Mongols invaded Europe. Poland was ravaged and plundered by the Tartars, yet some of them interspersed into the population, leaving their genetic makeup. The Mongolian spot isn’t that rare around the world. In fact, American Indians often exhibit the blue color patch, especially with their children, where it would be more easily noticed.” For a split second, the term *Indian* seemed to strike a chord with Jack, however, it was short-lived and further pursuit seemed blocked.

“You never cease to amaze me,” Jack asserted while moving closer. Then he asked, “How much time do we have?”

Chapter Seventeen

A long train ride is an unusual human experience. You sense traveling in a midway state of being in which you're not anywhere, but everywhere, moving past place to place, toward a final destination.

Fortunately, the remainder of the trip to Nashville went without incident. Abigail and her father were occasionally stopped at roadblocks and questioned by Union troops although they were sympathetic to their mission and were never detained for any length of time. Apparently, the minister and his daughter were not seen as a material threat and held no longer than the time required to ask the nature of their business, inspect the carriage, and pet Miracle. Considering the fact good horses were at a premium, there was speculation as to how the travelers came by one such as the brilliant mare; nevertheless, no effort went into further investigation.

"As I recall, the governor's building is in the center of town," Hyrum stated as he clucked Miracle into an ambling gait. Hyrum took notice of churches they passed along the way and made mental notes of their location. If need be, he can get directions to the governor's office and secure a place for them to spend the night.

"I never realized Nashville had so many churches. It's like there is one on every corner," Abigail commented while viewing the stately architecture. One in particular had Gothic arches, Jacoby stained glass windows, and what appeared to be a domed ceiling, compelling her to say, "Oh, Father, that's the most beautiful church I've ever seen."

"It's a Catholic church, dear, and I agree. It truly is beautiful."

Only a block or so from that cornerstone, the new Methodist Church's sanctuary had been started three years before. However, as almost everywhere, the stress of the Civil War had infiltrated and stopped construction. Tin portions of the roof had been removed to make canteens for soldiers and now the structure was used as a hospital for the sick and wounded. He could see that a portion of the building was still maintained as a sanctuary, and Hyrum decided to find the pastor.

"It looks as though most of the newly freed slaves have come to Nashville and makes me wonder if they'll still attend the Methodist Church," Abigail stated as her father directed the carriage toward what appeared to be the parsonage.

"John Wesley was an ardent opponent of slavery, but the Methodist Church was split on the question. While most ministers held positions against it, they never seemed to get a resolution by the general conference. The directors were always reluctant to oppose slavery. Their indecision resulted in serious friction among the clergy, and consequently, many groups broke away.

Before other groups came on board, they had ruled that slaveholders could not be members. This confounded the internal problem even more. Now, Mr. Lincoln has made the decision for us all, and no matter what opinions are held, our church must acquiesce. I expect, in time, free black people will eventually want their own identity and a church more sensitive to their own cultural and social issues," Hyrum replied. Noticing a hitching post, the Statesville minister pulled in front; and both passengers stepped down from the gig, secured the mare, and took the path leading to the parsonage door.

"Good afternoon, I am Rev. Adams from the church in Statesville. This is my daughter, Abigail Leffingwell. We need to speak with Rev. Parrot," Hyrum explained to the woman opening the parsonage door.

"Please come in and take a chair. I'll let the reverend know you all are here," she answered and left for a moment.

Harold Parrot was a tall man with dark thinning hair combed straight back. He had been pastor of the largest Methodist church in Nashville for over ten years. Well known for his charity work with the underprivileged, Parrot was one of the first persons Andrew Johnson needed for an ally when Lincoln appointed him governor of the occupation. Since then, the governor's wife was a regular at each Sunday service. However, the governor himself didn't accompany her very often. Hyrum rose from his chair and walked to meet Rev. Parrot as he entered the room. Extending a handshake in greeting, he explained his purpose for being in Nashville and solicited the Methodist minister's help. Rev. Parrot agreed to accommodate their need by writing a letter of introduction to the governor and requesting them an audience.

"I recommend you take this letter of introduction to the governor's office this afternoon. Just tell the soldier at the front desk your purpose for the visit and hand him the letter. Tell him you will be spending the night as my guest and will return in the morning. The young soldier and his wife were married here in the church about a month ago, and if I know human nature, he will secretly read the letter, and noting it has my signature, make certain Governor Johnson gets it."

"I can't tell you how much I appreciate what you're doing for us," Abigail said honestly.

"Think nothing of it, my dear. In these trying times, we do what we can. I do want you to spend the night with us. We have two guest rooms, and you're welcome to them. Paula, the lady who received you at the door, is my housekeeper and will show you the way. You may want to freshen up before dinner."

Abigail sat on the guest room bed and looked about in order to acculturate herself to the new surroundings. Things were happening so fast her emotions were keyed at their highest level. While sitting on the bed, the brief respite made her weary; and lying back, for just a moment, she quickly fell asleep.

"Miss Abigail, are you awake? Supper will be served in a half hour," the voice came from the other side of the door. Abigail's heart raced as tiny particles of awareness seemed to be floating in the air. Gradually they came together for her to acknowledge the present time. She rose from the bed and walked over to the dresser in hopes that the ewer and basin, resting on top, had water in its pitcher. Apparently, Paula anticipated their stay and filled it before they went upstairs. Thankfully, Abigail refreshed herself and combed her hair before proceeding to the dining table.

The meal was ample, in spite of shortages, and the conversation centered on conditions brought about by the war and occupation.

"The governor and I basically share the same sentiments, we just arrive from a different direction. He is not entirely antislavery, yet he is a strong believer in preserving the Union. Me, and most people like me, abhor slavery; and as far as the Union is concerned, states' rights are just as important. From the look of things, we both win. Slavery has ended, and the Union will be preserved," Rev. Parrot conveyed.

"Then, you think the South will lose the war," Hyrum stated hoarsely.

"Yes, I do. I pray every day for its end to come quickly."

"For some time now, I've believed the Union will ultimately win, in spite of their incompetent generals. My greatest fear is what beholds us once it's all over. We Tennesseans are getting a taste of postwar problems from the occupation, and many are resentful and have sworn retribution. Southerners are steadfast in their beliefs, and I fear many good citizens will answer that call, even if they have to disguise themselves."

"You're right, Brother Adams. It will be our responsibility to oppose it and condemn it from the pulpit."

The following morning, Abigail and her father arrived at the governor's office at 9:00 a.m., only to find it nearly full from those with appointments and others who were merely hopeful. They were able to find two chairs, placed them together and sat, planning for an extended wait. The young soldier acknowledged their presence, walked over to them, and bending down, whispered, "The governor will see you today."

Each time the governor's door opened and someone walked out, Abigail had a nervous spell and, up till now, all for naught. Finally, the young soldier announced, "Rev. Hyrum Adams, you may go in now."

In March 1862, Andrew Johnson was appointed military governor of occupied Tennessee. When the Volunteer State seceded from the Union in 1861, Johnson was the only Southern senator not to resign his seat. In fact, he held it during the entire Civil War. As a Southern War Democrat in the U.S. Senate, he was somewhat of an anomaly, supporting Lincoln's military policies, a staunch Unionist, yet proslavery. At the time of his appointment, his destination, Nashville, had been evacuated by the Confederates and the government, which he was displacing, had fled to Memphis. He quickly reorganized an administration and set about performing the required duties. One of the first acts to set him apart from those he replaced was to establish the conception that traitors must be punished and treason crushed, by moving resolutely to eradicate all pro-Confederate influences in the state. Married with five children, Johnson also was sympathetic to those disenfranchised by the war and extended the hand of friendship often. Although never a member of an established church, he read the Bible and occasionally attended Methodist services.

"As I understand, your husband is in Robertson Hospital, located in Richmond, Virginia, and you wish to travel there to be with him. How serious are his injuries?"

"He has retrograde amnesia as a result of an exploding artillery shell."

"Then physically he is in no danger. Your concern is because of the amnesia. How long has it been since you've seen your husband?"

"We haven't seen each other for two years. Jack has a son he has never set eyes on and a daughter who can't remember what her father looks like. I take that back. Jack mailed us a picture in his most recent correspondence."

"From what I know about amnesia, the memory will eventually return. Nevertheless, two years is a very long time for a family to be separated without a single visit. Do you know what regiment he is in?"

"Yes, the Seventh Tennessee regiment from Wilson County."

"I'm aware of them. They were sent to Virginia, along with a couple other regiments, to be part of Robert E. Lee's Army of Northern Virginia. They're damn good fighting boys and give the Union forces more than they ask for." Governor Johnson paused for a while and pondered the situation, finally saying, "I'm not sure how much help this office can give. I'm willing to do whatever is in my power. I understand you wish to travel by railroad train. That's going to be pretty troublesome, considering the war conditions. A pass under my name is respected from Nashville to eastern Tennessee; however, in Virginia, it may not carry enough weight. These things you're just going to have to find out by yourself," the governor conveyed.

"I'll be eternally grateful for whatever you can do to help me to see my husband," Abigail said bravely.

"I'll draft the letter of passage and have it ready for you in the morning. You come back tomorrow, and by then, I may have more ideas."

Abigail left the governor's office filled with both anticipation and hope. She will soon be with the first man in her life, the Tennessee mountain man, her husband, Jack Leffingwell. Ironically, she was no longer weary; and sleep, which found her before, had vanished, replaced by a fitful night of toss and turn, refreshed on occasion by the other side of the pillow. Morning found Abigail and her father waiting again in the governor's office, this time, exceedingly more hopeful.

"Mrs. Leffingwell, here is your letter of passage," Governor Johnson handed her the envelope and continued. "With regard to railroad travel, I've learned a few things yesterday, after we met, that won't make it any easier, but should transport you to the Virginia state line. A lot will depend on the condition of the tracks. The North understood the value of the railroad better than us here in the South. We Southerners were less enthusiastic about the railroad industry, preferring an agrarian living, and left the mechanical professions to men from the North. We also believed railroads existed solely for the purpose to get our cotton to the ports. Accordingly, what lines we do have are short, relatively speaking, and not designed to interconnect. They sometimes lack a standard gauge, so trains of different companies ran on tracks anywhere from four to six feet wide. Freight had to be transferred from one railroad to another to continue the conveyance."

"As a result, the Union enjoys its benefits a great deal more than us Southerners. Fortunately, what rail centers we do have connect to Richmond. Unfortunately, between Nashville and Richmond, it seems like both armies take turns destroying the tracks. Have you ever heard the term *Sherman's neckties*? It's likely such information would never reach your tender ears. Nevertheless, as Union troops moved South, they sabotaged the rails by pulling them up and heating them until they could be wrapped around a tree. Lucky for you, most of that activity occurs farther south. When will you be ready to make the journey?"

"I'm ready to leave today. My father will return to Statesville and alert the rest of my family," Abigail replied earnestly.

"Very well, we have a detachment from my office leaving for Knoxville today, and they will travel by train. You may accompany them as part of the group, and safety will be provided by Union soldiers acting as security guards. The next leg of your journey takes place in Knoxville, and my people have telegraphed ahead to alert them as to your needs. I trust they will be helpful once you arrive."

Abigail could not restrain her tears as she embraced the governor, whose eyes also glistened a little more than usual.

That afternoon, Hyrum watched his daughter board the train while one of the soldier guards carried her portmanteau and placed it securely near her seat. The engine was an old wood burner. In fact, nearly all Southern locomotives were fueled by wood, and since wood had become scarce, train crews had taken to stopping along the route to chop and load wood, as it was needed. The poor conditions of the tracks were another cause for concern. Crossties became rotten and rails broke along the way. At times, the train crews walked in front of the engine in order to guarantee safe passage. These were some of the factors that forced the engineer to dramatically reduce the speed of his engine. The distance between Nashville and Knoxville was about 180 miles.

With frequent stops for fuel, a slowdown to inspect the rails, and an occasional repair, the trip would take nearly two days. Abigail had opened a dialogue with the women in the governor's group, making the time seem to go by faster. Some of the women, however, had taken the same trip in better times and reached Knoxville in a little over five hours. Today, they exhibited frustration at every delay and inconvenience. After the discussion with Governor Johnson, Abigail knew some delays were to be expected and not that unnerving, as long as they continue moving toward the ultimate goal. When the conversation became aggravating, she simply closed her eyes and feigned sleep. Their complaints continued, but the clamor became softer, out of common courtesy.

The Knoxville Depot sign improved the traveler's demeanor, and as they departed from the passenger coach, one of the women blurted, "Isn't that our carriage driver holding up a placard?"

"It most certainly is. What does it say?" asked another.

"It just reads Leffingwell."

Once the carriage driver noticed Abigail stepping down from the railcar, he hurried to her and took hold of the portmanteau. "Mrs. Leffingwell, I presume? My name is Waters, and I'm here to take you to the mayor's office." Noting the resentment revealed by her fellow travelers' expressions, Abigail quickly recognized the taxi driver as genuine and released her grip on the suitcase.

James Churchwell Luttrell was the mayor of Knoxville, and in many ways, his household epitomized the divided sentiments of the Civil War era. He was a solid supporter of the Union, and his son, Samuel, fought for the Union army. His other two sons, John and James, Jr., both fought on the Confederate side. In spite of Luttrell's Union sentiments, he was reelected mayor in a city dominated by Confederate sympathy and loyalism.

"I've got to admire your courage in taking on such a journey, Mrs. Leffingwell. It would be arduous in peacetime, let alone during this terrible war. There's no better letter of transport than the one you have in your possession. Governor Johnson is highly regarded in East Tennessee and thought well of along the route you plan to travel. If I may be so bold, how did you ever get to see him? I've been trying to have an audience with him for over a year. He just sends a congregation of his staff, and they take back a message. Naturally, I reserve the personal aspects that would be revealed if we were face-to-face."

"I met some of the ladies on the train," Abigail said blandly. "They seem to be nice people."

"They probably are, but that isn't my problem. Knoxville has zealots on both sides of this war, many of which propagate violence. I believe that is the foremost reason East Tennessee isn't occupied. I know who these people are, and I feel that information is important for when the occupation takes place."

"Well, maybe Governor Johnson is waiting until that day becomes clearer."

"I hope so. I shouldn't belabor you with my problems, but since you are from middle Tennessee and know the governor, I hoped to find a sympathetic ear."

Abigail didn't explain her true relationship with Governor Johnson and how she came by her travel document, resolving herself with not doing so wasn't a lie, just the truth held in reserve. Her silence was interpreted by the mayor as a positive sign, elevating his hopes of an invitation in the near future.

"I believe you'll find rail travel in Virginia better than here in Tennessee. But before you can experience it, you have to get to Kingsport. That's going to be similar to what you've experienced coming here."

"I didn't find the trip here overexasperating, so perhaps, it won't be that bad."

"I hope you're right. We tend to equate travel today as it was before the Civil War, and with that in mind, annoying delays are apt to strike a nerve."

"How far is it from here to Richmond?" asked Abigail.

"Oh, Mrs. Leffingwell, you have over four hundred miles to go before reaching Richmond." Abigail was silent. The expression on her face said it all. It was only a momentary pause; however, she stiffened her resolve and told the mayor she was ready.

"You're welcome to spend the night with my wife and me. With three sons fighting in the war, it's awful quiet at home nowadays. A little company will do wonders for Eliza." Abigail accepted his offer and was entertained overnight by a grateful pair of lonely hosts. Eliza Luttrell was an avid reader and became delighted when she learned her visitor taught school back in Statesville. The two women conversed well into the night, while Mayor Luttrell stood by, just enjoying the sight of his wife being happy. The following morning, when it became time for Abigail to depart, Eliza handed her a small bag and said, "It's a little something to eat and the book we talked about yesterday. Reading always helps us women pass the time during the dull periods in life."

The train pulled from the Knoxville depot at 8:00 a.m. and traveled for about an hour before stopping at a wood station to replenish its supply. Unfortunately, there wasn't a stick to be found. It took over an hour for the railroad hands to go into the woods and collect enough to get the locomotive to the next stop. Traveling at a speed of twenty miles per hour, about sixty more miles were covered before stopping for water. By 2:30 p.m., the engineer yanked the steam whistle chain and gave a piercing blast to announce their arrival in Kingsport. Abigail's portmanteau was stored in the luggage area; however, she carried a small bag given to her by Eliza Luttrell and kept it beside her. It contained a light lunch and the novel *Adam Bede* by George Eliot. Eliza's only request was that Abigail mail it back to her after reading it. Hardcover books were rather rare and costly. Newspapers tended to serialize them and publish portions weekly for the general population.

Adam Bede was the first novel written by George Eliot, the pen name of Mary Ann Evans, a highly respected scholar of her time. And though anxious to begin reading, Abigail planned to wait until they were in Virginia and on the longest part of the trip. The itinerary, written by Mayor Luttrell, called for her to change trains in Kingsport due to the different track size in Virginia. Many passengers were traveling to the Old Commonwealth that day, and all Abigail needed to do was stand in the queue and follow its movement. Two station hands pushed the luggage cart to the entrance of the waiting train and helped carry the belongings aboard. The repetitive sounds of exhaling steam and hullabaloo of well-wishers melded into the general din, forcing Abigail to shout to a station hand while pointing to her suitcase. Soon it was safely secured on board, and she took a seat after placing a dime in the hand of her helper. This train had more cars than the previous transporter and, information rumored by newsboys, indicted some of them were hospital units conveying wounded soldiers to Richmond.

It took nearly two hours for the wounded soldiers to be situated on board. Some entrained under their own power, and others were carried on stretchers. The other travelers occupied themselves in conversation and reading newspapers purchased from the aforementioned newsboys. Most of the early afternoon passed by, and the train hadn't moved an inch. Passengers began to fall under the spell of ennui and became restless; some left their seats to stroll from car to car. Looking through the window, Abigail saw that the depot platform was nearly deserted. Well-wishers had apparently gone home, and the baggage handlers have stowed their carts and were now sitting on benches counting tips. At that moment, the train jerked forward, causing a chain reaction of couplers tugging against each other and brought about the return of the wandering riders. At last, the iron horse was pulling a long chain of rolling carriages into Virginia. For safety purposes, a slower pace is anticipated, out of fear that Union forces may have sabotaged the tracks. Top speed of ten miles per hour, in all likelihood, would be the train engineer's goal.

Looking out the window, Abigail observed the fading sun making its decent into the horizon. Soon lanterns will be lit to provide illumination within the carriage car. The rocking motion of a moving train can cause a traveler to suffer from kinetosis—motion sickness. The jerky movements tend to provoke the condition, and Abigail knew that once a traveler began to suffer, there was no easy cure. Therefore, every precaution needed to be brought to bear. She purposely took a window seat facing forward and made certain not to attempt reading Eliza's book while the train was in motion. So far, so good.

Dining cars hadn't been invented yet; and water, basically, was the soup du jour. Unfortunately, the source was retained in barrels located in a recess behind the locomotive. Every two hours or so, one of the conductors would walk through the carriage cars carrying a bucket and drinking ladle. Thanks again to Eliza, a collapsible folding travel cup was placed in the bag for just that purpose.

Abigail didn't recall falling asleep, but suddenly, she realized the train was no longer moving.

"Is there anything wrong?" she asked the elderly gentleman in the seat facing her.

"Not really, young lady. I believe we've just stopped for wood," he replied. "I think we are at the Abingdon fuel station."

"Do you make this trip often?"

"You might say that. My name is Horace Waterman. Before the war, I taught history at Richmond College. Now, I'm a senior editor for the *Richmond Dispatch*. They called on me after the younger men joined the army. There are quite a few of us retirees back working since the war started. Several of my former colleagues work for the Richmond newspapers as competitors. We, at the *Dispatch*, offer Richmond the best possible source for local, state, and national news. I'm returning from interviewing James and Eliza Luttrell. He is the mayor of Knoxville, and they have sons fighting on both sides in the war. It's quite a human interest story."

"I can't believe this. I spent last night with the Luttrells. It's certainly a small world after all. They talked to me about their sons. Eliza packed my lunch and loaned me a book to help pass the time away. I think they're wonderful people."

Waterman nodded in agreement and continued, "I've been working again since the war started. The *Dispatch* is a four-sheet newspaper selling for a penny. We started off nonpartisan. The war changed all that. We're pro-Confederacy, yet try to stay away from the vitriolic political propaganda of our daily rivals."

After a short pause to gather his thoughts, the senior newsman asked, "You must excuse my interest, still, it's unusual to find a woman like yourself traveling without an escort. I don't mean to pry, and if you think me meddlesome, just tell me. I'm curious as to your mission."

"I guess I do appear irregular to those unaware of my mission. I am traveling to the Robertson Hospital in Richmond to visit my husband. He is a wounded soldier and needs my presence to help him recover."

"That makes a lot of sense, and you are to be congratulated for the effort, especially with the war going on. From where did your ordeal begin?"

"We live in Statesville, Tennessee, and my junket began in Nashville. That was where I received a travel letter from Governor Johnson." Their conversation ended with the train once again on the move and heading for the water station at Marion.

A new day was unfolding, and the first blush of morning flashed sunlight against the windows on the other side of the carriage car, forcing those passengers to pull their shade. When the water bucket made the rounds, the conductor also extinguished the lantern flames. Abigail took advantage of the opportunity to use the toilet room. Many men benefited from the stops for fuel and had briefly left the train for a similar purpose. Much to her delight, she found the metal pitcher recently filled with freshwater. "Almost the comforts of home," she whispered good-naturedly to herself.

When she returned to her seat, the elderly cotraveler remarked, "Make sure you pull open your collapsible cup. They'll be around soon with hot coffee."

No sooner had they become comfortable with their coffee, the train began to slow down and gradually come to another stop. Waterman, having ridden the line before, knew of no scheduled stops until Marion and asked the conductor, "Is there a problem?"

"I'm told that there are damaged tracks up ahead, and a crew is making repairs as we speak."

"Any idea of how long it's going to take?"

"I'll try to get you an answer when I finish my rounds," the conductor replied.

With a few hours' delay now promised, Abigail reached into the bag and withdrew the hardcover novel loaned by Eliza Luttrell. Perusing the title, *Adam Bede*, she flipped through a few pages looking for illustrations. Eliza had told her that the author, George Eliot was, in actuality, Mary Ann Evans—a woman and respected scholar. Her first novel, *Adam Bede*, found instant popularity among the female gender.

> *The story takes place in the fictional village of Hayslope in 1799. It revolves around a beautiful but self-absorbed girl named Hetty Sorrel and Capt. Arthur Donnithorne, a young squire, who seduces her. Adam Bede, a local carpenter and forthright member of the community, is also in love with Hetty. Hetty's cousin, Dinah Morris, a fervent, virtuous, and equally*

attractive Methodist lay preacher, secretly is in love with Adam. When Adam interrupts a tryst between Hetty and Donnithorne, the two men fight. Arthur agrees to give up Hetty and returns to the militia. After he leaves, Hetty agrees to marry Adam but discovers she is pregnant. In desperation, she departs in search of Arthur. She cannot find him, but is unwilling to return to the village because of her shame. With the help of a friendly woman encountered along the way, she delivers her baby. Later, the child dies when abandoned in a field. Unable to endure the child's cries, Hetty returns to the field, however too late and finds that it died from exposure.

Hetty is subsequently caught and tried for child murder. She is found guilty and sentenced to be hanged. Dinah visits her in prison and promises to stay with her until the end. Her compassion brings about Hetty's repentant confession. When Arthur Donnithorne, on leave for his grandfather's funeral, hears of the impending execution, he races to court and has the sentence commuted to transportation to Australia. Ultimately, Adam and Dinah become mutually aware of their love for each other, marry, and live peacefully with his family.

Abigail's concentration was broken by the sound of a ruckus along the side of the carriage, and peering through her window, she beheld a throng of humanity attempting to sell their wares. Several enterprising peddlers, standing on the track embankment, were holding up placards that read Fried Chicken, while others carried buckets of lemonade and waved the tin ladle. Several Negroes, recently freed by Lincoln's mandate, were shouting, "Biscuits and eggs." Apparently, they were practicing their new independence as free merchants.

"Is this done often?" Abigail asked Horace Waterman.

"Yes, quite a bit nowadays. They usually ply their wares at the station. It appears some wanted to get the jump on the competition. For the most part, vendors concentrate on the hospital cars, and to a wounded soldier, they're angels of mercy. Many are unable to fetch water by themselves and are more than willing to pay for it. Would you care for any of the merchandize?" Waterman asked.

"Those apples look good to me," she responded.

The elderly journalist raised the window and shouted, "How much for the apples?"

"Three for a nickel," came the reply.

"Make it six for a nickel," bartered Waterman.

"Four for a nickel."

"Make it five and you can forget the sack."

Waterman shined one of the five apples on the leg of his trousers. When he felt it lustrous enough, he broke it in half and cut out the core with his penknife.

"Here you are, madam," he said, handing her the two pieces.

"I thank you kind, sir," Abigail replied coyly. She didn't need Ithuriel's spear to know that the old newsman was a perfect gentleman. The wrinkles of kindness in the corners of his eyes gave him away. His offers to help were truly from the milk of human kindness, for he saw Abigail as likened to his favorite daughter, who, at that very moment, was progressing hand over hand on the seat backs until she stopped by her father, sitting down with a plop.

"How are the wounded doing?" he asked, once she regained composure.

"Not very well, Father. These miserable delays make it worse for them. Many are in pain, and the medicine they need is in Richmond. I try to bring them water, and that sometimes is a full-time job. Seven cars are positioned to contain them. You have to travel the length of them all in order to get to everybody. Doctors and nurses are constantly passing back and forth through the cars. It's a wonder the soldiers get any rest at all. The vendors were a godsend, but at times, you'd think they were Yankees. Money has to be paid before any water is poured, and if a soldier uses paper money, he never sees his change. When the train whistle blows, the peddlers run away faster than the soldiers who need to get back on. I'll swear some of them are Yankees in disguise." Waterman gave his daughter a hug of encouragement and turned to Abigail, saying, "This angel of mercy is my daughter, Hope. You won't find anyone more sweet, kind, or gentle. Hope, this lady is Abigail Leffingwell who is traveling to Richmond to see her husband, a wounded soldier at Robertson Hospital."

"I'm happy to make your acquaintance. Robertson's is the best hospital Richmond has to offer. I'm sure your husband is in very good hands," Hope said assuredly.

"Are you a nurse?" asked Abigail.

"No, ma'am, all the same, I always try to do what I can to help the soldiers. I volunteer at the hospitals when we are home in Richmond. They used to tell me that nursing isn't the work for a lady. Even so, their minds are changing. Miss Sally Tompkins has done a lot to bring that about. Do you know Captain Tompkins? If not, you will real soon since she runs Robertson Hospital. In Richmond, most of the real nursing is done by older women. They usually assign me to the more menial tasks. I think they still forbid women to nurse in the field hospitals, and that too may change some day. A woman's role in society isn't what it used to be. The Civil War has changed it for us. With the men away fighting, we women have taken their place here at home. If we had the vote, there wouldn't be any wars. Don't you agree, Mrs. Leffingwell?"

"Please call me Abigail. And yes, if we had the vote, wars like the present one would be a distant memory." Hope was grinning from ear to ear. She had found an ally on her youthful march into adulthood.

Much to the delight of all on board, the news from the front end was that the tracks were repaired and they were about to get underway. As a safety measure, a handcar had gone ahead of the locomotive to inspect the tracks. The two-man pump trolley led the train to the Marion depot without further incident. The hand trolley was then reloaded on a flatbed car, and enough water and fuel was taken on to last until the next station, about forty miles away. Hope Waterman went up front to the hospital cars, her father got off for a brief time to buy a newspaper, and Abigail found her place in *Adam Bede*.

Chapter Eighteen

Valentine hearts beat more passionately than everyday hearts.

—Anonymous

When Maj. Gen. Walter Shaw appeared for his routine visit, he found the hospital exuberant over the forthcoming Valentine's Day. The usual hustle and bustle seemed to have more of a kick to it. The general attitude was noticeably more uplifting; and the nurses, with giggles and titters, went about their duties more willingly. Each time they visited patients, on unrestricted diets, chocolates were left in the room. Their cheerfulness was infectious, and soon Dr. Shaw found himself whistling as he walked into Sally Tompkins's office.

"What's going on around here? Everybody is acting like the war is over," the doctor said as he took the seat by Sally's desk.

"Don't you know? Saturday is Valentine's Day. It's a tradition here at Robertson's to celebrate the best we can.

We all make candy and distribute it to the patients. It does wonders for their morale."

"You're on to something there, Sally. I've always believed the patient's attitude had a great deal to do with their recovery. It's even biblical, Proverbs 17:22, 'A merry heart doeth good like a medicine, but, a broken spirit dries up the bones.' Positive thoughts give positive results. Speaking of results, how is our amnesia patient doing? Any changes since my last visit?"

"There's been nothing significant to speak of. I do have a bit of news. I received a letter from his wife the other day. She is on her way here to see him. That might help his condition," Sally reported.

"I would like to be here when she arrives. She must be traveling by the railroad, albeit, with the war, there's no telling how long it will take. It would be appreciated if you got a message to me. Your news gives me something to tell Stonewall Jackson. He gets a little testy when I've nothing to report."

"You can count on me, Doctor," said Sally.

"By the way, do you still have his Whitworth rifle? I want to give it to him this visit. It may jog his memory," he stated frankly.

The jubilant surroundings were not lost on Grazyna. She too was gay as a lark and quickly entered Jack's room to hand him a valentine envelope. Noticing they were alone, the radiant charmer pulled the curtain around Jack's bed and kissed him tenderly, saying, "That has to hold you until this afternoon at the cabin. Oh, yes, one more thing. Make sure you shave before we meet. My face is so chaffed, the other nurses are kidding me."

"Are you sure that's the only place you're chaffed?"

"Darling, that's the only place that shows," Grazyna replied and left the room.

Jack removed the card from the envelope and admired its beauty. It had paper lace around a heart with an image of cupid in the center. The poem read, "Weddings now are all the go, will you marry me or no?" Jack smiled to himself and planned to answer in the affirmative later in the day.

Grazyna's card was an Esther Howland Valentine's Day greeting card. Miss Howland was an artist and businesswoman who was responsible for popularizing Valentine's Day cards here in America. Shortly after graduating from Mount Holyoke College, a liberal arts college for women, in 1847, Esther received an ornate English Valentine from an associate of her father. She was nineteen at the time and intrigued with the idea of making similar cards. Since her father operated the largest book and stationery store in Worchester, Massachusetts, it was easy for her to import paper lace and floral decorations from England. She made a dozen samples for her brother to take on his next sales trip. When he returned with so many orders, Esther needed friends to help make them all. A thriving business had begun. She later became known as the Mother of the American Valentine.

Witnessing Dr. Shaw walking through the corridor carrying a Whitworth rifle turned a few heads. Yet nothing close to the shock to Grazyna when she was told about Jack's wife coming to Robertson's. The day feared most of all had finally come. Grazyna felt as though she was drowning in deep water. For a moment, she stopped breathing and struggled to maintain composure. She raised her hand to tuck her hair and missed because of trembling. Scolding herself not to be seen in this state of mind,

Grazyna entered a women's toilet and locked the door. Her thoughts were spinning. The shaken beauty knew the time had finally arrived when she must confirm the fact that Jack was married and had a family. She settled on waiting until they were alone in the caretaker's cabin before disclosing the painful reality. Time seemed to be at a standstill, and the minutes took forever to pass. The day finally came to an end, and Grazyna stole her way to their cabin rendezvous. Her nerves had settled enough to practice several ways of announcing it to Jack, with none totally acceptable to her. Weary from the different scenarios, she resolved to just play it by ear and lit the candles. Busying herself with mock housekeeping concerns, she feigned straightening and dusting until hearing Jack's key turn in the door. His tall shadow moved across the wall until it met with hers and ended in an embrace.

"Did I shave close enough for you?"

"Oh, darling, I don't mind your beard, it's just that it chaffs my face and makes it red. People know how that happens, and keep asking me who is doing it."

"Tell them. We don't have anything to hide."

"Yes, we do. After what I learned today. Darling, I've betrayed you, and I won't blame you for hating me. You are married, Jack, and your wife is on her way to see you." Grazyna's voice was fading as she tried to hold back her tears. "I fell in love with you knowing the truth. What kind of woman does that make me?"

"Darling, I love you. I've no recollection of any other woman. You gild all my dark places and make me come alive. I need you as I need to breathe, and to stop loving you is not within my power. We'll see our way through this, somehow, so dry your tears, my sweet."

The sex that night was different. Not the hard-driven emotional release, instead, much softer, gentler, and in its own way, even better. Grazyna's sleep was restless and wakeful. Jack slept soundly, with little thought of a woman he couldn't remember. As the adage goes, "Reason is the enemy of love. It's like water to fire."

* * *

With their comrade in the Robertson Hospital, responsibility of keeping up on the news fell on Abel Strawn. He had written Abigail, telling her about Jack's being wounded and in Robertson's. Also, assured her Jack suffered no serious injury, only amnesia from the exploding cannon shell. She, in turn, had written Abel thanking him for all he has done and alerting him of her plans to travel to Richmond. Her handwriting was steady and well organized and came as no surprise, since Jack had told him about her teaching school. Her handsome script made Abel wish to be better educated and have taken more interest in attending school. Abel was no match to Jack when it came to reading the *Enquirer*. Obvious to all, each time he did so, he showed an improvement.

Camp life around the Fredericksburg winter quarters was, basically, each day a repeat of the previous. The activity can never be completely told at one writing and bears repeating some of the nuances.

As reveille trumpeted the call to rise, a thousand soldiers struggled to don their uniform and rush into the morning formation. The snapping voice from under a gray military hat barked, "Fall in for roll call," and the names were enumerated. A camp at rest from the fighting sometime responded with a variety of phonation. For the most part, they were comical, though, others came across as callous and mean, when they sounded out the monosyllable, "Here!" When satisfied no one had ran away, the orderly announced those assigned to guard duty for the next twenty-four hours. The others were informed as to the drills of the day. Once dismissed, soldiers broke ranks and ran back to their tent to grab tin basins, soap, and towels, then headed for the nearest pump. If the pump was too crowded, they sometimes dashed to the closest stream. When perfunctory hygiene was completed, breakfast followed. The menu seldom changed, and if it did, it's still eaten from a tin plate with a metal fork. After breakfast came company drills, bayonet practice, battalion drills, and the heavy work of the day.

In the afternoon, the foot soldiers had target practice, skirmishing drill, and then a tent inspection was performed by the officer of the day. Attendance for supper was usually less than breakfast for a multitude of reasons, mainly because of the Post's sutler tent offering tobacco, sweets, and other edibles not provided by the army.

The Tennessee sharpshooters still received preferential treatment in spite of the absence of their leader, Jack Leffingwell. And as long as Jack was recovering, the aegis of Stonewall Jackson would continue.

Marksmen gathered around Abel who was now reading for the group. Abel, not as proficient as Jack, took longer to peruse an article and comprehend its true meaning. On the face of it, the story of President Lincoln replacing General Burnside's command of the Army of the Potomac appeared straightforward. Headlines didn't always convey the underlying truth which was often buried deep within the article. Replacing Burnside was purely a political move. His failure at Fredericksburg drew the wrath of public opinion and the press, subsequently, reflecting on the administration. Lincoln's appointment of Gen. Joseph "Fighting Joe" Hooker was a case of replacing one general with another, whom he liked even less. Lincoln felt as though Hooker and others did whatever they could to openly criticize and undermine Burnside. Lincoln later wrote Hooker a letter stating that opinion.

"A lot of good that's going to do him—replacing one general with another," stated Lomas. "They don't do any fighting."

"One Southern soldier is worth about six Yankees," Melvin bragged.

"The bluebellies ain't that bad, Melvin. Remember how hard they fought at Fredericksburg?"

"Sure I do. You remember how bad they got whipped?"

"Jack got it right. The Yankees have an unlimited amount of soldiers, and we don't. Now the Negroes are wearing blue uniforms, and soon we'll be fighting them as well. We seem to be doing well here in Virginia. The Yankees are like an octopus—their tentacles reach out all over the whole South. Each time we beat them back, both sides lose men. They replace theirs right away, and our army gets smaller," Abel explained.

"And every time Lincoln replaces a general, it proves we're winning," assured Melvin.

"Lincoln is looking for another Bobby Lee. Heaven help us if he finds one," returned Abel.

"Here's something of interest. The first claim under Lincoln's Homestead Act went to a fellow named Daniel Freeman in Beatrice, Nebraska."

"What's the Homestead Act?" asked Melvin.

"It's an act signed into law by President Lincoln in which he is giving away 160 acres of land west of the Mississippi. The law requires three steps: file for an application, improve the land, and file for deed of title. Anyone who had never taken up arms against the U.S. government, including freed slaves, could file an application to claim a federal land grant. As long as the occupant is twenty-one or older, lives on the land for five years, and can show evidence of having made improvements, he gets a deed, free and clear."

"You forgot the most important thing. As long as he can survive constant Indian attacks," added Melvin.

"Most of the hostile Indians have been removed," Abel said frankly. "If a fellow was enterprising enough, he could have his family lay claim to the land next to his and grow a farm of over a thousand acres and free of charge."

"And all of us in the Confederacy don't qualify," Lomas added bitterly.

"What do you care, Lomas? You wouldn't last one day out in the wilderness—building a dwelling, clearing the land, and planting crops. You've got to have people around. There wouldn't be any neighbors within miles. No women! And worst of all, no poker games!"

"I suppose you're right," admitted Lomas.

Abel felt as though all important news items had been discussed. Folding the *Enquirer*, he handed it to Melvin Kaufman, saying, "Pass it along to the next tent."

"There is something I think we should consider. When Mrs. Leffingwell gets to Robertson's, it would be nice to visit Jack and get to meet his wife. Having everybody there might jog Jack's memory faster."

"Great idea! Just let me know a couple of days in advance and I'll take care of everything," Lomas promised. Considering how well their previous trip came off, there wasn't much skepticism this time.

Chapter Nineteen

Good company in a journey makes the way seem shorter.

—Izaak Walton (1593-1683)

After the problem of damaged tracks near Marion, Virginia, the next leg was to Pulaski. It went without incident. Leading with the hand-operated pump car ensured the safety of the locomotive and made passengers more comfortable. That is, those not residing in the hospital cars. Abigail was well into *Adam Bede* and liked it very much. The even ride changed quickly when the train rolled over previously repaired rails, bumping too much for her to continue. She also found stretches of track smooth enough to read while the train was in motion. Horace Waterman, however, kept reading the *Richmond Dispatch*. Finishing the front page, he neatly folded the four-leaf section and continued his perusal. Looking up, Abigail noticed the picture of a ship. She couldn't focus on the print with the current rocking of the train in motion.

Often, while we concentrate elsewhere, we sense the stare of another and look up to find our premonition accurate. Such was the case that very moment, and as Horace lowered his gazette, he discovered Abigail attempting to read the back page.

"How's your novel going?" Horace asked politely.

"Oh, I love it. I believe it would be an excellent read for Hope. She's at the age where it would be appreciated."

"I always appreciate the opinion of the other gender when it comes to books. Mrs. Leffingwell, you've forced me to buy it for her," he said with a smile.

"On the back page of your newspaper is a small picture of a ship. Is it one of ours?"

"Actually, my dear, the larger picture is on the front page of the *Dispatch*. And yes, it was one of ours, and an important one, I might add. The article is quite interesting. Let me read you some of what it says. She was called the CSS *Nashville* and originally built as a side-wheeled steamer. Some claim she was the fastest passenger liner and mail carrier on the coast and capable of reaching a speed of over thirteen knots. The steam liner was plying her coastal trade near Charleston, South Carolina, at the precise time Fort Sumter was shelled. Her owners offered to outfit the ship as a privateer for the South; however, the Confederate government had other plans. We needed a fast water transport to bring in supplies and carry our government commissioners back to England. Accordingly, it was purchased for $100,000, and we appointed Robert B. Pegram her captain. She became the first vessel commissioned by the Confederacy and began her initial combat cruise by sailing to Bermuda, then set course for England. Unfortunately, a severe storm at sea caused some damage; nevertheless, her courageous captain continued on course. Arriving off the Irish coast, she encountered the American clipper, *Harvey Birch*. Moving alongside the ship, Captain Pegram ordered gun ports open and demanded surrender. Allowing for the evacuation of passengers and crew, Pegram ordered the vessel burned. The next day, captives were taken to Southampton and released to the custody of the American consul.

"Initially, the ship was greeted by a hostile crowd proclaiming the aggression on the *Harvey Birch* an act of piracy. Their attitude changed a few days later as news spread of the Trent Affair. A diplomatic outrage and crisis was created when the U.S. Navy forced the removal of Confederate commissioners Mason and Slidell from the British frigate.

"Naturally, such action angered the English parliament; however, they desired to maintain a careful course between the new Confederate government and that of the United States. The Confederacy, on the other hand, continuously sought help from both England and France and constantly worked to gain their favor. Either on the side of the Confederacy would dramatically change the war in favor of the South.

"The *Nashville* received a hearty send-off from a large and cheering crowd as she slipped her moorings and headed for open waters. A Union vessel, *Tuscarora*, watched the departure and was constrained from chasing after the Confederate craft before its appointed departure time, due to the presence of the British frigate, *Shannon*. England made certain of enforcing their regulations, requiring specific staggered departure of belligerent vessels from her ports.

"Back in American waters, the *Nashville* encountered the Yankee schooner, *Robert Gilfillan*, and hoisted an

American flag, ran alongside the schooner, and began conversing amiably, while reviewing the captain's papers. They caught the Yankee officer totally off guard, and the boarding party announced the seizure of the vessel. The *Gilfillan* was fired as soon as those aboard got out all their personal effects.

"Despite attempts by the U.S. Navy to track, capture, or sink the notorious Confederate ship, she continued to beleaguer the enemy. When the CSS *Nashville* successfully ran the Union blockade of Beaufort, North Carolina, to deliver its three-million-dollar cargo to the safe harbor, a flurry of dispatches and reports were exchanged among Union leaders trying to explain the success of our vessel. Their explanations varied from the use of deception as well as its outstanding speed.

Finally, after the Union army was again strengthened at the blockade, the Confederate government struck a deal with private parties in Charleston, South Carolina, to sell the vessel. The new owner's plan was to outfit the ship as a privateer. When the plan was set in motion, the immediate departure of the ship found the Charleston harbor blocked by sunken vessels and heavily guarded by Union gunboats; nevertheless, she escaped into the Georgetown, South Carolina, harbor.

"Once the sale was completed, the 1,221-ton battle steamer was renamed the *Thomas L. Wragg*, again, successfully escaping any Federal blockading ships. The *Thomas L. Wragg* continued to run Union impediments, carrying cotton out of Southern ports and bringing needed supplies into Confederate hands. She constantly frustrated the Federals by deftly escaping every attempt to trap her.

"Eventually, the vessel was modified and renamed the *Rattlesnake*. Fearing another escape, the Federals sent in the Union ironclad, USS *Montauk*, to destroy the elusive ship. Finally, withdrawing from another attempted escape, the *Rattlesnake* backed full-steam upriver and ran aground just beyond the protective guns of Fort McAllister. Repeated attempts to float her were unsuccessful, leaving the schooner stranded at the bar. The USS *Montauk* approached the marooned ship and began heavy bombardment. It took fourteen rounds before the helpless former *Nashville* was set afire and sank. The exploits of the legendary liner stood as a symbol of superiority in the eyes of England and France. Its diminishing loss resulted in their reconsidering any direct involvement, without which, the Confederacy was doomed to fail."

"Do you believe we're going to lose this war?" Abigail asked.

"Please don't misconstrue my comments as any form of disloyalty. Still, if the Confederacy doesn't find a European partner, the odds favor it," the erudite newsman replied.

"My father has felt that way for some time now. Being a man of the cloth, he always puts the future in the Lord's hands. Ironically, the Yankees are Christians too, and I imagine their ministers are doing the same thing. It's insane. Both sides can't be right. Or can they?"

"Perhaps God is testing us all, both North and South, so that we develop a better understanding of mankind and human purpose. It may take this horrible war in order for us to finally come together as one people," reasoned Waterman.

Abigail rearranged her pillow and laid her head back. The monotonous rolling movement of the train had the tendency to make her drowsy. It didn't take long before an afternoon nap had captured her. When Hope returned from the hospital cars, she saw that Abigail was sleeping and talked to her father in a subdued tone so as not to awaken her.

"How are things up front?" her father asked.

"About as well as can be expected. The soldiers are encouraged by the train's continuous movement forward. Those unscheduled stops are terrible for them—both physically and emotionally. The boredom of confinement is tough enough for them to handle, whereas, prolonged stops to repair tracks brings back images of the war and what got them here in the first place. Some begin to fear the train will be bombarded by the Yankees while it's stranded and helpless to move."

"Every hour that passes uninterrupted takes us that much closer to Richmond. One of the conductors told me that the stop at Big Lick will be a two—or three-hour layover. He said there wasn't any problem, and this is normal for the run. I was wondering if you and Mrs. Leffingwell would like to go into town and look around. Perhaps we could have something to eat," suggested Horace.

"I would love to. Have you suggested it to Mrs. Leffingwell?"

"I don't want to disturb her now. When she awakens, I'll ask her." After a wordless period of time, Horace questioned his daughter, "Do you remember the fairytales your mother and I read to you when you were a little girl? Wasn't there one in particular you liked best of all?"

"Oh, yes, Father, the one about Tom Thumb."

"Precisely, I believe they were written by Charlotte Yonge or perhaps Dinah Mulock, both English novelists. Well, the reason for my asking is there's an article about P. T. Barnum's Tom Thumb getting married and a picture of the happy couple," Horace said as he unfolded the *Dispatch* and found the piece.

> (Tom Thumb was the stage name of Charles Sherwood Stratton, a dwarf who achieved worldwide fame under circus pioneer P. T. Barnum, a distant cousin. Born to parents who were of medium height, Charles was a relatively large baby, weighing nine pounds eight ounces. He developed and grew normally the first six months of his life, and then, he stopped growing.
>
> At four years old, Stratton had not grown an inch in height or put on a pound in weight from when he was six months old. Apart from this, he was a totally normal, healthy child, with several siblings who were of average size.
>
> Phineas Taylor Barnum was an American showman, scam artist, and universally remembered for promoting celebrated hoaxes. When he heard about Stratton, Barnum saw a potential gold mine. After contacting his parents, he taught the boy how to sing, dance, mime, and impersonate famous people. The diminutive Stratton made his first tour of America at the age of five, with routines that included impersonating characters such as Cupid and Napoleon Bonaparte, as well as singing, dancing, and comical banter with another performer who acted as a straight man. It was a huge success, and the tour expanded. A year later, Barnum took young

Stratton on a tour of Europe where he became an international celebrity. Stratton appeared twice before Queen Victoria. He also met the three-year-old Prince of Wales, who would become King Edward VII. The tour was a huge success, with crowds mobbing him wherever he went.

In 1847, he started to grow for the first time since the first few months of his life, but with extreme slowness. In January 1851, Stratton stood exactly 2'5" tall. On this eighteenth birthday, he was measured at 2'8.5".

Stratton's marriage on February 10, 1863, to Lavinia Warren became front page news. The wedding took place at Grace Episcopal Church, and the wedding reception was held at the Metropolitan Hotel. The couple stood atop a grand piano in New York City's Metropolitan Hotel to greet some two thousand guests.

Following the wedding, the couple was received by President Lincoln at the White House. Afterward, Stratton and his wife toured together in Europe as well as Japan. Now, admirers flocked to see not only Tom Thumb but his wife as well.

Under Barnum's management, Stratton became a wealthy man. He owned a house in the fashionable part of New York and a steam yacht, and he had a wardrobe of fine clothes. He also owned a specially adapted home on one of Connecticut's posh Thimble Islands. When Barnum got into financial difficulty, Stratton bailed him out. Later, they became business partners as a way to discharge Barnum's loan. Stratton made his final appearance in England in 1878.

On January 10, 1883, Stratton was staying at the Newhall House in Milwaukee when a fire broke out, which Milwaukee historian John Gurda would call "one of the worst hotel fires in American history." More than seventy-one people died. Tom and Lavinia were saved by their manager, Sylvester Blaker.

Six months later, Stratton died suddenly of a stroke. He was forty-five years old, 3'4" tall, and weighed seventy-one pounds. Over ten thousand people attended the funeral. P. T. Barnum purchased a life-sized statue of Tom Thumb and placed it as a grave stone at Mountain Grove Cemetery in Bridgeport, Connecticut. Lavinia Warren is interred next to him with a simple grave stone that reads, "His wife." The cause of Stratton's extreme shortness was and still is unknown.)

Horace had to smile when he saw Hope hold out her hand to measure two feet above the floor. She quickly withdrew her hand when she realized her father glanced her way.

"In the stories you and Mother read me, Tom Thumb was only the size of his father's thumb," Hope expressed. "And he had all kinds of adventures, like being swallowed by a cow and again by a fish. He tangled with a giant and found favor in King Arthur's court. Father, the Tom

Thumb in your newspaper article isn't anything like the real one."

"You're right, darling, nothing like the real one," said Horace in a patronizing manner.

The engineer decided not to stop at the Blacksburg fueling station, continuing on to Big Lick. The train traveled unimpeded since the last refueling and plenty remained to reach the depot by the Roanoke River. The scheduled layover provides ample time to inspect the engine, take on water, and restock the wood supply. In addition, it gives a couple of hours for passengers to stretch their legs and visit the local community.

Abigail began to stir. As she opened her eyes, it took a moment for her consciousness to respond and return her among the living. The first object of concern was her hair. After touching it with both hands and assuring it remained presentable, she spoke, "Have I been sleeping long?"

"You had a good nap," Waterman replied.

"I don't know why I was so tired. I'm usually a very light sleeper, but for some reason, I just passed out."

"More than likely it's the company," he said, smiling.

"Not at all, you're my lifesaver. I don't know what I would have done if we hadn't met."

"I'm happy you feel that way. Hope was here a few minutes ago, and we discussed the next stop at Big Lick. There's going to be a couple of hours of layover, and I've invited you both to tour the town with me and have a bite to eat," he stated.

"You're so kind, that would be wonderful, and most certainly, I accept your offer," Abigail answered and returned both hands to her hair, thinking, *I've got to find a mirror.* She excused herself and walked briskly to the toilet room. Luckily, it was unlocked and empty. Her image in the mirror pleased her. Apparently, she slept without much head movement. A quick combing returned the coiffure to her satisfaction, and just as quick, she returned to her seat across from the senior newsman.

"Mrs. Leffingwell, this particular area has a very interesting history. It dates all the way back to colonial Virginia. Would you care to hear about it?" Waterman asked.

"Yes, I would, but only if you call me Abigail."

"All right, Abigail. Virtually from the beginning, the colonial government of Virginia sought to find a gap in the Allegheny Mountains for passage to reach farther west. Maps at the time didn't give much information concerning the Allegheny's relief or other natural positions. Up 'til then, the mountain's topography and native inhabitants had previously blocked any settlement. The colonial government of Virginia organized several expeditions to find a suitable passageway. The opening was finally discovered when British American explorers, led by Abraham Wood, reached the present-day location of Blacksburg, Virginia—a few miles west of Big Lick.

"Wood, a fur trader, made his base of operations out of Fort Henry. Remember, this was a time when the British and French were vying for control in the New World. While hostilities began on European soil, it eventually involved the American colonies. Their animosity was commonly called the Seven Years War although it lasted longer. Our portion of the conflict is called the French and Indian War.

"Have you read James Fenimore Cooper's book, *The Last of the Mohicans*? You might recall his tale included the fall of Fort Henry and the atrocities after the surrender. The fort was constructed in 1755 and located on a small hill at the southern end of Lake George in upstate New York. The French were at the northern end of the lake. Obviously, it was built to counter their presence. The fortress marked the legal frontier between the white settlers and the Indians. Fort Henry was the only point in Virginia at which Indians could be authorized to cross eastward into white territory or whites west into Indian land.

"You must excuse me. Sometimes I digress when discussing our history and get off on a tangent, more than likely, due to my years as a history teacher at Richmond College. The war has ended that for a while since the college facilities are being used as a military hospital. Let's see, we were talking about colonial Virginia and the region around Big Lick," apologized the newsman.

After a short pause to catch his breath, he continued, "The American Indians, who lived in the area, had fought each other to the point of exhaustion and left the territory unoccupied. Therefore, because the area had no effected claim upon it by hostile Indian tribes, the Virginia legislature authorized Wood to claim it for the colonies.

"During the next three generations, Wood, various Virginia expeditions, and a large number of settlers fought, secured, and finally built a fledgling, if tenuous, settlement there. As time went by, additional large portions of land were obtained and sold to Virginians as well as migrating Irish, Scotts-Irish, and English settlers.

"The settlement found itself between various Indian nations that took sides with either French or British, whichever suited their interests. The area's development as an American colony was viewed with increasing apprehension by the French and their Indian allies. Thus, in the final phase of the French and Indian War, Indians, supplied by French colonials, descended upon the settlement. Caught by surprise, the frontier pioneers retreated into their fortified homes, fighting back as best they could until, eventually, all were overwhelmed. Their valiant stand gave others time to escape to a larger fort from which they hoped to find safety. Ultimately, that fort also fell and the Indians murdered the surviving men, women, and children. Thousands of Americans were killed in the region and more along the frontier in the earlier stages of the war.

"During the period between 1755 and 1757, Virginia militiamen, under the command of Major George Washington, conducted operations in the frontier areas of Pennsylvania and New York. Our future president distinguished himself in our war for independence, yet back then, never won a single battle. It wasn't until William Pitt came to power in England that a noteworthy change took place. Pitt significantly increased British military resources in the colonies, while France was unwilling to risk larger convoys to aid the limited forces it had in North America. Between 1758 and 1760, the British military successfully penetrated the heartland of the area colonized by France, with Montreal falling in September 1760.

"Afterward, the western region of Virginia began to repopulate and continued to do so from that point until today. Unfortunately, history tends to hide itself in the present, and its benefit usually goes unnoticed. I believe our lives are enriched by learning what preceded us."

"I agree, the young people today just live for the moment with little concern for the past. Of course, today, the war takes center stage with us all," Abigail said honestly. Their conversation was interrupted when the conductor walked through the car, alerting the passengers to the fact they were approaching Big Lick and the extended layover.

"Just enough time for the boring history professor to finish his story," Waterman said.

"You're quite far from boring, Professor. I've learned more on this trip than all my years back home. Please, go on," Abigail urged.

"Big Lick was established in 1852 and named for a large outcropping of salt, which drew wildlife to the site near the Roanoke River. During colonial times, the area was an important hub of trails and roads. The Great Wagon Road, one of the most heavily travelled roads of eighteenth-century America, ran from Philadelphia, through the Shenandoah Valley, to the site of Big Lick, and the point where the Roanoke River passed through the Blue Ridge. Beginning at the port of Philadelphia, where many immigrants entered the colonies, it became the main route for settlement of the Southern United States."

The arrival of Horace's daughter Hope interrupted his history lesson, and at the same time, the locomotive started braking as the train approached the Big Lick depot. Passengers began to stir, with a few actually leaving their seats to stand near the exit doors.

"They sure are anxious to get off and walk around," Horace cracked. "It's going to be fifteen or twenty minutes before we reach the platform and open the doors. I guess they don't want anybody to be ahead of them once we disembark."

The conductor squeezed through the standing crowd and asked that they return to their seats, saying, "Those doors won't be opened for a half hour. We're still five miles from the depot. I'll let you know when we arrive."

Horace often wondered what it is about people who struggle to get ahead of others. Having traveled this route many times, he couldn't help noticing those rushing to be the leaders out the door. It reminded him of the first screaming pigs off Noah's Ark.

As promised, the train reached the Big Lick depot in the prescribed time; and once it secured the platform, the passenger car doors opened. Just as before, the same crowd jostled and shoved to be the first off. Depot personnel extended a hand to assist the women as they stepped down the carriage car metal steps. That courtesy had to wait until the initial crowd rushed by for fear of being trampled by the stampede.

Once standing on the platform, Horace Waterman said, "We have two choices. I could try to flag a hackney cab or we could walk uptown."

"Walking sounds good to me. After riding for days, a good walk would do me a lot of good," replied Abigail. Hope was smiling, since Abigail took the words right out of her mouth. That pleased all three because Horace always walked when he got off at Big Lick. He raised his hand to shield the sunlight and noticed some dark rainclouds to the west.

"If we're lucky, the rain won't get here for a couple of hours," imparted Waterman. Looking to the west, both women assured themselves Horace was correct, and the stroll commenced toward town. The landscape was beginning to morph into spring. Multicolored flowers had popped up along the river, and the Blue Ridge was not to be outdone. The activity in Big Lick was no different from any other town its size. Feed and hardware stores lined the street, along with a blacksmith shop near the stable. Freshly painted churches were located at the end of the next two blocks. Horace recalled a tavern on the side street ahead and alerted the women it was a place to have something to eat. When they entered, he noticed that others had the same idea although patrons were primarily drinking their lunch. The barkeep hurried to their table once they sat. Wiping the surface of the table, he asked their pleasure. It was apparent the train stop at Big Lick appreciably increased his business, and his ready smile was freely given.

"Can we get something to eat?" asked Horace.

"There isn't much. With the war and all, the food supply is growing kind of short. My wife did make egg salad and baked some bread this morning. How does an egg salad sandwich sound to you all?"

"Sounds pretty good to us," replied the women.

"Fine, that's what it will be. And there's a pitcher of lemonade sitting in the cellar, and it should be real cold by now."

Twenty minutes later, the barkeeps wife delivered a tray sporting the sandwiches and the pitcher of lemonade. Beads of moisture began running down the pitcher due to the temperature change from the cellar to the crowded tavern. She quickly poured two glasses until Horace held out his hand, saying, "I think I'd rather have a beer."

The tangy taste of cold lemonade made the women's lips pucker, and both smacked their approval. When you're cooped up on a train for a couple of days, the food was like a king's feast. Horace wanted to continue with his history lesson, but the expression on his daughter's face made him only relate the fact that Daniel Boone traveled through the area, blazing a trail to Kentucky. The rumbling sound of thunder off in the west compelled the customers to decide the time had come to return to the train. This time, our traveling trio had left the tavern earlier and was on board long before the crowd was jostling to climb the metal steps.

When the train began its journey, there's always a gratified sensation for those traveling by rail. The initial jerk of the locomotive engine and the echoing sound of metal couplers pulling against the car behind were familiar to a railroad traveler. The sensation was unmatched by any other mode of transportation. It took a while before movement steadied and the train to run more smoothly. At that point, passengers became satisfied their journey had begun and their thoughts, now, concentrated on the destination.

"There's only one more scheduled stop between here and Richmond. That would be the fueling station at Lynchburg," Waterman informed Abigail. "If all goes well, we will be in Richmond about this time tomorrow."

"That would be in the early afternoon. I'm happy it won't be at night since it is unfamiliar territory for me, having never been there before," Abigail replied.

"I've been meaning to ask you about that. Are you going to be met at the station?"

"No, I planned to ask for the location of Robertson Hospital and, perhaps, secure a hackney to take me there."

"You're a very brave lady, Mrs. Leffingwell . . . er, Abigail. Don't give it another thought. Hope and I will take you there. We will have a carriage waiting. Where do you plan to stay during your visit?" Horace was concerned and looked upon Abigail as another daughter.

"I planned to find a hotel once I arrived," she stated.

"Nonsense, you must stay with my wife and me. We have a guest room that should suit you perfectly. Hope does charity work at Robertson's, and you can accompany her to and fro."

"I couldn't accept. You have done too much for me already. I would be an imposition for your family." Abigail tried politely to refuse his generous offer.

"I'll hear no more on the subject. You're staying with us, and that ends the discussion," Horace insisted.

Abigail was reminded of the hymn by William Cowper in which the first two lines are "God moves in a mysterious way, His wonders to perform." She has felt blessed by the Lord most of her life. Never more so than at this very moment. Her eyes were closed again. Not for catching winks. This time in a Christian prayer of thankfulness.

* * *

Call it women's intuition. Without official notification, Sally Tompkins anticipated her amnesia patient's wife would be on the next train from Tennessee, due to arrive tomorrow afternoon. The day after was Major General Shaw's scheduled visit to examine the patient's progress. Contented that all the stars were in line, Sally felt tomorrow should be a fortuitous occasion and, hopefully, would mark a significant time of improvement for Jack Leffingwell. For some time now, Sally has observed the relationship between Grazyna and Jack. The way they looked at each other, mysterious gift exchanges, and long absences from the hospital when walking for exercise removed any doubt about their relationship. Sally's main concern was for Grazyna, who she saw as the daughter she would never have. Grazyna was the only one to be hurt, especially now that Jack's wife would soon be on the scene. Recognizing that it had to be played out, she decided to continue as though nothing was happening and remain innocent to the whole affair.

Jack had taken Dr. Shaw's advice and gone to the rifle range to practice with his Whitworth rifle. He left the range with the knowledge that he was an excellent marksman—nothing more than that. He had no memory of how it came about.

He and Grazyna sat on a bench in the hospital's ornamental garden to share the sandwich she brought for lunch. The doe-eyed beauty hadn't felt very well the past few mornings, attributing it to pent-up tension, awaiting the arrival of Abigail. Jack held Grazyna's hand and assured her that he had no recollection of a wife and nothing could change the love they shared.

"Isn't the parterre beautiful," she stated, while trying to muster courage for facing the inevitable meeting. It's actually glorious in the summer. People come from all over just to walk the paths and behold the flowers."

"I've always thought nothing could rival the Blue Ridge Mountains in springtime," Jack replied then caught himself and thought, *How did I know about the Blue Ridge spring foliage?* Passing it off as unimportant, Jack questioned, "Are we meeting at the cabin tonight?"

"Yes, dear, I'll bring you something special."

"No need to do that. Just being with you is something special for me," he replied, while elevating her chin with his forefinger and daring a kiss.

That night, Jack sensed that Grazyna was out of sorts. He understood her anxiety in confronting the wife, of whom he has no memory, and felt there was no reason to be overly concerned. The only woman he could remember intimately was the exotic beauty lying next to him.

Jack's psyche held but one memory, that being his first love—the love for Grazyna. He emphasized that fact in their lovemaking tonight and slept soundly after. Grazyna, on the other hand, slept on tenterhooks. Try as she may, it was impossible to prevent waking between dreams of confrontation with the only one innocent in the whole affair. Finally, unable to block her foreboding thoughts, she lay facing the man she adored and watched his chest rise and fall in his deep slumber.

Chapter Twenty

One's destination is never a place but rather a new way of looking at things.

—Henry Miller (American author and writer)

A gentle Virginia rain fell on the sharpshooter's tent. It was one of those intermittent showers that suggested it's better to change any plans for outside activities. Thanks to Melvin Kaufman, Abel was in possession of the latest edition of the *Richmond Enquirer*. Melvin particularly enjoyed having Abel read articles of interest to them. Growing up poor in rural Tennessee, writing one's name was the extent of many, when it came to schooling. He naturally knew newspapers existed, but they never interested him much, until now. Before passing the paper to the next tent, Melvin found a secluded place and practiced reading, an exercise that gradually improved his level of literacy. Both Lomas and Abel had a surprised look on their faces when he asked, "Read us the story about the battle at Thompson's Station."

"When did you learn to read?" Lomas remarked.

"I just read the headline," Melvin informed.

"You are definitely getting smarter. Must be from hanging around me," Lomas surmised. Abel ascertained that Melvin had been secretly studying to improve his reading ability and took the paper from him and read aloud the article in question.

"On March 4, a Confederate Cavalry Corps intercepts and defeats a Union brigade on their way to reconnoiter south of Nashville, Tennessee. Apparently, the 5,000-man contingent, under the command of Union colonel John Coburn, was on their way toward Columbia, Tennessee, the home of John Knox Polk, our eleventh president and favorite son. Four miles from Spring Hill, the Union army attacked the Confederate force and was repelled. Then, the Confederates swung into action and took the initiative. Brig. Gen. W. H. "Red" Jackson's division dismounted and made a frontal attack while Nathan Bedford Forrest's division swept around Coburn's left flank and took a position behind the enemy troops. After three attempts, Jackson carried the Union hilltop position as Forrest captured Coburn's wagon train and blocked the road to Nashville, preventing escape. Now, surrounded and out of ammunition, the Yankee colonel surrendered, along with most of his field officers. Union casualties ran high with 1,906 reported killed or wounded. The Confederate losses totaled 300, marking another victory for the proud sons of the South."

"I wish we were fighting back home in Tennessee instead of here in Virginia," Melvin said.

"I think we all would rather be defending our own soil. Apparently, the Confederacy needs us more here," Abel replied. "Considering the Yankees occupy the middle of the state, it's good to see that we can still put a hurt on them."

"Do you think Jack's wife has arrived in Richmond by now?" Lomas asked Abel.

"I would put money on it, Lomas. Maybe we should see about another leave and go visiting again," Abel suggested. And so the wheels were put in motion. Having taken part in such a scheme a month ago, the preparations fell into place much easier. And with the luck Lomas always claimed for the Irish, he was able to obtain a seventy-two-hour pass this time. Such a pass could only be approved by Gen. Stonewall Jackson—bringing Lomas' Irish luck into question.

* * *

The journey of life is unending, as long as we live and breathe. Without experience in traveling any great distance, or the knowledge by which it could be done, Abigail set out with fixed determination to be with her husband. Her resolution focused on the goal despite the obstacles that came her way. Stephen Covey, the great writer and teacher, got it right when he said, "We are not human beings on a spiritual journey. We are spiritual beings on a human journey." The young mother from Statesville, Tennessee, trusted in the Lord her whole life, and it would be difficult to argue against his presence during this arduous trip. It was that trust that allowed Abigail to concentrate on the pilgrimage itself rather than its destination. In doing so, she met many interesting people, who gladly helped to achieve her goal. Horace Waterman and his daughter Hope were certainly not the least of all.

Excitement and eagerness could be sensed throughout the railroad carriage when the conductor announced, "Richmond Station." Passengers began the search for their belongings and gathered possessions in preparation to depart.

Horace, his daughter Hope, and their guest Abigail stood ready to disembark once the doors opened. A swoosh of air signaled the doorway gap, and soon the trio found themselves standing on the depot platform.

"Over here," Horace shouted when he recognized his carriage driver, who quickly dismounted and rushed to shake his employer's hand, welcoming them back home.

"This lady is Mrs. Leffingwell. She will be our guest for a while. That's her portmanteau next to Hope's." With the luggage secured on board, the barouche quickly headed to the street. Initially, progress was slowed due to the crowd. Once the street was underfoot, the horse's gait increased to a jog.

"Hope and Mrs. Leffingwell will be getting off at Robertson Hospital," Horace announced to the driver. Since it was early in the afternoon, the two women agreed upon stopping there first because the Waterman home was within walking distance. Things were happening so fast, it kept Abigail in a daze. One thing was certain. It won't be long before she would see Jack. The carriage turned on the driveway leading to the hospital entrance and came to a stop.

"Robertson Hospital," the driver stated.

"We'll be home in time for supper," Hope said to her father before stepping down from the carriage and extending a hand to Abigail. Walking to the front door, all Abigail thought about was, *This is no time to panic*. Once inside the building, the odor of alcohol greeted the pair.

Hardly noticed by Hope, it caught Abigail unawares and, for a moment, took her breath away.

"Follow me," Hope said as she grasped Abigail's hand and proceeded down a corridor. When they came to a door with Maj. Sally Tompkins painted on the opal glass window, Hope tapped softly three times, and a voice from inside the room returned, "Please enter."

Sally Tompkins sat behind her desk and Dr. Walter Shaw directly across from her. When they saw who the visitors were, both quickly stood. Sally didn't wait for Hope's introductions. Instead, taking Abigail's hand, she said, "You must be Mrs. Leffingwell. I'm so glad you were able to come. This is Dr. Shaw from the government's military medical office. We all know Hope and the wonderful work she does here at Robertson's, as well as most of our military hospitals. Ladies, please be seated."

At that point, Dr. Shaw stated sympathetically, "I know you are anxious to see your husband, but there are a few things you will need to be aware of. First, Jack is in very good health. His problem has to do with recalling his past. Don't be surprised if he doesn't recognize you. Try to be comforted in the fact his condition is temporary and one day he will fully recover."

"Can you venture a guess as to how long it will take?" Abigail asked.

"We're in unfamiliar territory here. Most of the research has been conducted in Europe. I've written to some of the more accomplished doctors in England, but as yet, received no replies. My own personal opinion had expected Jack to have regained his memory by now, and that hasn't happened. From this point, it's anybody's guess. All I can tell you, Mrs. Leffingwell, is I expect a full recovery. Shall we pay a visit on the patient now?"

"Doctor, I've asked for his nurse to join us," Sally added.

Jack was standing near the window when his guests entered the room. He slowly turned to face the visitors and noticed one in the group to be a stranger. Though never seen before, there was something unusual about her, something that gave him a momentary pause. During that rare interval before introductions were made, he determined, *This must be she*. The newcomer had singular beauty despite beginnings of facial lines brought about by the ripening of age. In no regard was she past her prime; hence, Jack observed a fully mature and appealing woman.

Jack's image began to blur as Abigail's eyes filled with tears. She hurried across the room to embrace her husband. It had been over two years since she saw him last. The tall mountain man's expression at first was blank, then as the woman claiming to be his wife kissed his hair and whispered words of endearment, he began to wonder, *Can this be true?*

Dr. Shaw gently guided Abigail from her husband and to a nearby chair. He asked Jack to take the seat next to her, while drawing another in front of them both.

"Jack, this is an important moment in your recovery. At this point in time, you may not recognize the woman sitting next to you, but orient your thinking around the fact that she is your devoted wife, who has borne you two children. I want you to think in terms of duty. Being a soldier, that shouldn't be too difficult. While there may not be an emotional relationship at the moment, you must consider the circumstance. Abigail will be staying here for a conceivable length of time, which will help you to regain memory. Do you understand what I'm saying?"

Jack answered in the affirmative and wondered how he and Grazyna could handle the pending situation being created before their very eyes. His principal desire, at this point in time, was to console her. He was confident that everything would work out over time.

Sally Tompkins insisted Grazyna be present during the reunion. Grazyna was naturally disinclined, but the wise nurse had reasons of her own. She hoped the stark reality of the situation would discourage her young friend from continuing a relationship with a married man. Sally, and no one else for that matter, fully understood the love they shared. It was their own special love of trust and utter submission against tradition and the world. They gave each other not only their hearts but also their souls. That love would never be destroyed whether standing before heaven or the gates of hell. Sometimes love is like a weed. It grows on its own without tending and resistant to any effort to rid it.

When Grazyna was introduced, her cheeks grew as red as the autumn dust in Georgia, and tension in the room was as thick as gorse on a Celtic heath. Their glance locked on each other's eyes. Instantly, they shared the primitive female intuition dating back to the time of creation. Here was the worthy rival staring back at me. Taken aback by the nurse's sheer beauty, Abigail grew sick in the pit of her stomach, but maintained composure. She now confronted the tangled web of human nature, with all of the intricate patterns flashing before her mind. Perhaps, this was the greatest obstacle of all on the path of the young mother's journey.

Major General Shaw suggested they leave Jack to his thoughts and collectively meet in Sally's office to outline and organize the new plan for treatment.

The rest of the day was a time washed by second thoughts. At times, we are all put to the test, but it never comes to the point we prefer. Such was the case of Sally's effort to put an end to the improper liaison. Grazyna did, however, only attend to Jack the necessary periods and remained taciturn each time. Then, as her shift came to an end, her resolve weakened and she made one last unessential visit.

Jack took the opportunity to say, "Why should we worry? We have each other, and life is too short to let anything stand in the way. Look outside at all those shining stars. We're told that once we see them, they too are dead. Soon I will have to rejoin my regiment and fight in this terrible war. You, of all people, know what that can mean. Darling, I have no memory of this woman and will convince her to return to where she came from."

Grazyna believed his words were heartfelt. The softness in his voice both caressed and reassured her. When Jack drew her near him and sensually kissed her parted lips, she knew they would spend another night at the caretaker's cabin. It has been said that a pleasure not known beforehand is half wasted. To anticipate it is to double it. That evening could stand as proof.

Chapter Twenty-One

What passes for woman's intuition is often nothing more than man's transparency.

—*George Jean Nathan*

The following day, the marksmen arrived in Richmond and paid another visit at the hospital. After making their presence known at the front desk, they walked to Jack's room. The look on his face said it all. Jack was delighted.

"We've come to take you back to camp with us," Lomas said. "You've faked this amnesia thing long enough, and we need someone who can read better than Melvin."

"Let me get my coat," Jack jested, and a good round of laughter ensued.

"We understand that your wife is here," Abel stated. "We definitely want to meet her."

"Yes, she's here, but I don't remember her. Fellows, this is the weirdest situation you can imagine. She's like a complete stranger, claiming me to be her husband and father of her two children."

"I know what you mean. I've had a couple of women make the very same claim and I couldn't remember them either," Lomas joked.

Abel gave his friend a derisive look and said, "That's not funny, Lomas. Jack has a serious situation here." Turning to Jack, he continued, "Maybe you need to give it more time. The doctor told us your memory will eventually return. When that happens, you don't want to have said or done anything to harm your relationship."

Jack wrinkled his brow, remaining silent. Abel was the only one in the room to notice his hesitation. Dismissing it for the moment, he pulled up a chair, as did the other two, and planned to visit a while.

Grazyna, still aglow from the night before, wheeled in two vessels—one, a glass pitcher containing water, and the other, a tin coffeepot with visible vapor wafting out its spout. She then placed white cups beside each container and said, "Gentlemen, help yourself to the coffee. Someone from the kitchen is bringing pastry." At that point, she turned to face Jack and gave him a knowing smile before leaving the room.

"That's the most beautiful woman I've ever seen," Lomas remarked. "What is she, an Oriental or something?"

"I believe she's Polish," Jack confirmed, with a lover's pride that she was all his. He continued, "I believe her husband was an officer who fought at Manassas."

"Those damn officers get all the best women," Lomas lamented, missing the past tense in Jack's statement.

Abel whispered, "Clean it up," as two women in street clothes appeared in the doorway. One was too young. The other had to be Jack's wife, Abigail. Melvin arranged two more chairs, and Abel approached the more mature lady and extended his hand, saying, "I'm Abel Strawn. Are you Abigail Leffingwell?"

"Yes, I am," she answered. "I'm happy to finally meet you, Mr. Strawn, and thank you personally for all you have done."

"Mr. Strawn is the minister of a Methodist church back home in Tennessee. Please call me Abel."

Abigail began to calm her tension because, now, she had found an ally. Instinctively, she sensed, by Abel's demeanor, that here was a friend whom she could trust. She walked over to Jack, kissed his cheek, and bade him a good morning. He stood as though in a stupor and, for a split second, displayed resistance in his expression. Abel noticed it immediately while it was completely overlooked by the others, except Abigail, whose tears began to wash her eyes.

At first, the conversation was stilted and stiff, but with Lomas Chandler in the mix, it soon began to loosen. It was obvious he was trying to impress Hope Waterman with his humor and self-proclaimed je ne sais quoi. Hope would later tell Abigail that she thought Lomas was cute. All the same, she would never risk going out with him. The quiet one, Melvin, was more her type.

It's been said that "fish and visitors smell after three days." Hospital visitors grow tiresome after two hours. Today's visit lasted about that duration and, accordingly, broke up much to the delight of the patient.

Upon leaving, Abigail asked Abel to meet with her privately. While Hope was entertained by Melvin and Lomas, she found a waiting room unoccupied and sat in a chair away from the direct sunlight. The room itself was a conservatory with hanging ferns and two of the most beautiful potted begonias ever to behold a visitor's eye. They proudly displayed their colors of white, pink, scarlet, and purple and, best of all, emitted a fragrance of apple blossoms. Today, however, the sunroom splendor escaped the attention of Jack's pensive wife.

"Abel, I'm frightened. I can accept Jack's not recognizing me because Dr. Shaw explained it to me. What concerns me most is the pretty nurse, Grazyna. We women know when things are not right. Body language gives it away. Something is going on between her and Jack, and it's killing me."

Abel also had similar feelings brought about from the way Jack responded when Grazyna was present. Not to mention, the way he acted when the subject of a wife came up. It's one thing not to remember. It's no reason to be overly angry about it.

"I've been close to Jack for over two years now. Our lives depend on each other, so I think he will listen to me. It isn't in Jack's character to be involved in a situation of which you speak. You can rest assured that I am your friend and will find ways to reinforce your marriage every chance I get."

"Thank you, Abel. Jack is my life. I don't think I could go on living without him. You must know that I'll forgive him for anything he has done without a memory of me or the children."

"I wouldn't expect anything less. Let's keep our thoughts to ourselves for the moment. The boys and I will be here tomorrow. That gives me some time to figure out how to talk to him and broach the subject."

* * *

Cats have an amazing homing instinct, as well as a variety of other wild creatures such as spawning salmon and carrier pigeons. They have the uncanny ability to find their way back home even after traveling long distances and over unfamiliar territory. I'm reminded about the story of Ninja, a tomcat who moved with his owners from Utah to Washington State. He disappeared shortly after arriving at his new home, only to turn up at the old Utah address some 850 miles away. It took him over a year to get there. I can recall my grandparents' old tomcat we named Bambi, after the Walt Disney character. Bambi howled so loud after returning from an evening of fighting and lovemaking that he woke the entire neighborhood. He sounded like a banshee and sent chills up your spine. My grandfather finally had his last sleepless night and drove the huge cat to a small town over 20 miles away and deposited him on a farm. Three days later, Bambi was sitting on the front porch meowing to come in.

Lomas Chandler had homing instincts when it came to gambling, card games, and beer. Leaving the Robertson Hospital, Abel was unsure where the trio would spend the night and tried to remember the location of the Methodist church. Lomas suggested they stop and have a beer before making any decisions and led them directly, on an unwavering course, to the Eagle Inn and Tavern. Once inside, surrounded by the familiar settings, Abel was beginning to relax and give credence to his pledge to Abigail. As yet, he could think of no way to convince Jack of his wrongdoing other than speaking directly and straightforward. That, he knew, would cause a confrontation and end his friendship with the Tennessee mountain man. He needed to conceive an alternate approach and would think about it later. The first beer washed down by continuous swallows. Then, Lomas returned from the bar, carrying a pitcher with excess foam, dripping to the floor.

"Guess who I met sitting at the bar," Lomas asked and, then answering his own question, said, "Clyde Johnson." Filling the three empty mugs, he continued, "He said he will be over in a minute."

"Maybe we can stay here tonight like we did the last time," Melvin conjectured.

"Let's not be presumptuous. We're not exactly beggars; however, if he offers, I won't refuse him," said Abel.

The *Richmond Enquirer*'s editor did just that and insisted he pay for their evening keep. Clyde Johnson's last few expense reports were approved without any scrutiny whatsoever. He had another reason to be generous. His son, working out of the Richmond headquarters, got wind of plans for significant battles to take place this spring. Central command was preparing and gathering necessary matériel and manpower. The names of Chancellorsville and Gettysburg were overheard. Johnson, ever the newsman, asked the sharpshooters if they knew anything about it. While not surprising, no official word had been given.

For Abel, the news had planted a seed in which a strategy was beginning to grow. He now knew how to save the marriage of his fellow companion and the loving wife. Direct confrontation would make an enemy of his best friend. Therefore, he must accomplish the deed surreptitiously and without the other's knowledge. Satisfied he found the key to the perplexing situation, Abel said, "I'll go get the next pitcher," as he pushed back from the table and grabbed the empty vessel. In the days to come, the debate would be, on which visit they had the most fun. For Abel's part, it would definitely be the later.

Not so much because he saved his comrade's marriage, until now, the visit that also saved his friendship.

The following day, Abel asked Sally Tompkins for a private meeting with her and Major General Shaw. While Lomas and Melvin entertained Jack, Abel used the toilet room excuse and, once out of sight, quickly shuffled to Sally's office.

Both her and the good doctor were waiting. After perfunctory social small talk, the discourse focused on more important matters.

"This is the second visit to Robertson's by me and the other soldiers from Jack's regiment. Everyone commented how beneficial our first meeting was for Jack. He seemed to come more alive the longer we talked. And now he truly is happy to see us again. Jack has been here at Robertson's for four months and still has no memory of his past."

"Yes, but you must understand, these things take time," Dr. Shaw interrupted.

"That I understand. But wouldn't a return to his old outfit hasten the recovery?"

"Not necessarily, it may not make a difference at all," Major General Shaw replied.

"You've told us he is in perfectly good health. Would a return to the regiment hurt him in any way?" Abel questioned, turning to Sally Tompkins for support. He hadn't missed her negative vibrations when Grazyna and Jack were in the room together.

This young soldier might be on to something. It's true. Jack's progress appears to be at a standstill. The change of scenery might do him better than remaining here with us, she speculated.

Turning to Dr. Shaw, she asked, "Could you still monitor him if he returned to his regiment?"

"Of course, but you must remember, I've got to deal with General Jackson," the doctor said in a pleading manner.

"I could write the general and explain it as my suggestion. No doubt, he will ask your opinion and you can confirm the positive aspects," Sally offered.

"You both seem to forget that Jack's wife has travelled nearly nine hundred miles to be with him. She wouldn't be able to see him as frequently if he returned to the base."

"From what I've observed, her presence has hurt more than helped Jack's recovery." Turning to Abel, she continued, "Have you noticed a difference in Jack's attitude with Abigail here?"

"He resents her being here. He withdraws whenever she is in the room." Abel had the feeling he had found an ally.

It was finally agreed that Sally would write Stonewall Jackson and suggest the move. When Dr. Shaw's opinion was sought, he, in turn, would agree with Sally Tompkins. It appeared as though Abel's contrivance would be put into play. He left Sally's office satisfied with his effort and did the hot foot back to Jack and the sharpshooters.

"We were beginning to think you fell in," Lomas joked.

"It must have been something I ate last night," answered Abel.

"I sure wish I could have been with you guys last night," Jack lied. He spent another evening with Grazyna at the cabin.

"You might be back with us sooner than you think. Just keep getting better, and before you know it, you will be back at the camp, reading the newspaper to us," Abel seriously chaffed. All eyes looked at the doorway as a nurse pushed the beverage cart into the room. The duty fell upon Rachel Crabtree.

"Where's Grazyna?" asked Lomas.

"The last I saw of her, she was losing her breakfast. I hope she doesn't come down with something, we're shorthanded as it is," she complained. "I brought enough for two more. Are you expecting Abigail and her friend this morning?"

"Yes, they should be along any time now," assured Abel while Jack remained curiously silent.

No sooner had Abigail and Hope arrived did Melvin escort the Waterman daughter to the same conservatory Abigail discovered the previous day. They seemed to be hitting it off, as they say. Hope had the inherent ability to becalm those in her presence, and it couldn't be better served when it came to Melvin. Lacking in confidence, the newest sharpshooter suffered from self-effacement, flushing in brilliant shades of red whenever a pretty girl was around. Not to say that Hope Waterman wasn't pretty; in fact, she was one of the prettiest girls Melvin ever met. It was the aura she maintained and the capacity for mellowing anyone out of their self-inflected shell. On the other hand, there was a different side of her personality for those less fortunate. She liked Melvin from the first day they met. She found him kind, the most important quality a man can have. While only in the early stages, their relationship would not be curtailed by Hope Waterman. They have exchanged mailing addresses and promised to meet again. From all indications, Melvin Kaufman would soon be improving his letter writing, though, Hope had explained that ability takes time and practice.

Abigail faced another unresponsive reception from her husband, Jack. Her treatment went beyond indifference.

Jack's impassiveness reached the point of being callous with a hardened heart. He offered no pleasantry of any kind, while Abigail attempted to display her love.

Lomas was entertaining Jack with the exploits of last night and relaying a couple of jokes he picked up at the bar.

Finding the moment right, Abel whispered, "I believe that which we talked about yesterday will soon lift your spirits."

"Oh, Abel, what have you done?" she questioned.

"We can't go into it here. I'll tell you later," he heartened.

Lomas finally realized Melvin and Hope weren't in the room and asked, "Where the hell did Melvin go?"

"I believe they went somewhere to talk privately. Remember two is company and three is a crowd," Abel said jokingly.

"Yeah, but I wanted to talk to her," moaned Lomas.

"Looks like you're a day late and a dollar short," Abel replied.

"The story of my life," bemoaned the Irish mischief-maker.

"No, it isn't. I overheard you making plans with the barmaid for tonight."

Rachel Crabtree returned to take Jack's vitals and removed the remains of the morning's refreshments. Without being asked, she offered, "Looks like Grazyna is feeling better and will be her old self by this evening."

That comment was like a stab in Abigail's heart. The only person unaware of its meaning was Lomas Chandler, who thought of another joke to tell Jack.

Never in her wildest dreams would Abigail expect a reception such as this. She undertook the dangerous journey from Tennessee out of the betrothal promise and devoted love for her injured husband. While there had been no physical presence for over two years, the marital conjugation was maintained through the written word and prayer. Once learning of Jack's affliction, the dutiful wife felt as though she must be by his side. Calling each day on a husband who becomes more morose and dolorous on each visit was an undeserved punishment for someone so loving and true. The weight of it all was slowly taking effect on the good woman's will. Jack still was central to her nightly prayers, and she believed his open rejection only highlights the guilt buried deep in his subconscious, but a yearning to be home with those who love her was growing stronger.

When Hope Waterman and Melvin reappeared, the days visit was coming to an end. Their buoyant spirit was in direct contrast to the atmosphere in the room. As the group stepped out into the hall, Hope stopped them for a moment to make the following announcement, "I want to invite you all to have supper at my house this evening. Melvin has already agreed, and I sincerely wish Abel and Lomas will join us." Abigail gave Abel a nod, since she was staying with the Watermans and it would be a perfect occasion to discuss what action he had taken.

"I thank you for the invite, but I won't be able to attend," said Lomas. "I have a previous commitment that must be tended to before we return to the base."

Abel knew what Lomas's previous commitment actually was and stated, "You can count me in as long as it isn't an imposition on your parents."

"None whatsoever, in fact, it was their suggestion that I ask you in the first place."

"What time do you want me to be there?" asked Abel.

"We plan to eat at seven p.m. It would be nice if you arrived beforehand so we can talk a while."

With that final comment, the group disassembled. Melvin chose to stay with Hope and walk her and Abigail home. Lomas and Abel strolled back to the Eagle Inn and Tavern.

"How does a pitcher of beer sound to you, my treat?" asked Lomas.

"Just one glass, I don't want to screw up the dinner at Hope's by being inebriated."

The pleasant sounds of conversation and laughter could be heard by those passing by the Waterman home. Such sounds tend to raise the spirits of the individuals hearing them. Before the war, the joyful noise was heard several times during the week as Grace and Horace Waterman frequently hosted dinners and faculty get-togethers. Tonight, no dignitaries would sit at the polished mahogany dining table; guests of that nature had diminished due to the war. This evening, the two visitors were common Confederate soldiers and not high borne as most of their predecessors, yet their hosts granted them the same courtesies, as if they were.

Horace's wife, Grace, was the daughter of William Scott Harrison, owner of one of the largest plantations in eastern Virginia. Like most daughters from wealthy Virginia families, Grace was well educated in the three Rs, music, and learned to speak fluent French. She also was taught how to sew and do needlework since most clothes were hand sewn at the time. Besides her natural beauty, she developed a soft-spoken, graceful manner that allowed her to become a true Southern belle and the apple in her father's eye. Under her father's vigilance, strict guidelines had to be followed when courting. Any impropriety could ruin a young girl's reputation; therefore, proper etiquette was a must. All this had prepared her for an advantageous marriage, but then she met Horace Waterman.

Horace, a young teacher at the Richmond school for girls, was an aesthete with very modest finances and little more to offer. Grace didn't care. Captivated by his wit and kindness, she fell head over heels in love, much to the displeasure of William Scott Harrison. The argument between Harrison and his daughter lasted for almost a year, during which time he got to know Horace Waterman better. As in most cases where love is involved, Harrison couldn't win. He finally gave up the ship. After all, Waterman wasn't a bad guy and he did idolize Grace. After forty years of marriage, Grace never woke a single morning regretting her union. The following morning and a new day were always very forgiving.

The dinner party reposed in an anteroom located at the immediate right of the foyer. Sometimes referred to as a sitting room, it served as gathering place for dinner guests to relax and converse, prior to the call to dinner in the formal dining room. A sofa rested in front of the bay window, armchairs encircled the coffee table, and a piano forte stood in one corner of the room. A chaise longue was placed by a writing desk to the side of the fireplace. Original artwork decorated the walls, and potted and hanging greenery gave the final touch to the delightful chamber.

Hope and her father toured the room with Melvin, giving Abel the opportunity to talk to Abigail.

"I've put a plan in place to have Jack called back to the regiment. But I'm faced with a growing concern. You might say I'm on the horns of a dilemma. In the beginning, I viewed this action as the lesser of two evils. We both can visualize what will happen if Jack continues to stay at

Robertson's. The problem for me is what if he eventually gets wounded again or, even worse, is killed during battle. I then will be responsible, and you will hate me for it," Abel explained to Abigail.

"Oh, Abel, don't think that way. You are my truest friend, as well as Jack's. I agree that the only way to save my husband from himself is to remove him from temptation. He will never regain his latent memory while at the hospital. I'm sure of that. This is my only chance to get him back, and the risk of him losing his life, let's leave to the Lord," she said sincerely.

"What are your plans once Jack is moved? It will be difficult to see him after he's back at the base and impossible when we're in the field."

"I've considered returning to Statesville. Those who love me are still there, and I miss my children very much," she said. "Mr. Waterman told me he would help me on the return trip. He knows some of the people who facilitated me getting here. I guess going back is basically just reversing the process."

When the touring trio returned to their chairs, Hope excused herself to go help her mother with the meal. Abigail offered her assistance, but Hope wouldn't hear of it. Abigail had helped in the kitchen from the first day. Apparently, Hope was showing off for Melvin Kaufman's benefit.

Appetites were honed to the sharpest edge when Grace invited them all to the table. The table setting was perfectly laid out with silver utensils polished to a gleaming luster. Abigail hadn't observed this fine dinnerware before; obviously, it was only used on special occasions.

It marked the first time Melvin Kaufman had ever seen true silverware, period—let alone actually use it. He was suspicious of the small white towel lying beside his plate, rolled up with a silver napkin ring around it. He planned to watch the others and treat it the same way they did. A rolled napkin wasn't the only thing new to Melvin. His attention was drawn to the way the table was set. There was a large spoon in front of his plate with a fork to the left and another fork and knife to the right. Cups and saucers were also to the right and a small bowl rested in the middle of his plate. Putting two and two together, Melvin determined the bowl was for soup.

At that moment, Hope entered the dining room, behind a small cart, topped with a large round tureen, having fixed handles and standing on an under tray. She began serving each guest as she traveled from chair to chair. Melvin couldn't decide what was most beautiful—the porcelain tureen, which was a family keepsake, or the lovely hostess now serving soup.

After returning the cart to the kitchen, both she and Grace appeared, took their seats, and asked Horace to offer the prayer of thanks. His amen was repeated by both Abigail and Abel, at which point you could hear the spoons begin their attack on the soup dish.

"I don't know when I've tasted more delicious soup, is it onion?" Abigail asked Grace.

"You might say that. With the shortages cause by the war, we are unable to find many of the ingredients necessary to make proper meals. In fact, I must apologize for such a meager supper. Many of our friends are experiencing the same problem. I fear for those who aren't as well-off," lamented Grace.

"I think there's going to be trouble. When you can't feed your family because of scarcity, riots can take place,"

Horace added. "In times of war, the army comes first, then women and children after the soldiers are fed."

"Coming from a farm background, I wasn't aware of the problem in the cities," Abel confessed. "When you're raised growing your own food, not much thought is given to city dwellers other than selling them the farm harvest surplus."

"That philosophy works well during peacetime, but the war has taken most of our able men away. Not enough manpower is left to plant, cultivate, and harvest crops. In areas where the crops are harvested, it's difficult to transport them to the cities, especially with the destruction of many of the railroad lines. The bottom line for all of this is a serious food shortage and inflated prices for what's available," continued Hope's father.

"I can't believe some of the prices the stores are charging," added Grace. The last time Hope and I went shopping, the price of beef went from 4¢ to 11¢ a pound. And that's not all, eggs are 20¢ a dozen and sugar now costs 8¢ a pound. You don't bake many sweets with the price that high."

"Our citizens here in Richmond are cutting a thin line. The average laborer receives 90¢ a day, and the boarding houses charge $2.50 a week. It may be a little less for women, but they don't get paid as much either," said Horace. "By the numbers, people are able to sustain themselves. Oh, they may need to conserve a little. It's the shortages they find most difficult to accept."

"Abigail, you asked me about the soup. It's basically celery, onion, parsley, and beans. To make it different from other recipes, I add the yolks of some hard-boiled eggs. When they get mixed into the stock, you get the special taste," Grace confessed while rising from her chair to bring in the main course.

"Do you need my help, Mother?" asked Hope.

"Aucuns merci, le chéri mais, je peux avoir besoin de l'aide avec la portion," Grace replied in whispered French.

"I'm learning French in college, and Mother is helping me," Hope chimed. "She speaks beautifully, don't you think? Mother said, 'No thanks, darling, but I may need help with the serving.'"

Hot damn, Melvin thought. *If only my kinfolks could see me now—eating high on the hog and talking French.*

The main course was actually pot roast surrounded with onions, potatoes, and carrots. It was brought out and served in the same fashion as the soup. The only exception involved the container. The cooking pot was less ornamented and much larger. On a second trip to the kitchen, Hope returned with another loaf of freshly baked bread, still warm from the oven. Plum pudding capped off the dinner, making it a complete success.

"I'll bring hot coffee to the sitting room, and Horace has brandy and cigars there as well," Grace conveyed. This time, Abigail was allowed to assist in the cleanup effort. With her help, the job was accomplished in less than a half hour; after which, the three women joined the men.

The dinner party now sat relaxing in the sitting room. Each lazily swirled a pear-shaped snifter containing brandy the color of burnt sienna. Their most fearful concerns seemed to have dissipated like the mountain fog in morning sunlight.

The unlikely pairing of odd personalities actually fit like a wedding ring to the new bride's finger. They were approaching the end of a perfect day, the memory of which would improve even more each time it was recalled.

Grace Waterman was able to entertain her guests as in antebellum times. Her daughter Hope could flush her feathers to entice a newfound suitor. Abigail basked in the prospects of winning back her husband and soul mate. And Abel rested assured his actions would never be distained by an undesired outcome.

Perhaps, best of all, each departed in a lighthearted air of determination for better days to come.

* * *

Not everyone shared in such promising prospects. Grazyna had missed her second cycle. Finding each morning accompanied with nausea, she still hoped against hope it was caused by something else. Now, she must accept the fact that she was pregnant with Jack Leffingwell's baby. Disconcerted as to revealing her condition, the prospective mother hesitated in telling Jack, for fear of his reaction to such a perplexing problem. She found herself in a state of flux. One moment she would tell Jack, the next she had better wait. It was like the wooden yoyo given her by an uncle when she was a child. Up and down, up and down. When she decided to tell Jack, her decision was withdrawn, and like the yoyo, it returned to her hand. Any woman in this situation needs a confessor. Grazyna finally decided to tell Sally Tompkins.

It would be a month of Sundays before you could find someone more compassionate than Sally Tompkins. The confession of the disheartened damsel garnered sympathy immediately. Sally had looked upon her as a daughter from the first day they met. And now, matronly instincts made her feel as though she, too, shared in the guilt. From the point of first noticing the two lovers together, she might have been able to prevent an unhappy ending. Like most mothers, her inaction allowed her to share the blame.

"I don't know what I'm going to do," the tearful maiden sobbed.

"Well, eventually you will need to tell Jack, maybe not today, but in the very near future," Sally replied, thinking, *It may have to be sooner rather than later because he is going to be ordered back to his regiment.*

"One thing is certain, you now must move into my house. You're going to need me more each day, and I will be helpful with the baby when it comes. Remember when you told me that you may surprise me someday? Well, that day is here," Sally thoughtfully remarked. "In the meantime, go about your duties as though nothing has happened. That will delay the schadenfreude which will eventually occur since the nurses around here have been envious of you from day one."

And so it came to pass, that afternoon Grazyna whispered to Jack, "I've got something to tell you." There's nothing more provocative than when the woman he loved whispered to him. It conjured up images of them in bed, memories of her aroma, and that exquisite blue birth mark which was the reoccurring subject in his dreams. Even after she left the room, her bouquet lingered and brought about the exciting thought of the pending rendezvous, once the night shade fell.

The wind blew steadily for most of the day. Looking through his window, Jack watched pieces of white paper and other debris bounce across the Robertson's courtyard, only to entangle in the hedges lining the walkway. Sometimes the gusts would bend the trees like the Japanese bow of greeting, and as they say, March is coming in like a lion. It's too soon to predict whether it will go out like a lamb.

Wind is caused by changes in temperature in the atmosphere and on the ground. Warmer air expands and rises; then cooler air rushes in to replace it. March is a month in which you're hot in the sunshine and cold in the shadows, creating the perfect situation for wind. Normally, as we enter into April, the spring weather grows warmer and the corresponding rain showers tend to equalize temperatures, thus allowing March to end up more calm. It's not unusual for the month of March to come in like a lamb and go out like a lion. In either case, you're going to get a lot of wind in March, often resulting in very destructive tornados.

By now Grazyna and Jack had their frequent tryst down to a systematic, well-ordered routine. A subtle smile or nod could be the signal for their evening of mutual pleasure. Secrecy only heightened the lovers' anticipation and desire. Tonight they met with differing purposes. Jack's, to satisfy his yearning caused by her absence, and Grazyna's, to tell her ardent flame the news that would dramatically change their lives. The uneasiness and tension in the room went unnoticed by the mountain man. Jack was too engrossed with other thoughts and deeds. Grazyna couldn't get past it; she needed to know how he would react when the subject was broached. Jack finally exhausted himself and lay back staring blindly at the ceiling rafters.

Grazyna rolled to face him and said, "Remember when I said I've got something to tell you?"

"Yes, I remember," he acknowledged.

"Well, *Jestem brzemienne waszym dzieckiem.*"

"Very funny, you know I don't understand Polish," Jack said drily. "Tell me in English."

"Brace yourself, darling, I'm pregnant with your child."

The silence was deafening. There's no better way of describing it than employing the old cliché. What seemed to be an eternity was, in reality, only a minute or so before Jack said, "Who else knows about it?"

"Only one person besides us," Grazyna answered. "I was afraid to tell you and needed to tell someone. I've told Sally Tompkins."

"What did she say?"

"She was very sympathetic and wants me to move in with her. I've told her I would. Don't look so glum, that won't affect us."

After another quiet interval, Jack surmised, "I have to ask that woman for a divorce. We need to get married as soon as possible."

"You have no idea what torture I've put myself through. I was afraid to tell you, not knowing what your reaction would be. I nearly had a nervous breakdown," she stated as the tears of joy began to fall.

"Grazyna, I love you with all my heart. I want to spend the rest of my life with you and, sweetheart, I want our baby."

Major problems still lay ahead for the two lovers, but the unknown and bewildering future had partially cleared their minds. The tension of it all had stifled any pleasure Grazyna might have sought beforehand, and now, it was as though she'd been released from a tether. Her emotions ran rampant as she instigated the acts of love.

For the next two days, Abigail didn't visit her husband. Instead, with the help of Horace Waterman, she made the necessary arrangements to return to Statesville, Tennessee. On the day before her departure, she paid a visit to Robertson Hospital to thank Sally Tompkins for what they have done to help Jack and the courtesies extended to her. After a short debate with herself, Abigail decided to tell her husband she was leaving.

He was standing with his back to the open doorway, looking out his window, deep in thought.

Abigail stood watching him for a moment before entering the room.

Here was the man who followed her to Statesville not so many years ago.

Here was the man who changed his life because of her. Who broke down and cried when he thought he had hurt her. Who built their home and worked from morning till night to make the farm successful.

Here was the man who fathered her two children, and the man she would love until death did them part.

Abigail removed a handkerchief from her purse, dried her eyes, and walked out of the hospital.

Chapter Twenty-Two

In three words I can sum up everything I've learned about life: it goes on.

—Robert Frost

Abel Strawn and the rebel sharpshooters have been back on the base for one week. As yet, there's been no word about a transfer for Jack Leffingwell. They all assumed that Abigail was on her way back to Tennessee, and each commiserated her uncompassionate treatment during the visit with Jack. Until now, they had always respected him, his wisdom, courage, and dedication to Abigail. But now, a different man resided at Robertson Hospital. He looked the same and enjoyed their company; nevertheless, it's not the same mountain man from Tennessee they previously looked up to. His wounded psyche and amnesia was the cause of it. All the same, his soldier friends were simple, honest men, not highly educated or schooled in medical science. Without intellectually understanding the symptoms of amnesia, they only saw things as they appeared before them. Jack Leffingwell's attitude was reality, and they disliked it. His only hope for redemption was to return to the regiment and be his former self. Abel Strawn had set the wheels in motion. All they could do now was wait.

Confederate president Jefferson Davis had called for another day of fasting, prayer, and thanksgiving. He firmly believed that in order to eventually win the secession experiment, national soul-searching and thoughtful reflection was required. Each time the South's effort suffered a major blow, he declared it was part of God's plan to test their faith and perseverance and called for citizens to humble themselves before God Almighty by fasting and praying for victory. There would be at least ten such days called by Old Jef before the war was over.

Abel was back reading the news of the day to the others, whenever Melvin obtained a current publication of the *Richmond Enquirer*.

"Hot off the press," Melvin stated as he tossed the most recent edition he could find to Abel. Again, the others moved in closer to fulfill their part in the ritual.

This day the headlines read, "Richmond Bread Riots," and went on to say thousands of people, mostly women, broke into shops and began seizing clothing, shoes, food, and even jewelry before the militia arrived to restore order. Jefferson Davis himself appeared before the crowd and spoke to disperse the angry mob. He even threw money, saying, "You say you are hungry and have no money. Here, this is all I have." His words had the opposite effect and incited them more; however, only when Davis threatened to have the militiamen fire on the crowd did they finally disperse.

Several factors figured into the cause of the civil unrest. If one could be singled out as paramount, it is the Confederate government itself. It was far more profitable for plantation owners to grow cotton and tobacco instead of food. The taxes on many activities were a mere 2 percent while taxes on agricultural produce were 10 percent. This created obvious tensions and robbed the farmer of his income and means of providing for his family. Because of this, food crops suffered tremendously through supply and demand.

The previous year, a severe drought resulted in a poor harvest when food was already scarce. The price of wheat tripled, and butter and milk prices quadrupled. Women began to protest the exorbitant price of bread, blaming the government and speculators. They turned to violence to show their displeasure.

Similar riots occurred in most large cities in the South. In fact, the Confederate army also suffered the same food shortages and took food stocks for its own needs, thus creating less for the general public and more inflation. Due to costs exceeding the tax revenue, the Confederate government moved to deflate the currency, a mistake that additionally inflated prices on items needed by the public.

"That sure makes Horace Waterman look like a prophet," Melvin stated.

"Yes, he did fear that would happen," agreed Abel, who scanned the remaining articles, finding nothing of mutual interest, folded it, and handed it back to Melvin. He, in turn, planned to read more of the tabloid the next time he was alone.

"By the way, Lomas, you never did tell us about your date with that barmaid from the Eagle Inn and Tavern," reminded Melvin.

"There's not much to tell. She said we couldn't have sex unless we were engaged," replied Lomas.

"I notice you're missing one of your rings," Abel said jokingly.

Quickly looking at his hand, Lomas answered, "I suppose you're right."

* * *

The winds of future conflict grow stronger each day. You can feel it in the air and see it reflected in the resolute faces of the rank and file. These were brave men who rose to a level of heroism each time they're called. Even the bravest of the brave tended to weaken as food, clothing, and the tools of warfare slowly diminished. Now, some slept outdoors without shelter, many of which were ill with fever, yet never hesitated to toe the line once the bugle sounded. These underdogs, sustained by pride, would soon defend the Confederacy against the superior forces from the North.

* * *

Sally Tompkins has alerted the mailroom to segregate any registered mail addressed to Jack Leffingwell. She wished to learn firsthand when his orders to return to the army winter quarters arrive. In her mind, it will prevent him from keeping the news from Grazyna, whom she would tell immediately. The enamored pair continued to secretly meet and conspire a way to release Jack from his previous nuptial bonds, proving more difficult because Abigail quit the visit and returned home without being confronted for a divorce. Jack now promised to write her seeking the agreement. At this point, Grazyna lived with Sally Tompkins. That didn't raise a single eyebrow, since the nurses knew Sally wanted her to move in from the beginning. And it certainly did the young nurse a world of good. She had never looked or felt better in her life, emanating that special glow of motherhood, a condition about which the others have yet to learn.

The interval between Christmas Eve and the day the tree was decorated seemed like an eternity. When we were children, time always dragged. In school, that last hour crawled at a snail's pace. Like waiting for the water to boil, Sally Tompkins was experiencing the same dilemma. She began to loiter around the mail room just to be present when it arrived. And ironically, the day she decided to discontinue the mailroom vigil, Jack's orders appeared.

It came in an official government envelope and a second letter, encased in a similar fashion, was addressed to her. Sally tore it open while briskly walking back to her office. The gist of it said that Jack was to report to winter quarters within seventy-two hours of receipt. He was being released from Robertson's under the authorization of both General Shaw and Major Tompkins. Although the conditions under which Jack's transfer had changed, Sally still felt like the world had been lifted off her shoulders. Her next move was to inform Grazyna.

* * *

After Jack opened the envelope, his first thoughts were about Grazyna. He wondered how she would receive the unwelcome news. She'd been so happy lately. News, such as this, might upset her too much and affect the baby. Jack would later learn that Sally received a letter of her own and told Grazyna. Notwithstanding her fear for his safety, Grazyna had plenty to occupy her mind in Jack's absence. She was confident in his love and devotion and the separation would have taken place even if they were married. The radiant beauty stood admiring her reflection in the glass door leading to the lobby. As yet, there was no outward sign of her pregnancy, with one exception—the fullness of her bosom. Smiling, she thought, *Yes, Jack Leffingwell is going to miss me the most.*

Under normal circumstances, the summoned soldier would be confronted with finding his own way back to the base camp, not so for the Tennessee mountain man. The Seventh regiment provided an escort. Actually, it was a wagon and driver; nevertheless, it relieved Jack of any worry as to how he was going to get back.

The driver was a trusted enlisted man who frequently played poker with Lomas Chandler. He knew all the sharpshooters, including Jack, who claimed to have never seen him before. Schooled beforehand as to what he might expect, the driver let it pass without offering a reply. A one-sided conversation helped the time pass on the wearisome journey back. Jack had very little to offer since his memory only encompassed his experience at Robertson and the high points of that he chose to keep to himself.

* * *

While performing her nursing duties, Grazyna felt a pull to her heart strings each time she passed Jack's door. She had already received a letter from him, telling her he had written Abigail to ask for the divorce. Sally helped her loosen up her uniform. It was growing too tight for comfort. A rumor circulated throughout the hospital that Grazyna had eloped and married Jack. His ex-wife Abigail was here to finalize the divorce. Neither she nor Sally said anything to discourage the chatter or invalidate it. If you tell a lie long enough and keep repeating it, no matter how ridiculous it may be, people will eventually come to believe it. Unfortunately, so will the one telling the lie. Over time, both Grazyna and Sally became rather comfortable living with it.

Even though he was welcomed back with open arms, Jack found it difficult to reintegrate into army life. He remembered the sharpshooters only from the point of their first visit at Robertson Hospital. Like the new kid in school, Jack had to personally explore the camp to relearn where the various facilities were located. And Abel Strawn cleverly pointed out superior officers without causing any undesired attention.

During the early days of Jack's return, Abel proved himself to be the most faithful friend of both him and Abigail. He argued against writing Abigail for a divorce until Jack had more time to recover the recollection of his past. That consideration fell on deaf ears because of something Abel was to learn later. Jack confided that Grazyna was pregnant and he wanted to do right by her, for he loved her with all his heart. That came as sobering news to his tried and true friend, and the only suggestion Abel could make was, "You've got to spend more time on your knees."

* * *

Abigail's return trip home had only one unscheduled stop for track repairs. Other than that, the journey was without incident. The Tennessee and Virginia railroad made much better time going west to Nashville than the eastward journey to Richmond. Perhaps, the main reason was no hospital carriages were attached, which, by their very nature, requires considerable time to properly supervise and maintain. Abigail lacked the interesting company she found on her way to Richmond. There was no Horace Waterman or any man of information on the return trip although fellow passengers were polite and considerate of each other. Hyrum met her in Nashville, and after spending another night with Rev. Parrot, they aimed Miracle in the direction of Statesville and slapped the reins. Fortunately, a small party of Union soldiers offered to accompany them during the trip and Hyrum readily accepted. The added protection allowed them to relax and gave Abigail the opportunity to continue giving her description of the Richmond visit to her father. She withheld particulars while Rev. Parrot and Paula Finefield, his housekeeper, were present. To do otherwise would be too embarrassing.

When Abigail returned home to the farm in Statesville, she was met with expressions of heartfelt love and endearment. Minnie Rosenthal had to use force in order for Sarah Jane to release her embrace and Little Jack had a firm hold in an act of emulation. As luck would have it, Maryellen Riberty happened to be there at the time and was the first to greet her, other than a family member.

"Have you seen your father yet?" asked Maryellen.

"Yes, he picked me up in Nashville," Abigail replied.

"Oh, Abigail, I knew that. You must forgive my stupidity, it's just that I'm so happy to see you," answered Maryellen.

"Maryellen, you're far from being stupid. By the way, how did you get here? I didn't see a gig."

"I walked. It's not that far," Maryellen replied.

"It's nearly three miles. You certainly are a good friend. Thank the Lord. You won't have to walk home. You're going to spend the night with me, and tomorrow, once things settle down, we can harness Miracle and ride into town," promised Abigail.

Minnie added, "I've got hot tea on the stove. Let's get off the porch and go inside. We want to hear everything about your trip."

The children finally settled down, and the three women took their tea into the comfort of the living room and relaxed. Maryellen and Minnie were anxious for Abigail to begin. Their smiling expressions quickly changed as she put her hands to her face and burst into tears. Her two friends rose in tandem to place consoling arms around Abigail's shoulders. As they comforted her, she took more control and, daubing her eyes, said, "I'm okay now," and relayed the story of the Robertson experience.

Returning from the kitchen with a wet rag, Maryellen said, "I don't think I ever want to get married. If a man like Jack Leffingwell can act this way, the rest of them have to be worse."

"He's not the same person. He has no idea who I am or of our life together. The doctor told me his memory will return. He can't say when. It may take years, and by then, it will be much too late."

"Well, the first thing to do is separate him from that woman," Minnie offered.

"That should have happened by now. His friend, Abel Strawn, wanted to help me and arranged for Jack to be called back to the army base."

"What are you going to do now, my child?" asked Minnie.

"There's nothing much I can do now. Besides just sit and wait for Jack to remember."

"You will always have us at your side, no matter what he does," assured both Grandma Minnie and Maryellen.

A week later, the second boot stomped down. Jack's letter arrived. Abigail was in town making arrangements to take over her teaching duties. She had thanked the mothers who filled in while she was away and walked to the post office to check for mail. She had a letter, and it was from Jack. She hurried to her father's so it could be opened privately. Hyrum and his daughter sat at the kitchen table as Abigail slid her finger between the top flap and the envelope back. Recognizing the hand as Jack's, she began to absorb the script.

March 25, 1863
Dear Abigail,

Sorry I didn't get to speak to you before you left the hospital. There is something of a serious nature we needed to discuss. Please understand what I'm about to say. You seem like a very nice lady, and I don't want to hurt you. I'm not a bad person either, but our lives have changed dramatically, for many reasons. The war has separated us for over two years. My injury has taken away any memory of a past life. When you were here, I didn't know who you were. Yes, I was told that we are married, but I have no recollection of it. Without any memory of a past life, I met a wonderful girl and fell in love with her. She is with child, and I will do right by her. I want to marry her before the baby arrives. I will never return to Statesville. Therefore, the farm is yours to do with what you may. All I ask is for you to agree to a divorce. This can be done through the mail.

I hope to hear from you soon. Considering her condition, it's best to finalize this as soon as possible.

Yours truly,
Jack Leffingwell

Abigail was in a state of shock. Not in a thousand years did she expect anything like this. She sat speechless as she handed the missive to Hyrum. He read it again and folded the letter and placed it back in its envelope.

"Father, what am I going to do?" she asked drily.

"Do you still love him?"

"With all my heart."

"Then for one thing, you're not going to give him a divorce. Time is on your side, so don't think about even responding to this letter for at least a month. Do you know this girl?"

"I've seen her, but I haven't talked to her. She's a nurse at Robertson Hospital and a lot younger than me. She's also more beautiful as well," offered Abigail.

"I'm sure that's just the woman in you thinking that. A man always has a different opinion when it comes to a woman's looks. So don't give that a second thought."

"Dad, you haven't seen her."

"You need to get back into the swing of things. You've a school to run, a farm to tend, and a family to take care of at home. Besides, your old dad can use a little attention. You've been away a long time," said Hyrum as he put his arm around his daughter and held her tight. She had controlled her emotions up till now, but that sign of affection opened the floodgates.

Chapter Twenty-Three

I object to violence because when it appears to do good, the good is only temporary. The evil it does is permanent.

—Mahatma Gandhi

All the domestic rioting was not concentrated only in Southern cities. The North had its share of civil unrest, but for a diametrically different reason. Abraham Lincoln had issued the Enrollment Act of Conscription, the first wartime draft law passed in the United States. The act shocked the general public who were already discouraged after reading about the bloodshed at Gettysburg. After all, they were initially told the war would only last ninety days. Today, the war seemed endless, and Lincoln's call for three hundred thousand more young men appalled them even more. They included those who, in the beginning, dramatically supported the Union cause, hitherto, now were taken aback by the new law.

The conscription law contained several exemptions, the most unfair being the payment of a commutation fee that allowed wealthier and more influential citizens to buy their way out of service. It permitted a person to pay $300 to avoid military duty. It became known as the rich man's exception and precipitated violent riots in the larger cities. The worst riots took place in New York City. Over one hundred citizens were killed before the riots were quelled by Federal troops.

The Irish were the most resentful group. Populating the slums of northern cities, they were poor and forced to compete for the lowest-paying jobs. Lincoln's $300 commutation fee was way beyond their means. Rabble rousers changed the dialogue of the law to a fight on behalf of the blacks. Many Irish knew very little to nothing about the blacks in America, only that they had to compete against them for the low-paying jobs. Irish themselves faced extreme prejudice from the first step on American territory.

While back in Ireland, most of the property was owned by wealthy landowners in England. They rented sections to the Irish farmers, who, in turn, worked the land and depended on it for food and meeting their rent payment. In 1845, a fungus hit the potato fields, their primary crop, causing a devastating famine. The food shortage killed nearly two and a half million people and, making matters worse, was followed by more crop failures in 1846, 1848, and 1851. Potatoes rotted in the fields, people were unable to meet the rental obligation and were forced from their homes, only to die from starvation. This horrible famine caused a mass exodus to the United States. Over time, nearly two million Irish immigrants came to America, most of whom were poor, undernourished, and defeated by their previous life.

Leaving Ireland was only the beginning of troubles confronting the immigrants. They faced the two—to three-month journey aboard ships comprising the most intolerable conditions one can imagine. The steerage compartments had ceilings so low a man couldn't stand up. As many as nine hundred men, women, and children were crowded together and expected to sleep on a narrow cot that won't be aired out or washed until the day before arrival, and then only to satisfy the government inspectors. The air became increasingly foul as the journey progressed, and food was improperly cooked and insufficient. Water was limited and toilets were inadequate for the number of people aboard.

Before 1847, there was no official reception area. Peddlers and tavern keepers boarded the ships to make direct deals with the newly arriving immigrants. Once they got to the dock, their situation worsened. They were cheated when making a money exchange and persuaded into paying for dilapidated boarding houses. It wasn't until 1892 before immigrant regulation was turned over to the Federal government and Ellis Island established for processing.

The majority of Irish immigrants remained in the port cities where they first set foot on American soil. Weak from the rigors of their journey and with little money, there was no other option. They mistrusted farming since the memory of why they initially departed was still foremost on their minds. Accordingly, relocating in smaller, less populated rural areas was an unacceptable notion. Remaining at the points of their inaugurate landing left them with limited job opportunities and terrible, overcrowded living conditions. As many as nine people lived in one room. A slum area in Manhattan had seventy-five people living in twelve rooms and paying $4 a month rent. The lack of indoor plumbing or running water was responsible for the spread of disease. Most of the children's death, under five years of age, was Irish.

As more Irish immigrants came to the United States, many Americans blamed them for causing economic problems. They felt that the great number of Irish workers would put Americans out of work or lower their wages. They also believed that the increased number would result in a tax increase to cover the costs for more police, fire, health, sanitation, schools, and poorhouses. It became acceptable to discriminate against the Irish. Job posters read, No Irish Need Apply. Hotels and restaurants had signs stating, No Irish Permitted in this Establishment. When Irish did get hired, the pay was lowered to about one-half.

The sum total of discrimination against the Irish set the stage for city riots. When the names of the draftees were drawn, groups of irate citizens, many Irish immigrants, banded together across the cities. The mob grew to nearly fifty thousand people and terrorized the East Side of New York for three days, looting stores and destroying property. Soon blacks became the target of their hatred and several lynchings and beatings occurred before Federal troops could restore order.

Lincoln's draft law did not produce nearly the increase he had hoped for. It did, however, reveal the length of where he was willing to go, to be victorious, in this unhappy war.

* * *

By now Jack has mastered the subtleties of the military camp. Even though most of the things he's learned seem like it was for the first time. His accuracy at the shooting range was astonishing to the others. For Jack, marksmanship came with the package and wasn't a learned activity. His adjusting for the wind is not inborn, and the fact that he did so was encouraging to the rest of the men.

The month of April rolled into camp announced by storm clouds and thunder. It was as through the earth was a little boy, and Saturday night had arrived. Amidst the rumbling roar of thunder and crash of lighting, the downpour came. The only place to be, on occasions like this, is safely inside where it's warm and dry. That safety won't last very long. There was reorganization at the top when Colonel Goodner resigned. John A. Fife was promoted to full colonel, and Samuel G. Shepard to lieutenant colonel. They would hold their positions for the duration of the war.

Activity began to surmount when the Thirteenth Alabama was added to the brigade. Even a lowly recruit could read the signs. Another big battle was in the works.

What the rank and file didn't know was that the Union army had crossed the Rappahannock River to make another attempt to capture Richmond. This time, Union major general Joseph Hooker had devised a plan to have his infantry concentrate near Chancellorsville and another force facing Fredericksburg, a double envelopment attacking Lee from both his front and rear.

The sounds around the camp were of military movement. The two-wheeled caissons were tested to make certain the turning wheels didn't squeal from lack of grease. In fact, a similar test was made on all the wagons with additional lubricant applied just to be safe. A marching army makes enough noise by itself. Any other sounds only compound the situation of moving without detection.

Some of the brigades were already on the march when the Seventh regiment got their orders. They will leave in the morning and tramp to Spotsylvania County and the village of Chancellorsville, a distance of about twenty-five miles.

The Union cavalry had already begun a long-distance raid against Lee's supply lines, but the operation was completely ineffectual. On May 1, Hooker's army advanced from Chancellorsville toward Lee and the abridged Army of Northern Virginia. Lee had split the Confederate army. He made the risky decision to divide it, leaving a force at Fredericksburg to confront and deter Maj. Gen. John Sedgwick and the Army of the Potomac. At the most critical moment, Fighting Joe Hooker lost his nerve and, against the advice of his subordinates, moved to a defensive position around Chancellorsville, ceding the initiative to Lee. Unlike the handwriting on Belshazzar's wall, Hooker's inaction didn't take Daniel to predict the outcome. Lee pounced on the opportunity, and the second bloodiest battle of the Civil War occurred that day. Multiple attacks were launched against the Union position. Confederate artillery found a favorable position on a rise a short distance to the southwest and battered the Union center.

The Seventh Tennessee regiment took a significant role in the assault. Jack Leffingwell and the other marksmen kept a constant fusillade of long-distance accuracy with chilling results. It was like death came out of nowhere, followed by the demonic whistle of the Whitworth bullet.

Abel Strawn purposely stationed himself close to Jack in case his amnesia affected his performance under battle. It didn't. Similar to a carnival shooting gallery, the blue-uniformed soldiers toppled over steadily, until Jack's rifle became too hot to hold. After cooling, by dipping it into a bucket of water located at his side, the decimation continued.

The stentorian noise from cannon fire was staggering. The air smelled of cordite and became a gray, cloudy fog. At times, so thick that the sharpshooters temporarily lost their target until a helpful breeze brought it back in sight.

Meanwhile, Lee had determined that the Union army had, as yet, not refortified its right flank. He believed they were susceptible to attack if it came as a surprise. In a bold and daring move, Lee divided his army a second time. Confederate general Stonewall Jackson was to lead his Second Corps of twenty-eight thousand men around the Union right flank and attack. It required a twelve-mile march via roundabout roads, and it had to be done without detection. Lee would personally command the remaining two divisions, consisting of twenty-four cannons and thirteen thousand troops, and face the seventy thousand Union soldiers at Chancellorsville. While Jackson's march didn't escape detection, he continued as though it had. The Union observation balloon *Eagle* had spotted the Confederate column although, apparently, made no report to headquarters. Once Hooker was apprised of the situation, he believed that General Lee was retreating; even so, he also wouldn't discount the possibility that Lee was conducting a flanking maneuver. His response came too late. Making matters worse, when Hooker warned the Union commander of the Eleventh Corps, Maj. Gen. Oliver O. Howard delayed following orders to make provisions for defending a surprise attack. His only defense against a side assault was two cannons pointing out into the surrounding fields of brambles, thickets, and vines known as the Wilderness.

When Jackson's rebels exploded out of the woods screaming the rebel yell, most of the Federal troops were sitting down to dinner and had their rifles unloaded and stacked. A few bluecoats noticed the rabbits and foxes fleeing in their direction but made nothing of it. Union general Howard made several futile attempts to redeem his inadequate preparation, to no avail. Several thousand of Howard's men retreated to a clearing across the road from the Chancellor mansion, where the cannons of the Union artillery gave them cover to reorganize for a defensive stand. By then, however, the momentum of Jackson's attack had passed.

Stonewall Jackson wanted to press his advantage before Hooker, and his army could regain their bearings and plan a counterattack. He was well aware of the disparity in numbers and how quickly the North was able to add more troops. The moon was full, and he led a small reconnaissance party out to determine the feasibility of a night attack. Traveling beyond the farthest advance of his men, they were incorrectly identified as Union cavalry on their return.

"Halt, who goes there?" shouted a guard of the Eighteenth North Carolina Infantry. Jackson's reply, out of the darkness, wasn't evaluated before Southern soldiers opened fire. Frantic shouts by Jackson's staff identifying themselves were mistakenly thought to be the enemy. Maj. John D. Barry responded with the retort, "It's a damned Yankee trick! Fire!" The second volley resulted in Jackson being hit by three bullets and several men in his staff killed. Confusion and darkness prevented Jackson from getting immediate care. The incoming artillery rounds from the guns defending the Chancellorsville Inn forced the stretcher bearers to lay Jackson down several times before receiving treatment. Once the doctors saw him, his left arm had to be amputated. He was then moved to Fairfield, a plantation near Guinea Station, Virginia, where he died from complications.

After Jackson was wounded, command of the Second Corps went to Maj. Gen. A. P. Hill. Hill was soon wounded himself; however, Brig. Gen. Robert E. Rodes, the next senior division commander, agreed to summon J. E. B. Stuart to take command. Stuart was a cavalry man and had never before commanded infantry; nevertheless, he conducted himself admirably that day. The attack on Chancellorsville began the next morning. Initial waves were beaten back by Union troops positioned behind strong earthworks. Additional artillery at Hazel Grove gave the Confederate gunners a decided advantage over the Federal counterparts. And the constant barrage slowly took effect. By then, the soldiers of the two halves of Lee's army had reunited, and the Union Army of the Potomac began a fighting retreat.

Union general Hooker had taken the Chancellorsville House as his headquarters. It was battered to ruin when Confederate guns blasted the Federal center. Southern artillery fire from Fairview, a rise a short distance to the southwest, spelled the end for the stately brick mansion. One shell actually struck a column against which General Hooker was leaning, causing a possible concussion and temporary confusion. On the night of May 5, he withdrew back across the river at U.S. Ford. His surprise withdrawal frustrated Lee's plan for one final attack against Chancellorsville.

Two days prior to his victory at Chancellorsville, Lee received some bad news. Union forces had broken through the Confederate lines at Fredericksburg and were headed toward Chancellorsville. Hooker had given orders for Gen. John Sedgwick to cross the Rappahannock and take the Chancellorsville road until he caught up with him. He was to attack and destroy any force he met on the road.

When Lee divided his army, a relatively small force, under the command of Brig. Gen. Jubal Early, defended Fredericksburg. His orders were to watch the enemy and try to hold him. If the numbers were overwhelming, Early was to retreat to Richmond. Should for any reason Sedgwick withdraw from the front, then he was to join Lee at Chancellorsville. On the morning of May 2, Early received a garbled message from Lee's staff that caused him to start marching most of his smaller force toward Chancellorsville, but he quickly returned when he learned of a Union advance against Fredericksburg. The next day, Early found himself confronted by four Union divisions. They formed a line in front of the town to a few miles north at Deep Run. Early's strength lay to the south of town, where the Federal troops had achieved their most success during the first battle in December.

Federal forces made two attacks against the infamous stone wall on Marye's Heights, and both times were repulsed with numerous casualties. A party, under a flag of truce, was allowed to approach to collect the wounded. While close to the stone wall, they were able to observe how meagerly the Confederate line was manned.

Upon their return, the Union soldiers shouted, "They got hardly anybody behind them walls. They are bluffing us."

A third Union attack was successful in overrunning the Confederate position, and Early was forced to organize a fighting retreat.

The road to Chancellorsville was now open. A confident General Sedgwick wasted time in forming a marching column although many of his men were delayed for several hours by successive actions against the Alabama brigade of Brig. Gen. Cadmus M. Wilcox. The crafty Confederate officer established his final delaying line at the Salem church. By then Wilcox was joined by three more Confederate brigades, bringing his total strength to ten thousand men.

Artillery fire was exchanged by both sides in the afternoon, and the Union attacks were repelled. Their advance only reached as far as the churchyard, then was driven back. The Union army could not break the Confederate line. Now, Gen. Jubal Early began a counterattack which eventually forced Sedgwick to withdraw across the Rappahannock.

Lee, despite being outnumbered by a ratio of over two to one, won arguably his greatest victory of the war. But he paid a terrible price for it. With only sixty thousand engaged, he suffered 13,303 casualties (1,665 killed; 9,081 wounded; 2,018 missing). Losing some 22 percent of his force in the battle meant the future army would necessarily be smaller because they could not be replaced, a profound example of the war of attrition.

Lee also lost his most aggressive commander, Stonewall Jackson. Jackson's death was a severe setback for the Confederacy in multiple ways. It impacted not only the military prospects but also the morale of both its army and the general public. Stonewall Jackson was perhaps one of the most gifted tactician commanders in the nation's history. General Lee said it was like losing his right arm. His words would prove prophetic as he went forward in his quest tilting at windmills. Unlike the imaginary giants Don Quixote faced, Lee's giants were real. In Cervantes's story, the Knight of the Woeful Countenance fought a lost cause. There were many now who felt Robert E. Lee was doing the same. His remarkable victories in Virginia demonstrated superior leadership and military skills. As the war continued, the sheer numbers of active-duty Union troops outweighed Lee's forces by nearly 300 percent. And now, 150,000 black soldiers had been added to Abraham Lincoln's military. While the Confederate army seemed to match the forces pitted against it, replacing those lost in battle gradually became impossible. The North controlled 90 percent of industry and weapon making ability. Its navy was able to block Southern ports, restricting the import of vital supplies. With 70 percent of the railroads, the North could move men and matériel greater distances and quicker. At this point, the only advantage Lee had was defending Southern soil. He knew the territory and could dig in against a Federal attack. Any hope for European intervention was gone. It became clear the South must carry on by itself, sustained by valor and pride.

* * *

After the costly battle, the Army of Northern Virginia encamped in order to recuperate from the intensity of combat, take care of the wounded, and reassign troops. Gen. H. H. Heth was now corps commander of the Seventh Tennessee regiment.

The sharpshooters' spirits were at a low level when they heard that their benefactor, Stonewall Jackson, was killed. They had never met him. Even Jack Leffingwell, who found favor with the legendary general, hadn't exchanged a single word. He was a myth. Nevertheless, nearly every rebel soldier felt marooned in a gloomy sea of gray uniforms.

The first week in camp went by without drills. It gave the men the opportunity to set up personal accommodations, clean and repair their weapons, and write letters to loved ones and friends. For the first time since being together, all four sharpshooters were busy composing an epistle. Even Lomas Chandler was occupied with pen in hand. From all appearances, his engagement to the barmaid at the Eagle Inn was more serious than anyone thought. No one questioned the union between Melvin Kaufman and Hope Waterman, and their correspondence was to be expected. The same went for Abel Strawn and Amanda. After all, they were already married before Abel joined up. The scribe garnering the most attention was Jack Leffingwell. They knew he loved the beautiful nurse. He was married to another—and a woman they all respected. As much as they coveted Grazyna McCracken, who now was pregnant, they wouldn't change places with Jack for all the tea in China. Be that as it may, when looking through Jack's eyes and unable to retrieve past memories, Grazyna was his first love. He was totally smitten and read her letters over and over again. Thanks to Lomas, the marksmen sleep in a tent. At the moment, you could hear a pin drop. Each was living in their own little world, oblivious to their surroundings. Jack's pencil was down to a stub, but he would replace it the first chance he got. Right now, he dated another letter to Grazyna.

May 9, 1863
Dearest Grazyna,

My regiment has returned to camp for recovery from battle. We successfully defended the South against Yankee aggressors at Chancellorsville. Abe Lincoln's boys put up a good fight, but I was told we had more cannons than them. Abel learned that it was the first time that ever happened since the war started. In the heat of it all, my only thoughts were of you.

To date, I haven't heard from Abigail. I can't think of a reason why she wouldn't agree to the divorce. I've offered her the farm and all that's connected to it. Darling, we will start from scratch. You don't need to worry. I can build a house for the three of us when this terrible war is over. All you need to do is take care of yourself and our baby.

In case you haven't heard, Stonewall Jackson was killed in the battle. We both lost a good friend. It's because of him I was able to meet you, my darling, and I owe him a great deal for that.

If we stay at rest for a while, I will try to get a pass to come see you. With General Jackson gone, it might be different, but I still have Lomas Chandler and he also has a reason to *come to Richmond. He got engaged to a girl he met at the Eagle Inn. Dearest, you are always on my mind from the thing I think of in the morning to the last at night.*

I love you with all my heart,
Jack

Jack rolled over on his cot and put both hands behind his head while breaking into a self-rewarding smile. He knew how resourceful Lomas Chandler could be and basked in the idea of being with Grazyna soon.

Chapter Twenty-Four

Life isn't about finding yourself. Life is about creating yourself.

—George Bernard Shaw

Abigail had followed her father's suggestion and didn't respond to Jack's letter. Instead, she went about her duties and attempted to put her life back in order. She did, however, receive more mail from Richmond. A letter came from the Robertson Hospital and Sally Tompkins, trusting she reached home okay and telling her that Jack had been released and was back with his regiment.

The other correspondence was from Hope Waterman. The two had formed a congenial relationship during Abigail's stay, and Hope viewed her as a reliable confidant. She looked to Abigail for advice on certain personal matters rather than her father. Her most pressing problem was, how best to handle her relationship with Melvin Kaufman. Abigail advised she not rush into anything. Love doesn't always conquer all, and if she and Melvin were meant to be, then things would work themselves out. A long-distance friendship with Hope Waterman had another benefit for Abigail. She couldn't explain it, but it tended to make her feel closer to Jack.

The farm took on a more redeeming appearance during springtime. Multicolored wildflowers popped up overnight and adorned the road. They also decorated the creek embankment as it twisted and turned through the rural property. This time of year, the creek was fully flowing from the spring rains and the fast-moving water was so clear you had to put your hand in it to make sure it was there. The icy compensation quickly stood as proof. Mountain men believed fast-moving water was the best to drink, as long as there's no evidence that animals had the same idea. In an era without crop chemicals, the creek water, on the Leffingwell farm, had quenched the thirst many times.

Abigail and Minnie have expanded their garden. It's been over a year since the Union occupiers bothered them, and they felt safe to plant more without having their harvest stolen. The excess would be taken to town and redeemed at the market, unless the hungry had no money. Then it was cheerfully given away.

Yalata and his wife Ailana visited about twice a month and, on rare occasions, took time to learn about Jack's activities. Abigail related her trip and told them about Jack's amnesia and recovery prognosis. No mention was made about the most recent unpleasantness. Minnie Rosenthal had grown more tolerant of the stoical pair, even to the point of sharing a recipe with Ailana.

Sundays was the time for the whole family to get together. After church, they shared dinner with Hyrum in the parsonage. During the week, the minister always found time to see his grandchildren at the farm. Today, there was an issue he wished to discuss with his daughter and Minnie. Shortly after eating a piece of Minnie's custard pie, Hyrum took a cup of coffee with him as he sat in a living room recliner and broached the subject.

"Some of the more influential personages in town have come to the conclusion that the war effort will have an undesirable ending. The Yankees already occupy middle Tennessee, and a majority in the eastern part of the state stands ready to acquiesce. It will be a different world when the South is forced to surrender and vitally important for us to retain the traditional Southern way of life. They refer to the old way of life as the noblesse oblige, which is based in traditional chivalry. They are calling it the Confederate *noble cause.*"

"After seeing the way these Yankees act, I think that's a darn good idea," Minnie said frankly.

"Do you find fault with it, Father?" asked Abigail.

"Not on the surface of it," Hyrum answered. "What concerns me is, they want me to agree and communicate it from the pulpit. I have always tried to keep politics out of my sermons and advocate prayer as the solution. The war will end when God wills it to be over."

"Do they really believe we will lose the war?" questioned Minnie.

"They claim the defeat will come about by overwhelming force rather than military expertise," Hyrum replied. "These men fear that once the war is over, the reconstruction will be an attempt by the North to destroy the traditional way of life."

Minnie thought for a second then responded, "I think they're right. Just look at us here in the occupation. People aren't allowed to speak openly against the Union. We have to denounce the Confederacy and are forbidden to fly the Stars and Bars."

Hyrum continued, "All this draws attention as to why we are caught up in a war in the first place. Those in the North claim the war is over chattel slavery. According to the group that talked to me, that's never been our contention. The importation of slaves ended years ago. The primary cause that led eleven states to secede from the Union was the defense of states' rights. The country's tax laws were bias against the Southern economy when it came to trade. For years, the entry of new states required congressional balance. If a slave state joined the Union, it had to be balanced by a free state. This policy became more perplexing as America's west expanded. In all likelihood, it, too, could ultimately be settled by Congress. For the men who have been talking to me, when Lincoln sent seventy-five thousand troops into the South to teach Southerners a lesson, that cinched the deal. Secession was a justifiable constitutional response to Northern cultural and economic aggression against the Southern heritage and modus vivendi."

"You must admit, Father, they do make a lot of sense," offered Abigail.

"Only from one side of the view," replied her father. "For them to discount slavery as part of the reason we're at war is patently dishonest. I might have a different opinion if they would acknowledge that fact and admit it was wrong. You both know firsthand how I've always felt about slavery. My church served as an Underground Railroad station house for years. We met Jack Leffingwell while conducting runaways to freedom. Slavery is against God's law. I've told the Lost Cause group that I needed time to think it over, and that's the way I plan to keep it."

"I know one thing to be sure, if the South loses this war, the Yankee occupation will stomp on our pride like a ton of bricks. It will be a double loss and engender hatred against the North that will last for generations. Maybe this Lost Cause idea can help Southerners make the adjustment less painful," Abigail stated.

Hyrum was silent. He was thinking, *Where did this wonderful woman come from? When did she mature into such a bright and logical thinker? How does she handle the misfortunes recently befallen her and continue as though nothing is wrong? Where was I when my little girl grew up?* Looking at his daughter, he took another sip of coffee, glanced at a smiling and proud Minnie Rosenthal, cleared his throat, and said, "Like I said, I need more time to ponder the matter. There may be some positive aspects to it."

* * *

It took Lomas Chandler nearly three weeks to circumvent second-level authority and receive a seventy-two-hour pass for both him and Jack Leffingwell. For the more curious, it had something to do with General Shaw and the Robertson Hospital giving credibility to his request. The shrewd Irish gambler never revealed his hand unless someone paid to see it, and his unorthodox tactics in everyday life were never revealed, period. By now, Jack had learned not to ask. It would make him sleep better if he didn't know.

Abel Strawn had located the Methodist church tent and met the minister. He also managed to persuade Melvin Kaufman to attend with him. When it came to Lomas Chandler, Abel's luck ran out. Raised in a Roman Catholic family, Lomas defied tradition. Organized religion wasn't for him. In fact, his reply to Abel was, "Being in a church doesn't make you any more a Christian than being in a barn makes you a horse." Anyhow, Lomas had other things on his mind. Right now he was thinking of being with Isabella Manfredi, the voluptuous Eagle Inn barmaid.

"You're right, my wayward friend. It's not just being in church that makes you anything at all; but when groups of likeminded Christians are together, there is a sense of closeness with the Lord. When we stand and sing his praises, I can feel the Holy Spirit among us."

"Abel, your father is a preacher. You've been brought up that way. I was brought up swatting and scratching. My old man was a drunk."

"How does your mother feel about it?" Abel rhetorically asked.

"She would probably agree with you. Let's talk about something else or don't talk at all," Lomas suggested before pulling the flap and leaving the tent.

While Lomas and Jack made plans to make a personal visit to Richmond, other plans were under discussion at Gen. Robert E. Lee's headquarters. Union general Hooker's failure to move Lee out of his Fredericksburg stronghold bolstered the Gray Old Fox to pursue greater things. His stunning victory at Chancellorsville was viewed as an opportunity to follow up and destroy the Union army on its own soil. Not all of his advisors were of the same opinion. There were those who argued for shifting resources from Virginia to Mississippi and relieve Vicksburg. Others advocated reinforcing General Bragg in central Tennessee.

Lee had learned that it was too late to affect the outcome at Vicksburg. The Union siege was already underway. As a practical matter, it didn't make a lot of sense to detach forces from the Confederacy's only successful field army, led by the only successful general, and send them to other generals, whose competence was questionable. Instead, Lee held that the best use of limited Confederate resources was to invade Pennsylvania. By the time the oil lamps were lit, the beginning of a strategic plan was underway.

Chapter Twenty-Five

To die and part is a less evil; but to part and live, there, there is the torment.

—George Lansdowne, English poet, playwright, and politician

Back at the Robertson Hospital, Grazyna was walking on air. The good news was contained in Jack's latest correspondence—the envelope residing in her apron's front pocket.

"You're acting like the cat that got the bird. What makes you so happy this morning?" Sally asked.

"Jack got a three-day pass and should be here on Thursday," she answered.

"No wonder you're all excited," Sally said thoughtfully. "I need to spend some time with him to discuss his future plans regarding you and the baby. I'm perfectly willing to provide for you both, but once the war is over, I deserve to know his plans."

"He has asked his wife for a divorce and thinks she will agree," Grazyna stated.

"Yes, dear, but there's many a slip between the cup and the lip, and I want to hear his plans directly from him. As far as anybody around here is concerned, you guys are already married, and we need to keep it that way. There will be no need for you to use the caretaker's cabin. He can stay with you at our house."

Never in a million years would Sally ever imagine she would say such a thing. The morals of her Christian upbringing strongly prohibited the relationship between Grazyna and Jack Leffingwell, yet Grazyna was like a daughter to her and her happiness is paramount. The only way Sally was able to abide their conduct was accepting the adage, "All's well that ends well," and trust Jack to make sure that it would. Until then, she would hold a candle to the devil and countenance that which was wrong.

* * *

Lomas was able to arrange their ride to Richmond on the ironworks wagon. It was the same wagon that carried the sharpshooters on their previous visits. The driver was more than willing to smuggle them aboard because of certain favors Lomas Chandler provided. The resourceful Irishman seemed to have broken the code when it came to official documents, passes for three—and four-day leaves being one of them. As to how high up the chain of command his corruption went was never asked—ignorance is bliss. If anything went wrong, you were better off not knowing. The fact that the authorizing signature was totally illegible might make a person wonder just a little. This trip featured a wagon drawn by six mules and skillfully handled by its driver.

"Looks like you have a heavy load this trip," Lomas remarked.

"Hauling some cannon to the ironworks for repair," he said. "I'd rather be doing this than what you boys have been up to. They told me that a six-mule wagon can haul four thousand pounds. I don't believe we got near that much today. We will, however, be traveling a wee bit slower. I hope that don't cramp your style much."

"When do you think we'll get to Richmond?" Jack asked earnestly.

"If the roads are good and we don't have any problems, we ought to see Richmond this evening sometime." The driver drawled.

In anticipation of a long ride, Jack settled back down in the wagon bed. He found a comfortable area between two large wooden boxes and relaxed to the tune of the bumpy ride. Lomas Chandler, always in a talkative mood, spent the morning hours gossiping with the driver.

"You all have family in Richmond?" asked the teamster.

"Sort of, we're engaged to a couple of gals there. My buddy's lady is expecting, and this might be the last time he can be with her before she delivers. As for me, I may have to get hitched this trip. In fact, if I'm going to have any fun, I definitely will have to get married this trip," Lomas said gravely.

"Well, congratulations," said the driver.

"Thanks," came a bland reply.

"Has the food shortage troubled you boys very much? All hell broke loose in Richmond. There have been riots and a lot of destruction and such. They had to call in the troops to stop the damage. Old Jefferson Davis talked to them. But it didn't do any good. Guess when you're hungry, nothing else matters."

"Our chow is so lousy, if there was a shortage, we'd never know it," Lomas said sarcastically.

"Well, they know it in Richmond. A couple of weeks ago, a mob of those rioters stopped me. They thought I was hauling food or something. You should have seen their faces when they pulled the tarp back. I believed they were going to shoot me. They did eye my mules though. I thought, oh shit, they're going to eat them. While they were standing around, I eased the team down the road and nobody followed. Needless to say, they had me kind of scared," the driver admitted.

At that point, the teamster pulled off the road to a small sward in order to rest the mules. The way the grassplot was trampled down gave evidence that this stop had been performed many times before. The driver extracted a jug from behind his front legs and took a prolonged swallow.

"This rheumatism medicine you got me sure helps on these trips to Richmond," he said with a wink. "How do you ever come by it?"

"You just leave that up to Dr. Chandler," Lomas answered formally.

"Word is that Chimborazo Hospital makes their own. They do everything else there, so I don't doubt it one bit."

"I heard they just brew beer," replied Lomas.

Jack poked his head out from under the tarp and asked, "How come we stopped?"

"Got to rest the team once in a while," the teamster said tersely.

"Say, Jack, you ever hear of Chimborazo Hospital?" Lomas asked.

"Yeah, I've heard of it. Why do you ask?"

"We were wondering if they had a still and made their own liquor."

"They may make beer, but I don't think they have a still on the property. Old Jeff Davis is pretty firm about strong drink in the military and its hospitals. Even the sutlers are careful when it comes to *sippin'* whiskey. I'm not saying they don't sell it, but they're darn careful who they sell it to."

The teamster guided his mules back on the road and stayed a little to the right side, avoiding some deep ruts caused by a recent rain and a previous heavy wagonload. Soon the main road evened out, and once again the muleteer had his cargo heading for Richmond. After traveling at a comfortable pace, he asked, "Where did they come up with a name like Chimborazo?"

"I believe it's called that because it was built on Chimborazo Hill, so named for Mount Chimborazo, a volcano located in Ecuador. When I was a patient in Robertson Hospital, it seemed like Chimborazo was all the nurses talked about. They said it was like a city all to itself," Jack conveyed.

Actually, the nurses were right. Chimborazo Hospital, at this time in history, is the most celebrated and largest military hospital in the world. It is located on an elevated plateau east of the Confederate capital and rests on nearly forty acres. From such a height and eminent position, it provides a grand view of the surrounding area. Directing your eyes to the south, one will see the James River spanned by many bridges, ships in the harbor, and the towns of Chesterfield and Manchester. Observing to the east, a view of the countryside appears with cultivated fields, forests, rolling hills and valleys, and the falls of the James River flowing to the sea. The city of Richmond lies to the west with its churches and majestic steeples, the capitol buildings, public dwellings, and various manufacturing plants.

The hospital came into being shortly after the war started. Confederate volunteers converged on Richmond for troop assignments and drills. Many regiments camped on and around Chimborazo Hill. They built extensive wooden barracks for shelter, only to abandon them when ordered to the front lines. In their absence, a hundred well-made wooded buildings were left on Chimborazo Hill. Dr. Samuel P. Moore, CSA surgeon general, commandeered the buildings for his department and, in doing so, established Chimborazo Hospital.

Because of its proximity to the significant battles and five converging railroads, the capital city of Richmond became the hospital center of the Confederacy. Of over fifty hospitals in the city, nearly all were dedicated to the treatment of wounded or ailing soldiers. Not only was it the largest hospital, Chimborazo was a city unto itself. Among its one-hundred-plus buildings were five soup houses, a bakery producing ten thousand loaves daily, a forty-keg brewery, soap factory utilizing grease from the soup houses (lye was imported through the blockade), and five ice houses. It also managed its own farm with nearly two hundred cows and five hundred goats.

The hospital never drew a dollar from the Confederate government, but relied solely upon money received from commutation of rations. The hospital canal boat navigated from Lynchburg to Lexington, bartering cotton, yarn, shoes, and the like for the provisions it needed.

Before the war ended, Chimborazo will have treated seventy-six thousand patients. About seventeen thousand were wounded soldiers. On occasion, almost four thousand men were being treated at one time. Most of the patients were sick rather than wounded. Those who were wounded had been injured several days earlier and already received emergency treatment. Soon thereafter, they were transported to Chimborazo by railroad or ambulance. The percentage of deaths for the wounded soldiers was about 9 percent. Considering the state of medical practice in 1861, a great deal of credit must be given to the hospital's doctors and staff.

"Don't get me wrong. I'm as loyal a Confederate patriot as they come, but there's something that troubles my mind for a few months now," the driver stated.

"What's that?" Lomas asked.

"Are we going to win this here war?"

Lomas turned to Jack for an honest answer since that was a subject he always avoided whenever possible.

"Nobody can win this war. When you got families fighting against their neighbors and one brother fighting against the other, there's never any real winner. Before it's over, we all end up losing," Jack explained. That wasn't exactly the answer the teamster wanted to hear, resulting in a very quiet ride the rest of the way.

They reached Richmond and their dropping-off location just as the sun was dipping below the horizon. From that point until it gets dark is called twilight time, or the blue hour, from the French *l'heure bleue*. There would still be enough ambient light for both men to reach their destination. Lomas accompanied Jack to the steps of the Robertson Hospital and nearby home of Sally Tompkins. The walk from there to the Eagle Inn and Tavern was a piece of cake for a rebel infantryman.

"Good luck with Isabella," Jack volunteered as the pair parted company.

"I'm certain I will be married before I see you next," Lomas resolved.

"Then Grazyna and I will meet you Saturday night at the Eagle Inn to celebrate."

"It's a date," Lomas snapped as he quickened his step and proceeded to his purpose and ultimate destiny.

Jack stood in front of Sally's house for a minute or two, seemingly to muster courage before mounting the steps. This would mark the first time he openly declared his troth in the presence of Maj. Sally Tompkins. Even though Grazyna assured him that Sally was sympathetic toward them both, he couldn't help the surprising twinge of guilt. His pause was no more than that, and dismissing the momentary pang, he took the steps and presented himself with three audible raps of the black iron knocker.

Having spent the day in anticipation of Jack's arrival, Grazyna quickly opened the door and threw her arms around her smiling beloved, uttering words of endearment and bestowing passionate kisses. Jack responded in like manner, and though locked in their mutual embrace, they somehow progressed into the foyer.

Grazyna was now six months along, and no effort was made to conceal her pregnancy. Jack felt her condition as he held her close, and his love for her was deepened with the mere thought of her bearing his child. Grazyna took hold of Jack's hand and led him into the anteroom, pulling toward a two-person settee. They sat down together. Grazyna couldn't control her happiness being revealed by a glistening smile and the pupils of her beautiful eyes completely dilated. The lovers' trance ended when Sally Tompkins entered the room carrying a tray holding cups of hot coffee and sandwiches. Jack rose from the settee as she placed them on a side table and said, "Welcome to our home, Jack." It was a clumsy moment for the mountain man. He was confused about the proper way to acknowledge her greeting; should he salute or shake hands or give a big hug. Thankfully, the question was answered when Sally gave him a hug and peck on his cheek.

"How was your trip coming over?" Sally asked.

"It took quite a bit longer this time. We hitched a ride on the ironworks wagon, and it was a six-mule load. The driver made several stops to rest the team, and due to the weight, he drove them a lot slower. Other than that, things went pretty well," Jack replied.

"You indicated *we*. Who else accompanied you?"

"Another fellow from my regiment named Lomas Chandler. I believe you have met him before."

"Is he the taller man with light color hair?"

"No, ma'am, that would be Abel Strawn. This fellow is kind of short with dark hair."

"I know him. He's the little Irishman with a devilish look in his eye."

"He's really not a bad sort, once you get to know him. I owe him a debt of gratitude for helping me get a pass to visit Grazyna. He's staying over at the Eagle Inn and Tavern," Jack retorted.

Turning to Grazyna, Sally said, "When Jack finishes his snack, have him take his duffel bag upstairs to your room. I'm going to my office and finish up on some hospital business before I turn in. Remember, breakfast is at eight o'clock, sharp."

After Sally left the room, Grazyna said to Jack, "Sally gave me time off while you are here. If you want to sleep in, it's all right. I can make you breakfast later."

"I think it would be better if we don't disappoint her. I can be ready for breakfast."

With a sly smile, Grazyna replied, "Time will tell."

Meanwhile, at the Eagle Inn and Tavern, Lomas received a similar greeting. Isabella had found a priest willing to marry them, forgoing the church's wedding banns due to the conditions brought about by the war. However, only with a promise of a traditional ceremony once the war ended and the country again at peace. The fact Lomas was born and baptized into a Catholic family was immeasurably helpful in winning the priest's consent. Things seemed to be moving along all by themselves. It was as if a compelling force was leading the young Irishman, and he traveled with it in a daze. Strangely, a confirmed bachelor, Lomas never gave one thought to resist. Isabella was possibly the most erogenous woman he had ever met, but that alone would not bring him to this point in his life, or would it? Perhaps, Lomas was about to have second thoughts, the condition nearly all men face a few moments before giving up their treasured freedom and pledging the marital oath.

Nevertheless, the Irish sharpshooter's bachelorhood could now be measured in hours as he took a chair at an unoccupied table and watched the activities going on around him. Isabella had brought him a hot dinner plate of roast beef and gravy, and the aroma alone set his juices flowing. He wolfed it down so fast that Isabella took notice and asked if he needed another. Lomas declined and held up his empty beer mug. It was replaced with a full one on her next trip around.

As the evening wore on, he noticed a card game taking place at a table in the far corner. The players were animated and in good spirit. They weren't playing for coins. There was plenty of folding money in the current pot, and nobody was dropping out. Under normal circumstances Lomas would have finagled a way into the game, but today he kept his powder dry and only watched.

Around midnight, the crowd thinned out and the card game was coming to an end. Isabella sat down at Lomas's table, reached for his hand, and whispered, "Il mio tesoro, l'amo." She had said it before, and he knew it meant that she loved him. At the moment, he was concerned about a place to sleep tonight and acknowledge it to his bride-to-be.

"Darling, you will sleep here at the inn. I have made the arrangements for the whole weekend."

"How long will it be before we can go up?" he asked.

"Oh, I cannot go up with you, dear. Tomorrow we will be married, and then I will sleep with you the rest of our lives."

Lomas thought for a while and asked, "How much is the room going to cost for the entire weekend? I don't have much money."

And with a grin, Isabella said, "Silly goose, it isn't going to cost us anything. My family owns the Eagle Inn and Tavern."

The following morning, at the St. Peter's Church on Grace Street, Father Anthony Sandino performed the rite of marriage. It marked the first time Lomas had been in church since he was a child. Due to the unusual circumstances, the ceremony was performed in a small chapel and outside of mass. Isabella's parents stood up for them, and the couple declared their consent to be married. The wedding rings, provided by Isabella, were blessed and then placed on each other's fingers by the couple. At the conclusion of the ceremony, Father Sandino gave a nuptial blessing. Then all in attendance recited the Lord's Prayer. At the end, he asked a solemn blessing over Isabella and Lomas and dismissed the assemblage with "Thanks be to God."

Isabella was elated. Her parents, however, were less so because the rite was performed without a mass. Their daughter consoled them by assuring a proper wedding once the war was over. For his part, Lomas was at sea with his thoughts. Yesterday, he was riding in a six-mule wagon footloose and fancy free. In less than twenty-four hours, he now was a married man. Who would have thought it?

* * *

Jack did not disappoint Sally Tompkins the next morning at breakfast. Both he and Grazyna were sitting at the table fifteen minutes early. Sally was pleased by the mountain man keeping his word, and his stock increased in her opinion of him. It might have increased even more had she been aware of Grazyna's effort to incapacitate him. She kept him wide awake most of the night with coquetry and dalliance and, in spite of her condition, found several approaches to express the *l'art d'amour qui fait.*

"I trust you had a good night sleep," Sally said drily. "I usually sleep like a log when I'm tired from a hard day at the hospital. I imagine the trip over here pretty much wore you out. It had to be boring, and sometimes, monotony can tire us most of all. I thought I heard someone go the toilet a couple of times during the night, and it worried me that Grazyna might be feeling ill."

"I must have slept through that," Jack stated and turned to Grazyna, saying,

"Were you having problems last night, dear?"

"Not really. I did have to pee a couple of times though," she replied as her ears began to redden at the tips.

"I learned from Dr. Shaw that the Yankees have vandalized the railroads to the extent we can't get food to General Lee's army. Have you noticed a shortage?"

"Not that much. We never do get enough beef meat, and bread and potatoes seem to be about the same. We get salt pork and bacon just about every day."

Sally had finished her breakfast and brought her dishes to the sink. The cooking utensils were washed and put away once they were initially used. Before she attempted to wash her plate, Grazyna interrupted, "Sally, you've done enough, I'll take care of the dishes when Jack is finished eating. We're just going to hang around here today. So I can start supper and have it ready when you get home."

"That would be nice. Maybe Jack can take a look at our screen door. It's hanging kind of loose," Sally suggested on her way out.

Grazyna clasped her cheek with her left hand, placing her elbow on the table, and seductively asked, "Do you want to go back to bed?"

Chapter Twenty-Six

By a continuing process of inflation, government can confiscate, secretly and unobserved, an important part of the wealth of their citizens.

—John Maynard Keynes, English economist, journalist, and financier

With Confederate money losing value almost on a daily basis, Hyrum was concerned for several reasons. Primarily, each time it lost value, the price of everyday commodities increased. The price of beef, potatoes, flour, and poultry had tripled, and all were in short supply. In Statesville, there was a shortage of the Confederate currency itself, and postage stamps were being used as legal tender. Most worrisome of all, however, was the possibility of losing the war. In that event, Confederate money would be worthless. Rumors were flourishing about the subjugation of private property throughout the South. Southern landowners lacked specie since their capital was mainly made up of land and Negroes. The government took private property for public use to pay for taxes and other debt.

If there was a benefit to the Union occupation, it was in this area. Private land, for the most part, was protected. The subject was raised during Hyrum's most recent visit to see his daughter and grandchildren.

"I think it is of the upmost importance to hedge against the worst things that can happen. At the moment, your entire savings is in Confederate money at the Statesville bank. You need to devise a plan in order to convert that to Federal greenbacks. Whenever the Union soldiers are in town, they pay with that money, and shopkeepers prefer it to Confederate paper," the father advised.

"How can we do that?" asked Minnie.

"Well, you can start by withdrawing money from the bank to pay for whatever you purchase in town. And only take greenbacks for whatever you sell from the farm."

"Union soldiers are always stopping by to purchase eggs and an occasional chicken," Abigail mentioned.

"And how do they pay for them?"

"They have been using Confederate money because I told them that was the only kind I will take."

"You can change that right now," Hyrum suggested. "How is your garden coming along? You might sell them any excess you have. If it were up to me, I'd plant some corn in that field next to the barn and consider it a cash crop. Your old dad is ready to help anytime other than Sunday."

"I don't think you will need to, Dad, I'll discuss it with Yalata and his wife. They're due to visit us anytime now. Jack's friend is very resourceful and may have more ideas to make money."

After supper, the entire family took a stroll across the road and along the creek. It was a pleasant time of day and a walk was fitting before it became too dark. Recent rains caused the water to be high and rapidly flowing. For the most part, they walked in silence. The only utterance came from the children as Sarah Jane skipped ahead and beckoned her little brother to catch up. Abigail was lost in thoughts of Jack, and the life they had lived thus far. Her sense of yearning grew with each step to the point she had to speak in order to terminate the melancholy mood.

"Watch out for your brother, Sarah Jane. Don't let him go near the water," she shouted. Shortly thereafter, the group turned around and slowly headed back toward the house. Abigail tried to talk her father into spending the night, only to hear he had church commitments for the evening and needed to return to town.

When deep purple surrounded the cabin, Abigail lit an oil lamp and sat at the dining table with Minnie Rosenthal in Rubenesque shadows and glow. They were brainstorming for ways to earn greenbacks. An hour later, they hadn't come up with anything more than when Hyrum was there and decided to give up the task.

Minnie recalled, "If Jacob was still alive, he could have thought of lots of ways to make money. When it came to turning a dollar, he was an expert. When we first bought the farm, it took all the money we had. That year the crops were poor, and Jacob chopped wood and hauled it into town to sell. People thought he was a real mensch and paid top dollar,"

"Our problem is that we are women. People think the things women make for trade are somehow worth a lot less than what men offer for sale. Alas, we're stuck with the image of being the gentler sex and caught in its purview. I think our last hope will rest on whatever Yalata has to offer," added Abigail.

Minnie frowned and said, "Just remember, Yalata is an Indian and will trade the whole farm for a string of glass beads."

"Oh, Minnie, how you talk. Things are a lot different today. It's 1863, and the Indians know the value of a dollar the same as anyone else," Abigail insisted.

Two days later, Yalata and Ailana made their routine visit to the farm. They arrived with gifts of food and a large red hen and rooster. The poultry was a gift from Ailana who stated, "The large red hen lays the biggest eggs you'll ever see. Keep her with the rooster, and soon you will have lots of baby chicks."

"Thank you, Ailana, I'm so glad to see you both. There's something I need your advice about." Abigail used the word *both* as a sign of respect for the Choctaw princess. What she really needed was Yalata's input.

"I must yield to my husband on serious or troubling matters as is our tradition. I will, however, listen to what you have to say," Ailana answered exactly the way Abigail had expected. Now that both women are satisfied with the formalities, they waited for Yalata to speak. Minnie had served steaming cups of hot coffee and Yalata blew the steam from the top of his, took a small careful sip, and asked, "What is the problem that seems to vex you?"

"It has to do with something my father said. He believes we need to protect ourselves in the event the South loses the war. If that happens, Confederate money will be worthless, and the only legal currency will be Federal greenbacks or postage stamps. He believes we should convert Confederate notes to greenbacks. Minnie and I can exchange our bank savings when be purchase items in town and take only stamps as change, but it won't amount to very much. We need to come up with an idea to make Federal money, and as yet, we are at a loss. I hoped you could help by offering suggestions."

"First, you must consider who has greenbacks to trade. I can only think of the Union soldiers with that type of currency. You have what they need most of all. You have horses and cattle. They would pay handsomely for either one."

"I could pay you half of the profit," Abigail offered.

"I will receive nothing. The livestock is yours in my safekeeping until your husband returns from the war," Yalata stated.

"But you are entitled to something."

"That will be determined in horses and cattle once Jack Leffingwell returns."

Abigail, clinging to her secret, said, "What if Jack doesn't return."

"Then I will deal with you in horses and cattle," he replied without expression. "Your husband's herd of livestock has grown since he went to war. The mare you call Miracle came from his herd of horses. His black stallion is an excellent breeder, and foals drop each spring. The same is true for the cattle. I suggest you tell the bluecoat soldiers you can provide a single head of beef to be traded for greenback dollars. Ask for half payment ahead of time and balance in one week. I will deliver the animal to you before they return."

Yalata had provided a solution to Abigail's enigmatic Confederate money conundrum. But as it so often happens, one solution creates another problem. She now had to convince herself that selling to the occupiers was not being unpatriotic to the Southern cause. This she must discuss with her father.

* * *

Before opening the door to the Eagle Inn and Tavern, Jack made certain that Grazyna was comfortable being there. After she declared her approval, he turned the brass knob and opened a different world to the young expectant mother. A gay din first met her ears followed by laughter and joyful shouting. The bridal party of Lomas and Isabella was well underway. Amid the shouts of *un'altra bevanda alla sposa e governa* and *è qui a una vita lunga e molti bambini*, Jack spotted the newlyweds at a large table with Lomas waving to catch their eye.

"Nice quiet little affair you have here," Jack said, laughing.

"Yeah, they keep shouting, 'Another drink to the bride and groom' and 'Here's to a long life and many children.'"

"And no doubt you are keeping up with them."

"I tried to partner, but I've met my match." Rising to his feet, he said, "Let me introduce my bride, this is Isabella Manfredi . . . er, I guess it's Chandler now."

Jack remained standing after positioning the chair for Grazyna and returned, "The other beautiful lady at this table is Grazyna McCracken, soon-to-be Leffingwell, and I am Jack Leffingwell, her fiancé." Isabella reached across the table to hold Grazyna's hand and sincerely said, "I am so happy to meet you both. Welcome to our wedding party."

While the two women were engaged in a conversation about pregnancy and childbirth, Lomas and Jack excused themselves and strode to the bar for another pitcher of beer. Along the way, Lomas remarked, "You're never going to believe this. Isabella's father owns the Eagle Inn and Tavern. This is a dream come true, and the girl is beautiful. Perhaps second to Grazyna. But there's a lot more of her, if you know what I mean."

"I couldn't help knowing what you mean, looking from the waist up."

"I think I'm in heaven," confirmed the Irish friend.

"Well, don't get too carried away. We have to meet the wagon driver day after tomorrow."

"Don't worry about me. I'll be picking you up at eight o'clock sharp," Lomas reassured. "We don't have to get up in the morning, so let's give it hell tonight."

"I'd love to, only I have to think of Grazyna's condition. We'll stay for another hour and make our excuses. I want to get her home as early as possible."

"I understand. How far along is she?"

"She's due the end of September or early October."

"If Isabella gets her way, she will get pregnant this weekend," Lomas lamented with a smile.

"Well, all I can say is, you know the only way to stop that from happening."

"You gotta be kidding me. You said yourself that you looked above the waist," chimed Lomas as they returned to the table.

The following day, Grazyna felt fine and Jack had a slight headache. No doubt his migraine was due to the one drinking contest Lomas was able to goad him into participating. Today, being present at Sally's eight o'clock breakfast table was an immense task; nevertheless, he made it.

"You two got back a lot earlier than I expected. How was the wedding party? From what I've been told, there's a lot of drinking at Italian weddings."

"Jack would only let me drink one glass of red wine. He's like a mother hen when it comes to the baby." Grazyna smiled. "He drank a little more though."

"That's why you have that headache," Sally said to Jack. "It's a wonder you got her home in one piece."

"Don't worry, Sally, I've drank a lot more than last night and managed to find my bed all by myself," Jack assured.

"Just the same, I'm against drinking all together. It's the devil's brew, and nothing good ever comes from it." Next to nursing, temperance was her second love and she never missed an opportunity to speak out about it.

Jack said, "Remember, Sally, the Apostle Paul wrote Timothy saying, 'Drink no longer water, but use a little wine for thy stomach's sake and thine often infirmities' [1 Timothy 5:23]."

Sally retorted, "First, he was talking to Timothy, not the people today. Apparently, the water in the area was unfit to drink. Wine for thy stomach's sake refers to using it as medicine. We stop taking medicine once the misery passes. If you want to quote the Bible, read Proverbs 23:29-35:

> *Who hath woe? Who hath sorrow? Who hath contentions? Who hath babbling? Who hath wounds without cause? Who hath redness of eyes?*
>
> *They that tarry long at the wine; they that go to seek mixed wine.*
>
> *Look not thou upon the wine when it is red, when it giveth his colour in the cup, when it moveth itself aright.*
>
> *At the last it biteth like a serpent, and stingeth like an adder.*
>
> *Thine eyes shall behold strange women, and thine heart shall utter perverse things.*

> *Yea, thou shalt be as he that lieth down in the midst of the sea, or as he that lieth upon the top of a mast.*
>
> *They have stricken me, shalt thou say, and I was not sick; they have beaten me, and I felt it not: when shall I awake? I will yet seek it again.*

With a sniff, Sally was out the door smiling, and then she gave a prayer to be forgiven for her pride.

"You can't quote the Bible in front of Sally. I think she knows it by heart," Grazyna sighed.

"You got to admit, she's as honest as the day is long. When it comes right down to it, you can't beat a good Christian upbringing," Jack asserted.

"She's a godsend with me being pregnant. I don't know what we would do without her. She watches over me like a mother hen and is as anxious about the baby as I am."

"Not to change the subject, but what do you think of Lomas's new bride?"

"She's very nice. I worry about her being married to somebody like Lomas Chandler. I see him just like a bumble bee skipping from flower to flower."

"Like a bumble bee, huh? I think he's found the perfect woman. And to top it off, she owns the Eagle Inn and Tavern. Lomas will never do anything to mess that up. He's living in the Garden of Eden," Jack affirmed.

As Grazyna's delivery time drew near, the beloved couple never spoke about the war and possible danger to Jack. Although Grazyna had sleepless nights fearing the worst, she did her best to dismiss tenebrous thoughts. Jack, on the other hand, felt certain he would escape the war unscathed and spent idle time planning their future. I'm always reminded that my highest expectations and worst fears never materialize, it's always something in between.

On the morning of departure, Isabella accompanied Lomas to meet Jack Leffingwell. She and Grazyna had said their personal farewells earlier and now walked with them to meet the ironworks wagon. For lovers, parting brings such sorrow and torment. Hope for the next meeting resides deep within until the time for reunion draws near. The pang of absence now occupied the two tender female hearts as the image of their departed dear one gradually disappeared into the horizon.

* * *

Once back in the Confederate camp, Lomas was the benefactor of back slaps and well-wishes. He also received good-natured jest about the wedding and how it came about. Primarily referring to and using the word *shotgun*. Lomas, still walking on air, took it all in stride. Abel Strawn brought them up to date on the latest camp scuttlebutt, and Melvin Kaufman couldn't wait to hear Lomas tell the story of everything that happened. That night, Abel's suspicions were confirmed when the Fredericksburg base camp was put on alert for immediate readiness to move.

After the death of Stonewall Jackson, Lee had reorganized the Army of Northern Virginia from two large corps into three smaller units. The First Corps was placed under the command of James Longstreet, the Second Corps under James Ewell, and Third Corps under A. P. Hill (Ambrose Powell Hill). The latter two assignments would give Lee pause later on, and he would sorely long for General Jackson.

Some say Gen. Robert E. Lee was riding high in a state of euphoria. If so, it was for a good reason. The Union had suffered bitter defeats, from McClellan's failure with his Peninsula Campaign, Pope's setback at the Second Battle of Bull Run, Burnside's disaster at Fredericksburg, and Hooker's overthrow at Chancellorsville. It appeared as though Lincoln changes generals with every defeat, and now, those in the North were calling for a similar fate for Hooker. Reluctantly, Lincoln resisted another change and decided to stick with Hooker one more time.

Without the usual pomp, Lee's army quietly evacuated the Fredericksburg camp and began a move west into the valley of Virginia. General Ewell's Second Corps led the way with Longstreet and A. P. Hill to follow. At this point, the destination was still remaining a secret to Jack Leffingwell and the sharpshooters. Rumors abound.

"We're heading the wrong way to be going to Pennsylvania," Abel conjectured.

"We'll know for sure if we turn north in a couple of days. It's got to be big because we're packed for battle," Jack replied. The Seventh Tennessee regiment infantrymen were toting nearly fifty pounds of gear counting their rifle. In addition to the musket, they carried double rounds of ammunition, blankets, clothing, a three-day allotment of food, and personal items. At first, they began marching in regular military order four abreast, but after a short while under the hot sun, they began to break down and disperse all over the road. Under such conditions and carrying heavy loads, the troops fatigued quickly and required several stops of an hour or more to rest, replenish loss fluids, and await stragglers who fell off along the way.

That night they camped in the open. Blankets were drawn from their rucksacks and spread out around a crackling fire. Firewood was plentiful, and looking down from a higher elevation, the area seemed to twinkle with fairy lights of red, orange, yellow, and white. The sharpshooters formed a partial arc of the soldiers circle, and Lomas had raked embers to the edge of the flickering flames, on which was placed the coffeepot. The steam and hiss emanating from the spout was music to their ears. Tonight, the fare would be cornbread in bacon grease, coffee, and as usual, a little extra provided by the newlywed Irishman. Soldiers at each fire gathering placed their weapons in a stand of arms which included their rifle and ammunition belts. Because of the costly and unique long-distance models, the marksmen slept with their rifles at their side. The regiment was up before the sparrows shook their feathers, and Melvin's frying pan stowed safely in his backpack. This morning, coffee, johnnycakes, and goober peas would make up breakfast.

"Where's Lomas?" Melvin asked while rolling his blanket.

"Out looking for the commissary wagon I suspect," replied Abel. "He mentioned he was running low on canned meat and fruit."

"Can a soldier just go get that stuff?"

"Not without a signed requisition order," said Abel

"I don't think Lomas has one," Melvin uttered.

"Don't bet on it," Jack interjected.

By the time the regiment was again on the march, Lomas had returned with a heavier rucksack than he carried the day before. Good weather was holding up for at least another day, and the Seventh regiment met up with General Ewell's corps at the Culpeper Court House before dusk. That evening, the cooking fires in the common area were doubled. Melvin Kaufman had extracted his skillet, and the sharpshooter's supper, along with steaming hot coffee, included tinned beef and canned peaches. They remained in camp for a few days while Generals Ewell and Hill reviewed maps and reported conditions and progress. Then, the two divisions separated again with Ewell continuing in a northwestern direction and A. P. Hill's corps marching due north, thus answering any questions as to where the final destination lay.

The northward march would once again necessitate crossing the Rappahannock River, a task Hill's corps faced at the beginning of the expedition. Culpeper County, Virginia, has several shallow fords from which a river crossing can be completed and, if the river is at low levels, done so without the need for a major pontoon bridge. The Blue Ridge Mountains, always a formidable challenge, lay ahead and must be crossed to reach the Shenandoah Valley. According to General Hill's maps, this was to be conducted via Ashby's Gap, a route often used by Stonewall Jackson when he conducted the Shenandoah campaigns. General Hill rested his division east of the Shenandoah River to await the arrival of Maj. Gen. J. E. B. Stuart's cavalry. Lee's plan called for Jeb Stuart to secure and hold the gap to prevent elements of General Hooker's Union army from interfering with the Confederate march toward Pennsylvania.

Unbeknown to Hill, Gen. Jeb Stuart had problems of his own. Aware of Lee's northern movement, Union general Hooker believed J. E. B. Stuart's cavalry was planning to raid the Northern army's supply lines and ordered his cavalry commander, Maj. Gen. Alfred Pleasonton, to disperse and destroy the rebel fighting horsemen. Unknown to Stuart, the Federals crossed the Rappahannock River in dense fog, pushed aside the Confederate pickets at Beverly's Ford, and surprised the drowsy Southern force. Upon hearing gunfire, the men in butternut attire snapped out of their sluggishness and responded in kind. Several Union charges were turned back, and before the day was over, Pleasonton called for a troop withdrawal. Although Stuart held his position, his superiority over the Yankee cavalry was now drawn into question. For the first time, the enemy matched the Confederates in skill and determination.

When Stuart reached Ashby's Gap, the weather had taken a turn for the worse. Storm clouds caused the sky to hide its most treasured possessions, the moon and stars. The wind had picked up, and rain came down in sheets. Soldiers scattered in all directions seeking shelter. Lomas Chandler was prepared for such events and produced two waterproof tarps under which the marksmen safely resided. At the glimpse of morning light, the rain had subsided, but the division faced the problem of fording the elevated waters of the Shenandoah River. While some attempted to wade across, the majority traveled over pontoon bridges built by the division engineers. It took most of the day for men and matériel to reach the other side and continue on the northern junket.

Ewell's division was ordered to attack the Union force at Winchester to clear the lower Valley of enemy opposition. The three-day battle (June 13-15) resulted in the defeat and rout of Union major general Robert Milroy's brigade, offering high hopes for the future success of Lee's Pennsylvania campaign. Soldiers in A. P. Hill's division could hear the battle, but their orders were to continue on the march.

And when they next made camp, they were joined by Gen. James Longstreet's First Corps. Moving up the Shenandoah Valley, Maj. Gen. J. E. B. Stuart's cavalry fought several skirmishes with his Federal counterpart, Maj. Gen. Alfred Pleasonton, in successful screening endeavors to keep the Union from learning the location of Lee's Army of Northern Virginia.

Continuing north, the Confederate army found farm crops plentiful and foraging unburdensome. Corn fields were in full tassel and fruit trees at early ripening stage. Many of the farms featured barns with colorful geometric decorations, painted in order to bring good luck and protection to its owner. These hex signs did nothing to stop the foraging of nearly thirty thousand rebel troops. Fortunately, for the farmers, they were troops on the march and soon to be gone.

Up to this point, General Lee and his cotton state compatriots had basically tramped according to the overall directive. Confronted with the axiom that, in the army, nothing ever goes to plan, Bobby Lee had managed to perplex Union general Hooker, who knew the Army of Northern Virginia was on the move, but couldn't find them. U.S. President Abraham Lincoln, concerned about protecting the capital at Washington and still skeptical of his general's ability, demanded Hooker stay between the city and the Army of Northern Virginia wherever it happened to be. This resulted in two armies, parallel to each other, and slowly moving northward. Lee, without his most capable commander, Stonewall Jackson, depended on Jeb Stuart's cavalry to keep track of the Union army's movement and developments. Fighting Joe Hooker's Army of the Potomac moved faster than Jeb Stuart expected, and it soon became lost to him. He found himself unable to give Lee the information he needed, resulting in both armies blind to each other's whereabouts. Upset, but undaunted, Lee continued to move his seventy-thousand-man machine steadily north.

Chapter Twenty-Seven

If your morals make you dreary, depend upon it they are wrong. I do not say "give them up," for they may be all you have; but conceal them like a vice, lest they should spoil the lives of better and simpler people.

—Robert Louis Stevenson

Abigail had discussed the morality of selling to the enemy for profit and greenbacks. Hyrum managed to dance around the principal issues to the point his daughter was still confused. She wanted a yes or no answer, but the subjects were too complicated for that. He focused on the main reason of the war in the first place: slavery. Southern Democrats viewed Negroes as chattel and believed their right to ownership was protected by the Constitution. After all, Thomas Jefferson took part in writing the Declaration of Independence with the statement that "all men were created equal" and, at the same time, owning hundreds of slaves. The argument that the South was fighting Yankee aggression was patent hypocrisy; it's being conducted to protect slave ownership.

"We Bible-loving Christians know that slavery in any form is wrong, according to the teaching of Jesus," Hyrum said.

"Yes, Father, but why doesn't the Bible speak out more about slavery being a sin?" asked Abigail.

While opening his Bible to 1 Timothy 1:8-10, Hyrum began to read aloud,

> *But we know that the law is good, if a man use it lawfully;*
>
> *Knowing this, that the law is not made for a righteous man, but for the lawless and disobedient, for the ungodly and for sinners, for unholy and profane, for murderers of fathers and murderers of mothers, for manslayers,*
>
> *For whoremongers, for them that defile themselves with mankind, for menstealers, for liars, for perjured persons, and if there be any other thing that is contrary to sound doctrine.*

Closing his Bible, the minister said, "I believe that covers it. I believe you can be loyal to your heritage and disavow slavery. Remember, daughter, it's more than likely the soldier who buys from you is also a devout Christian."

Returning home, Abigail had made up her mind to act in the best interest of her family even though the loyalty issue still gave some misgiving. She mentally flashed back to the day a young Union soldier stopped on the road outside her gate to watch her pumping water at her well. She had finished giving a ladle to Sarah Jane and was in the process of holding it for Little Jack when she noticed him. She could tell he was dusty, hot, tired, and most of all, thirsty. He didn't look to be a day over sixteen years old, and her feminine instincts moved her to ask, "Are you thirsty, young man?"

"Yes, ma'am, terribly so," he replied.

"Well, I think the farm can spare a ladle of water. Come in, and I'll pump one for you."

"I can't come inside your fence, ma'am, General Sherman's orders."

Abigail realized that the order had to be because of the incident a year ago when the Union lieutenant was killed by a Choctaw arrow. It explains why the Yankee soldiers had never bothered them since. Holding up a dripping ladle full, she asserted, "I'm not going to carry this over to you, so if you want a drink, just tie up your horse and walk over here."

The young soldier refused to budge and said, "I'm sorry, ma'am, but nobody's going to defy the general's order, least of all me."

Abigail dropped the ladle into the bucket and carried the water to her fence with the children in tow. The Northern youngster drank three ladles full and thanked her between each one. At that point, the chickens began to make a fuss by high-pitched squawking. Looking back toward the barn, Abigail said, "There must be a snake around the henhouse."

"Seems like every time I pass by, I can hear the hens cackling and all I can think about is fresh eggs. I can't remember the last time I ate real eggs. Back home, Mom used to have them nearly every morning. I'd be forever obliged if I could buy some from you, ma'am," asked the young bluecoat.

From that day forward, Abigail sold eggs to the young soldier and did not give much thought to Southern loyalty. The transactions took place with buyer and seller on opposite sides of the fence, an ironic symbol of the times. In the past, she had insisted on Confederate money, and now, she asked for greenbacks. And Jack Leffingwell's wife would also make the first attempt to try to sell a beef cow.

Abigail was now on a mission. Last week she had learned that the Confederate Congress levied a tax in kind on farmers and families dependent on the land for subsistence. The new tax would take 10 percent of all agricultural products and livestock raised for slaughter. It was easy to see the injustice such a law would be for her and Minnie Rosenthal. Fortunately, no government agent would assess the farm due to Middle Tennessee being under Union occupation. Thinking forward, once the war was over, most of the reconstruction costs would necessitate a tremendous amount of money. Property owners would be taxed, and payment would require legal tender of which Confederate money won't qualify. She arrived home with her jaw set solid in determination.

That evening, the conversation between Abigail and Minnie Rosenthal focused on how much to charge for a beef cow. In Statesville, the cheapest beef prices had risen to $1 per pound; and calculated from that number, plus an erroneous guess as to the weight of imaginary beef cattle, the blind leading the blind came up with $60 a head. The wisdom of the most experienced tradesman, using exact numbers, would, in all likelihood, arrive at the same price. The old saw, ignorance is bliss, had hit the bull's eye, no pun intended. All that needed be done at this point was await the next visit from the young soldier. He appeared two days later.

"Good morning, ma'am," he greeted as he dismounted his horse and walked to the fence. Abigail was holding the handle of a small wicker basket with a layer of straw to protect the dozen eggs nestled on top. The young soldier exchanged its empty willow-made twin with a Federal greenback in place of the eggs.

"I've been meaning to ask you if there was an interest in purchasing a beef cow?" Abigail questioned with a slight quaver in her voice.

"That's as certain as the law of gravity," he replied. "How much will you be asking?"

"My lady friend and I were thinking $60, greenback dollars."

"That's a little too big for me to swallow, but let me talk it over with some of the guys in the unit. One of them is a cook at the post, and if we pool our money, we can handle it."

"I don't have cattle on the farm. I just know of someone who has one to sell. I'll need a day or two to tell them and for them to bring the beef over here. Let me know what you decide the next time you get eggs."

"We won't need to wait that long, ma'am. I already know what they'll say. I'll be back in two days with the money. There will be a couple more of us, so don't be frightened."

"All right then, you will find the animal staked in the field behind you. You can leave the money in that knothole in the fence post."

For the next two nights, Abigail lay in a sleepless bed. She pondered how in the world Yalata would get the message and what would happen if he didn't. He had assured her not to worry, but that was impossible. On the appointed day, both women peered through the window facing the road. It continued to fog up from their excited exhale; and they, in turn, constantly wiped it away with the flat of their hands. Finally, as the morning mist began to subside and the day lightened, they beheld the large beef cow staked at the edge of the field. Shortly after sunrise, the young cavalryman and three others cantered down the quiet road and threw another rope on the rust-and-white-colored beef. Confident the animal was secured, they immediately returned in the direction in which they arrived, but not before the young bluecoat leaned down at the fence post to deposit the agreed-upon sum.

Inside the house, two gleeful women, in each other's arms, bounced in a circle dance of happiness. When the riders were out of sight, Abigail ran to the fence post and returned with a roll of greenbacks secured by a rubber band. That morning breakfast was most enjoyable in spite of the uneasiness in their stomach. The children ate as though they were starved. Abigail and Minnie decided they weren't really that hungry and needed to lie down.

The following week, the young soldier appeared at the fence to buy eggs. The familiar routine of exchanging baskets was repeated once more.

Abigail thanked him and said, "You have been buying eggs for some time now, and I don't even know your name."

"My name is Landry Sinclair, ma'am, Corp. Landry Sinclair, but my friends just call me Lanny."

"How did that beef cow work out?"

"Real good, ma'am. When we brought that big beef back into camp, it caused quite a commotion. You see, our cattle pen has been empty for going on three weeks, and the only fresh meat we had was goats. I don't know if you ever ate kid meat, but it sure ain't the same as beef. Well, one of the fellows that came with me is a man named Joe Monk. Joe is a butcher by trade and one of the posts' cooks. He told us what to do when it came to butchering the cow. We got to it right away, and when we were finished, soldiers were lined up wanting to buy some meat. Joe suggested we sell half to them, and when it was all over, we collected $100. Not only was your beef cow delicious, but it paid for itself and earned us another $40 to boot. You could smell steak cooking all over the camp. That was a dream comes true."

"Do you think you might want another sometime?" Abigail asked. "I believe I can get one more."

"I definitely think we can use another. There were a lot of disappointed fellows the last time. As big as that beef cow was, there wasn't enough meat for everybody standing in line."

"Come back in two days. The beef will be where you found the first one, and it might even be a little bigger." She grinned.

At the end of the following week, the Leffingwell family visited the Statesville bank to purchase a safety strong box. Accordingly to Maryellen Riberty, many of the ladies in Statesville used these metal deposit containers to store their jewelry. Neither Abigail nor Minnie Rosenthal had an abundance of jewelry, but they did have $130 greenback; and when they left the bank, the money was securely placed inside one of the lockboxes with each woman holding a key.

The Union soldiers were having breakfast at their camp outside of Nashville when Corporal Sinclair was approached by Lieutenant Haggard.

"Are you the soldier with a horse to sell?" he asked.

"Not exactly, sir, I just know of one for sale."

"Who's selling it?"

"The lady I buy eggs from," Lanny replied.

"Is she the same person you got that beef from a while back?"

"Yes, sir, her name is Mrs. Abigail Leffingwell, and she has a farm about ten or twelve miles from here."

"I know that farm. That's where Lt. Jason Cartwright was killed. That farm is off-limits. What the hell are you doing there?"

"I've never been on the property, sir. My dealings are from the road."

"And she is the one with a horse for sale? Why should I pay for one when all I have to do is just take it?"

"There are lots of reasons, sir. She doesn't keep the horse on the farm, and nobody knows where it is. General Sherman's order won't let anyone go on her property, and she's been honest with her business dealings."

"Well, my mount was shot out from under me during the last skirmish. I had to put him away. The horse I'm on now isn't near as good, and I need to find one better. Do you think this woman has a better animal?"

"Yes, sir. She tells me it is young and spirited and carries his tail high," replied the younger soldier.

"How much does she want for it?"

"She told me $200 greenback."

"Too much," exclaimed the lieutenant. "Do you realize that's what the best saddle horse brings, and this one is a pig in a poke."

"You don't have to buy it sight unseen. It will be outside her fence line and, if you don't like it, we just ride away."

"What if I just take it?"

"Remember what happened to Lieutenant Cartwright?"

"I see what you mean. Tell her I'm interested," the lieutenant declared as he walked away.

When Lieutenant Haggard set eyes on the high-spirited gelding, it was love at first sight. The shiny black charger had both ears straight up and shook his head as if to say ride me. Standing almost sixteen hands high, with rippling muscles that shouted speed and endurance, the Union lieutenant handed Landry Sinclair the money and switched his saddle. On the way back to camp, it took a great deal of self-control not to challenge the young corporal to a race.

Before the week was out, Abigail had $330 Federal greenback in the safe deposit box. This was more money either she or Minnie Rosenthal had ever seen at one time. It also marked the end of her business venture with the enemy since Corporal Sinclair and his troop were ordered to join Union forces in Alabama.

Chapter Twenty-Eight

If I had eight hours to chop down a tree, I'd spend six sharpening my axe.

—Abraham Lincoln

By mid-June, all three corps of Lee's Army of Northern Virginia came together outside Hagerstown, Maryland, forming an expansive camp of seventy-five thousand soldiers, nearly two thousand wagons, and over twenty thousand horses, mules, and other livestock. The view from above was like a sprawling city made up of campfires and pup tents. A chief goal of the campaign was for the Confederate army to accumulate food and supplies outside of Virginia with minimal negative impact on civilians. An army of this size would consume five hundred tons of food and other supplies daily. The replacement for food, horses, and the rest was not seized outright. However, disgruntled farmers and merchants were maddened when reimbursed with Confederate money. General Lee felt disappointment by the attitude of the populace in Maryland, a sister slave state. Apparently, the principled military leader had expected a more generous contribution to the cause. Americans, no matter what their bent may be, have inherent independence and resent anyone willfully taking their possessions, especially with payment in foreign currency. Maryland, a slave state, voted not to secede from the Union and resented Federal troops passing through its sovereign territory in order to reach the national capital at Washington, D.C. Having contributed troops to both the Union and the Confederacy forced Lincoln to arrest and imprison outspoken secessionists, including about one-third of the state's general assembly. Yet very little deference was given the Southern army of Gen. Robert E. Lee, compounding the paradox.

Even though on the march, the arrangement of tents was set up according to standard military practice. Laid out in company streets, perpendicular to the regimental colors, they lined on either side with openings facing outward, about ten feet across from their neighbor. There were no large fires for an army in the field, but hundreds of smaller ones. The marksmen shared a cooking fire with the occupants of a tent beside them, resulting in no more than eight men at the fire any one time. Lomas Chandler produced a colorful banner to hang above the entry flap, confusing officers as to its purpose. It did, nevertheless, relieve the sharpshooters of any latrine duty. Free time was consumed with writing letters, touring the area to find freshwater and, for Lomas Chandler, hunting the nearest poker game. Since the rebel soldiers hadn't been paid for the last two months, a strange assortment of articles make up larger poker pots. Rings and watches didn't make Lomas unhappy. In fact, he'd rather win tangible items than Confederate paper money. A good ring could always be used for specie in remote territories. Besides, the crafty Irishman also feared the value of Confederate money in the event the wrong side would win the war.

Jack Leffingwell wrote two letters. The first to Abigail, reminding her of a decision he requested in the earlier correspondence, and the second to Grazyna, keeping her apprised of his whereabouts and activity.

June 21, 1863
My Darling Grazyna,

There hasn't been a day go by that I haven't thought about you and our child-to-be. You are in my dreams every night. We've been on the march since returning from my visit. It's pretty much decided that General Lee has us heading for Pennsylvania. Thus far, we haven't seen any action, but heard plenty of it around us. They split us up into three corps, and now we've come together here, close to the Pennsylvania state line. It looks like we'll stay here for a couple of days and then Katy bar the door.

Don't worry, sweetheart, the Lord is watching over us. I've never been more confident of anything in my life more than that. You just need to take care of yourself and the baby. I have a feeling this old war will be over soon. And when it is, we will find a place to spend the rest of our lives, where I will dedicate mine to making you happy.

In the meantime, I have written to Abigail again asking for a divorce, just in case she didn't receive the first letter. No matter, if she refuses, we will ignore the world and live our lives for each other and the baby. This is a big country and getting bigger, especially out West. No one will know us. We can get married when we find the right place. I promise you one thing, my love, you will have a wedding ring on your precious finger before it's over. I'm going to close now to hit the hay and dream about the most wonderful woman in the world, a beautiful girl with a blue dot on her behind.

With all my love forever,
Jack

* * *

The word around the camp was that General Ewell's Second Corps had pulled out and, along with Gen. Albert G. Jenkins's cavalry brigade, continued north into the Keystone State. Actually, Jenkins cavalry acted as a screen for Ewell's marching army. He led his men through the Cumberland Valley into Pennsylvania and captured Chambersburg, burning down railroad structures and bridges before accompanying Ewell's column to Carlisle.

Union general Hooker was still at sea when it came to figuring out the crafty Robert E. Lee's intentions. He was sure of one thing. He knew the Confederate capital at Richmond, Virginia, was left unprotected with Lee's army gone. It was a tempting prize waiting to be won and help repair a damaged reputation. President Lincoln, ever mindful of Hooker's recent activities, sternly reminded him that Lee's army was the true objective. His orders were to pursue and defeat Lee while staying between Lee and Washington, D.C., and Baltimore.

On June 24 and June 25 the other two corps of the Army of Northern Virginia returned to the march. General Longstreet headed due north to Chambersburg, then turned to the east, and advanced to Gettysburg. Gen. A. P. Hill's corps also initially preceded north then, they and Jack Leffingwell's sharpshooters, trudged toward the fateful battle yet to come.

Confederate general Ewell had pushed deeper into Pennsylvania while his cavalry division, under the command of Jubal Earley, rode over the Southern mountain range and attacked the borough of Gettysburg. After chasing off some newly raised Pennsylvania militia, they occupied the town overnight, yet found meager tribute. The soldiers burned several railroad cars and a covered bridge before calling it a day. The following morning, disappointed in the town's lack of supplies, Earley's horse soldiers destroyed additional rails and telegraph lines, then departed for York County where they observed, for the first time, many unusual churches (Lutheran and Mennonite), lush green pastures, neat rolls of baled hay, immaculate farm buildings, and heard a strange dialect spoken that few Johnny Rebs could understand: Pennsylvania Dutch. They did, however, understand the expression on the faces of those ordered to pay indemnities in lieu of supplies.

Up until now, Jeb Stuart's cavalry had been circumnavigating the Union army. Stuart, awaiting Lee's orders, also needed to erase the embarrassing stain on his reputation by his surprise and near defeat at Brandy Station. When his instructions arrived, they directed him to guard the mountain passes with part of his force, while the Army of Northern Virginia was still south of the Potomac, and stipulated that he cross the river with the remainder of the army and screen the right flank of Ewell's Second Corps. Instead of taking a direct route north near the Blue Ridge Mountains, Stuart chose to reach Ewell's flank by moving his three best brigades between the Union army and Washington, traveling north through small towns on his way into Pennsylvania, hoping to impress General Lee by capturing large amounts of supplies and causing havoc near the enemy capital. Stuart certainly didn't sleep in a field of four-leaf clover. Because the Union army's movement had already been underway and his proposed route was blocked by columns of blue jacket infantry, forcing him to veer farther to the east than he originally planned. This unwelcome adjustment prevented him from linking up with Ewell as ordered and deprived Lee of the use of his prime cavalry force, the intelligence wing of the army, while advancing into unfamiliar enemy territory. After several skirmishes along the alternate route, Stuart finally reached General Lee at Gettysburg on July 2, the day after the battle began.

* * *

Prior to the Gettysburg attack, the cat was out of the bag, and Lee's offensive strategy had become clear. President Abraham Lincoln called for one hundred thousand militia volunteers from adjoining states to serve for six months and defend potential Pennsylvania targets.

The response was rather limited; however, it did cause a great deal of fear among the populace. Many sought refuge in cities farther north.

Union general-in-chief, Maj. Gen. Henry W. Halleck, planned a countermove in order to take advantage of the lightly defended Confederate capital of Richmond. He ordered two corps under Maj. Gen. John A. Dix to move on Richmond, but he made the mistake of not explicitly demanding Dix to attack the city. Instead, the confusing order called for Dix to threaten Richmond by seizing and destroying their railroad bridges and doing all the damage possible. While Dix was a respected politician, he was not an aggressive general, yet he still contemplated attacking Richmond directly. Due to both the vagueness of Halleck's orders and his own officers' concern about their limited strength, Dix finally decided to employ only threatening gestures. The net effect did force Lee to hold back some troops from the offensive in order to guard the capital.

The bickering between Hooker and Halleck persisted until the contention about defending the garrison at Harpers Ferry. General Hooker requested additional troops from the garrison and was refused by the War Department. In a state of pique, he asked to be relieved of the army command. His request was immediately accepted by President Lincoln, an, a surprised Gen. George Meade was ordered to replace him and assume command of the Army of the Potomac. In all likelihood, it was Lincoln's response to Hooker's embarrassing defeat at Chancellorsville and his weakness in reacting to Lee's second invasion north of the Potomac. President Lincoln was still looking for that fighting general and now placed his hopes on George Meade. Meade had previously stated he had no interest in the army command, nevertheless promptly accepted.

* * *

The lack of intelligence from Stuart's cavalry kept Lee in the dark as to how far the Union army had moved north. In the past, the Federals were less organized and slow to react. Assuming their progress to be sluggish, he was startled to learn that the enemy was nearby. Making matters worse, Lee's army was strung out and miles away from coming together. He immediately ordered his forces to concentrate around Cashtown, a village located at the base of South Mountain and about eight miles from Gettysburg. Many Confederate officers and staff, including Gen. A. P. Hill, took up residence in the Cashtown Inn.

The Battle of Gettysburg Begins

Gettysburg Combatants

South Army of Northern Virginia	North Army of the Potomac
Gen. Robert E. Lee	Henry W. Halleck (general-in-chief)
Gen. James Longstreet, First Corps	Gen. George Meade
Gen. Richard Stoddard Ewell, Second Corps	Gen. Joseph Hooker
Gen. Jubal Earley, Cavalry	Maj. Gen. John A. Dix
Gen. Ambrose Powell Hill, Jr., Third Corps Brig.	Gen. John Buford, Cavalry
Gen. Jeb Stuart, Cavalry	Gen. John F. Reynolds
Gen. Henry Heth	Maj. Gen. Lysander Cutler
Brig. Gen. J. Johnston Pettigrew	Gen. Daniel Sickles
Gen. Joseph Davis	Col. Andrew Harris
Gen. James J. Archer	
Gen. H. H. Walker	
Maj. Gen. George Pickett	

On June 30, a brigade of Hill's, led by Brig. Gen. J. Johnston Pettigrew, ventured toward Gettysburg and stumbled upon the Union cavalry, under Brig. Gen. John Buford, arriving south of town. Pettigrew hurried back to Cashtown to inform Generals Hill and Heth. Despite Lee's orders to avoid a broad engagement until the entire army was concentrated, A. P. Hill decided to mount a significant reconnaissance in force to determine the exact size and strength of the enemy legions. The following morning, July 1, two brigades of Heth's division advanced to Gettysburg. One of the brigades, General Archer's, included the Seventh Tennessee regiment; and shortly, Jack Leffingwell and the other marksmen, would be engaging in the battle.

General Buford now knew the rebel forces were at the gate and fell back to establish three defensive lines on ridges west of town. Since his cavalry division was small, compared to the Confederate infantry forces, his main purpose was to confront them by a delaying action. He planned to buy time until Union infantrymen could set up stronger defenses on the hills south of town.

As Heth's division moved forward, the two brigades met with light resistance from outposts of Union cavalry and deployed a standard military line for attacking. Eventually, his troops reached dismounted Yankee cavalry troops who raised determined resistance from behind fence posts with fire from their breechloading carbines. (Such weapons are used by cavalrymen because they are shorter and easier to maneuver than a rifle or musket, which is much longer and clumsy. Carbines use the same ammunition as their longer counterparts, but less accurate and powerful, due to the shorter barrel. Resembling the sawed-off shotgun, carbines are very effective when fighting in close quarters.) Buford's delaying tactics were proving successful; and the vanguard of the Union's first corps, under Gen. John F. Reynolds, soon arrived, adding more defensive troops.

The other rebel brigade, commanded by Confederate general Joseph R. Davis, gained temporary success against Maj. Gen. Lysander Cutler's blue jackets north of the road leading to town; but they were unable to maintain the advantage and were driven back with heavy losses. South of the pike, Archer's brigade with Jack Leffingwell and the Tennessee sharpshooters launched out through McPherson's Woods. The Southern men in gray were moving in double step. Their muskets shining from the reflection off the sun appeared as an undulating wave to those bracing behind cover. At first, the rebel yell was masked by an acoustical shadow, then as they drew nearer, exploded to a ringing pitch resounding in the ears of the defenders in blue garb. For most, it was the first time they heard the famous head-splitting yell. They certainly knew of it since Union soldiers had come to the agreement that it was very unnerving and frightening as well, though few would admit it in public. Jack Leffingwell and the sharpshooters took positions so they could concentrate on Union artillery units. Their accuracy proved effective in keeping cannon fire at a minimum. Any bluecoat on horseback automatically became prime targets. Union general John Reynolds fit the description and fell victim, while directing his troops and artillery placements east of the woods.

Archer's charge also met stiff resistance from the Yankee troops, who held their line. With the initial onslaught stopped and bolstered by rapidly arriving Union infantry soldiers, the Federals counterattacked, quickly pushing the Confederates back across Willoughby

Run, where the exhausted rebel general took cover in a thicket and was subsequently captured. Archer became the first general officer of the Army of Northern Virginia taken prisoner while under Lee's command. Now Heth's entire division was brought into action along with two divisions of Ewell's Second Corps. The additional manpower turned the tide, forcing the Federal positions to collapse, with their soldiers retreating to the high ground south of town.

At day's end, General Lee deemed it a Southern victory, with the enemy routed and in retreat. The facts tend to speak otherwise. It was true that once the Confederates had superior numbers, they were able to push the first line of Union defense to higher ground, but not without sustaining heavy losses. By the second day of battle, most of both armies were assembled and in position. General Lee's cup was never half-empty, it was always half-full. He honestly believed that valor can conquer overwhelming forces. It's usually only a matter of time before those tending the garden of fancy illusion are faced with the shock of reality. For Robert E. Lee, the most able general in the Civil War, it would happen in less than forty-eight hours.

Newly appointed Union commander George Meade had army strength of 93,921 men while CSA Gen. Robert E. Lee relied on 71,699 men ready to fight. Under most tactical warfare techniques, the aggressor needed two to three times that of a defender, especially if they were entrenched or held a higher elevation. Obviously, Lee's forces didn't fit that category; and without the required numbers, the task of dislodging determined resistance is beyond just being unlikely.

With General Archer captured, the brigade was consolidated under Gen. H. H. Walker's command and held in reserve during the second day. Although not in the battle, the Seventh Tennessee regiment had to remain alert and ready to resume at a moment's notice. Infantry soldiers cleaned their rifles and refilled ammunition packs. Some assisted those less able to make preparations in order to be ready for the next call to action. Jack Leffingwell, satisfied that his Whitworth rifle was clean and operational, leaned back against a tree and took a bite of hardtack. Abel Strawn walked over to him, leaned his weapon against a stump, and sat down beside him.

"Old Billy Yank has turned into a much better fighter," Abel said with a sigh.

"Seems that way," Jack replied. "I think some of them have Henry rifles." At that point, Melvin Kaufman joined them and questioned, "What's so good about Henry rifles?"

"It can fire off fifteen rounds without being reloaded. That makes it perfect for fighting at close range and a good weapon against an infantry attack. When that kind of rapid fire is against you, it makes one man seem like five."

"How come our boys don't have that rifle?" Melvin asked honestly.

"I don't think it is officially adopted for service by the Union army. The bluecoats using them probably bought the rifle with their own money. We've captured a few Henrys, but there isn't any good way to resupply the ammunition. Nevertheless, a couple of our units use 'em, especially the cavalry boys."

"Besides, they're not very accurate at long range," Abel interjected, and Jack nodded in agreement. "Say, where is Lomas Chandler?"

"They got him doing sentry duty," Melvin replied with a smile. "Word is that General Archer got himself captured."

"How'd that ever happen?"

"I guess when we pulled back in the woods, he rested for a while and a Yankee found him. That is what I heard anyway," Melvin replied.

"He always seemed a little peeked and frail to me. Like he had the fever or something. He was tired all the time," Abel stated. "Well, he's going to get a lot of rest now. But it sure as hell won't be a vacation."

"I heard officers go to a better prison camp."

"Maybe so, but it ain't like being free," Abel expressed.

At midnight, Lomas Chandler returned to the three-man group sitting around a small fire. No one commented on where he had been. From the look on Lomas's face, that subject was best left alone.

"Grab yourself a cup. The coffee's still piping hot," Jack said blandly.

"Thanks, don't mind if I do."

The sharpshooters sat in silence, looking up at a cloudless sky. Both armies have taken the evening off. Occasionally, a crack of rifle fire was heard, but they were unsure if it was from anger or accident. At the moment, the scene was surreal.

Sounds of human pain and misery came from the hospital tents as more of the wounded were brought in from the battlefield. The dead would not be buried this evening, as neither side could claim victory. That unsavory task must wait at least one more day. A similar scene was probably going on all through the South this night. At times, the rebel forces, fighting in Virginia, lost sight of the fact that in the West, major battles took place. Letters from home let the Seventh Tennessee regiment know of on-goings in their home state, but that was a small part of the war.

Early on, the Confederate forces won the majority of skirmishes. Their officers were better trained and more experienced. They also were fighting on their home turf, making it an advantage and disadvantage at the same time. The paradox gave the Southern soldiers an advantage in being familiar with the territory, which provided them the edge when it came to mountain terrain and location of freshwater. On the other hand, it resulted in a serious disadvantage, since the battles were being conducted in Southern towns, homes, and farms, many of which were burned and decimated.

The battles fought in Virginia, however, received the most attention in the newspapers. Most likely due to the fact they took place closer to the capitals at Richmond and Washington, D.C., and the two largest armies in the war were pitted against each other. Gen. Robert E. Lee was respected by the North and renowned in the South. President Abraham Lincoln believed if the Army of Northern Virginia was defeated, the war would be over; accordingly, his attention, as well as the general population, focused on Virginia.

"This sure is pretty land around here," Melvin stated. "All those tidy farms, green fields, and hardwood trees make a fellow kinda envious."

"They're pretty all right. I'll take my farm back in Tennessee over them anytime," Jack replied. A surprised expression reflected in the faces of the others. Abel, looking at Jack, said, "You said, your farm back in Tennessee. Do you remember it?"

"Not really, I don't know why I said that," Jack answered. Hearing that, the marksmen, who were holding their breath, exhaled and unrolled their blankets.

Chapter Twenty-Nine

Battles are won by slaughter and maneuver.
The greater the general, the more he contributes in maneuver, the less he demands in slaughter.

—Winston Churchill

The Second Day, July 2, 1863

Troops on both sides continued to arrive during the night and took their positions on the field. The Union line ran south of town and extended for nearly two miles. Men in blue jackets were atop elevations with such names as Cemetery Ridge, Culp's Hill, and Little Round Top. Lee's Confederate line, nearly five miles long, paralleled the Union delineation with men in butternut uniforms curving around the interior defenders. Lee's battle plan called for General Longstreet's First Corps to attack the Union left flank and move up the enemy line. The plan may have been a good one if the Gray Old Fox had recent information. Jeb Stuart was still absent, and the available intelligence proved to be faulty. As a result, Longstreet's forces failed to circle beyond the Federal left flank. Coming up short of the desired position, they ended up finding Gen. Daniel Sickles's Third Corps directly in their path. Dissatisfied with the position assigned him, Sickles had moved his troops to higher ground in order to make his artillery more effective. Without orders, and unbeknown to Lee, General Longstreet and the officers of the cotton state brigade were taken by surprise when they discovered Sickles's new position, which met the Confederates head on.

Nevertheless, Longstreet's division drove into Sickles's Third Corps with such force that they needed immediate reinforcements. Union general Meade, without hesitation, responded with twenty thousand more troops in blue. The rebel juggernaut pressed against positions with such names as the Wheatfield, Sherfy's Peach Orchard, and Plum Valley. They even reached the crest of Cemetery Hill, but could not hold their position in the face of counterattacks. One of which was that of the First Minnesota regiment that charged the rebels with bayonets. This attempt was almost suicidal as they lost 215 of their 262 participating, plus the regimental commander and all but three of his officers. It did, however, buy needed time for other forces to arrive and support the hill.

At the extreme left of the Union line stood an elevation named Little Round Top. The site was a vitally important position, as it gave cover for the Federal left flank. A brigade of four small regiments was able to resist repeated Confederate assaults; however, after continuous heavy fighting, those holding the hill were running out of ammunition. While the rebel infantry was forming again for another attack, the desperate soldiers atop the hummock made a fixed bayonet charge, surprising the stunned Confederates. Rebel soldiers panicked and scattered in retreat with many being captured. Had Little Round Top fallen into rebel hands, the defeat of the Union left flank would be guaranteed. And in all probability, the Battle of Gettysburg would end in the Gray Fox's victory column.

As darkness drew near, the Lincolnites managed to hold on to the major portion of Culp's Hill. Union army's interior lines were laid out so that commanders were able to shift troops quickly to critical areas. On East Cemetery Hill, Union colonel Andrew Harris, of the Second Brigade, First Division, lost half his forces but managed to hold on until Jubal Early and his cotton state cognates were forced to withdraw. Neither side was enthused about fighting at night. The second day ended with heavy losses and neither army with a victory.

During the evening, the irrational reality of bands playing music echoed across each campsite. The sounds of the banjo, fiddle, guitar, fife, and bugle came together, easing the stress of the hours before. This dreamlike expression was accompanied by the voices from a hundred different cities, singing such songs as "Battle Cry of Freedom" and "John Brown's Body" in the Union camp and "Dixie" and "Lorena" in the other. It was as though fighting was not enough and the battle had to be continued with song. Once the marital and patriotic ballads ended, a more sentimental attitude prevailed; and before the music stopped, both sides seemed to join in singing "Home! Sweet Home!" Men with iron will and hearts of stone had tears shining in their eyes when they repeated in unison,

'Mid pleasures and places though I may roam,
Be it ever so humble, there's no place like home;
A charm from the sky seems to hallow us there,
Which, seek thro' the world, is ne'er me with elsewhere.
Home! Home! Sweet, sweet home!
There's no place like home!
There's no place like home.
An exile from home, splendor dazzles in vain,
Oh, give me my lowly thatched cottage again;
The birds singing gaily, that come at my call;
Give me them, with that peace of mind, dearer than all.

To thee, I'll return, overburdened with care,
The heart's dearest solace will smile on me there.
No more from that cottage again will I roam,
Be it ever so humble, there's no place like home.

* * *

"They say tomorrow's going to be the big day," Lomas stated as a matter of fact while poking an ember in the fire he shared with the adjoining tent.

"From the steady stream of wounded coming back, it doesn't look like we're doing too well either," Abel returned. "What do you think, Jack?"

"I think we better make sure we have identification in our pockets," the tall Tennessean soberly said.

"What do you mean?" That got Melvin's attention.

"He means we should have something to identify ourselves in case we get killed. It will tell them who we are," Lomas answered. "Just write your name and where you're from on a piece of paper and put it in your shirt pocket."

"Is that what you did?" Melvin asked Lomas.

"Not exactly, I also wrote a note to Abraham Lincoln telling him I'll see him in hell," Lomas said, drily. "Just think, Melvin, you would finally get a chance to see the fairies."

"Yeah, but I don't want to rush into that experience."

"Fellas, we only got two or three hours before daylight, better get some shuteye," Jack said as he unrolled his bedding.

Reveille found the sharpshooters half-awake from a night made shorter and disrupted by their thoughts. For many of the Southern faithful, it would be the last time they'd hear the bugle. The camp began to stir as men went through the paces. Years of training allowed them to go through the motions while their senses were dulled by anxiety and the task that lay ahead. Some of the men expressed nervous smiles, others had a deadpan look. Most were simple farm boys, raised to fear the Lord and never been this far from home. All of them wished this cup would be passed from their lips.

General Lee's previous attacks on the Union's flanks had failed the day before. It only made him more determined to continue his battle plan against "those people." On the third day, Lee ordered General Longstreet to continue his offensive on the Union's left and directed General Ewell's boys in butternut to resume their assault on Culp's Hill. The Federals anticipated that would be the case and were prepared for it. Union troops atop the hill were reinforced and began an artillery bombardment, driving back multiple Confederate attacks. With no progress made, and heavy casualties realized, the futile assaults were discontinued.

Lee was forced to change his plans. General Longstreet would now command divisions of his own First Corps plus six brigades from A. P. Hill's Third Corps and strike at the Union line on Cemetery Ridge.

About the same time the rebels gave up the ghost at Culp's Hill, all the artillery the Confederacy could muster was brought to bear on the Federal positions at Cemetery Ridge. Over 150 Confederate cannons began the largest bombardment in the war. Designed to weaken the enemy, the cannonade failed to materially affect the Union position. In fact, it made Lee's situation worse, since the assault was ineffective, and his low ammunition supply was diminished further. The Union army held its fire for a short time, allowing the rebels to initiate the contest, then opened up with about eighty cannons of their own and braced for the rebel infantry attack that was sure to follow. In the early afternoon, about 12,500 Confederate soldiers moved from the ridgeline and advanced over a battle-strewn field to Cemetery Ridge. The Light Brigade of Alfred, Lord Tennyson, who charged into the valley of death, was not over or above these heroic young farm boys from the South. They charged through fierce artillery fire from Union positions on Cemetery Hill and Little Round Top along with musket and canister enfilades from Federal infantry troops. Rebel soldiers were being devastated. Federal cannon balls were bounding through Confederate lines killing whomever they met. Screaming shells of canister and grape shot brought down eight or ten men at a time; in addition, many were hit by the torrent of nearly two thousand musket and rifles being fired in unison. Nearly half of the attackers lay on the field either killed or wounded. Many joined those who fell during the first two days; some now only torsos without arms, legs, and faces. The desperate drive later became known as Pickett's Charge. Jack Leffingwell and his comrades took part in a line to the left of General Pickett's men. Their unit penetrated the Federal line momentarily, but was unable to hold the position. Two of the marksmen were wounded. Abel Strawn was struck in the shoulder by a minié ball, and Melvin Kaufman took a piece of shrapnel in his leg when a canister exploded nearby. Both were helped to the field hospital by artillery soldiers. Jack Leffingwell and Lomas Chandler managed to escape injury. That couldn't be said for 50 percent of those who took part in the charge. Total losses during the attack were 6,555, of which over 1,100 Confederates were killed on the battlefield. An additional 4,019 were wounded, and an estimated 3,750 men captured and taken prisoner. Three of Pickett's brigade commanders and all thirteen of his regimental officers were casualties. The Union lost a total of 1,500 killed and wounded.

The luster is off the shine for Gen. Robert E. Lee. His trusting soldiers would follow him through the gates of hell if need be. Today, they did just that. Such awesome loyalty can be dangerous in the hands of an enthusiast determined to defeat the enemy and believing he is invincible. The King of Spades now knows that to be true and took full responsibility for the defeat. As the third day of battle came to an end, the clouds turned dark and a steady rain came down. The two armies watched one another while the heavy drencher washed across the bloody battlefield. That night, Lee evacuated the town of

Gettysburg and reformed his lines into a defensive position on Seminary Ridge. General Meade, cautious against the risk associated with an attack, would not take the bait. Both armies began to collect their wounded and bury some of their dead. Nearly eight thousand soldiers had been killed and their bodies still on the battlefield. They should have been buried quickly since exposure to the hot July sun made burial duty even more unpleasant. Men became violently ill due to the sickening stench. Up to three thousand dead horses also dotted the ghastly scene, and their disposal required burning. The many pyres added another odor to the already-putrefied surroundings.

General Lee's next strategic move was to organize the mass retreat of his Army of Northern Virginia. Indication began on the evening of July 4, when the initial movement of troops started heading toward Fairfield and Chambersburg. The dramatic fallback consisted of a miles-long wagon train of supplies and wounded men, two of which were Abel Strawn and Melvin Kaufman. The minié ball imbedded in Strawn's shoulder was painfully removed at the field hospital. Melvin Kaufman's injury required more serious surgery. The jagged shrapnel was dangerously close to a major artery in his leg. A mistake in its removal would likely result in his bleeding to death. Fortunately, Melvin must wait longer to see the Irish fairies, the existence of which Lomas had assured. The surgeon needed over an hour, but was able to remove the iron shard without disturbing the blood vessel. Had the shrapnel been located below the knee, it would be a simple procedure of just removing his leg. Both men now face another danger. That being a killer just as ruthless: infection.

Lee's retrogression used the route through Cashtown and Hagerstown to reach Williamsport, Maryland. Heavy rainfall created another obstacle. Some of the Confederate soldiers were trapped on the north side of the rain-swollen Potomac River. The pontoon bridge had been destroyed by a Union cavalry raid. General Meade's army followed the retreating rebels, unenthusiastically. Once the weather cleared, the river fell enough to allow the construction of a new bridge and Lee's army began crossing after dark. Aware of Meade's pursuit, Lee entrenched a line to protect the river crossings and waited for the Union advance. By the time Meade finally reached the area, he probed the Confederate line resulting in heavy skirmishes; however, the cotton state contingency had begun fording across. Union general Meade postponed any attack until he first performed reconnaissance of the rebel positions. By the time he decided to advance, the Gray Fox was long gone. During the next several days, Lee's retreating army was harassed, on route, by Union cavalry. The bluecoats on horseback destroyed or captured many wagons, plus hundreds of horses and mules. They also seized numerous prisoners, some of which were previously wounded at Gettysburg. All in all, Lee's rear guard proved reasonably effective, and by the end of the month, the Army of Northern Virginia was beyond pursuit.

The Gettysburg Campaign cost Lee's army twenty-seven thousand casualties at a time when there were few replacements. He would no longer engage in any major offensive, but concentrate primarily on reaction to Union initiatives. While the myth of his invincibility was burst, he continued to skillfully outmaneuver and frustrate General Meade's attempts to defeat him.

The Battle of Gettysburg, Pennsylvania—July 1-3, 1863*

	Total Casualties	Wounded	Killed	Captured/Missing
Union	23,055	14,531	3,155	5,369
Confederate	23,231	12,693	4,708	5,830

*The largest number of casualties in the American Civil War. (Numbers derived from wikipedia.org/wiki/Battle_of_Gettysburg.)

At the same period Lee was beaten at Gettysburg, Union general Ulysses S. Grant captured Vicksburg, Mississippi, and took control of the Big Muddy. For many observers, governing the Father of Waters, coupled with an effective navel blockage of Southern ports, virtually guaranteed a Federal victory. It's now only a matter of time. A similar conclusion could be drawn when considering active troop strength. As it now stood, the Union had 611,250 men available for duty while the Confederacy could only muster 233, 586. In Virginia, men of the Confederate coalition still held Lee in the highest regard, while in the West, due to the many hardships, the Southern army morale was becoming depressed. Especially, after they received the news of losing Vicksburg and over one hundred thousand black men now wearing Union blue.

Outside of two minor battles, in which the Seventh Tennessee was held in reserve, Lee's army returned to their camp near Fredericksburg to quarter for the winter. The white-haired general, tormented by his defeat at Gettysburg, sent a letter of resignation to President Jefferson Davis, only to be refused by the Confederate head of state.

* * *

The coming winter would allow for returning soldiers to heal from the rigors of war. Not only to mend actual physical wounds, but those invisible as well. Camp surgeons and medical officers knew there could be mental wounds that would go unseen, yet cause unwelcome behavior. As in the case of Jack Leffingwell's amnesia, doctors treating bodily injury knew very little about mental damage. It would take years before the full involvement of prolonged exposure to combat-related stress was understood. In time, they'd learn that it might be disproportionately high compared with the physical injuries of combat. Today, however, all they could prescribe was rest. Returning troops also had to suffer the agony of defeat—a new experience for the rebels in Virginia. Again, in time, that too would pass. After a short period, the general mood of disappointment began to subside.

Saint Martin of Tours must have watched over Abel Strawn and Melvin Kaufman, as both returned to duty without complications from their trauma on the battlefield. Abel's shoulder was a little tender, and Melvin walked gingerly with a slight limp. The doctors assured them that, in a few days, they would be as good as new. The defeat at Gettysburg made them think retrospectively as to their individual roles and what they could have done differently.

"My conscience is clear," Lomas asserted. "I did everything I was asked to do. Besides, General Lee took full responsibility. He even wrote a letter of resignation."

"It takes a hard man to eat boiled owl. If that old man asked me to suit up and have another go at *those people*, I'd be there in a heartbeat," Melvin added.

"We all would, Melvin. General Lee is one of the three people I hold high respect for," Jack Leffingwell said frankly.

"Who are the other two, Jack?" Abel stressed.

"I don't know. It's gone now. I think I knew a second ago, but I can't recall it. I believe one of them might be a minister," Jack conveyed.

"It's hard to accept that we got whupped," uttered Melvin. "We always could send the bluecoats a-runnin' before."

"Maybe we were lucky before. When you piss your pants, it feels warm for only so long," Lomas replied. "Maybe we finally saw the elephant." Melvin didn't understand a word Lomas said. It was all mumbo jumbo. He planned to ask Abel about it when they were alone.

"We haven't changed, but they sure as hell have. That was a different army in Pennsylvania. Their generals are getting smarter, and the Yankees have a lot of them. I don't know about you guys, but I ended up scratching for ammunition. Yesterday, I overheard a couple of officers talking, and they said we are having a tough time getting resupplied because of the ports being blocked. They also said that Vicksburg surrendered to Gen. Ulysses Grant, and that means the Yankees control the Mississippi River and our forces are split in half," Leffingwell lamented.

* * *

The prospects for a Southern victory were tenebrous. Superior numbers of troops alone made the Union indefatigable in the war of attrition. Early successes in the West were now being reversed. Battles in Ohio, Kentucky, Tennessee, Georgia, Mississippi, and Louisiana had turned in favor of the Union. As news from the battleground gradually improved, President Lincoln's confidence grew from a glimmer of optimism to self-assurance of the ultimate victory. He finally could turn his attention to the power struggle between Congress and the executive over the process connected to a military triumph. One war was replaced with another as to defining the status of secession states. Many in Congress wanted them to be considered new territories, and in keeping with the Constitution, this gave them the authority to delineate the terms of readmission. Conversely, if the states were enduring and secession was the acts of individuals, President Lincoln had the power to set the terms for restoration, deriving from his constitutional authority, to suppress insurrection and to grant pardons and amnesty. The argument would continue during the coming months; and since the war would last for another year, Washington, D.C., would have another bloodless political battle of its own.

As the fortunes of the North improved, the influence of the Copperheads began to wane. Opposed to the Civil War, some Democrats from Northern states wanted an immediate peace settlement with the Confederates. The most famous Copperhead was Ohio's Clement L. Vallandigham, a congressmen and leader of the Democrat Party. He also led the more extreme wing of what was known as the Peace Democrats. They sought to damage the Union war effort by fighting the draft and encouraging deserters. When Union armies were doing poorly, their impact grew. Conversely, just the opposite happened when the Union army did well.

The largest Copperhead group was the Knights of the Golden Circle, later renamed the Order of the Sons of Liberty with Vallandigham as commander.

Under his leadership, they sought to overthrow governments in Illinois, Indiana, Kentucky, and Missouri, targeting Southerners who settled north of the Ohio River. The conspiracy was thwarted after President Lincoln's investigation. Smoldering beneath their facade of peace, their true agenda was obvious. They held violent anger against the abolition of the slaves.

The bloom was off the rose for a few discouraged Confederate states as well, North Carolina in particular. While officially a slave state, there were no plantations and few slaves in the mountainous region to its west. North Carolina was also reluctant to join the seceding states when Abraham Lincoln had won the presidential election. Farmers who didn't own slaves were hesitant about the Confederacy and, if push came to shove, would be just as happy to remain in the Union. Accordingly, because of this confliction of sentiment, North Carolina was the last state to secede from the Union. That being said, North Carolina contributed nearly as many troops to the Confederacy as Virginia and suffered more causalities than any other, save Old Dominion.

Dissatisfied with the Confederacy and the war, influential North Carolinians formed a peace movement and sought independent negotiations with the Union. When this proved impossible, they formed a peace party and unsuccessfully ran against the standing governor. Like their sister states, the frustrated residents of North Carolina suffered from runaway inflation causing food riots in the spring of 1863.

Most of the fighting in North Carolina occurred on the coast where the Union made several attempts to capture Fort Fisher. As the war was coming to an end, Gen. William T. Sherman led a large Federal force into the state and occupied a good portion. Considering the previous stance North Carolina held regarding the Confederacy, Sherman's forces refrained from the devastation they wrought in South Carolina and Georgia.

Chapter Thirty

Give sorrow words; the grief that does not speak knits up the o-er wrought heart and bids it break.

—William Shakespeare, Macbeth

Fall weather in Virginia is a mixed blessing. Half the days the sun is never seen, the other half exhibits brilliant illumination and a balmy temperature around eighty degrees during the day. It also rains half the days. It's as though the elements refuse to accept the actuality that the growing season is over and ignoring the fact that the wind has taken the leaves from the trees. Some say that's Mother Nature's way of washing down the ends of summer and carrying it to the sea. The importance of this natural descent cannot be overstated. Progressing via small rivulets to streams, then rivers, the water's flow carries components much-needed by life in the ocean.

At the Confederate winter quarters, the rain gave relief to loyal gray coats by cancelled drill sessions. Even though they were there to heal and recover from the stress and fatigue of battle, military discipline requires a drill routine for over all readiness. At the moment, a pattering of rain could be heard by the sharpshooters taking shelter in their tent. Another gray day had given rise to their inactivity as they lolled within, reading and writing letters to those foremost on their minds.

"Isn't it getting close to Grazyna's time to have her baby?" Melvin asked Jack.

"Pretty close, I'm going to ask for a furlough to be with her when the time comes," Jack replied.

Lomas, miffed because he couldn't find a poker game nearby, lay on his cot with his hands behind his head and added, "I've put in for a two-week leave for the both of us." Late last week, Lomas heard that Maj. Gen. Walter Shaw was visiting the camp and made certain to corner him for about fifteen minutes. What was said between them was unknown, but one could surmise it had to do with Jack Leffingwell since the furloughs were requested the same day. By positioning himself as sort of an intermediary regarding Jack's recovery from amnesia, Lomas's own vested interest could be served. His yearning to see Isabella grew stronger with each passing day. This had never happened to the Irish trickster before, and there's no telling what he might do if the furloughs didn't come through. Fortunately for Lomas, the request was approved, eliminating the need for him to become a deserter. Although scores of furlough leaves were being granted during this inactive period, there's no question that General Shaw's recommendation had greatly influenced the final decision.

Over the next two days, Lomas devoted his attention on procuring two horses from the cavalry corral. One of the cavalry officers was indebted to the Irish sharpshooter due to his frequently holding the second best hand.

Lomas retained a watch as collateral against the officer's previous losses. Apparently, it was a family heirloom, and the indebted lieutenant was willing to exchange the use of a couple of mounts for return of his watch. Once that transaction was completed, the marksmen were able to clear post security, note the date of departure, and direct their horses toward Richmond.

By leaving early in the morning and traveling at a leisurely pace, they arrived several hours sooner than the ride in the ironworks wagon. Their horses were not prime stock, but adequate for the trip. This marked the first time Jack Leffingwell had ridden since joining up, yet he rode like a seasoned pro. That didn't escape Lomas Chandler, and he said, "You look like you were born in the saddle. Did you do a lot of ridding before the war?"

"Yes, I've ridden ever since I was a little shaver," Jack answered without forethought.

"You probably had your own horse before you enlisted. What was its name?" Lomas asked to draw him out more.

"For the life of me, I can't remember. I don't know why I even said what I did. That's happening to me a lot lately. I say something then can't remember why I said it."

Lomas, thinking he might have discovered a breakthrough, catalogued the incident for later. He needed more time to determine its value and what he could ask for in return. There's no question that Jack Leffingwell was his friend, and there wasn't much he wouldn't do for him, but . . .

The pair glimpsed Richmond's skyline of church steeples late in the afternoon. Anticipation of seeing their loved ones invigorated them from the long ride on horseback. Muscles, needing to remain centered in the saddle, were tired and beginning to ache. They would walk bowlegged in the morning. Two Confederate soldiers, atop CSA horses, with military insignia on the saddle, and properly signed furlough permits, had no problems with army sentinels at the outpost leading to town. In fact, Lomas struck up a conversation with one of them and revealed he was a part owner of the Eagle Inn and Tavern, inviting him to stop by and play a little poker when he wasn't on duty.

As they rode on, Jack commented, "Lomas, someday you will either be a millionaire or get hanged. I hope it isn't the latter."

"Thanks for the support," he returned with a chuckle.

Arriving at Sally Tompkins house, the two parted ways, but not before Jack agreed to visit the newlyweds in a day or two. Jack led his horse to a small barn behind the house and removed the saddle. The little shed had previously been used as a stable before the war effort took the horse. He felt his animal would be safe, belonging to the Confederate cavalry, and shut the doors. Turning to the house, he saw Grazyna standing in the back entryway with the door open. She appeared tired, pale, and definitely ready to deliver. She also was beautiful. Her beauty was something even illness couldn't hide. They held each other, with their eyes closed, in a lovers' embrace. Neither saying a word for the longest time before Grazyna led him into the house.

That evening, they slept holding hands. It was a sound sleep for Jack, who was tired from the trip. Grazyna slept in silken repose due to the hypnotic sedative of undisturbed protection. The next morning, Jack remembered how Sally felt about breakfast and rose without disturbing his dearly beloved. Taking a place at the breakfast table, he noticed Sally's slight smile as she poured him a cup of hot coffee.

"How did Grazyna spend the night?" she asked.

"She seemed to fall asleep as soon as her head hit the pillow," Jack answered. "She was still sleeping soundly when I came downstairs."

"That's good. Jack, I'm glad you were able to be here now. I've been concerned about her. The last week or so, she seemed extremely frail and overly tired. I insisted she see her doctor, and he said she was in good health, but weakened from the pregnancy. He also said she could have the baby any time now."

"Is there anything I can do to help?" he asked.

"Just be here for her is all I can think of," Sally said.

At that moment, they both heard activity in the room above and smiled knowing Grazyna was getting up and about. Sally had other questions to ask the Tennessee mountain man; however, they would have to wait for a more convenient time.

Jack held her chair as she sat down, and Sally recognized the look of a good night's sleep. While still weak, Grazyna appeared rested.

"This is the best I've felt in a long time," Grazyna stated while resting her hand on Jack's arm.

"A good night sleep can cure a multitude of ills," Sally confirmed, while in the back of her mind, she had to admit it was the presence of Jack Leffingwell that gave a sense of security to her *adopted* daughter.

"What are your plans for today?" Sally asked.

"There's nothing special planned, we'll just stay here and enjoy each other's company," Grazyna said. "Maybe later I'll take a nap while Jack catches up on the *Richmond Enquirer*. I've saved the last ten or twelve editions."

"I had promised Lomas Chandler that we would visit him and his new wife in a day or so, still, it all depends on how Grazyna feels. It might be best if I cancelled out and have them come visit us, that is, if you don't mind." Jack said thoughtfully.

"Not at all," Sally replied. "I can have the hospital courier get a message to them and save you the walk. Considering the way things are right now, I wouldn't recommend you taking your horse. It's a lot safer where it is."

Sally left for the hospital, and Jack helped Grazyna clear the table and wash the breakfast dishes. Her happiness brought a soft melody to her lips, and she hummed a tune while putting the dishes back in the cabinet. The final days of being with child had been hard on the beautiful expectant mother. Her energy had been sapped along with her spirit; however, with Jack being there, her inner self was vastly improved, especially in the current domestic setting. Satisfied the kitchen chores were finished, they walked to the sitting room and made themselves comfortable. The newspapers were neatly stacked on the table in front of the divan; nevertheless, before reading them, Jack had to tend to the horse.

"I'm going to pull down a little hay and pump a bucket of water for the horse. It won't take long, and I'll be right back," Jack explained.

"Darling, it's so comforting having you here with me. Do you see what I'm knitting? It's for the baby," Grazyna proudly expressed, while holding it up for him to see. Jack had no idea what it was, even so, told her it was beautiful before departing out the back door.

Near the end of the first week on leave, Lomas and Isabella stopped by, making a social call. Grazyna appeared brightened by the visit; though after their company left, she nearly collapsed with fatigue. Jack, initially concerned about her health, now began to worry, disallowing any unnecessary excitement.

The following week, Grazyna began to have contractions and, under Sally's direction, went immediately to Robertson Hospital. Jack wanted to carry her, but since it was located practically next door, Grazyna insisted she could handle the short walk herself.

Sally had prearranged a room, and the hospital staff was waiting when Jack pushed the front door open. Directly across from her chamber was an alcove with a glass ceiling. The recess was used as a small solarium and proudly displayed its greenery. It also contained a few chairs, one of which proved enticing to the anticipant soldier. Not only was it comfortable, it faced directly at Grazyna's doorway, giving him a glimpse of the inner activity each time it opened.

Looking upward, Jack watched the sky change from light wispy clouds to a more ominous overcast. Rolling darkness was now viewed above and a thunderclap echoed from a distance away. A flash of lightning signaled the pending storm, and soon intermittent raindrops turned into a downpour. Jack had always enjoyed rainfall. Probably due to his rural background where it was life-giver to crops and necessary for animals via ponds and shallow streams. Today, however, he could do without it, since it only served to dim his general mood.

The hours passed with activity in and out increasing. He kept listening for the cry of a baby, all the same, realizing he wouldn't hear it this far away.

Around midnight, a nurse came into the waiting area carrying a bundle and said, "Mr. Leffingwell, here is your son. Grazyna insisted that I bring him to you and show you his bottom. I have no idea what she meant," she said as the bundle was gently opened exposing a diminutive backside with a bright blue mark just above where his tiny cheeks met.

"Thank you, Nurse, I know exactly what she meant. Here, let me hold him," Jack replied as he received the testament to their love. Jack was holding his son when the doctor entered the waiting area. His expression changed the general feelings in the room.

"Mr. Leffingwell, you have a fine healthy boy, but I'm concerned about your wife," he said.

"What's wrong with Grazyna? Is she all right?" the startled father asked.

"It appears as though she had a preexisting heart condition. She was able to tolerate her pregnancy without demonstrating any unusual effects, and it went unnoticed. The stress of childbirth weakened her heart to the point of serious dysfunction," the doctor explained.

"Is she going to die?" Jack's heart was pounding like a drum.

"I honestly don't know."

"I need to be with her," Jack pleaded.

"Normally, I would say no, at this time. She's very weak. You must not excite her." The doctor saw that Jack was determined to be with Grazyna and it would take a great deal more than he and two nurses to stop him. Rather than have the explosion then and there, he authorized Jack to be in Grazyna's room.

Jack sat by Grazyna's bed holding her hand. It seemed so small and fragile, engulfed by the mountain man's gentle grip. Her face was pale and ashen in a vain attempt to hide her beauty, but it failed. She slowly began to stir and open her exotic eyes.

"Oh, Jack, I'm so glad you are here with me. I think that I am dying. You know I've loved you since the first day I saw you. And I know that you love me too."

"Darling, you're not going to die. You just need lots of rest," Jack said assuredly.

"You once told me that life is short. And even the stars have died by the time we see them. I have prayed to God for forgiveness for the things I've done, and I know he heard me. Promise me that you will do the same."

"Falling in love with you, Grazyna, is the best thing that ever happened in my life. I will love you forever, sweetheart. You and I are now, and always will be, one flesh, one heart, and one soul. I pray every day and thank God I have you. When you are well, sweetheart, we will pray together."

"Have you seen our little boy? He has a blue dot on his butt. The Lord put it there so you will never forget me."

"I now have two treasures with a blue dot." Jack's cheeks glistened from the tears of intense emotion.

"I know, darling, but there's something I need to say to you. I want you to go back to Statesville and be with Abigail and the children. She is a good woman, and I know she will accept our son into your family. While we are still holding hands, say that you will. Promise me that you will. Promise me . . ." Her words faded, and heaven had another angel.

For a few seconds, Jack couldn't breathe. He was paralyzed from the shock of witnessing her lifeless body. His most priceless treasure was stolen before his very eyes, and the rebel sharpshooter had no way to prevent it. It was like a vague and clouded dream from which he could not waken and force this bitter truth from his existence.

"No, no, don't die. You can't die. My god, this can't be. Grazyna, don't leave me," Jack sobbed.

The nurses, standing near the door, could hear Jack's plea and felt his grief. Even the doctor had shameless tears.

Sally Tompkins was the first to enter the room. She sat on the other side of the bed with her hand on her *adopted* daughter and prayed for her salvation. When it came down to it, she had always resented Jack Leffingwell. Witnessing his grief, ostensibly deeper than her own, she rose from the chair and silently walked over to Jack and placed her arm around his shoulder in consolation.

God's greatest gift to man had been redeemed. Those were the last words Jack would hear from Grazyna, except in his dreams. He was still holding her hand when the nurses came in the check for signs of life. There were none. Jesus forgave a thief from the cross. A loving God could do no less for the beautiful angel with a blue dot.

The mountain man was overcome with heartache and in no position to think clearly. Recognizing this, Sally took charge and made necessary arrangements for handling Grazyna. She knew from experience the stricken soldier would require time to pull through his present state of mind. With her every action, Sally demonstrated why she was called the Angel of the Confederacy.

That night, at her kitchen table, she explained to Jack what was happening and why.

"Jack, if you don't object, I would like for Grazyna to be buried in my family's plot. She has been like a daughter to me, and my guess is, you are unable to provide anything better," she stated firmly. "I'll make a stipulation that you will always have free access."

"Thank you, Sally. I believe this is what she would have wanted," he said quietly.

"There is another issue even of more importance. You have a son now, and you're still in the army fighting this terrible war. Let's look at the best-case scenario. The war ends, and you are still alive. Will you want to take responsibility for him?"

"Yes," he answered. "I made a promise to Grazyna to go back to Statesville, Tennessee, after the war. She thought Abigail would accept him into the family."

"How do you feel about that?"

"From what I've learned about Abigail, I think Grazyna is right. As for me, I love Grazyna, but there may be a way to live on the farm platonically. No matter, I will fulfill my promise."

"Then let's look at the worst-case scenario. I want your son to be mine. I want to raise and provide for him like he was my own."

"That would be fair. At this point, Abigail has no knowledge of my son."

"We need to refer to him by his name. Grazyna has named him Jozef. In Polish, it means God will add another son."

The weather had cleared the day Grazyna's funeral was held. Services were conducted at the Protestant Episcopal church near Robertson Hospital. The ceremony seemed strange to the Methodist from the hills. Not so to Lomas and Isabella, whose Catholic rituals were similar. Jack, absorbed with the beauty and splendor of it all, went through the motions as if in a trance. The interment took place in the Tompkins burial ground with Grazyna placed beneath a majestic oak tree. Sally mentioned to Jack that the gravesite was next to her own. That evening, when all the mourners and well-wishers were gone, Jack could ponder about the tragic loss he now suffered. His tears had run dry, there were none left to shed. Sally had engaged a wet nurse for Little Jozef, and after feeding him, she brought the tiny bundle to his father. Sally stared at Jack to see his reaction. Not so much about having the baby presented to him, but the fact that the wet nurse was black. Looking up after receiving his son, all Jack could say was, "Thank you."

* * *

In October, as the harvest moon shone brilliantly over the Confederate army winter quarters, President Abraham Lincoln sat at his desk in Washington, D.C., and designated the last Thursday in November as Thanksgiving Day.

Although Lincoln was always open to opportunities to unite the citizens of the Union, he knew there would come a day when both North and South must reunite in a common loyalty. A letter written by Sarah Josepha Hale the previous month might have been the trigger for issuing his proclamation when he did. Sarah Josepha Hale was editor of *Godey's Lady's Book*, the most influential women's magazine of her day. A poet and accomplished novelist, she was respected as an arbiter of taste, fashion, cooking, literature, and morality. Born in New Port, New Hampshire, she was raised in the New England tradition of celebrating an annual dinner of thanksgiving. It dates back to the Pilgrims, who suffered that first cold winter of starvation and sickness. Nearly half had died, but the next year brought a bountiful harvest, and along with their American Indian friends, they celebrated a three-day feast to praise and thank God. In the northeastern corner of the United States, such a day was set aside for a similar celebration each year. In fact, when New Englanders eventually moved to new territories in the southwest, many returned for the annual day of thanksgiving.

Sarah Josepha Hale had advocated for a national thanksgiving holiday since 1846. She had written the last four presidents—Zachary Taylor, Millard Fillmore, Franklin Pierce, and James Buchanan—without success. Finally, after seventeen years, her poignant letter to Abraham Lincoln convinced the Republican rail-splitter to support legislation establishing a national holiday of Thanksgiving. It would become the third national holiday celebrated in the United States, after Washington's Birthday and Independence Day.

While Sarah Josepha Hale was one of the most accomplished women of her day, she probably was most remembered for the following children's poem:

Mary had a little lamb, whose fleece was white as snow.
And everywhere that Mary went, the lamb was sure to go.
It followed her to school one day which was against the rule.
It made the children laugh and play, to see a lamb at school.
And so the teacher turned it out, but still it lingered near,
And waited patiently about, till Mary did appear.
"Why does the lamb love Mary so?" the eager children cry.
"Why, Mary loves the lamb, you know," the teacher did reply.[*]

* (http://en.wikipedia.org/wiki/Mary_Had_a_Little_Lamb)

Chapter Thirty-One

I will honor Christmas in my heart, and try to keep it all the year.

—*Charles Dickens, A Christmas Carol*

On Thursday, November 19, 1863, Abraham Lincoln gave a three-minute address at the Gettysburg battlefield cemetery. He sat for nearly two hours listening to Edward Everett, one of America's great orators of the Civil War era. Then, when the president's turn came, he rose to his height of six feet four inches and walked to the speaker's platform. Over 1,500 citizens had gathered for the outdoor dedication of the seventeen-acre cemetery. And as he stood looking out over the crowd, most had their first glimpse of the man they elected president three years prior. Lincoln had written his speech while still in Washington, D.C. He arrived by train in Gettysburg the night before the dedication and stayed at the home of David Wills, the lawyer promoting the event. The next morning, the president joined the procession atop a gray horse provided by his host. Standing at the dais, he looked tired. His complexion, normally the color of butternut, was pale. Heavy eyebrows shielded his stare, and his coarse black hair appeared uncaring. A rumor began to circulate that he might be ill, but that was short-lived as Lincoln began to speak. The crowd was taken aback when, for the first time, they heard his sharp, high-pitch tenor, perfect to carry across the open-air dedication.

In his speech, Lincoln referred to the American Revolution as to when the founding fathers established the principles of equality of all men. The Civil War was a struggle not merely for the preservation of the Union, but for a "new birth of freedom" that would bring true equality to all citizens. He not only consecrated the grounds of the Gettysburg cemetery but also exhorted for the survival of a representation democracy using the words, "government of the people, by the people, for the people, shall not perish from the earth." It was clearly a sharp distinction against the constitutional argument for state rights. Using just 273 words and speaking less than three minutes, Lincoln had perfectly defined the central idea and purpose of the gathering.

The audience, in general, was unreactive. There was no wild exuberating, instead, only a tepid response. Perhaps, it was due to the brevity of his words after a two-hour oratory by the main speaker. Lincoln turned to a companion and said, "It was a flat failure," before the customary handshakes with those dignitaries standing on the platform.

The band struck up a loud marching tune; and the crowd, realizing the event was over, began a noisy departure. Many were heading to taverns to continue their celebration. None were aware that they had just been witnesses to the most quoted speech in American history.

* * *

It had become common practice for both armies to rest during the winter. The Army of Northern Virginia, while at their winter quarters, reassigned troops and stockpiled weaponry and supplies. Due to General Archer's capture at Gettysburg, the Seventh regiment of Tennessee was placed under the command of Brig. Gen. H. H. Walker. All four marksmen had received a promotion in rank, likely due to their conduct during General Pickett's Charge. Melvin Kaufman seemed to be the only one excited by the news. The other three were unmoved. It did mean a slight increase in pay, but when you haven't received anything for over two months, it's not a big deal.

Grazyna had been gone for about three months. Jack still had a hard time accepting her death. She came to him nearly every night in his dreams. His promise to her rested foremost on his mind; and he knew, for that to take place, he must write Abigail. Tormented by what to say, he found reasons to postpone the correspondence. He demurred primarily because, in his last letter, he asked for a divorce.

Meanwhile, back in Statesville, Abigail and her father were on the hunt for the right-size evergreen. November was long past, and a light dusting of snow covered the untended fields as Miracle pulled a small wagon, at the present empty, over the crusty terrain.

"Let's take a rest on that log," Hyrum suggested while pointing in the direction of the fallen timber. "Your old dad isn't as spry as he used to be, and it's a pretty far piece from the house."

Abigail felt invigorated by the exercise and a crisp morning breeze, but could see that her father was winded. They sat in silence for a minute or two. Looking back at the farmhouse, she saw the feint plume of smoke rising from the kitchen fireplace and was reminded to gather any fallen wood they came upon. Winters are usually mild in Statesville; however, the nights can get pretty chilly and a good fire is always welcome, especially by Minnie Rosenthal. Before the children came along and Jack joined the army, she enjoyed those frosty nights cuddled up when both were in bed together. Her reverie ended when Hyrum stated, "I sure needed that. Let's head toward the creek. There are plenty small pines located as the water makes the bend."

Her father was right, and soon the proper-size conifer was located and succumbing to the ax. Its branches were full when viewed from every direction and, once placed in the stand Jack had made, would require Abigail to climb on a box to position the star, a gift from their first wedding anniversary. It took them both to load it in the wagon. Abigail found other branches she would use to decorate the house and, on their return trip, loaded enough fagots to last a month.

When they arrived back at the farm, Abigail guided Miracle to the front steps and helped her father bring the fir tree inside. The stand was already waiting in the chosen corner, and once accommodating the tree, father and daughter stood back to admire their handiwork. Sarah Jane's happy eyes were big as saucers; and Little Jack, with his rear end in the air, was bent over clapping his hands.

"I've got hot chocolate waiting at the kitchen table," Minnie announced, much to the delight of the children.

The family gathered around the polished oak table that Jack had made the first year he and Abigail were married. At the time, she thought it was too big; but as the family grew, she realized her husband had just planned ahead. In fact, were Jack at home this day, he most likely would insert one of the three leafs he made to accommodate both family and guests during special occasions. After the Union occupation, the walnut-stained table mostly stood glistening in sole support of an oil lamp, while Abigail and Minnie plotted their scheme for survival. Today, the mood was more festive, and after the children left the table to have a second look at the tree, Hyrum blew across his second cup of steaming chocolate and asked, "Have you figured out what to give the youngsters this year?"

"Pretty much, however, Minnie and I have spent most of the time on how to decorate the house," Abigail answered.

"Well, the reason I asked is, we have a man in the congregation who is quite handy with wood. He lives alone on a small piece of land with several hardwood trees. He salvages any tree damaged by storms and fashions all sorts of things to sell. I made a sketch of your house, and he's going to make a dollhouse replica. That will be my gift for Sarah Jane. It's something she may keep forever. He made me a toy wagon for Little Jack. One he can pull around by a string."

"Oh, Father, those sound like wonderful gifts. Minnie and I found coloring books at Riberty's general store and had them laid away. Sarah Jane is at an inquisitive age and is already searching the house for presents. Some of the girls at school have got her suspicious about the existence of Santa Claus."

"That's the way it goes, dear. Children lose their belief when they reach a certain age, then once they become parents, get it back again," the minister reflected.

The fragrance of pine now permeated throughout the house. The traditional aroma served to alert those within that the Christmas holiday was forthcoming. The two women had tastefully decorated the house with boughs of evergreen, mistletoe, and holly. As usual, strings of dried fruit, popcorn, and pine cones were undulating around the evergreen tree. This year, something new was added. Minnie Rosenthal had opened her family trunk and found silver foil as well as spun glass from previous years when Jacob was still celebrating Christmas with her. Those items, plus a few colored paper cutouts hanging from the branches, gave a perfect final touch. Everyone agreed, this was the most beautiful tree they ever had. Minnie was especially proud of her contributions and made certain all visitors were taken past the tree before offering them a chair.

And so it went, that Christmas of 1863, in which the Statesville family gave a prayer of thankfulness and praised the blessing of the birth of Christ. Abigail asked the Lord for strength to help her face the awesome tasks ahead: raising two children and living without the husband she still loved and conversed with in her dreams.

* * *

The Christmas meal for the soldiers in General Lee's winter camp was sparse. The Confederacy was having a difficult time in feeding the troops at all. However, Lee did manage to provide a somewhat-better holiday meal.

Dinner consisted of tinned meat, bean soup and bacon, hot coffee, hard tack, and apples for dessert. Thanks to Lomas Chandler, a few superior comestibles were added to enhance the meal once the sharpshooters returned to their tent. He provided a loaf of bread and a small tub of butter, plus generous amounts of ham and turkey. In keeping with the Chandler Rules, no one was allowed to question where the largess came from. The men realized one thing for certain, considering the paucity of supplies. It had to cost their Irish friend a great deal of money. Melvin Kaufman lay back on his cot, unbuckled his belt, gave a sigh, and said, "I betcha Abe Lincoln's boys ain't eating any better'n us today."

"The way things are going, they sure as hell will next year," Abel asserted.

"Why do you think that way, Abel?" Melvin asked.

"Well, as I see it, the Yankees have our ports blocked so no supplies can get in. Their army just gets bigger while ours gets smaller. In fact, we are still losing fighters every day. Men are tired, hungry, and fed up with the whole shebang. They're leaving every night and heading home. And to top it off, we got whipped up north, no matter what anybody says."

"If the newspapers are telling the truth, a hundred thousand black men have signed up for Lincoln's army. That might be more than the army out West and ours combined," Jack added. "I agree with Abel. We're going to be fighting on defense for the rest of this war."

"We got colored that will fight for us. If this here war is about their freedom, give it to them if they join up," Melvin determined.

"Marse Robert thinks the same way you do, Melvin, but old Jeff Davis isn't so anxious to make the move,"

Jack stated. "Has anybody taken a good look around here lately? We have details just digging trenches and creating networks of battlements. You don't do that if we're on the attack. Yesterday, I saw some troops sharpening poles for making abatises. The bluecoats think they're on a roll, and from what's going on around here, they may be right."

"They're gonna need those big numbers if'n we're dug in," Melvin said with authority.

"Yeah, Melvin. But remember this, if we're dug in, there isn't any place to go."

The next two months saw continued work on fortifying the base camp and areas southwest of Fredericksburg and the Rapidan River. The Union expected General Lee to make winter camp in Culpeper County. Instead, the crafty Gray Fox retreated to Orange County and positioned his army along a thirty-mile front behind the Rapidan River. Finding the location more suitable for defense, he built observation posts on the higher ground of Clark's Mountain, to keep watch over the Union troops on the other side of the river.

Union general Meade, discouraged by several failed attempts to out flank Lee, moved his Army of the Potomac to Brandy Station for winter quarters. He had no plans to resume fighting until spring, much to the chagrin of President Lincoln. Feeling that General Meade had missed the opportunity to finish off Lee's army, the Yankee president began to mull over the idea to bring Gen. Ulysses S. Grant to Washington and have him take over.

At Lee's Confederate camp, troops were drilled twice a day and target practice was discontinued, most likely to conserve ammunition. While military exercise was intended to condition and maintain battle readiness, a specter haunted the camp from inside and served as a danger equal to any on the battlefield. The camp doctors struggled to treat the large numbers of soldiers suffering from disease before they were claimed by the grave. Cramped, unsanitary conditions were the perfect breeding grounds for malaria, typhoid fever, and dysentery. Confederate soldiers were more prone to catch even the more routine illnesses. Men from rural areas were sometimes less exposed to many of the germs and had not developed adequate immunity. Other country boys had never even had measles.

* * *

Once the new year arrived, Jack could put off writing to Abigail no longer. He thought for a while as to the proper way to inform her of his plans and then decided to tell the truth, come hell and high water.

January 7, 1864
Dear Abigail,

I trust this letter finds you in good health and agreeable temperament. That which I had previously requested is no longer urgent. The wonderful lady I had given my heart to had sadly passed on after the birth of my child, a boy she named Jozef. While on her deathbed, she made me promise to return to Statesville after the war. With your permission, I plan to keep my promise to her. I have no memory of you and me before my injury, and I still suffer the loss of my love,

Grazyna McCracken, but there's no reason why I might not prove helpful around the farm. It would give us an opportunity to become friends and allow Jozef to grow up in a family. This war has created a separation of both country and families. When it's finally over, it will take years to repair the damage it has caused.

There's still a good chance I may not survive it because a great deal of fighting is yet to take place. In the event that happens, arrangements have already been made for the proper care of Jozef. Regardless of your decision, I will return to Statesville to fulfill my vow. I guess this letter will mainly serve to make you aware of my plans. God be willing.

Yours truly,
Jack Leffingwell

It took well over a month before the letter arrived at the Statesville post office. Recognizing a military envelope, Abigail's heart hammered in her chest as she struggled to tear it open. Her first thoughts were that Jack had been killed. Then after reading it, she was stunned by what it said. What did it say? She had no immediate answer and, at that point, rushed to see her father.

As soon as Hyrum answered the door, she burst inside and said, "I got a letter from Jack, and you have to read it. I don't know what to do about it." Her hands were shaking as she presented the missive to his outstretched grasp. They both walked to a table where Hyrum retrieved his eyeglasses and calmly asked his daughter to sit down. In his usual deliberate manner, Hyrum slowly read Jack's letter, folded it, then unfolded it, and read it a second time.

"It looks as though Jack will be coming back to Statesville."

"Yes, but under what circumstances?" she plaintively asked.

"That's going to be up to you, daughter. Do you still love him?" the wise minister asked. "Remember you can't lie to your father."

"Yes, I do love him, no matter what has happened. I will love him for the rest of my life," she honestly replied.

"Then take him back. Let him live on the farm and help him make it as beautiful as it was before he left for war."

"But we don't share the same feelings for each other. He has no memory of our lives together," Abigail stated. "And now he has another son."

"Put it all in the hands of the Lord. He has a purpose for everything, so don't fight it. Keep your prayers in the forefront, and let his will be done," advised her father.

"Should I answer his letter?"

"I don't believe so. What could you actually say? He stated that he will come no matter what, so just let it be."

Abigail taught the children that day with her thoughts elsewhere. She was conflicted with images of an incompatible situation: a husband who, in his own mind, was not her husband and a little boy who wasn't hers. Naturally, in this type of situation, the time passed at a snail's pace; still eventually, the day came to an end and she hurried home to tell Minnie Rosenthal.

The octogenarian's first reaction was to get a broom and run him off the place. But she quickly changed her mind and told her adopted granddaughter that her feelings were all that mattered. If Abigail was happy to have him back, under these circumstances, then it was perfectly okay with her. That night, alone with her thoughts, Abigail realized her counsel had only come from family members. She needed to talk to someone outside the household. Tomorrow she would run it by Maryellen Riberty.

* * *

The January weather took a turn for the worse the day after Jack posted his letter. Harsh winter conditions beset the camp. Cold drizzling rain, followed by snow, sleet, misty fog, and mud, made the life of those with only a canvas tent for shelter more miserable. This was especially true for boys from farther South who were unaccustomed to so cold a climate. Fortunately, Lomas Chandler had provided the sharpshooters with woolen stockings; but at night, even with feet encased in wool, they shivered until the morning.

Melvin Kaufman made the discovery while on picket duty. He noticed that sometime during the evening, a large stack of long timbers had been removed, probably for use in erecting abatises. Their absence exposed a log hut, previously hidden under the pile of wood. A closer examination revealed a shed, measuring twelve square feet, with a stone chimney on one side. Lomas forced open the plank board door and found it dry inside. Quickly, he left his post to alert his fellow marksmen. It didn't take long before the other three were moving their cots and valuables to the newly acquired home. Concern for the blustery frigid wind was put aside until the former canvas residence was empty. Once inside their new domicile, they noticed it had a singular window with six small glass panes, of which two were missing.

Lomas had the answer when he said, "Don't worry about the missing glass. Just cover it with anything, and I'll have replacements before the day is over. Hey, Jack, how does that fireplace look?"

"I think it's operable," the mountain man replied. "I'm going to need some clay mud to patch the chimney before we can start a fire. We can't do that until it stops raining. Nevertheless, it's a hell of a lot warmer in here than in the tent."

"I know what clay mud looks like," Melvin asserted. "I'll fetch it the first chance we get."

That night, they all agreed that Melvin was the man of the hour. They could hear the howling icy wind outside, but behind the log walls of the hut felt a lot warmer than before. In weather like this, the men would just wile away the time reading, quarreling, and relating the latest rumor from what they called the grapevine. When conditions improved, they would attend prayer meetings and religious services on Sunday. After Jack Leffingwell had tucked and patched the chimney, the sharpshooters would light candles at night and draw around a crackling fire. Lomas Chandler would come in later, once the last hand in a poker game was played out. The Irishman had poker percentages down pat. If they played him long enough, he'd end up with all the money.

* * *

Back in Washington, President Abraham Lincoln was often beleaguered with spells of deep depression and hadn't slept the night before. He had developed one of his familiar sick headaches and fought against these maladies in an effort to, as they commonly said, *think straight*. Until now, he hadn't developed a war strategy. He was operating by *leading from behind*, a technique of reaction rather than action. Lincoln knew the war couldn't be won until he took the lead.

> (His military experience was lacking; however, he did volunteer in the Illinois militia when Chief Black Hawk broke his agreement and reentered the state, causing panic among the white settlers. The actual reason for Black Hawk's actions was unclear since his trespass included the aged, women, and children, along with his warriors. Such noncombatants are never included if intensions are warlike. Nevertheless, the militia ultimately drove him out of Illinois and farther north in the Michigan Territory. Abraham Lincoln saw no action and mustered out after about two months' duty.)

In the beginning, one of the stumbling blocks for Lincoln to take the lead was his general-in-chief, Winfield Scott. Old Fuss and Feathers gave Lincoln conflicting information, making it more difficult to formulate the correct strategy. Scott was not entirely the blame since he, too, was kept in the dark by those subordinate to him. Lincoln quickly realized his chief general was not physically in condition to oversee the Union war efforts.

His age and weight made it difficult for him to stand and walk, much less review troops in the field. He needed pulleys in order to rise from his chaise or bed and could never ride a horse. After the defeat at Manassas on July 21, 1861, Lincoln appointed Gen. George B. McClellan as general-in-chief. He, too, disappointed the president, as well as those who followed, until the present moment in early 1864. With General Lee's Army of Northern Virginia bottled into a defensive position, Lincoln's thoughts were increasingly focused on his most successful army leader, Gen. Ulysses S. Grant.

* * *

The president's cabinet consisted of political appointees, chosen to satisfy and balance patronage between the states. He really didn't personally know any of them, and of course, they viewed him as a backwoods hick lawyer and usurper to the throne. A position many of them believed rightfully theirs. To make matters worse, they disliked each other. Naturally, Lincoln's primary concern was the conduct of the Civil War; and while his cabinet secretaries continued their own war against each other, Abraham Lincoln remained calm, equable, and uncomplaining. Some had come to the president offering their letters of resignation. Lincoln, always pleasant and cordial, dismissed the idea and sent them back to their duties of office; however, their letters remained in the lanky president's pocket.

Foremost of those opposed to Lincoln's presidency was Secretary of State William H. Seward, the leading candidate for the Republican presidential nomination in 1860. Seward's bid was harmed by his support of parochial schools, while serving as governor of New York, a decision earning the enmity of nativists.

(The debate over using public taxes to support Roman Catholic schools was a point of contention since the early years of the new republic. Wealthy New Yorkers could afford to send their own children to private schools and didn't want to pay for other people's children to attend public school. The less fortunate, or working class, needed their children to work, rather than attend any school, and didn't want to pay taxes for a school system they would never get to use.

Nevertheless, the ardor for public schools continued to grow, based on the understanding that an educated citizenry is necessary for the betterment of the country. An organization called the Public School Society of New York was created to make available free schooling for poor children who were not provided for by either religious or private institutions. The PSS was a private group, dominated by Protestants and heavily anti-Catholic. They also were given the responsibility for dividing up New York City's portion of the state education fund among the city's schools. Accordingly, the common school attendance was compulsory, tax-supported, free, and Protestant. In spite of the obvious, the common schools were considered nonsectarian and eligible to receive public money.

> The Roman Catholic Church objected to their children being taught under the Protestant version of the Bible. In fact, if the truth be told, the common schools were responsible for the establishment of Catholic schools in the mid-nineteenth century.
>
> In 1840, the governor of New York was Lincoln's Secretary of State, William H. Seward. Back then, Seward promoted progressive political policies such as prison reform and increased spending on education. He was sensitive to the growing political power of Catholic voters. In his annual message to the New York State legislature, he supported state funding for schools for immigrants, operated by their own clergy and taught in their native language. This support, which included Catholic parochial schools, came back to haunt him in the 1850s when anti-Catholic feelings were high, especially among nativists and ex-Whigs in the Republican Party. In 1860, the same groups turned against him, blocking his nomination as the Republican candidate for president. They made the claim that his radical reputation in support of parochial schools and antislavery stance disqualified him as a candidate.)

Seward, angry over losing the nomination, refused Lincoln's appointment to become secretary of state until inauguration day. And then only because he felt he would still be able to influence events as if he were the president. It didn't take long before Seward realized that the backwoods lawyer from Illinois was a formidable leader whose policies agreed with many of his own. President Lincoln understood the difficulty for someone like Seward to accept a subordinate role and often sought his counsel on matters beyond his normal duties. They became good friends, much to the annoyance of other cabinet members.

Chapter Thirty-Two

When March comes in like a lion it goes out like a lamb.

Winter slowly passed with the marksmen enjoying the comfort of their log cabin home. The month of March is a time of transition from winter to spring. March was the first month in the Roman calendar and began the year for Western civilization as well, until 1752, when England changed to the Gregorian numbering structure. After that, the year started on the first of January. For the men in the Confederate winter camp, March came in with relentless blustery winds. At night, whistling through trees just beginning to bud, the gusty whine sounded eerily human. Unnerving at first, it didn't take long before Jack Leffingwell and crew got used to it and performed their duties without giving it a second thought. That's not to say it didn't bother them. The wind and idleness was getting on Lomas's nerves to the point that he signed up to drive hospital wagons taking wounded soldiers to Richmond. Obviously, his ulterior motive was being with his wife,

Isabella. Jack Leffingwell arranged to tag along for a week at Robertson's under the pretense of doctors checking on his amnesia progress. It had been four months since he had seen his son although Sally Tompkins had written him twice to report Jozef was in excellent health.

Two rebel soldiers, one of which was Lomas Chandler, sat on top the front seat taking turns driving the six-horse team. Three wagons made the trip this time. The wounded rode in the wagon bed, protected by its canvas bonnet. The ambulance wagons were designed to accommodate three or four patients lying down and another six in a seated position and one recumbent. At least two junior medical attendants accompanied each unit to provide care and comfort to those inside. Jack Leffingwell traveled as a patient. Obviously, in top physical health. Having the two sharpshooters along was comforting for the men should they run into a Union cavalry patrol. Fortunately, the journey was completed without incident. Several stops were planned. The soldiers were assigned to various Richmond care units. Most, however, were to be taken to Chimborazo Hospital. Jack Leffingwell hopped down in front of Robertson and stated, "I'm here for a week."

"Not to worry, someone will pick you up right here next week. They'll let the hospital know about what time it will be," the driver said.

With that, Lomas jumped off and said, "I'll be waiting here with him."

Apparently, a deal had been struck and Robertson Hospital was the perfect stop off point, since it's only a few blocks from the Eagle Inn and Tavern.

"Stop by when you get a chance, the drinks are on me, or on me and Isabella," Lomas offered as he walked in the direction of the friendly hostel. Jack could hear his friend whistling before deciding to bound up the steps and open the hospital door. Once inside, he gave a nod to the receptionist and quickly proceeded to Sally Tompkins's office. Her door was ajar enough for Jack to see that she was at her desk and alone. He gently tapped on the door before requesting, "May I come in?"

"Of course, Jack, come take a seat. How long can you stay?" she seemed happy to see him.

"I have one week here for follow-up on my amnesia problem," Jack answered with a smile.

"We can finalize the examination right now. Have you had further recollection of your past before the injury?"

"Not that I know of," he replied.

"Then your progress is moving along satisfactorily and we need to see you in about a month or so," she amusingly stated. "I'll notify Dr. Shaw of my examination."

"How is the baby doing?"

"You can see for yourself in about an hour, unless you want to go over to the house unescorted," Sally answered.

"No thanks, the wet nurse scares me," he honestly replied. Then pointing to the newspaper on her desk, he asked, "May I borrow the *Richmond Examiner*?"

Jack found a waiting room empty and took up residence for the time Sally needed to finish her duties. It required nearly two hours. The mountain man hadn't read the *Examiner* for the past three weeks, and once engrossed, the time flew by.

Upon arriving at Sally's residence, they were greeted by the same wet nurse Jack was afraid of, Lavinia Robertson. Lavinia was born a slave on a nearby plantation. When the Civil War broke out, she was loaned to the Robertson Hospital, a common act during the war. Sally was pleased with her from the beginning. Her willingness to help and give comfort to the wounded impressed the major to the point she bought her from the plantation owner. The purchasing price was unknown, but no sooner than the transaction was finalized, Lavinia was freed by an act of manumission. She had worked at the hospital ever since and most recently in the domestic employ of Sally. The liberated woman disliked the rebel soldier from the start. She viewed him as someone fighting on the side of the South and against abolition. Her attitude began to mellow somewhat after learning the Tennessee mountain man abetted runaway slaves when working as a conductor of the Underground Railroad. With that knowledge, yet still a little reluctant, she has agreed to tolerate him.

"Lavinia," Sally said, "guess who's going to be visiting with us for a week?"

"I can see him," she answered stoically.

"Remember, he is my guest and deserves our best hospitality."

"Oh, he'll get what he deserves all right," she returned.

Sally let it pass and inquired, "How has Jozef been? I kind of thought he felt a little warm this morning."

"That was just waking up heat. He's fine and taking a nap right now. Do you want me to wake him?"

Sally turned to Jack, who shook his head no, and responded, "Not now."

After waiving Lavinia off, the duo walked into the living area and Jack sat on an overstuffed chair while Sally stood in front of the credenza and asked, "Would you like a before-dinner drink? I usually have a glass of wine to help end the workday and relax me before eating."

"Yes, thank you, I'm feeling sort of nervous. All this is new to me. Maybe a little wine will help relax me as well."

Handing Jack a glass of red wine, Sally proposed a toast, "Here's to ending this terrible war soon, no matter who wins it, so that Little Jozef grows up in a peaceful environment."

"I'll drink to that," Jack responded.

While they raised their crystal wine glasses, Lavinia walked in holding an active bundle and speaking in a mignon voice. She cradled the animated swaddling, ignored Jack, and unhurriedly walked to where Sally was standing, then handed her the baby. Recognizing Sally, Little Jozef broke out in a big grin and reached for her glasses.

"He's started on solid food now and seems to love rice cereal. It appears to serve him well because he has more than doubled his weight since being born and grows more alert every day," informed Sally as she handed the infant to his father. Jozef's eyes moved smoothly back to Sally with a questioning expression, but rather than cry, he looked up at Jack and made gurgling sounds. As the tall stranger bent down to kiss his forehead, Jozef reached up and took hold of a handful of Jack's hair and wouldn't let go.

"You can see for yourself that he does a lot with his hands. The hands are now working together to take hold of things," Sally continued. "In fact, those tiny hands will grab for just about anything within reach including a stuffed animal, your hair, and any colorful or shiny object nearby. We have to be watchful because anything he picks up will likely end up in his mouth. Tasting is another way a baby explores the world; therefore, it's crucial we don't leave small items lying about that he could choke on."

"What color eyes do you think he'll have?" Jack questioned.

"It's anyone's guess right now. They've started to change, but we won't know for a few more months. What color do you prefer?"

"Oh, I don't have a preference. It's only that Grazyna had such unique and beautiful eyes, I was just wondering if his would be like hers."

"I don't think so, Jack. If I had to make a prediction, I would have to say that they will be more like yours, or just dark brown," she presumed.

Jozef finally released his father's hair and began looking around. Obviously, he could see across the room but preferred close-up and returned his gaze to Jack, attempting a toothless bite on his cheek. With Jozef snuggled in his arms, Jack had the oddest feeling that he had held a baby before, but again, like other similar situations, couldn't remember when.

"It's his suppertime. Would you like to feed him?" Sally asked.

"I've never done that before. I'm willing to give it a try," Jack answered.

The trio proceeded into the kitchen, and Jack pulled out a chair and sat at the table. A small dish of rice cereal was placed in front of him, and he automatically situated Jozef in a position where one arm was restrained and the other held by his father. Jack picked up the tiny baby spoon with his free hand and began to feed his son. Each spoonful eagerly received when placed at the cherub's lips.

"You obviously have fed a baby before. You're doing it like an old pro," Lavinia stated.

"I don't remember ever doing it," he insisted while using the edge of the spoon to gently remove a small amount of cereal that missed the target.

The two women gave each a knowing smile and sat at the table until Jozef was finished. Lavinia prepared a bottle and took the baby from his father. After making him comfortable in the nearby crib, the adults began to dine on the meal Lavinia had prepared earlier.

* * *

Isabella was overjoyed when she looked at the doorway and saw the outline of Lomas standing in her view. The tavern, kept in subdued light, made his image appear gossamer due to the daylight behind him. She dropped whatever she was occupied with and dashed to her husband's arms and whispered, "Lomas, il tesoro che le mie preghiere sono state risposte. Come lei è riuscito a avere un congedo dal campeggio?" (Lomas, darling, my prayers have been answered. How did you manage to have a leave from the camp?)

The Irish Confederate kissed the tears on her cheek and said softly, "Darling, you know I don't understand a word of Italian. Please talk to me in English."

"I'm just so excited to see you, sweetheart, I forgot." And taking him by the hand, she led Lomas up the stairs to their apartment. For the next hour, the mattress took a beating. It's impossible to tell which of the lovers was the happiest. At this moment, they shared an equal joy, and all doubt was removed regarding Lomas surrendering himself to Isabella for the rest of his life.

"Darling, you must be tired. Just rest here for a while. I need to go downstairs and help my parents, but I'll be back before you know it."

Lomas lay on the bed with his arms and legs stretched out and apart while Isabella made a quick trip to the bathroom before speed stepping back down the stairs. Ten minutes later, Lomas was out like a light and slept soundly until his lovely bride returned.

"*Amante*, are you asleep?" she inquired. Isabella soon realized that it was fruitless to attempt waking her husband at this point; therefore, she removed her clothing and snuggled for the night.

Mornings were not nearly as active as the evenings at the Eagle Inn and Tavern. Usually, only one family member could handle the obligations of supervising the clean-up crew, composed of cousins and aunts, and receiving any early deliveries. Taking turns, the remainder of the Manfredi family could sleep late, all but one day a week. Isabella performed her early-morning responsibilities the day prior, leaving the rest of her week idle until lunchtime. Now that Lomas was home, she made certain to have his breakfast ready for when he woke up. When he did wake up, he wanted something other than breakfast, and Isabella found herself back in bed for another hour.

"Your breakfast is cold, and I made it special for you," she whimpered.

"Honey, being separated from you as long as I've been, breakfast is the last thing on my mind," said Lomas hoarsely. "It ain't going to go to waste. All you got to do is ask if your cousins are hungry."

Having Lomas under their roof made the entire Manfredi family elated because Isabella was no longer melancholy. The effect of her happiness, like a broad brush, washed over everyone; and the cheerfulness was recognized by even the strangers. The day seemed to fly by, with each family member spending time talking to their new addition. As we all knew, Lomas could be very ingratiating when he put his mind to it; and no one left his table without positive opinions of the Irish version of Robin Goodfellow, the character in Shakespeare's play, also known as Puck. In *A Midsummer Night's Dream*, William Shakespeare referred to him as the shrewd and knavish sprite, a side of Lomas he made certain was not revealed.

As the afternoon turned into evening, the bar patrons began to fill the stools and, once all were taken, moved over to the tables. Lomas kept an eye peeled on the table in the far corner. The one in which the nightly poker game took place. Soon, that also began to fill in and Lomas edged closer, waiting for an invitation. They now knew who he was. They knew he was Isabella's new husband, they knew he was a Confederate soldier, they knew he was of Irish decent; but there was one thing about Lomas Chandler they didn't know. They didn't know that he was the best poker player in every city he resided, including Richmond.

"Hey, Lomas, come join us for a few hands," shouted the one shuffling the cards.

"Your game's too rich for my blood," the Irishman replied.

"We'll go easy on you, come on over," another insisted.

"There is one thing though. We don't play for Confederate money anymore. The value has dropped too much. Most of us buy chips with gold and redeem the gold when we turn in the chips," the first explained.

"Some of us redeem the gold," said the second player to a resounding round of laughter.

"I don't have any gold," Lomas stated.

"What do you have?" questioned the dealer.

"I got some jewelry Isabella doesn't know about," Lomas answered.

"Bring it over, we'll tell you what it's worth and you can draw the agreed-upon value in chips," the second player promised.

That was music to Lomas's ears, and he bounded the stairs to retrieve the small leather pouch he safely hid from Isabella. The men at the table determined the jewels to be worth $200 and suggested he only draw $50 in chips, in order to play it safe, until it was decided what level player he was. The ante was $5, and Lomas was in heaven. For the first hour, the men at the table coached Lomas as to when to drop out or raise the bet and he held his own. The players set an eleven o'clock curfew, and it was only minutes before the last hand. The cards were passed to Lomas who called for seven card stud poker and tossed in a $5 chip. His hole cards were a jack and three of diamonds and the next card up an ace of diamonds. When the player directly across from him had two kings facing, the price of poker increased appreciably. Only one player dropped out. When the last card was dealt, a pair of kings was the highest hand showing and its owner raised the previous bet twenty dollars. Another player folded. It was now between two kings showing and the dealer, with what appeared to be a possible pair of aces. Lomas called and raised twenty dollars. The player with kings showing turned over his hole cards and placed the third king on top the others saying, "Three kings.

Lomas flipped over his two hole cards and declared, "Diamond flush, ace high."

"I don't think we need to teach you anymore," said the one holding the second best hand. "Just make sure you're here next week so we can get a shot at winning it back."

"Sorry to disappoint you, gents, but my leave is only for one week. I would be happy to give you your money back, if there are any hard feelings," Lomas offered, reasonably sure they would have to refuse.

"No, that won't be necessary. You got to come back sometime. Just make sure you play poker with us."

"You can bet on it," Lomas honestly stated.

That night, the Irishman cashed in over $300 in chips for exchange in gold. In fact, two of the players asked permission to take jewelry in lieu of gold in order to create a good impression with their wives upon returning home. Isabella surmised that her husband came out of the game big winner and didn't say anything about it, waiting for Lomas to bring up the subject. And much to her satisfaction, he admitted to winning over $200. He also told her to hide it in a safe place because, if things keep going the way they are, the South would lose the war and Confederate money would be worthless. That much gold would save the business and even their lives if it would come to that. He had plans for the rest of the gold. It would be loaned to Jack Leffingwell for when he returned to Statesville. Jack was the most honest man he's ever met, and a loan to him was safer than money in a bank. Of course, it all depended upon their getting out of the army alive. Right now, the odds were pretty good.

It has been said that there are two things that should never be wasted: time and money. As their furlough came to an end, our sharpshooting friends could not be accused of wasting either. Jack Leffingwell made the most of his visit getting better acquainted with his infant son. When he held Little Jozef, he secretly wished that time would stop; but the relentless pendulum of the clock continued to follow its arc, day and night, rain or shine, and asleep or awake. Because of Jack's injury, the baby with a blue mark on his posterior was his first experience with a father's love for his child. There's no remorse or memories triggering a painful longing for his other children. While wanting the week to never end, Jack realized his salad days had now become watermelon time, and he must leave Jozef to the care of the two women who also loved him.

Lomas Chandler battled his strong desire to desert the military. Others had done it. *We're going to lose the war anyway.* He could think of several reasons why he should walk away from the army, but there was always the one reason to remain—the respect of Isabella and her family. This week was the happiest he had ever been in his entire life, and now, it was coming to a close. The pain of parting made him realize how much he loved Isabella and began the unfamiliar hollow feeling in the pit of his stomach. Leaving the Manfredi family standing at the door, Lomas and Isabella walked part way to the Robertson Hospital when he stopped and said, "Let's say our farewells here. I don't want to cry in front of my friend, Jack Leffingwell." They lingered in each other's arms for the longest time, and finally, Lomas turned without looking back and made his way to the appointed location for the return trip to camp.

Chapter Thirty-Three

Tell me what brand of whiskey that Grant drinks.
I would like to send a barrel of it to my other generals.

—Abraham Lincoln

In the eyes of President Lincoln, Gen. Ulysses S. Grant was now his favorite commissioned officer. Not so much because of his strategic military skills (although he had ample), but at last, here was a general willing to fight. After removing McClellan for his timid approach to engage in battle, Lincoln acted as his own supreme commander. In so doing, he found himself trying to manage the war from arm's length in Washington, D.C. While the Union army scored victories at various points, they operated independently of one another; and many times, the elusive Confederates escaped to fight again at another battle. The simultaneous victories at Gettysburg and Vicksburg highlighted the need for an over-all strategic plan, and a general who could carry it out.

Lincoln's mind was made up. A compatriot from Illinois, Ulysses Grant, was his man.

Earlier, Congress had revived Winfield Scott's old rank of lieutenant general; and on March 9, 1864, Grant was promoted to that position and ordered to come to Washington. Lincoln previously relieved Gen. Henry Halleck of the post, making room for Grant. Halleck's strengths lay in administrative issues, training, and deploying thousands of troops. He was not the grand strategist the president now needed. Upon Grant's arrival in Washington, he met with both President Lincoln and the brusque, hot-tempered Secretary of War, Edwin Stanton. The outcome of the meeting resulted in command, staff, and communication tools all ceded to the new general-in-chief. When the meeting ended, Grant made a tour of his newly acquired White House staff. Later, after Grant had left the building, the president returned to his office accompanied by Stanton.

"What do you think of our new chief general?" Lincoln asked, once the two were comfortably seated. It was important to the president that Edwin Stanton was completely on board with the appointment. Remarkably, after a shaky beginning, the two men had become good friends. At first, Edwin Stanton was skeptical of Lincoln's ability. Now, his opinion had changed. The manner in which Lincoln took ownership of the war and how he skillfully handled his political opponents in the Congress had garnered a deep respect for the former Illinois rail-splitter.

"I'm very impressed with his public reputation," said the quick-tempered Stanton. Silently, Stanton demurred before giving his answer. The hesitation did not escape the president.

"Yes, he has done a great deal to earn it, but I'm surprised he isn't much heftier," Lincoln stated as he leaned back in his chair, stretched his long legs, and tapped the toes of his size 14 shoes.

"Wasn't it you who told me it's not the size of the dog in the fight but the size of the fight in the dog?" Stanton replied.

"I don't believe so. I'm not one to use aphorisms or clichés during these difficult times," Lincoln said with a smile. That brought a rare chuckle from Stanton who rose from the chair, shook the president's hand, and walked to the doorway.

"Only time will tell," Stanton remarked as he withdrew from the room.

* * *

Grant physically removed himself from the politics of Washington and established his headquarters with General Meade in Northern Virginia. Meade, the victor at Gettysburg, chafed at the idea of Grant's proximity to his own and offered his resignation. A career officer, Meade would accept any assignment that might be given. Grant refused Meade's offer and told him that he had no intention of replacing him. Furthermore, he only chose to be with Meade to be closer to the real action and Lee's army. Grant made his headquarters with Meade for the remainder of the war and made the appropriate effort to give him due diligence.

By mid-April 1864, Grant had finalized his grand strategy and issued specific orders to each commander of four Federal armies. While Meade's Army of the Potomac, along with Burnside's independent corps, represented the major attack column under Grant's personal purview, the other armies would operate in a simultaneous and coordinated effort to his overall plan.

> First, Gen. Benjamin Butler's thirty-three thousand bluecoats were to skirt the south bank of the James River and menace Richmond, taking it, if possible, and destroy the railroads below Petersburg.
>
> Then, Maj. Gen. Franz Sigel's twenty-three-thousand-men army was to act as a rear guard in the Shenandoah Valley and advance on Lee's rail hub at Lynchburg, Virginia.
>
> Gen. William T. Sherman's one hundred thousand Federal troops were to march on Atlanta, defeat Confederate general Joseph E. Johnston's sixty-five thousand soldiers, and then move to devastate the resources of central Georgia.
>
> Gen. Nathanial Banks's forces were to disengage along the Red River and, with Rear Admiral David C. Farragut, make a limited amphibian landing against Mobile, Alabama, with the day to advance announced in May.

Back in Washington, Gen. Henry Halleck operated a war room for the new general-in-chief. By preparing brief digests of the several army commanders detailed field directives, Grant was saved hours of reading their meticulous reports. In addition, Halleck had a major job in keeping Grant informed about supply levels at base depots and advance dumps in various cities. Under Secretary Stanton, Quartermaster Montgomery C. Meigs dispatched men and munitions to Grant's subcommanders according to his strategic timetable. Together, they formed a rear-area team that understood the balance between theater objectives and the logistical support necessary to achieve them.

Lincoln's wish for a general, who could pull all the threads of an emerging strategy together and then concentrate the Union armies and their supporting naval power against the Confederacy, had finally come true.

* * *

The first combat of Ulysses S. Grant's strategic Virginia Overland Campaign took place in the Battle of the Wilderness, fought May 5-7, 1864. Under the watchful eyes of Confederate scouts, Union forces camped to the north of the Rapidan River gathered in strength until an aggregate of nearly 120,000 men in blue jackets stood ready.

The Battle of the Wilderness

On the morning of May 4, the Army of the Potomac, commanded by Gen. George Meade, crossed the Rapidan at three separate points at the edge of the Wilderness of Spotsylvania in central Virginia. The execution of Grant's overland plan to defeat Robert E. Lee's army of Northern Virginia had begun. At Grant's direction, the huge fighting force was to test Lee's right flank instead of his left. In order to do so, however, he must lead his troops through a dense and tangled wooded area known as the Wilderness of Spotsylvania. The unwelcome terrain of bramble, briar, and thicket prohibited Grant from bringing his artillery to bear. In addition, beginning in the wilderness worked in Lee's favor since Grant's superior numbers meant less. Actually, they became an encumbrance due to the narrow pathways and trails. And with limited visibility, it was nearly impossible for officers to exercise effective control over formations, leading to even more confusion. To make matters worse, the overcast sky might be the harbinger for a spring rain.

As mentioned earlier, the movement of Union troops came as no surprise to General Lee who had conducted constant surveillance from atop Clark's Mountain, an excellent observation post and signal station. He watched as the Federal army grew in size and looked for heightened activity that would indicate the advance to battle. During the night of May 3, Lee was informed of the Union army's movement. It was too dark to determine their direction; however, Lee responded by ordering Gen. Richard Ewell's Second Corps to be ready to march at dawn. The Gray Fox now knew that Grant was on the move although perplexed as to what direction he planned to take.

By the following morning of May 4, his questions were answered. Yet he still found it difficult to decipher the wisdom for such a maneuver. Nevertheless, by noon, he ordered General Ewell's waiting troops to move east along the Orange Turnpike, a gravel toll road connecting Fredericksburg with the Orange County Court House. And at the same time, Gen. A. P. Hill's Third Corps was to move east from the Orange Court House area, leaving one of his divisions, under Maj. Gen. Richard Anderson, to watch the river in case the enemy tried to slip behind him. With Gen. James Longstreet's First Corps, moving up in Hill's right flank, Lee anticipated the three corps forming a continuous north-south line.

Still unsure as to what General Grant's plans were, Lee sent a note to Confederate president Jefferson Davis admitting two possibilities. Gen. George Meade, under Grant's direction, could either turn his army and attack or move away toward Fredericksburg.

Marse Robert, forever cautious, hesitated to risk a direct confrontation without a better understanding as to what Grant had on his mind. At this point, General Lee's orders were for his corps to probe the enemy positions, but not bring on a general engagement. The Old Man was emphatic that he did not want a major skirmish until Longstreet could come up, and that wasn't expected before nightfall.

On the morning of May 5, Federal forces attacked Ewell's Second Corps on the Orange Turnpike. And as the Union troops continued to grow in size, Ewell's men erected earthworks on a commanding ridge west of the road. While preparing his defensive position, Ewell observed a column of Union troops heading south across the well-traveled thoroughfare and sent a dispatch rider to immediately inform General Lee.

The Federals hesitated making a full frontal attack because Ewell's line extended beyond the Union right, subjecting them to enfilade fire. Grant, driven by his compulsion to engage and defeat General Lee's army, underestimated the size of Ewell's forces and ordered General Meade to assail the enemy regardless of the length of their line. For the remainder of the day, both sides attacked and counterattacked as they stubbornly refused to give quarter. Visibility was limited to sometimes only a foot ahead. Soldiers were forced to thrash noisily and blindly forward through the underbrush, making them perfect targets for the concealed defenders. Sporadically, the jungle would open up to a small clearing favoring no one due to the corresponding confusion. At times, the fighting was hand to hand, turning the skirmish into a melee, with soldiers in blue and gray firing their weapons a foot apart from each other. Exploding shells ignited the woods, and both sides witnessed the horror of their wounded comrades being burnt to death. By the end of the day, neither had gained the advantage. If there was an edge in this near jungle, the Confederates had to be given points for being better woodsmen and more familiar with the terrain. The Union maps were worthless.

Gen. A. P. Hill's approach was detected by the Federals and Union general Meade sent his cavalry to defend the important intersection of the Orange Plank and Brock Roads. Using repeating carbines, they were able to briefly stall the Confederate advance until more troops arrived.

Initially, Gen. Henry H. Walker's brigade was stationed in a backup line of support, but as the opposing Federals continued to increase in strength, they were moved up to a frontline position. Although Jack Leffingwell and his sharpshooters were retained in the rear of their regiment, the terrain of dense stunted trees and twisted prickly bramble worked against them by camouflaging the enemy. Accuracy had taken a back seat as both sides rapidly fired blindly in the general direction of the other.

"Can you see the enemy?" Lomas Chandler shouted over the sounds of hiss and zing as bullets cut through the leaves of stunted trees.

"I can't see anything. I'm just shooting in the direction the bullets are coming from," Abel Strawn hollered back.

"Aim a little high," Jack added. "There's a steady stream of wounded coming back, and we don't want to hit our own men."

"It seems like the smoke is increasing. Which way is the wind blowing?" asked Melvin Kaufman.

"It's at our back," shouted Lomas. "Our artillery must have caught fire to the woods somewhere. I'm sure as hell glad we're not downwind from it."

"Oh shit," bellowed Melvin.

"What happened?" Jack shouted over the constant din of gunfire.

"I got hit in the arm," Melvin returned.

"Can you walk?" yelled Lomas.

"Hell yes, I can walk. I got hit in my arm, you dumb son of a bitch," Melvin thundered. The young soldier was obviously in severe pain.

"Are you bleeding badly?" asked Jack.

"Not too bad. I'm tying a shoelace above where I'm hit," Melvin yelled.

"Keep low and walk back to the field hospital. It's about a half mile behind us," ordered Jack.

Hiding behind earthen works, none of the marksmen saw Melvin's departure and could only hope he got to the field hospital in one piece. Soon they began to hear screams of the wounded caught by the fast-moving flames. Those who could walk were withdrawing rapidly. Those unable to walk were being burnt to death. Abel Strawn, the son of a Methodist minister, had always feared hell, but maintained a vague understanding of its true meaning. Now, here in the Spotsylvania wilderness, he was witnessing hell firsthand.

Confederate general Lee had set up his headquarters about a mile to the west at a small farm known as Widow Tapp. He also stationed Lt. Col. William T. Poaque's sixteen-artillery cannon east of the farm. The rebel artillery continuously fired canister after canister into the Union position to hold back their attack until Confederate reinforcements could show up. Finally, the vanguard of General Longstreet's column arrived, and the eight-hundred-man Texas Brigade helped stem the Union push.

At dawn on May 6, Grant's Federal forces attacked along the Plank Road, driving A. P. Hill's Third Corps back to near the Widow Tapp's farm. The Confederates' day was saved when Gen. James Longstreet's First Corps finally arrived. Lee's Old War Horse had rested his troops the day before, after a long march, and appeared on the field ready for action, driving the bluecoats back to the Brock Road. Longstreet's fresh forces mounted a surprise attack on the Union left flank and rolled up the Yankee's line even further. While riding forward to inspect his recently won skirmish, Longstreet encountered some of his own men returning. Believing Old Pete's mounted party to be the enemy, they opened fire, severely wounding the Confederate general in the neck and killing a brigade commander. Fierce fighting continued until nightfall with neither side gaining an advantage.

The two-day battle was inconclusive, but very damaging to both sides. General Grant did not retreat from the battle like his predecessors. Instead, he sent his army to the southeast and, coursing in an arc, began a campaign of maneuver that kept Lee on the defensive through a series of bloody battles, all the time moving closer to Richmond. Grant knew that his larger army and superiority in manpower could sustain a war of attrition better that Lee and the Confederacy.

Battle of the Wilderness (May 5-7, 1864)*

	Total Casualties	Wounded	Killed	Captured/Missing
Union	17,666	12,037	2,246	3,383
Confederate	11,125	7,690	1,495	1,940

*As stated by Bonekeeper, Victor, and Not a Butcher—wikipedia.org/wiki/Battle of the Wilderness.

At the beginning of Grant's Overland Campaign, the total Union army had 611,250 troops available for duty compared to 233,586 able Confederates soldiers. With three times as many troops, the outcome tilts heavily in Grant's favor. In order to prolong his ultimate fate, General Lee must avoid fighting in the open at all costs and do battle behind heavily fortified earthworks. In so doing, Marse Robert was winning the military tactics, and General Grant's strategy was winning the war.

On the morning of May 7, Grant was faced with the prospect of continuing the attacks against strong Confederate earthworks, rifle pits, parapets of abatis, artillery in position, and entrenched infantry. Instead of slugging it out, he chose to keep up his maneuver strategy. By moving south on the Brock Road, Grant hoped to reach the crossroads at Spotsylvania Court House, which would interpose his army between Lee and Richmond, forcing Lee to fight on ground more advantageous to the Union army. He ordered preparations for a night march on May 7 that would reach Spotsylvania, ten miles to the southeast, by the morning of May 8. Unfortunately for Grant, inadequate cavalry screening and bad luck allowed Lee's army to reach the crossroads before sufficient Union troops arrived to contest it. Once again faced with formidable earthworks, Grant fought the bloody Battle of

Spotsylvania Court House (May 8-21) before maneuvering yet again as the campaign continued toward Richmond.

The Battle of Spotsylvania Court House was the second major battle in Lt. Gen. Ulysses S. Grant's 1864 Overland Campaign. Following the bloody Battle of the Wilderness, Grant's army disengaged and moved to the southeast, attempting once again to lure Lee into battle under more favorable conditions. Elements of Lee's army beat the Union soldiers to the critical crossroads and began entrenching.

Fighting occurred on and off from May 8 through May 21, 1864, as Grant tried various schemes to break the Confederate line. Lee had established an advantageous position on an elevated area called Laurel Hill and blocked the Union army from their goal. Efforts to dislodge the rebels from Laurel Hill were both unsuccessful and costly. The frustrated Northern general ordered attacks across the Confederate line of earthworks that extended over four miles, including a prominent salient known as Mule Shoe. It became apparent that with each failure, General Grant, unlike those before him, became more determined. In the back of his mind, the Galena Tanner knew that ultimate victory would be his even if it would take dogging Lee all summer.

Thus far, Lee's rebel line of defense had proven to be impenetrable. A scheme proposed by one of Grant's officers caught his attention. It consisted of a tactic wherein several columns of massed infantry would rush across the open field and assault a small part of the enemy line, without pausing to trade fire, and, in so doing, overwhelm the defenders and achieve a breakthrough. At that point, fighting would be hand to hand until more troops arrived to widen the breach and expand their advantage. Union general Meade, among others, opposed the plan because of the unnecessary casualties it would bring upon their soldiers. The standard infantry assault over a wide battle line called for advancing more slowly and firing at the enemy as it moved forward. Grant, however, was intrigued and willing to risk casualties for the possible reward.

On May 10, Union colonel Emory Upton, the one who devised the strategy, led a group of twelve handpicked regiments or about five thousand men against an identified weak point on the west side of the Mule Shoe salient. The plan worked well in the beginning, and the defensive works were broken with rebel soldiers thrown back, suffering heavy casualties. However, with no Union support units arriving, General Lee was quick to organize a vigorous counterattack with brigades from all sectors of the Mule Shoe. Upton's men were driven out of the Confederate works and forced to retreat.

In spite of the reverses, Grant viewed Upton's failed assault with a degree of optimism. It was a partial success by the sheer fact that the rebel line was breached and the failure stemming from the lack of support. Grant reasoned that by using the same tactics with an entire corps, he might be successful. Gen. Winfield S. Hancock's Second Corps was assigned to repeat the assault on the Mule Shoe while other corps attacked the eastern end of the salient and applied pressure to Laurel Hill. As Hancock gathered his men, it began to pour down rain, a condition normally favoring defensive positions. Both officers and men were poorly prepared regarding the nature of the ground being covered and what obstacles to expect. Nevertheless, this time, the attack consisted of fifteen thousand infantrymen who crashed through the rebel works effectively destroying a defensive brigade, still the early success began to stall because of poor planning. No one had considered how to capitalize on the breakthrough. Hancock's Second Corps found itself crowded into a narrow front about a half mile wide and soon lost all unit cohesion.

Following the initial shock, Lee's army began to react to the Union onslaught. Reinforcements raced to the gaps that previously collapsed and, suffering heavy casualties, fought their way to regain their entrenchments.

Grant also sent in reinforcements that headed for the western leg of the Mule Shoe. Due to the intense fighting, this sector would become known as the Bloody Angle with Union brigade after brigade slamming into the Confederate line. The rain came down in buckets, and both sides fought on the slippery rebel earthworks amid their artillery exchanging fire on each other. As the day wore on, it became evident that the two armies were stalemated. The furious fighting continued day and night with neither side gaining the advantage. The entire landscape was flattened, all foliage was destroyed, and bodies were piled up one on top the other. The ghastly scene was made worse by the twitching of bodies among the dead, signifying that some were still alive within the heap of decaying corpses.

The Seventh Tennessee regiment lost another leader when Gen. Henry H. Walker was severely wounded by a Yankee minié ball, while he encouraged his soldiers from horseback. His left foot was shattered and later amputated in the nearest field hospital. Subsequently, command was assigned to Col. B. D. Fry from the combined rebel brigades.

Lomas Chandler learned that Melvin Kaufman was intercepted by medics and escorted to a surgeon's tent. The fact of him still being alive came as welcome news to the marksmen. What they didn't know was that their friend had lost his left arm. Such amputations were routine and, considering the state of medical practice in 1864, the safest treatment.

Throughout the battle, General Lee's engineers were busy creating a new defensive line about a quarter mile farther south. On May 13, the Confederate infantrymen were notified that the new line was ready, and they withdrew from the original earthworks unit by unit.

Jack Leffingwell and the sharpshooters were more than happy for the move to a new line. Besides the assurance of fighting from behind new undamaged earthworks, it would relieve them from the growing odor of decaying bodies and, temporally, the sickening sounds and sight of the vacated remains of war.

Despite the significant casualties of May 12, Grant remained undeterred and took this opportunity to reorient his own lines. He ordered a shift to the center of Lee's defenses east of Spotsylvania where he planned to renew the battle. On the night of May 13-14, Union troops began a difficult march in heavy rain over the nearly unnavigable muddy roads. Having endured five days of almost constant rain, Grant's army was too scattered and exhausted to undertake another assault against Lee's rebel line. He sent an element of his Second Corps to occupy an elevated position called Myers Hill, a point at which overlooked most of the Confederate line. Then, somewhat uncharacteristically, Grant waited for the weather to improve.

On May 17, the weather cleared enough for the Yankee general to resume the offensive. Assuming the original Confederate line was now lightly defended, Grant ordered another major attack on the Mule Shoe. He was in store for a big surprise. The works were still occupied by General Ewell's Second Corps. Ewell had used the intervening time to improve the earthworks and still retained his artillery. When the Union soldiers attacked, they were caught up in newly placed abatis and artillery fire so intense that infantry rifle fire was not necessary to repulse the assault. After yet another repulse, Grant decided to forget about the Mule Shoe as a battlefield and ordered General Hancock's Second Corps to move south in hopes Lee would fall in behind them to attack, at which time the remainder of the Union army would move and catch the crafty rebel general's troops away from their trenches. Lee refused to be fooled into open combat and took a parallel path to Grant's movement and beat him to the North Anna River, where only a series of small actions took place.

On May 23, Grant's V Corps forded the river at Jericho Mills and held their beachhead against a division from Gen. A. P. Hill's Confederates. That night, Lee and his engineers devised a masterful scheme for defensive earthworks in the shape of an inverted V that could split the Union army when it advanced, thus reducing the amount of attackers and allowing the Confederate interior lines to defeat one wing.

Grant initially fell into this trap, but soon avoided his frontal tactics and, after two days of minor skirmishes, ordered another wide movement to the southeast. His objective was the crossroads of Cold Harbor. From these intersections, the Union army was positioned to receive reinforcement, sailing up the Pamunkey River, and be able to attack either the Confederate capital or the Army of Northern Virginia.

Battle of Spotsylvania Court House (May 8-21, 1864)*

	Total Casualties	Wounded	Killed	Captured/Missing
Union	18,399	13,416	2,725	2,258
Confederate	13,421	6,285	1,467	5,719

*As stated by Bonekeeper, Victor, and Not a Butcher—wikipedia.org/wiki/Battle of Spotsylvania Court House.

The Battle of Cold Harbor

Despite its name, Cold Harbor was not a port city. Rather, it described two rural crossroads named for the Cold Harbor Tavern located in the Mechanicsburg area. Old Cold Harbor stood two miles east of Gaines's Mill and New Cold Harbor, a mile southeast. Fought from May 31 to June 12, the battle represented one of the final major clashes in Grant's Overland Campaign. Thousands of Union soldiers were killed or wounded in a desperate frontal assault against Gen. Robert E. Lee's well-fortified positions. The outcome resulted in one of Lee's most lopsided victories, and ironically, it was also the Gray Fox's last major triumph.

On May 31, as Grant's army once again swung around the Confederate right flank, Union cavalry seized the crossroads of Old Cold Harbor and held it until the blue jacket infantry arrived.

On June 2, both armies were in place, and the Confederates built an elaborate series of fortifications seven-mile long. Lee's engineers constructed an ingenious defensive configuration of earth-and-log barricades with artillery posted on every avenue of approach. Even stakes were driven in the ground to aid their gunners' range estimates.

At dawn on June 3, three Union corps attacked the Confederate works on the southern end of the rebel line and was easily repulsed, sustaining heavy casualties. Similar attempts on the northern end of Lee's works were also unsuccessful. Waves of Federal brigades charged into the face of Confederate firepower without any gain. The recklessness of Billy Yank's self-destruction was a testament to their bravery, but begs the question as to their leader's wisdom.

Grant would later rue the day he ordered the last assault on Cold Harbor. Not only because it lowered the morale of his remaining troops, but it caused a rise in antiwar sentiment back home, with some referring to him as the "fumbling butcher."

In the final analysis, no matter how ill advised the attack on Cold Harbor was, Lee had lost the initiative and was forced to devote his attention to the defense of Richmond and Petersburg behind his fortified trench lines.

The Battle of Cold Harbor*

	Total Casualties	Wounded	Killed	Captured/Missing
Union	12,737	9,077	1,844	1,816
Confederate	4,595	3,380	83	1,132

*Estimates of casualties sometimes widely differ. The numbers presented are those of Bonekeeper, Victor, and Not a Butcher given in wikipedia.org/Battle of Cold Harbor.

After the slaughter, Grant launched no more attacks on Cold Harbor. For the next nine days, the opposing armies confronted each other in trench warfare. Sharpshooters worked continuously, killing many who braved the open field of battle. An occasional rush pit the foes only yards apart, but with the artillery bombardment from both sides, a return to the trenches deemed the most rational judgment. Grant employed several Coehorn mortars that lobbed their shell in a high arc over the rebel trenches before exploding in scattered fragments—its effectiveness limited, since the Confederate soldiers could see them coming. Lee responded with a twenty-four-pound howitzer, depressing a sinister trail within the Union positions.

The trenches were hot, dirty, and miserable. Conditions were worse between the lines, where thousands of wounded Federal soldiers suffered horribly without food, water, or medical attention. General Grant, stubborn as a mule, refused to ask for a formal truce that would allow him to recover his wounded because, in his obstinate view, it would acknowledge he had lost the battle. When he finally requested a two-hour truce, it was too late for most of the unfortunate wounded.

Once again, recognizing another stalemate, the Federal general withdrew from Lee's front and moved across the James River. This time he was able to disguise his intentions as the bluecoats crossed on a 2,100-foot bridge of pontoons erected by Union engineers. Uppermost in Lee's mind was a forced siege of Richmond. Grant, however, determined a more efficient way to get at Richmond and the Old Man straddling an iron gray horse named Traveller. (Ironically, it would be the same horse that followed the caisson bearing the Confederate general's casket during Lee's funeral procession in 1870.)

A few miles to the south, the city of Petersburg contained crucial rail links that supplied the capital. Grant determined that if the Union army could seize it, for all practical purposes, Richmond would be taken. Lee anticipated the Federal maneuver and quickly moved his Confederate army to reinforce the impregnable defenses already in place.

Both sides settled in for a siege that would last for the next ten months. It's somewhat a misnomer to call the next battle a siege, since Lee's supply lines remained open, even though the two sides fought behind trenches.

After Grant unsuccessfully assaulted Petersburg, he then constructed his own trench lines, eventually extending over thirty miles, from the eastern outskirts of Richmond to the southern outskirts of Petersburg.

Over the next few months, Grant conducted numerous raids in attempts to cut off the railroad supply lines between Petersburg and Richmond. However, the Confederates were able to repel the attacks.

In order to maintain his supply route, Lee was forced to lengthen the trench lines to the point of thinning his already-inferior manpower.

Grant's armies continued to be significantly larger than Lee's rebel columns. After Cold Harbor, Lee was outnumbered two to one. He managed to replace most of his twenty thousand casualties with veterans from inactive fronts. Grant, on the other hand, had lost twice that amount and another twenty thousand who went home after their enlistment ended. While a temporary setback, the Union had many men available and reinforced with troops pulled out of Washington, D.C. Although some were either raw recruits or artillery crews unfamiliar with infantry tactics, there were now over one hundred thousand black troops ready for assignment. In a war of attrition, it's the numbers that count, and Grant held four aces.

Casualty Estimates for the Overland Campaign*

	Total Casualties	Wounded	Killed	Captured/Missing
Union	54,926	38,339	7,621	8,966
Confederate	32,631	18,566	4,206	9,861

*Estimates of casualties sometimes widely differ. The numbers presented are those of Bonekeeper, Victor, and Not a Butcher given in wikipedia.org/Battle of Cold Harbor.

The Siege of Petersburg

The siege that wasn't a siege lasted nine months with a series of unsuccessful attacks on Petersburg and constant trench warfare. At the time, Petersburg was a prosperous city of eighteen thousand inhabitants and the railroad supply base for the entire area, not to mention, General Lee's army and the capital city of Richmond. As late as 1862, Petersburg was an unfortified city. In August of that year, Confederate general Lee ordered his engineers to examine the area and establish a line of works to defend that position. It was decided to encircle the town with a ring of partially enclosed forts, connected by trench lines. Its construction required over four thousand rebel troops helped by as many as one thousand conscripted slaves from nearby plantations in Virginia. It was completed under the supervision of Capt. Charles Dimmock; hence, the line was known as the Dimmock Line. The finished line consisted of fifty-five numbered batteries connected by entrenchments completely encircling the town south of the Appomattox River, even so, there were some important defects. Some of their projected salients were vulnerable to enemy attack. Too many guns were exposed above the parapets and insufficient fields of fire had been cleared in front of the line. An attacking army would be able to approach the fortifications and establish trench lines of their own. This is exactly what General Grant did.

Attempts to Cut Off the Railroads

Failing to capture Petersburg by assault, Grant's next objective was to secure or disable the three remaining open rail lines that served Petersburg and Richmond: the Richmond and Petersburg, the South Side Railroad, and the Weldon Railroad. By cutting these supply lines, he could starve the two cities already suffering from extreme shortages in food, clothing, medicine, and everyday items necessary to conduct even a meager existence.

The Weldon Railroad, with over 160 miles of track, was the longest in the world when first completed in 1840. It now was the most vital supply and transportation route for the Confederacy.

On June 21-23, under Grant's orders, General Meade sent elements of his Second Corps on a probing mission against the Weldon RR. The Confederates, more familiar with the area's terrain, hid in a ravine and emerged behind the Federal troops, catching them by surprise. The startled bluecoats ran for cover and rallied around earthworks they had previously constructed.

On June 23, after stabilizing their line, Meade's Second Corps took back lost ground after the Confederates had pulled back, abandoning the earthworks previously captured. A second attempt by Meade's forces was driven back with only minimal damage to a short segment of track. While the rebel troops retained control of the Weldon Railroad, the siege lines were stretched farther to the west, weakening Lee's thin line even more.

On June 22 to July 1, Union general Meade, undaunted by previous failures, intensified his raids to destroy as much of the South Side Railroad as possible. His assault consisted of two cavalry divisions commanded by Gens. James A. Wilson and August Kautz. General Wilson took his contingent seven miles south of Petersburg and commenced destroying Weldon Railroad track and cars at Reams Station. Kautz's men moved to the west to Ford's Station and began destroying track, locomotives, and cars on the South Side Railroad. Wilson proceeded to the junction of the Richmond and Danville Railroad where he encountered Rooney Lee's cavalry. Leaving a brigade to fend off the Confederate cavalry element, Wilson followed Kautz along the South Side Railroad, destroying about thirty miles of track as they went. On June 24, while Kautz remained skirmishing around Burkeville, Wilson crossed over to Meherrin Station on the Richmond and Danville line and began destroying track. The tactic of two separate divisions seemed to be working. While one confronted the Confederates, the other continued destroying the railroads.

On June 25, Rooney Lee's mounted soldiers closed on the Federals from the northeast and skirmished with Wilson's rear guard. At that point, the two Union generals decided to abandon their mission and retreated back to the safety of their own lines in the east. Confederate general Robert E. Lee saw an opportunity and sent more cavalry troops to pursue and attack the retreating Wilson and Kautz.

Wilson had received assurances from Meade's chief of staff, Maj. Gen. Andrew A. Humphreys, that the Army of the Potomac would be immediately taking control of the Weldon Railroad, at least as far south as Reams Station.

With this understanding, it made sense to the former topographic engineer that that would be an appropriate place to return to the Union line.

Wilson and Kautz were caught off guard when they drew within ten miles south of Reams Station. Blocking their path from behind well-constructed earthworks were hundreds of Confederate cavalry and infantry awaiting their arrival. Kautz's division, following Wilson's, had taken a back road and approached Reams Station from the west. Once the two joined up, they found themselves virtually surrounded. Wilson's men tried to break through, but had to fall back when the rebel soldiers began to envelope their left flank. Kautz attacked along the Depot Road and was driven back by another Confederate counterattack.

Wilson, dogged by Robert E. Lee's son Rooney Lee and his cavalry division, now found himself confronted by main Confederate forces. He managed to slip a messenger through the lines, urgently asking General Meade for help. Meade, realizing that foot soldiers would take too long to arrive, requested that Gen. Phil Sheridan's cavalry division send aid.

The Wilson-Kautz railway raiders were hopelessly caught in the Confederate trap. Not knowing when or, even if, help would arrive soon, they burned their wagons and disabled their artillery pieces before fleeing to the north. The two Union cavalry brigades ended up losing hundreds of men as prisoners and suffered nearly 1,500 casualties or about a quarter of their forces. At least three hundred escaped slaves, who had joined the Union cavalrymen along their route of wrecking flat bottom rails, were abandoned during the retreat. Their mission resulted in the destruction of about sixty miles of railroad track which took several weeks for the Confederate gandy dancers to repair.

Grant was not happy over the outcome of the Wilson-Kautz raids. Designed to only tear up Lee's *permanent way*, he figured it was too big a loss for what little was accomplished.

Tenacious as a hyena, Lincoln's top general never gave up on the objective of drawing Lee out into the open or at least diluting his forces positioned behind earthen works and trenches. To that effect, Grant devised a plan by which he would feint another attack on Richmond in hopes that Lee responds by taking troops from Petersburg to reinforce the capital's defenses. On July 27-29, he ordered Gen. Winfield S. Hancock's Second Corps and two cavalry divisions of Gen. Philip H. Sheridan to cross the river at Deep Bottom and advance on Richmond. (Deep Bottom refers to a horseshoe-shaped bend in the James River that offers a convenient crossing point from the south side.)

When Lee found out about it, he ordered the Richmond lines to be reinforced, taking troops from the defenses at Petersburg. Grant's plan worked, and after a few skirmishes, the Union expedition was terminated and the Federal troops were recalled.

Chapter Thirty-Four

There's anxiety, battle fatigue, lack of sleep and they're miles from home. Any of those is difficult, but all of them together is bad.

—Robert Davis

During the Union's siege of Petersburg, the Seventh Tennessee regiment fought continuously in the trenches. The Second Maryland Battalion was added to beef up forces that were in very poor condition. The casualties resulting from the Battle of the Wilderness, Spotsylvania Court House, and Cold Harbor had taken a terrible toll on both manpower and morale. Making matters worse, conditions in the trenches were lacking in proper sanitation. Soldiers were being lost to common infections including dysentery, typhus, and cholera. Many suffered from fungal infections and others even from rat bites.

Burial of the dead was something neither side could agree on; therefore, bodies would lie in no-man's land for extended periods of time. (This created more of a problem for the Federals since Lee's soldiers remained in the trenches as the Union men attacked.) The Confederate main fortifications weren't of the closed type and had an opening that faced the town, giving limited egress to the troops. Still, many latrines consisted of holes dug in the ground and were located nearby. After any rainfall mud was prevalent and flat boards had to be lain over puddles to allow soldiers to move about and not sink in sludge over their ankles.

While Jack Leffingwell and his sharpshooters were stationed on the western end of Lee's defenses, General Grant had captured enough of the eastern area to deploy artillery and fire on the citizens of the town. Petersburg's factories, public buildings, and dwellings became targets. More than six hundred structures sustained some kind of shell damage, and civilian evacuees were driven from their homes. Ironically, on the western side of town, out of range of Federal guns, people walked about in everyday activities, dodging an occasional shell. On a much smaller scale, it was sort of reminiscent of London during the Second World War.

The rebel riflemen gave visible evidence of the present state of affairs. They now sported scraggly beards, not having shaved in weeks, and clothing that would erupt in a dust cloud, should they receive a pat on the back. It was impossible to eat without biting down on grains of sand, with the shock followed by concern that it might be a piece of broken tooth, since dental hygiene rode the back seat of the personal care engine, now in general decline. Each man had lost at least twenty pounds of flesh, making cheekbones more evident. A premature aging was reflected by a more furrowed brow and faces that appeared to always display a frozen grimace. All things considered, they had held up remarkably well after nearly four years in deadly combat.

"You know what I really miss right now?" Abel asked no one in particular. "Remember when we spent the winter in the Shenandoah Valley at the base of the Blue Ridge Mountains?"

"I sure do," Lomas replied. "It was at the Berryville winter camp two years ago. That was where we built our own log cabin."

"That's right. Remember the mountain stream located behind the cabin?"

"I think I know where you're coming from," said Lomas. "That mountain creek was where we took a bath."

"You got it, Lomas, and I sure wish I was back there now so I could take another one," Abel stated.

"That was when we first met Melvin Kaufman. We sure gave him a rough time and, as I recall, made him take a bath before we let him come in the cabin," Lomas added.

"Do you remember some of that, Jack?" asked Abel.

"Nope, I don't remember any of it," Jack answered.

Abel Strawn slowly shook his head. Even now he still had difficulty accepting Jack's amnesia. The doctors said that eventually Jack would get his memory back. After this long of a period, Abel doubted it would ever happen. Nevertheless, he would continue praying for a miracle.

"Hey, Jack," Lomas shouted over the rumble of artillery from both sides. "How many colored did you take to freedom when you were part of the Underground Railroad?"

"Oh, I don't know exactly, I got no memory of it. It could be around fifty or sixty," the mountain man replied. "Why do you ask?"

"I was just wondering what you thought about it now that they're over there with the bluecoats and trying to kill you," Lomas said blandly.

"It all seems crazy, doesn't it?" Jack said. "I have thought about it. I've thought about it a lot. The only way I can reconcile it is that we are fighting for two different things. I'm defending the South against Northern aggression, and they are fighting for their freedom."

"So if they kill you, it's okay?"

"No, it's just a mistake."

"And people say that I'm crazy," Lomas imparted cynically.

The sharpshooters were silent again and peered over their trenches, looking for the slightest movement in the Union line. They had worked out a system. If the movement was on the right side of the enemy's line, Abel Strawn took the shot; on the left, it belonged to Lomas Chandler; and any movement in the center would fall victim to Jack Leffingwell's Whitfield rifle.

* * *

Back in Washington, it was beginning to look like Abraham Lincoln would be a one-term president. The North had become very war-weary and lacked enthusiasm to continue the fight. It was a time of depression for the president and a gloomy period for the Union cause. Many newspapers published a continuous stream of invective criticism pandering to those in opposition and agreement. The president himself was caught on the horns of a dilemma: General Sherman, stalled outside Atlanta, and, in the east, Robert E. Lee had Gen. Ulysses S. Grant in a stalemate. At the same time, the country was calling for peaceful negotiations to end the war.

Even though the national election loomed a short time ahead, Lincoln stood his ground.

Pressure continued to mount. The price of gold rose to the point it affected national credit. A few months earlier, the president's call for more army volunteers failed. Left with no other choice, Lincoln instituted a draft order for a half million more recruits and riots resulted. The Democratic opposition began naming those whom they felt would defeat the incumbent; and from all indication, they will settle on George Brinton McClellan, a nemeses previously removed of command by Lincoln early in the war.

The president had lost the exuberant look of confidence as he worried with regard to winning reelection in November. He walked about with a sorrowful and sad face, not unlike his usual appearance, but now without the fire to accompany it.

Lincoln often suffered from bouts of depression, dating back to his youth. When witnessed in the public purview, it was referred to as his being melancholy. It was more than that. There were periods when he was bedridden for days and sometimes longer.

Young Lincoln wrote and quoted maudlin poetry and defended suicide, especially after the untimely death of Ann Rutledge. The evidence of a love affair between Lincoln and Rutledge was lacking, but when you take note of his actions in the aftermath, you're led to believe it did exist.

The evidence that our sixteenth president suffered from clinical depression is indeed a different story. It became a lifelong battle and a testimonial to the old adage, "If the stick doesn't break your back, it will make you strong." Lincoln dedicated his life to overcoming any mental imperfection by substituting humor in place of despair, generosity over parsimony, and humility over arrogance, on his way to becoming the greatest president in U.S. history. (Sadly, in today's environment, were he to run for the same office, Lincoln couldn't make it past the vetting process.)

Battle of the Crater

No one was more aware of Lincoln's need for change in the present status of the war than Union general-in-chief Ulysses S. Grant. So much so that he was willing to entertain almost any innovative ideas to alter the situation. One of the most bizarre proposals put forward was from Lt. Col. Henry Pleasants, a mining engineer from Pennsylvania. He proposed digging a long mine shaft underneath the Confederate defenses and planting explosive charges directly underneath a fort in the middle of the Confederate First Corps line. If successful, when the explosives were ignited, it would open a gap in the rebel line big enough for the Federals to rush in and attack from behind the enemy's fortifications. At first, Grant was leery of the scheme and considered it folly. As the pressure continued to mount in Washington, Grant had no choice but to give it a try.

Digging began in late June. It took about a month to create a mine with an approach shaft 511 feet long and, at its end, a perpendicular run of 75 feet extending in both directions.

The cotton state allies above the project could feel occasional earth movement beneath their feet, but attributed it to the incessant Federal guns firing shells and lobbing mortars.

The passageway was filled with eight thousand pounds of gunpowder buried twenty feet underneath the Confederate works.

Union general Ambrose Everett Burnside had trained a division of colored troops to lead the assault. General Meade, lacking in confidence in the operation from the beginning, had issued an order not to use them. He feared that, if it failed, they would be killed needlessly, creating a political repercussion in the North. He asked for volunteers. None were forthcoming. Finally, a replacement white division was selected by drawing lots. While the black troops were trained for the assault, the white replacements weren't even briefed as to what was expected of them.

Early on the morning of July 30, the charges exploded in a massive shower of earth, men, and guns. The thunderous sound awakened sleeping citizens in the town of Petersburg and stunned any soldiers not privy to the project. The assault group of white soldiers, startled and shocked by the magnitude of the blast, lingered for several minutes before leaving their own entrenchments. Once they moved forward, they proceeded down into the crater instead of around it as the original plan detailed. Accordingly, no ladders were provided to assist those some thirty feet down to use in exiting the enormous hole. The Confederates gathered as many troops they could and staged a counterattack. In less than an hour, they formed around the man-made cavern and began firing their rifles and artillery down into it.

The Union plan had failed. Making matters worse, instead of cutting their losses, General Burnside sent in additional men, only to be faced with considerable flanking fire as they went down into the crater and were slaughtered in their attempt to escape. Grant was mortified. Union losses after the explosion were significant and unnecessary.

Casualty Estimates for the Battle of the Crater*

	Total Casualties	Wounded	Killed	Captured/Missing
Union	3,798	1,881	504	1,413
Confederate	1,500	900	200	400

*Many of the Union losses were from the U.S. colored troops who were originally trained to lead the assault. Had plans gone unchanged, the outcome would have been different. In all likelihood, Union troops would have proceeded into the town of Petersburg from their advantage.

Chapter Thirty-Five

The best and most beautiful things in this world cannot be seen or even heard, but must be felt with the heart.

—Helen Keller

Hope Waterman was going over the list of new arrivals at Chimborazo Hospital when her eyes fell upon a name familiar to her—Melvin Kaufman. Could it be the same Melvin Kaufman she grew fond of over a year ago? She had written him two letters without a response. It was obvious to her that he didn't share the same affection. Still, reading his name and the fact he had been wounded increased her heartbeat. She decided then and there to find out why he hadn't written her after promising to do so. With a quickened gait, Hope walked to the nearest receptionist and asked in what section his bed resided.

Chimborazo was a very large convalescent medical facility. Without knowledge of an exact location, a visitor could spend the entire day in the hunt, without success. Up to four thousand patients resided there at any one time, and without foreknowledge, finding a specific person would certainly be like the old adage, "Hunting for a needle in a haystack." Melvin was quartered in a building facing a small common, exhibiting a green lawn, shade trees, and a few benches. Discovering him away from his bed, Hope asked if the patients on either side knew his whereabouts.

"You should find him outside," answered one of the soldiers. "He spends a lot of time sitting on the benches."

Hope raised her hand in order to shield the brilliant sunlight as she stepped outside and visibly searched the grounds. Every bench was in use, making her concentrate on benches with only one occupant. She saw him sitting alone with a woebegone expression and staring straight ahead.

"Good morning, Melvin, do you remember me?" she asked, startling him out of his reverie. He was struck dumb for a few seconds and couldn't answer.

"Yes, I remember," Melvin finally stammered.

"Why are you here? Have you been wounded?" Hope questioned.

"Because of this," Melvin replied, while raising the armless sleeve of his shirt.

"I'm so sorry. Do you mind if I sit beside you for a while?"

Melvin moved to the end of the bench allowing Hope to sit down. His heart pounded until there was a ringing in his ears. Pretty girls always did that to him, and Hope was a rose among flowers.

"Care to tell me how you got injured?" Hope asked after positioning herself on the seat and straightening out the wrinkles in her skirt.

"I got shot," he answered tersely.

"As I recall, you were part of a group of sharpshooters. Did any of them get shot," the young girl questioned. "I believe their names were Abel Strawn and Jack Leffingwell. I know about Mr. Leffingwell from correspondence with his wife Abigail. We became the best of friends while she was visiting here in Richmond."

"I don't think my friends were hurt, at least not in that fight. I had to leave them because I was bleeding a lot, and Captain Leffingwell told me to head back to the field hospital," Melvin answered.

"Did it hurt terribly?"

"It hurt at first. It hurt a lot, and then it just got numb. I was bleeding awful so I took off my belt and pulled it tight around my arm and it slowed down some. The medics found me and helped me to the field hospital tent. The surgeon took one look and cut off my arm. They gave me something to put me asleep, but it didn't work. It hurt when he was cutting. I must have been in a state of shock because I passed out. When I woke up, I was lying on a cot, and a little later, they loaded me in an ambulance and brought me here to Chimborazo. That just about sums it up," Melvin drawled.

"I think you are about the bravest man I've ever met," Hope asserted.

"Heck, there weren't any bravery to it. What I did just come natural like. I've seen lots of bravery in this here war, and what happened to me don't qualify."

"I don't care what you say, Melvin Kaufman. To me, you are a very brave man and gave his arm to prove it. I call people like that heroes."

Her words seemed to improve Melvin's outlook. Hope had the inherent ability to becalm those in her presence, especially the young soldier from Watertown, Tennessee.

Melvin never quite overcame his self-effacement; and now, missing his left arm, self-esteem couldn't be any lower. When they first met, Hope appeared to choose his company over Lomas Chandler's. Something he found hard to believe and impossible to explain. Today, in his presence, she acted totally natural, as if the space of nearly two years were only two days. They sat on the bench together and talked until the Virginia sun, once high overhead, began to slowly decline toward the west. Most of the benches were now empty, save a few couples still oblivious to their surroundings. Somewhere off in the distance, a bell began to peal. It was a doleful sound signaling the end of visiting hours.

"I guess visiting hours are over. It's close to your dinnertime, and you must be getting hungry. How are the meals here at the hospital?"

"Not too bad. Better than in the field. I think the Yankees are sitting to a much better table than we are. How about here in Richmond?"

"It's considerably worse since the last time you were here, but we are able to make do," Hope said sadly. "I'm going to visit Robertson and a couple others in the morning. I'll be back here in the afternoon. I have a question that I must ask you, so save me a seat."

With that she gathered her things, and the two walked slowly back to the building and said their adieus. For the first time since being at the Chimborazo Hospital, Melvin exhibited a smile and took a lot of guff for it, from the patients near his bed.

"How come you guys from Tennessee get all the good-looking women?" a soldier from Alabama wanted to know.

"He's so damn ugly that with part of him gone, he looks better to them," another chimed in jest.

"If that's the reason, I would have cut mine off by myself," squalled another.

Melvin now realized that the others actually liked him and were only waiting for the opportunity to break their silence.

"If you guys are serious, I know a surgeon that I can recommend," he said jokingly.

To a man, the wounded rebels began to moan loudly, and finally one said, "They rang the dinner bell a long time ago. Let's skedaddle before it's all gone."

That night, Melvin slept without the interruption of a nightmare. He did wake up and reach for the corner of his blanket with his missing arm, only to chuckle quietly to himself. Old habits are hard to break. This one would take longer than most.

The thought that Hope would visit him later in the day made time crawl. Anticipation has a way of making one pensive, sort of sitting on pins and needles. It's a human emotion involving several of our senses such as pleasure, excitement, and anxiety, awaiting an expected event. At times, anticipation is nature's way of relieving stress by looking forward to a desirable outcome. It also is one of the central ingredients in a human's sexual desire.

Growing older, I've come to understand that my greatest expectations and worse fears never materialize. It's always something in between. If we take the time to think about it, it's that way for all of us.

A scattered shower was the majority of opinion for today's weather. Thus far, they were spot-on. Rain appeared just before daylight and came down heavily an hour before lunchtime. Melvin stood in the doorway leading to the grassy common and grudgingly accepted the fact that Hope would not call on him today. Surrendering to that unpleasant actuality, he joined the others at the lunch table.

"Do you think your girlfriend will show up with it raining so much?" asked the soldier wearing a bandage over his right eye. He was a candidate for an ocular prosthesis (commonly called a glass eye) but not at Chimborazo, since the procedure is quite complicated and requires a specialist. In all likelihood, he would end up wearing a black patch for the rest of his life.

"She probably won't, women aren't usually out and about when it rains this hard," Melvin answered as he pushed his plate forward. He wasn't hungry.

"Hey, don't give up too soon. The way she was looking at you, she may show up in spite of the rain," another piped up from across the table.

It didn't take much to resurrect Melvin's hopefulness; and shortly after leaving the lunch table, he found himself once again standing at the doorway, facing empty benches. At that point, he saw it. Standing on the right side of the glistening green sward was a small pavilion and a lone table positioned underneath. From a distance, it appeared dry. Braving the gentle shower, he dashed across the common and found the structure protected from the elements. If Hope decided to chance the rain, she would at least stay dry during her visit. Melvin sat on the seat facing the doorway and settled in for a long wait.

Hope found him with his head lying over his arm and sound asleep. She shook her umbrella free of water and laid it beside her, after taking the seat across from the sleeping soldier. She couldn't help smiling to herself. Melvin was the only man, besides her father, with whom she had ever felt a connection or bond. She accepted the intellectual differences between them because of his tenderness and kind heart. Due to her youth, Hope hadn't grown sensitive to social status, and the fact Melvin came from a poor background meant nothing to her. She had never felt more comfortable with anyone of the opposite gender, and the happiness she experienced at this moment could only mean one thing.

"Melvin," she said as she placed her hand on his arm.

He woke with a start. It took a few seconds for Melvin's mind to clear, and then he said, "I'm sorry, I must have dozed off. What time is it?"

"Around three o'clock. Have you been waiting long? This weather has slowed me down quite a bit today."

"I was afraid the rain might keep you away today," Melvin confessed.

"No chance of that. When I told you I would be here, a little rain wasn't going to keep me away. Besides, there's something I need to ask you," Hope seriously stated.

"Ask me anything, I'm all ears," Melvin volunteered.

"When you were here last, I thought we hit it off pretty well. You seemed to have taken a liking to me, and I tried to let you know I felt the same way about you. You promised to write me. I wrote you two letters, to which you never replied. I need to know why. Perhaps I was wrong to think you looked upon me affectionately, but if so, you must tell me now."

"I tried to write you back, but I wasn't able to put the thoughts in my head down on paper. I tried several times. I'm not as smart as you, and the more I thought about us, the more I came to realize that nothing would ever happen between us, no matter how much I wanted it."

"Then the matter is settled. We must plan for the future. What do you plan to do after release from Chimborazo? You cannot go back to the field; therefore, you must serve in other ways. I will talk to my father . . . We will talk to my father about it. You can plan on having dinner with us this Saturday. I will see to your pass and pick you up at the allotted time," Hope said excitedly.

I can think of no two people less alike than Hope Waterman and Melvin Kaufman. They say opposites attract, but that only applies to magnetic poles, certainly not to people. Hope was young, ambitious, and knew what she wanted, always on the mark to take action. Melvin, on the other hand, lacked self-confidence, was slow to act and reticent about moving forward. They made quite a pair, like two birds flying against the wind. Reason dictated that they won't make it, but their love spoke otherwise and shouted, yes, they would.

* * *

About the same time Union general Grant suffered the debacle at the Crater, Confederate general Jubal A. Early was burning the town of Chambersburg, Pennsylvania. Operating out of the Shenandoah Valley, Early threatened northern towns in Maryland and the Keystone State as well as the District of Columbia. General Lee knew his Northern nemesis would not allow Early to continue to operate freely and would take action against him. With that in mind, Lee sent an infantry and cavalry division to Culpeper, Virginia, where they could either help Early or return to the Richmond-Petersburg front if needed.

Grant misinterpreted this movement and assumed that the entire corps had been removed from the vicinity of

Richmond, leaving only 8,500 men north of the James River. He deemed it the perfect opportunity to attempt another advance on the Confederate capital.

Second Battle of Deep Bottom

On August 13, a bluecoat cavalry division crossed pontoon bridges from Bermuda Hundred to Deep Bottom. The Yankee Second Corps infantry were delivered that night by steamships. Even though the month of August in Virginia is usually quite warm, for the past few days, it had been especially hot, a period often referred to as dog days. The nighttime landing of troops was scheduled to give a modicum of relief; nevertheless, the conditions were stifling and caused many Union soldiers to die from heat stroke during the operation.

The following day, the Union army made contact with the Confederate defenders. Yankee generals were surprised at the strength of the rebel forces. The Union army attempted several attacks, but for the most part, they were unsuccessful. On the night of August 20, suffering losses two to one, the Federals withdrew back over the James River.

Another Attack on the Weldon Railroad

On August 18-21, while the Second Corps fought at Deep Bottom, Grant planned another attack against the Weldon. At dawn on August 18, the Union Fifth Corps marched to the south and reached the railway at Globe Tavern around 9:00 a.m. Parts of the division began to destroy track while another branch moved north and formed a line of battle to block any Confederate advance.

Confederate general A. P. Hill sent three brigades to meet the advancing Union divisions. At first their rush was able to push the blue jackets back to near the Globe Tavern, but then, the Federals were able to counterattack and regain lost ground. After which, they entrenched for the night. The next day, it began to rain heavily; yet both armies continued to fight back and forth, advancing and retreating. Finally, unable to improve against the entrenched Union position, the Confederate army withdrew.

Neither side actually gained an advantage. General Lee felt as though no material harm was done to his troops, and Grant wasn't entirely happy with his general's claim of victory.

Casualty Estimates for the Attack on the Weldon Railroad*

	Total Casualties	Wounded	Killed	Captured/Missing
Union	4,296	2,897	251	2,897
Confederate	1,600	900	219	419

*The Confederates lost a key section of the Weldon RR and were forced to carry supplies by wagon for thirty miles in order to bring supplies to Petersburg.

The Second Battle of Reams Station

Grant was not satisfied with the results of the previous raid. He wanted the Weldon closed permanently. He assigned the task to Gen. Winfield S. Hancock's Second Corps, selected primarily because Major General Warren was busy extending the newly claimed fortifications at Globe Tavern.

Hancock's troops were exhausted from their efforts north of the James River and forced to stomp a measured tread without rest. They were augmented with General Gregg's cavalry division and, on August 22, began destroying railroad tracks to within sight of the Reams Station.

Confederate general Robert E. Lee understood that the Federal troops at Reams Station posed a threat not only to his supply line but also to the county seat of Dinwiddie County. If it were to fall, he would be forced to evacuate Petersburg-Richmond. Dinwiddie was a vital point on the army's potential retreat route.

The wise rebel commander saw an opportunity. If he could impose a stinging defeat on the Union army ahead of the pending election, it might lead to Lincoln's defeat and a victory for the Peace Democrats. At this point, it was the best of a fast-dwindling list of options.

Lee ordered Gen. A. P. Hill to take the overall command of a ten-thousand-man expedition, consisting of both cavalry and infantry. On August 25, the rebels launched two coordinated attacks. The first assault on the Union troops manning the Northern earthworks was stalled and driven back. In the South, the Confederate cavalry swept around the Union line. By that time, replacements had arrived to bolster those fighters who were screeching the unnerving rebel yell and lifting standards with flags having stars and bars for an emblem. With rebel artillery softening the Union position, the soldiers in mustard colors broke through the lines and bluecoats either ran or surrendered. By this time, the Confederate cavalry launched a surprise attack with dismounted troops, keeping a galling fire on the Yanks until it brought similar results as achieved by their comrades north of Reams Station. Sometime that night, under the cloak of darkness, the Union division made an orderly retreat to the safety of their lines at Petersburg.

It was a clear victory for Lee, but he lost the Weldon Railroad as a stage of supply, leaving only the South Side Railroad left to provide for Petersburg and his army.

Casualty Estimates for the Second Battle of Reams Station*

	Total Casualties	Wounded	Killed	Captured/Missing
Union	2,747	439	117	2,046
Confederate	814	75	16	3

*General A. P. Hill's infantry received the majority of Confederate casualties.

The Beefsteak Raid

On September 5, Sgt. George D. Shadburne came dashing back from reconnaissance behind the Union lines. Five miles east of Grant's headquarters, there was a plantation with three thousand beef cattle guarded by only 120 troops and a few citizens. Ironically, just two days earlier, Robert E. Lee had suggested to General Hampton that Grant's rear area was lightly defended and open to attack. On September 14, while the Federal's general-in-chief was in the Shenandoah Valley conferring with Sheridan, Hampton led about four thousand men in gray on a looping course to circumvent the Union army and approach their destination by crossing the Blackwater Swamp* at a point where the Cook's Bridge once stood.

* While the drainage basin of the Blackwater River contains many swamps, the upper Blackwater River is called by that name. In fact, in this region of Virginia, many streams are called swamps even though they are long and linear with moving water from one end to the other.

Knowing that an attack from there would go undetected, he had his engineers reconstruct the damaged arch over. Hampton, still undiscovered, was able to position himself and launch a three-pronged attack: Rooney Lee's division on the left against Union soldiers camped at Prince George Court House, Brig. Gen. James Dearing on the right against Cook's Mill, and a sizable detachment in the center to seize the cattle herd. Meeting only minimal resistance, Hampton's men soon were driving 2,486 head of cattle south to the Confederate lines. An attempt to intercept the rebels was unsuccessful, as Hampton retraced his steps back to Petersburg.

The total Confederate losses were forty-seven wounded and ten killed, while 304 Union soldiers were taken prisoner.

For days, the emaciated Confederate troops, existing on half rations, feasted on beef earmarked for the boys in blue. Word of the slick cattle rustling carried quickly to the North and even found the President's ear.

Lines leading to the latrines were doubled with soldiers dancing on one foot, then the other, while awaiting their turn. After days of meager rations, the ingestion of rich beef put their digestion process in high gear. Cramps and Borborygmus ruled the day. Lomas Chandler appeared to be the only sharpshooter affected. Jack Leffingwell cautioned the others to go easy on the beef until their system could handle it. Abel Strawn understood; however, Lomas Chandler ate half of Jack's portion and an equal amount from Abel's plate.

"You guys just don't know what you're missing. For myself, the Irish have cast iron stomachs. I can eat all I want, and it will never affect me," he boasted.

"Beef is hard to digest in the first place. If you're not used to it and load up, you run the risk of getting the trots and not making it to the latrine. I was completely unaware that the Irish are unaffected by such things," Jack returned with a sly grin.

Lomas unloosened his belt to the next hole and magically produced a thin panatela and lit up.

"This is the life. If the army fed us like this every day, I'd consider reenlisting," Lomas said while blowing an aromatic ring into the air.

"I sure wish I could have eaten more," Abel bemoaned.

"Don't worry. You can eat all of Lomas's tomorrow, he won't be hungry," Jack whispered.

About an hour later, a rumbling or gurgling noise was heard from the position Lomas now occupied. The young marksman turned pale, staring straight ahead. Seconds later, he made a mad dash in the direction of the latrines, shouting, "Out of my way. I can't hold it any longer."

"Do you think he made it in time?" asked Abel.

"Nope," Jack replied tersely.

On the night of September 28, Maj. Gen. Benjamin Butler crossed the James River, his army of the same name. The following morning, he assaulted the rebel defenses north of the Confederate capital. While the attack was contained, Lee decided to shift troops from Petersburg to meet the increased threat now being posed against Richmond.

Things were working out as Grant had anticipated, and once Lee moved to strengthen Richmond, the Union general extended his left flank to cut Petersburg lines of communication southwest of the city. The moves were performed under extreme caution since reports of rebel troop strength appeared to be inaccurate. It was confusing to Grant that with a sizable amount relocated to Richmond, none were missing from Petersburg. General Lee did not earn the title Gray Fox for nothing. He returned all extra duty personnel back to the Petersburg trenches. This included cooks, clerks, and fatigue details. In addition, he called small detachments and second class troops back to cover the holes his fighting body was about to create by marching north of the James. Looking across at the entrenchments of the Cockade City gave the appearance that nobody had left the Petersburg entrenchments.

On September 30, a Federal attack overran Fort Archer; but when Confederate reinforcements arrived, the blue coat push was quelled. For the past few days, most of the Union sorties resulted in limited success; however, a new Federal line was entrenched from Weldon Railroad to the southwest at Pegram's farm. Grant's forces were like a giant reticulated python, slowly encircling its prey, in this case, the traumatized city of Petersburg.

Other than the constant banter that took place between the picket lines, the month of October primarily featured skirmishes and lesser confrontations. The most notable were the Battle of Darbytown and New Market Roads (October 7), the Battle of Darbytown Road (October 13), and the Battle of Fair Oaks and Darbytown Road (October 27-28).

Jack Leffingwell and the Seventh regiment sharpshooters remained in the trenches while most of these encounters took place. That is, until the end of the month, when they left the Petersburg defensive entrenchments to join Gen. Henry Heth's counterattack during the Battle of Boydton Plank and Fair Oaks Roads.

The Battle of Fair Oaks and Boydton Plank Road

Three Union divisions and a cavalry legion, under the command of Winfield Scott Hancock, withdrew thirty thousand men from the Petersburg lines and marched west to operate against the Boydton Plank Road and South Side Railroad. Their initial advance gained the Boydton Plank Road, one of the campaign's main objectives; however, shortly thereafter, a counterattack by Gen. Henry Heth's division, aided by cavalry, forced a Union retreat. Control of the vital road remained in Lee's hands for the rest of the winter.

More often than not, both armies stopped fighting during the winter. It was used as a time for rebuilding fragmented units, planning their strategic maneuvers, and resting battle-worn troops. The winter of 1864 was mood changing for the two competing generals. During the siege of Petersburg, Ulysses Grant had taken up the area at City Point for his headquarters. The sector was ideal as it overlooked the James and Appomattox Rivers and soon to become one of the busiest ports in the world. A large supply depot was constructed along with the Depot Field Hospital, capable of holding ten thousand patients. The facility offered each patient his own bed and wash basin and a regular exchange of fresh pillows and linens. Laundries, dispensaries, special diet kitchens, dining halls, and log barracks during the winter made the compound the finest in America.

Outside of a colossal explosion in August that shook the city itself, Grant had things going his way and the news was uplifting. Gen. William T. Sherman had finally broken the siege and took Atlanta, making it a Christmas present for Abraham Lincoln. Lincoln, largely due to Atlanta's conquest, won reelection, defeating former Union Gen. George B. McClellan, a Democrat running on a peace platform, calling for a truce with the Confederacy.

Regarding the explosion, mentioned above, after the air was clear of falling pieces of wood, iron bars, chains, and missiles of every kind, it was determined that a barge loaded with ammunition had detonated, destroying the wharf, killing 45 and wounding 126. Laden with thirty thousand artillery shells and over seventy-five thousand rounds of small arms ammunition, a saboteur had placed a time bomb aboard the barge and remained elsewhere as the weapon ticked to the allotted point.

The morale at Lee's winter quarters had turned to its lowest point of the conflict. Any hope of a negotiated peace was dashed by Lincoln's reelection. As the year's end approached, even the gentlemanly Robert E. Lee found it difficult to conceal his feelings. His elegant moral aptitude and patience had met their depths of despair. Like soup on a stove, the heat will eventually bring it to a boil. With so many victories won and those people defeated at almost every turn, the noble general stared in disbelief and saw little hope for the future. It's only a matter of time. The disparities in numbers had finally taken its toll. Many of his soldiers had deserted, dreading a continued stay in the trenches. What troops remained suffered from reduced rations and clothing unfit for the cold, hail, and sleet of winter.

Only a few yards away from the rebel pickets, the Union soldiers were well fed and clothed for the conditions. Their biggest problem during the winter recess was overcoming boredom or ennui. Unlike the ragged foes across from them, the material needs of the boys in blue were well attended to. In fact, Grant's army shared a Thanksgiving dinner in honor of Lincoln's national holiday. The citizens in the Northern states conducted food drives and collected funds in order to send dinner packages to the Union troops. President Lincoln added 6,000 turkeys and had them sent to the siege lines. Grant's army supply routes were used to deliver food packages, and he even utilized the James River to transport items, i.e., barrels of oysters packed in ice. Before it was all over, 120,000 turkeys and chickens were received and prepared by the division cooks, along with ham, potatoes, peas, fruit, nuts, pies, and pudding. It was a virtual banquet bonanza, while the cotton collaborators were entrenched behind their fortifications and starving. Out of respect for the Union holiday, Confederate soldiers ceased fire until the following day.

Early the next predawn morning, Lomas Chandler was on the picket line shouting across to a Union sentry, "Hey, Yankee, how 'bout a trade for some of that turkey you all ate yesterday?"

"You Johnny Rebs ain't got anything to trade with," he replied.

"Don't be too sure about that. What would it cost me for say five pounds of turkey?"

"We don't take any Confederate money. It ain't worth anything."

"Who's saying anything about Confederate money? I'll make you an offer, and you think about it for a while. I offer you a twenty-dollar gold piece for five pounds of turkey and one of them fruit pies."

After a minute of thinking about it, the blue jacket asked, "How do we make the exchange?"

"You put it in a bag and tie the end with a length of string or rope. Make it long enough to reach our line. Tie something heavy on the end and throw it to me. That way I can pull it over here."

"How do I get my money?"

"Don't worry about that, I got a good enough arm to throw the coin to you," Lomas answered.

"I get relieved in an hour. It'll take me that long to get the turkey. So look for me in two hours. Another thing, there better not be any shootin' until the exchange is made."

"You got it."

When lunchtime rolled around, Lomas Chandler appeared before the other sharpshooters with a large bag over his shoulder, saying, "I got something to make our half rations of hardtack taste a lot better."

Chapter Thirty-Six

Success is not final, failure is not fatal: It is the courage to continue that counts.

—Winston Churchill

In the cities of Petersburg and Richmond, it was as though the mythical Greek goddess Oizys was working her talent in high gear. History tells us that she was the spirit of misery and woe. One of the malevolent children of the goddess Nyx, she walked among mortals dispensing distress and suffering, deceiving us with what appears to promise happiness, but ends up with pain and misery.

The conditions in the siege cities during the harsh winter were horrible. Heating fuel was in short supply and food prices out of reach. Flour was selling for $200 a barrel, and merchants were asking $30 for a bushel of beans. Few were able to pay. Many of the families were refugees from outside the area and had no local ties. They were compelled to go among the soldiers and beg for bread. Both crime and desertion were increasing.

When deserters were caught, they were either hanged or shot. It was a severe penalty, but not enough to stop the steady stream of soldiers going home to care for their own starving families.

Nearly all rifle fire had stopped as the men in the trenches settled in for the seasonal downtime. Artillery fire continued, but at a much lesser degree. There was, perhaps, one exception. Union general Grant had taken a liking to a mammoth artillery gun they called the Dictator. It was a thirteen-inch seacoast mortar mounted on a railroad flatcar to accommodate its seventeen-thousand-pound weight. By moving the car along a section of railroad track, different points along the Confederate lines were brought under fire. It could lob a two-hundred-pound explosive shell nearly two and a half miles. There was a problem. When charged with fourteen pounds of powder, the mortar would recoil a minimal amount on the flatcar, but the car itself recoiled a dozen feet up the track. The Union engineers corrected this by using a curved section of track and widening the mortar's traverse. The amount of damage it actually caused was up for debate. The fact it was only employed for three months indicated it might not have been worth the effort, considering all that was entailed in its operation.

The winter standstill was a period of less fighting; even so, the Confederates continued to receive supplies, though they were limited and meager. Grant knew that for a siege to be successful, no supplies could be allowed to pass through to the enemy. On February 5, 1865, Gen. David McMurtrie Gregg led his cavalry division out to the Boydton Plank Road in an attempt to intercept Confederate supply trains. The Union general, a native of Pennsylvania, had narrowly escaped death two years earlier when he came down with typhoid fever. Today, after three loyal years of Civil War service, his nerves were frayed and he wished to be home with his family. While he presented himself tall in the saddle, a letter of resignation rested on his table, dated January 25, 1865.

Gregg was aided, in his current mission, by Maj. Gen. Gouverneur K. Warren's Fifth Corps, taking up a blocking position to prevent interference from the rebels. Two other divisions of Maj. Gen. Andrew A. Humphrey's Second Corps shifted west to cover Warren's right flank, thus completing a strategy unworthy of any criticism.

As daylight dwindled, Confederate general Lee and his Southern supporters set about to disrupt the Union plan. Confederate general John B. Gordon, plantation born and of Scottish lineage, made an attempt to turn Humphrey's right flank but was repulsed. During the night, Grant sent in two more divisions to reinforce the Federal troops. On February 6, Gregg's cavalry was attacked by elements of Brig. Gen. John Pegram's rebel horsemen. Shortly thereafter, when Union general Warren was performing reconnaissance, he too was set upon by Pegram, joined by General Mahone's division. The Union mission was stopped; however, their siege works were extended, tightening the chain another link.

Unfortunately, Confederate general Pegram was killed in the skirmish. Pegram, while serving in western Virginia, participated in the Battle of Rich Mountain on July 11, 1861. After a two-hour combat, the Confederates were split in two. Half escaped over a mountain trail; but Pegram, whose regiment included students from Hampden-Sydney College, was overpowered by McClellan's forces and surrendered his entire regiment. He became the first Confederate officer to be captured.

Held prisoner for six months, he was paroled in a prisoner exchange and traveled back to Richmond. It was there he met prominent socialite Hetty Cary, and they became engaged.

Ironically, on January 19, 1865, Pegram married Hetty Cary in St. Paul's Church in Richmond. Many celebrated persons were in attendance, including Confederate president Jefferson Davis and his wife, Varina. Less than three weeks later, his funeral was held in the same church, with many of the same people who attended his wedding.

It seems as though many of the Civil War battle plans were drawn up by those with their fingers crossed behind their backs. A typical plan was successful in the beginning, then the unintended consequences came into play, and the initial success was reversed. The Union, with its overwhelming advantage in manpower, could continue such plans even though suffering with lopsided losses. General Lee, on the other hand, had to be spot on most of the time. Even then, in a war of attrition, the wisest strategies will gradually succumb to the imbalance in numbers. So it was with the distinguished gentleman general from Old Dominion.

The month of March found General Lee's army weakened by desertion, disease, and undernourished from weeks on half rations. They were outnumbered three to one and prospects calling for an even greater disparity. Union general Sheridan was returning from the Shenandoah Valley with fifty thousand troops and Gen. William T. Sherman, parading through the Carolinas, commanding even more. Both were on their way to team up with Grant at the siege lines. Lee's options were fading faster than cut flowers out of water. He soon would be unable to sustain defenses of either city.

Spending another sleepless night, his thoughts were muddled and devising the proper plan, at this point in time, just wouldn't come into focus. As the shadows from his oil lamp danced on the canvas walls of his field tent, Lee decided to seek suggestions from his most trusted living general, John B. Gordon. Together, they agreed that only three options remained: First, they could offer peace terms to Grant. The humility and embarrassment associated with that idea was unacceptable to both men; besides, the political implications were too great for either one to shoulder. The second possibility was to retreat from the Petersburg-Richmond defenses and link up with Gen. Joseph E. Johnson's army in North Carolina. A combined army might allow them to defeat Sherman and then go after Grant. Finally, they could stay and fight to the last man.

Lee thanked Gordon for his input and bid him a good evening. He had already erased the first option from his mental chalkboard. The third choice was obvious along with its outcome. Lee concentrated on a plan to escape the fortifications.

On March 6, Gordon was summoned back to headquarters, and Lee told him that there seemed to be only one thing they could do.

"Keeping things as they are means a certain death. Escaping the fortifications would only be death if we failed. We must formulate a plan to break through those people's line and move our army south," Lee stated.

"The sky is blue no matter where anyone stands. I, for one, would rather see it away from the trenches," Gordon replied.

It was settled. Now, General Lee would labor night and day to find the proper plan that, in all likelihood, would be the last hope for the life of the Confederacy.

After two weeks of endless detail, General Gordon had devised the steps of action, and Lee's plan was ready for execution. It called for a surprise attack on the Union lines to force Grant to pull troops from either side in order to confront the Confederate push, thus weakening his right flank. At that point, Confederate general John B. Gordon would assault Fort Stedman, one of the Union fortifications now encircling Petersburg, by passing through the Confederate obstructions. It was an area with less cheval-de-frise to circumvent (basically, a long log with projecting iron or wooden spikes and, principally, intended as an anticavalry obstacle). The intended target, a Union supply depot on the U.S. Military Railroad, was located less than a mile behind the fort. Gordon's collective force, nearly half of Lee's Army of Northern Virginia, would then move north and south along the Union lines to clear the way for the main attack—that being the Union supply base of City Point and Grant's headquarters.

* * *

Soldiers are not always uninformed as to the overall plans of their generals. A pervading underground line of communication remains open around the clock to pass along both rumor and fact. Something big was about to happen, and scuttlebutt reached the receptive ears of Lomas Chandler well before any movement was noticed by those in the ranks.

"Marse Robert has a big one brewing," Lomas commented when all three were together.

"What have you heard?" Abel asked.

"We're soon going to break ranks and attack the bluebellies for a change."

"That doesn't make sense, Lomas, the numbers are wrong for us to attack in force. There's got to be a lot more to it. Have you heard what regiments might be involved? I sure would like to breathe fresh air for a while," Jack expressed.

"If I got to be in the trenches, out here on the left is the safest of all. I think we're the farthest away from Petersburg, and up till now, the Yanks haven't tried to take our line," Abel added. "We've lost most everybody in the Seventh regiment, hell, I don't recognize anybody anymore. Maybe they'll keep us in reserve so we all don't get killed off."

"I'm just tired of eating mud and being stuck in it up to my ankles. I long for the mountains and open spaces. I got an Indian buddy that I used to go hunting and fishing with. I sure wish I was with him right now with my line in the water," Jack reminisced.

"That was before you lost your memory. Do you remember his name?" Abel asked frankly.

"No, I've tried to recall it, but seem to always draw a blank. Funny, things come back to me until I think hard about it, then it all disappears."

"I've noticed it happening more frequently. One of these days you'll get it all back, and when you do, heaven help you," Able said with conviction.

"The way you make it sound, I hope I never get it back," Jack said as he raised his Whitworth to aim at an object slightly moving behind the Union works.

* * *

Gordon's attack started in the chilly dawn with lead parties of sharpshooters and engineers, acting as deserting soldiers, out to overwhelm Union pickets and remove obstructions that would delay infantry advance. They were crouched low and walking like a duck through dry corn stalks. The Union sentry in front of Fort Stedman could hear the rustle and cocked his weapon.

"I can hear you moving about, Reb, what you are up to?" he called out.

"Just getting a little corn to parch, we don't receive all the goodies y'all are given," a voice came from the stalks.

"You better hurry up, Reb. It's going to be daylight soon," the sentry cautioned.

It was not unusual for sentries to converse across each other's line—a distance as close as four or five hundred feet. Such fraternization led to occasional swaps of items that one side had over the other, a transaction that could never take place during the daylight hours with sharpshooters drawing a bead on the slightest movement.

On this crispy morning, the banter appeared to be between the Union sentry and a rebel soldier picking corn. What the sentry didn't know was that most of the noise he heard was the sound coming from farther back when Confederate abatis was being pulled aside in order to make way for the infantry.

A second group, consisting of three one-hundred-man teams of marksmen, was to storm the Union works and stream back into the Union rear area. The sharpshooters waited until the colloquy continued then moved as close to the Union pickets line as they dared before lying flat. The early morning still hung on to its predawn darkness, and with fog starting to gather, it was impossible to see very far ahead. Each man wore a white strip of cloth drawn over the right shoulder and around the body and tied, a gift from the general's wife and distributed by Gordon himself, so that the men could recognize each other in the darkness.

Once the obstructions were moved, a signal was given. Several sharpshooters stood and began moving forward, ignoring the noise they created as they pushed through the corn. They were acting like deserters as they progressed toward the Union pickets. It wasn't unusual to see armed rebel deserters at the picket line, and the sentinel was more focused on the reward of capture than a possibility that it might be a sham. He was quickly overpowered and knocked senseless, and most of his compatriots were captured; still, the scene was witnessed by others who shouted the alarm.

Behind them, only a few hundred yards away, the three divisions of Gordon's 7,500-man Second Corps were formed into columns. He had just over ten thousand men in his assaulting force, with about half that many held back in reserve. It was an open question if the men from the First Corps would arrive on time. They had encountered problems with the Southside Railroad and suffered delays.

The general drew his revolver and fired three quick shots—the signal for the attack.

By now, the officer responsible for the Fort Stedman sector heard the sounds of attack and rode to his battery at Fort Haskell nearby. Finding the fort on alert and ready to defend itself, he continued riding north to Fort Stedman. Crossing the parapet, he met some men coming over the curtains and assumed them to be part of the picket. Accordingly, he gave directions to establish them inside the earthworks with regard to position and firing. He suddenly realized that the men he was ordering were

Confederate soldiers who, after recognizing him as a Union general, captured him and took him back across the unoccupied area where he surrendered his sword to Gordon.

When Gordon arrived at Fort Stedman, he found his attack had so far exceeded all expectations. The batteries at the fort had been seized, and a gap of one thousand feet opened in the Union line. Now, the rebels were using captured artillery guns from Fort Stedman to open up enfilading fire on the entrenchments to the north and south.

The attack began to bog down in the north when Union troops formed a battle line and the Confederates were too confused by the maze of trenches to attack it effectively. Gordon turned his attention to the southern flank and Fort Haskell, but the bluecoats successfully employed canister rounds from three cannons, halting the assault. Southern farmers have a saying, "Early ripe, early rotten," which is beginning to describe Gordon's well-designed battle plan. More trouble was developing. His three one-hundred-man detachments were wandering around the rear area in confusion, and many had stopped to eat some of the captured Federal rations. As a result, the cavalry had not found an avenue through which to advance into the rear. A major part of Gordon's army had problems with rail transportation and didn't arrive until midday, too late to take part in the battle. And making matters worse, the main Union defense force was beginning to mobilize.

From the instant Union officers received word that Fort Stedman had fallen, they worked furiously to limit any further penetration. Once that objective was achieved, they concentrated on the pocket of rebels trespassing within their lines. Union defense forces were organized to completely encircle the Confederate penetration, bringing it to a stop. Recognizing that rebels were controlling Fort Stedman, the Union artillery launched continuous fire against them. The punishing fusillade quickly taught the Southern invaders that remaining there would be fatal. They joined their comrades in a frantic dash back to their own lines and safety.

Expecting much different results, General Lee had arrived earlier to watch the battle. Instead, he witnessed those soldiers who led the attack, franticly returning in haste. They fled under solid Union crossfire suffering heavy casualties, claiming that Federal resistance was too strong for them to continue.

Lee's pained expression said it all. Disappointment was not a strong-enough word for his heartfelt affectations. Gordon interrupted his general's despondency with a request to retreat his forces to safety. The attack had failed with no impact on the Union lines, and Lee was out of options, save one. He was now faced with ceding the Richmond-Petersburg defenses and, as they say in the hills of Kentucky, "make a run for it."

Union general Grant's noose pulled tighter on April 1, when his Federals dislodged rebel troops from the crossroads protecting their Southside Railroad supply line. It was a decisive Union victory that resulted in over 4,500 Confederate soldiers either surrendering or being captured.

The next day, April 2, Grant's army achieved a breakthrough of the lines at Petersburg. It became obvious that Lee no longer had the strength to defend the fortifications. He advised the Confederate government to abandon the cities. That night, Lieutenant General Longstreet's corps crossed the James River to team up with the Confederates in Petersburg, and the capital city of Richmond was evacuated.

At that point, Lee planned to move his collective forces across the Appomattox River, where he could be resupplied from stocks now held in Richmond. He would then proceed to meet up with the fleeing Confederate government before heading south to join Gen. Joseph E. Johnson.

Events were changing rapidly. The Seventh regiment of Tennessee, or what was left of it, was held back to defend the Petersburg fortifications. At first, the sharpshooters were miffed for not being selected to join the attack on Fort Stedman. Later, when retreating soldiers rejoined the trenches, they changed their minds.

"When we started out, things were going okay, but those Yankees ain't like they used to be. Before long, they were coming at us from all sides. It was like they wanted to fight hand to hand, and the bullets were so thick a fellow couldn't hear himself think. My buddies were falling right and left, and some of us took off running as fast as we could and didn't look back. I heard that before it was over, everybody retreated, even Marse Robert himself," a returning soldier exclaimed.

"Do you think they were tipped off that we were coming?" Lomas questioned.

"Nah, we surprised them all right, they just got too many men."

"Did you see General Gordon?" asked Jack. "How did he take it?"

"Hell, I saw them both."

"Both? Who was the other person?" Lomas asked hoarsely.

"General Robert Lee himself," returned the soldier. "The word is that he was there to watch the victory, but that sure ain't what happened."

"How did he look?" asked Jack.

"I only glimpsed him as he rode past me. He was staring straight ahead and riding that gray horse. He sure wasn't happy."

While the friendly interrogation was going on, a messenger dashed by, shouting, "Prepare to depart the trenches. You will be given orders directly." Stupefied for a moment, the sharpshooters gave each other a quizzical look. Jack Leffingwell recognized the messenger as someone from the Seventh regiment and grabbed his arm as he passed by returning through the trenches.

"What's going on, Friend?"

"Don't know for sure, Jack. I hear we might be going to Lynchburg. One thing I do know for sure. We're leaving these damn trenches."

On April 4, Lee managed to move his army across the Appomattox River to Amelia Court House, the destination for receiving supplies, only to find that the expected rations had not arrived. They had not been placed on the trains escaping Richmond. Those traveling in supply wagons had been captured by pursuing Union cavalry. The commissary general had promised he would send eighty thousand rations to Farmville, another fifty miles away. With thirty thousand hungry men to feed, Lee lingered an extra day to send out foraging parties. They returned with few provisions. By waiting to hunt for food, the frustrated Confederate general lost the advantage of a head start.

It was like looking at objects in the distance through a magnifying glass. Nothing was clear now. With Grant's

Union army pursuing relentlessly, Farmville, and the promised rations, a three-day march, any expectation of joining Joseph E. Johnson in North Carolina was beginning to fade like the morning mist.

The avenues of escape were systematically being blocked, and on April 6, Lee's army suffered a significant defeat in a battle along Sailor's Creek. Nearly a fourth of the Confederate army was cut off by Union cavalry and bluecoats on foot. Confederate soldiers were hammered by artillery and demoralized by Union cavalry cutting through their lines. Soundly defeated, most of the 7,700 troops in gray surrendered along with nearly a dozen of Lee's generals.

The encounter along Sailor's Creek, like most of the Civil War battles, was called by different names, i.e., Sailor's Creek, Hillsman Farm, or Lockett Farm. Call it what you may, it was the last significant confrontation between the armies of Robert E. Lee and Ulysses S. Grant.

On April 7, Grant sent a note to Lee suggesting that it was time to surrender the Army of Northern Virginia. Lee's answer refused the request but asked what terms he had in mind.

On April 8, Union cavalry captured and burned three supply trains waiting for Lee's army at Appomattox Station. Now, the Union Army of the Potomac and the Army of the James were closing in on the defenders of the Confederacy.

On April 9, Gen. John B. Gordon took the offensive and launched an early-morning attack on the Union general Sheridan's cavalry. He was successful in forcing the first line back; however, the next line held and slowed the Confederate advance. Gordon's troops charged through the line and took the ridge, but as they reached the crest, they saw blankets of blue as far as the eye could see. It was the entire Union Twelfth Corps in a line of battle with the Union Fifth Corps to their right.

Upon seeing these Union forces, Lee's cavalry immediately withdrew and rode off toward Lynchburg. At the same time, the Union troops began advancing against Gordon's worn and frazzled corps, leaving Lee with no alternative other than to go and see General Grant.

Chapter Thirty-Seven

A crowd is not the sum of the individuals who compose it. Rather it is a species of animal, with language or real consciousness, born when they gather, dying when they depart.

—Gene Wolfe, The Shadow of the Torturer

The Evacuation of Richmond

President Jefferson Davis was attending Sunday services at St. Paul's Church when he received a dispatch form General Lee stating that it would be necessary to evacuate the city that night. Davis read the message twice, neatly folded it, and slipped it into his suit pocket. While General Lee's telegram gave detailed reasons, one sentence had remained prominent in Davis's mind, *I advise that all preparation be made for leaving Richmond tonight.* The Confederate president composed himself, slowly rose to his feet, apologized to the gentleman sitting next to him, and left the church. On his way to the executive office, he envisioned the work ahead. Always aware that this day could possibly come, he always hoped it would never arrive. His wife and family had left Richmond a few days before and were now either in Raleigh or Charlotte, North Carolina. Most importantly to Davis, they were safe at the moment.

Sunday was a bad time to call for a cabinet meeting; however, the situation definitely demanded one. About a half-dozen cabinet members responded to the call, and when they reached Davis's office, a brief session was held. They were informed of Lee's telegram and reminded of the action plan for such an event. Staff members began to destroy official documents. Most of them were burned outside the government building. Passersby thought it queer to be done on Sunday, but took no serious notice. Later in the day, President Davis had presence of mind to pen an official statement.

The following morning, President Davis and his cabinet fled south on the last open railroad line, the Richmond and Danville.

The citizens of the city had little knowledge of what transpired at the lines of defense and went about their daily activities, ignorant of their pending fate. They had grown accustomed to the sound of artillery fire from fortifications a few miles away.

Official word of the government's departure was announced around four o'clock in the afternoon. From that point forward, all hell broke loose. The rest of the day and throughout the night the exodus continued. All means of transportation were utilized as a steady stream of humanity began to cross the James River on the old Mayo Bridge. Viewed from a distance, it brought to mind the image of hungry Marabunta on the move. In this case, it wasn't army ants, only people on horseback, cart, carriage, and on foot. And, those not fleeing by other means were making preparations to do just that.

Confederate lieutenant general Richard S. Ewell was in charge of the city's defenses, and as the fall of Petersburg became imminent, he was alerted to the task of destroying anything of military value before leaving the city. The city came alive with rumors spreading mouth to mouth. Crowds gathered in front of General Ewell's office seeking answers. Ewell's staff was uncommitted. Finally, a soldier hinted that the city might be occupied before morning. Pandemonium ensued as crowds began to turn into mobs. Recognizing the added danger of uncontrolled riots, the city officials ordered all liquor to be destroyed, a herculean task with little time remaining, and the activity of Ewell's soldiers carrying out their mission. In the need for haste, those charged with going through the stocks of every saloon and warehouse found the most expedient way was to smash the bottles and pour kegs into the gutter. It was only natural that such activities drew a crowd. They scooped up whisky in their hats, boots, and some actually gulped it while on all fours at the curbside. The activity to prevent a Union rampage created one of their own. Not with Federal soldiers, but people of the city.

Early Monday morning, ammunition warehouses were set fire, and the sound of their powder magazines exploding resounded across the rooftops. In addition, Lt. Gen. Richard S. Ewell was ordered to destroy the city's tobacco, cotton, and foodstuffs so that the Yankees couldn't have them. Ewell had tobacco moved to buildings he could burn without setting the rest of the city on fire. In their search for suitable buildings, a startling discovery was made. They were surprised to find that speculators had brought up their supplies to capitalize on the shortages. While women and children were in rags, barefoot and starving, the speculators' commissaries teemed with smoked meats, flour, sugar, and coffee. Enraged, the crowd snatched the food and clothing and turned to the nearby shops to loot whatever else they found. The crowd had now turned into a rioting mob; and General Ewell, on his mission for departure, didn't have enough able men left over to bring them under control.

* * *

The doors of the Eagle Inn and Tavern flew open as Isabella's cousin, Luigi Marciano, burst inside, shouting, "Tutto l'inferno scappa in città. Le plebaglie rompono delle finestre, rubando e regolare degli affari sul fuoco."

"Speak English, Luigi, you're in America now," Isabella chided.

"*Scusarsi*, Isabella, all hell is breaking loose in town. Mobs are breaking windows, stealing, and setting business on fire."

"Quickly, we must tell Father," Isabella stressed.

Senior Enzio Manfredi was in conversation with a patron sitting at the bar and couldn't help from overhearing the disturbance at the door. He calmly took off his apron and motioned Luigi toward a secluded table. Luigi Marciano repeated the news to Enzio who kept an unemotional stare straight ahead.

"Notify our cousins and their families. We own the building across the street. I want every window filled with an armed Italian and the same here at the inn and tavern. Put our people on the rooftops, and give the order to shoot anyone attempting to harm the properties," directed

Enzio. Soon men with names like Alfonso Agrusa, Gianni Siragusa, and Cosimo Battaglia, along with their cousins, were guarding the buildings. The news spread like the waves from a large rock tossed in the middle of a lake. Pedestrians avoided the sidewalks in front of the inn and tavern as armed Italians stood guard awaiting the rioting mob.

They finally appeared in force acting in the manner reported by Luigi, breaking storefront windows and raiding the contents inside. Their march came to a halt at the sight of armed resistance on the block containing the Eagle Inn and Tavern. It was only a temporary pause, however. The mindless mind of the mob ignited the rioters once again, and they crossed the street ignoring what lie ahead. A barrage of rifle fire, sounding like firecrackers, stopped the crowd for a second time. What's more, the pop-pop-popping of gunfire resulted in mob members collapsing to the street. A decision was made on the spot to avoid the block, and the rioters changed their route to another direction, leaving their injured and dead. Enzio's family held their ground until the following morning when Union troops took control of the city.

"I wish Lomas was here," mewed Isabella.

"You do know, *figlina*, that Lomas Chandler wasn't my favorite man for you. Your *Madre* and I had hoped he would be a fine Italian boy. We put your happiness over our wishes, and now only time will tell who is right. *Inoltre, è Irlandese!*" the proud Italian retorted.

"He's not an Irishman, Father, he's an American Confederate," Isabella chimed.

"Not for long. From the looks of things, he's soon to be a prisoner of war," said Enzio in parting. His back was to the daughter for only three steps after which he turned, rushed back, put his arms around Isabella, and whispered softly, "They won't keep him, dear. Your husband will be with you before you know it. And I will take my son-in-law around to meet the vendors or those who are left."

* * *

The wind picked up, carrying embers from the street fires and unintended sparks from buildings burned by Ewell's troops. One burning building ignited the other next to it until the whole business district was aflame. Leaving nothing left to ransack, the rioting mob disbanded.

When the last Confederate soldier rode across the pontoon bridge to catch up with Lee's troops, city officials traveled to the Union lines and formally turned over the city and asked the Federal officers to help quench the fires.

Early Monday morning, April 3, the Union cavalry entered the town and flew their regimental flag above the capital building. They were followed by infantry troops with orders to put out the fires. While making preparations to do just that, it became known that the city's two fire engines were in good working order. Considering their task, the engines were put to use at once. Bucket brigades were formed, utilizing the Negroes who congregated around the Federal troops. Legally no longer slaves, they had no choice in the matter as men with rifles sternly issued a command. Ironically, blacks would be forbidden to gather in groups and remain off the streets unless on particular business. Such restrictions did not divert their joyful optimism. Thousands of contraband men were put to work tearing down ruined buildings and cleaning up debris while others labored on the docks loading and unloading Union vessels. Negro women were assigned work as cooks and house cleaners. The pay for the contraband was food and shelter. Money, if there was to be any, would be determined at a later time.

The famed city of Richmond was now a ghost of its former self. The capital city of the Confederacy is now rendered unto the hands of its Union enemy. Richmond—the city that remembers a vast amount of historical events: when Capt. John Smith landed at the falls of the James River in 1607 and the city where Patrick Henry rang freedom's cry in 1775, shouting from St. John's Church, "Give me liberty, or give me death."

It was once a city of culture, enlivened by the likes of Charles Dickens and Edgar Allen Poe. Its many theaters featured programs from such stars as Jenny Lind. People paid over one hundred dollars a seat to hear the Swedish Nightingale sing and only a quarter for a ticket to watch burlesque.

This city of destiny now lay in smoldering ruins, yet somehow, one felt it would rise up for a second time. Like the mythological sacred firebird, Richmond also would rise from its ashes to live again.

Chapter Thirty-Eight

Peace is normally a great good, and normally it coincides with righteousness, but it is righteousness and not peace which should bind the conscience of a nation as it should bind the conscience of an individual; and neither a nation nor an individual can surrender conscience to another's keeping.

—Theodore Roosevelt

Gen. Robert E. Lee Surrenders

After exchanging several messages leading up to face-to-face contact, Lee and Grant met in the parlor of the brick house owned by Wilmer McLean. McLean had moved to Appomattox from Manassas Junction after a shell passed through his house during the First Battle of Bull Run. He wanted to get farther away from the conflict. General Lee arrived first and was greeted with the cordiality of someone respected of their position. He was led to a spacious sitting room on the first floor. There was a large marble-topped table in the center of the room and a smaller oval stand near the window. Lee took a seat beside it.

Shortly thereafter, Grant came in and Lee rose to shake hands. General Grant entered the room alone while his staff respectfully waited on the front lawn. As the two men stood clasping their right hands, there was an obvious difference between them. Grant, much shorter than Lee, had come directly from the field. No time was taken to change clothes. It was as though the occasion was just another event in the execution of his duties in winning the war for Lincoln. Dressed in a rumpled military tunic with mud-spattered trousers stuffed into his equally muddy boots, Grant resembled the workman that he was, and this was just another day on the job. Lee, on the other hand, was a resplendent figure standing six feet tall and in his finest dress gray uniform. His tunic was buttoned all the way up. He wore a sash around his waist and, at his side, carried a long sword of fine workmanship with jewels studding its hilt. This was not just another day to the gentile general from Virginia. After four years of arduous effort defending the Confederacy and its noblesse oblige, Lee dressed to receive the bitter taste of defeat with dignity. After a short conversation, Grant's staff was summoned to the room.

The terms of surrender were not what Lee had expected and better than he had feared. Grant allowed Lee's officers to keep their small arms and horses, and as long as they didn't take up arms against the North again, they were paroled without punishment. Aware that his artillerymen owned their own horses, Lee asked permission for them to retain theirs as well. Grant agreed.

"I only ask that your men pledge allegiance to the United States after which they are free to travel," Grant stated.

"My men call that 'swallowing the dog,' but I'm confident the offer of freedom will make them comply," Lee replied.

"With your permission, General, I would be most happy to send rations to the Confederate troops."

"That would be gratefully accepted. My men are in dire need," Lee said.

Then, the elder general shook hands with Grant and, bowing slightly to the other officers, left the room. Out on the porch, Lee signaled to his orderly to bring up his horse. Standing on the lowest step, the sad general, overwhelmed by his own thoughts, gazed in the direction of where his army lay. The arrival of his horse seemed to recall him from his reverie. As he mounted Traveler, General Grant stepped down from the porch and saluted by raising his hat. Lee answered by raising his own and rode off to break the news to the brave soldiers of his command.

* * *

Jack Leffingwell and the sharpshooters were paroled as part of the Seventh Tennessee Infantry Regiment under Lt. Col. Samuel G. Shepard. Only forty-seven men remained from the original unit. As part of the surrender agreement, all had to take an oath to uphold the United States with their loyalty and pledge never to take up arms against it. The swearing took place in tents set up throughout the Appomattox campsite, after which they were released on their own cognizance. For many of the rebel soldiers, this was the most unpleasant part of the war; however, the rations provided by General Grant lessened the sting of it all. Jack, Abel, and Lomas were processed as part of McComb's brigade and Gen. Henry Heth's division from Ambrose P. Hill's Third Corps. The procedure moved slowly with long lines of gray uniforms stacking their weapons and moving through the tents. They were prisoners of war as they entered, and free men when they left. The soldiers were issued printed parole passes which served as evidence that they had laid down their arms at Appomattox Court House and had the right to return peaceably to their homes.

Inside the tents were tables butted end to end in order to accommodate the equally protracted queues of rebel soldiers. Union soldiers sat behind the tables to process the oath and inspect personal knapsacks. Standing behind, with their back to the tent walls, were additional soldiers to guarantee a peaceful process.

"What's in your knapsack, Soldier?" asked the officer who was standing behind the table.

"Just some clothes and my Bible," Jack replied.

"Move on," the officer ordered before turning to Abel Strawn.

"If I may, I'd like to retain my Whitworth rifle," Jack requested.

"Only officers have that privilege, now move on," he replied.

Call it fate or kismet or whatever you like, but General Grant himself had entered the tent to witness the procedure, primarily to make a report to President Lincoln as to when all prisoners would complete the process. Grant looked Jack in the eyes as if studying him to read his mind. He saw the vestige of a real man, standing erect with his head unbowed and thought, *If only I had an army of this sort*. Pausing for a few seconds more, Grant had made up his mind.

"Why do you want the Whitworth," he asked.

"I will need it to provide food for my family," Jack avowed.

"Where is your family?"

"The farm is in Statesville, Tennessee, but I have to pick up my son in Richmond before going home. Back home, I have another son I've never seen and a little girl who I haven't held or kissed for four years. You'll get no more trouble from me, General," Jack stated.

"Give him his rifle and a bundle of ammunition. I sense a man of honor here," Grant ordered. Turning to one of the soldiers standing at the tent wall, he imparted, "Let him pick out a horse and one of those captured wagons. I got too many damn wagons as it is."

"Thank you, General. My friend will be traveling with me," Jack added.

The general narrowed his eyes as he assessed Abel then said, "Okay, let him pick out a horse as well."

The soldier Grant had assigned to help was a black man. Leroy Littlefield had recognized the Tennessee mountain man immediately and followed him outside the tent.

"Do you recognize me?" he asked.

"Can't say that I do," Jack replied.

"You might remember my mother and father, Marie and Wilbur Littlefield."

"I'm sorry, I only draw a blank."

Leroy stood staring with a puzzled look when Abel interjected, "He has amnesia ever since he was wounded at Fredericksburg."

The black soldier's expression changed as if to understand, and he said, "I was there. I know firsthand how terrible that battle was." The three were quiet in their thoughts as they walked toward a corral of horses.

"You all can pick out a couple of horses from that corral over yonder and hook up to the wagon by the big oak tree. I personally inspected that one, and it's the best of the lot. While you're picking out the horses, I'll go fetch the Whitworth."

Jack and Abel stood with one foot on the bottom rail and arms across the top bar of the makeshift corral. They observed the movement of the captured horses until Abel said, "Look at that big chestnut, he sure looks good to me."

"I think it would be best if we chose the best-looking mares. That way we would be assured of getting another in less than a year," Jack suggested.

"You're right, I wasn't thinking along those lines. You best pick them out, and I'll gather a couple of those saddles straddling along the top bar of this fence."

Jack vaulted the top rail and pushed his way through horses until he grabbed the halter of a dark brown mare. He led it to the gate where Abel slipped on a bridle. The animal, about five years old, calmly stood while a blanket and saddle was thrown on its back. Jack pushed his way again while looking for the large buckskin he noticed earlier. After finding her, he returned to the gate. By this time, Corporal Littlefield had returned carrying the Whitworth and a canister of ammunition, shouting, "I'm going to put these in the wagon. Bring the horses on over."

"We took the saddles off the top rail. I hope that was okay?" Abel questioned.

"If somebody complains, they can talk to General Grant about it," said a smiling Leroy.

Meanwhile, back at the tent, Lomas had tossed his duffel bag on the inspection table and declared it contained clothing. Because of the trouble he had hoisting it up, the officer behind the table asked for him to open it. He was in amused surprise as Lomas removed a skillet, coffeepot, a waterproof canvas, several tins of potted meats, canned fruit, an extra pair of boots, and five decks of unopened playing cards. Lomas also removed a small leather bag with pull strings. Holding it up, he said, "This has my wedding ring and money."

The Union officer called some of his cohorts to come over and take a look at the accumulation on the table.

"You guys ever see so much packed in one duffel bag?" he said, laughing.

"I guess it's okay. None of it can be considered weaponry," returned another. "Maybe that skillet. I remember my grandmother used to use one like this on me and my brothers when we acted up," he added jokingly.

"Okay, card player, move on. As far as your money goes, I don't think it's going to buy you very much from now on."

"I can save it to show my grandchildren someday," Lomas replied as he repacked the backpack. The leather bag with pull strings did contain his wedding ring, but the money wasn't Confederate. The little leather bag also held over one hundred dollars in gold coins. Once everything was replaced, Lomas left the tent and began to hunt for Jack and Abel. He found them arranging a harness for the recently acquired wagon.

"When are you going to Richmond?" he asked.

"We won't go until the morning," Jack replied. "You are coming with us, aren't you?"

"Certainly, I just needed to know how much time I had before we left."

Jack and Abel didn't need to ask. Their crafty French friend had noticed Yankee soldiers playing poker. It won't be too long before Lomas would be in the game.

"I read somewhere that poker is the national pastime here in America," Abel commented.

"If that's true, then Lomas must be a national hero. I fear that he won't be after he takes money away from the boys in blue," Jack conveyed.

"As long as he doesn't get himself shot," imparted Abel.

* * *

The news of General Lee's surrender had a special effect on Sally Tompkins. She knew that with the war over, they won't be receiving any more patients, and as those in her care recover, there would be less to take care of. It won't be long, now that the city was occupied, before the Robertson Hospital would be shut down. It had been her life for the past four years, and thoughts of what she would do next frightened her. She was a person who had to be active in an endeavor in which she was eminently needed. Her time at Robertson went without saying, and the last few months taking care of Jozef was rewarding for both her and Lavinia Robertson, even though the imminent fact of his father's return was constantly in the foremost of their minds. They attempted aloofness so as not to become too attached to the child and lessen the heartache when his father would take him away, all the same, it was a failing struggle.

Concerning the father, Jack Leffingwell's welfare was as yet unknown. For all they knew, Jack Leffingwell might not return; however, up till now, his name was not on the list of slain soldiers.

The two women sat in Sally's kitchen and commiserated over a hot cup of tea. Lavinia just finished feeding Jozef and struggled to continue holding the precocious little boy as he wiggled to get free.

"Jozef Leffingwell, you are the fussiest little tyke your aunt Lavinia has ever seen. Sit still for a minute so I can wipe your face and hands," Lavinia scolded as she wiped some cereal from his cheek and chin. After she put him down, Jozef crawled away at top speed in an aimless direction. Just as sudden, he came to a complete stop and sat up flashing a self-satisfying grin that melted the hearts of both women.

"I can always hire out as a cleaning woman when the hospital is closed," stated Lavinia.

"There's no need for that, Lavinia. I still have much of my inheritance left, and we can go on with our charity work. We've got the Episcopal Church work, and there will soon be lots of veteran associations that will need our help."

"Sally, for years I never thought there was people like you. You never took a penny for all you did at Robertson's, and most of the time you paid for the supplies out of your own purse," Lavinia stressed.

"That's what charity work is all about. I'm just glad that I was able to do it. And remember, I couldn't have done as much without your help. Let's pray and give thanks for what we have and ask the Lord to watch over Jozef's father and bring him home safely."

* * *

The early-morning air was crisp and aromatic from the blossoms of nearby fruit trees. A mountain mist still draped the area, and a blanket of dew covered everything including the wagon. Jack had greased the wagon wheels from a keg of lubricant given by Leroy Littlefield the day prior. The large buckskin mare was given the first chance to pull, and while Abel was attaching the harness, a shadowed figure came into view. It was Lomas Chandler astride a magnificent exhibition of horse flesh.

"I hope you didn't steal that animal," Abel asserted.

"Not to worry. This fine specimen belonged to a Yankee cavalry officer who thought he was a good poker player. There were five of them all together, and after they saw a twenty-dollar gold piece, they couldn't wait to take it away from me. Fortunately for them, they hadn't drawn this month's pay, or my purse would be stretched even tighter," Lomas remarked as he dismounted.

"Did you buy the horse with your winnings?" Jack questioned.

"Buy him, hell no. A Yankee officer was out of money and held a good hand. He put his horse and saddle up to cover the pot and raised the ante. The others dropped out, and I knew what he was holding and could see I had him beat. It took a while for us to convince him that a flush beats a straight. He went ballistic, but his buddies finally quieted him down. I did invite them all to stop by the Eagle Inn and Tavern, but they probably won't. I think they're from Illinois. When are we hitting the road?"

"Everybody got their parole paper?" Lomas and Abel gave an affirmative nod. "Then, let's roll," Jack snapped with vigor.

April in Virginia can reach temperatures of seventy degrees during the daylight hours and drop well below freezing at night. Even with the wide range of temperature alternation, the morning sunlight brings out the brilliant display of mountain colors from the woodland wildflowers. Such beauty begins at the lower elevations and progresses upward as the season lengthens. The spectacular flowering, normally a breathtaking attraction, had gone unnoticed while war occupied both land and mental awareness. Today, however, the thought of war was the last thing on the sharpshooters' minds as they traveled east to Richmond and a renewed future. The eighty-five-mile trip would take the better part of a week. Thanks to Corporal Littlefield, the wagon larder was full. Unsure as to when he did it, the food rations in the wagon and the little extra provided by Lomas guaranteed a more pleasurable trip. It came as no surprise at the density of traffic on the way. After all, it was the main road, and migrants wearing blue and gray seemed to be moving both east and west, all with a common purpose. Union soldiers were either escorting larger groups or marching to a new assignment; and civilians, apparently, were returning to their previously vacated homes.

The first day on route the former marksmen were energized by a traveler's enthusiasm. Their pace was slow; however, it was sustained until nightfall. When purple shades began to descend, the wayfarers found a convenient green glade and pitched camp. Horses were allowed to graze for a short time on April's new grass and then given oats from the barrel in their tent. Lomas had located a rill nearby and led them to drink before tethering for the evening. Their soft nickering served to tell the world they were content.

The sky was speckled with tiny dots of bright illumination, and as Jack Leffingwell lay on his blanket near the fire, he was reminded of a nest holding robin eggs. The reason for such an analogy became muddled in his thoughts. He knew one thing, like recent glimpses into his past, it had to be related to events before his injury. As the remainder of the evening unwound, the spent travelers slept soundly until the predawn hours. The stars were no longer visible. A depressing blackness had taken their place, and as Jack Leffingwell stoked embers of their fire, the sound of thunder echoed from a few miles away.

"Sounds like we got rain coming in," Abel stated as he tossed a faggot of wood on the restarted flame.

"Can't rightly tell how bad it's going to be for a couple of hours. Once the coffee gets hot, we best get back on the road. Might be able to put a few miles under our belt before it hits," Jack conveyed.

Hot coffee gave the needed boost, and soon wagon wheels were turning and heading east toward Richmond. As anticipated, the rolling dark clouds caught up with them after two hours on the road. The wayfarers began to search for a sheltered area, hoping not to be completely exposed once the downpour arrived. Lomas Chandler had galloped ahead, acting as a one-man scouting party, and returned with good news. There was a small grove about a quarter mile up front, with a brook nearby. In all likelihood, it was an extension of the rill from the previous day.

Rain began to descend with a smattering of large drops falling heavily from the sky. Shortly thereafter, the raindrops modified smaller and increased in volume. A flash of lightening reached the ground a short distance ahead of the travelers, followed by a resounding boom of thunder, just as Abel directed the wagon to the parcel of land suggested by Lomas. The trio took cover in the nick of time as the rain turned into a torrential downpour and fell to ground in buckets. The road glistened at first, from the falling water, but then gradually became a quagmire of muddy earth.

The marksmen initially sought shelter beneath trees, however, soon moved to the wagon and its protective canvas cover.

"Back home we call this a gully washer," Jack stated. "It comes up fast but doesn't stay long."

"It's still going to take a whole lot of sunshine before the road is dry enough to travel on," Abel remarked.

"It might not take as long as you think. We've marched in weather worse than this," Jack replied.

"Yeah, but the wagons had a hell of a time keeping up," Abel reminded.

"Nevertheless, we best stay here until the road dries well enough for the wagon wheels to take hold," Jack suggested. "I'm for staying until we see how other wagons fare. There are plenty of them heading east."

By noon, the sun was beginning to do its work. A couple of hardy souls went by struggling with their wagons even with two horses pulling the dray. That was enough for the paroled Southerners to give up on the idea of a quick return to their journey and set about fixing something for lunch. Old habits are hard to break. With a larder full of options, hardtack was the first item that came to mind.

"I kind of miss ole Melvin," Lomas lamented. "He seemed to brighten the day."

"You just liked to bullshit him. Telling him that fairies really existed," Abel retorted.

"They do exist, Abel, but a person has to have a kind heart in order to see them," Lomas chided.

"That would explain why you've never seen them," Abel said laughingly.

"I've made a point of looking him up once we get to Richmond," Jack interjected.

It was around four o'clock in the afternoon before General Grant's gift was back on the road. The wagon driver's seat was occupied by Jack Leffingwell, who needed to take special care in order to avoid any mired sections. Thus, travel was slowed to a snail's pace. Because of Jack's concern for the horse, they stopped early and made camp. Evening temperatures began to be more comfortable, and the cooking fire proved adequate for sleeping in the open on their bedrolls.

The next morning, roads were much drier, and it was Abel's turn driving the wagon. Morning chores completed, they were on their way as the sun broke free on the eastern horizon. Their steady pace was interrupted by three horsemen who approached from behind and took an unusual interest in the wagon and horses. After an impolite ogle, the trio galloped forward and stopped at a bend up road and waited under a yellow canvas.

"What was that all about?" Abel asked Jack.

"Looks kinda suspicious, doesn't it?"

"I don't think they're soldiers, and they look too mean to be regular folks," Abel stated.

"I'll mosey ahead and see what they're up to," Lomas said calmly as he heel-kicked his mount. When Lomas drew nearer, one of the strangers responded by trotting to meet him.

"Morning, Friend, we sure had good rain last night. Is there anything I can do to help you?" asked Lomas.

"Yeah, as a matter of fact, there is," the stranger replied. Drawing his pistol, he added, "You can start by giving us your valuables and horses, and if you do it fast enough, I might let you live. Just get off that pony and back away."

Jack Leffingwell had been observing the activity through the telescope mounted on his Whitworth, and once the stranger drew his weapon, he knew they were some sort of road bandits.

The shock of impact was emphatic and without resistance as the revolver flew from the highway robber's hand and landed on the roadside. The bandit's eyes were the size of saucers and, in a state of shock, looked at his hand half torn from his wrist. Lomas walked to the roadside and retrieved the revolver while the wounded man rolled from side to side holding his wrist and howling. Under the yellow canvas, a second pirate raised his rifle toward Lomas, only to hear the eerie whistle of a Whitworth bullet and fly backward off his horse, dead from a shot to his chest. The third bandit tossed the canvas aside and kicked his horse to a gallop, riding hell-bent for leather.

"You better have somebody look at that hand before you bleed to death," Lomas said before trotting to where the second man lay and taking hold of his horse's reins to lead him back to the wagon.

"Tie your kerchief around your arm real tight," was the only help Lomas offered.

"They sure were an ornery bunch," said Abel. "I've heard tell about road pirates, but this is the first time to actually see one."

"They did seem to be a tad unfriendly," Jack added.

Lomas tied the bonus horse's reins to the wagon and, shaking his head, said, "This animal looks like it's of no account, but I did pick up a good revolver from the hullabaloo."

"It looks to me like it has only been mistreated. Hard to tell if he's any good until more meat's put on his bones," Jack asserted.

Four years actively fighting a war had a way of hardening a man's feelings. The life-threatening situation that took place just minutes before passed as though it was inconsequential. And when the wagon rolled past the bend in the road, no thought was given to bury the body lying face up under a tangle of briar, a callousness unthought-of four years earlier. Alternating the mares pulling the dray kept both well rested, and fair weather followed them for the remainder of the trip. Little was spoken that final day. The marksmen, being occupied with their own personal thoughts, conspired in daydreams of positive results for the future. Only the Tennessee mountain man had occasional trepidation, and well, he should, considering what lies ahead.

Union outposts blocked entry into the city from main thoroughfares. There still was a general nervousness only days after Lee's surrender since fighting continued elsewhere. The surrender of Confederate general Joseph E. Johnston's armies on April 26 marked the *official* end of hostilities.

"Make sure you have your papers ready," Jack told the others.

A bluejacket sentry approached the wagon and ordered, "State your business." His tone made the marksmen bristle. Handing him their papers, Jack Leffingwell said, "I'm here to pick up my son and visit a friend in Chimborazo."

"I live here," Lomas stated drily.

"We're going to be heading back to Tennessee, and I'm traveling with them," Abel added.

"What's in the wagon?" questioned the sentry as he pulled back the flap and peered inside.

"Comestibles," Lomas answered.

"What the hell is that?" he snorted.

"That's food," Jack answered.

"You Southern assholes better learn to talk American." The Union soldier was showing his frustration. "I'm about ready to have you unload the whole kit and caboodle."

Jack leaned about two inches from the sentry's face and drawled softly, "Son, you're about ready to start this damn war all over again. I think you ought to call for your superior officer."

The Yankee soldier stood for a moment, biting his upper lip, then handed Jack the papers and shouted, "Okay to go ahead."

Passing the charred black skeletons of former buildings, the city had taken on an apocalyptic appearance. Most of the street activity consisted of Union soldiers and former slaves. Large gangs of black men were tearing down burned—out buildings and hauling the debris away. Working with a rhythmic chant, the scene was unchanged from antebellum days. The Union occupiers seemed to have little veneration for the blacks and made them toe the line in every respect. Unless working, they must dance to the tune of very strict discipline and were not allowed to loll about in the streets. There's one major difference. Today, they extemporized in a pleasant-sounding chorus, celebrating freedom.

When the sharpshooters reached to the corner of Third and Main, they were relieved to find the area had escaped the terrible fire. Lomas Chandler was especially encouraged and, after telling Abel and Jack to make sure they get together before leaving, galloped down the street toward the Eagle Inn and Tavern.

"What was in the bag that Lomas gave you?" asked Abel.

"Let's take a look," Jack replied as he spread the top and poured out its contents. In addition to the wad of greenbacks, Jack held $100 in gold coins. Their Irish friend had given them nearly $200 to help pay for the return to Tennessee. The two former rebel soldiers just stared at each other without speaking. Their silence told it all.

Chapter Thirty-Nine

With the new day comes new strength and new thoughts.

—Eleanor Roosevelt

News of General Lee's surrender had reached the state of Tennessee, receiving mixed blessings. In the eastern part of the state, it was met with celebration, not too surprising due to the majority of its populace having a Union bent. The hoorah was considerably less in the central and western parts. Abigail Leffingwell, the bruised wife of the Tennessee mountain man, accepted the news with prayerful thanksgiving. She and Minnie Rosenthal burned the candle's wick to its very end, discussing how they would be affected by Jack's return.

"Funny how things turn out," Minnie said. "Just when it seems the darkest, the good Lord brings the light."

"I keep telling myself not to get too hopeful. Jack doesn't remember me or the life we had before he got hurt.

And now, if he really comes home, he'll bring another woman's child with him."

"That woman is dead. Only the Lord can judge her now. You must try to forget about her and be the generous granddaughter I know you to be."

"Oh, Minnie, how could I have ever made it without you?"

"Darling, it's all part of faith. When Jacob died, I was at my wit's end. Then your husband came along. When Jack went to war, you invited me to come live with you: all part of God's plan. Shortly thereafter, Little Jack was born, and with divine help, we made it through four years of this terrible war. He watches over us now as we sit here in the light of that candle," Minnie smiled reassuredly.

"Well, that candle is about burned out," Abigail said softly. "We best turn in and finish our conversation tomorrow," Abigail yawned.

The following morning, Abigail woke with a start. She had slept the night without disturbing dreams. The house seemed unusually quiet for this late after sunup. Slipping on her house robe, Abigail padded into the hallway and called, "Minnie, are you awake?"

Receiving no answer, she gently pushed open the door to the elderly saint's bedroom. Sometime during the silence of night, Minnie Rosenthal had joined her husband Jacob. There was no pain as evidenced by her calm expression. Dylan Thomas would possibly disapprove since she did not "rage against the dying of the light." Instead, Minnie Rosenthal gently took the Lord's hand as he led her to paradise.

"Oh, Minnie, why now when I need you the most?" Abigail whispered as she woke the children and prepared for the trip to visit her father.

"Isn't Grandma Minnie coming with us?" Sarah Jane asked.

"Not this time, dear, we're going to see Grandpa by ourselves."

Noticing his daughter and grandchildren without Minnie in the carriage, Hyrum sensed something wrong. After Abigail drew close enough for him to see her tears, he knew the little saint was gone.

"She died last night in her sleep," Abigail whimpered.

"We need to give thanks for the time she was with us," Hyrum said softly. "I'll contact the doctor, and we'll follow you back to the farm."

"I want to leave the children with Maryellen Riberty so they don't see everything."

"That's fine, I'll ride back with you in the carriage," Hyrum replied. "The last I heard, Minnie wanted to be buried next to Jacob in the family plot. That is likely part of her will. Dr. Campbell has her last testament in his safekeeping."

"I never knew Minnie had a will."

"She was adamant about it after Jacob passed on. I suggested she see Doc Campbell, and he told me she did. In fact, the last time you all visited Statesville, she brought her will up to date."

"Minnie told me she saw him to get something for her cough," stated Abigail.

"I guess she didn't want you to know."

Making a will wasn't the only business Minnie handled during her visit with Dr. Campbell. She also arranged for the purchase of a coffin at Riberty's general store. While Statesville had local craftsmen able to build cabinets, and yes, toe-pinching coffins, Minnie chose an artisan from Lebanon, a town twenty-five miles to the northwest.

Statesville didn't have a funeral parlor; therefore, burials were handled by the families involved. In some cases, especially in the more remote rural areas, the deceased was laid to rest directly into the ground sans a casket.

Hyrum suggested they acquire Minnie's casket when the children visit Maryellen and take it back with them.

"She must have had a premonition," Abigail stated flatly as the pair began the short trip to the farm.

"I think not, her actions were typical for a woman at such an advanced age. Not wanting to be a burden, they take care of this business themselves, while they remain healthy and still of sound mind," Hyrum explained.

Once the cedar coffin was secured in the wagon, Miracle began the return journey to the farm. She never failed to get excited on the homecoming trip, probably because a bucket of oats and fresh hay awaited her arrival. Another reason could be the fact of being set free from the burden of the wagon and released to run loose in her corral. Those who have experience riding horses can recall the animal at the end of the ride and return to the stable. The somewhat-lethargic creature became energized and full of spirit on the way back.

Dr. Campbell and Sheriff Williams were sitting at the kitchen table when Abigail arrived. Sheriff Ezell Williams had served in that capacity for nearly twenty years. A congenial man, over three score in age, he was never elected to the office. Actually, the office didn't really exist. Everyone knew that Williams was the sheriff, but no one recalled how he got the job. He owned a revolver that lay in his desk drawer. It was unused for over five years, and then only for target practice or varmints. His demeanor of authority worked most of the time, and when that rarely failed, there were always others who came to his aid. When the war broke out, he was discouraged from enlisting by the town leaders. They did so because of his age and saving him the embarrassment of being rejected. Ezell reluctantly agreed to stay and let the younger men have the honor.

"We brought Minnie's casket back with us," Abigail uttered as she plopped on the corner chair.

"Come on, Ezell, let's give Hyrum a hand," the doctor said while sliding his chair from the table. "Abigail, now's the time to gather material for lining the box 'cause we'll be putting her in it when we come back in."

Abigail went to Minnie's room to fetch her feather tick and blanket. A quick glance at the sweet lady was all her emotions could handle before returning to the kitchen.

Even with Minnie inside, the wooden casket seemed no heavier than it did empty. Though physically diminutive, Minnie Rosenthal's weight was expanded by her unfailing faith in God and the steel of her moral fiber. The heft of her kindness knew no bounds.

Hyrum presided at her graveside funeral services two days later. Men from the congregation had arrived the day before with shovels and dug the grave next to her husband, Jacob. It was a day with continuous sunshine, and over seventy-five people attended the burial. That in itself is not unusual since church congregations pay respect to their fellow members. This day, many others had come in reverence to a pioneer in the territory—one who shared the experience of settling the land and defended it against storm, drought, pestilence, and Indians.

Maryellen Riberty helped Abigail arrange tables on the lawn, under hardwood trees, whose green leaves days before were merely buds waiting for their vernal promise. The two friends were up all night preparing for the traditional country meal after a farm funeral. It was only a short stroll from the gravesite to the Leffingwell farm and the results of Abigail and Maryellen's nocturnal effort. The tone of the guests was predictable, solemn at first then, as time went by, the event took on a happier deportment.

"Abigail, the next time you're in town, I'd like you to come see me. I have in my possession Minnie's last will and testament," Dr. Campbell said formally.

"I didn't know Minnie even had a will. We never talked about that sort of thing," Abigail replied.

"I guess Minnie would rather have it that way. Your father knew about it. In fact, Hyrum sent her to me so that it could be properly handled. It's probably in bad taste to discuss it here and now, so let's wait until you visit Statesville."

By midafternoon, those that lingered longest had finally departed, leaving Maryellen and Abigail to their own thoughts. Church ladies helped with the cleanup, and their men stacked the tables in Maryellen's wagon to be returned to her father's general store.

"I would appreciate it if you spend the night," Abigail suggested.

"I plan to, honey. You're going to need me for a while. By the way, with the war over, do you think that rat husband of yours will really come back?"

"I hope so. I'm sorry, Maryellen, but I still love him."

"Even after all he's said and done?"

"Yes."

"Well, you'll just have to forgive me for hating him," Maryellen replied. "The farm needs work, so maybe you could hook a plow up to his sorry ass and let me have a whip."

It was the first time Abigail laughed since finding Minnie gone. Her friend had a way about her that never failed to cheer her up. The farm did need a man's work, and the fields hadn't been touched since Jack left four years ago.

When Abigail visited Dr. Campbell, she learned that she was Minnie's only heir. Minnie's farm and all her earthly possession were left to her. Now she had two farms badly in need of a man's strength, effort, and sweat.

Chapter Forty

Of all sad words of tongue or pen, the saddest are these, "It might have been."

—John Greenleaf Whittier

Jack and Abel hitched the horses and wagon along the side of Robertson's entrance and climbed the steps to the front door. Inside, they looked about finding everything unchanged from their last visit. Amidst inquisitive glances of nurses and orderlies, the pair found their way to Sally Tompkins's office and gently rapped on the door.

"Come in," came the voice from inside.

Jack reached for the knob and gave it a twist. The door swung open, and he and Abel entered Sally's office and also her life. Obviously, both men survived the war, and now she was about to lose Little Jozef, entrusted to her safe keep until this very moment. The reception was formal and without exuberance as Sally said drily, "Your son is well and doing fine. I have to be here for at least another hour, so feel free to go to the house. Lavinia is there with Little Jozef. I'll be along once I finish here."

The three found conversation difficult. Hopefully, later today, things would be more comfortable and the ice easier broken. Jack walked the short distance to Sally's home while Abel led the mare behind the house. Lavinia had been in the kitchen watching him maneuver the horses and wagon and didn't hear Jack knocking at the front door. The sight of Abel made her realize that dreaded day had arrived, and without hearing him, she knew Jack was at the front door. It would be impossible to determine which reception was the coolest. Nevertheless, Jack felt empathy for both women. The situation couldn't be avoided. Jozef was Jack's flesh and blood given to him by the woman he deeply loved, and nobody had claim on him except his natural father. In spite of that fact, the pain Sally and Lavinia shared was just as deep as if the little boy was their very own.

"Do you plan to stay in Richmond for a while?" Sally asked.

"Yes, if you don't mind. We plan to visit Chimborazo and see Melvin Kaufman. You might remember him from past visits," Jack answered.

"Now that you mention it, I believe I do. He was sort of a quiet sort, if I recall properly," said Sally. "Why is he at Chimborazo?"

"He got wounded at the Wilderness battle, and we heard they took him to Chimborazo," Abel chimed in.

"Where do you men plan on staying?"

"We thought we'd look around, and if push comes to shove, there is always the wagon," Abel added.

"Nonsense, you will stay here with me and Lavinia. Jack can stay with his son, and you can have Grazyna's old room."

"We don't want to put you all out any more than we already have," Jack said honestly.

"The matter is closed. What's for supper, Lavinia?" asked Sally.

Supper was meager although considerably better than what was had by most inhabitants of the city. Since Union forces entered, no one was starving due to daily rations provided by the military and converted shopkeepers; nevertheless, it would take months before something resembling *normal* would return.

"It would please Abel and me if you let us pay for our stay with you. We are in possession of a few gold coins and greenbacks," Jack offered.

"Our problem isn't money. We have money, including greenbacks, but right now there's no food to be purchased, and with so many freed slaves, it's going to get worse before it gets any better," Sally replied. "So far we've been able to feed the patients at Robertson's even with the beggars that appear daily. The mayor promises conditions will improve. I certainly hope he's right."

"We don't want to take food away from people who are hungry," Abel stated.

"My Momma always told us children, there's always enough for another plate and there were fourteen at our table," Lavinia added. "Ain't nobody starving 'cause you all are here."

"Ever since you arrived, there's a question that's puzzling me. How did you come by three horses and a wagon?" Sally asked.

"It's a long story."

"I'd like to hear it."

"Well, when General Lee surrendered at Appomattox, we infantry soldiers were made to stack our weapons and line up to take the pledge. Most of us were glad it was all over, and we made it through with our skin. Others called it *swallowing the dog* and faked it. When the line was moving, I asked if I could keep my Whitfield rifle, and the officer said my rank doesn't allow it. Just then General Grant entered the tent, and one of his soldiers explained to him what the delay was about. He was a colored soldier, and he told the general that he knew me from far back. I don't remember him, but apparently, it had to do with his mother and father. The general asked me a couple of questions, and before you know it, they gave us two horses, a wagon, and my Whitfield rifle. That young black soldier helped us find everything you see, including a paper signed by the general himself. Lomas Chandler came back with us, but he won his horse in a poker game."

"That's quite a story. You're lucky General Grant showed up when he did, or you men would be on foot," Sally reasoned. "You only accounted for two animals, and I see three."

"The other one we got off a renegade pirate on the way over here."

"I think you took that soldier's parents to freedom back in your Underground Railroad days," Lavinia surmised. "He found a way to repay the good deed."

"You could be right, Lavinia, but I don't remember any of it," Jack concluded.

"One of these days it'll all come back to you. Right now I best fetch Little Jozef and bring him to the dinner table."

* * *

Lomas Chandler received a hero's welcome. The Eagle Inn and Tavern made it through the riots and fire without visible damage, and his return was cause for celebration. To the Italian family, it was like their native son had come back from a long ordeal; and tonight, when he laid his head on a familiar pillow and saw his beloved's smile, Lomas also would know he, too, was home.

The gaiety lasted well into the night and early morning hours as various families dropped by once they heard the news of Lomas's return. For many, it was their first time to meet Isabella's husband; and with his easy manner and quick wit, Lomas captured each and every one. He also was drawn to the way Isabella was treated. No queen ever born was treated with more tender regard, and as his eyes became fixed to her presence, he was absorbed with her stunning south European beauty. Her olive skin and hazel eyes reminded him of how lucky he was to be married to such a woman.

Finally, alone in their room, they lay together without speaking. In less than two hours, a glimmer of daylight would appear in the east; and Isabella's heart rate was still slightly elevated from the celebration. She whispered, "I still have the money you asked me to hide."

She must be clairvoyant because, at that exact moment, Lomas was thinking of the very same thing. Exhaling deeply, Lomas replied, "That's good, dear, but we can talk about it in the morning. We both need a couple of hours to come back down to earth."

"Then you don't want to make love tonight?" Shortly thereafter, Lomas found out that he wasn't very tired at all.

The sun was well past its apogee when the young pair descended the stairs to be greeted by Isabella's mother and father. The bar was well attended, and two tables had men playing dominoes—a game Lomas was unfamiliar with.

"Isn't anyone going to play poker?" he asked.

"Sì, i giocatori di carta arrivano dopo la cena," a domino player answered before he placed a tile on the table and shouted, "Cento!" Lomas, confused by the language, gave Isabella a pleading glance.

"The card players arrive after supper," she translated, much to her husband's delight. Taking Lomas's hand, Isabella led him to a table away from others, and food arrived moments later. By now, the rebel soldier was famished, and what appeared to be stew was wolfed down in short order. Isabella, just as hungry, took her time displaying more ladylike manners.

"That tasted great. What was it?"

"*Stufato italiano*, Italian stew," Isabella replied.

"Tell your mother that it tasted great."

"You tell her, she and Father are coming to join us," Isabella said frankly. Enzio and Maria took chairs from a neighboring table and turned the gathering into a foursome.

"You two look well rested from last night. I hope we didn't frighten Lomas with so many family members. We Italians, especially those from Sicily, tend to be rather clannish, but once you get to know them, everything seems normal," Maria said while patting Lomas's arm.

"I thought everybody was very friendly considering that I'm not Italian. My kinfolk came over because of the potato famine. I personally don't remember it, but my mother and sainted grandmother told me all about it. More than one million people starved to death and another million emigrated elsewhere. They said that living in Ireland was a life of poverty and prejudice. Nobody owned the land they farmed, and the setup England established made matters worse. Rent was paid to the overseer who disliked us because of being poor and, most of all, because of our foreign faith. Being Catholic in England was viewed as belonging to an alien church. My grandfather brought us all to New York. That's where most of the Chandler family resides," explained Lomas.

"How in the world did you ever end up here in Virginia?" asked Enzio.

"Well, I reached a point in my life where the time had come to get married. The local girls, although very pretty, were not the right ones, so I set out hunting for Isabella. I traveled over land and water hunting for her. Each time I thought I had found her, shortly after, I realized it wasn't her and continued my search. Finally, she couldn't elude me any longer because I found her here in Richmond, Virginia."

"That's the biggest line of applesauce I've ever heard in my life, but I love you for it," said Maria. Isabella ogled her husband in adoration and could only smile since her words were lost for a moment.

Enzio broke the three-way circle of admiration by saying, "There's something I want to talk to you about. We will need to discuss your future employment. There's no rush for that because you are now part of the Eagle Inn and Tavern. I want to take you around to meet all, or most all of the family. Richmond is in a state of turmoil right now, but it won't stay that way. Lomas, you obviously have a great gift of gab, and I want you to consider running for precinct captain this fall. You can't lose since 80 percent of voters are blood related. I've given this a lot of thought, and I truly believe you have a future in politics. Give it some thought and maybe next week we can take a tour of the neighborhood."

With that being said, Isabella's parents excused themselves and returned to their preparations for the suppertime crowd. Lomas's thoughts were being bombarded with ideas based on what Enzio had proposed. He had never given any consideration for a career in politics. In fact, he never had to think about any actual work to make his living, as long as a poker game could be found. Now, his biggest task was to figure out how to merge the two together and enjoy the best of both worlds. That night, when the card players arrived, they congregated around their favorite table and drew cards to see who was first to shuffle the deck and deal. Once they noticed Lomas, one shouted across the room, "Hey, Lomas, come play and give us a chance to win our money back."

"Thanks anyway, but I only arrived yesterday and still don't have my sea legs under me. Give me 'til tomorrow, and I'll join you. Right now, I couldn't even hold the cards."

"We'll hold you to your promise," he replied, and subdued laughter encircled the table as most believed Lomas previously won by beginner's luck. Next time, the shoe would be on the other foot.

"If you don't mind, Isabella, my other friends plan to come by tomorrow, and the three of us will go and visit Melvin Kaufman at Chimborazo Hospital," stated Lomas.

"How could I mind that? Did he get hurt in the war?"

"Yes, and I believe he also lost an arm," he replied as the poker table erupted with shouting and laughter. In the midst of the din, Enzio tapped on a beer glass and announced, "Now that my son-in-law is back from the war, the Eagle Inn and Tavern will have entertainment on Friday nights. In about an hour, Pasquale Piatanesi will entertain us with his Italian accordion."

Before the doors were locked at day's end, festive accordion music wafted into the air in front of the building. It attracted a small crowd outside, listening to the pleasant sound. Word spread quickly, and the following Friday, there wasn't enough tables to handle the customers. From that point on, Fridays required reservations. The inn became a hot spot for dining, with evenings in which the dining room was half-occupied by troopers wearing blue jackets, taking their dates out for dinner and causing a constant ring of the cash register.

While the three sharpshooters were planning their visit to Chimborazo, a devastating rumor circulated around the city. Unfortunately, the shocking gossip turned out to be true. On Good Friday, April 14, President Abraham Lincoln was assassinated five days after General Lee surrendered to Ulysses S. Grant. According to the newspapers, the assassination was carried out by a stage actor named John Wilkes Booth, who was still at large. The president and his wife were watching the play *Our American Cousin* at Ford's Theater in Washington, D.C. Booth and his co-conspirators aimed to simultaneously eliminate the top three people in the administration in hopes of severing the continuity of the United States government and revive the Confederate cause. The plot failed. Authorities had launched a comprehensive manhunt and were confident that Booth's capture was imminent.

"Well, what do you know about that? Most folks are going to believe it was the work of the Lord for starting the war in the first place," Lomas stated.

"People up North are convinced we started the war when we fired on Fort Sumter," Abel replied.

"We didn't send seventy-five thousand troops up North to teach them a lesson. That was Mr. Lincoln, and to most of us Southerners, that's what caused the war," Jack added. "It doesn't make any difference now, we lost the war and Lincoln is dead. It's all kind of sad when you think about it."

"What happens now?" Lomas asked.

"Tennessee's own Andrew Johnson is now the president of the United States," Abel answered. "I only have one thing to say about that. When it comes to slavery, Johnson is no Abraham Lincoln and might give the newly freed slaves something to think about."

After church services the following Sunday, Jack Leffingwell and Abel Strawn teamed up with Lomas and rode in the direction of Chimborazo Hill. The hospital's elevation made it recognizable from most city points facing east. Lomas's mount tossed his head and snorted in appreciation for being untethered and had to be under a strong hold in order to keep him from a spirited gallop. The two mares were much better mannered. When the three riders neared the hospital grounds, a blue-clad soldier with a black armband stood in the road and raised his hand as a signal to stop. Federal forces occupy not only the city of Richmond but also the hospitals therein. It was a priority to investigate them all in search of wounded Union prisoners and transfer them into one of three selected institutions. At one time, Union wounded soldiers were dispersed into nearly fifty hospitals and care units. Once they were located and placed in the selected infirmaries, it became easier to identify the men as well as their status. The search revealed one important fact: the

Yankee enemy prisoners were treated the same as rebel soldiers and given identical care and food.

The Union sentry found it suspicious that three rebel soldiers could blatantly ride to Chimborazo as if on a Sunday afternoon stroll. Most visitors arrived either on foot or in a carriage and never atop fine-looking equines.

"State your business," he ordered.

"We're here to visit a friend," Jack replied and handed him the travel papers. Apparently, the blue trooper found difficulty reading and insisted the trio dismount and accompany him to the post. After which, the duty officer read Jack's documents and remarked, "It says that General Grant gave you two horses and a wagon and signed it himself. Where did you see the general?"

"At Appomattox," Jack answered.

"How about that galloper?" the soldier of rank questioned while pointing at Lomas Chandler.

"He won it in a poker game and has the paper signed by the Union captain that lost it."

Shrugging his shoulders, the Union officer handed back Jack's papers and sighed. "Now, I think I've seen it all. You guys are okay to pass." The puzzled sentry was visibly disappointed and asked his superior, "Are you just going to let them go?"

"Yeah, how would you like to explain it to Gen. Ulysses S. Grant as to why you didn't honor his signature?"

Chimborazo was divided into five units, ostensibly to separate soldiers by regiment and home state. As the war progressed, patients increased to nearly four thousand and orderly separation became more difficult. Treatment mainly focused on the sick and those recovering from their wounds. Such was the case of Melvin Kaufman who received initial treatment in a field hospital and sent to Chimborazo for convalescence. The sharpshooters tied their mounts to a rail located at the main entrance and walked to the admissions counter. They learned that Melvin was in section 3, but away on a weekend pass. He wasn't expected back until sometime Monday before noon. The butternut threesome retraced their steps and stood in front of Chimborazo pondering their next move.

"We can always go back to the Eagle Inn and Tavern and spend the rest of the day drinking beer and preventing kidney stones," Lomas suggested. "Beer isn't just for breakfast anymore. You can drink it anytime you want."

"I didn't get dolled up in my bib and tucker just to drink beer all day," Abel replied. "Where do you think Melvin is?"

"If it was me, I'd be either at a poker game or with a colleen," said Lomas.

"I think Lomas has got something. What was the name of that little gal Melvin was sparking when I was in Robertson's?" Jack questioned.

"Hope Waterman," Abel offered. "Remember, we had supper at her house. And I recollect where she lives."

Agreeing that the Waterman house should be their next destination, the trio mounted their chargers and backtracked at a faster gait than the pace used on their arrival. Passing the sentry, who stopped their earlier approach, they each gave a cheerful wave and, as they cantered by, suppressed the desire to give him the rebels' yell. With Abel leading the way, their journey took a couple of twists and turns, but eventually led them to Robertson Hospital. The Waterman house was located nearby. Pulling up in front, they found Melvin and Hope on the porch swing holding hands.

"So you thought you could hide from us, huh?" Lomas chided as the trio dismounted. Melvin was elated and skipped down the front steps to receive hugs from his fellow marksmen. Even Lomas had tears in his eyes from the emotional reunion.

"You all remember Hope. She and I are engaged," Melvin stammered earnestly. "Jack, I don't believe you've ever met her. This is Hope Waterman, my intended."

"The honor is all mine," Jack said graciously. "I'm pleased to meet you."

"Thank you. You're too kind. Won't you all please come inside so we can sit together and talk. You can tie your horses behind the house."

The visitors languished the day in pleasant conversation without mentioning Melvin's missing arm. Finally, the subject couldn't be held back any longer. Lomas naturally was the first to speak.

"There's something different about you from the last time I saw you, but I can't figure out what it is. Are you combing your hair differently?"

"Okay, okay, they cut my arm off in the field hospital," Melvin explained.

"You're kidding me. I never noticed until you mentioned it," Lomas said jokingly.

"Look at the bright side, the police will never be able to handcuff you," Abel said, laughing.

"That ain't the worst part. You won't be able to hold your beer and scratch your ass at the same time," Lomas added.

"You forgot to say that I can't get a job as a paper hanger," Melvin said.

"Hell, two hands aren't enough to hang wallpaper," Jack imparted. And with that things began to feel normal and Melvin back in the fold.

"What are your plans for the future?" Abel asked seriously.

"It's kind of up in the air right now. Hope wants to get married right away. I can sense her parents are against it. I've considered looking for a job in town, but I feel folks will see me as a gimp because of the arm. Things can't stay the way they are. I know that I have to do something," Melvin said frankly.

"Have you given any thought to returning to Tennessee?" Jack queried. "There should be plenty work around Statesville with the war over and farms needing to be tended. Most of them won't have a man on the place. Our regiment lost nearly one thousand soldiers, and less than fifty will be coming home."

"I won't leave Richmond without Hope, and she'll want to stay here," Melvin conjectured.

"That's not exactly true, Melvin. I'll go anywhere you go. I just want us married, that's all I care about," Hope piped up, adding her two cents.

"Well, here's the deal, we plan on leaving in about a week. They'll be one spare horse and a wagon. I'll have my son Jozef with me and Abel, so you two would make it perfect. You'd be another hand to help drive the team, and a woman's touch to help take care of Grazyna's and my little boy," asserted Jack.

Hope was excited by the prospective adventure and knew she must explain it to her father first to have an ally when her mother was told. She also knew neither parent would readily accept their daughter's decision to live so far away from home, but her father could best explain it to her mother and lessen her shock and pain. After all, she mused, the railroad would be restored soon and they could visit for extended periods of time. Right now, the important thing was getting married before leaving. Hope would talk to her father this evening after supper. At this moment, she would write Abigail Leffingwell, telling her of the good news. The two women had retained their initial friendship through correspondence and, hearing from each other in that fashion, strengthened their bond.

As expected, Grace Waterman fainted on the news of her daughter's plans. Horace had learned early on that, when dealing with Southern belles, aromatic spirits of ammonia (smelling salts) was to be kept on hand for just these occasions. One pass under her nose did the trick. Any more would make her eyes sting, water, and turn red. Like the fragile belle she claimed to be, Grace trained herself to recover with just one whiff. And with a solemn promise to visit for at least a month at a time, Grace agreed to call the minister.

During times of war, it wasn't unusual for weddings to be performed hastily for fear of undesirable delays and the dreaded permanent postponement. Rev. Sylvester Smith had known the Waterman family for over ten years. In his own mind, Hope would not want a quick ceremony for the reason most people thought and, after talking with Horace, was reassured by the facts. That condition which beleaguered many young women would not affect Hope if she was married beforehand.

The wedding was conducted in the Waterman home with Melvin's friends as guests. Hope's little sister Suzan acted as maid of honor; and Horace, her father, gave away the bride. Excited by her role in the wedding, Suzan was yet to realize her sister's absence. In two days, the nine-year-old would be faced with that special ache when she waved at the departing wagon. Grace would be unaware she was holding Suzan a little too tight when signaling her own farewell. The next two days were filled with activity. Hope assisted Jack preparing his son for the pending journey. She also became better acquainted with the little boy, making the transition much easier. The fact Jozef was a happy child helped it all come together more willingly.

Jack and Abel adapted the wagon's tongue to accommodate the harnesses of two horses. A trip of nearly seven hundred miles would be too much for one animal to pull, especially with the total of Hope, now Kaufman, and Jack's baby son, Jozef, added to the weight of the wagon.

Melvin hoisted aboard a portmanteau filled with Hope's clothing and asked Jack, "How long do you figure the trip will take?"

"If the weather holds out and we don't run into any problems, we ought to reach Statesville in about six weeks. Otherwise, it will take us longer. You best figure it taking two months. That way the delays won't be too disappointing," Jack replied.

"It shouldn't take that long. We used to march twenty miles a day for General Lee and think nothing of it," stated Melvin.

"You forget the times we sat by the road waiting for it to stop raining so the wagons could catch up."

"I guess you're right. I wasn't counting on that," Melvin confessed.

At the end of preparations, it was agreed that everyone would meet at Sally Tompkins's house the next day at six o'clock in the morning. That night was filled with restless sleep in anticipation of the following day's departure. At the appointed time, they all said their farewells and wheels began to turn at half past six.

The wagon became a blur to Horace as he put his arm around Grace and gave her a loving hug. Blinking away his tears, the retired professor mentally calculated the time by which the railroad would be repaired. Satisfied with his answer, he softly said to Grace, "We should be visiting them in about six months."

Sally and Lavinia shed their tears for the loss of a tiny child who was their own for over a year. They would never see him again.

Chapter Forty-One

We travel, some of us forever, to seek other states, other lives, other souls.

—Anaïs Nin

The morning sun was at their back, once the small caravan left the outskirts of Richmond and set a steady pace on the earthen highway. Spirits were high and the sway of the wagon induced Jozef to fall asleep in Hope's arms. She had located his bed directly behind the wagon cover flap for easy access. It worked perfectly, and the sleeping tot was laid in his bed without disturbance. Early haze still dominated the sky, but a feint crescent daylight moon could be seen by those looking upward. It's much too soon for anyone to contemplate what would happen at journey's end; therefore, Melvin's main concern was keeping the wagon aligned to the road. He did give thought to his missing arm since he needed the one he had to hold the reins and lacked the other around his new wife, sitting beside him. With the baby asleep behind them,

Hope's free arm found its way around Melvin's waist, so as Lomas would have said, "pot's right."

Jack and Abel were riding a few yards in front. Abel's mount was the renegade's horse, changed completely from the nag of a couple of weeks ago. A little care and regular feed did the trick. Jack was astride the charger Lomas won in a poker game. He insisted Jack take the horse because being tied up in Richmond wasn't the best life for such a spirited animal. Of course, Lomas was right; but in Jack's mind, such an altruistic gesture of generosity was uncharacteristic of a person like the crafty Irishman. The equine was first-rate, and making a gift of it for the Tennessee mountain man was the least Lomas could do. After all, it was Jack and his Whitworth rifle that saved his life only a few short days ago.

Abel wheeled around and trotted back to the wagon, turned again, and walked his pony alongside of Melvin, saying, "We've been on the road over two hours, and Jack thinks it's time to find a proper resting place. He's gone ahead in search of one now and will let you know where to pull off the road. How's the arm holding up? Driving a team is tiring if you have both arms."

"I'm doing all right. It was difficult at first, but once you get the knack of it, you learn to hold on and rest at the same time," Melvin replied.

The sun was straight overhead when the travelers spotted Jack Leffingwell standing in the saddle and waving toward a group of trees on the road side. The area had a shallow-moving stream winding through and a startling display of windflowers beneath its budding trees. The surrounding land boasted of new green grass from which the animals would receive a springtime treat. When the wagon arrived, Jack dismounted, grabbed the reins of the lead mare, and walked the canvas-covered dray to a desirable resting spot.

Little Jozef had been awake for the past hour and entertained himself until movement of the transporter came to a halt. Now his curiosity got the better of him, and he crawled through the covered portal for a better look. Hope took possession of him and handed the tyke down to his father.

"We're going to be here for a couple of hours, so let's free the team to drink at the creek," Abel said to Melvin. While the mares were walked to the water, Jack returned from his little stroll with his son and handed him to Hope, who by now had gathered the tot's foodstuffs.

"I'm going to build a fire circle for lunch. I spotted some nice-sized rocks when I was walking with Jozef," Jack said as he hiked toward the rill. Abel found enough dry kindling to make a decent blaze, and soon the aroma of hot coffee filled the air. After Melvin poured everyone the steaming brew, the iron skillet rested atop the flames and the sizzle of bacon stimulated the appetite of them all. Hot coffee, oven-baked bread, and crispy fried bacon seemed to fit the bill for the first meal on the long journey home. The scene was truly idyllic, having the travelers sitting with their backs to hardwood trees and a gentle breeze keeping the temperature well below that in direct sunlight.

Jack interrupted the languor when he declared, "There's still plenty of daylight remaining, and we need to take advantage of it. We can cover another ten or fifteen miles before making camp for the night." Good-natured moaning followed as the mares were brought in line to be hooked up to the wagon tongue and utensils washed and replaced in their allotted crate for travel. Jack Leffingwell inspected the wheel hubs before mounting the gift from Lomas and leading the group back on the highway. When daylight finally faded, the travelers had gained another fifteen miles. Jack suggested the men take shifts on watch while the others slept. Instinctively, he wanted to guard against any unsuspected visitors, even more so since the incident on the way to Richmond. Remembering the pistol obtained that day, he retrieved it from the wagon and offered to take the first two-hour watch. The moon was high and bright when Abel appeared for his turn. The two men sat and talked for a better part of the next hour and kept the cooking fire alive by tossing occasional kindling into the sputtering flame.

"I'm not a bit sleepy," Jack said. "Let's let the newlyweds have a good night's rest. I can doze in the saddle."

"You act as though you've done it before. Can you remember when?"

"Sort of, it had to be before the war," Jack replied.

"Were you married then?"

"I don't think so. It must have been before that."

"Do you remember being married?"

"Sometimes I seem to recall it, but then everything gets real fuzzy."

"You going back to Statesville is definitely the right thing to do. Grazyna must have been a wonderful woman to make you promise," Abel said emphatically.

"She was all that and a whole lot more." Jack sighed.

Engrossed in their own thoughts, the two friends sat silent staring at the hypnotic flames until it began to lighten in the east and the sparrows started to shake their feathers. After sleeping the night, the newlyweds owned all of the morning's energy. Jack and Abel tended the necessary chores by rote, and the migratory group was soon rolling west.

By midafternoon, the converted artillery wagon reached Amelia County. Jack directed Melvin to leave the road and rest the horses. Melvin found shade under a stand of oaks and hopped down to assist Hope and Little Jozef descend to the grass. While Hope and Melvin were still savoring the evening before, Jozef screamed with delight and ran at top speed until a flower caught his attention.

"Don't eat that!" Hope scolded as the tot dropped his treasure and dashed in another direction. "You need to watch this little guy every minute he's awake."

"I believe all two-year-olds are the same, especially boys," Melvin commented.

"Well, ours won't be like Jack Leffingwell's son."

"I'm afraid you're in for a big surprise, sweetheart," Melvin replied.

"Then I'll only have girls," she chided.

Jack and Abel stood atop a slight rise and scanned the pleasant countryside. Less than a month before, the serenity of their idyllic purview was a veritable dynamo of warfare. The air was filled with the resounding roar of bursting shells and canisters, the agonizing snapping of simultaneous rifle fire, and chilling screams of the wounded.

"You might say that this is where the war actually ended. The Yankees whipped us over yonder at Sayler's Creek," Jack continued, pointing with a waving motion to the west. "After that, General Lee realized he couldn't win."

"It all seems like a bad dream," Abel stated.

"More like a nightmare to me," the mountain man replied.

Walking back to join the others, they couldn't help but notice the darkening at the base of the western horizon. Jack had hoped the weather would hold long enough for them to reach Farmville by tomorrow evening. From the looks of things, that might not be possible. He could, however, keep pushing toward that destination until a storm would call a halt to their progress.

"Let's keep at it for as long as we are able. Once the storm hits, we're going to be stuck for a while," he announced to Melvin and Hope. "About ten miles ahead is a good-sized wooded area. We can make it our shelter if the wind picks up."

It now became a slow race to see who reached the forest first. The horses were getting nervous as dark rolling clouds became more evident. A feint rumbling roar was now being heard and, as the storm came nearer, grew louder and louder. The forest refuge lay straight ahead as the booming cannonade was upon them. Jack motioned for Melvin to drive the team along the tracks of earlier wagons leading deeper into the woods. The mixture of oak, hickory, and pine gave protection from the brunt of the wind, and the canopy of tree leaves acted like a porous umbrella. Once the travelers heard the crack of falling timbers however, Hope and Jozef found safety under the wagon. The storm lasted for about an hour, but the rain continued throughout the night. Progress had ended until it would quit raining and the heat of the sun would bake the muddy road dry. That night, the animals were fed oats and hay from the wagon's larder, but the wayfarers had to settle for hardtack and water. A crease in the dray's canvas cover made a path for rain to run off. Jack placed empty buckets underneath and soon had their water casks replenished. The yellow tarp, taken from the highway bandits, served as an adequate awning for Jack and Abel to sleep under. Melvin, Hope, and Jack's son Jozef spent another night in the wagon.

The new dawn reflected the previous day's rainfall. Bushes and greenery drooped from the watery pounding, and even the oaks and hickory branches seemed to sag while waiting for the sun to restore them to their natural height. The surface of the road glistened with slimy mud, and it only took one glance to understand no wagon travel could be conducted under such conditions.

"Might as well get comfortable because we won't be traveling today," Jack announced. Turning to Abel, he said, "I think that colored Yankee soldier put a couple of bamboo poles in the wagon, and if he included line and hooks, I'm gonna do a little fishing this morning. There's a small lake not far from here, and the rain caused a lot of night crawlers to come up."

"If he gave us two poles, I'd be happy to join you," Abel grinned.

The lake was a little farther away than Jack imagined, but the walk gave the marksmen a chance to stretch their legs and dry off in the bright sunlight. The surface of the lakelet was still agitated from the storm. Insects and tree leaves covered its edge.

"I don't think we'll do any good fishing on top after the rainstorm. We best settle on catfish eating on the bottom," Jack conveyed.

Soon their lines were in the water and cork bobbers undulating with the movement of the waves. Abel brought along the yellow tarp and spread it on the ground at the lakeside. Both men lay face up, with their hats covering their eyes, and fishing poles supported by a V-notch sapling sunk deep into the ground.

"Now this is the life," Abel sighed, while trying to stifle a yawn.

"In my younger days, I spent many a happy hour doing this very same thing," Jack stated.

"I suppose it all had to stop when you married Abigail," Abel tested.

"You're probably right. I don't recall that part of my life." That being said, Jacked noticed his cork bobber dipped underwater and jumped up to grab his pole. Giving it a sharp tug, he walked to the lowest level of the sandy bank and pulled a flipping two-pound blue catfish out of the water.

"Now that's a nice-looking fish," said Abel just as his own cork went under. Two hours later, they walked back to the wagon carrying a stringer heavy laden with the species.

"The fish we caught are just babies. A blue catfish can reach over five feet long and weigh 150 pounds. They're actually predators and will eat any fish they can catch, along with frogs and crayfish. Mainly a river fish, they were either put in the lake or found their way from the Appomattox or James River during flood stage," Jack surmised.

"Nevertheless, they're gonna make a great supper," Abel declared as they walked back to the four-wheel transport and the rest of the crew. Melvin and Hope had not been idle the time the other two were fishing. Returning, Jack and Abel were treated to a lively cooking fire and stacks of wood fagots drying out nearby.

There were smiles all around when Jack held up the stringer. He then walked to the dray and grabbed a bucket of water, saying, "There are some large rocks a little farther in. I'll clean the catch there, so get the skillets ready for when I get back."

Jack had cleaned and removed the head and skin, but left the bone in the fillets. While they were sizzling in the frying pan, he turned them from time to time until browned to his satisfaction. Then, using his knife, he made a cut from tail to head and removed the backbone, leaving the meat in one piece. Meanwhile, Hope fried potatoes in the other skillet using bacon grease to prevent burning. Jozef had eaten earlier, but Jack wanted his son to at least taste the mild, sweet flavor of a catfish's dense meat and commented, "I want him to grow up and become a mountain man like his daddy."

"Times are changing, Jack. Maybe Abigail will want more for him. Last I heard, she was teaching school," Abel said as he popped in the last bite of fish and reached for another.

It sounded strange. Abigail's name mentioned when it came to Grazyna's son. Jack didn't speak. He only shrugged his shoulders.

"Was there any traffic on the highway while we were gone?" Abel asked.

"A few horsemen, but no wagons. And they rode on the side of the highway," Melvin replied.

"Let's just kick back until tomorrow, or when we see other wagons handle the conditions," Jack suggested.

The next day, it was nearly noon before the travelers heard the creak and moan of wagon wheels as a lumbering Conestoga passed by. It left a rather-deep rut. Perhaps it was due to a very heavy load. In any case, the journey was resumed with Melvin dodging obvious areas of mire. Naturally, the pace was slow; however, they reached the outskirts of Farmville before darkness took them off the road. Jack had inquired how Jozef's food was holding up, and Hope assured him that the milk was still sweet. Other than that, the tyke ate whatever the rest of them were having. Recalling a farmhouse and cows across the fields from where they now rested, Jack planned to ride over to it and offer to buy fresh milk, if it was available. After breakfast, the mountain man tied a covered container to his saddle and rode to the farmhouse, now active with a woman feeding chickens and her children fetching water from a well. She stood erect as the stranger approached, wondering about his purpose.

"Good morning, ma'am, I'm with the wagon parked up yonder and was wondering it you might sell me some milk for my little boy," he asked calmly.

"I might, but I don't take no Confederate money anymore."

"I have Yankee greenbacks."

"Show me the money and give me your pail."

Jack did as she ordered and followed her to the barn where a cow was standing, ready for milking. In fifteen minutes, Jack's pail was filled with warm fresh milk.

"How much do I owe you?" he asked.

"Normally, I wouldn't take a penny, but times are very tough for us now. Is a dollar too much to ask?"

"I understand the fix you're in. What would it cost me to have one of those fat hens over there?"

"Since you're paying a dollar for the milk, I'll toss in the chicken."

"I'll tell you what, give me a fat hen, and I'll pay you a total of five greenback dollars."

"God bless you, young man. You are the answer to my prayers."

Riding back to the idle wagon, Jack held up the squawking bird for all to see.

Chapter Forty-Two

But men often mistake killing and revenge for justice. They seldom have the stomach for justice.

—Robert Jordan

Back in Washington, D.C., more was learned about the plot to kill President Lincoln and the co-conspirators involved. Apparently, John Wilkes Booth had become angered when Ulysses S. Grant suspended the exchange of prisoners of war in March of 1864. In his own mind, Grant had a good reason. He realized the exchange was prolonging the war by returning soldiers to the outnumbered Confederate army only to have them reappear on the front lines and resume their battle against the North. Booth, a Southerner and radical sympathizer of the cotton king cohorts, came up with a bizarre plan to kidnap President Lincoln and deliver him to the Confederate army who would then hold him until the North agreed to resume exchanging prisoners. In order to pull off the plan, he recruited six others to help him.

They included Samuel Bland Arnold, a schoolmate from St. Timothy's Hall, a military academy, and Booth's early friend and neighbor, twenty-four-year-old Michael O'Laughlen, both dropping out of the conspiracy after the prisoner exchange program began. Other conspirators included George Andreas Atzerodt, a thirty-year-old German immigrant who repaired carriages for a living; David Edgar Herold, a pharmacist's assistant and only son to reach adulthood in a family of eleven children; Lewis Powell, son of a Baptist minister; and John Surratt, whose mother owned the boarding house, where much of the conspiracy was planned.

It was also learned that the scheme to kidnap Lincoln fell through after two failed attempts in which the president's expected location and route of travel failed to materialize. At the same time, the Confederacy was in a shambles. Richmond had fallen and General Lee's army was on the run, soon to surrender. A kidnapped president now served no purpose. While the war-weary South prepared to accept defeat, the zealot, John Wilkes Booth, conceived a more devious plan: assassinating Abraham Lincoln.

His proposed plot of high treason included former kidnapping accomplices Atzerodt, Powell, and Herold. On April 14, Powell, accompanied by Herold, was to go to the home of Secretary of State William H. Seward and kill him. At the same time, Atzerodt was to assassinate Vice President Andrew Johnson. Booth, in turn, gave himself the responsibility to murder Abraham Lincoln.

Powell entered Seward's house claiming to have medicine from the secretary's doctor while Herold waited outside in the shadows. Seward was convalescing from injury in a previous carriage accident. Powell broke into his bedroom and stabbed Seward several times. Though suffering from a broken right arm, broken jaw, serious bruises, and concussion caused by the accident, Seward fought for his life, while a jaw splint deflected the blade away from its target: Seward's jugular vein. Seward's two oldest sons were also injured defending their father. Herold, hearing the screams of Seward's daughter, ran away and abandoned Powell. Failing in his attempt on Seward's life, Lewis Powell fled the home and hid, shuttering for three days in a large tree. Later, during the night, he sought sanctuary at Mary Surratt's boarding house and arrived there just as she was being arrested for her part in the sinister scheme.

Atzerodt failed his assignment to kill the vice president when he lost his nerve and tried to drown his cowardice by getting drunk. Booth, on the other hand, was successful in completing his task. At first, the theater audience believed the commotion to be part of the show, but soon learned something more serious was taking place. After shooting the president, Booth leaped from the balcony box and shouted something loud, but imperceptibly confusing, before limping across the stage. He had landed awkwardly and broken his leg from the twelve-foot drop. Some in the audience claimed Booth yelled "Sic semper tyrannis!" in Latin, meaning, "Thus always to tyrants." Others stated he also uttered, "The South is avenged!" Some of the men in the audience chased after the limping assassin, but with all the confusion, failed to stop him. Booth ran out the side door to a horse he had waiting and rode away toward the Navy Yard Bridge to meet up with Herold and Powell. Finding neither one there, he dashed across the bridge into Maryland.

David Herold caught up with Booth less than an hour later, and the pair retrieved weapons and supplies previously stored at Surrattsville before visiting Samuel A. Mudd, a local doctor who determined that Booth's leg had been broken and put it in a splint.

After a day at Mudd's house, Booth and Herold were guided to the home of Thomas Jones near Zekiah Swamp, a narrow stretch of greenway composed of hardwood trees and interlacing water. The fugitives hid in the swamp for five days until they could cross the Potomac River into Virginia.

On the afternoon of April 24, they arrived at the farm of Richard H. Garrett, where Booth claimed to be a wounded Confederate soldier. They lingered at Garrett's farm for two days when Union soldiers arrived and surrounded the fugitives in the barn.

Herold surrendered right away and walked out of the farm building with his hands behind his head. Booth refused to come out and vowed that he would not be taken alive as he scrambled for the back doorway. A Union soldier, looking through the space between the barn side planks, sighted Booth approaching the rear portal. The bark of his weapon broke the silence, and the killer of Lincoln fell mortally injured from a head wound near the spot that proved fatal for the president. Booth died on the porch of Garrett's farm two hours later.

On May 1, 1865, eight subjects were tried by a nine-member military tribunal. At the end of seven weeks, all of the defendants were found guilty. We would later learn that on June 30, Mary Surratt, Lewis Powell, David Herold, and George Atzerodt were sentenced to death by hanging. Samuel Mudd, Samuel Arnold, and Michael O'Laughlen were given life sentences. Edmund Spangler, an employee of the Ford's Theater, who held the horse for Booth's escape, received a six-year sentence.

The verdict to hang Mary Surratt stirred the conscience of five jury members, who signed a letter asking for clemency. Andrew Johnson, now president, refused to stop the execution.

The hanging took place on the grounds of the Old Arsenal Penitentiary on July 7, 1865, after which, the nation's focus could return to the reconstruction of the South.

* * *

The weather remained bonny and travel unimpeded for the next three days. The covered wagon pulled off the road at Appomattox, so named for the Appomattox River, and familiar to Jack and Abel since it was where they became United States citizens again. Progress had slowed due to the gradual incline in elevation. The resting place was a welcomed sight to the travelers and especially two mares pulling the load. The area sported no fishing lake. However, scenic springs provided plenty of water for their temporary needs, some of which was used to give baby Jozef an unwelcomed bath. Afterward, he became so enlivened with boundless energy that Hope couldn't resist the opportunity and placed a couple of buckets of spring water on the fire. Once they became steaming hot, she retired to the privacy of the wagon's protective canvas cover and bathed away the remnants of a week on the road.

With supper over and velvet shades of purple settling down on the deeper parts of their wooded area, the image of three riders came into view. Jack gave Abel the look of suspicion and rose from the fire, walking slowly toward the wagon. Once they arrived, their spokesman asked gruffly, "State your business here in Nebraska, mister. What are you doing here tonight?" (The town was first named Nebraska in 1855. Ten years later, those living in the area continued to call it by its older name.)

"We're just travelers heading for Tennessee," Abel replied. "We'll be back on the road tomorrow."

"Are you deserters?" he asked

"Deserters, hell no, we've been pardoned and have papers to prove it. The war is over, haven't you heard?"

"We got rumor to that effect, but this war will never be over for us until the Yankees are driven off Southern soil. I think you all are toting way more than you need, and I have men with the wolf in their bellies. You best divvy up what you got," he ordered.

"My grandma always told me that there are two sides to every argument. There's a man in that wagon yonder with a Whitworth rifle aiming directly at your head, ready to send you to the promised land. Now, this here war may not be over for you all, but it is for us. Unless, of course you don't saw that animal around and take your war somewhere else," Abel replied with conviction.

The rebel soldier had a pained expression and, just for a second, wanted to put it to the test. But better judgment made him wheel around and depart, giving the rebel yell.

"Looks like we spend another night on watch," said Abel.

"I believe you're right. We're probably going to run into die-hards like him all the way to Tennessee."

"Do you think he'll come back?"

"No way of knowing, it all depends on how hungry his men are. He's aware we are prepared for a shoot-out, even though there aren't many of us. Maybe he hasn't seen the elephant, so the romance of the thing hasn't worn off yet. My guess, he'll think long and hard before he tries anything. Moreover, if it was me, I'd be concerned a Yankee patrol would hear the fracas and come to investigate. To my way of thinking, that would present too big of a risk, since the Appomattox railroad depot is nearby and probably crawling with bluecoats. Just to be safe, we best have Melvin stand watch with us," replied Jack. "Did you take a good look at him?"

"All I remember is he was gimlet-eyed, with a piercing stare and scared the bejesus out of me."

That night, the wayfarers were on tenterhooks and didn't sleep a wink. They had a clear view of the rolling pasture across the road, but the woods with its dense timber could hide someone creeping up on them. Any attack would most likely come from that direction. Melvin was assigned to watch the hills, and Jack and Abel took positions farther into the wooded vicinity of oak and pine. There was no chance of dozing off. The routine activity of the forest after dark kept their nerves on edge. The snap of a twig, flapping swoop of a horned owl, and grunts of wild pigs rooting the grass aided their alertness. At the crack of dawn, Little Jozef ate breakfast in a rolling carriage, heading west, with horses at a lively pace.

Reaching Lynchburg before dark, the journeyers found the community bustling with activity, in spite of Federal occupation. Located on the banks of the James River, with a populace of nearly seven thousand inhabitants, the town had become a major transportation center. In addition to the James River, both the South Side and Orange and Alexandria railroads made the City of Seven Hills an important supply base for the Confederate army.

During the antebellum days, Lynchburg became wealthy from the manufacture and sale of plug tobacco and its related products. Their tobacco factories used rude technology, but enslaved labor kept costs at a minimum and profits soared as the product was eagerly purchased in the north.

Accordingly, it stands to reason that most of the white inhabitants were less than enthusiastic when it came to secession. And as matters grew worse, they began to blame the Confederate government for the hardships bestowed on them because of the war. Many civic leaders blamed congregated rebel soldiers for the rise in crime and public acts of disorder. It came as no surprise that when Union soldiers marched in, white residents joined the slaves in welcoming the occupation by men wearing blue uniforms, even though the poor were mistreated and former slaves conscripted into the military as common laborers.

Melvin guided the horses and wagon alongside the combination merchandise-and-feed store before shouting the familiar, "Whoa, Team, whoa!" Several men were sitting on benches lined on either side of the entrance door. From all appearances, they had been resting there for some time and, in all likelihood, only visited the inside to purchase soda pop and tobacco. Jack Leffingwell and Abel Strawn pulled their horses up to the store's front steps and swung a leg over their saddles. Stepping to the ground, they tied the reins to the hitching post, located off to one side of the porch steps.

"Good afternoon, fellows," Jack greeted as he slowly ascended the steps. A chorus of nods and greetings were given in return. Abel pinched the front brim of his hat acknowledging the friendly reception and followed Jack inside. The temperature inside the emporium of assorted merchandise was ten degrees cooler than on the porch. The owner's inventory was abundantly displayed on tables and shelves. Seemingly, they stocked more than the marksmen could imagine, impressing Jack to say, "Go get Hope and Melvin. It's been a long time since she's seen a fully stocked store."

"May I help you boys?" asked the proprietor.

"We're going to need some things. First, I've asked for our friends to come in and have a look around. You have a very fine store here, mister," Jack stated.

"Thank you, the wife and I are proud of what we've done with it. You all just look around as much as you want. Give a whistle when you're ready to be waited on."

Hope entered holding Jozef, and Melvin at her side. She was drawn immediately to the haberdashery and bolted cloth. She had convinced herself that, in her new rustic life, she would be making her own clothes. With only a vague idea of how it's done, she asked the storekeeper's wife about patterns. The lady reassured it was within her capabilities and laid some pattern packages on the counter, of which Hope selected her favorite. Next, Hope carefully chose a light blue material with tiny white flowers.

"You're not a large woman, so I think three yards is enough; however, since this is your first dress, maybe a half yard more would be wise," she suggested.

"How much will all this cost?" Hope asked softly.

"It comes to a dollar and a quarter," she replied.

"We'll take it," Jack interrupted. "Just put in on my bill. There's going to be a lot more before we're finished. Lest I forget, would you happen to sell newspapers?"

"No, we don't sell them, but I happen to still have yesterday's *Lynchburg Virginian* in the back. If you'd care to have a day-old paper, I'll go fetch it."

The mountain man was true to his word. The travelers were able to restock the wagon with supplies and feed for the animals. Jack also had the wagon wheels examined and well-greased, while the horses were watered and fed. By the time they were finished, the sunlight was fading in the west. Jack suggested they go around the city and make camp on the other side. A suitable site appeared under bright moonlight when Melvin pulled off the road.

Foothills of the Blue Ridge Mountains now slowed their pace. The range got its name because of the blue-green color when viewed from a distance, primarily due to the rapid evaporation of *isoprene* produced naturally by the trees. While colorless, the mixture in the atmosphere gives the mountains its bluish appearance.

By now, Melvin Kaufman had become proficient driving the team and wagon; however, managing wheel brakes and reins, in undulating mountain valleys, would present a new experience. The horses require resting more often and for longer periods as they tire during uphill pulls.

"It's going to be slow for the next few days, or at least until we reach Roanoke. Thereafter, the road flattens out for a stretch and is a lot easier on the horses," Jack said to Melvin. "How's Jozef doing?"

"He's doing fine. The little guy can't keep his eyes open when the wagon is moving," Hope replied. "Was that thunder I heard a while back?"

"Yeah, I was hoping we could make Bedford County today, but it might be best if we find a suitable spot to spend the night before the rain comes. I'll ride up ahead and see what the mountain has to offer."

Hope never thought she would like Jack Leffingwell after what he did to Abigail. Abigail was so sweet, honest, and caring from the first day they met on the train. They became friends instantly. Now, after being in his company, she sees, firsthand, what Melvin always said about him. Impressed with the mountain man's gentler side, the young bride observed the way he interacted with Jozef and understood why the baby boy idolized his father. There's no doubt that his physical presence commanded respect. Standing well over six feet, he walked erect. Most tall people Hope had seen walked with a stoop, trying to appear shorter. Jack never spoke to anyone while staring at his shoes. He looked you straight in the eye, at times, creating an emotional provocation that stirs excitement, overwhelming the young girl's composure. At these times, Hope knew why Abigail and Grazyna, for that matter, fell in love with him. She would never trade Melvin for him, and besides, he was a much older man.

The sounds of turning wheels and squeak of harness leather kept the newlywed entranced, until the subject of her thoughts returned from his scouting mission.

"Three miles ahead there's a good spot to make camp and sit out the storm," Jack shouted as Abel rode up to meet him. The location Jack selected was across the road from a mountain farm. He could see in the distance a barn and log cabin home with a faint wisp of white smoke escaping the chimney—most likely from either cooking or a guard against the evening chill. At this elevation, even in May, temperatures could drop into the fifties at night. The prairie schooner came to a rest after fording a shallow stream, bubbling along the roadside, and finding a stand of foothill oak and pine. Unharnessed, the team of mares were led to the brook to water and then tethered in the copse for protection against the pending elements. All three men scoured the woods for fallen branches, twigs, and bark dry enough to start their cooking fire, knowing full well, once it rained, it would be nearly impossible. There would be another need for a fire tonight. After the sun went down, the air would have a bone-chilling temperature.

The first booming lighting crack made everybody jump. An eerie darkness had fallen around them as the rain began in spatters before the hard downpour. The yellow tarp was put to good use. Jack had suspended it above the fire, high enough so as not to scorch, yet still keep the campfire dry. His mountain background taught him to look for a dead tree, still standing. It could be cut down easily and, with a few swings of an ax, made into very combustible logs.

While the rain found its way through the canopy of treetops, the yellow tarp extended over a large-enough area for Jack and Abel, protected by their new-bought Stetson hats and canvas dusters, were kept dry and warm as toast. Melvin and Hope stayed in the wagon but needed extra clothing against the nippy air. Little Jozef slept comfortably with as additional blanket.

Eventually, the sky presented a speckle of stars unseen by the two marksmen who rested their heads on saddles and soundly dozed. The midnight hour silently ushered the death of another day and quietly greeted a new diurnal with the birth of dawn. Beneath the dripping trees, Jack began to stir and added more wood to the fire, taking note he could see his breath in the air. By the time he checked on the animals and returned to the campfire, Abel had risen and placed the coffeepot on the edge of the flames.

"I think we got some hail last night," Abel asserted.

"Yeah, we did, but I can't find any damage to the wagon cover. We found shelter just in time."

Hearing the conversation outside the covered carriage, those inside began to come to life, and soon the aroma of bacon frying delighted the senses. Hope fed Jozef while holding him on her lap and, much to his dissatisfaction, prevented him from running around and getting wet. His father, in turn, mounted his charger and trotted in the direction of the cabin across the road. They moved near the log structure; and an older female, covered by a shawl, opened the door and walked out on her porch.

"Can I help you?" she drawled, with her teeth clenched on the stem of a corncob pipe.

"Yes, ma'am, I'd like to buy some cow's milk, if you have any to spare."

"There's a cow in the barn ready for milking, but my husband still has his lazy bones in bed. You're welcome to whatever you can get by yourself," she said.

Jack returned from the barn carrying two pails of fresh milk and placed them on the porch. He had earlier filled his own and tightened its lid. The old woman opened the door again and exclaimed, "You must be a farm boy. That's the most we ever got from that bossy. You can take some for yourself at no cost."

"I've already got mine and willing to pay for it. How much would you be asking?"

"I declare, that cow-critter gave even more than I first thought. There won't be a charge, son. I now have a gauge when my husband is milking. It only proves what I've always thought, he quits too soon. Not to change the subject, but you look like a soldier boy. How's the war going?"

"The war's over, ma'am."

"Did we win?"

"No, sorry to say that we lost," Jack replied.

"That's too bad. I never did like those Yankees."

"You might also be pleased to hear that somebody shot President Lincoln."

"Lordy be, I've learned more today than I did in grade school. Excuse me, son, I've got to break the news to my husband."

With that, Jack turned his horse and headed back to the land schooner, but not before slipping a greenback under one of the buckets.

The teamsters maintained a steady pace the remainder of their way to Roanoke, Virginia, stopping only to rest and feed the horses and camping for the evening.

Once named Big Lick because of a large outcropping of salt near the Roanoke River, the area attracted animals from miles around. The natural mineral deposit provided essential nutrients required by deer for bone and muscle growth. While most animals were drawn to the natural lick by the taste of sodium, or salt, the benefit of several minerals filled a basic need for good health. Hunters, also, were always on the lookout for such deposits. They rarely departed the area without bagging meat for the smokehouse.

Big Lick became a stop for the Virginia and Tennessee Railroad linking Lynchburg to the Tennessee border. In later years, the Roanoke Valley served as a hub for commercial activity in the surrounding area of western Virginia. The historic Wilderness Road began in the Roanoke Gap, but its pathway consisted of rough steep hills and deep declines, making wagon travel a perilous adventure.

Jack Leffingwell and his friends chose to take a less risky route that runs near the old highway, however, a great deal flatter and much safer. After crossing the

Roanoke River, they traveled about five miles out of town and camped for the night. Travel on the highway had increased a great deal, and several other small Conestogas passed by while our wayfarers ate supper and a slight amount of limited daylight remained. Jack held his son, who was fascinated with his father's hat, failing several times to take hold of it. They had just returned from a stroll along one of the perpetual mountain brooks and its contents, so exciting for a precocious two-year-old boy.

A cloudless sky, aided by shining moonlight and coupled with an active campfire, gave enough illumination for Jack to read the nearly forgotten newspaper acquired back in Lynchburg. Melvin Kaufman, hoping it would be read aloud, volunteered to retrieve it from the prairie schooner. While the others sat attentively, Jack unfolded the *Lynchburg Virginian* and narrowed his eyebrows when he saw the headlines: "Tragedy on the Mississippi—*Sultana* Explodes, Thousands Die."

On April 27, at two o'clock in the morning, the steamboat *Sultana* exploded and sank in the Mississippi River a few miles north of Memphis, Tennessee. It carried 2,300 passengers, most of whom were discharged Union soldiers, recently released from Confederate prison camps. Over 1,700 people died, losing their lives on a frigid spring night when boilers aboard the overcrowded steamer erupted and caught fire.

The explosion occurred in a wide portion of the river with no land for a mile on either side. Those near the boilers were scalded to death immediately, while others panicked and jumped overboard into the foreboding deep waters of the mighty Mississippi. For miles around, the horrific scene consisted of floating people and the glow of the burning boat. Cries for help seemed to glide over the water, as women screamed and those wounded by the blast groaned in pain.

Another steam boat, the *Bostona,* was on her way downriver about a mile above the *Sultana* and heard the explosion. Observing the light of the burning vessel, it made all haste to the scene of the disaster. And hearing the cries and struggles of the drowning passengers, she sent out her yawls and threw stage planks overboard. Everything that could float was thrown into the river to render aid.

When additional boats arrived in the early-morning darkness, they could barely see ten feet ahead and had to listen for screams of help in order to locate survivors. The strong current made rescue more difficult as many people were carried downstream in the blackness.

When the sun came up, more than 1,700 were dead. Of the six hundred passengers that survived, another two hundred would die later. What was left of the *Sultana* drifted downriver and sank near Memphis to a mud-covered grave.

It was learned that corruption by the steamboat captain and army officers played a role in the paddle wheel steamboat being overcrowded. The government paid $5 per man, and boat captains kicked back $1.50 to the army officers in charge if they filled the boats with men.

After departing New Orleans, with one hundred passengers, the *Sultana* headed north on the Mississippi River. As the boat steadily moved upriver, an engineer noticed a leaking boiler and, once the boat pulled into port at Vicksburg, sought out a boilermaker. Learning that two sheets of the boiler had to be replaced, the captain, torn by time and money, told the boilermaker to patch the boiler and promised to finish repairs when he reached St.

Louis. Reluctantly, the boilermaker made a patch for the *Sultana*.

While docked in Vicksburg, the owners hoped to find former Union prisoners of war from Cahaba and Andersonville prisons and receive the $5 per enlisted man and $10 per officer, the government bounty. Fearing other steamships would come to Vicksburg and pick up Union prisoners of war, the owners managed to persuade prison officials to let their steamship take all the soldiers back North. Had the owners chosen to make the proper repairs, they would have lost the opportunity for such a large bonanza. As it was, army officers knew about the *Sultana*'s kickback and loaded 2,300 POWs aboard. The three decks of the steamship were packed like sardines, so tightly that soldiers were unable to sit down or sleep. After their experiences in Southern prison camps, they would accept anything to get home as soon as possible. For most of them, it was their last day on earth.

The month of April 1865 was filled with events that alter our understanding of life and the times in which we live. On April 9, Gen. Robert E. Lee surrendered. President Abraham Lincoln was assassinated five days later. His killer, John Wilkes Booth, was captured and slain on April 26, the same day Gen. Joseph Johnson surrendered the last large Confederate army. It's only a matter of days before Union troops would capture Confederate president Jefferson Davis and, now, the worse maritime tragedy in history. The country had faced both celebration and sorrow; unfortunately, all emotional traumas didn't end with the war. The Southern states must face the rigors of reconstruction. A conquered foe, whose cities were destroyed, must endure the oppressive effort to reshape them in the image of the north. The transition would take years and only time would tell if it could be done successfully.

"That steamboat captain should have stayed three more days and had the boilers repaired properly," Melvin stated.

"My father preached that money is the root of all evil, and the *Sultana* proves him right," said Abel.

"Lomas used to say that God must love poor people, just look at how many of us he made," Jack quipped as he folded the paper and handed it back to Melvin.

Hope had held her husband's arm during the reading. And though she listened intently, she couldn't help feeling a little homesick. She was reminded of her father, who read articles to her ever since she was a child. At that moment, with the reflection of campfire shadows dancing in her eyes, Hope wished her parents were there to enjoy the exciting journey as much as she did.

The campsite conversation grew steadily stunted and unsuppressed yawns gave evidence the sandman was hard at work. Soon the travelers would be in the arms of Morpheus, logging another day in their adventurous journey to Tennessee.

Chapter Forty-Three

O God, I could be bound in a nutshell, and count myself a king of infinite space—were it not that I have bad dreams.

—William Shakespeare

The cannon gave a resounding boom as it discharged its load and recoiled backward from the velocity, coming to rest against its mooring. Cordite filled the smoky air as the bodies of Melvin Kaufman and Abel Strawn lay face up with the vacant stare of death. Jack was on all fours frantically searching for his Whitworth rifle to no avail. At that point, he shouted for help and woke in a cold sweat. For a few moments, the mountain man believed he was still on the battlefield, but soon realized it was only a bad dream. Glancing in the direction of their night fire, Abel was curled in his saddle blanket and snoring softly. Melvin, he remembered, was sleeping with Hope and Little Jozef. All was right with the world.

Jack picked up a leafless branch and poked the fire, sending sparks of glowing embers skyward into the dark predawn air. Sunrise would take at least another hour. He placed the branch on top the embers and watched while it ignited, then added another log to guarantee the morning cooking fire and lay back with his hands behind his head.

Losing two days due to rain, the land schooner reined in at the village of Lovely Mount, near the New River. The area had always been a gathering place for travelers heading west because of the freshwater. Once the Virginia and Tennessee Railroad came through, establishing a depot, it had a major population increase and the amount of trade and business to match. It was also encouraging to see Union troops repairing the tracks, a familiar scene along the wayfarer's route. Hope was especially happy since it served to assure her parents would be able to visit her sooner rather than later.

The tedium of travel has begun to take the edge off the excitement involved in their adventurous journey. Melvin and Hope no longer rise while it's still dark outside and now spend the night in a deeper relaxing slumber. Jack and Abel accommodate this by making enough noise to wake up Jozef. The rest takes care of itself.

"Looks like it's going to be a good day," Abel suggested while biting half of a strip of crispy bacon.

"I'm in love with this place," Hope said as she wiped Jozef's face from his breakfast leftovers. "The flowers are remarkable, and there seems to be a million butterflies."

The second Jozef was let down, he made a dash for his father. At these times, the serious look on Jack's face melts into one of satisfaction and pleasure.

"You're right, Hope, the Appalachian Valley is noted for monarch butterflies and the New River area is loaded with them. I think it has to do with the flowers. They become an excellent source of nectar for the fluttering creatures. The monarchs migrate long distances from Mexico to North America, a range up to three thousand miles."

"Have you ever fished the New River?" asked Abel.

"Yes, I have," answered Jack. "Don't ask me when, but I know that I've caught plenty of fish in it. The New River isn't new at all. In fact, it's the oldest river in North America. Some say, when considering the world's oldest, it's second only to the Nile. You probably noticed that the river appears to flow uphill. Well, there's an answer for that. I learned it from an Indian pal, sometime back. He told me that when God made the mountains, he lifted the river's source along with them. So the point of origin was elevated, and its water flows downward from a higher beginning."

"Who was your Indian pal?" asked Abel.

"I don't remember his name. It had to be before my hospital stay," Jack replied, knowing Abel took every opportunity to help him remember the past. At times it became a little frustrating.

"Please go on," Hope implored, with the knowledge that her father could explain the phenomena in scientific terms, but preferring the homespun version told by the Tennessee mountain man. His was a little more down-to-earth and a lot more romantic. Jack smiled knowingly and continued.

"The ancient New River begins in the Appalachian mountains of North Carolina, near the Tennessee state line. It flows generally north westward across the Blue Ridge and cuts through the Appalachian Valley to the Allegheny front in western Virginia. Then, it loops through the Appalachian Plateau in West Virginia and flows to the Ohio River and, finally, down the Mississippi to the Gulf of Mexico. There always seems to be a modicum of scientific fact behind Indian lore. In this case, the New River was probably flat at one time. Three hundred million years ago, when the continents collided, rocks were crushed and, with no place to go, forced upward creating the mountains and folds in between, which we now call valleys," Jack concluded.

The tall mountain man rose to his feet and, with his son in his arms, walked to the highway. Contemplating the distance covered thus far, he determined they were halfway to their final destination.

Chapter Forty-Four

The truth is, we know so little about life, we don't really know what the good news is and what the bad news is.

—*Kurt Vonnegut, A Man Without a Country*

Abigail had concluded the teaching session and, with her own children in tow, stopped by Riberty's hardware store for a visit with Maryellen before returning to the farm. Sarah Jane and Little Jack loved the emporium. Going on ten years old, her daughter loved to inspect the colorful bolts of cloth, and her three-year-old son was always drawn to the candy counter. They both were taught to never ask. The decision whether to purchase or not rested on how well they behaved the previous day. Apparently, they conducted themselves well because Little Jack ended up with a small brown bag of hard candy and Sarah Jane got to pick out five yards of beautiful material.

"Maryellen, will you keep an eye on the kids while I run to the post office and check the mail? It'll save them a trip to the farm tomorrow."

"Of course, I want to come over tomorrow and help lay out the patterns for the dresses, if that's okay."

"I was hoping you would. The last time I laid one out I ended up with a piece I never did figure out where it went."

"I remember," Maryellen said with a smile.

The Statesville post office was part of the print shop. Neither had enough business to warrant an individual establishment on their own merit. Together, the proprietor managed to survive by printing weekly bulletins for the churches, weddings, and other forms of announcements, i.e., farm sales and the like, plus a stipend for managing the post office. Old Robert Snell, the owner, liked to wear a green eye shade visor, believing it legitimized his position. He had tried to print a weekly gazette, but never could find enough original news to continue past his initial attempt. The first edition was so filled with annoying errors that Abigail offered to proofread and edit the next, free of charge. There never was a second edition.

The bell above the door gave its familiar jingle as Abigail turned the handhold and stepped inside.

"Good afternoon, Mr. Snell, did I receive any mail today?"

"Yes, I believe you did," he replied as he straightened his visor and walked behind the floor-to-ceiling, chain-link wall allotted for the postal service. Handing Abigail a letter through an open portal in the door, he continued, "This letter came this morning from Richmond. It looks like it's written in a female hand."

Abigail thanked him and left without acknowledging his statement questioning the author's gender and quickly returned to the hardware store, waving the epistle for Maryellen to see. The two women took chairs in the back room of the store; and Abigail, in spite of trembling hands, managed to open it without ripping the contents.

"Would you rather be alone?" Maryellen asked.

"No, I need you here with me. I recognize the penmanship from my young friend in Richmond, Virginia, but can't fathom the subject of the letter." At that point, Abigail began to read.

April 27, 1865
Dearest Friend,

I have the most wonderful news to report. Remember the young soldier I favored when you were here in Richmond? Well, I'm proud to say that I am now his wife. We were married in my parents' house this afternoon. I've never been happier, and that's only the half of it. Our relationship renewed when Melvin was at Chimborazo Hospital, recovering from a wound he received at Fredericksburg, costing him his left arm. Needless to say, he was pretty low when I found him. We had decided to wed once the war was over, until your husband and Abel Strawn visited us and talked Melvin into coming to Tennessee with them. I couldn't go unless Melvin and I were married. We will be on the road for at least six weeks, and it just wouldn't be proper. After that, things moved quickly. I was married one day and will help Melvin drive a prairie wagon the next.

Your husband has his little boy with him. I plan to take custody of him on the trip and free up the menfolk. Oh, Abigail, he is the sweetest little boy. I can't wait for you to meet him.

We've been led to believe there will be plenty of work for us at, or around, Statesville and promised help in finding a place to stay. It's going to be a new experience for me, as you know. I've never lived outside of the city. Right now, everything seems so exciting, but I realize that once reality sinks in, I might feel differently. Nevertheless, I'm looking forward to being with you again. You, dear lady, are my only female friend, and it's been too long since we chatted over a cup of tea.

Thank God this horrible war is over. Union soldiers have taken control of the Richmond hospitals, and soon there will be no need for me to visit. If there's one thing I've learned, it's nothing stays the same. My fervent hope is that future changes in our lives will be more agreeable. It's funny, you know what a fraidy cat I've always been. Well, I'm not a bit frightened by this adventure. I'm sure it all has to do with Jack Leffingwell, your husband. He has a way about him that settles our nerves, making us feel safe. He still has the amnesia but determined to return to the farm. He doesn't talk about it, so I can't quite figure out why. Perhaps, we can study that together. I'm too excited to write more, so until we meet face-to-face, I remain.

Your friend in heart and thought,
Hope Kaufman
P.S. Jack's little boy is named Jozef.

Abigail sat silently staring straight ahead until Maryellen spoke, "Well, it looks like Jack Leffingwell will be sniffing round your door in a couple of weeks."

"Not only him, but several others as well. I need to talk to my father about this. Will you watch the children for a few minutes more?" Abigail asked while holding her friend's hand.

Hyrum had dozed off, sitting in his rocker, when wakened by the rapping outside his front door. It took a minute or two before he was able to piece events together, rise from his favorite chair, and answer the visitor standing on the stoop.

Opening the door, he invited his daughter inside. She, in turn, recognized his mussed-up hair to be the result of interrupting an afternoon nap.

"I'm sorry to have wakened you, Father, but I got serious news and need your advice."

"That's perfectly all right, I wasn't sleeping anyway."

Smiling at Hyrum's statement, Abigail walked to the table and read again the letter from Hope aloud. Afterward Hyrum said, "It looks like Jack will soon be home."

"Yes, but what shall I do? So much has changed in the past few weeks. Minnie is gone, and I now own her farm. Yalata has been asking about Jack and when I expect to have him home. I've never told him the truth about Jack and me. Now, this letter, I'm at my wit's end."

"Your life is in good order. As far as you're concerned, these people are friends coming to visit. Handle it that way."

"I still love my husband, Father."

"Then you can only pray and wait for the Lord to answer," Hyrum suggested.

By the time the rooster crowed the following morning, Abigail had read Hope's letter five times. Furthermore, her sleep was disturbed by the various scenarios concocted in her dreams, none of which gave the perfect solution. She was determined to stay busy until Maryellen arrived and try not to think of the pending visit. The kitchen, always neat as a pin, received a complete scrub down, and the floor washed a second time. She was standing outside sanitizing the windows when Maryellen's rig pulled up in front.

"What the hell are you doing? We washed those windows two days ago," Maryellen quizzed.

"I know, I'm just trying to keep busy," Abigail responded.

"Well, you can stop for a while. I brought some more material and a couple of new patterns. We're going to spend the day making clothes." And make clothes they did. From her time of arrival until well into oil lamp time, Maryellen and Abigail took turns operating the sewing machine and its foot treadle. They made a dress for themselves, two for Sarah Jane, a shirt for Little Jack, and a dress for Abigail's friend, Hope Kaufman. Sitting at the kitchen table, with the final cup of tea, both women wept and laughed from sheer exhaustion. Needless to say, Maryellen spent another night in what used to be Minnie

Rosenthal's bed. After saying their evening prayers, each whispered, in the darkened room, "Thank God, tomorrow is Saturday."

The children were up and about long before their mother. In fact, Sarah Jane made several visits to her mother's room to make certain she was still breathing. Once assured that was the case, Sarah Jane peeked into Maryellen's room and observed a similar condition. Unsure of what to do next, Sarah Jane said to her brother, "Come on, Little Jack, let's go gather the eggs."

Children are very observant and, unfortunately, too candid. Sarah Jane noticed right off that her mother and Maryellen were not near as joyful as they were the day before. It must be an allergy or a condition close to it because both women had puffy eyes and neither smiled. They sat for the longest time just stirring their coffee cups without a spoken word. Finally, Abigail said blandly, "You look terrible."

"Have you looked in the mirror lately?" Maryellen asked irreverently. With that remark, morning sunshine returned to the Leffingwell breakfast table, and a few of the newly gathered hen fruits were sizzling in the remaining grease after frying the bacon. Maryellen mixed the ingredients for biscuits, rolled out the dough, and asked Sarah Jane to help by handing her the biscuit cutter. The cutter was the young girl's favorite kitchen tool, and she prided herself in her ability to twist it into soft dough, remove the biscuit, and place it onto a greased cookie tray. After her ninth birthday, she was allowed to open the oven door and slide the tray onto the top rack, wait fifteen minutes, then repeat the process in reverse. Little Jack could care less how the biscuits were made. His main concern was the strawberry preserves his mother put on top.

Once breakfast was over, Sarah Jane's only other chore was to stack the dishes and take them to the kitchen sink where her mother and Maryellen stood ready to wash and dry.

"Have you given more thought to the pending visit?" Maryellen asked as she handed Abigail a dish to be dried.

"Yes, at first I was in a panic as to where they all would sleep."

"That shouldn't be hard. The newlyweds could have Minnie's old room, and Jack can sleep in the barn," Maryellen said sarcastically.

"That is a possibility, but then I remembered Minnie's house. She always kept it neat as a pin, and even though nobody's been in it for over two years, it should be rather easy to spruce it up for company. I was hoping we could walk over there after breakfast and check it out."

"It's probably loaded with varmints," Maryellen said gravely.

Their outside inspection was encouraging. It revealed no broken windows or any sign of animal intrusion. The front door, however, was swollen shut and impossible to open without tools. Peering through windows, they could see the arrangement of furniture exactly as Minnie had left it when she moved in with Abigail after Little Jack was born.

"I'll tell you what, when church is over tomorrow, I'll see if I can get a few ladies to help us give the place a proper scrubbing," Maryellen offered.

"In the meantime, I'll see if Father will bring his tools to open the front door," Abigail added as she relocked the immovable entry.

Walking back to the Leffingwell farmhouse, Abigail's steps were much lighter, in that her inheritance might provide a wonderful place for her company to stay, no matter what her husband had decided prior to getting here.

* * *

Jack Leffingwell and his fellow travelers had reached the town of Wytheville, Virginia, and were obligated to stay for two days due to heavy rains and flooding of their mountain road. Still following a route along the foothills of the Blue Ridge Mountains, the heavy spring rains frequently made wagon travel challenging while passable on horseback. Rather than run the risk of the prairie schooner mired to its hubs, discretion was the better part of valor. A little lost time at the moment was better than several days stuck in the mud and needing additional help to free the wagon. Thus far, they had traveled more miles faster than Jack had expected and, at that pace, would be in Tennessee by the end of the month.

> *The town of Wytheville (pronounced* with-ville*) is named in honor of George Wythe, an early patriot and signer of the Declaration of Independence. Born in 1726, in Hampton, Virginia, he began his education at home, taught by his mother, an accomplished and educated woman. At the age of thirty, Wythe started reading law and became a legal apprentice. Shortly thereafter, he was admitted to the bar and, from then on, made law and scholarship his life's work.*
>
> *In 1754, Wythe was appointed to the Virginia House of Burgesses and served*

intermittently until 1768, after which he served one term as mayor of Williamsburg, Virginia, before being elected to the Continental Congress in 1775.

The first Continental Congress consisted of fifty-six elected delegates representing twelve of the thirteen colonies and meeting in Philadelphia, Pennsylvania, to coordinate an official protest against recent parliamentary acts issued out of England. The missing colony, the Provence of Georgia, had troubles with Indians on its frontier and needed British help, fearing England's reaction if they attended the Philadelphia meeting.

Wythe, along with other patriots the likes of George Washington, Patrick Henry, and John Adams, would later vote in favor of the resolution for independence and sign the declaration that would give birth to the United States of America.

In 1779, Wythe was appointed to the chair of law at the College of William and Mary, making him the first law professor in the United States. Thomas Jefferson and James Monroe were taught, during his tenure, and became American presidents. Another student, John Marshall, would later become chief justice of the U.S. Supreme Court.

Thomas Jefferson assisted in Wythe's law office as a legal apprentice, acting as his law clerk for five years. The two men were eclectic readers and became friends studying a variety of books from political philosophy,

English literary works, and even the ancient classics.

Originally, a planter and slaveholder, Wythe began to oppose the repressive institution and, after the Revolutionary War, freed most of his slaves, as did many others in Virginia. He earned the sobriquet, Father of American jurisprudence, in no small measure, by arguing to end slavery based on judicial interpretation of the 1776 Virginia Declaration of Rights. And on that basis, all men should be considered presumptively free when considering the first article, stating, "That all men are by nature equally free and independent and have certain inherent rights."

Wythe became an abolitionist, not only freeing his slaves but also providing for them during their transition to freedom. After the death of his second wife in 1787 (his first wife died after only eight months of marriage), the widower moved to Richmond in 1791, taking his housemaid and cook, Lydia Broadnax, and a youth, by the name of Michael Brown, with him. Lydia Broadnax was freed the month after Wythe's wife passed on and Brown, a mixed-race youth, had been born free in 1790.

By 1797, Lydia Broadnax owned her own home, where she and Brown lived, and supported her livelihood by taking in boarders, plus continuing to work for Wythe as his cook.

By 1805, Wythe's grandnephew, George Wythe Sweeny, moved in with him. The seventeen-year-old was incorrigible by all standards. He had trouble with alcohol and gambling and stole his uncle's books to sell along with forging checks to fund his wicked habits. On May 25, Wythe, Broadnax, and Michael Brown all became violently ill. At first, doctors diagnosed the illness as cholera. Two days later, the grandnephew tried to cash a $100 check drawn on his uncle's account. Wythe claimed that Sweeny had tried to murder him. Michael Brown died on June 1, 1806, and Wythe on June 8, but Lydia Broadnax survived the poisoning. Broadnax said she had seen Sweeny put powder in their morning coffee, resulting in Sweeny being charged with murder. However, Virginia race laws prohibited her from testifying at the trial. Blacks were prevented by law from testifying at trials against whites. The jury acquitted George Sweeny. All the same, Wythe had changed his will before his death and disinherited him.

In his will, Wythe left his large book collection to Thomas Jefferson. It later became part of the collection which Jefferson sold to create the Library of Congress. Wythe's funeral was the largest in state history at that time.

---

* Adapted from http://en.wikipedia.org/wiki/George_Wythe.

Chapter Forty-Five

I have learned now that while those who speak about one's miseries usually hurt, those who keep silence hurt more.

—C. S. Lewis

On the third day of the Wytheville layover, morning broke to a crystal clear sky. Remnants of a two-day rain were evaporating before their very eyes as Jack Leffingwell returned from an inspection of the highway. He had ridden a couple miles ahead and saw that the drying effect had rapidly improved prospects for resuming travel, at least after lunch. The mood of the rest of the wayfarers now changed from ennui to mild excitement. Even the horses became more animated as they seemed to anticipate a return to the road. Or possibly just expecting breakfast. Nevertheless, once harnessed to the wagon tongue, they definitely knew what lies ahead.

Jack drove the land schooner on this leg of the journey, exchanging a saddle for a wooden seat. Melvin gripped the reins of the spirited charger while Jozef sat on Hope's lap and stared in worshipful adoration at his father.

Thunderstorms in southwestern Virginia are an accepted fact, especially during spring and summer. And they most likely occur during the warmest part of the day, frequently beginning at 4:00 p.m. and continuing until midnight. Mountain thunderstorms also produce a complex pattern, in that some areas receive heavy rainfall while the section next to it gets little to none. The Tennessee mountain man was aware of this fact and explained why he rode ahead to check out highway conditions even though the present path was saturated.

By late afternoon, the sun became hidden behind the higher elevations; and although still daylight, the view was somewhat dimmed from the Blue Ridge's shadow. Once Melvin became more adroit handling the spirited steed, he returned to the wagon several times to ride alongside his wife.

"Have you ever come up with a name for this horse?" Melvin asked Jack.

"No matter what you call him, he'll take a bite out of you if you turn your back on him," Jack replied drily.

"Thanks for the warning. I don't think he can do much damage with the bit in his mouth."

"You're probably right. Just don't try to put Hope on him. He can be a load if he wants to be. She should have a palfrey."

"You sure know a lot about horses, Jack," stated Melvin.

"I used to raise them before the war," the mountain man admitted.

Were Abel in the conversation, he would question Jack further, but Melvin only kicked the horse with the heels of his boots and rode ahead to look for a suitable area to spend the night. Considering their present location, an area with a slight rise was preferred in case the stream, flowing parallel to the highway, flooded from a flash rain. Such a place did exist, on the opposite side of the road and, from the looks of it, had been used in the past for similar purposes. Jack took a steady hold of the horse team reins and negotiated the slight incline with the skill of a muleskinner hauling his freight.

That evening, sitting in the familiar campfire circle, the travelers listened as Abel Strawn gave the daily thanks for another day granted by their Savior and repeat of the Lord's Prayer. For many in the South, the Bible held equal importance to the rifle, and the returning Tennessee natives were no exception.

"Are you anxious about seeing Abigail?" Abel asked while poking the fire and causing ember sparkles.

"I can't say it hasn't crossed my mind," Jack replied in his usual dull and distant manner.

"I'll bet it has crossed your mind. This whole damn trip is dependent on the attitude of one woman, and you're telling me that it's occasionally crossed your mind," Abel stated with a trace of emphatic anger in his voice.

"Okay, okay, don't get so riled up. I think about it all the time, but there's not much I can do until we get there."

"You sure as hell have done enough before now to have her greet us with the sheriff and a shotgun. And I wouldn't blame her none either. In case you don't know it, I think the world of your wife and consider her a friend. It was me that got you transferred out of the Robertson Hospital and away from that woman. My only regret is I didn't do it sooner," confessed Abel as a great deal more glowing embers sparkled in the night.

"You just don't understand, Abel, I don't remember Abigail. I don't know her to this day. That woman you refer to is Grazyna. I know her, love her, and will remember her until the day I die. We have a child together, and had she not passed away, we would have married and this trip would never happen. I'm going back to Statesville only because I promised Grazyna that I would. Apparently, she thought it will be better for Jozef to grow up with a family. I plan to confront Abigail with my begging bowl in hand and plead for what Grazyna wants. I can do no more than that," Jack explained before getting up and disappearing into the blackness.

There's an old saying that people are more truthful in the dark. Whether that's true or not, I can't say with conviction; however, it stands to reason that we humans, all of us with a neurosis of one kind or another, would be less self-conscious if we believed others, in the conversation, were unable to see us.

Abel remained sitting by the fire. His face, between the intermittent illuminations from the flickering flames, gave the expression of concern. Jack Leffingwell is his best friend, and as Abel confronted the possibility of losing him, he began to realize an emotional letdown. Perhaps the words spoken that night would be best unsaid. Abel was reminded of what Jack told him about the weight of words, "Words are so heavy that if the sparrows could speak, they wouldn't be able to fly."

At that moment, the Tennessee mountain man returned from his stroll of self-contemplation and unrolled his night blanket. Stretching out and looking at the stars, he said,

"Good night, Abel. It looks like we're going to have a clear day tomorrow."

"Jack," Abel began.

"No need to talk further, you are now and always will be my truest friend," Jack replied.

* * *

The following morning, after breakfast, Jack guided the wagon team back down the incline and straightened it out on the road heading to Tennessee. He delighted in the time spent with Jozef, even if he was held by Melvin's wife and kept immobile.

"Melvin told me the stream flowing at the roadside is named Hungry Mother Creek. That seems such an unusual name, but Melvin didn't know why and said to ask you," Hope conveyed.

"There are stories as to how it came by that name. The most common and probably retold in these parts of southwestern Virginia dates back nearly a hundred years.

"A raiding party of Cherokee Indians attacked settlers around New River and killed the husband of Molly Marley, taking her and her little boy captive. The Indians returned with their captives to their settlement in the Tazewell area. Life as an Indian captive was deplorable with beatings and other tortures of debasement. All Molly could think of was to escape. Shortly thereafter, she did just that and slipped away with her child. She had no way of knowing where she was, but it didn't matter as long as she was free from the camp. Eventually, after eating only berries for many days, Molly collapsed at the foot of the mountain now known as Molly's Knob. With his mother lying dead, the little boy wandered down a creek and came upon a group of houses. He could only repeat, “Hungry, Mother,” due to his being half-starved.

“Searchers found the body of his mother by the creek. From that point on, it became known as Hungry Mother Creek.”

Hope thought on it for a second then said, “I’m sure glad Indians are no longer attacking and killing settlers.”

“Not around here so much, but farther West, it still goes on. We haven’t heard about it much because of the Civil War. Now that it’s over, the government will probably send the army West to confront them,” Jack surmised as he glanced at his sleeping son.

“I guess the Indians have a right to resent people moving in on their territory. They were here long before us,” pondered Hope.

“I agree, but it has more to do with their way of life. The settlers do just that. They find a good source of water and arable soil, build a house, and stay put. Many Indians are nomads, especially the plains Indians. They followed the migration of the bison, their main food source. The land on the American plains has the best soil for planting, and unfortunately for the Indians, pioneer farmers flocked to the plains to build their farms. Our government played a part by making it easier to settle the land. In fact, as recently as 1862, Abraham Lincoln passed the Homestead Act that made 160-acre tracks practically free for those who farmed it.

“The railroad people always encouraged foreign immigration resulting in thousands of European immigrants coming here to take advantage of the land being offered.

“Indians witnessed the depletion of bison herds and were forced to travel farther for food each year. They resented white trespassers on their property and fought back the only way they knew how."

"You seem sympathetic toward the Indians," Hope stated.

"It's not that so much, it's that we could have done it better," Jack replied while looking straight ahead.

* * *

The journeyers traveled to the other side of Abingdon, Virginia, before the evening rains forced them off the highway and required finding shelter. Much to their disappointment, because the roads were smoother, easier on the horses and allowed them to cover more distance in less time. Another reason might have been that they were only about forty miles from the Volunteer state line and anxious to be in their home territory, a milestone on their trek. Nevertheless, the rain became a deluge, and it would take a while before returning to the highway. Fortunately, the shelter was adequate and all they could do now was make the best of it.

Once the waterproof tarp was positioned over the stone firebreak, a crackling flame caught hold soon, allowing for the other dampened branches to dry out and ignite. Jack Leffingwell had also poured a little lamp oil on them to hasten the process. There was no evidence of others having camped on that very locale, and plenty of fallen branches remained, but they needed drying out. Therefore, the travelers gathered and stacked a supply near the fire, protected by the tarpaulin.

In the absence of sunlight and presence of a mountain thunderstorm, the temperature made a precipitous plunge. Heavier clothing was no longer an option. With a fifty-degree chill, it became a necessity. Soon, the heat from the campfire dried the area under the waterproof cover, making it suitable ground on which to sleep.

At first, Melvin and Hope sat in front of the fire with a blanket over them and eating a raw potato. It had finally become dry enough to cook supper, but considering the hour, a decision was made to forego supper in favor of a big breakfast. Naturally, an exception was made for Little Jozef, who remained under the protective cover of the prairie schooner and presently enjoying the company of his father.

"Funny how things turn out, this here tarpaulin we got off those road robbers has sure come in handy. I wonder where they came by it in the first place," Melvin mused.

"Most likely, they stole it off some farmer's haystack," considered Abel.

"You're probably right. Do you want a tater?"

"No thanks, this hot coffee will do me till the morning," Abel answered.

"Hope was telling me how Jack explained the origin of the name, Hungry Mother Creek. How does he come by knowing all these things?"

"Being born in the mountains of Georgia gave him exposure to a particular lifestyle. His parents originated from Pennsylvania and went to Georgia when his father was drawn to the gold fields. Before Jack was married, he met a man named Tobias Taylor, a true mountain man, who got Jack interested in the Underground Railroad. He also became friends with a Choctaw Indian named Yalata, who shared the life of hunting, fishing, and trapping. The pair traveled miles on horseback, exploring the wilderness and learning about the local game and customs. Jack was the better trapper and accumulated many animal skins during the course of their adventures. When enough pelts were gathered, he delivered them to a trading post for sale. Many such mountain men would meet at the trading posts in a seasonal reunion, bringing in their wares from a period of hunting and trapping. Some came as far as the Rocky Mountains with a variety of furs and stories of their experiences. Not only did Jack earn money for his beaver pelts, but he also gained a great deal of knowledge about how the others lived and the distant terrain with its various types of plants and animals. It was sort of like a mountain man jamboree that lasted for a week or two. These folks are men who preferred the singular life of restless exploration, but looked forward to visiting friends at the trading posts. They always avoided the white man's town and settlements. They did, however, sometimes live with the Indians for a spell, most likely because of the women.

"Once Jack married Abigail, he gave up the mountain man life and settled down with his own farm. The Civil War changed that as well, and like the rest of us, he joined the Seventh Tennessee regiment," Abel explained.

"I ain't seen no land unless a Yankee gun was aiming at me," Melvin bemoaned.

"Well, I ain't seen much either. That's just the half of it. Jack's read more books, seen more places, and talked to more people than all of us put together.

"I used to dislike him, especially when Abigail was in Richmond. Now that I see him with his son and watch him more closely, I know why Abigail fell in love with him. I sure hope things work out once we get to their farm," said Hope.

Morning brought sunshine. However, the roads were too wet to chance wagon travel. The area didn't offer much for a diversion, so the travelers took inventory of their larder and basically sat around reminiscing about their lives. An assessment of their location put them near the foothills of the Southern Appalachian Mountains, yet still in the Blue Ridge area with its high elevations and rugged terrain.

On June 1, the pioneers crossed the Tennessee state line and entered Sullivan County, giving a hardy shout while doing so. The area was sparsely populated with only cabins dotting the landscape. It's a region with a wide diversity of both plants and animals, frequented primarily by hunters and others with a rugged disposition. Jack Leffingwell had chosen to make camp near the border village of Bristol. Melvin Kaufman came galloping back to the slow-moving wagon with news of a good location just a half mile ahead. The site was definitely to the mountain man's satisfaction. A flat area for parking the prairie schooner trailed into the wooded foothills, and a fast-moving stream brought a rare smile to the sharpshooter's face.

Preparations for making the evening's camp had now become routine. Each traveler assumed their particular duties and went about the task in mutual confidence. As nightshades fell, the journeyers sat around the crackling flames of the campfire digesting their evening meal. The sky was clear, save the twinkle of brilliant stars, and the full moon gave enough illumination for Jack to read his shirt pocket Bible. Still unable to understand why he could automatically turn quickly to certain verses. Hope Kaufman sat holding Little Jozef and was trying to get him to look up at the giant moon.

"It's no use, he won't do a thing I ask of him," surrendered Hope. "I can't remember ever seeing the moon that large before."

"It appears large because it's closer to the earth," Jack affirmed. "Its fullness signifies it has completed the waxing cycle. It will now begin to wane before it starts over again."

Looking up into the lunar light, Hope said, "My father told me the moon regulates the tides by gravitational pull."

"He's right. In fact, the American Indians took notice of the moon phases and gave a name for the full moon each month. They believed it was a symbol of fate and time granted by the great Mother Earth. It not only governed their daily conduct but also influenced hunting, fishing, and planting. While various tribes gave different names, the Cherokee called the waxing moon of May the *planting moon*. Their medicine men declared when the moon is full, Mother Earth exhales, and when the moon is waning, she inhales. A coincidental statement of fact as it relates to gravitational pull.

"Behind many early people's superstitions lay scientific fact. We know that the gravitational pull of the moon affects the tides as well as our bodies. High tide and full moon tend to increase the moisture in the earth's soil, allowing plants to absorb more water. Correspondingly, more moonlight stimulates leaf growth. Most farmers understand this and coordinate their planting with a waxing moon."

"Jack Leffingwell, you are a world of knowledge. How did you ever learn such things without attending college?"

"Much of it was learned from my Choctaw Indian friend Yalata and his wife. She is a Cherokee princess and explained these things to me," Jack replied. He also had her name momentarily, but it slipped away without recall.

Abel Strawn could see Jack's frustration in not remembering Ailana's name, taking pleasure in the fact he remembered Yalata and an episode in his past. When Hope and Melvin retired to the wagon, he turned to Jack and suggested, "This looks like a pretty good hunting area. In the morning, let's take a gander in the woods and check out the game. Dinner might just be waiting for us somewhere in those pines."

Morning dew was dripping from the scrub oak and pine trees when the two marksmen ventured into the dense forest. Intermittent patches of fog disrupted visibility; however, the experienced hunters were able to navigate by intuition and their sense of hearing and smell. They had been stalking for about a half hour when the familiar gobble sound of a wild turkey was heard in a thicket about fifty feet ahead.

"You better take the shot, Abel, my Whitworth won't leave enough to eat," Jack whispered.

The male turkey gave a series of short staccato clucks then a couple of single putts as it wandered into the open in search of food. Feathers flew after the report from Abel's long rifle, and dinner was now flopping about in the clearing. Holding the tom by its feet and extending it at arm's length, Abel declared, "It must weigh over twenty-five pounds." Jack congratulated him on the fine shot and said, "I'll get some water boiling as soon as we get back."

When the hunters returned to camp, with a bounty for their efforts, there was cause for rejoicing. Melvin recognized the turkey as soon as Abel's image cleared the dense trees and gave out with the rebel yell. Hope, somewhat confused by it all, knew her husband's reaction was a good thing and presented a female version.

"Looks like we're going to have roast turkey for dinner," Melvin conveyed to his wife while trying to hide the disappointment in his eyes for not being on the hunt. Hope held Jozef until Jack was nearer the camp, then lowered him to the ground allowing his little legs, already in motion, to touch the earth and propel him across the grass.

"Keep an eye on Jozef while I put some potatoes and carrots in the cooking pot," Hope said as she walked back to the wagon.

"Don't worry about Jozef, Jack's got him now."

Abel laid the large bird on some rocks near the fire and turned to Jack as if to say, "What do we do now?" The Tennessee mountain man stood alongside his fellow hunter as if pondering the next move then asserted, "There won't be a need to pluck the feathers. This guy isn't like a domesticated bird that's penned up and fed corn all day. He's going to taste a little gamey because he's lived on the run, eating insects and whatever else he could find. The best part of a wild turkey is the breast, their legs are too skinny and tough as leather, so I'm going to remove the breast and we can dig a hole and bury the carcass."

None of Jack's fellow travelers had eaten wild turkey, therefore accepted any disposition he had regarding the manner in which it was cooked. Rolling the bird on its back, Jack found the breast bone then removed his hunting knife from its sheath. He made an incision from top to bottom and ripped open the chest cavity, deftly removing both sides of the breast, and declared, "The best way to prepare the meat is to fry it. We can use bacon fat or lard and maybe some chopped onion to lessen the gaminess."

"I'm already boiling some potatoes and carrots," Hope mentioned.

"That's fine, it will go good with the fried turkey, and what's left over will make a hearty stew with the turkey meat added to it."

Melvin grabbed the shovel and began to dig into the soft earth. Since losing his arm, he had grown stronger with the remaining appendage due to its additional use. Jack brought the turkey remains and dropped it into the shallow grave, saying, "If nobody objects, I'd like to spend another day here and do more exploring of the woods. Deeper in, I saw signs of water. Maybe a hidden lake is waiting to be found and fished."

"What signs tell you there might be a lake?" Melvin questioned.

"I spotted some big nests higher up in the trees. That's a sign of good-sized birds like bald eagles. If they are eagle's nests, there has to be a big lake nearby, since eagles need large bodies of water in order to thrive. Abel shot the turkey and told me he would watch over Hope and Jozef, if you cared to join me tomorrow."

"Yeah, I'd like that," Melvin replied.

"Then we'll leave first thing in the morning. Bring along a rifle, just in case, and I'll tote the fishing gear."

That evening, the group agreed to spend another night at the current campsite and make ready for departure a day later. Curiosity forced Hope to ask Jack what he hoped to find when he and Melvin go off together in the morning.

"I believe I saw signs of a lake, and we plan to explore the possibility. That's the reason we're bring the fishing poles. This whole area is special in that while we're on the eastern edge of Tennessee and foothills of the Blue Ridge Mountains, other mountain forms tend to surround us. The Great Smoky Mountains and Bald Mountains are nearby from where we stand. We're in a fertile valley with wooded ridges, but within a short distance, there are massive caverns running for miles. Not too many years ago, hostile Indians would attack the settlers then disappear like ghosts. They would follow the underground river back into the caverns where no one could find them. Settlers never knew the caverns existed until years later. During the war, one of the largest caves became a saltpeter mine—the main ingredient in gunpowder—and was active until the surrender at Appomattox. If we find a big lake, chances are it doesn't appear on any map."

"Every so often, the mountain man in you comes out. I'm amazed that you stayed put for any length of time," Hope asserted.

"Oh, I can stay put if I have to, but the urge is always there," Jack confessed.

The next day, Hope took the time to write to her parents, bringing them up to date at this point in her journey. She also penned a letter to Abigail with similar news. Both missives would be dropped off at the first community they'd come to with a post office.

Jack and Melvin never found a large lake although the mountain man still believed it was nearby, perhaps within a ten-mile area. They did, however, find smaller lakes and caught several fish for supper. Melvin spotted a deer, but too far away to warrant a shot. Jack determined a black bear was nearby by tell-tale signs, i.e., claw marks on trees and fresh scat droppings. When the breeze was in the right direction, Jack told Melvin that he could smell him. When asked what a bear smells like, Jack said, "Like a wet dog, but worse."

* * *

The travelers were on the road at dawn and progressed well into the area of natural springs before calling it a day. There were no sizable communities directly on their path; and Hope, obviously disappointed, had to hold on to her letters. She did receive encouragement when Jack told her that the town of Greeneville would be near the following day's camp. He planned to replenish the covered wagon with food for themselves and also hay and grain for the animals.

True to his word, after spending the night on the roadside, the mountain man made a slight detour toward Greeneville.

"In years past, the Cherokee Indians claimed this area as part of their hunting grounds. They had hunted and camped in the Nolichucky River Valley and its confluence with Big Limestone Creek long before any settlers arrived. There's a lot of history in the area. Davy Crockett, the famous frontiersman, was born around here, and nearby Jonesborough is considered Tennessee's oldest town. The Great Indian Warpath is only five miles from Greeneville," Jack explained to Hope while clicking to the team with the side of his mouth.

"Was the Warpath for attacking the settlers?" she asked.

"Not really, it's also called the Great Trading Path. It was a main travel route to the east coast and Great Lakes and consisted of many branches and trails."

Melvin dropped back to ride alongside his wife, and Jack suggested he drive the team for a while. After changing places, Jack rode ahead to talk to Abel Strawn.

The two rebel veterans rode side by side in silence until Jack remarked, "Make sure you bring that pistol when we get to Greeneville."

"Do you think there's going to be a problem?"

"I'm just concerned. East Tennessee has consistently had a strong abolitionist movement ever since their Quaker population grew. They migrated from Pennsylvania, claiming that biblical scripture forbid slavery and were always ready to help the runaway slaves. Back in 1861, when we joined up, about thirty counties of East Tennessee met in Greeneville to seek a separate pro-Union state and remain in the Union. The government in Nashville refused it and sent Confederate troops to occupy East Tennessee, and, I suspect, there's been animosity ever since. I'll never hide the fact I am a pardoned Confederate soldier. All the same, it's better to be prepared for trouble."

Traffic on the highway increased considerably the closer the wagon got to town. Most likely due to business conducted to and from Knoxville. With eyes peeled for a general feed store, their wagon wheels slowed to a much lesser pace. Passersby appeared to give unfriendly stares even though Jack and Abel tipped their hats. At Jack's suggestion, Hope held Jozef on her lap, giving the prairie schooner a more pleasant family appearance. To the onlookers, it didn't seem to matter. Finally, they came upon a group of buildings offering exactly what was desired. A general store for hard goods and food, whereas the building alongside was a blacksmith shop having a stable barn offering hay and oats. Connected to the general store was a tavern. It wasn't unusual to find such combinations in smaller towns. As the wagon came to a stop, Jack noticed a cow tied to a tree across from the general store. It reminded him that his son hadn't had milk for three days.

Jack dismounted in front of the store and tied his horse to a rail for that purpose. Several other mounts acknowledged the others inside. Abel retrieved the revolver and tucked it under his shirt before tying his equine's reins to the rail. Managing to fix a smile to their faces, the two slowly climbed the steps to the porch and opened the screen door. As soon as they entered the store, the hair on the back of their necks began to stand up. Tension was so thick you could almost cut it with a knife. Walking up to the counter, Jack had to squeeze between two men refusing to move an inch.

"We would like to buy some provisions," he stated in a voice louder than the din of the room.

"What's your business here in Greeneville?" the storekeeper asked.

"We're just passing through and need supplies," Abel replied before Jack could speak. He could tell Jack's breathing was increasing.

"We don't take Confederate money," the storekeeper snarled.

"We don't have that, we have greenbacks," Abel said.

"We only take gold," the storekeeper snapped.

"That's okay, I've got gold," Jack replied as those in the room turned to see the man making that statement.

The person behind the counter was stumped. His eyes darted from side to side, and as he nervously licked his lips, Jack handed him a list of what he wanted and laid a $20 gold piece on top the shop board. At that moment, a very large man entered the room from the tavern.

"What's the problem here?" he shouted with authority.

"There's no problem. We just want to buy some supplies and return to the road," Abel explained.

"What are you people, Secesh?"

"The war's over, mister, and we don't want any trouble," Abel said.

"The war ain't over in East Tennessee," he replied while reaching over and grabbing Abel's shirt.

Jack slapped his hand away and said, "Let it go, mister, we carry our own storm wherever we go. You don't want bad weather today. It's best you go back to the tavern and sit in the sunshine."

Behind a full black beard, the aggressor's eyes were blazing. Accustomed to being feared, he found himself unsure of the present situation. His backwoods instinct told him to attack, yet there was something different about the tall mountain man standing before him. A hesitation of only a second decided his fate. Jack Leffingwell's right hand punch was as quick as a rattlesnake bite, and it landed between the eyes with the force of a mule's kick. The burley giant tipped a pickle barrel over before landing flat on his back ten toes up. Dill pickle brine slowly soaked into his bib coveralls as he lay unconscious.

"Sometimes it's better to bend with the wind than stand firm and break in half. Someone better go fetch the law," Jack said firmly as two other men entered from the saloon and gaped incredulously at their large friend lying out cold.

"Now wait a minute. Next thing you know, the place will be full of Union soldiers and bothering us for a week. You boys just stay put, and I'll see that your order is filled. All I ask is no more trouble and your partner put his sidearm away," stammered the owner. At that moment, Jack remembered Hope's letters and mentioned, "The sign says you offer postal service. If it's possible, I'd like to have these two letters mailed."

"Not a problem," the storekeeper replied.

Jack laid Hope's correspondence on the countertop, and as he glanced out the front window, he noticed someone pushing a cart toward the wagon loaded with a keg of oats and three bales of hay. When it came time to settle the bill, greenbacks were now acceptable. The two comrades of the unconscious giant had dragged him into the tavern, and Abel was concerned about his health. He looked through the doorway and saw that Black Beard was still out cold.

"How's your friend?" Abel asked.

"He's still breathing," was the reply.

Jack, in the meantime, inquired about the cow tied to a tree. The storekeeper sent the blacksmith to fill Jozef's pail, after which the journeyers paid their bill and were back on the road. The two rebel veterans rode side by side for quite a spell without a word being spoken. Abel's admiration for his mountain friend was augmented by his realization that still water actually does run deep.

"Sure was an unfriendly town," imparted Abel.

"There's prejudice and evil the world over, it's just easier to find it in a small town."

Melvin surmised there was a ruckus back in Greeneville; all the same, he would have to wait until they'd camp before asking Abel about it.

Chapter Forty-Six

The worst thing in the world is to try
to sleep and not to.

—F. Scott Fitzgerald.

It required two more days for the single wagon caravan to reach the outskirts of Knoxville. Making camp for the night, Hope noticed how warm and sultry it became and commented about it, saying, "It's like we crossed a line, and it became hot as August all of a sudden."

"With all the water around, it tends to get hot and very humid, though not as hot as the area to the South. We're in a subtropical zone; however, the higher elevations prevent it from getting even hotter," Jack stated.

The city was located about halfway between the Great Smokey Mountains to the east and the Cumberland Plateau to the west, an area referred to as the Great Appalachian Valley or the Tennessee Valley. The Tennessee River was formed by the Holston River flowing from Virginia and the French Broad River racing westward out of North

Carolina. Supported by the additional tributaries, i.e., creeks and streams, the collective river now courses directly through the center of town. As one would expect, the combination of three major rivers brought flatboats and steamboat traffic to the city's waterfront, making it a way station for travelers and migrants heading west.

During the early days, the Cherokee Indians were the dominant tribe in East Tennessee. When the Revolutionary War ended, there was a rush to settle west of the Appalachian Mountains. The land belonged to the Cherokee by treaty; therefore, the government ordered the illegals out. They wouldn't budge, and all the while, more settlers continued to take Cherokee land. Hostilities grew beyond the boiling point as Indians attacked settlers and the pioneering immigrants returned the favor, forcing another treaty and adjustment of Cherokee hunting grounds.

After the arrival of the railroads in the 1850s, Knoxville grew to become a major wholesale and manufacturing center. While East Tennessee was both antislavery and pro-Union, the Knoxville business interests were connected to the cotton-growing centers to the South. As a result, the city tended to be prosecessionist, favoring it by a 2-1 margin. Confederate troops were able to hold the city until the summer of 1863, after which, the Union was in control.

With the exception of Little Jozef, the day trippers spent a restless night. The men slept away from the campfire, yet fidgeted with blankets in an attempt to cool off. The night breeze was nonexistent, and even with the covered wagon flaps wide open, Hope also found it difficult to sleep though the night.

First light found the prairie schooner crossing a bridge over the Tennessee River and heading west. The sheer fact that they were moving seemed to have a cooling effect as they pushed against the tepid morning air. Whether imagined or not, temperatures seemed to drop the longer the wayfarers continued on the highway. Accordingly, they kept the wagon wheels turning for an hour after sunset.

Finally, the party came to rest on the edge of Roane County and the small community of Harriman. Having tossed and turned the evening before, the group made up for it this night and slept as sound as a twenty-dollar gold piece.

When the eastern horizon began to glimmer with a morning sun, the travelers had a cook fire started and their coffeepot steaming from its spout. It's a wonder what a good night's sleep can bring.

Beginning at the end of April, the westward land expedition was now approaching mid-June. There had been a few impediments on the way to their ultimate destination, however, none to cause a serious setback. Thunderstorms were the main culprit although that only delayed travel time waiting for the roads to dry. More importantly, the animals and equipment had held up well, thanks to the efforts of the Tennessee mountain man. And as the sun slipped behind the western elevation, the wayfarers found themselves at the gateway to the Cumberland area and the sparsely populated portion called Crab Orchard. It was given that name when pioneers passed through the region and took notice of the abundance of crabapple trees.

The campsite was picturesque, featuring oak and hickory trees as well as a grassy glade for the horses to graze. Initially unnoticed by the travelers, a small creek meandered nearby. The horses, sensing water, alerted Jack to the location by their actions. It wasn't uncommon for pioneers to depend on their animals to help locate a waterhole.

The region was a gap between a subrange of the Cumberland Mountains, with the shadowed outline of Big Rock Mountain to the north and Haley and Black Mountain governing the view to the south. Collectively, they're referred to as the Crab Orchard Mountains.

"This area has an exceptional fragrance in the month of May when the crabapple trees are in blossom," Jack mentioned to Hope.

"Are the tiny apples edible?" she asked.

"Yes, but not like the apples you're used to back in Richmond. Most folks think it's not worth the effort for what you end up with. You can make jelly out of them if you're willing to add a lot of sugar. I personally seek out the chestnut crabapple trees. They produce the largest apple and have a desirable nutlike flavor. The fruit tends to get real sweet when it ripens."

Hope devised a harness for Little Jozef and attached a tether string to it. Actually, the string was more like a thin rope and served her intended purpose to a tee. The crabapple campsite was the perfect location to give it a try. She tied one end to the wheel of the wagon and said, "Okay, Junior, go for it." And Jozef did just that, running full speed to the end of his rope. His leash was long enough to provide a rather-large area for him to explore and, best of all, gave Hope's back a rest from carrying the rambunctious tot.

Jack and Abel set about looking for dry branches to start the campfire while Melvin picked out the place to put it. Crabapple wood makes excellent kindling, since it burns slowly and gives off a pleasant scent.

With the evening meal completed and communion with their creator at the closing amen, a sensation of anxiety had taken hold. Their goal was near. The mornings were filled with enthusiasm, and returning to the highway could not come fast enough. The next night found them beyond Crossville and the following evening at Burgess Falls, an area noted for its natural beauty.

The spectacular falls are situated along a steep gorge, in which the Falling Water River drops 250 feet during a one-mile stretch, culminating in a series of three cataract waterfalls. The last of these falls is the most spectacular and begins where the water comes to a sharp edge of the riverbed and plunges more than 130 feet into the deep cut ravine. Protruding rocks halfway down break the curtain of water and spread a mist around the base of the falls. Sheer limestone bluffs rise on each side of the gorge, framing the falls in rough gray rock.

Cherokee, Creek, and Chickasaw tribes shared the region as a hunting ground before the early settlers arrived and established a gristmill and sawmill on the river above the falls, providing meal and lumber to newcomers to the area. An expanse of diverse forest surrounds the region, featuring an assortment of trees, including eastern hemlock, umbrella magnolia, and the cucumber magnolia tree. Basswood, buckeye, sugar and red maple, oaks and hickories, white ash, tulip poplar, and beech are readily found along with an array of bright showy wildflowers.

Jack Leffingwell had seen the falls several times before; however, the impression made on the travelers would be an image never forgotten. Hope claimed to have never seen anything more beautiful, and it served as a fitting climax to the journey because the good Lord willing, they would be in Statesville tomorrow.

Chapter Forty-Seven

Together again, my tears have stopped falling. The long lonely nights, are now at an end. The key to my heart, you hold in your hand. And nothing else matters now, we're together again.

—Buck Owens

"They're coming, they're coming," shouted Sarah Jane, running to the house to tell her mother. Jack Leffingwell's daughter had anticipated the visit for over a week. Each morning, while gathering eggs, she stood at the roadside and stared toward town in hopes of seeing the covered wagon. Today her dreams came true. She would see her father for the first time in four years.

"Calm down, dear, they'll be here soon. Where is your little brother?" Abigail asked.

"He's standing by the road."

"Have him come in so we all can wait on the porch together," asserted her mother, whose hands were trembling as she attempted to pull back her hair and remove her apron.

Once the wagon came to a stop at the front steps, Hope jumped down and ran to embrace Abigail. It was a tearful greeting of two friends who previously had only communicated by mail. Abigail pushed back and said, "Let me have a good look at you. You're a grown woman now, and married too."

"And you are more beautiful than ever," Hope replied, turning to Melvin and extending her hand. "This is my husband, Melvin Kaufman."

"I remember Melvin from when I was in Richmond. Congratulations, young man, you couldn't have picked a better wife than my adopted sister."

Abel Strawn had dismounted and stood by awaiting his turn to greet the sweet lady who became his friend. Their eyes met in knowing friendship as they hugged, both beginning to cry. Abel's tears glistened on his cheeks as he searched for his handkerchief to wipe a running nose.

For a fleeting moment, Sarah Jane became timid as she observed the man sitting on the wagon's wooden seat and holding a small child younger than her brother, Little Jack. She recognized his face as belonging to the father she hadn't seen for four years, but she was overwhelmed by the feeling that she beheld a stranger. Only time would tell if the mountain man could win her over to the love they shared before leaving for the army.

Looking back at the wagon, Jack remained seated and holding Little Jozef. "This is my son. His name is Jozef," Jack stated. Abigail was aware of all from Hope's letters. At last she said, "Well, Jack, aren't you going to bring him inside so he can meet his family?"

It was an odd homecoming with the return of a husband and father who had no memory of the loving familial bond. Nevertheless, Abigail now trusted in a homelike environment to return things to their proper place. She held to the belief that the separation by distant miles could more easily be overcome when the object of her heart was now nearby.

The previous morning, in anticipation of their arrival, Abigail had plucked and cleaned three chickens which now hang in her outside root cellar. Always a splendid host, she was prepared to feed visitors and guests, an age old custom in rural homes. Once everybody was seated and comfortable in the living room, she took Hope's hand and led her into the kitchen.

"The men seem settled for a while. Would you care to help me prepare a meal for everybody?" Abigail asked in softened tone.

"I would love to," Hope replied. Then remembering Jack's little boy, she asked, "I haven't seen Jozef lately, do you know where he is?"

"Yes, he's with his big sister. Sarah Jane thinks he's the cutest little boy she's ever seen and asked to take him outside and show him the farm. Right now the three of them are probably looking at baby chicks."

"I'm so happy you are accepting Jozef into the family. Not that I had any doubts, I'm truly blessed to have such a wonderful woman as my best friend."

"Well, remember that I'm a preacher's daughter and brought up to forgive, but I'm also a woman, and in that way, it didn't come easy. I can't change what has happened although I'd certainly change it if I could. You see, I still love Jack with all my heart and will pray every day for his memory to return. In the meantime, I'll just hide my hurt behind a happy face and be like a circus clown. Do you know the story behind the clown's smiling face?" Abigail quavered.

Hope was in tears and hugged her friend until her sobs were controlled enough to say, "If there's a god in heaven, things will work out. They just have to."

A few moments later, while the girls were wiping their eyes, Abel Strawn poked his head in the kitchen and said, "We're going outside to take care of the animals."

"When you see the children, tell them to come in. We'll have supper ready in about a half hour," Abigail declared.

The dining room table was the one built by Jack Leffingwell and presented a grand display of competent workmanship. It was large enough to accommodate the household and even more if the handmade leaf was utilized. Made from oak and hand rubbed with oil until a bright luster became a permanent sight, the table received more than one compliment from those seeing it for the first time. Today was no exception, as Melvin and Abel praised the craftsmanship and asked how it was made. Ironically, Jack could explain how it was built, despite the fact he didn't remember making it. Needless to say, it accommodated a sumptuous fried chicken supper and all the side dishes, with room to spare.

While Sarah Jane was disappointed in not sitting at the main table, she did agree it was necessary for someone older to sit with the younger boys, especially Little Jozef, at the table in the kitchen. By now, Jozef has accepted Sarah Jane as his little mother and cooperated with whatever she told him. Hope could only chuckle at him and say, "And now he finally minds."

After supper, conversations continued until the time for oil lamps to be lit when Hope suggested that she and

Melvin could sleep in the wagon. They had done so for nearly two months and grown rather used to it.

"There's no need for that. I have a surprise for you both. Remember the elderly woman who lived with me? She was like a mother to me while Jack was in the army. Sadly, she passed away this spring and willed me her farm. The house is in tip-top condition and is ready for you two to move in. We still have enough light to walk over and show it to you."

The key opened the door with ease, and all could see how neat and tidy Maryellen and the other ladies from the church had cleaned and polished every room.

"There are fresh linens on the beds, and I'm sure this will be much better than another night in the wagon," Abigail said with a smile, handing the key to Hope.

"I'll keep another key back at my house in case that one gets lost."

"Abigail, I'm in a state of shock and disbelief. You do work miracles," said Hope as she turned to Abel and added, "You can stay with us tonight and let our benefactors have some peace and quiet."

When Abigail and Jack walked back to the farm, they needed the lantern to find the path. They walked in silence for a short while until Jack spoke, "I don't remember Minnie Rosenthal, but she must have been a wonderful woman."

"Wonderful woman is an understatement. I've never met anyone like her."

No one spoke until they reached the porch, and before entering the house, Abigail said, "You can have Minnie's room. I've changed that bedding as well. There's a hamper by the door. You can put your dirty clothes in it, and I'll do a wash on Saturday." Out of sight of Abigail's eyes, Jack was counting on his fingers the days until washday.

Checking in the children's room, Abigail found Sarah Jane sleeping with Little Jozef and Jack Junior, dead to the world, alone. The scene brought a smile; however, a better arrangement must be made in the morning. There were two rooms in the loft. She would put the boys together, and Sarah Jane could have the other.

After extinguishing the lighted oil lamps, Abigail retired to her bedroom and changed into a sleeping gown. She left the door ajar in case someone cried out in the night. It was unlikely tonight, since the children were exhausted from the excitement of the day and deep in their gentle state of slumber. A condition not shared by their mother who found sleep wanting. Abigail was constantly stirring, agitated by the present conditions in which she was a stranger to her husband. Even though the restless pillow turned through the night, she sought fortitude to stay the course until a better situation would come about.

Hopefully, she listened for any sound of encouragement from Minnie Rosenthal's old room. But none was heard because, after sleeping on the ground for nearly two months, the coolness of sheets had fully tranquilized the mountain man. Abandoning further effort to sleep, Abigail relinquished the bed in favor of rising early. While making her bed, she heard the grandfather clock in the living room strike its chimes four times. Donning her housecoat, she padded to the kitchen and lit the kindling under the stove burner. At this moment, the only form of sanity was a steaming hot cup of coffee. As the pungent aroma traveled from room to room, it soon reached the chamber occupied by her sleeping husband. It served as a wakeup call, and soon the tall form of Jack Leffingwell appeared in the kitchen doorway.

"Nothing like a hot cup of coffee to start the day off right," said Abigail as two cups were placed across from each other.

"What time is it?" asked Jack.

"A little after four," she answered while filling both cups with the steaming brew. "It's too early to start breakfast. I don't expect the others before eight o'clock. Abel plans to leave for Lebanon this morning, and I want to make sure he has something to eat before he takes off."

"You're quite a woman, Abigail. I had a lot of apprehension on the trip from Virginia coming over here. As it turns out, my reception is nothing like the one I feared," Jack confessed while stirring his coffee.

"You belong here, Jack, whether you remember it or not, it was you who built this farm, this house, and fathered our children. I'm hoping we have passed the bottom of our friendship, and the only way to go now is up. I love you, Jack, no matter what has happened. Please understand the past four years have been a nightmare for me, living in limbo not knowing whether you are dead or alive. I wanted to kill myself when I learned you loved another, and only my fear of the Lord stopped me. It's important for me to tell you that I don't hate Grazyna, however much I dislike what she did. We all have goodness in us as well as evil, and you wouldn't be here without her goodness.

"I realize that your amnesia has taken away the memory of our life together, and because of it, you can't share the love I have for you. But when it comes to a man and a woman, love alone is not enough. You need trust, honesty, and a sharing of the noble spirit. These things require time, a long time, maybe years. All I know is, it doesn't just happen. You must work at it, without requital, and I'm willing to do so and wait, if it takes forever.

"We now have two farms and soon your friend Yalata will be bringing the livestock back. The farm has direly missed you for four years and got pretty run-down. It's a good thing Melvin and Hope are here to help out. We will need to work something out to pay them for their effort. Not now, but soon, so they have more to look forward to. And last, but certainly not least, we have three children to take care of and rear properly. There's plenty of work ahead of us, and our future will be determined only by God and time. I do need to know one thing. This morning is as good a time as any to have your answer. Are you going to stay and help me?"

Jack sat staring at the woman before him with a serious expression frozen on his face. It seemed like an eternity to Abigail before he finally spoke and said, "Do you need any help making breakfast?"

* * *

About an hour later, Hope Kaufman appeared ready to help Abigail prepare breakfast and was quite pleased to see Jack Leffingwell lending a hand. She waited until Jack went outside with a wicker basket before commenting, "Things are looking rather domestic around here."

"It's not exactly what you think. Jack has agreed to stay and help put the farm back to where it was before the war," Abigail said formally.

"It's okay to take baby steps as long as you're moving forward. Where was he going with the basket?"

"I asked him to go to the root cellar and get potatoes. When he returns, maybe you can peel them and we'll have fried potatoes with the morning meal. Jack would probably use his big hunting knife," Abigail replied jokingly.

"Melvin and I love your other cabin. Everything is so comfy and handy. Even the pump in the kitchen works. The three of us had a drink of water, just to see if it was operational."

"How was it?"

"It was ice-cold and tasted wonderful."

"I always thought Minnie's kitchen pump was the best part of her house. Her husband Jacob must have dug the well before building the cabin. Women who helped spruce up the place told me they got it working and made tea.

"The pump we have in this kitchen is for water from a cistern. It's great for doing the wash; however, since it's soft rainwater, it must be boiled before we drink it. Regular cooking and drinking water comes from our well in front of the house. I still have to bring it in each day. Now that Jack's back, maybe he can figure out something to make it easier," Abigail imparted.

Noise at the kitchen door indicated Jack's return. He sat his wicker basket on the countertop and said, "The root cellar held up quite well. I've got a couple of ideas to improve on what you already have. Nothing major, but it should keep food longer and fresher."

Abigail wore the smile of satisfaction as she added, "Hope also has a root cellar."

"Yes, but I don't have anything to put in it," she replied innocently.

"Oh, you will, dear, once we plant a garden."

"I'm so excited about everything. It's like I'm in a dream," Hope uttered.

Jack noticed that Hope picked up a paring knife and began peeling a potato, so he took a chair and said, “From the looks of things, there’s going to be plenty of work for all of us. Not only planting a garden for ourselves, but also planting a corn crop for the animals. Fruit trees will need picking in a month, and pecan and walnuts later this fall.”

“It all seems thrilling to me,” said Hope.

“We’ll see how you feel when we’re doing the canning for the winter,” threatened Abigail teasingly.

* * *

The embarking breakfast for Abel Strawn was a success, and his departure allowed, only through the valediction of returning soon, with his wife, Amanda. Obtaining Melvin’s approval beforehand, Jack handed Abel a small leather pouch containing five double eagles in gold, and those remaining on the farm were shocked to see the Tennessee mountain man with tears swelling in his eyes as he gave his fellow marksman and friend an embrace, prior to Abel swinging a leg over the saddle and mounting his horse.

Standing like a silent sentinel, Abigail watched her true ally gradually disappear down the road leading to Lebanon and another life.

A few moments later, it was as if someone gave the signal for all to blow their noses at the same time.

Walking back to the house, Jack turned to Melvin and remarked, “Let’s mount up and take a ride around the property. I’d like to inspect the parcel to the west of us. It looks like abandoned pasture with a pond on it.”

The riding tour proved the land in question did actually have a spring-filled pond, ideal for raising cattle and horses. On their own property, they found a parcel with hay ready to be cut and stacked. A good hay field lasts for years since it's cut down, leaving six inches to regrow. This one contained alfalfa and timothy, making a sweet grass loved by both cows and horses. On their journey back to the barn, Jack asserted, "I want to go into town and find out who owns that grazing land. Maybe they will sell it or at least rent it to us."

"When do you think we need to cut hay?"

"We have a little time. You can tell when it's ready by the heavy-perfumed smell in the field. We don't want to cut it when it's too wet. Hay gets hot as the moisture evaporates and could catch fire."

Abigail wanted them all to go to Statesville so that the newcomers could meet her father. Jack wasn't too excited over the idea but realized it had to happen sooner or later, and he did need to find out about the pastureland.

Reuniting with Rev. Hyrum Adams proved to be a seminal experience without a hint of accusation or reproach. The wise man of the cloth treated him as the welcome son-in-law returning from war and, with his comforting manner, put Jack at ease. He did, however, ask for a private meeting, ostensibly to hear more about the war and discuss the possible justification from the Christian viewpoint. With all eyes focused on the mountain man, he yielded to the only option available and promised to visit the following day.

Regarding the rental or purchase of the pastureland, Hyrum believed it was owned by an older couple, now living in town, and offered to intercede on his behalf in making a proposal. He promised to have an answer by the time Jack returned for his visit the next day. For a split second, Jack was reminded of the Irish trickster, Lomas Chandler, by the manner in which he was bamboozled into agreeing. Unsurprisingly, Hope and Melvin were favorably impressed with Abigail's father; and while he had his two grandsons straddling a knee, they pledged to attend Sunday services. Before heading back, Abigail made a short detour so that she could bring Maryellen Riberty up to date on the recent happenings. She found her friend all smiles due to the announcement of a new Union officer who took headquarters in the building across the street. At this point, she only knew that he was about her own age, a widower, and from East Tennessee.

She loved Maryellen, but there were times when their friendship was vexing; and today pointed out that, basically, people really never change.

On the return trip to the farm, Jack reminded Melvin that half of what was left of Lomas's gift belonged to him, a little over $100 in greenbacks and gold. They decided to give the money to Hope for safekeeping in a glass jar on the top kitchen shelf. As far as Abigail was concerned, she planned to convince Hope to open an account at the same bank she and Minnie used, leaving only ten dollars for an opaque glass jar.

That night, the coolness of sheets didn't help. Jack found sleep elusive as he pondered various scenarios of the pending meeting with Hyrum. He was actually frightened over the possibility of losing the minister's friendship. Anguishing over his inability to determine the cause of such fears, he searched his mind for a plausible meaning. Was it guilt? Was it fear of losing the farm now that he has seen it, or was it actually losing the respect of Abigail's father?

The morning coffee was made, compliments of the man in the house, when a puffy-eyed lady sat down in front of a vaporous cup.

"You're up early," she stated.

"I know, I found it hard to sleep. It must have been something I ate," he replied.

"Or something about having to meet my father alone." She grinned. "You have nothing to worry about, Jack. My father is the most congenial person I've ever met. You two were the best of friends. Sometimes I thought he preferred you over me." Abigail was grinning when she said that and looking down stirring her coffee.

"I hope you're right. I guess I'll find out once we meet," he said resolutely. Changing the subject, she revealed, "Hope is making her first attempt to cook breakfast using a kindling fired stove, so they won't be joining us this morning. It's going to be just the five of us."

The mountain man was subconsciously pleased whenever Jozef was mentioned as part of the family. No less than at that moment when the words came from the woman seated across the table. He noticed her puffy eyes were slowly retaking their original shape and found them appealing at every stage.

"I plan to take the wagon this morning. Melvin is going with me. We need to pick up items from the feed store, and it will do him good to be involved. Naturally, he won't be around while I'm talking to your father," Jack asserted.

"What are you getting from the feed store?"

"Last I remembered, no pun intended, we can have two plantings here in Tennessee. I think we can still put in a crop of corn. It won't be as good as one planted in the spring, but should yield thirty or thirty-five bushels per acre. The field next door had corn on it years back, and it should serve the purpose. The other seeds will be primarily a garden variety, and their produce should be ready for harvest before cold weather."

"You better buy some fruit jars at Riberty's. It looks like Hope and I will be doing a lot of canning this fall," Abigail added.

"How many do you think we'll need?"

"Better get a hundred quarts and at least fifty pints for a start. We can always get more if they are needed. You will have to examine Hope's root cellar to make sure it's workable."

"I've got a couple of ideas that will make them both better."

Having only her own family at the breakfast table felt natural to Abigail. The banter among the children and questions for their father was pleasing for Jack as well. There was one argument about the seating arrangements, but once Jozef had to sit in Jack Junior's highchair, things settled down. When the grandfather's clock chimed nine times, Melvin and Jack were on their way to Statesville. They entered Hyrum's cottage so Melvin could give his greetings and shake his hand, then make excuses to run errands and buy what was written down on Jack's list.

Jack followed Hyrum to the living room. Hyrum sat in his favorite chair by the lamp table and motioned Jack to sit in the one across from him.

"Before we get into other subjects, let me tell you what I know about the pastureland. It does belong to the couple mentioned at your visit yesterday. Mr. and Mrs. James Wright own the property. They never farmed it and loved the fact it had a spring lake. Just before the Civil War broke out, they considered selling it. They're in their eighties, and it's too hard to go there now. As you are aware, once the war started, prices on farmland begin to rise but wooded property took a precipitous fall. Taxes, however, stayed the same. Nobody was interested in buying, so they took it off the market. About two weeks ago, a stranger approached them to buy the land and offered fifty dollars. They believed it was worth much more and told him so. He then invited the two black men he had with him to come in while he restated his offer. Obviously, it was a ploy to frighten the elderly couple. It worked, and you couldn't find anyone more eager to sell when I talked to them about you. Here is the deal I offered, and they accepted. You will rent the pastureland for three years at $25 a year. The selling price of $250 will then come due, with the previous rent to apply to the balance. That means you will owe them $175."

"I should be able to pay it off before then."

"Tell them that. I'm sure they will appreciate it," Hyrum said as he handed Jack an envelope containing the agreement. "Old Dr. Campbell and Sheriff Williams helped write it and have already signed as witnesses. All you need to do is go to their house, have them sign it, and give them twenty-five dollars as payment for the first year. Do you have the money?"

"Yes, it will be completed before we leave town."

"Now then, let's discuss the problem facing all of us, now that you're home from the war. Abigail has told me about your amnesia, caused by a war wound. And a little about the girl named Grazyna whom she met on her trip to Richmond Hospital. If not now, you will certainly someday be faced with your actions and the need for redemption."

Those thoughts hadn't taken priority considering all that had happened up till now, but Jack knew the minister was right. Someday he would need to face it.

"The Bible has always been a mainstay in the critical times of my life. I truly believe the answer to every human malady can be found there. It teaches us that King David and Bathsheba had a son they named Solomon, who followed his father as king. God gave Solomon wisdom surpassing any in the past and eclipsing any in the future. Solomon was a great king, forming alliances with surrounding nations to both protect and develop trade. He built the temple and a great palace protected by a chain of forts. He constructed a fleet of ships to extend the overall trade routes. His riches were unsurpassed. But two evils lurked behind the brilliance of Solomon's empire. They were the curse of polygamy and the curse of dictatorship. These evils eventually brought spiritual ruin to both the great king and the people. While there is disagreement as to the author of the book of Ecclesiastes, most Bible scholars agree it is an interpretation of life as seen through the eyes of Solomon, perhaps a melancholy reflection in his later years," Hyrum stated as he rose to his feet, walked over to a nightstand by his rocker, and picked up his Bible.

"Do you remember the book of Ecclesiastes?" he asked.

"Not really. That's not to say I haven't been reading my Bible, it's just mainly the New Testament that I've read," replied Jack.

"Let me read it to you. Not the whole thing although it's rather short, but chapter 3 verses 1 through 8." The minister opened the well-worn book to within three pages of his destination and began reading aloud,

> *To every thing there is a season, and a time to every purpose under the heaven:*
>
> *A time to be born, and a time to die; a time to plant, and a time to pluck up that which is planted;*
>
> *A time to kill, and a time to heal; a time to break down, and a time to build up;*
>
> *A time to weep, and a time to laugh; a time to mourn, and a time to dance;*
>
> *A time to cast away stones, and a time to gather stones together; a time to embrace, and a time to refrain from embracing;*
>
> *A time to get, and a time to lose; a time to keep, and a time to cast away;*
>
> *A time to rend, and a time to sew; a time to keep silence, and a time to speak;*
>
> *A time to love, and a time to hate; a time of war, and a time of peace.*

"I remember that chapter, but what does it mean for me?" Jack questioned.

"Where it might apply is the concern about polygamy and the relationship you've had with Grazyna. Solomon, in his old age, may have been admitting to the sins of life as a natural process to the ultimate goal. Now, Old Solomon makes you a piker in this area. He had seven hundred wives and three hundred concubines, but the issue isn't how many. Only one is a sin. The fact you have amnesia will not excuse you in the Lord's eyes. The minute you learned of your marriage to Abigail, the sin began. Recognizing this will mark the beginning of redemption. The rest will be determined by the way you live your life from this point forward," offered Hyrum.

"If God is supposed to be so loving of mankind, why does he allow wars and disasters? I don't understand how horrific events can be part of his plan. How can the terrible things such as murder and rape of children be part of his plan? How could he allow Grazyna to die? How do you explain that?" Jack asked passionately.

"That's a tough one, son, and it bothers nearly all of us. God is always with us when we're most in need. He helps us to survive the tragedies in life. God doesn't cause those things as part of his plan or purpose. It would be like if you were walking with your two-year-old son, Jozef, and you had hold of his hand. Suddenly, he trips and skins his knee. You didn't plan for that to happen or cause it, but you're there to help comfort him. To help dry his tears and heal the hurt. That is the way God's plan works. He is always with us to perform his miracles; however, his promise to us is everlasting life if we repent our sins and come to him."

"That's too easy, there's got to be more to it."

"It's not easy at all. In fact, it's the hardest thing, for my part, I've undertaken. I was personally shaken to devastation when Abigail's mother died. Marian and I both had lived our lives by his Bible dictates, yet my wife was taken away by fever illness, leaving me with a nine-year-old daughter. I searched the Good Book for answers, all the same time unable to give a sermon without breaking down in tears. Then one day, I took special notice of Ecclesiastes and what its true meaning was for me. The time had come to give up my sorrow and live with the responsibilities given me. Her memory is always with me, and I confess there are times I wake up and feel as though she is there beside me. I even talk to her at times, but I'm resolute now that the time for us to be reunited, and that time will come, is in the Lord's hands."

"I still love Grazyna. We have a child as a testament to our love. She was my fire in winter, my breath and truth beyond the blood. We had a marital relationship, and I'm glad we had it. Perhaps, Grazyna and I couldn't work out, but I'm forever beholden to have met her. I know now, it all was wrong, but considering I had no memory of my past, the sin needs the Lord's interpretation. She's still in my dreams, and most likely, her enchanting beauty will be there forever."

Hyrum showed no emotion to Jack's words although they had to hurt deeply. Any man would resent a dialogue that presented a negative effect on his daughter. He finally told Jack that he believed he was on the right track to redemption. Moving back to the farm and taking responsibility for the family was a good start.

"We need to see more of each other. It will be good for me as well as you. The changes brought about by the Reconstruction will not go well with most citizens of Statesville, or Tennessee for that matter. We will need all the levelheaded men we have to help guide us through it."

"How long will this Reconstruction period last?" questioned his son-in-law.

"It's going to take years."

Melvin was sitting atop the wagon seat, with a full load behind, as Jack departed his father-in-law's house and bade him a proper farewell.

"I've got one more stop to make," he said while waving the envelope above his head and walking the two blocks to the Wright's home. "Just stay where you are, this won't take a minute."

A few minutes later found Jack quick-stepping back to the wood-sided wagon with a smile on his face and a copy of the executed document in his pocket.

"We own it," he told Melvin, who snapped the reins on Miracle's rump and guided the mare to the highway.

"Once we get unloaded, we can saddle up and take a good look around. That stand of woods is mighty dense and goes for a long way. No telling what we might find in there. My guess, it's loaded with plenty of game," surmised the tall Tennessean.

"Are we going to bring our rifles?"

"Maybe yours, we're only on a scouting mission this time, but could use one for protection, just in case."

The men received an old-fashioned front porch welcome on their return. A small table stood by the screen door as if announcing a pitcher of cold lemonade and plate of sandwiches by its side. Like the accumulated dust on clothes and shoes, the mountain man grew more appreciative of the decision to revisit the farm. Every time he saw Abigail, he noticed something new about her. This time, with both women standing with the children, he wondered, *How does she keep her teeth so sparkling and white?*

Melvin managed to jump down and beat Jack to the porch, gave Hope a quick kiss, and grabbed a glass of refreshing citrus drink. Jack had a brief urge to do the same with Abigail but managed to reserve his surprising temptation. He did, however, give her a friendly hug and said, "We now own the property next to us. Your father worked out a plan for us to rent for a while and buy it after three years." Reaching into his back pocket, Jack produced the contract and handed it to his wife for safekeeping then said, "Melvin wants to explore the place before it gets dark, so I thought we might saddle up and give it a look-see."

With the men in the barn saddling their horses, the women and Sarah Jane cleaned up the early lunch and removed to the kitchen.

"Melvin wanted to explore the place? What a liar Jack can be. We both know who couldn't wait to look the land over. Melvin could have waited until next week."

"I thought the way he said it was kind of sweet."

"Oh, you just say that because you like him."

"Not the same way you do," Hope replied as she finished drying the last glass.

* * *

Riding around the circumference of the large spring-fed pond, the plaintiff cry of small frogs could be heard. It was music to Jack's ears from latent memories in his past.

"Mrs. Wright told me they used to fish this pond and catch yellow bellies. Some of them were very big, according to her." At that moment, the surface broke farther out and a small frog disappeared. "That weren't no yellow-belly catfish. We got ourselves something else in there, probably a blue catfish."

"How could they ever get in there?"

"My guess it comes from the wild ducks. They swim in one place and pick up fish eggs on their bottom feathers and land on another, leaving the eggs. That's how most ponds get their fish around here. Anyway, it's going to be fun some night seeing what we can catch, and there ain't no better place to teach the boys how to fish."

They turned the horses and rode toward the dense forest. Finding no obvious path, Jack suggested they dismount and explore on foot. After fifteen minutes of reconnoitering, Jack uttered, "There are enough loose brambles and branches to provide firewood for this winter. It's got to be loaded with brambleberries. I'll wager that there are enough raspberries and blackberries to load the root cellars for years."

"Yeah, but there wasn't much indication of game," stated Melvin, sounding disappointed.

"On the contrary, my friend, there are plenty of deer droppings and a bent grass path that can only be made by a bear," Jack assured. "The bear track concerns me some. Let's hope the cattle make him leave. They're not noted to be meat eaters, but sometimes they do just that. Maybe with us poking around, it might decide to leave by itself. If not, you and I will need to go hunting."

Both men were satisfied with the survey of the newly acquired property, but for different reasons: Melvin's blood got hotter thinking of a possible bear hunt and Jack with the obvious bounty the pastureland offered in timber and an excellent oversized pond for watering the cattle. He believed parts would eventually need to be fenced in, however, not at the moment. The cattle, or horses for that matter, won't go far into the woods with their water nearby, and Yalata would probably bring the horses first, giving time to erect a small fenced area to be enlarged later. Depending on how much help Yalata had with him, the fence could go up sooner.

As far as the bear was concerned, it won't be the first time he had encountered black bears.

Jack's thoughts had already turned to planting corn. He remembered seeing a rusty three-bottom tillage plow in Minnie Rosenthal's barn—it's still hard for him to think of that farm as his own—and if the wheels were operable, it won't take much to get it working again. He could harness the biggest mare and operate the plow while Melvin helped the women dropping seed and covering it over. They won't be able to keep up, so after a few passes, he could rest the horse and help out.

Later that day, the plow proved workable. Plans were made to mow the field before any other planting took place. With a horse-drawn mower, the task was accomplished in less than a full day, even with cross mowing a second time. The following morning would begin the big day.

A disappointed Sarah Jane was assigned the task of tending to the little boys. All she said was, "They better mind me."

Hope Kaufman had taken to the rural life and seemed to enjoy every minute of it. Her enthusiasm reached new heights when she overheard Jack tell his wife the men would help them with their gardens.

The cornfield measured slightly less than thirty acres and promised a decent fall crop depending on the weather. No-till planting usually required extra water once the seed was in the ground. Jack seemed confident because, should a drought turn things from bad to worse, the winding brook stood nearby.

It required three days, in the hot summer sun, to complete the planting. When the last seeds were covered, Hope's tempered enthusiasm was noticeably lessened. Both she and Abigail stood with slumped shoulders and straggled hair. Lines of perspiration ran down their faces, leaving skin-colored paths in the direction of descent. The mountain man brought a cake of soap ostensibly to once more use the creek as a bathtub. Ignoring respectability and feminine disposition, the tired pair walked to the creek; took off their shoes, shirt, and workpants; then sat in the fast-flowing burble, dipping their heads and washing hair free from the remnants of labor. With each other's women naked in the water, masculine courtesy forbid either the right to watch; however, for a fleeting second, Jack did observe Abigail, but quickly averted his eyes. By the time they completed their bath, Jack and Melvin had loaded the box wagon and was waiting patiently for them to climb in.

"Toss me the soap," Jack said once the girls approached the wagon. Abigail obliged and asked, "Do you want me to drive the wagon back to the barn?"

"Yes, Melvin and I will be along rightly."

In the center of the rivulet, the water was over their knees. When the sharpshooters sat on the brightly colored stones, worn smooth by the constant and abrasive rush of liquid, only their heads poked above the running course. The runnel moved rapidly and washed away the foamy soapsuds as fast as they were created.

"I could stay here all night," Melvin claimed.

"I know what you mean. This creek is perfect, and I can't think of a better one. We're damn lucky to have it on our property. If it had wider banks, it could be a running road."

"Do you think it has any fish in it?"

"Not where we are. The water is moving too fast. There might be some where it slows down. We got mainly crayfish and turtles. Now that you mention fish, I've been thinking about the spring-fed pond. It's big enough to be a tiny lake, and we know there's fish in it. I've been working out a way to pump the water into troughs for the livestock rather than have them drink directly from the water's edge. They would turn the banks into solid mud. Do you remember Ihme Mueller from our original group? Now there was a guy who could solve my pump problem quickly."

"Yeah, he knew his beans when it came to engineering. A darn good shot as well. I loved the way he pestered good old Lomas. He couldn't tell if Ihme was serious or not, and it drove him wild." At that moment a rumbling reverberation was heard from the west, drawing the attention to the dark rolling clouds. They observed twisting billows, colored from black to gray with dangling ragged ends similar to tattered cloth.

"Looks like we're in for it," Melvin said abruptly.

"Yeah, it couldn't have come at a better time. Let's head back."

That evening, the two families ate in communal fashion at Abigail's table. Conversation was clipped due to everyone being tired from the strenuous day. There's a saying that the best employee goes to work every day, on time, and goes home tired. This certainly could apply to those at the present taciturn table. Even the children were quiet after a day of running, jumping, and tossing a ball, especially Sarah Jane, who spent the day trying to keep the rambunctious miniature rebels in line.

Rain fell steadily now with an occasional flash of lightning and booming thunder.

"It appears as though tomorrow will be a day of leisure. This rain is exactly what we need to start the corn seed," remarked Jack. "It's also going to make the ground easier to plant the gardens."

Heavy rain tapered off by midnight, nonetheless, continued to fall in a gentle patter most of the next day. For the two women, the *physique de jour* was sore muscles and an aching back, resulting in great difficulty for them to rise and shine. The soothing sound of rain, softly tapping the rooftop, and darkness due to the sunless sky was more conducive to just stay put. Unfortunately, the splendor under the sheets couldn't last, and they soon found themselves in front of the stove with a frying pan in their hands.

Henry Wadsworth Longfellow is quoted as saying, "The best thing one can do when it's raining is to let it rain." Ever the pragmatist, Jack Leffingwell apparently agreed as he sat in the front porch rocker, with his second cup of coffee, and viewed the wetting of the realm. He turned his attention to the squeak of the screen door as Abigail joined him with a second cup as well.

"A penny for your thoughts," she said softly.

"Oh, nothing in particular, I was just thinking about some things your father said, and the wisdom of his advice."

"Daddy has been a rock for me these last four years. Nevertheless, I often don't like to hear what he recommends, despite the fact he is seldom wrong," she acknowledged while walking to the porch swing.

"What are the kids up to?"

"Don't talk so loud. Right now they're being quiet. Jozef has found a little mother and follows her all over the place. Sarah Jane is at the right age to enjoy every bit of it. Jack Junior sees no reason at all to mind his big sister. My only hope is that he doesn't upset the applecart."

"You're a very special woman, Abigail, and I'm a lucky man to be here with you."

Chapter Forty-Eight

One day at a time—this is enough. Do not look back and grieve over the past for it is gone; and do not be troubled about the future, for it has not yet come. Live in the present, and make it so beautiful it will be worth remembering.

—Ida Scott Taylor

Golden sunshine of July followed the rain burst, making vegetable planting an easier task. They put in every leaf and tuber imaginable along with a variety of beans. Secretly, most felt things were overdone. Abigail suggested it by saying, "Jack, there's enough here to feed an army. What will we do with it all?"

"Have a little faith, dear. Next spring we won't need to plant as much." The mountain man knew the yield from fall planting would give a reduced harvest, and while there might be a little extra, it's better safe than sorry.

The larger barn on the Leffingwell farm accommodated equipment better than the other. It was another example of considering the future when being built. Up till now, a sizable portion had never been needed and was left empty during the war. Jack presently planned to use it for maintenance and repair of their implements and wagons.

"Hope, how would you like to have a couple of brooder hens and a rooster?" he asked out of the blue.

"I'd love it," she answered. "I think we have a small chicken house already."

"Mind you now, I'm thinking of increasing our egg production, so whatever is produced will be sat on by the hens. It shouldn't take long before hatchlings show up. You don't want to keep many roosters."

"We can always eat them," she suggested.

"From a business standpoint, that wouldn't be very profitable. They eat too much food to keep them all. Some will need to be culled out when they hatch."

The expression on her face said it all. Jack realized that Hope Kaufman would never be able to cull baby chicks, so he assured her someone else would perform the despicable chore. Nevertheless, it was something necessary, if one intended to raise chickens for the purpose of selling eggs. Wartime inflation had increased the cost of most foodstuffs, especially in the South, due to a host of causes. With many men in the army, farm production was left to those few remaining at home. Shortages were the natural byproduct. The Union blockade guaranteed less imports, and the destroyed rail lines made it nearly impossible to bring what did exist to market. Eggs, for example, rose in price from $1.44 a dozen when the war started to $3.60 at its end. On the surface, it seemed to be an activity Hope and Melvin could employ and provide a steady source of income.

"There are basically two methods to sex chickens other than waiting until they consume grain for three or four weeks," Jack began. "It can be done a day or so after they hatch." He had the attention of both Kaufmans.

"You can grab the chick, turn it upside down, and squeeze until a rudimentary male sex organ appears near its vent hole. That procedure is the most difficult and usually adopted by the more experienced sexers. My personal preference just involves examining the baby chick's rudimentary wing feathers. With hens, the primary wing feathers are longer than the secondary or covert feathers lying behind them. In males, the covert wing feathers are either the same length or longer than the primary feathers. The method is quite accurate, and it doesn't take long before the sexing becomes second nature. Disposal of the culled chicks can be done out of sight of anyone squeamish over the process."

"We won't be able to eat any of the eggs?" she asked.

"You can eat them all if you want to. I'm just suggesting a way to make extra money. Farm life doesn't provide a steady income like other occupations. Considering the times, we'll need to tighten our belts while waiting for the year-end harvest. A little cash money coming in makes the wait a whole lot easier."

* * *

Melvin and Jack had been working together in the main barn, greasing wagon wheel axles, when Abigail appeared in the sunlit doorway and said, "Jack, there's a rider coming. I believe a visit from your friend Yalata is imminent."

Jack had taken time out to be defeated by Jack Junior in a wrestling match in which the four-year-old had thrown his father to the ground and was sitting on top his chest.

All the while, Jozef was kicking him in the side to help out his slightly larger brother. Melvin stood by encouraging the youngsters, and both were embarrassed when Abigail found them conducting horseplay during the serious working hours of the day. On the other hand, Abigail was happy to see her husband bonding with his unfamiliar son. Jozef made a heroic attempt to deliver the coup de grâce with a kick to the leg, but missed and landed on his tiny behind.

Both families were standing on the front porch when the rider approached, leading a muscular stallion, which Jack recognized as his own favorite charger, Rambler.

The proud Choctaw swung his leg over a beautiful pinto pony and landed on the sun-hardened earth without breaking a constant stare. Speaking in formal Cherokee, the language of Ailana, his wife, Yalata said, "O si yo, Jack Leffingwell, o-gi-na-li, I bring your so'-qui-li. The wind spirits have told the medicine man you are home from your war. These same spirits also tell many things about you I do not understand. We must talk of it, as in the old days, and smoke the pipe and watch the stars."

"O si yo, my friend. Your spirits speak the truth. It is good to talk the truth at night, while the campfire shines its honest light. The wind spirit knows many things about me, I, too, do not understand. An evil ghost has stolen part of my memory. The image of your presence, here today, has gotten some of it back. I look forward to our private meeting. First, I must pay my debts," declared the mountain man.

"I have already taken my compensation. Half of the offspring reside in my corral," the unexpressive friend stated. "Does Jack Leffingwell consider it fair?"

"That is much more than fair, I have a greater reward."

"Where will you keep those of which I bring today?" Yalata questioned.

"I have purchased the pastureland with the little lake. I wish to keep them there, but I ask another favor. How many braves are with you today?"

"Enough to drive the horses," replied the cautious Choctaw.

"What will it cost for your braves to build a fence?" asked Jack.

Yalata replied, quickly saying, "Two colts that you select or one colt I choose."

Respecting the keen eye of his ochre friend, Jack opted for two colts from his own choosing.

"We will make a small rail-fence for the horses and be prepared to enlarge it when the cattle arrive. When we return, you must provide post-hole diggers and two saws to cut the timber."

By the end of the succeeding day, with Yalata's share removed, Jack ended up with six additional colts and three mares. Nineteen horses now nibbled grass inside the temporary wooden corral, and Rambler galloped along the interior periphery with his tail held high.

Jack and Yalata sat cross-legged in front of a crackling fire made from waste wood left over from the temporary fence construction. The reflection of the flames could be seen by those braves resting on the other side of the small lake. Savoring the moment, the two friends did not speak. As if in deep thought, each one seemed to be waiting for the other to break the silence. Finally, Yalata said, "Tell me more about the evil ghost who stole your memory."

"It happened during mid-December 1862 at Fredericksburg, Virginia. Yankee Gen. Ambrose E. Burnside had planned a surprise attack on the capital city of Richmond, whereas General Lee's troops dug in to stop him. We sharpshooters took a defensive position along the line confronting the railroad and right flank of the Union brigades. Both sides were in a continuous contest of dueling artillery, and the noise was so loud you couldn't hear yourself think. I was told an exploding shell wounded me and killed a fellow marksman named Ihme Mueller. I woke up in the Robertson Hospital in Richmond and remembered nothing of what put me there. Doctors called it amnesia from shock. Still and all, they said my memory should return in time."

"Let us now talk about the woman who made you disrespect Abigail, your wife."

The word *disrespect* made Jack wince as if being prejudged by his friend. In an effort to gain understanding, Jack replied, "Remember, at the time, I had no memory of being married."

"That doesn't change the fact."

Exhaling deeply, Jack continued, "Her name is Grazyna Kaminski-McCracken, the most enchanting and beautiful woman I have ever met. She was a nurse at the hospital. Her husband was killed in the battle at Manassas, without consummating her marriage. I think I fell in love with her from the first time we spoke. We planned to marry. Abigail came to Richmond, even though I did not know her and, after two weeks, traveled back to Statesville. I wrote her to ask for a divorce; however, she didn't answer me. After learning Grazyna was with child, I became resolute to our life together, whether married or not. Fate intervened, and Grazyna died after giving birth to our son. The doctor told me she must have had an unseen heart condition. She made me promise to return to Statesville so that Jozef could have a family life here on the farm. Somehow, she correctly assumed Abigail would accept him, if I returned. Now that I'm here, I think of Grazyna every day and dream of her every night."

"If she is such a wonderful woman, why do you insist on keeping her spirit from its final rest? Each time you dream about her, you evoke her soul to come to you. From the way you describe Grazyna Kaminski-McCracken, she deserves better. She deserves to be untroubled at her final repose. Many of our tribes never speak the name of one who passes on so as not to evoke their essence and keep them from the Great Spirit in the sky. The white man does just the opposite, preventing the spirit from reaching its natural destination. I will talk to the old ones when I return, though I know what they will tell me. You must go back to Abigail's bed, make love to her, and change your dreams."

"Lately, I have thought of that often, up to now, afraid of her reaction. She is a woman of strong Christian faith, and I may be rejected," Jack said in good conscience. Yalata stood and tossed more wood on their fire, ahead of sitting again near his mountain friend to say, "Let us speak the rest of the night without words."

When dawn broke in the eastern sky, Yalata and his braves were gone. Jack awoke covered in a multicolored wool trading blanket with symbols known only to Yalata. After a quick glance at the corral, he slowly began the trek back to the farmhouse wrapped in the decorated mantle. Abigail had risen and had a cup of hot coffee steaming on the table when he walked into the kitchen.

"What do you enjoy most, sleeping on the ground or between clean sheets?" Abigail said with a smile.

"Each has its finer points," he answered, sipping a little hot coffee from the cup's surface.

"What all did you two talk about?"

"Nothing special, just about things in general, the animals, corral, and items he will need when he returns with the cattle. The fence will be a major project since the pastureland covers nearly three hundred acres, counting the wooded part. We plan to make four separate pastures and deliver water to troughs by a siphon pipe. That way the spring-fed lake can continue to be unspoiled," Jack explained, unable to hold her stare with his own.

Abigail pushed back from the table and slowly walked back to the stove. Jack brought their empty coffee cups to the kitchen sink and, standing behind her, breathed the fragrance of her newly washed hair. Her bouquet had a singular essence belonging to no other. Within the mountain man, the flames of passion were awakened. Jack, aroused and unashamed, placed his trembling hands on Abigail's shoulders and turned her gently to him. Their kiss was the culmination of Abigail's wishes and prayers. After four long hurtful years, at last, she was where she belonged. In the arms of her husband, nothing else matters now, they're together again. Sexually aroused, Jack whispered hoarsely, "Let's finish this in bed."

"There is nothing I would like better. That being said, there is something I want first. I want us to repeat our wedding vows."

"I understand, and you are right. I'll talk to your father, and maybe he will conduct the ceremony on Sunday."

"Darling, I'm certain he will be happy to do so."

Abigail walked on air the rest of the day, recollecting the exquisite moment that culminated her desires and dreams. Jack went about his chores actually humming a tune. Hope and Melvin were dumbstruck by the change. Even the children, most certainly Sarah Jane, could sense something special had taken place. The planets were aligned in perfect order, and that night would be the last they would sleep alone for the next forty years.

They say it's good to change the place where one sleeps from time to time because it gives one more interesting dreams. Abigail slept soundly in the miracle of a husband who actually fell in love with her twice. Across the house, in the room once occupied by Minnie Rosenthal, Jack softly snored in gentle puffs. Not once did the image of a blue dot enter his mind; instead, he was standing at the Cumberland Caverns, beneath Caldwell Mountain, waiting for the next conductor to arrive in order to deliver Wilbur Littlefield and his family to the following leg of their escape to freedom. Two days had passed, and it was beginning to appear as though he would be required to conduct the runaway slaves to the next station. Just at the moment, when Jack was about to explain the situation to Wilbur and his family, a horse and box wagon pulled up.

The driver's hat brim was turned down and coat collar turned up, hiding the transporter's face. Jack walked toward the wagon to get a better look, and a woman's voice asked, "Are you Jack Leffingwell?"

"I might be. Then again I might not be. Who the hell are you?"

"My name is Abigail Adams. I am Rev. Adams's daughter. My father couldn't make the trip. The Good Lord took Pastor Simmons day before yesterday, and the council had to meet for succession talk. I volunteered to take his place."

Jack tilted his head to see her face better.

"You people must be crazy. There are renegade Indians between here and there. Nobody risks a trip like that alone."

"I ain't actually alone," she said, holding up a rifle in one hand and pistol in the other. "And I can use them better than most men."

Jack saw he had ruffled her feathers and replied, "I suppose you could. Let's go meet the folks you'll be taking to Statesville."

Even though Abigail made an attempt to hide her face, Jack saw enough to determine she had handsome looks. In fact, he found her pretty. After she took off her hat to wipe her brow, he saw she was beautiful.

"Your husband couldn't make the trip either?" he asked.

"I'm not married, but if I was, he wouldn't need to come along. I can take care of myself."

Jack had made up his mind. He wanted to get better acquainted. So he decided to join them on the trip back. Various excuses ran through his mind. He knew if any of them offended her, she wouldn't allow him to come along.

"I understand Statesville is where all the cotton mills are located," he said casually.

"Yep, and that ain't all. We got seven stores, three blacksmiths, a wood shop and harness maker, and a boot and shoe shop as well. We also have a problem—what you'd like most of all—five saloons."

"The saloons don't interest me none since I don't drink hard liquor," he lied. "But I sure would like to see the boot maker. These old brogans are about to give out, and there ain't any good cobblers where I come from."

"Statesville has a good one."

"Would you mind if I tagged along on the way back? I need to have a pair made."

She was about to answer when the mountain man opened his eyes. It was a dream of perhaps the first time he met the smiling woman, asleep in the room soon to be theirs. Another piece of his memory puzzle put in its proper place and slowly creating the picture of his past life.

On Sunday morning, those watching the road witnessed the Leffingwell families arrive in town seated in their carriage drawn by a somewhat larger mare. Abigail's little mare, Miracle, was given the day off and reposed in their barn, nibbling an extra ration of oats. Jack felt that with Melvin and Hope aboard, it would be a lesser burden for the stronger horse to transport the coach. Sarah Jane and Hope had decorated the mare's mane with petite blue bows in celebration of the ceremony to be conducted after regular services.

Hyrum's sermon was about redemption, a fitting subject considering the day, and even more poignant, when standing in Jack's shoes. After the announcement for the repeated marriage vows, very few people left the sanctuary. Maryellen Riberty and her friends prepared punch for those who stayed and served it in the hallway. She concluded the occasion would be perfect to introduce her new beau, Lt. August Manfred McKnight, to Abigail and Jack.

The McKnight family owned iron foundries in and around Knoxville, a vital industry during the war. The work was hot, laborious, and free since Manfred McKnight also owned many slaves. While the majority of Tennessee slaves resided in the middle and western part of the state, about 10 percent lived in the east. Excluded from Lincoln's plan to free slaves in 1861, Tennessee was the only state to emancipate the captive minions by popular vote, a decision directly affecting McKnight's fortunes. Now, as well-wishers sipped their punch, about 25 percent of the population consists of free blacks.

"This is my best friend, Abigail Leffingwell, and her husband, Jack," introduced Maryellen. "And he is my steady, August McKnight." Cordiality prevailed as Hope and Melvin were presented, and they all shook hands during the introductions.

"Maryellen tells me you have a large ranch and several good horses," the lieutenant implied.

"It's more of a farm than a ranch; however, we do have several quality animals."

"Well, I now know where to look should I need a good mount," stated the man in blue.

"We'd be happy to show you around," said Jack.

"What brings you to our little town?" Melvin questioned.

"Basically, it is a routine changing of the guard, so to speak. I'm lucky they did because it gave me the opportunity to meet Maryellen," he said with a smile and brief hug around her waist.

"Well, it's nice to have met you, but I must gather the children. Please visit us anytime. Maryellen can show you the way," expressed Abigail, ahead of walking outside and calling for Sarah Jane. Hope took that opportunity to do the same and walked with her, descending the sanctuary steps.

"There's something I've been meaning to ask you," confessed Hope.

"What is it, dear?"

"Have you noticed the birthmark Jozef has above his little behind?"

"Actually, Sarah Jane saw it first. I asked Jack about it, and he told me it was something he got from his mother," relayed Abigail.

"I noticed it on the way over here from Virginia. Jack told me the same thing. Grazyna must have had one as well," Hope stated seriously.

"I don't want to think about it. God has answered my prayers, and in some regard, I feel like a newlywed."

"I think you mean a newlywed on her honeymoon," Hope said with a suggestive inference and a grin from ear to ear.

* * *

On the drowsy ride to the homestead, the adults were stifling yawns. There's something about the active period of preparing themselves for church attendance and the natural letdown once it's over. It's nothing that a good Sunday afternoon nap won't cure. Abigail tested the men about August McKnight, saying, "Maryellen's new beau seem like a nice fellow."

Hope agreed; however, Abigail was only interested in what Jack and Melvin thought. Finally, Melvin stated, "He's awful short. I think your friend is an inch taller. What do you think, Jack?"

"I think he believes wearing that blue uniform makes him taller."

That brought a chuckle from Melvin who asked, "I wonder if we ever faced each other in battle?"

"Definitely not," Jack responded.

"What makes you say that?" Melvin queried.

"He's still walking the earth."

As the carriage stopped at the Kaufmans' door, Abigail was contemplating the manner in which the men could be subdued when Maryellen and her suitor come to visit. Agreeing on the necessity of a nap, they planned to get together later in the day. Hope made certain that visit never took place. After all, this day was their honeymoon of a sorts, and privacy was the least she and Melvin could offer.

Each with thoughts of what awaits them, the children changed their Sunday clothes and ate a light lunch before being ushered to their rooms, with an admonishment not to disturb their parents until naptime was over. With only the occasional sound of the log home bracing against the summer wind, Abigail and her husband consummated their reunion amid the pounding of their eager heartbeats.

Midway during the following week, Yalata and his feathered crew arrived with twenty head of cattle and energy to finish the fence. Jack's Indian friend had discussed many subjects with the elders of his village, not the least of which was building a siphon pipe from the lake to animal water troughs. While Jack knew of lead or iron pipe, none was immediately available to him. Like the early settlers, he planned to build with wood, since he had plenty to choose from nearby. Water pipes would be made of bored-out logs. His hemlock and elm trees should serve the purpose well. The trees having trunks about nine or ten inches thick would be cut into seven- to nine-foot lengths.

As it so happened, a pair of log borers happened to pass by the previous week. Jack hired them to demonstrate their skills on the Leffingwell farm. The colorful characters traveled from town to town, bringing news and gossip as they went about their job. They each were armed with a five-foot steel auger. Fixing the log by eye, they would drill or bore out the center. Butting one end to make a conical shape, they would jam the logs together in a series using a bituminous-like pitch to caulk the joints. (They have been known to split the log, dig out the center, and rejoin each half, then securing it with iron bands—a process requiring a blacksmith.)

Disinclined to have the wooden pipe below ground, Jack found a sloped portion of the landscape where the gravity water system would be elevated, yet slant enough to function properly.

* * *

As the summer shadows grew longer, Jack and Abigail sat together on their front porch, each captured in their own thoughts. This tranquil scene, having been disrupted by four years of brutal war and personal despair, gave no indication of what had transpired. The fall crops were in, livestock resided behind what appeared to be an endless fence line, and the Leffingwells were married for a second time. Jack Junior and Little Jozef had managed their father's lap, and Sarah Jane sat with her head on her mother's shoulder. If only our lives could remain at the most pleasant occasions. Unfortunately, such hopes could not come true.

There were times, during long periods of silence, Abigail sensed they were not alone. She was aware of a gap between their mutual thoughts, and her intuition articulated that she was joined by the presence of Grazyna. It's a situation she had no control over, and neither did the mountain man. In one way or another, the beautiful paramour would always be with them. Each time Jack cast an eye on Little Jozef, he's reminded of the young mother. And yes, on occasion, Grazyna came to Jack in his dreams, in which he relived precious moments of their past.

That's not to say his waking thoughts were completely void of the lovely woman with a blue dot. The frequency lengthened with each passing month. Still, her image came to him without warning and at no special time, leaving the pain Jack worked so hard to eliminate. He accepted the fact Grazyna's memory loomed somewhere in the depths of his psyche. It is there the dragon dwells for all of us.

Abigail, in her feminine wisdom, recognized such times and did her best to distract her husband from remorseful thoughts. It is said that fate always has one eye open to allow for change. It permits us to amend destiny and change as individuals, both our circumstances and ourselves.

The hazards of Reconstruction loomed in the future. The years of 1865 to 1877 would see the Southern states, and all their inhabitants, presented with enormous political, social, and economic changes.

If the ancient cave artist could imagine the future, his symbolic drawings would extend beyond swimmers in the desert and cover every inch of the stone walls within which he lives. Perhaps the concept of a spinning earth is beyond his native aptitude, yet such happenings still existed, even then.

And change also ruled at that time, as well as now, conceivably unnoticed by those living at any particular period. Nevertheless, alterations continue to occur deep and permanent in the ways of the world around them. Jack Leffingwell was frequently called a fixed point in a changing world, yet he too had transformed. It's been said that a passing boat leaves no trace upon the waters;

a bird's flight leaves no trail in the sky. Be that as it may, within us human beings, there are events that do leave a permanent mark. However, when fleeting success, failure, gain, or loss leaves no lasting trace upon the heart, the great wisdom of liberation and redemption has been achieved.

Whether or not Jack Leffingwell completely regained memory of his past life could not be told. Bits and pieces seemed to crop up each week; nevertheless, he had safely crossed his Mara River. Yes, the Tennessee mountain man had been absolved and, finally, emancipated.

The End

Epilogue

The Reconstruction period after the Civil War is one of the most controversial and debated segments of our history. Whether or not it was successful still divides scholars and historians today. It took place under the guiding hand of four United States presidents: Abraham Lincoln (1861-1865), Andrew Johnson (1865-1869), Ulysses Grant (1869-1877), and Rutherford Hayes (1877-1881) and in a time of national alteration and divisional strife.

While the Civil War was still raging, President Abraham Lincoln wrestled over the proper procedure to bring the defeated rebels back into the fold. He knew of the innate Southern pride and wished to avoid further animosity by instituting too harsh a requirement for their return.

Before his assassination, Lincoln announced moderate plans for reconstruction to reintegrate the former Confederacy as fast as possible. Lincoln chose not to punish the South. He wanted to preserve the Union and start rebuilding the wealth and prosperity of the country. His model for reinstatement was called the 10 percent Reconstruction plan. It decreed that a state could be reintegrated into the Union when 10 percent of its 1860 vote count had taken an oath of allegiance to the United States and pledged to abide by emancipation.

At the same time, there was a loose faction in the Republican Party, who felt as though nothing was too harsh for the Confederacy. Radical Republican leaders argued that slavery and the Slave Power had to be permanently destroyed and all forms of Confederate nationalism suppressed. After all, their felonious act of treason had resulted in over one-half of a million deaths, mostly Northerners. They called themselves Radicals and stood in opposition to Lincoln, as well as moderates within the party, who wanted to reunite the nation painlessly and quickly.

While Lincoln considered an oath that "in the future" the rebels would support the Union, the Radicals found that unacceptable. They wanted more stringent requirements for Southern states' readmission, fashioning what became known as the Ironclad Oath that required a person to have never borne arms against the Union or supported the Confederacy. It went on to necessitate the pledge that no aid, countenance, council, or encouragement was given to persons engaged in armed hostility before receiving any consideration for reinstatement. Obviously, such an oath would eliminate every soldier, Southerners holding office, as well as most Southern citizens. Both Lincoln and, later, President Andrew Johnson opposed such strict measures; nevertheless, the Radicals won the critical midterm election of 1866 and overcame Johnson's vetoes.

Thereafter, in 1867, Congress removed the civilian governments in the South and put into effect the Radical Republican's Reconstruction plan under the supervision of the army, allowing an immoderate coalition of freed slaves, scalawags (local whites), and carpetbaggers (recent arrivals) to take control of the Southern state governments. Many of which were unqualified for positions of authority and ill prepared for the important task that lay ahead. Some say the sinister plan was to have the cobbled state governments continue special interest spending and raise taxes to the point landowners were unable to pay, thus forcing them to either sell off portions or have them confiscated.

The South's economy was in ruins. Massive war effort costs took a high toll on its financial framework. Many of its major cities were either destroyed or severely damaged. Their courthouses had burned to the ground, along with the documents for the various legal relationships in the communities. And beyond the obvious physical destruction, losses in human capital, such as knowledge, useful social attributes, and desire, had reduced the ability to perform the required labor to produce economic value. Furthermore, slaves were now free under Federal mandate, and white planters lacked necessary capital to pay the freedmen workers to bring in the crops.

Farms were in disrepair. The prewar stock of horses, mules, and cattle was much depleted. In fact, 40 percent of the South's livestock had been killed. In the struggle to survive, hapless landowners began to section small parcels of land and rented them to former slaves and their families. As a result, a system of sharecropping was developed. The concept of a tenant farming agricultural system began to take root.

* * *

The transportation infrastructure was in a state of destruction, with little railroad or riverboat service available to move crops and animals to market. For all intents and purposes, over two-thirds of the South's railroads, bridges, repair depots, and rolling stock were damaged by the Union army. In areas away from the Federal troops, equipment suffered from overuse and lack of maintenance and repair. Under the influence of Northern investors, it came as no surprise that restoring railroad systems became a high priority for Reconstruction state's governments.

They made the argument that railroads were the pathway to haul the South out of isolation and poverty. Accordingly, every Southern state was forced to subsidize the building and expansion of the permanent rolling iron network. Most of which were owned and directed overwhelmingly by Northerners. Millions of dollars in bonds and subsidies were fraudulently pocketed by those taking advantage of the federally enforced circumstances, leaving the Southern states holding the bag. Taxes skyrocketed across the South in order to pay for it.

Despite the poverty, those in control of Reconstruction changed the tax structure in the South. In some states, it increased to ten times the previous tax obligation. The new tax system was designed to force owners of large estates, with huge tracts of uncultivated land, to either sell or have it confiscated for failure to pay the levy. Such actions served as a market-based system for redistributing the land to the landless freedmen and, to a lesser degree, poor whites. Property taxes that formerly fell on the slave-owners now fell on the landowners. Many of whom were already in dire straits. Family property, and in turn, fortunes, were lost because of their inability to pay the higher assessments. All the while, the newly installed governments continued to borrow heavily, which incurred even more financial obligations for the already-bankrupted and vanquished states.

The second major indebtedness was the cost to build schools. In the past, the South had little commitment for public works or public education, keeping taxes historically low. Now, with over four million newly emancipated slaves, even more borrowing was necessary to accommodate and educate their children. Here again, new spending on schools, coupled with fraudulent disbursements, ran up huge deficits, causing the Southern states' credit to collapse.

* * *

Vice President Andrew Johnson's Reconstruction policy had evolved to more sympathetic and moderate stands, no doubt, due to the influence of Lincoln. It infuriated the Radical Republicans bent on retribution. After Lincoln's assassination, President Andrew Johnson's policy would be known best for nonenforcement of laws passed by the U.S. Congress, which kept him in constant conflict with the Radicals. The Tennessee Tailor, a slaveholder himself, was resigned to the abolition of slavery; however, he understood the unwillingness of the defeated South to accept social changes and political domination by former slaves. He envisioned a lenient policy for the return of Southern states and found himself at odds with Republicans in Congress. Johnson let it be known that wholesale land redistribution from the planters to former slaves would not occur. In defiance to the wishes of the Radicals, the self-educated vice president ordered that confiscated or abandoned lands be returned to their pardoned owners. Johnson's lenient positions led to a clash of power between the executive and legislative branches of government as to who had the authority over the Reconstruction. The midterm election of 1866 decisively changed the balance of power, giving the Republicans two-thirds majority in both houses of Congress and enough votes to overrule presidential vetoes. Indeed, once in control, they impeached President Johnson and almost removed him from office in 1868 were it not for a single vote.

After Congress failed to remove President Johnson, he infuriated the Radical Republicans further by officially granting amnesty and pardoning the Southern soldiers before leaving office.

* * *

Former slaves were now granted freedom, something they had only previously dreamed about. The change left them both jubilant and perplexed. Now that they have it, what do they do with it? While some slaves remained on the plantation, many others migrated to the cities only to find themselves relegated to the lowest-paying jobs for unskilled labor and domestic work. Ironically, the large population of subjugated artisans during the antebellum had not translated into a significant number of emancipated skilled workers during the Reconstruction. This came as a surprise to those now in power. Part of the North's restoration plan was to utilize the skillful blacks into their rebuilding program. Over 25 percent of the South's white workforce died during the war, leaving a sizable void in experienced manpower. The remaining families were disillusioned, discouraged, and destitute—locked into a system of poverty lasting well into the twentieth century.

* * *

From the beginning, many Southerners felt as though the Radical Reconstruction policies were counterproductive and only in place to further punish the South. Especially since black males could now vote and those whites who supported the Confederacy, and their military officers, were forbidden.

Most white members of the planter, business, and common farmer class opposed black power, carpetbaggers, and military rule. They sought a return to the policy of white hegemony. Like the cleft created by the constant drip of water, the planters and their business allies eventually dominated the self-styled conservative coalition that finally took control in the South. Paternalistic toward blacks, they feared the freedmen would use their power to raise taxes and slow business development. They further contended, the project to make voters out of black men was not so much for their social elevation as for the further punishment of the Southern white people.

In retrospect, their claim might be right. The Republican Radicals believed, by capturing government offices and entrenchment of the Radical Republican party, for a long time to come, would extend their castigation of the South. That's not to say that men of goodwill didn't take part in restoring the Union. There were plenty of altruistic motives; however, emotions ran high during this period in history. And the more negative viewpoint seems always to win out and last longer than the positive. As humans, our minds work that way. The human brain handles positive and negative information in different hemispheres. Negative emotions require more thinking and are processed more thoroughly than positive. Bad impressions are quicker to form and more resistant to renounce than good ones. Considering their situation, it's little wonder their attitudes were what they were.

Reaction by the angry whites included the formation of violent secret societies, especially the odious Ku Klux Klan—an infamous group who disguised themselves and threatened anyone opposing their views.

* * *

Tensions built as violence occurred in cities with Democrats, Conservatives, and other angry whites on one side and Republicans, former slaves, and coalition state governments on the other. The victims of this violence were overwhelmingly African Americans. Rising tensions not only built up among Southerners, but also political pressure began to build up inside the Radical Republican Party, as they were continuously criticized by the Democrats.

* * *

By its Reconstruction acts, Congress was correct not limiting the right of suffrage to whites. But wrong in the exclusion from suffrage certain classes of citizens and all who were unable to take its prescribed ex post facto oath. Also wrong in the establishment of despotic military governments in the states, plus authorizing military commissions for the trial of civilians in time of peace.

In 1868, Georgia Democrats, with support from some Republicans, expelled all twenty-eight black Republican members, arguing blacks were eligible to vote but not to hold office. In several states, the more conservative scalawags fought for control with the more radical carpetbaggers and usually lost. The Radical Republican party lost support steadily as many scalawags left it and few recruits were acquired. Meanwhile, the freedmen were demanding a bigger share of the offices and patronage, thus squeezing out their carpetbagger allies. Finally, some of the more prosperous freedmen were joining the Democrats, as they were angered at the failure of the Republicans to help them acquire land.

By 1870, the Democrat-Conservative leadership across the South decided it had to end its opposition to Reconstruction and black suffrage in order to survive. They moved on to new issues. Not all Democrats agreed, and the insurgent element continued to resist Reconstruction, no matter what. Eventually, a more levelheaded group called Redeemers took control of the party in the Southern states.

* * *

A worldwide economic depression began in 1873 and ran through the spring of 1879. It severely affected the United States and Europe and especially the fragile Southern economy. Republicans, who had gambled that railroads would pull the South out of its poverty, were now disillusioned. The price of cotton fell by half. Many small landowners, local merchants of cotton, and wholesalers went bankrupt. Others, seeking a way of spreading the risk, turned to sharecropping with both blacks and whites.

The hard times, caused by the recession, forced many local black leaders to give more consideration for cooperating with white elites rather than focusing on their own racial political progress. While blacks had an increased voice in the Republican Party, it was divided by internal bickering and rapidly losing its cohesion.

Nationally, President Grant was blamed for the depression. The Republican Party lost government seats in all parts of the country in the 1874 election. Democrats took control of the House and were confident of electing the next president. President Grant appeared as though he was losing interest in the South and declared he would not seek reelection.

In the midst of national uncertainty, secret societies continued to grow in popularity in the South. By now, the Ku Klux Klan was able to elude existing law enforcement, while serving as a pseudomilitary arm of the Democrat Party. Its principle aim was preventing blacks from voting and destroying the Republican Party by assassinating local leaders and public officials.

Both parties, Democrat and Republican, agreed that Confederate nationalism and slavery were dead. War goals were achieved and further Federal military interference was an undemocratic violation of historic Republican values.

After the election of Rutherford Hayes, the national compromise of 1877 was reached. White Democrats in the South agreed to accept Hayes's victory if he withdrew the last Federal troops. By this point, the North was weary of insurgency. Blacks considered the Reconstruction a failure because Federal government withdrew from enforcing their ability to exercise their rights as citizens.

Booker T. Washington, born into slavery, was a noted scholar, educator, orator, and artful politician advising Republican presidents. He later concluded that the Reconstruction experiment in racial democracy failed because it began at the wrong end, emphasizing political means and civil rights acts rather than economic means and self-determination. His solution was to concentrate on building the economic infrastructure of the black community. Others claimed that it took freedoms and rights from qualified whites and gave them to unqualified blacks, who were being duped by corrupt carpetbaggers and scalawags.

Well into the 1930s, scholars argued that the Radical rhetoric of equal rights was mostly smoke screen, hiding the true motivation of its backers—Northern industrialists and financiers who would own the South economically by controlling the railroads.

On the positive side, one only has to look at the establishment of universal public education, suffrage, legal marriages for blacks, the Thirteenth Amendment (outlawing slavery and involuntary servitude), Fourteenth Amendment (broad definition of citizenship and equal protection clause), and Fifteenth Amendment (the right to vote).

Whatever the historic view, it's reasonable to conclude that Reconstruction had many successful aspects although never fully completed. To bring change about through severe punishment has long proven to be ineffective. Resentment and hatred always boils beneath the surface. That fact holds true for parents and children and, yes, both slave and master. Most of us agree there is always a better way to do practically everything in life. Had Abraham Lincoln's policies been chosen by the North, a more noble-minded approach for statehood unification would have been put in place. Whether or not magnanimity could have accomplished the desired result cannot now be answered. In the face of turmoil and tribulation, an American president recently assassinated and the countrywide clamor for justice, it's a wonder the republic survived not only the Civil War but also the civil peace thereafter.